# TOMORROW
# AND
# TOMORROW
# AND
# TOMORROW

Other Virago Modern Classics published by The Dial Press

# M. Barnard Eldershaw

# TOMORROW AND TOMORROW AND TOMORROW

*With a new introduction by*
*Anne Chisholm*

*The Dial Press*
*DOUBLEDAY & COMPANY, INC.*
*GARDEN CITY, NEW YORK*
*1984*

Published by The Dial Press
Censored edition first published in Australia by
Georgian House, Melbourne, 1947
Copyright © in this uncensored edition
Marjorie Barnard 1983
Introduction copyright © Anne Chisholm 1983
Manufactured in the United States of America

Library of Congress Cataloging in Publication Data
Eldershaw, M. Bernard, pseud.
Tomorrow & tomorrow & tomorrow.
(A Virago modern classic)
"Censored edition first published in Australia
by Georgian House, Melbourne, 1947"—Verso t.p.
I. Title.   II. Title: Tomorrow and tomorrow and
tomorrow.   III. Series.
PR9619.3.E418T6   1984      823      84-7748
ISBN 0-385-27980-9

# *CONTENTS*

Tomorrow, and tomorrow, and tomorrow,
Creeps in this petty pace from day to day,
To the last syllable of recorded time;
And all our yesterdays have lighted fools
The way to dusty death.

—Macbeth.

# INTRODUCTION

In 1938, M. Barnard Eldershaw, a two-woman writing partnership that had been active for ten years, produced a book of criticism called *Essays in Australian Fiction*. The opening lines are:

Year by year the numbers of women novelists increase. Writing has become quite a recognised feminine profession—like nursing. . . A certain tardiness in recognising the novel as a form of art allowed women to establish themselves in the practice of it without opposition. They did not have to combat a strong tradition. The sex has not developed an inferiority complex in regard to novel writing as in most of the other arts. Women had won their spurs before anyone thought of telling them they were incapable of doing so.

They went on to give first place in their selection of eight writers to two women, Henry Handel Richardson and Katharine Susannah Prichard. They included two more women, Christina Stead and Eleanor Dark, making an even balance between the sexes. It is striking that today all four women have major reputations in Australia and two, Richardson and Stead, enjoy international standing. The four men writers come some way behind. (Frank Dalby Davison, Vance Palmer, Martin Boyd, Leonard Mann.)

M. Barnard Eldershaw, as novelists, were part of the extraordinary flowering of writing talent which they were among the first to recognise; but, curiously, it is only of late that the extent of Australian women writers' achievement between the wars has begun to be appreciated. In particular, Drusilla Modjeska's outstanding book, *Exiles at Home: Australian Women Writers 1925–1945*, (Angus and Robertson, Australia 1981) combines new material and fresh insights to bring the period and characters into focus. Curiosity about and respect for women's achievements, inspired by the women's movement of the 1960s and 70s, combined with the wish, in Australia, to revalue neglected aspects of their own literature have led to exciting rediscoveries of which the work of M. Barnard Eldershaw is surely one.

When *Tomorrow and Tomorrow and Tomorrow* was published in Australia in 1947, the two women who wrote it, Marjorie Barnard and Flora Eldershaw, had been working together in an unusually productive and successful literary partnership for nearly twenty years. They were born in the same year, 1897; Marjorie Barnard in Sydney, and Flora Eldershaw in the country in New South Wales. Both were children of middle-class professional families and went to good schools; they met at Sydney University during the First World War. Marjorie Barnard has described her encounter with Eldershaw as "a piece of good fortune. . . She had ambitions to write, and we used to talk about the books we would write, and it occurred to us that it would be much more fun to write together." But writing at first seemed impractical for two serious-minded young women with no connections to the Sydney literary world who both needed, and wanted, to be professionally and financially independent of their families.

Flora Eldershaw became a teacher and eventually head of a leading Sydney girls' school, the Presbyterian Ladies' College; Marjorie Barnard reluctantly became a librarian. She had graduated in 1919 with first-class honours and the University medal and was offered a place at Oxford; she longed to go, as academic life appealed to her, but her father, an accountant, refused her permission and she felt she could not defy him. During the 1920s she lived at home, and Flora Eldershaw lived at her school. Marjorie Barnard was always the shyer of the two, but neither had much social life nor any contact with other writers. Both women worked hard and lived quiet, dull lives. They published nothing until they were over thirty.

In 1928 the Sydney magazine *The Bulletin* offered a prize for an Australian novel. According to Marjorie Barnard, this prompted her and Flora Eldershaw to turn their dream of writing a book together into reality. They wrote *A House is Built* which shared the first prize with *Coonardoo* by Katharine Susannah Prichard, became an instant success and has remained in print ever since. "After that," Marjorie Barnard has said, "we felt ourselves to be writers."

During the next ten years the two women were to write five more novels, eight historical studies, and a book of criticism; both were to become leading figures on the Sydney literary scene. They were to play their part, as writers and as individuals, in the crises of conscience and loyalty that gripped writers everywhere as the social and political problems of the 1930s gathered momentum.

By the time *Tomorrow and Tomorrow and Tomorrow* was written, their attention had shifted from the purely Australian scene, past or present, to the world stage and the part Australia could or should play on it; and their interest, which grew steadily until the late 1930s, in exploring in particular the situation of women, expecially single women, was overtaken by concern for the plight and the future of humanity.

The success of *A House is Built*, a novel about a quartermaster's family and business in Sydney in the early nineteenth century, led to changes in the lives of the two authors, but only slowly. In the early 1930s they both continued to work full time and to write as and when they could. Their collaboration, which the leading historian of Australian literature, H.M. Green, has called "among the most successful in literature" was, according to Marjorie Barnard, easy and harmonious from the start. "We never had any trouble," she says,

and the reason for this is that we talked things over very thoroughly before pen was put to paper . . . nothing was written until we'd decided just what we were going to do and how we were going to do it, and those preliminary talks were most valuable. The collaboration began in them. It didn't matter very much who did the actual writing. We both contributed the ideas and we both criticised whatever one another did, and there was no harm done, either to the book or to our friendship.

Flora Eldershaw told H.M. Green that either of them could draft a chapter in which the other would usually find little to change. This was just as well, as both of them used to write mostly at night.

It was primarily through correspondence and eventually friendship with another remarkable woman that Flora Eldershaw and Marjorie Barnard gradually acquired confidence in themselves as writers. This was Nettie Palmer, about ten years older than they, who after aspiring to be a poet had decided to combine marriage to the novelist Vance Palmer and the raising of two children with literary journalism and criticism. Nettie Palmer came from a middle-class Melbourne family with connections in politics and literature; she dedicated herself to encouraging Australian writers to invent their own strong national tradition and not to feel inferior to the British. She was interested in socialism and broadly on the left, but remained deeply suspicious of communism, which attracted many of the younger writers of the decade. Above all she believed in education, the exchange of ideas, and the benefits that a network of writers and thinkers could bring to Australian intellectual life.

Nettie Palmer's allegiance to Australia and her belief in an Australian literary tradition were immensely important to struggling young writers like Barnard and Eldershaw. The pull of Europe and America was strong, and not resisted by the early women writers. Miles Franklin, whose first book, the feminist classic *My Brilliant Career*, came out in 1901, had found her position so awkward that she left the country in 1906 and did not return for twenty years. Henry Handel Richardson lived and wrote in London. Christina Stead starved herself for three years to earn her fare to Europe, and sailed in 1928, the year that Barnard Eldershaw started to write. Those who decided to stay at home needed not only advice, but also reassurance that they were doing something worthwhile especially if, like Barnard Eldershaw, they were working in isolation.

By the end of 1930 a regular and detailed correspondence had begun between Nettie Palmer and Marjorie Barnard in particular. They discussed at first writing and publishing; but gradually the letters became more personal. Barnard felt able to tell Nettie Palmer how arduous she found her work and how she resented the demands on her time made by her parents, for whom she worked as an "amateur housemaid". In 1931 Barnard Eldershaw published their second novel, again about a family, *Green Memory*; the story of a daughter at the time of the gold rush who sacrifices herself and her lover in order to restore the family's position after her father's disgrace. By 1935, both women had made trips to Europe with their families, and the long sea voyage produced their third novel *The Glasshouse* (published 1936), about a woman writer on a similar journey observing her fellow passengers.

In the same year, Marjorie Barnard consulted Nettie Palmer about an audacious step; should she yield to her longing to abandon her work as a librarian in order to write full time? Encouraged by Palmer, she did so, and embarked on what she later described as the best and most productive time of her life—"seven years without a job, living at home and working practically from nine till five". She joined the Fellowship of Australian Writers, began to take a serious interest in politics, and met, thanks to Nettie Palmer again, probably the most important person in her life (apart from Flora Eldershaw), the novelist Frank Dalby Davison.

Together, Marjorie Barnard, Flora Eldershaw and Frank Davison formed "the triumvirate" which was central to the intellectual and political debates among Australian writers in the later 1930s. Remote though Australia sometimes seemed from Europe, both economic disaster and international tensions reverberated there. The depression of the 1930s, the Egon Kisch affair of 1934 (in which a German Czech communist writer was refused permission to land in Australia), and the formation of the Popular Front whereby communists joined non-communists in opposing fascism, shifted many writers towards the left.

Both Flora Eldershaw and Frank Davison became presidents of the Fellowship of Australian writers and helped to move that previously staid and conservative body towards more radical views; Marjorie Barnard, although less publicly prominent, was close to the arguments; she became a pacifist and, in 1940, a member of the Australian Labor Party. During these years Barnard and Eldershaw for the first time secured a room of their own. In 1936 they rented a small flat at Potts Point on Sydney Harbour, where at last they could entertain away from parental or professional scrutiny.

Marjorie Barnard wrote to Nettie Palmer in 1937: "I've only made friends quickly twice in my life—you and Frank." This was a prolific period. In the same year Barnard Eldershaw published their fourth novel, *Plaque with Laurel*, about the relationships and ambitions of a group of writers. In 1938 they produced not only a life of Governor Phillip but the book of critical essays which Green calls "a landmark in Australian fiction"; and in 1939 they brought out two more books: an analysis of the Australian identity, *My Australia*, and a biographical study of Captain John Piper, one of the founders of Sydney.

The outbreak of war brought this full and exhilarating period in Barnard Eldershaw's life to a close. In 1940 Barnard's father died, leaving her responsible for her ailing mother. In 1941 Flora Eldershaw took a government job and moved to Canberra. Frank Davison remarried and moved to Melbourne. By 1942 Marjorie Barnard was compelled for financial reasons to resume work as a librarian. In her loneliness and unhappiness, she first turned inward and produced, under her own name, a remarkable collection of short stories on the theme of isolated, frustrated women, *The Persimmon Tree*. Then in 1942, at a depressing point both in her life and in the course of the war, with the support of Flora Eldershaw but without her day to day collaboration, she began to write *Tomorrow and Tomorrow and Tomorrow*.

*Tomorrow and Tomorrow and Tomorrow* is both the culmination of Barnard Eldershaw's previous work and a radical departure from it. It expresses all their knowledge and love of Australian history and their deep concern for the part Australia had played and might play in world affairs; yet it is also a book about ordinary people, full of insight and sympathy. As a novel, though, its structure, and themes, were something quite new. It is written as a book within a book, with events and characters in the "novel" at its core realistically and directly expressed.

It opens in the twenty-fourth century, with future Australians living in a highly-ordered, technologically-advanced society. A writer and outsider, Knarf (Frank spelled backwards, a tribute to Frank Davison intended,

Barnard said later, as a joke), has written a novel exploring the history and everyday life of Australia in the twentieth century, based on fact. He reads his book over a period of several days to his friend Ord. Meanwhile Knarf's young son Ren is caught up in a hopeless struggle to break the power of the state and win more freedom of choice and action for the citizens.

It is a deeply political book and a brave one, considering that it was written at the height of World War Two. At the heart of it is the story of how the aftermath of the First World War—the Depression and the rise of Fascism in Europe—impinged on the lives of a group of working-class Australians in Sydney, in particular on Harry Munster and his family and circle. But Barnard Eldershaw do not stop the story at the outbreak of World War Two. Writing before the war was half over, they postulate a series of events leading to an invasion of Australia by a right-wing international police force, a revolutionary uprising by left-wingers and the destruction and abandonment of Sydney.

It is hardly surprising that the book, when it came to the attention of the war-time censors, caused them concern. Although they confined their cuts to the fictional ending and aftermath of the war and the build up to the rising, the whole book is in fact provocative in the extreme. It reveals Barnard Eldershaw's deep hostility to capitalism, materialism, and competition, and to the way Australia, as they saw it, had been exploited and manipulated by Britain and the United States. The opening pages contain this passage about twentieth-century Australians:

They had been a very strange people, full of contradictions, adaptable and obstinate. With courage and endurance they had pioneered the land, only to ruin it with greed and lack of forethought. They had drawn a hardy independence from the soil and had maintained it with pride and yet they had allowed themselves to be dispossessed by the most fantastic tyranny the world had ever known, money in the hands of the few, an unreal, an imaginary system driving out reality. . . They loved their country and exalted patriotism as if it were a virtue, and yet they gave a greater love to a little island in the north sea that many of them had never seen. . . The small people was prodigal of its armies; generation after generation, they swarmed out to fight and die in strange places and for strange causes. Tough, sardonic and humorous, they were romantics the like of which the world had never seen.

The censor's cuts in 1944 were made mostly in the second half of the penultimate section of the book, "Afternoon". The original typescript, placed by Marjorie Barnard in the Mitchell Library in Sydney, shows the censors' clearance stamp on 145 pages out of a total in that section of 276. The deletions, in red ink, add up to some 393 lines. Sometimes a word or two is deleted, sometimes several pages. It is hard to follow the workings of the censor's mind; frequently he cleared passages that seem as challenging as those he removed.

The first cut is one of the most significant. The authors, still sticking close to the facts, describe the Russo-Finnish war of 1941.

The Finnish war, the ideological confusion and its stirring up of enmity between left and right, had its consequences. The Government, perceiving a cleavage, proceeded, under cover of the State of War, to sew it together in their own way. Parliament passed the National Security Act. It looked short and meek enough in the statute book, pages of dry legal jargon, but it severed at its root that democratic principle of goverment for which the war was, presumably, being fought.

The Barnard Eldershaw theme which most provoked the censor was undoubtedly that the Australian government, in order to keep the populace in line and willing to fight, manipulated the flow of information and concealed or distorted facts that would have allowed people to think for themselves about the war. And yet, many lines survived to support this theme; for example, on page 310: "When fear receded, the leaders and politicians must bring it back, for it was a powerful lever to advance the war effort." It seems curious that these lines were passed, while two sentences on the same page about Japanese attacks on Darwin and nearby islands were cut.

The first long cut occurs at a crucial point in the narrative, when Barnard Eldershaw abandon any basis of historical fact and launch into the climax of the book. The censor's other aim, apparently, was to weaken and blur the impact and credibility of the account of how large numbers of people, sick of war and propaganda, followed the Peace Party and withdrew from the war machine.

In the novel, when the war in Europe was over, Australians were divided and uneasy about continuing the war in the Pacific. The censor cut lines such as,

The British Navy did not stream into the Pacific to end the stalemate of the Japanese war. . . Doubt was in every heart, unease. . . The news that Hitler had hanged himself in Berchtesgarten scarcely raised a cheer. He, after all, was not the enemy, the enemy was everywhere.

The most substantial and significant cuts in the book occur at the point where Barnard Eldershaw are brilliantly and imaginatively constructing their scenario of dissension and revolution, of an Australia invaded by international forces of the right and torn apart by civil war. Essentially, the cuts reveal the deep nervousness caused by the suggestion, even in a work of fiction set four centuries ahead, that a Peace Party based on the refusal of Australians to compete or fight might win popular support.

It must be said that the censors' efforts were only partly successful. Enough was left for the authors' intentions to be visible, but in a confused and muted way when compared with the detail, passion and clarity of the original.

Even in mutilated form *Tomorrow and Tomorrow and Tomorrow* has stood as something rare in Australian fiction—a novel of political ideas which sees Australia not as a remote country apart from the world's upheavals and problems but as a place both affected by, and with responsibilities to, the rest of the world. In its intense love of Australia, its concern for lost innocence and wasted energy, its love for the ancient landscape and its fear of the impact of modern industrial technology, the novel touched on concerns which are still painfully live, posing questions without answers. And the account of a right-wing invasion from outside, in the wake of the traumatic intervention of 1975 by the Governor-General, Sir John Kerr, that ended the Labor Government of Gough Whitlam, strikes with added force.

By the time *Tomorrow and Tomorrow and Tomorrow* was published, which was not until 1947, the war was over. The postwar mood was not sympathetic to the novel. Its reception ranged from the lukewarm to the hostile and it has been neglected ever since. Marjorie Barnard has said recently that in her view the censors ruined it, and that she feels it to be her best work, better than the far more popular *A House is Built*. Deeply discouraged by the failure of their most ambitious book and with the Cold War and the start of the long years of Menzies' conservatism in Australia offering them little hope of a change of mood, Flora Eldershaw and Marjorie Barnard wrote no more fiction, returning instead to history and criticism. Flora Eldershaw died in 1957; Marjorie Barnard now lives near the coast north of Sydney.

She has recently seen her work praised by a new generation of women who have learned to look again at the lives and works of her colleagues and friends and to learn from them. It has always been her wish that *Tomorrow and Tomorrow and Tomorrow* should be republished in its uncensored form. Here it is.

*Anne Chisholm, London, 1982*

# NOTES ON CUTS

A comparison of the typescript of *Tomorrow and Tomorrow and Tomorrow* (given to the Mitchell Library, Sydney, by Marjorie Barnard) with the Georgian House edition published in Melbourne in 1947 results in the list of passages given below which were deleted from the previous published edition and have been restored in this one.

Certain problems have arisen in preparing the list which should be pointed out to the reader.

In the Mitchell Library typescript each section of the book is page-numbered separately. Although the censors' stamp first appears on page 132 of the section entitled "Afternoon", the first deletion apparently by the censor appears on page 18. There are six deletions before the stamp appears. It has not been possible to discuss these deletions with Marjorie Barnard, nor with the original publishers, nor with the censor concerned; it is therefore possible, though given their content not likely, that some of the deletions on the unstamped pages were not made by the government censors but by the author or publishers for other reasons.

The censors' intervention affected the placing of the passage concerning the outbreak of plague on the Japanese ship, which appeared slightly later in the narrative in the Georgian House edition. We have followed the original typescript version.

The Georgian House edition was published as *Tomorrow and Tomorrow*, the third "Tomorrow" having been dropped by the publishers without the authors' permission. At the request of Marjorie Barnard we have reverted to the original title.

# LISTS OF CUTS RESTORED

# AUBADE

# I

The first light was welling up in the east. In the west a few stars were dying in the colourless sky. The waking sky was enormous and under it the sleeping earth was enormous too. It was a great platter with one edge tilted up into the light, so that the pattern of hills, dark under a gold dust bloom, was visible. The night had been warm and still, as early autumn nights sometimes are, and with a feeling of transience, of breaking ripeness, of doomed fertility, like a woman who does not show her age but whose beauty will crumble under the first grief or hardship. With the dawn, sheets of thin cold air were slipping over the earth, congealing the warmth into a delicate smoking mist. Knarf was glad to wrap his woollen cloak about him. Standing on the flat roof in the dawn he felt giddily tall and, after a night of intense effort, transparent with fatigue. Weariness was spread evenly through his body. He was supersensitively aware of himself, the tension of his skin nervously tightened by long concentration, the vulnerability of his temples, the frailty of his ribs caging his enlarged heart, the civilisation of his hands. . . . Flesh and imagination were blent and equally receptive. The cold air struck his hot forehead with a shock of excitement, he looked out over the wide sculptury of light, darkness, earth, with new wonder. For a few moments, turning so suddenly from work to idleness, everything had an exaggerated significance. When he drew his fingers along the balustrade, leaving in the thick moisture faint dark marks on its glimmering whiteness, that, too, seemed like a contact, sharply intimate, with the external world where the rising light was beginning to show trees dark and grass grey with that same dew.

Behind Knarf the lamp still burned in the pavilion and the dawn had already diminished and sickened its light. Only one wall, the west, was folded back. It was empty save for the low broad table with its piles of manuscript, a chair in the same pale unornamented wood, the tall lamp, and a couch where Knarf sometimes slept on a summer night with all the walls folded back, like—he told Ren, but his jest had fallen flat—an antique corpse under a canopy. There was no colour except in the bindings of the books piled on the table and spilled on the floor. The frame of the pavilion stood up dark against the golden sky and within the frame the lamplight, at variance with the new daylight, was clotted and impotent. The vapours of a night of effort and struggle could not escape. The empty room was like a sloughed skin. Knarf had been born from it into this new day of which he was so keenly aware.

In this pause between darkness and light he was between two worlds, a reality between two ghosts, a moment of sharp individual consciousness in the drift of centuries. His imagination had been living so vehemently in the past that the present had become only half real. He was standing at a nexus of time. Four hundred years ago, a thousand years ago, dawn among these gentle hills would have seemed no different, to any living eye that had seen it, than it did to him. In a few minutes, so quickly was the light growing, the world of to-day would be back, incontrovertibly, in its place. But now, for a moment, the old world, the past, might lie under the shadows just as easily as the present. A thousand years ago the country had been covered with bush, a thick mat of it, unending, breaking into natural clearings, closing in again, a shaggy pelt existing for nothing but itself, unknown except to the wandering tribes of the First People, and they, measured against the world they lived in, were newcomers and sojourners. They lived in it according to its terms without changing it or penetrating it. The pattern of their lives wound, like a kabbalistic sign traced in water, through the bush. Their apparently free roaming had followed a set tide. Their food supply, since they did not intervene in nature save in the spearing of game, was bound upon the seasons. Within this cycle of nature was the human cycle, the pattern of contacts, the linking invisible trade routes, the crossing and recrossing of tribe with tribe, the circulation of thought and knowledge as natural and primitive as the circulation of the blood in the body. Within the human cycle was the mystic cycle, the linking of rites and places, of ceremonies that were symbols of symbols forgotten even in the beginning of time but that continued to draw men through old, remembered ways. He thought of the anonymous and indecipherable tracks of the First People which had lain so lightly on these hills. Far away, reduced by distance of time to outline, theirs was only another arrangement of the eternal pattern, of eating, communicating, and reaching out into the unknown. They were gone, completely and utterly, nothing was left of them but a few rock drawings, a few spearheads in rosy quartz, some patterns incised in wood, the words of some songs, soft, melancholy, their meaning forever sealed. Their dust was in this dust, nothing more. In the north, where they had not perished but had been absorbed, their docile blood had mingled without trace and no overt memory of them remained.

Four hundred years ago this country was stripped bare. The delicately moulded hills were naked to the sun and wind and rain, their hoarded fertility broken into and flowing out of them. Knarf remembered the old barbaric name of the river—Murrumbidgee. It had not slipped quiet and full between canal-like banks, tame and sure, as it did today. It held the rich lands in a great gnarled claw, its red banks sculptured into canyons, carved, pillared, eroded, littered with the flotsam of old floods, an ancient tribal river that ruled like a god in these parts. The countryside had been called the Riverina, a gentle fruitful name, a propitiatory name perhaps, much better than Tenth Commune; Knarf would have liked to see the old name in use again. To divide up the earth into squares with a ruler was too arrogant. This earth was not like any other earth, it had its spirit still, even if old god Murrumbidgee was tamed and made to serve it. All that had happened was written in the dust, it didn't end and it wasn't lost, it was woven in.

The river had been a frontier. At the beginning of the dark ages, there had been a migration along and beyond it,—the people who would not make terms thrust out by the pressure from the coast. They had mustered their flocks, piled such goods as they could salvage on to their trucks, and with their families sought the interior. It was here, probably almost at this very spot, that their final decision had had to be made. The waterways had been secured so that they could no longer push along the comparative safety of the river frontages. From here they had struck west and north for the safety of the bad lands. When the trucks had foundered for want of petrol, which happened sooner or later, (nowadays whenever a farmer turned up a rusted shard of metal in the paddocks by the river, he'd claim it was from one of the abandoned trucks—they must have been pretty thick about here, like the detritus of a routed army) they had taken off the wheels, cut down the famous Murrumbidgee gums, the old-man trees, and made themselves rough drays to which they harnessed their horses or their bullocks and they had gone on. No one pursued them, but their needs drove them further and further out. As they reached poorer country they needed more and more of it for their sheep. They could not stick together, they had to scatter. It was every man, or every family, for himself. The years of the migration were good, the country was in good heart and so were the men. They were the descendants of a peculiar people called the Pioneers and, only two or three generations earlier, their forbears had gone out into the wilderness, had come down here from the coast and the city, and, driving out the First People and cutting down the bush, had made a life for themselves. It had been hard and many had perished but others had prospered, grown wise, tough, and rich. They hadn't been afraid of the country and its irregular rhythms. The sons thought they could do it again, or rather they wouldn't believe that they couldn't. They were the great-grandsons, the grandsons, and even the sons of Pioneers, so close was the end to the beginning. History melted down the years between and these followers of a forlorn hope became one with their successful forbears, and were also called "The Pioneers." They left their foundered, mortgaged runs, where they had been feeling the long wars like a drought, and set off in a sort of cheerful desperation. If they lost a lot they got rid of a lot too. What had been done once they could do again—but this time it was different. There was not only no way back but there were no resources behind them. For a year or two it was not so bad, while the few things they had brought with them lasted and the seasons were good. Then the situation began to tell on them in earnest. At first they shore their sheep but there was no market for the wool. It decayed and stank and burned in bark sheds. A little of it they made shift to spin into yarn for their own use. Several risked a journey to a southern port with a drayload or two, but it proved too dangerous and unprofitable. They could dispose of the wool readily and secretly but there was little or nothing they could get in exchange. It was useless to keep the flocks save a few small ones to provide meat, yarn, leather, and tallow. They let them go, it was better than confiscation. The sheep wandered over the fenceless pastures. They lambed and wandered on. Their fleeces grew and blinded them, the burden of wool dragged them down till every morning there were some that could not rise and must starve where they lay. Summer and drought pressed hard on them. The waterholes dried up. The sheep died in hundreds and then thousands. Dumb and helpless death was everywhere. The Pioneers had great difficulty in keeping alive the small flocks that were necessary to their own survival. Beside that the death of a myriad sheep meant nothing to them. Even on the coast where there was water and feed people starved and went in rags. One dry summer was enough for the sheep laden with wool.

The men were much harder to break. Others had come after them, a motley crowd of the dispossesseed, the angry, the frightened, the hungry, but they had had no staying power, they began to die like the sheep as soon as they had crossed the Murrumbidgee. But the Pioneers endured, long and incredibly. Like the First People, they learned to move from scanty resource to scanty resource, they valued nothing but water and food and perhaps the antique fetish, liberty, but that would not be a word they ever troubled to speak. It was something they could not help having and for which they had no use. They were as tough, as thin, and almost as black from the sun, as the First People had been, but, unlike the First People, they had no festivals, no corroborees, no old rites. They were scaled down to something below that. It is said that as a people they stopped breeding.

They could not or would not return and no effort was ever made to bring them back. Such people were useless for the building of a new world. A few may have straggled back, but very few. The great majority was lost. After twenty or even thirty years there would be a few survivors, madmen living in caves with their phantom dogs beside them, men gone native with the last of the tribes, gone crazy.

That wasn't the history you found in history books, it was local legend. Knarf believed it and Ord said it was true. He had known it for a long time but only this morning did it seem completely real. He was smitten, he supposed, with imaginative conviction. It was often like that. Knowledge lay dead in his brain, so much ready-made merchandise on its shelves, and then, often for no obvious reason, it quickened and became part of the small, living, and productive part of his mind. In the shadowy morning light he could trick himself into seeing the Pioneers moving down to the river in neutral coloured cavalcade, flocks of sheep travelling over the brown plain beyond in a haze of dust, tall, brown, laconic men in dusty clothes, their heterogeneous belongings piled on the makeshift vehicles already weathered to drabness, the slow flight into country without cover. . . . There were people far out west, in the next commune, old or lonely or simple people, who in unguarded moments told stories of the Pioneers. Solitary travellers had seen camp fires in the bush. When they approached, the fire had been burning brightly with a skeleton sitting beside it, bushman fashion, on his heels. Their ghosts are thick round waterholes, and if you spend a night there you cannot sleep for the rattle of hobble chains and the stamping of horses that will have left no trace in the morning. The strange dog seen at twilight is no mortal dog but the mythical folkdog, the Kelpie, "too faithful to die," as they say. When cattle stampede in the night they say "It's the Pioneers." Sometimes, it is said, they pass through on a moonlight night, you hear the rustle of sheep's feet in the dust, the creak and clatter of riders, and even men's voices singing in an archaic dialect, and in the morning there will be broken fences and eaten out paddocks but not a mark in the dust of the road or a single dropping of dung. . . . But no one ever caught up with this legend, it had always happened farther on. It was like the Hosting of the Sidhe, Ord said, thrusting it farther back into the world that was his own province.

There must be a good deal of Pioneer blood about here still, Knarf thought. He'd often noticed, though it wasn't a thing anyone talked about, that the inlanders were taller, looser, leaner than the men on the coast, with less of the orient in their faces. Blood mixed slowly even after all this time.

With his back to the east Knarf had been straining his eyes into the west. The light had grown imperceptibly. It collected on objects like dew. The river was already a broad silver band. At his feet there was still a well of darkness, a well full of sleep, but farther away the white houses of the square and along the bank of the river were visible. By concentration, sight could rescue the dark lines of trees and even pick out, across the river, the black and grey pattern of the irrigated orchards and gardens. As yet there was no colour, only assembling shapes. The river was quicksilver between dark banks.

In a few minutes now the past would be buried again under the present. The scene he knew so well and loved so deeply would cover and supersede the figment of his imagination which had had for the moment the intense overstrung reality of things that pass. He would see, not the shaggy olive green hills of the beginning, nor the bare hills of the twentieth century with their chromatic swing from the new green of the rains through silvers and browns to the naked brown purple of the earth, stripped and compressed by drought; not the irregular wasteful pattern of land overdriven and under-used, but the lovely design of safe and steady fruitfulness. It was a bright picture, where there had never been a bright picture before. If a man of the First People had stood here he would have seen only a monotone, or perhaps no more than the mazing pattern of narrow leaves against the sky. To the Pioneer it would have been a variation in pale colours, country under threat, a threnody for the wind. And yet—it must have been lovely. It might even have had something the present lacked. Eyes that had known it would be homesick to-day. Man might turn away from surfeits to pine for hard and meagre fare. To think of the Pioneers as a people who had ravaged the country, left it denuded and helpless and then had gone out, irrationally and obstinately, to die with the country, to become in the last resort place-spirits, the half-evil genii of the soil, was a poet's conception. Life was lived as fully then as now, now as then. This, that looks so sleek, is only an approximation too.

The Australians, of whom the Pioneers were part, had been the second people. They had been so few, never more than eight or nine million in the whole continent. They had been a very strange people, full of contradictions, adaptable and obstinate. With courage and endurance they had pioneered the land, only to ruin it with greed and lack of forethought. They had drawn a hardy independence from the soil and had maintained it with pride and yet they had allowed themselves to be dispossessed by the most fantastic tyranny the world had ever known, money in the hands of the few, an unreal, an imaginary, system driving out reality. They had their hardbitten realism and yet they co-operated in the suicidal fiction of production for profit instead of for use. They thought of Australia as a land of plenty and yet they consented to starve among the plenty. They lost the reality of their land to the fantasy of the Banks. They looked always to Government for redress and assistance but they were always scornful of their governments and with a persistent lawless streak in them. They loved their country and exalted patriotism as if it were a virtue, and yet they gave a greater love to a little island in the North Sea that many of them had never seen. They were hard drinkers and yet had puritanical prejudices and made difficulties against the purchase of their drink. Inherent gamblers, they legislated against gambling and then broke their own laws systematically and as a matter of course. Lovers of horseflesh, they had no feeling for the animals, sheep and cattle, by which they lived. They praised the country but lived in the cities, or they grumbled eternally of the land but would not leave it. There was no measuring their pride and yet they were unsure. They tried to live alone in the world when their whole civilisation was in the melting pot. They called the North the East and the Near North the Far East and it was to them an unknown place of mystery and menace. They were a fighting people —but not at home. They settled their differences at home by other means. The small people was prodigal of its armies; generation after generation, they swarmed out to fight and die in strange places and for strange causes. Tough, sardonic, humorous, they were romantics the like of which the world had never seen. Crusaders without a crusade, they fought for any cause that offered or for the simulacrum of a cause. They went to South Africa to fight against a people small and liberty loving as themselves. They fought in France and Flanders, Egypt, Palestine, Mesopotamia, for an imperial design from which they themselves sought to escape. Within a generation they were fighting throughout the world, for what they scarcely knew, for brave words and a coloured rag, for things that were only names being already lost. They fought with tenacity and élan, the bravest of the brave. Or was that the incurable romanticism of history? Knarf didn't think so, there were facts and figures to support it.

All that, and yet they weren't a belligerent people. It was as if there were two people, indistinguishable in peace time, the fighting tribe—the Anzacs, as they came to be called—and the others who didn't fight. At the first drawing of the sword the cleavage showed and apparently they accepted it. The armies were volunteer, both sections of the community joined together to refuse conscription. It was one of their gestures of freedom, the curious truncated liberty to which they held.

Knarf could think of the Australians as living in a perpetual high gale of unreason. Their whole life was stormy and perverse. They were city-dwellers and their cities were great vortices of energy that carried them nowhere. They strove enormously for the thing called profit. In competition men's efforts cancelled out, one against another; they could succeed only, one at the expense of another, but when competition merged into monopoly they were worse off, for as the forces became more powerful they were more destructive. A terrible logic worked itself out. There were those who saw the end coming and cried their warnings, but helplessly. When a man is caught in a conveyor belt he is not saved by realising his danger.

Life went like a cart on square wheels. Their houses were choked with useless objects and meaningless ornament, their shops with wasteful luxuries. Yet men were hungry. There was always too much and too little, never enough. Nothing was secure, neither bread nor faith, and man's confidence in himself and in his fellows was at last ruined by the cajolery of the advertiser and the propagandist, for advertising and propaganda were spokes in the wheel whose hub and circumference were profit, the iron wheel that ground men into gold which cannot nourish. It was all mad and strange and wanton, it poisoned itself and had issue in violence and violence begot death. "The Australian Fairytale" Lunda had called his book, a story so fantastic and remote that it was difficult to think of these people as fully human. That was the trouble with historians. They dealt in curios. They wanted to surprise their readers and to flatter today. The queer things had happened but they weren't the whole, any more than the stone stripped of its rosy pulp and glowing skin is the fruit. It had been life in a different key, it had been transposed not lost.

The Australians coming after the First People, disinheriting rather than inheriting from them, had laid a different pattern on the earth, a free pattern, asymmetrical, never completed, because their life was so disrupted, complex, and unreasoning. They had brought in the rhythm of flocks and crops, but that had never quite formed because the seasons to which they were bound were irregular then as now; there must always have been a sort of counterpoint. The imported beasts and grains must have striven with the blind instinct of their life to fulfil each its immemorial cycle, only to be thwarted by the irregularity of the climate, the unstable incidence of the rains. The pattern had been pulled aside, crazed, until after centuries of effort an adjustment, not perfect, but adequate, had been reached. The life of the Australians themselves had been based in part on this new fertility pattern which they had brought and were holding to the land rather by their obstinacy than by their reason, and in part on their political and economic conceptions, a flow of opposites, wealth and poverty, freedom and slavery, till you had a design in cross currents, in negations, in contradictions, that reflected itself, as it must, in the patterns traced by civilization on the earth itself. Knarf could see it from the watchtower of time—the clotting of life into cities, the irregular scattering of habitations over the country, the thousand and one reasons, apart from the main scientific reason—the only legitimate one, people would tell you—that were allowed to influence or even direct development, the haphazard network of the roads, the inequality of the dwellings, the movements of people and goods based on the fantasy of supply and demand. . . . After the simple incised pattern of the First People the Australians had left a sunken maze. Each people had reflected its own way of life in its design. The First People had lived scientifically, following a rational, adjusted, permanent design. The fragments of the handiwork and ornaments that survived were in the likeness of their lives, simple arrangements of lines and dots, naturalistic representations of animals, designs fed not by shallow conceptions of beauty but by deeper fountains of meaning. They were few or repeated. The Australians, having overthrown reason and ignored adjustment in the interests of their fantastic conceptions, begot a multiplicity of hybrid, unco-ordinated patterns and left upon the earth itself a half-meaningless scrabble. Their movements had been turbid and without rhythm. There had been a constant flux through the country of men looking for work, the need constant, the opportunity fluctuating with times and seasons. Few, even of those who were "settled," could retain their place for long; economic forces levered them out, sent them circulating rootless through the country or gravitating towards the cities. Then would come a change of wind, a thing called Depression, and many of those who had been drawn into the cities would be driven out again, travelling the roads looking for bread, to die on the roads as the last of the Pioneers died in the deserts but unsentimentalised, unregarded. . . .

The Australians had brought a new sort of death to the continent, —not overt violence but the unregarded, unrecorded death of dumb men and beasts, bound luckless upon the machine. Death as the unplanned by-product, the leakage of the system,—animals caught by drought on overstocked pastures, men caught by depression in overproduced cities, a needless repeating pattern—the softfooted death with the look of accident was not accident, but a part of the relentless logic of a way of life: the loneliness of condoned death.

All this side by side with pride and courage and independence, unvisualised for what it was. Knarf shivered in the dawn. This was one of the moments when, his spirit worn thin, he was oppressed by all the suffering that there had been in the world, especially the pitiful unrecorded suffering of those who died without redress or drama. It was as if he saw it still, like a lava stain upon the hills he loved so much. We may be just as blind, he thought, and because blind, cruel—or because secretly cruel, blind. They weren't inferior to us in mind or heart.

They loved this place, Knarf thought, they were the first to love it for it wasn't possible to think of the First People formulating an emotion so explicit and detached. He caught a glimpse of the landscape he could as yet hardly see, through the eyes of his imagination, as they must have seen it four centuries ago. He was brushed for a moment by that excitement of the spirit which was the secret manna of his gifts. These hills, these wide horizons, these aboriginal contours, unchanging and unchangeable, must have had an added lustre against the background of a more turbid world. We don't know peace, he thought, because we take it for granted. Life is not so fiercely indented as it used to be, more evenly spread, and so even our eyes cannot know the quality that this earth once had. It wasn't only the loveliness of peace, it was peace over against turmoil, it was refuge, it was home. If the sky was empty and the horizon unbroken, that was rest. These were not hills, they were the gentle breasts of the earth. Like a man suddenly realising that his retreat is cut off by the tide, Knarf thought "I belong as much with them as with today, with the Australians as with my own generation of a people who have no name."

It was nearly seven years now since he had gone down with Ord to the Centre on the coast because of the excavations. Ord and all the other registered archaeologists had been invited to view some fragments dug out of the channel of the old underground railway. The official circular had described them with dry enthusiasm as "of unique interest, probably part of a memorial pavilion which, as the result of bombing from the air, was carried through the crust of earth on which it stood into the railway excavations beneath, and then being covered with debris was completely forgotten until rediscovered in the course of tunnelling for sewage works. The exhibits include a stone figure, seated, almost intact, fragments of other figures possibly similar, portion of bas-relief and other exhibits which, although incomplete, are of the first importance." Because Knarf was in the constipated and dreary state of a writer temporarily deserted by his desire to write, Ord had said "Why don't you come too?" He had gone, more than anything else, in the perverse hope of pinning on Ord the responsibility for the tedium in which he was becalmed. To begin with, he had not been able to resist the pleasure that he always felt in the sea. From the first glimpse of it from the air, a dark blue band on the horizon, his heart had lifted, he had been stirred by the drama of its immensity and his sealed mind had become receptive again. The panorama of the coastline, the great procession of treeless headlands north and south, green, brown, bronze, dust, smoke, in diminishing tone, old and dogged; the scallops of apricot sand, the highlights of white surf, the voluminous blue of the ocean, the jewel-like harbour, the Centre so compact where once a great city had sprawled, invaded his brain like an intoxication of light. To walk upon the ground and perform the common routine had, in the hour after their arrival, been curiously unreal. His mind had been washed clear in that great draught of light.

As soon as they had eaten they went to the enclosure to view the relics. Knarf had first seen the colossus, that they now called the Brooding Anzac, as a dark shape against the sky. It had been raised upon a plinth, a sketched fragmentary reconstruction of the original pavilion. The construction of the figure, the curator of archæology pointed out, indicated that it was meant to be seen from below and it could not be justly estimated unless shown in a setting which at least sketched the original. It was possible to ascend to the platform on which the statue was set, should they wish to make a more detailed examination. Ord, who was in a vile temper, complained at once that headquarters took too much on itself; that the curator was an arrogant, insolent fellow who tried to score off all his colleagues by presenting them with a ready made arrangement on which he had the audacity to lecture them; that he took on his shoulders decisions which should be communal.

The colossus sat, looking straight before him, his stone arms resting on his stone knees, a soldier after battle, accoutred, his battle dress a rough swaddling on his tired limbs, an infantryman in a slouch hat, hard, lean, far-sighted, one who had covered great distances, a man worn down to bedrock, an immortal ghost in stone.

Knarf stood looking up at it, eliminating Ord's grumblings from his attention as something accustomed and meaningless. He was at once irrationally convinced that this stone figure had survived holocaust and time, not by chance, but because of some inherent quality in itself. The stone was charged with life. Just as its substance was harder and more enduring than the flesh of man whose likeness it held, so too the spirit that had been in him, dogged, enduring, obstinate, unfailing, was transmitted unchanged into stone. It endured because it embodied endurance. This was the thing itself, the surviving principle of man, grasped by the sculptor and set down in stone. As the stone preserved the life it copied, so the tension of the artist's imagination preserved the stone. This brooding, unheroic figure was immortal man. Knarf had one of those moments when his mind made what seemed to him a direct contact with reality, dead knowledge came to life in him, a world co-ordinated about this focal point. The thing that was illuminated in his mind was a truism, something that his mind had never doubted and his imagination had never before accepted. The men of the lost world, four centuries sunk in time, were as fully matured in their humanity as any man living, cut from the same living, continuous tree of life—only their circumstances had been different. Trapped in a failing world they had still had the strength and temerity to beget a new world, or there would have been no new world, no now.

There had been a frieze of these stone men, a wide-spaced hollow square. It guarded a shrine, an altar with the figure of a naked boy crucified upon a sword. The curator was working on that. He was making a marvellous job of it, piecing it together almost out of dust, you might say, with only an old fragmentary inscription that no one had been able to trace before to guide him. "He gave himself a good long start," Ord said bitterly. But Knarf could see the stone men up on their rampart, obstinate and brave, outfacing a world they could not save, defending the symbol of death and sacrifice, which was all they had to defend, against death and destruction. It moved him enormously—because, he warned himself with the residuum of his mind, I am a romantic which is the synonym for an untrustworthy person, one who is emotionally avaricious, as Ord would say. He hid everything that was in his mind from Ord.

Presently he followed Ord up the rough steps at the back of the plinth to the platform on which the statue stood, but proximity blotted out the whole conception. He was aware only of the roughness of the stone and of a certain disproportion introduced to counteract the height. He could not understand how a sculptor could work in the close disillusion of proximity and yet achieve the compelling long-distance effect. The height, though it was not great, disturbed him and he came down to walk on the grass among the scattered blocks of stone, stooping now and again to see if his awakened imagination could force any secret from them, and letting the images that had assailed him seep into his mind.

When Ord came down again he was in a better temper. "That sculptor knew his stuff," he said, "the detail's pretty accurate."

Knarf flared. "Do you know more than a contemporary? That thing was done from life."

Ord gave him one of those quick glances which reminded him of a delicate and prehensile tentacle thrust out for an instant from beneath a horny shell.

"*You* said that, did you?"

"I can't see anything else? It's the work of a great artist."

"Nevertheless artists by their very nature are inaccurate. I'd sooner trust a trained archaeologist of any period."

"Meaning yourself?" said Knarf with childish rudeness.

"Exactly," Ord answered imperturbably.

Knarf came back later alone. The gatekeeper who remembered him made no demur although he was about to close for the night. The enclosure was empty. From the wooden shed where the curator still worked with his long patience, piecing together the dust, a powerful blue-white light sent its diamond rays into the dusk. Knarf stood for a long time among the elegiac debris, staring up at the Brooding Anzac. The figure grew larger against the fading sky, the outline more fluent. The thought of flesh imprisoned beneath stone shook Knarf's heart. Touching him on the shoulder the gatekeeper told him in a subdued tone that he must lock up now.

Knarf returned again and again in the next few days, sometimes with Ord, sometimes alone. Ord was very busy examining and measuring the piece. This seemed almost perversely profitless to Knarf. What was there to do with such a thing but to look at it? It had no secret, no mystery, except the imagination that had informed its making and that could not be captured by any foot rule or by anything else except another imagination of the same quality. Knarf was developing some of the fetichism of a man in love. Between him and Ord there had developed a competition in vanities which masked the deep feeling to which one, if not both, was a prey. It was, in its very pettiness, a relief.

Ord was certainly at his worst. He had embarked with great gusto on a controversy as to the authorship of the Brooding Anzac with another archæologist, Lunda—a man, as he said privately, who had sold his honest trade of archaeologist to the arts by becoming also a writer. Ord, with a great display of pedantic learning, maintained that it was by a Dutchman named Hoff, who had been official sculptor or laureate and who had died sometime in the nineteen thirties in the narrow gulf between two great wars. "One of the fortunate," Ord said, coming, surprisingly, out of character and as quickly retiring into it. Lunda contended, with a more showy virtuosity, that it was by Raynor, an Englishman, famous for his bas-reliefs, the head of a famous academy. He lived on far into the troubled century, forsook his art for public affairs, became a guerrilla leader in the Blue Mountains, and there came to an unrecorded end. One man, thought Knarf, who became the thing he imagined. He didn't believe that either of them had sound evidence, this was just a game they played, building such patterns as they could conceive out of the fragments of evidence that they had. History is a creative art, a putty nose. You can make what you like of it. Event, immediately it is past, becomes a changing simulacrum at the mercy of all the minds through which it must seep if it is to live, memory passed from hand to hand, coloured with prejudice, embroidered with fantasy, flattened with pedantry, and finally served up in all seriousness as history. Ord made him think these things. It was impossible to be sure whether Ord believed his own thesis or whether he was perpetuating some sort of solemn joke, burlesquing the whole controversy, or whether he did believe it and mocked himself as well as his colleagues as a sort of insurance against being made a fool.

Knarf didn't know or care. He had seen with his own eyes history pegged down at one point. He had trodden in the footsteps of another man's imagination and it did not matter at all that there were four centuries of time between them. The impact had engendered that excitement in his mind which meant further creative effort. His unattached imagination had found its host. Slowly, in the years since, he had beaten that moment into shape and fashioned from it something that was his own. The book that was just finished was not obviously related to its source and yet it was rooted there and the Brooding Anzac had been its touchstone. What had been begun in that moment was finished in this, as far as processes can finish. This book was like an island of reality in his life. The poetry that he had written as a young man, the dramatic work of his maturity, seemed to him now uninhabitable, like stiff garments upon cold limbs. He believed that his life would not accumulate enough energy for another major work. His writing had caught up with his living and had consumed all that the years had hoarded. The shock of finishing a book is almost as great as the shock of beginning it. He had been safe in it, uneasy but safe, and now he must go out again into objectless living and expose his newly stripped mind to the harsh light of a world he had not made. The book was finished and yet his mind was not discharged. It was as yet unshared. Today he would talk to Ord about it, they often had talked about it but never as a whole. Ord, who knew perhaps all that had been salvaged of the old Australia, had been his quarry. He, at least, had come, long ago, to take the work for granted and that was a help. Knarf must talk to someone, get this book that was still and finished into the world. A book is as implacable as an unborn child, a rising day, inevitable in its demands.

It was as if the light were coming not from the east only, but quickening in the earth itself, like a flush of blood beneath a transparent skin. The river was no longer like steel in the primitive darkness, it was silver-blue. The whole picture was developing under his gaze like a photograph in the acid bath. He could see everything as far as the horizon in an unearthly quiet clarity; first it was shape, the empty mould of form, and now the colour was flowing back into its accustomed channels. Following the horizon north to south as far as the eye could see, was a broad dark blue band, the rain reserve. Through the west there was one of these five-mile belts of trees in every hundred miles so that from the air the country had a wave pattern. From the river almost to the rain reserve stretched the irrigation garden. It was like a great sampler in the dark frame of its wind-break, corduroy of vines, groves of deciduous fruit-trees among which autumn had begun to burn, the bas-relief of vegetable gardens, threaded with blue where the water channels lay. Farther away, to the north, lay the fodder crops, a solid mass of intense green. It was the focus of the whole scene, and yet it was a relief to look away, to comfort the eyes with the tranquil hills. They appeared empty but for the roads with their double line of trees and the clots of greenery that marked the presence of a house here and there. They were pasture land. The countryside was, of course, much more thickly settled than it had been, since the hundredfold improvement of the pasture, the larger flocks on smaller areas, and scientific culture generally had concentrated the population. The wool, with the better pastures, had deteriorated, it was said, but that was the sort of old man's tale that usually got about.

If we looked back at today instead of living in it, we would say it was the Golden Age, Knarf told himself pedantically. There has never before in the whole history of man been anything like this, peace and plenty. The river was once the last refuge from the desert. In the worst times the desert reached the river itself, running long red fingers into the good lands, its dusty breath carried blight for hundreds of miles. The river itself was half silted up, the excoriating dust ground the faces of the hills. Rabbits, driven by the desert into the cultivated lands, devoured everything before them. Men went out to massacre them because both could not survive in the denuded land. They killed and killed but hunger was stronger than fear in the creatures, and despair than will in men. For over a century the land had lain dead, virtually deserted, but towards the end of the twenty-second century, because it had been left alone, it began very slowly to rejuvenate itself. It had taken more than a hundred years of conscious effort of replanting, of vast engineering schemes that tapped the snows of the Alps and brought water into the dredged and deepened channels of the old rivers, to rehabilitate it completely. Knarf told himself the story, bricking in the hollow spaces of his mind with it. Would the desert ever come again, was the possibility of it still there, giving the brilliant scene its phantasmal quality? Had it the sharp-edged beauty of something threatened? Or was that only a suggestion of the restless imagination? Nothing is lost, nothing ends. I don't know that, I only feel it. Didn't the desert pass like a sponge over the land, wiping out all that had gone before? So that this is a new beginning? This place has never been standardised either because it is too new and cannot catch up to the older places—or because it cannot forget that it was once a frontier. Frontier people are different. A part of life has gone underground here like the old rivers. We don't quite fit the world pattern, we accept the mould but we don't fit it.

The past isn't dead because it left so few material traces. It excites the imagination the more because there is so little evidence. It has gone back into the earth. The bark huts and the slab houses, the weatherboard and the mud walls have all gone back. The earth accepted them as it would never accept us. Our houses don't really belong. They come from the north, but where the northern houses were flimsy, of wood and paper, these are solid, of concrete and glass, but it's the same pattern essentially, with a hint or two brought back from Egypt by the Crusaders. No, the earth wouldn't receive us back so willingly and we're as much of the earth as of civilisation. We're a frontier people, all this doesn't fit us or we it.

That's heresy, Knarf thought suddenly. Of course we don't fit, nobody does. Men have to be held to good ways. Civilisation isn't natural. It's an art and a science. Left to nature this would be semi-desert, left to ourselves we would be semi-barbarians. To go our own way would be to go back. Engineering must help nature and laws must help man. Anything else is degeneracy.

The Centre, because his house was a part of it, did not come fully within Knarf's survey. It was small, one of the smallest, because there was no industry here, only the irrigation gardens to be tended and the few jobs there always were about a Centre. The workers' dormitories usually such a feature in any Centre, were only miniature. It was looked upon as a health camp because the work was easy and the dry air so good, and it was usual to send here young people who had some defect, or those who had overstudied or had recently suffered an illness. For this reason they were on the whole less high-spirited and played a smaller part in the communal life, than was usual. There was, of course, the school and the Service House, the clinics for man and beast, the library in its grove—how many hours had he spent there in a perfect daze of tranquillity, lifting his eyes from the printed page to stare between the columns and the tree trunks at the broken panorama of the river, to listen to the clock ticking like a pulse, to consider the shafts of sunlight thick as honey pouring through the bookish air from the high windows, till he sickened—the Pavilion where every citizen had the right to exhibit, for a period not longer than one week in any year, anything that he had made or grown, whether it was a flower, a cake, a picture, a statue, or a toy. In some of the big Centres the Pavilion was a vortex of criticism and emulation, but here it was quiet enough. Few came to exhibit their work and because they were few they were embarrassed. Knarf thought he might take the manuscript of his book and lay it there for a week as a matter of principle. On the communal altar, he thought with a wry smile. No one would have the curiosity to turn its leaves, not even Ren. Least of all Ren. Something failed to ignite. The citizens of the Centre weren't interested in Making and the wisest provisions of the authorities could not force them to it. When he said that to Ord, he'd asked in his dry way "Aren't you the obvious person to breathe life into the Pavilion?" And then, with the way he had of ignoring his own remarks he had gone on to point out that the Pavilions were the last vestiges of the old Country Shows and that they had been hotbeds of competition and were themselves vestiges of much more ancient orgies. "Of corroborees, too?" Knarf had asked, accepting the red herring and responding to the interest old things always had for him. "No," Ord had grunted, "they were collaterals."

The face Knarf turned to the light was the face of an individualist. It had become, in a moment and for a moment only, bitter and brooding. His mind had returned from its wide half-feverish excursion through the ages to its narrowest base, himself. The sight of the Pavilion just now in his exalted state had uncovered an old distress in his mind. He could not bring down fire to his own altar. To his wife, to his son Ren, he was a dead man. He had standing but not here. His life did not mesh with the life of his community. Of all the people here most might be expected of him and he gave least. He was a prisoner in himself. If he cared only—as he sometimes thought he cared—about his work, he could not expect it to be otherwise. That he was so frequently now, in his forty-seventh year, a prey to desolation and doubt, did not matter to anyone. A man who by his work as a writer sought an audience found himself without an audience for his personal drama. It was as if he had given his power to his work and now was bereft. This form of depression descended upon him with peculiar violence whenever he finished a book. This last book had sustained him for a long time; now it was finished, his mind had rocketed into the blue only to fall back into emptiness, an emptiness that was worse for being familiar. In these moods he had tried going into one of the big

Centres but it had not helped him. If he attracted attention it irritated him, hampered his movements, gave him the sense of being a prize animal in a stall; if he avoided it he felt neglected and the velocity of life in the city left him utterly lonely. He would return but only to dullness and emptiness. He would be haunted by a vision of the country, by the belief that there was a ritual assuagement to be drawn from the earth. He would walk out into the hills, walk till he dropped and then lie unresisting in the grass, breathing its warm sappiness, feeling under him the beating of a heart greater than his own, waiting for peace to storm his nerves and possess him. But the moment never came. The ants bit him, the sun went down and he had to rise and make his way back, dog-tired.

The Centre now looked drugged with quiet, no one stirred although this was to be a most unusual day, a meeting of all citizens for a consensus of public opinion. Soon enough there would be plenty of bustle, even if it were only of the domestic order, and by eleven o'clock the first infiltration from the countryside would have begun. Ord would be here and, although he was exasperating sometimes, he was stimulating, his mind dry and sharp like herbs rubbed between the hands. Sardonic and combative, there was something comforting about him. They would talk about the book. Ord was the only person he could talk to about his writing. Ord infuriated him, drove him to defend and justify himself. Many an idea he'd beaten out in the heat of opposition. Ord had no leaks in his mind, none that Knarf had ever discovered. It was as strong, unsentimental, impersonal, as an anvil; as an anvil he would use it. It was flattery enough that he had his place in Ord's uncompromising world, for he wasn't a friendly man or liked, as little a respecter of prejudices as of persons. For that reason people were all the more ready to believe that he excelled in his subject. But for Ord the book would never have been written—without the long walks through the countryside, the unearthing of relics the more stimulating to the imagination because so naive, the circles of crumbling cement which Knarf had thought the last remnants of forts but which Ord said were silos or wheat reservoirs, the depressions in the grass that Ord told him were the traces of dams, a form of water storage so primitive that it suggested thirst rather than plenty, the just discernible trace of some homestead among the grass or close growing trees. It was Ord who had traced the course of the old railway, who had dragged him fifty miles to the site of some once flourishing town and with immense erudition had located the important buildings, mostly banks and hotels. There was nothing to be found, no treasure, no museum pieces, no relics of cultural interest, only the blind hieroglyphic of a life long lived and effaced, scattered among the undulating hills and on the banks of the river. It was different in the great cities of the coast. There the light had never been extinguished, but here it had been rekindled. There was a hiatus, a snapping of the thread, so that our life had a beginning and theirs an ending. And it was here, in the least remunerative field, that the great scholar, Ord, the archaeologist, was happiest. The purest essence of his science was to revive these vestiges, and so he was content to live on the family holding ten miles out from the Centre and neither to bear any part in the work of the place nor to comply with the requirements of the Bureau of Statistics from which he drew his allowance. This worried them, but not him. He resisted all their persuasions to work on what they called "assignments of universal importance" and continued indefatigably with the compilation of his big book "Riverina in Australia," making of it an excuse for standing aloof from all the local interests, at once a claim and a refusal, a life work and an alibi. Knarf knew that under this pose of stubborn rationality there quickened a strong imagination, that Ord could not have held to his task without this secret nourishment of the spirit, yet that it was so hidden made their friendship easier. There was no competition and yet it was open to each to mask his strongest feelings under an assumption of hostility or even contempt.

Today would mean different things to many people, an excursion, a rare taste of political excitement, a break in routine, but to Knarf it meant that Ord would come and that they would talk about his book and that in the passion of conflict the book would come alive to him again, or so he hoped. He looked forward to it with eager trepidation. He wished he were not so tired. He weighed his reserves of strength and endurance against the day. Sometimes he got more out of himself when he was tired than when he was fresh; a night without sleep keyed him up when a good night relaxed his nerves and left him spiritually foundered in a featherbed of indifference. He had made today his sticking point. After years spent on the book he had suddenly, a couple of months ago, determined that it must be finished by today, that this was the final outpost of endurance. If he allowed it to run on longer, after the peak of his effort was passed, it would spoil. Last night he had made the final effort to gather the whole into his imagination and synthesize it in a single flame, subjecting it once again to the melting fire of his imagination in a last effort to anneal its weakness. And today was important because he knew Ord would be forced to come into the Centre for this fantastic business of the vote, and, although he would have come at any time, grumbling perhaps, but never for a moment hesitating or delaying, the formal occasion made the whole affair easier and more natural. Secretly these subterfuges were important to Knarf. He made his way through life by a series of little concealed artifices, as a fugitive might cross this undulating country, taking advantage of every fold in the ground, every tree and bush — as doubtless fugitives had in the days of the melting pot. Knarf's mind was brushed with homesickness for a world in which overt or objective danger gave man peace from himself, the world of his book with its driving necessity, its heroic extremity. He had thought so long on it that he belonged there now, more than here where the *tabula rasa* of his life frightened him. Ord had hit on some kind of truth when he said, "You're writing your own autobiography, aren't you?" Now it was over, the book was closed against him and he was a man shut out. "I am shut out of mine own heart," one of their poets had written. Our thoughts, like our blood, root deep in the past. Knarf was none the less alone for that thought. The work of years had left him, he was alone, he was forty-seven years old and life had been too simple. There had not been enough pain and distress, not even enough event. His lot as a man was still unfulfilled. If it were not behind him then it must be before. His foot was on the brink of an unseen trap. Something will fill this vacuum in my heart, some folly or pain. I have done nothing but write. I have never even loved any one except Amila—and Ren. His son's name was a stone blocking the channel of his thought. A shaft of real pain shot through the vapour of his not altogether unpleasing melancholy. Through the boy he was vulnerable as he no longer was in his own person. Ren was involved in today's business, he didn't know how far or how deeply. Knarf reproached himself because he knew so little. He had taken no trouble to find out. Because he had been so wrapped up in his own work he had come to this day, which he suspected of being a crucial one for

Ren, quite unprepared. He must talk to Ren—but perhaps it was already too late. A relationship could not be built up in a conversation. The chances were that he could neither help nor understand at the eleventh hour. He knew very little of what Ren thought or felt, only suspected that he did both abundantly. On one of the few occasions when Lin's grudge against him had become articulate, she had accused him, with a bitterness that suggested that the idea had been working in her mind a long time, of keeping everything, all his thought and energy and emotion, for his books. She even seemed to think it was because of this that they had had no more children. He had grudged the giving of life and blind nature had recognised it. His fatherhood, as a spiritual relationship, had always seemed to him accidental and precarious. Nor was there much that was motherly in Lin, though always now her eyes went past him to Ren and he had seen a dumb greed in them that horrified him. Lin, in a way, had remained immature. Though she was over forty her youth had not left her, it had hardened, so that she was like a fruit turned woody. She was still waiting for heaven knew what improbable spring. She was disappointed, vaguely, envelopingly, and she blamed him for it. Opportunity, both before and after her marriage, had been as much open to her as to any one else, but she had not risked taking it. She had wanted her husband, home, and children to absorb her, and when it hadn't been like that she blamed Knarf for her inability to deal with her own life in her own way. The situation was chronic and insoluble. He had nothing to give. Even with the best will in the world he could never have given her what she wanted. He didn't know if Lin had ever loved him; if she had, she lacked the power to make that love a reality, a cogent force. He knew her so well and yet she had never come into the full focus of his mind. She was not quite as real as the characters his imagination had created.

Lin would not like today because the house would be full of his friends, people she did not understand and with whom she was painfully awkward. Awkwardness at her age was an ugly thing and she knew it. Above all she disliked Ord. But she would do her part by preparing them a good meal and supplying all their wants—only it would be without grace or kindliness. Her hostility never rose beyond a certain point. All through their married life it had been rising to this point just short of danger and falling ineffectually away again. Today, too, she would resent and comply and both would be valueless. Knarf found that he had no idea what Ren thought of his mother, how much he loved her or how much she irked him. He might have been Amila's child for all he resembled Lin.

The rim of the sun was showing above the horizon like the edge of a golden coin. A few small clouds had collected like flecks of fire on the background of golden light. The day had rounded out, it was bright, fine, and still. Knarf turned slowly, sweeping the wide circle of the horizon with his eyes. Deep in his heart he saluted the day. He was alive. He was a creator and had completed his task. He stood alone and the miracle of light lifted his spirits. The myriad thoughts of the last half-hour had not so much passed through his mind as stood in it; all were of things with which he had long been familiar. They came to him as the scene slowly came out of darkness into light. They had evolved as the unborn child evolves and as, his imagination believed, the country before him had evolved from past to present in the changing light. In half an hour, following a natural process, his life had co-ordinated, with himself as pivot, the world of his imagination and the unresolved pattern of his life. He had laid three worlds one on top of the other, like three plates, and each was his. He had to steady himself with his hands upon the balustrade.

## II

Ren came lightly up the stairs to the roof. When he saw his father leaning on the parapet he had an unexplored impulse to turn back. His bare feet had made no sound on the stone. It was simply his unwillingness to have his mood destroyed by contact with an immovable object. All people over forty were immovable objects, even when you were proud of them as he was, sometimes, of his father. Often his father made him feel flimsy, papery, and above all he didn't want to feel that today. He went and stood beside his father. Knarf didn't greet him but shifted into a more companionable attitude and smiled with his eyes at his son.

"It's going to be fine," Ren said. You could tell he felt proprietary towards the day.

"You'll have a good day for it," Knarf agreed.

"A lot will be riding in as the weather is so good. Some will have started now."

There was a little movement in the square below. Someone was dashing water on the flags, a boy with a basket of flowers in one hand was crossing it, whistling and seeming to shuffle up the new sunlight with his feet, doors were standing open and a fine reticulation of sound was beginning to invade the air. More distantly, the roads were empty and in the hills, sculptured in full relief by the morning light which left blue shadows in every small valley and depression, later to be flattened by the full sun, nothing moved. But Knarf could see in his imagination the little groups already assembling in the courtyards of distant farms, the smell of coffee and hot cakes in the air, the horses stamping, the crisp freshness that touched faces and voices to brittle sharpness, the riding away, the closing in of sunny silence on deserted buildings. He saw the boys and girls wrapped in their oatmeal-coloured cloaks, looking alike, cropped heads, straight slender bodies. Only when you had watched them for some time would the girl betray herself by some softer, more fluent movement. Behind would come the older people and the man would often have a child in front of him, tented in his cloak. Citizens coming in from their farms to vote in the city would not have looked much different, nearly three thousand years ago, riding over the thymy hills of Greece. People travelling didn't change much. They would have looked the same, too, in the Middle Ages, going on pilgrimage or riding to fairs, only then the clothes were brighter. The chief difference now was that here were no young men and women, only adolescents and older, steadier people. Knarf was not really thinking about these things; the images just flashed up at him, first of people riding immemorially through the sunny autumn morning, and then of the roads at mid-day beginning to prickle with flashes of light where the glass and metal of speeding watermobiles caught the sun.

"What's the order of the day?" he asked Ren. "At what time is the vote to be taken?"

There was just a hint of patience in Ren's voice as he answered. His father must be the only man in the commune who did not know all about today's great experiment and who was not stirred by it. He could almost hear Sfax say in his negligently hearty way,

"Practise on the home circle, laddie. If we can't even get the intellectuals, where are we? It's your job, you know." He didn't appreciate how much easier it was to talk to strangers and how much more readily they listened.

"The vote is to be taken at four o'clock. The workers will knock off at 2.30, which will give them time to bathe and change. They'll line up on the north side. The citizens will stand on the other three sides. Everyone's asked to be in their places at ten to four. The loud speakers will warn them. There'll be a sort of cordon round there. The votometer will be on the platform beside the library. Those are the indicators under the tarpaulin, they will show the automatic result. At four o'clock the motion will be read from the Library steps and everyone will be asked to keep silent for two minutes and record his vote. Think it, you know. You see how simple it is, absolutely foolproof? No one has to do anything but stand still and just make a mental affirmation or denial, no possible interference. Sfax says people won't even be able to cheat themselves. They won't be able to think one way and vote another, because it is the strongest element that will record. Sfax says that democracy always fell through before because it wasn't scientific. The votometer records the unadulterated will of the people."

"How?" asked Knarf.

"I don't think I can explain how. It's very complicated. I don't suppose anyone but Sfax really understands it. He did try to explain it to me a bit, in general terms you know, but I don't think I'm very good at passing it on. It depends on the recording of thought waves. Wireless telegraphy was the first crude exploitation of wave records in the ether. Later it was possible by a refinement of the apparatus to record the thoughts of the individual. Scientific justice. That must be a century old. Sfax has carried it a step farther. He can record mass thinking. As far as I can make out, thinking isn't, well, just gelatinous, it's words, and when you think words it's a physical as well as a mental process. You say it in an inaudible truncated sort of way, your larynx contracts infinitesimally but enough to make what you're thinking tangible and therefore record-able. Thinking is a bit more than that. It's words in jelly, so to speak, and even the jelly weighs. It's awfully confusing when you think of complicated things, but when it is just 'yes' or 'no' it's possible. You might put it this way. No is bass and Yes is tenor.

They're different weights. Poor old Sfax would be just about green if he heard the mess I was making of this."

"I do at least make something of what you're saying. I don't suppose I'd be able to understand Sfax at all."

The boy took it seriously. "No one can touch Sfax," he said, "he beats them all. The instrument records its finding on a graph and the purport is passed on in terms of light—I don't know how but Sfax says that's quite simple—and it's the light that works the indicators. They are photosensitive. There!" he grinned, "It's really instantaneous, but two minutes is a good round figure. Anyone could keep his attention focused for two minutes."

"Two minutes' silence was an old custom. People used it to mark great occasions. Two minutes' silence and everything stopped in the cities, the noise suspended, the workers immobilised. Thinking of the glorious dead. A million and a quarter people in one place. That must have been a tidal wave in the ether. But perhaps they didn't think at all, or only a few of them did. It's a far cry from that to this, but it's curious to see the same ideas crop up again. It would be an interesting job to tabulate the ideas in the world, there wouldn't be so many, and trace their permutations and combinations. It would be possible but," his enthusiasm flagged, "unprofitable."

"Yes," said Ren, and Knarf could see that this academic excursus into the past had damped him. Only today was important, and to suggest that it was not fresh minted in time was heresy.

"How are you going to prevent multiple voting? I mean enthusiasts will just keep on shouting Yes or No inside their minds for the whole two minutes, recording hundreds of votes and upsetting the calculation."

"That has been thought out. The instrument works with a shutter, rather like a camera. There are going to be three exposures during the two minutes, each one just an instantaneous flash, three sections of public opinion. Of course some people will give more of their attention than others and their vote will be recorded three times, some perhaps will only record once. But public opinion is like that, isn't it? It isn't even and flat. This is going to be truer than all those old crude forms like the ballot. Each flash will be recorded in detail on the graph and, in general terms, on the indicators. The indicators are just long glass cylinders stood on end, golden fluid will rise in one to record the yes's, silver fluid in another to record the no's. In an affair like this you have to take psychology into account. The graph wouldn't mean anything to a lot of people."

"Is every one to have a vote — men, women, children?"

"Men, women, children, and dogs. An all-in vote. It's simplest. There will always be a few people, too old or too young or too stupid, to understand or be bothered. To forbid them to vote would be, well, invidious, so we've provided for them another way. There's a third indicator with black fluid — the discard, the extraneous stuff will be recorded in that. It's not important, of course, just keeps things tidy."

"The informal vote."

"It won't amount to anything here because in a small commune we've been able to prepare every one. In some of the big places it won't be so easy. That's one of the reasons why the Tenth was chosen for the first try-out." Knarf thought guiltily of the little pile of literature lying somewhere unopened and unread under the papers on his desk. "The indicators, Sfax says, aren't really scientific, but they give an approximate idea of the result. People can see it at once and know there hasn't been any tampering with results."

"Couldn't some one tamper with the instrument?"

"I don't think so, it's so complex, and they would have to understand it before they manipulated it. No one does understand it completely except Sfax. He'd rather die than tamper with *facts*." Ren said that proudly.

Sfax was his hero. Knarf remembered how, when Ren was a little boy, he used to trot round after Sfax, who was five years older and a great man in a little world even then. Ren had been so eager and loyal, content with very little and not even getting that. Occasionally, if he could be useful, Sfax would take notice of him, and then the little boy would be wild with delight. Sometimes Knarf had wanted to knock Sfax's clever head on the wall, but he knew Ren would never have forgiven him. That had made him want to knock Ren's gullible little head on the wall, too—when he noticed, which wasn't often. He'd treated Ren a bit like that himself. He could remember moments in his childhood that had been warm and sweet—when the child had been out all day and he had had to carry him home, asleep in his arms. That warm confiding young body had comforted him. There had been other times when Ren had turned to him in trouble,

or with his quick charming smile had wanted to enlist his interest
in some treasure. When Knarf wanted consciously to repeat these
moments they had generally fallen flat and he had lost patience.
He'd decide that Ren was too young to be a companion, he'd have
to wait, and for months, wrapped in his work, he'd take no interest
in the child. Adolescence had made each shy of the other. Perhaps
the boy had wanted help, understanding at least — he had not
troubled to find out. It was just another troublesome phase he must
wait for the boy to out-grow. Ren was nineteen now; in four months
he would go for his compulsory social service. For eight years Knarf
would see little of him and when he came back, if he did, he would
be a man established in his own life and independence, very likely
with wife and child. They would meet cordially, but as strangers.
When Ren had wanted him he was too busy. It was too late now.
What could he do in the matter of getting to know his son in four
months, when nineteen years of indifferent intimacy stood between
them. Lin's bitter taunt came back to him, "A man who keeps
everything for himself doesn't father children." He glanced quickly
at Ren, who was looking out across the hills, barely holding in a
smile, young, frank, and undefeated. "I love him," he thought
ashamedly, his heart turning over with pride. He wasn't listening to
what the boy was saying.

"The workers' vote was a much more difficult nut to crack. Some
of the committee wanted workers' electorates, I mean for them to
vote as workers and not as part of the general commune. But that
wouldn't do. It'd just make a hard and fast division, and, besides,
we'd hamstring ourselves. It's the young people against the old, the
people who want change and an open road against those who don't.
If the young people, my people, are shut up in a few electorates
they'll be outnumbered in the whole, but if they vote wherever they're
stationed they'll have the chance to swing a lot of others. That's
tactics. But that's in the future. It doesn't really come up yet."

"You're on the council of this Union of Youth, aren't you?"

"Yes," Ren buttoned down his pride. "Of course, knowing Sfax
helped me there," he admitted. "We're strong, father. It's — it's new
life."

It was evidently Sfax's show, and this time Sfax was letting Ren
play. Ren wouldn't always be a suppliant. It was time he had his
part in things, however he came by it. That it was in Sfax's gift was

only a fiction, a generous fiction. Knarf couldn't bring himself to like Sfax. Too many brains, chocked with brains, and not enough of anything else. At twenty-five, although he was still in his compulsory social service, he was already a figure. He'd go on and on. Some day he would be one of the top ones. A genius for mechanics, and that was everything, the way things were now. What Knarf couldn't make out was why Sfax should interest himself in a movement that wanted to bring in change, because the world as it stood was just made for men like him. The will to dominate, probably. Men's vanity often took the form of wanting to do something they weren't fitted for. A chance to unload this fancy machine of his. Sfax in the long run would prove a poor end to enthusiasm, the too smooth, too clever, young man. . . . Oh God, I am thinking about Ren, not listening to him, and it's a listener he wants. It's not really me he's talking to, though, I mustn't run away with that idea in my vanity. He's so full of this thing he'd talk to any one.

Ren was saying "Today's only an experiment, a sort of dress rehearsal, and the votometer isn't important in itself, only a means to an end, but we wouldn't have got this chance without Sfax and his votometer. It was something tangible to put before the Council. They gave permission to hold the test on the grounds, I suppose, of scientific enquiry. The right sort of facade and all that. Sfax is one of them and one of us. That's tactics. It lulls them until we get the whole movement under way, and then — well, it will be too late to head us off, we'll have captured public opinion, and that's important even in a scientific state. It's going to begin here today, in the Tenth Commune. We're fighting them with their own weapons and they're too stupid to know it. It's scientific revolution. You think it's just a gadget, don't you?" It was the quick, suspicious thrust of one who has uncovered himself dangerously.

"No, Ren, no. I can see farther into a stone wall than that."

"Look at the way things are now. Everything is in the hands of the Regional Council, and the Regional Council is drawn from the branch of the Scientific and Technical Congress, not even by ballot, by lot—and the Congress itself only represents about eleven per cent of the community. The greater the power the narrower its basis. I know the theory. It sounds all right, but it isn't. Man's first need is to eat. His second need is to be clothed and housed, and so on throughout all the items of the good life. The rational means of achieving these things is through the ordered functioning of the scientist and technologist. The good life can only be assured by the specialists, they are the guardians of civilisation. The work of the world is done by men and women between the ages of twenty and twenty-eight. You're called up for service and you're processed, more or less, given the once over by the experts. The bright ones get the good jobs, the dull ones get the dull jobs. And while you work, you may slave to improve yourself, pass examinations, build up a record, sweat blood, and pray to mumbo jumbo that you've chosen the right branch of technology, and that, when it's time for you to be passed out, there'll be a vacancy for you in the next hierarchy and you'll be kept on. There mightn't be a vacancy, or it might happen that there's a lot of talent about just then, or you might have a black mark against you for something quite irrelevant. Then out you go, and there's no getting back. The door is shut. You've earned your keep for the rest of your life, and you've a whole fortune in leisure to squander at will. It's all right for some who know what they want to do. But most of us are in the discard, waste stuff. The best have been selected and will carry on in the managerial jobs, the research labs, the higher teaching jobs, and from among them the ruling class will be chosen by chance. Fine, isn't it? Foolproof."

"And the voice of the demagogue was heard in the land," thought Knarf. For all that Ren was so passionately in earnest he was speaking with other men's voices. He was getting his ideas in cardboard cartons, but they were real ideas.

"That would be all right if it were all. But it isn't. All these things that we get, the minimum standard of well-being, isn't the good life. Not all of it, anyway. We've just got the habit of puffing out our chests and saying, 'Isn't it marvellous how every one has everything he needs? That never happened in the world before.' It isn't marvellous, because we're used to it and every one *ought* to enjoy a high minimum standard of well-being. It's the set speech on *all* public occasions, and we — all the young people everywhere — we just get bored sick with hearing it, because we haven't everything we want and we don't see why the works should stop just because everyone has enough food and blankets. The Rule of the Best was necessary when everything was in a frightful mess, but the mess has been cleared up and the Best aren't good enough. I mean they only look Best from one angle or for one purpose, and the same sort of people always being at the top and choosing the people who come after them, and not being responsible except to other people just like themselves, jolly well brings civilisation to a standstill, doesn't it? And it's not as if they didn't cheat. They do. The whole thing is supposed to be an open go, but it isn't. If you've got influence, if you've got a father or an uncle or a father-in-law in the Congress or the Council, you're safe. If you haven't you have to be a raving genius like Sfax or out you go. Running the machine — and the machine's pretty good now and doesn't take much running, I'll grant you the technicians have done that — it shouldn't be the only thing that matters. It's hell being young and knowing you're going to be knocked on the head when you're twenty-eight, and it's hell the way we're forced to compete, shove past one another, if we are going to get through."

Ren spoke of the young as if they were a separate people. So they were. Eight years of compulsory social service broke the family bond, opened a chasm between those who worked and those who had settled down into the final mould of their lives. Middle age came early and lasted a long time. Youth was a time of great activity; for eight years there was little intercourse between the young — the workers — and the older people. The young were a world in themselves, then suddenly on reaching a birthday, an artificial point, they were thrown out of that world, superseded, and dispossessed. They had had a communal life and now must build up an individual life. Often they married during the eight years and their wives or husbands were allies of the old life, now shut to them, against the new, which opened on nothing in particular. The departure of the young and their mating in a new place, that surely was a very old pattern repeating itself. But it should be a preparation and it wasn't.

If they belonged to a farming family their position was better, they had something to return to, provided that their work had not vitiated their taste for the soil. The system of privately owned farms, which to some seemed a grave anachronism in the socialist state, worked tolerably well. Ownership was hedged about by safeguards and restrictions, and filled a certain spiritual need in the community without becoming a menace to the structure of the state. Ownership was vested in the family group, not in the individual, a farm could be surrendered to the state, but not sold, ownership of land might not in any way interfere with the ordinary duties or rights of citizenship. It had been discovered that collective farming was not always economic, some land, some crops, were suited to it, others were not; hence the mosaic of small family holdings as auxiliary to the enormous state-owned farms. On them were produced the small crops and the difficult crops, and in them a continuous, hereditary feeling for the land was maintained. The farms were an element of plasticity in an already too rigid system.

But for the great majority of the young, the end of their compulsory service meant that they were thrown clear of life. The Technical Bureau absorbed the fortunate few, the family farms a few more, the creative arts still fewer.

"The end of life," said Ren, "isn't comfort, it's fulfilment. And most people are cut off from fulfilment, and only a limited number of sorts of fulfilment are allowed. The whole system is going into a coma. Don't you feel it? Don't you feel it is?"

"I haven't thought enough about how other people were getting on. I've lived in a specialised world."

"Your book." A little silence fell on Ren. The thought of his father's writing embarrassed him a little. It was something secret and unsharable. For so many years this book had been like another presence in the house. It was always there, it was the most important thing in the house, and yet he knew nothing of it and was too shy to ask. Some of his mother's hostility clung like mud to his mind. Was his father going to retreat behind his book now, leaving him to feel like a childish fool?

Knarf had spoken humbly. He only feared that Ren would withdraw this new confidence, so real, despite its stereotyped garb.

"What can you do about it, what is this practical programme?" The shining walls of the world had never seemed so unscalable.

Ren drew his brows together in a frown. "The essence of the programme is that there is none. It's no good countering one patent remedy with another patent remedy. We've got to break new country. It's so difficult to get people to see that. It's easy enough talking about this reform or that reform, but a radical change. . . ." He brought down his fist on the balustrade. "We've got to break down the wall first. That's rather another gadget like the votometer. The first objective is to establish and have recognised by public opinion another ruling body, co-existent with the Council. We're going to apply the plebiscite like a battering ram to that point — a supplementary council to represent all the interests not included in the Congress of Science and Technology, a debating club with a watching brief, if you like, to act as the mouthpiece of the general public. Unlimited publicity, no censorship. It might not be a success, but it would be a breach in the wall. It would have to learn how to function. There would be plenty of trial and error, but it would be something got going, a beginning that could be enlarged." Ren looked Knarf full in the eyes, the flush on his face was not from the sun, his thought had gathered momentum and he spoke more softly with a new bloom on his voice. "We must bring liberty back into the world, because life is poor and narrow without it. It's not a new idea, I know. It has been tried again and again. Our generation has to try, too. Even if we fail we'll be better off than if we had never tried. I know it all seems strange and wild, and if you say, 'What will you do with this liberty?' I won't know what to answer. There isn't anything to do with it till it exists. It's a state of mind and it makes its own content. The longing for it has never quite died out. There's that to work on, deep in everyone's heart. There'll be sacrifice and suffering, and a lot of people will say it's unnecessary and unscientific and just sheer perversity. But there are slaves and dispossessed people, for all the smooth and shining look of things. The young have hungry hearts and they don't mean to go unsatisfied. This council we want — it isn't the real thing, it's just a bar to pull on, to hoist ourselves up. People aren't going to be content with being useful. Even being fed and clothed makes a vacuum. We don't have to struggle for those things, so we've more strength and energy to struggle for other things. The unfulfilled can't be held down by the fulfilled even for their own good. Not for ever."

Knarf answered in the same tone. "One of the ancients, Laski, defined liberty: 'Liberty, therefore, cannot help being a courage to resist the demands of power at some point that is deemed decisive, and, because of this, liberty also is an inescapable doctrine of contingent anarchy. It is always a threat to those who operate the engines of authority that prohibition of experience will be denied. Where there is respect for reason there also is respect for freedom. And only respect for freedom can give final beauty to men's lives.' "

He asked himself, "What does Ren want? What drives him to this? We are all driven. Lin wanted me to make great demands on her, so that she would be freed from the responsibility of framing her own ,life, and I made none. I have built myself another world, a world of pain and struggle, and I have escaped into it, or half escaped. When I was Ren's age I sought the adventitious strength of a grand passion. Ren has found a great cause. He would live a poet's life. O life, carry me for I cannot walk by myself."

Ren said, "They thought everything there was to think and they said everything there was to say, but they didn't accomplish much. They made a sad mess of doing, didn't they?"

"There are so many by-products to whatever you do. It's hard to know where you are going."

"But we are going to be cautious, take it slowly."

"And today is going to be a test? You'll take a sample of public opinion and if it is favourable you'll have a platform, just a little one, to build on?"

"Yes. It will be a success. We are calling on something real in people."

"And then?"

"We'll go on building up public opinion and using the votometer to register it. We'll push this votometer in front of us like a screen. Today's only the beginning."

"The begining was ten thousand years ago. No one ever got past the beginning."

"We shall." He had the air of putting his certainty out of Knarf's reach, in a safe place known only to youth.

"I'm to read the motion before the vote, did you know?" The boy was obviously pleased. "I thought I wouldn't read it, I'd speak it. It's quite short."

"Are you used to hearing your own voice?"

"Not very."

"Say it to me now."

Ren did, without self-consciousness, standing very straight against the parapet, his back to the wide view.

My son, you look like a standard bearer.

"Citizens of the tenth commune, is it your will that the deliberations of your government be assisted by an auxiliary council, representing those elements of the population, both the workers and the private citizens, who have at present no direct voice in what vitally concerns them, to the furtherance of public liberty and private fulfilment. I call upon you to register your vote thoughtfully and sincerely by silently affirming or denying this proposal during the next two minutes."

"That's all. We don't want to stampede or cajole any one. We've taken care beforehand that they should know what it is all about. Now we ask a simple question. It's fair, isn't it?"

"You're very trusting," said Knarf, drily. "Fair to what? To whom? To human nature?"

Ren looked for a moment confused and hesitant. He had a conception of the whole as clear and complete as a soap bubble. It had withstood no shocks yet. It stood. He could find no flaw in it.

"To human intelligence."

"I suppose you've been about, canvassing this idea?"

"Yes, only inside the commune. Next year I'll be able to do more."

"What sort of response did you get?"

He was eager again. "Every one listened, they were very nice to me."

Of course they were, thought Knarf. Who wouldn't be? He could see Ren's eager face and confident eyes as he spoke his set piece. Who would want to rebuff him?

"Did they take fire?"

"No. We didn't expect them to. We've tried to keep emotionalism out of it."

"I don't think you'll find it as simple as you expect."

He could feel the boy stiffen and the thought was so clear in his mind, "Have you the right to criticise when you're the one person who hasn't taken any interest?" that he almost answered him aloud. "I haven't any right. Rights be damned. I don't want you to take a toss, that's all." Instead he said, "There were people who thought as you do in the old days. Do you know what they were called?"

"No."

"Liberals." I'm a pedantic fool, Knarf thought to himself.

Ren said very quietly, "You're thrown clear, father. But that doesn't hold for the rest of us."

They stood side by side in silence. Ren repaired in himself whatever damage had been done. The pause prolonged itself and they became aware that it was now full day. The world below them was awake and had taken on its usual aspect. The timeless interlude when they might exchange confidences had gone. The barriers were up again. It was as if a wall had moved back into place. They were both aware of it — with sorrow and relief. Knarf found himself looking at the familiar prospect with different eyes. The hill, the sky itself, had solidified, the Centre, the irrigation gardens, the firmly drawn road, were immutable. The flux of time was stilled.

He followed Ren's gaze, which was fixed upon an intermittent flash far out on the highway. As they watched, it resolved itself into a fast moving object, and presently became a covered truck painted in the green and gold of the Technical Bureau.

Ren said a little hurriedly, "I meant to tell you before, father, but you have been so busy. Sfax is making this his headquarters for today. It was the least I could do."

"Of course, Ren, of course."

"Oran is coming down from the Technical Bureau to watch the experiment."

"Oran, no less."

Ren grinned at him. "You didn't believe it was an important occasion, did you?"

"Does Oran make it important?"

"Sfax thinks so. He's practically life and death. If we can convince him . . . ."

"Convince him of what, Ren?"

"That we've public opinion behind us and that we've a perfectly genuine foolproof means of measuring it."

"I see. I've met Oran once or twice. Not a bird of very good omen, I should think. But he's Sfax's pigeon, of course."

"But we'll have to entertain him. Sfax'll have a heavy day, the instrument to install and test by four o'clock. It could not be done overnight, the adjustment is so delicate."

"Four o'clock is late for the vote. People from far out will have difficulty in getting home."

"We thought of that. It can't be helped. Sfax must do everything himself. You see, his reputation is at stake; he cannot trust anyone else to help him."

"In theory, everything a worker does during his period of compulsory social service belongs to the community. That evidently doesn't apply to Sfax."

Knarf regretted having said that. In a moment he had swept away all that had been built up between them. The waggon had disappeared from sight. In a minute it would be stopping in the square.

"I must go down," said Ren.

Knarf turned away from the parapet and went slowly into his pavilion. He did not want to watch Ren bring Sfax in triumph into the house.

# MORNING

Knarf heard Ord's step on the stairs, heavy and unhurried. He always imagined that Ord accentuated his brusqueness and clumsiness in protest against the matt stillness and synthetic tranquillity of this house. He broke through the garnered serenity as casually as if it were the wrapping about some carton whose contents he wanted to use. Ord, with his subtle mind sunk deep in his forthright flesh, its awareness as natural as sight, its steadfastness like the easy strength of his body. . . . Behind Ord was his brother's farm, unprotected white buildings in a brown paddock, the doors forever open, farm implements in the courtyard, motherless lambs in the kitchen, everything about the place used and worn with use, a smell of tar and baking bread and sun-dried linen, great joints sizzling in the big black oven, dogs as universal and as much at home as the children; Luza, the sister-in-law, her small merry eyes disappearing in her fat cheeks when she laughed, bearing her children without fuss, bringing them up with a fine cheerful impartiality, casual, plentiful, useful, slovenly, easy; Ord, setting out on his expeditions into the country, commandeering a couple of horses and one of his nephews or nieces at random, looking, in his shabby old cloak, a bundle of food in a knotted cloth before him on the saddle and a child riding beside him, oddly, disconcertingly, like one of the prophets; Ord, strangely formidable, coming slowly up the stairs with the heavy tread of fate. Nervousness started in Knarf like an acrid sweat. His face was no longer plastic flesh, but a mask of clay.

Knarf remained standing by the table in the pavilion. He saw Ord pause at the head of the stairs and look about him, take a deep breath of the day. It was not yet ten o'clock. He had come early as he had promised. He cut short Knarf's greetings, his eye had fallen on the pile of papers on the table.

"So," he said, running his thumb up their edges, leaving a dog-eared track, a gesture casual and familiar that Knarf did not fail to resent. "Finished? I thought that would be why you wanted to see me." He took the manuscript into his hands, weighing it as if it were Luza's latest baby, a pleasant, natural phenomenon that yet demanded his tolerance. But his words were from a different font. "I, too, have lived with this book for a long time. The thought that it was growing here, expressing a world we share and giving it back to life in a way I never could have done, has meant a lot to me. Now you are going to show it to me." The smile in his deep-set eyes made a trifle of Knarf's absurd nervousness. It was as simple as this. With Ord things always turned out more simple or more complex than you expected. "I may as well be comfortable." Ord stretched himself on the daybed, rumpling it to suit him.

Knarf began, "I've chosen the antique form of the novel, it is contemporary with the subject, and it gives the maximum room. There's been an all-round shrinkage of literary forms. . . ."

"Never mind that. We haven't a month."

With the thin crackling of paper, Knarf, without more ado, opened his book and began to read from his novel in a voice that gradually warmed to its task and modelled to what he read.

It was half-past seven on a Friday evening in November 1924. The year was precociously hot, the air heavy and tired, as if it were the end and not the beginning of summer. A woman was threading her way with exhausted haste across the great vestibule of Central Station. She carried a child in her arms, a little boy about seven months old. He was asleep, a deadweight, a big child but pasty, his face old and troubled even in his sleep, his head rolling uncomfortably to his mother's jerky movements and one arm dangling flaccidly against her side. It wasn't easy for her crossing the station in the crowd, hampered as she was with the child, a basket, and a number of parcels. It was a busy time, too. Travellers were arriving for the night expresses. Here and there they stood waiting, surrounded by luggage, inconvenient islands in the swirl; porters, shabby, seedy men with the anxious faces of those who perpetually lift and drag heavy weights, pushed their loaded barrows as best they could; the miniature yellow car with its long string of trailers, like the tail of a kite or the barges of the Danube, piled with mail bags and luggage, honked its way through, the mechanic python, the place spirit of the enormous cavern. Brisk streams of people, the crowd for the eight o'clock picture session, were being discharged from suburban trains and crossing the vestibule diagonally to the trams on the arched terrace beyond, many of them young people, dressed for the evening. They met another stream, laden, sluggish, tired, and sated, returning from late shopping. Most had parcels, packages of some sort, poor spoil from their sack of the city, unwieldy things, potplants, bags of fruit, household oddments; many dragged or carried their children. People clotted round the indicators, searching the boards with dazed, slowly comprehending faces for the times and platforms of their trains. They waited, impatient or phlegmatic, under the big clock, which hung as impersonal as a moon from the domed roof; they leaned on the sticky counters of the milk bar, which smelt of spilt milk, hot metal, and washing up; they sorted themselves onto platforms, pigeon-holed themselves in the lighted cylinders of the waiting trains, glad at last to be sitting down. Wheeled stalls with pyramids of oranges, pyramids of last year's apples wrapped in wisps of tissue paper, bags of peanuts, medleys of brightly packaged sweets and tobaccos, blocked the way and caught the passing traffic. The two big bookstalls flaunted coloured reading matter tier on tier, high over the heads of the people. Hard, searching light beat down. Noise, the clash of the trains, hiss of steam, the more distant whining of trams, made a false oppressive roof, and the close patina of innumerable feet on asphalt, of voices pulped into one long susurration, filled and distended the very air. The faint stir and excitement from the platforms where the streamlined engines waited and the bright compartments of de luxe travel received handsome or experienced luggage, and travellers distinct as individuals by right of the magnitude of their journeyings, and heard farewells touched with possible drama, soon expended itself in the great tepid listlessness that pervaded the homing crowds. For so many of the people the apex of the week had just passed — Friday, payday, the shopping night, was over, they were returning in a sluggish tide to their small homes and circumscribed orbits, carrying with them such fragments, often tawdry and lifeless, as they had been able to break off or capture in the course of their communal hunting. It was all without pattern or direction; no common purpose or thought held the crowd together, an infinite crisscross of destinies, in the mass illegible and insignificant. If there were a common denominator it must have been a sort of passive, unregistered disappointment, the inevitable concomitant of lives passed in the sight but not the possession of plenty. The seconds dropped off the clock like invisible, abrasive sand.

The woman had to stop, put her basket and parcels on the ground, while she rummaged in her worn handbag for her ticket. Her train was due to go in four minutes. The baby woke and whimpered, his tam-o'-shanter cap was falling off; she pulled it down ungently over his ears, picked up her luggage and hurried on. She had hoped to have time to go into the Ladies' Room to change the baby and feed him, but everything had taken longer than she had planned. He'd have to wait. She wasn't going to miss the train. Carrying him round all day had fairly dragged the heart out of her. If he went on sleeping it would be all right, but she felt an unreasoning black resentment against the child's inert weight, his complete dependence on her. She had only one thought and that was to escape this clearing-house of Babel, to go home. It had been an awful day. A day in town — the sort of thing she dreamed about — and this was how it had turned out. Childish disappointment blotted out everything else, and brought her to the edge of tears. To *want* to go home at half-past seven, to want that hole. That was what she'd come to, that was the measure of her misery.

The promised land was a mirage, she had been shown the delights and told roughly, "None of this is for you, go back where you come from and stay there." She had seen thousands of people enjoying themselves, Sydney on Friday night, and she was going home even before the shops shut. Behind her was the dream, the phantasmagoria, the only reality with which the poverty of her mind could clothe her need. Sydney lay behind her, its deeply channelled streets rimmed with light; from the air snakes of light belly-pressed to earth and the dark buildings piled over them; here and there a soaring facade with every window lit, neat, pale squares, or the crackling front of a motion-picture theatre. The streets thronged with people, spilling over from the narrow pavements on to the roadway; trams, tame juggernauts, easing their way through, coloured taxis moving at footpace through the whirlpool, then reaching its edge and flying out, released upon their journey, like sparks thrown out into the darkness. Crowds moving with interior currents, fast and slow, drugged, enchanted, eager, people living for an hour or so outside themselves, a hunting pack, hunting with eyes, with febrile, stunted imaginations, with unattached fishlike appetites, rather than with hands and purpose. Bright shop windows, endless wish fulfilment, emblems of paradisaical, unattainable living—model rooms in machine-made taste; eternal sylphs of papier mache arrayed in Fashion's dictates for spring, brides who will never go to bed with their waxen bridegrooms; wooden legs that will never lose their line in stockings that will never ladder, lingerie for a harem with no afterthought of the washtub; food voluptuous and ornate beyond the compass of any stomach; mumbo jumbo of perfumery, secrets of eternal youth and fadeless beauty at bargain prices; no promise too large or improbable, the constant titillation of every gambling impulse, bargains, lay-bys, hire purchase, everything under glass, men and women divided from the millennium only by a price ticket; trade far beyond commodities, selling hope and love and faith, battening on the living, tender substance of humanity and, unexpected retaliation, humanity feeding on this display as on a new pasture, satisfying eye and imagination for nothing, taking the bait and leaving the hook. The shops themselves half empty, whole departments blazing with light in garnished emptiness, marshalled and waiting, should some whim bring in the omnipotent crowd. Our Motto is Service. Just a few, a very few, serious customers. But if those great departments were closed and dark the occasion would be different. The whole system is soliciting the people. Only the floors where the bargain tables stand, the cheap arcades, the basements, are full. The shoddy of Japan looks like the wealth of the Indies. All the glory of the world is there in the cheapest and grossest terms. Plenty, plenty, plenty. These are not real things the people are buying, they are tokens. This is not a late shopping night for the public's convenience, it is a ritual, an orgy, but nobody knows it. It is a mystical sharing in the world's plenty, because there is no sharing. Its banality brings it within everyone's reach, its blatancy lifts it into the realms of religion, of mysticism. It is vastly, impressively unreasonable. The people do little that is reasonable. They eat certainly — out of paper bags as they walk, standing first on one tired foot, then on the other at soda fountains and milk bars, in restaurants, waiting behind the chairs of other diners to slip into their places at the dishevelled tables as soon as they vacate them. . . . The whirl of activity is clearly marked and restricted. Beyond it are empty streets where the wholesale business is done, closed buildings, street lights, shooting motor-cars, policemen in white gloves at the intersections, or the parks with their regiments of light and dark trees just breathing, lovers and loungers on the grass, curiously invisible in the mingling of light and shadow, or the harbour with its ferries, like shuttles of light, headlands powdered with lights, sky with stars, dark anonymous water, full and deep, full stop, or the great morass of the suburbs half denuded of life, with their small nuclei repeating the theme.

"That fabulous city," said Ord, "that fabulous city."

. . . . . . . . . .

It was this on which the woman turned her back. She did not know, did not consciously think anything of the kind. She was hurrying for her train. She was intent on getting home. She wanted to draw the country darkness, like a poor thin blanket, over her head. Young and not ill-favoured, her face was coarse and ugly with fatigue and rebellion.

. . . . . . . . . .

"I see what you are doing," said Ord, "you are creating the world. The molten magma and this woman, one bubble in it, part of it thrown up in the natural process. We follow her, don't we?"

"Yes." Knarf resisted the temptation to explain and extenuate. "It is turgid and chaotic, now, but soon, you will see, it will take shape." He was not willing to discuss the book till it had established itself further.

. . . . . . . . . .

The train was waiting at the platform, a long train, a collection of old rolling stock, shabby box carriages painted a faded, grimed red, worn and scratched with a thousand insignificant journeys. Each box held the passengers, seats of woven cane lumpily upholstered, official photographs of beauty spots, luggage racks, a massive water-bottle, and two thick tumblers on a bracket, shiny yellow wood, unshaded light. The distant engine relieved itself of steam piercingly. The train looked like illuminated vertebrae, separated knobs of hard yellow light beside the dingy platform.

The second-class carriages were crowded. The woman had to make her way almost the length of the platform to the engine before she found even a possibility of wedging herself in.

The train was due to start. The guard already stood with lantern raised ready to signal the engine-driver, the platform was empty, doors banged finally all along the train. As if breaking the spell of a protracted nightmare in which she seemed to have been ranging the platform for hours rather than minutes in the vain search for a place, the woman bundled herself and her child into a compartment which appeared a little less full than the others. There were already five on each side, but one was a thin shaver of a boy who took up as little room as a child. There was a fraction of seat visible. The woman sat on it and slowly pushed her body back with a powerful and not unrehearsed movement of the buttocks. The line gave; she had won a seat from the elastic flesh of her fellow passengers. The train started with a long co-ordinated jolt. The six were wedged indissolubly together. On one side the woman was pressed tightly against a girl. She was young and thin with a pert plain little face, on which she had painted a large voluptuous dark mouth and fine black Japanese eyebrows, curiously at variance with her sharp chin and nose and her quick green eyes between sandy lashes. She did not raise her eyes from the woman's paper she was reading, but her whole body became wooden with obstinacy and she forced her elbows back against the seat, ensuring her rights. The woman on the other side was stout with large, cushiony, pneumatic hips. She took up more than her fair share of room and, in her dark serge dress, she gave out heat like an oven. As the racks were full there was nowhere for the newcomer to put her basket and parcels but on the floor, and there was little enough room there. The woman had to tuck her feet away as best she could, resting them uncomfortably on the tips of her toes. She scrimped herself together as much as she could. If she was determined to have her rights she was also determined not to give anyone else cause for complaint against her. Cautious and resentful, she drew herself together for an hour's siege if need be.

The hot air of the stuffy carriage was charged with a good deal of ill feeling. Every one resented, in varying degrees as it impinged upon his comfort, the intrusion of the woman and child. The fat woman obviously considered it primarily her grievance. Her face, goodnatured in most circumstances, was not so now; she was tired after a long day shopping and cross because she wanted her tea. She was in no mood to be put upon, had given ground unwillingly, and now, by the exercise of lateral pressure and heavy rolling movements, sought to recover some of it. The thin boy beside her, her son, was pressed so hard against the wall of the carriage that he could scarcely move his arms to manipulate his comic. He did not hesitate to jog his mother with his sharp elbow, in the knowledge that she would, if humanly possible, see him righted. The girl with the painted lips was neither angry nor much concerned. Her attitude proclaimed that she was only perching for the moment in this grimy second-class carriage, that her interests were all in another and more glamorous world, but she wasn't, purely as a matter of principle, going to allow anyone to infringe her rights. The two men beyond her were not much concerned, poultry farmers returning from a meeting of the Co-operative. The one by the window allowed himself to be jolted to sleep almost at once, and the other took a phlegmatic but not hopeful interest in the girl's silk-clad legs and allowed himself to enjoy, as one who had few pleasures, the more intimate contact with her which was forced upon him. On the opposite side of the compartment the question of the intrusion was more academic. The very old woman in the corner, a shapeless mass in her worn black clothes, her brown jaws continually working, chewing either words or some more palpable substance, made a few clumsy overtures to the baby, only to be suppressed by her daughter. She thought women with babies ought to travel in the carriages reserved for ladies and not endanger the comfort of the general public. She always gave children a wide berth. Ma was bad enough. She saw in the little boy an imminent threat to her neuralgia. The middle-aged, prosperous looking man merely looked up from his sporting paper and grunted when the basket came down on his foot. Women always had plenty of encumbrances. The woman beside him took a more active interest. She was sister and counterpart to the fat woman and of a forthcoming partisan disposition. Her daughter in the window seat, a child of thirteen or fourteen with large, round, dark eyes in a round freckled face, took everything in with insatiable curiosity. She was a great one for staring, as her mother pointed out. Her intent gaze and drawn-in cheeks gave the impression that she was sucking like a ju-jube each of her fellow passengers in turn. The girl with the painted lips evidently intrigued her most, for she was one who had entered into the kingdom which she herself, stimulated by the pictures and the women's press, already hoped one day to possess.

"I'm that hot," said the fat woman, "I'm just wet."

"I don't wonder," said her sister sympathetically, "open the window a bit. Geoff, your poor mum's suffocating."

"Don't you move, Geoff. If he got up he'd lose his seat, we're that squeezed."

"You do it, Shirl."

The little girl got up self-consciously and began to fiddle ineffectually with the windows.

"Push it up, then down, Shirl."

"Mind your fingers, love."

The little girl didn't really try. She rattled the window and her cousin sniggered. The prosperous man put down his paper and heaved himself up. The woman with the baby had to snatch her basket from beneath his feet. He lumbered to the window, opened it, and a waft of sooty air came in. The fat women were wreathed in smiles, they thanked him effusively. With a grunt of surly good nature he returned to his newspaper. Shirley, blushing scarlet, sank back into her seat. Her cousin made a face at her as if he considered all this a score to him in the war between them.

It was nearly dark outside. The train ran through the vast railway assembly yards, a disjointed nightmare of black and silver — grimed sheds, embankments of cinders, hills of coal, unlit trains like dead leviathans, cruising locomotives, watering equipment as sinister as gallows, white patches of steam, maze of steel rails. It emerged into the city's rind of slums, inextricable confusion of shops and streets and dwellings, half-melted into the darkness, on which floated the bright patches of advertisement hoardings; it told off the trite stations; it shook its passenger contents, in a jumble of sound and motion, as if intent on digesting them.

By sheer weight the fat woman settled herself more comfortably and began to discuss with her sister the fortunes of the day.

"The blue at three-eleven-a-half was a bargain. It ought to make up real nice."

"I don't know whether to make it myself or to let Miss Higgins."

"I'm not too pleased with Miss Higgins. She made this and it girt me under the arms something frightful."

"That's her fault. She cuts too skimpy. Thinks we're all bits of girls." The sister laughed richly. The fat woman laughed and her stays creaked. She overlapped her neighbour so that the last comer was forced to sit at an uncomfortable angle and came in contact with the girl's stony shoulder. She tried to elbow back the great soft bulk, but under her softness the woman seemed to be filled with concrete. The baby, awake, tried to crawl round on her lap. She hated the fat woman with an implacable hatred. She hated her because of her bulk, her self-indulgent, complacent fatness. People oughtn't to let themselves get like that, and if they did they ought to be punished for it. This new anger was like a sudden tongue of flame in the smouldering resentment that had filled her heart all day, against her lot, against the child, against her husband, who was the author and prime cause of them both.

The train ran through Suburbia. The pattern sorted itself out, took form and coherence, villas in gardens, tree-lined streets, garages with red and yellow bowsers, cinemas bedizened with light, shopping centres, churches and little parks, schools and fire-stations, clean and separate like the grains of well cooked rice. Strathfield, first stop — a panting, reverberating moment in the covered station, the departure of those who claimed by any surviving fiction to live in the great world, the degradation of the train from a "through" to a "slow," the guard shouting, "All stations to Penrith;" west into a larger, sparser darkness, flat country. No one left the compartment, they relaxed and spread against one another. The boy ate an orange and the smell of its spirity skin was added to the close air. The poultry farmer sitting next to the girl took out his pipe and asked her if she minded smoking.

"It won't worry me," she answered, summing him up from behind her lashes.

"S'pose you're used to men about," he asked with the suggestion of gallantry.

"I smoke myself."

"In that case. . . ." he slapped his pockets and finally produced a packet of cigarettes. With a half-defiant glance about her the girl took one, stuck it between her lips and let him light it.

The faces of the fat women withered, as if their mouths had filled with acid, they looked meaningly at one another and nodded almost imperceptibly. The woman in black ostentatiously opened her window one inch. The baby made a sudden grab at the cigarette, almost springing out of his mother's arms. The girl shrugged away with a glance of irritated disgust.

The train skirted the saleyards at Flemington, that wilderness of wooden pens, those arid grassless enclosures where the city's meat supply is brought and sold en route to the slaughter yards. They were empty now, but the smell of hides and animal sweat and cattle trucks crowded with suffering beasts, hung over the place and came into the carriage like a blast. The woman felt sickness, like a small, cold worm, stir in her stomach. The baby propelled himself from side to side in her arms, she could hardly hold him. There was no room. His clothes were getting bundled up round his neck, he was hot, sticky, thoroughly uncomfortable. His discomfort affected everybody. He was whimpering and might at any moment begin to cry. His clothes smelt sour, and he flapped the odour all over the carriage. The girl was now talking to the two poultry farmers, who were both smoking, but a side glance every now and then showed she was aware of the danger to her blouse from sticky fingers. The baby made a lunge at the pink sporting paper and succeeded in knocking it out of the owner's hands; he patiently picked it up again. The mother was too tired and angry to apologise, she merely jerked the child back, and he squealed with disappointment. Next he turned his attention to the fat woman's handbag, but his mother was determined not to give offence there. She turned the baby about and dumped him tightly on her knee. She wanted to smack him and he was more than anxious to kick her. Both were angry, they had worn each other out. No one offered to help, and if they had there was little they could do in that confined space. She held him with all her strength and didn't care if she hurt him.

The train ran beside Rookwood Cemetery, the great burying ground of the city, acre upon acre sown with stones, so that as far as the eye could see they rose like unwholesome grey bristles out of the ground. It was quite dark. The train was a string of yellow beads drawn through the acquiescent night. Another twenty minutes, the woman thought blindly.

The baby slackened in her arms. He was quite still. Something had caught his interest. On his troubled, yellowish, little face was a look of anxiety increasing to pain. The old woman was nodding at him, smiling grotesquely. Slowly she raised a clawed hand and waved to him in the parody of a gesture that was, long ago, arch and gay. The baby's face fell together, he doubled his body back sharply and yelled with all his might. His mother was taken by surprise and her nerve broke. Darkness rushed at her. With one hand she tried to stifle his screams, with the other she beat furiously at his wildly-threshing legs. Her face was white and distorted with fury. A shock of horror ran through the compartment. The man opposite seized her wrists.

"Now, now, missus. He's only a little fellow."

In a second she relaxed trembling, and he let her go. Everybody was profoundly and sincerely shocked. They stared in silence. Only the child continued to scream as if he were being murdered. The girl, her pert mask dropped, looked at her with wide-open eyes, dewy with reproach. Shirley stared through this peephole into life, white-faced, on the point of tears. The fat woman pressed her heart, her face was mottled, it had given her quite a turn. Later when she told the story, she always added, "If we hadn't been there I do believe she'd have murdered that poor little baby." The old woman wavered, uncomprehending, "What's it? What's happened?" Her daughter hushed her down. She didn't like children, but seeing them ill-used was another matter. Poor little helpless brat, some women weren't fit to be mothers. The prosperous man continued to look at the culprit sternly. That was a fine termagant for a man to come home to. He was sorry for some poor devil. The other men and the boy were acutely embarrassed. The ugly little episode had shocked them all in their finer feelings. Humanity had been outraged at its very font. Trembling, the woman tried to rock the baby into quiet. She looked from face to face and saw anger, fear, disapproval, horror. She was in the dock before these people. Hysteria rose in her. The pack was after her. She wanted madly to explain that what had happened was not her fault. She'd had an awful day, she was trapped, caught, everything was against her, it was her husband's fault. On that her mind reached its dead end, ran into the buffers. She looked from face to face, she must make her defence, but that would be the whole story of her five years' marriage. It was his fault that she had disgraced herself in public, everything was his fault. She groped helplessly for reprisal. Her mouth widened in a sickly propitiatory smile, still trying to soothe the child.

"He has his father's paddy."

They took no notice. The poor arrow fell away blunted. The baby began to choke dangerously on his sobs. The fat woman peered at him with informed curiosity. "He don't look too good to me," she reported to her sister. The sister shook her head as if to say, "Do you wonder?"

The mother bent low over him to hide him from their staring eyes. In desperation she opened her blouse and put him to her breast. For a moment his cries continued, then dropped to hiccoughing gurgles.

The train pulled into Parramatta. The girl and the prosperous man got out. One of the poultry farmers changed to the other side. No one made any move to take advantage of the extra space. The woman could have it all. She was alone. Her heart was like iron. She waited for the minutes and the miles to pass. No one spoke. They were ashamed. The shame should have belonged to the woman only, but it did not. They all felt it. It embarrassed them to be ashamed, they wanted to be rid of it. The mushroom rights of private property in virtue had been infringed, the thin partitions of individuality pierced. By abhorring they had not freed themselves; in whatever had happened they had participated. They would deny the sharing that denial was killing everywhere. It was fixed only in the air and time, and the train could be trusted to carry them away from it.

Westmead. Wentworthville — almost a country town — more sulkies than motor-cars in the main street. Quiet, flat country under the night, paddocks, weatherboard cottages, dusty roads, unsculptured landscape, barren, but with a sort of cumulative beauty. Pendle Hill. The family party got out in a sudden, exaggerated bustle, as if released. The baby was asleep, his cheeks red and glazed with his tears, his breathing still uneven. Next station, Toongabbie. The woman gathered together her things. Harry would be at the station to meet her. And he'd get it all.

The train stopped. She got out awkwardly with the baby and one of the men followed with her basket and parcels and put them down on the platform beside her. Harry was there. He acknowledged the service, "Thanks, Dig," took the baby from her and picked up the basket.

"I thought you'd be on the last train."

"I missed it."

"Get on all right?"

"No."

When she stopped to get out her ticket he held the baby under one of the station lights.

"Been crying, hasn't he?"

"I should say he has. Fair excelled himself. We was packed like sardines and everyone nasty about it."

"Not one of his attacks, was it?"

"No, just temper."

They were out in the station yard.

"I've got young Archie in the truck. He came on the last train. Mrs. Castles asked me to look out for him."

A tow-haired youngster of about ten was sitting in the driving seat of the battered old utility.

"Hullo, Archie."

"Hullo, Mrs Munster."

Well, she couldn't let Harry have it, not yet, because of the kid, and that gossiping, old busybody, his mother. The repression disappointed and sickened her, actually, pressing like a clumsy weight on the nerves of her stomach.

The boy was eating something out of a greasy cone of paper. Fish and chips. Harry had bought them for him, of course. The kid had been hungry. You'd look a fool and worse, raising hell over threepennorth of fish and chips for a kid, but that was Harry all over, all the time doing something for somebody in his soft way. Getting on for him would always be like storing water in a leaking tank. She climbed into the cabin, Harry handed her up the baby and stowed the basket.

He went to crank the engine. As he bent to it the sickly, yellow light of the headlamps fell across his face and shoulders, a long head with deep temples, dark hair cut very short, greying and wearing back from the temples, dark eyes deeply set, mouth drawn tight with effort, skin burnt by sun and wind, but a skin that had taken them kindly and naturally. It was a face deeply marked, if there had been anyone to notice it, with prolonged effort — an effort that antedated his physical maturity — to keep his nose into the wind; the flesh was set and moulded upon the bones.

The engine was old and hard to move, but at last it burst into life, leaping like a loose and aching tooth in its agony. Harry stood up, panting with effort, steadying himself with his hands on mudguard and radiator, and the light took in a new swathe of his body—faded, patched blue shirt, trousers hanging loose on his lean narrow hips. His wife's eye fastened on the patch.

A man lounged over to them.

" 'Night, Harry. What cheer, Mrs Munster? Bess wants to know what the doctor said about Jackie and will you come over and have a cup of tea. The kettle's on the boil. She'd have come herself only she's just getting the kids to bed."

Harry answered him: "Thanks, Pete. But we've got to be getting along."

"What's the hurry?" Mrs Munster, thwarted of her outburst by Archie's presence, was disposed to be contrary about ever getting home at all.

"We don't like leaving Wanda and Ruthie alone in the house, not any longer than we can help."

"Give Bess my love and say I'm sorry I can't wait. My husband won't let me." The attempt at facetiousness was none the less sorry for its barb.

"Right oh. But how's the kid?"

"Doctor says he'll do. I got to change his food. That's all."

"I'll tell Bess. Cheerio."

"Goodnight, Pete. Thanks all the same."

Harry swung the truck out of the station yard expertly, despite its ineradicable jarring rattle.

"That true about Jackie?"

"Yes."

He saw she wasn't going to tell him anything yet and so he left it. They drove in silence, off the macadam on to a rutted country road, away from the lights into the country darkness. Archie leaned against the man, inert, half asleep. The man made the best of the familiar road, humouring the ruts and achieving a steady pace. Their world was narrowed down to the segment of light from the lamps and the glimmer from the dashboard. The woman was aware of the man's strong thin hands on the wheel. She hardened her heart against those hands but she knew that they had always meant and always would mean her security, and that, despite herself, she'd go on trusting them.

Once she roused herself to ask a question, the inevitable one. "Anything happen while I was away?"

"Four more chicks dead out of that last lot. Dunno why. Some clutches seem unlucky. Grant came over about the Rhode Islands. Said his son was thinking of getting married about Easter. He wants a place. I thought it was a sort of feeler. Let him know there was nothing doing without saying so."

Her interest fell away. Harry's idea of something happening. She hated poultry, dead or alive, the smell of them, and their scaley feet and the feckless way chickens died. Poultry farmers got to look like them. Billy Grant looked just like a battered old rooster and his sandy wife was the image of a Buff Orpington.

They left the road for a wheel track. The gate hung listlessly open. They stopped by a verandahless wooden house in the middle of a paddock. Mrs Castles came running out.

"I thought you were lorsted," she cried, in her loud jovial voice. Archie scrambled down and came in for a genial cuff from his mother to make him say thank you. Harry kept the engine running as a hint that he wanted to get on his way, but undeterred, Mrs Castles leaned her fat arms on the window of the cabin and began a torrent of enquiry. Mrs Munster, who disliked her for her close range, larded speech, and avid eyes, made no effort to conceal it. She answered ungraciously.

"You're fair tuckered up, love, come in and have a cup o' tea, do."

"We've got to get back on account of the kids, thanks all the same, Mrs Castles." Harry put in the clutch.

Mrs Castles removed her arms. "If that's how it is, go you must, but it fair grieves me to have you go without a bite or sup and you the best neighbours I ever had."

Harry raised his hand in salute, breaking as best he could the harshness of departure, and the truck roared away across the paddock.

Mrs Castles waded through her offspring into the house. "Ally Munster was in a devil of a temper," she informed her old man. "Talk about a monkey on her back. Did anything happen while you was with them, Archie?"

"Nope."

"Was they quarrelling in the truck?"

"No, ma."

"What was they saying to one another?"

"Nuthin' "

"Sulky. That's what she is. They're the worst sort. I'm sorry for Harry. Devil a bit of supper he'll have had and her gadding off to town. And would she let him come in here for a cup of tea? Not she."

The familiar smell of the house, boxed in in the warm weather, hit Ally Munster like a wave of sickness as she pushed open the door —the peardrop smell of cheap varnish, the oiliness of the new Bolton sheeting curtains, hot stove polish, and the bran and pollard mash that had recently been mixed. She put the baby down on the bed, just as he was, and went through to the kitchen with the other things. When Harry came in from putting the truck away she had taken her shoes off and was rubbing her feet. He felt the heavy murk but tried the old doomed strategem of ignoring it.

"It's good news about Jackie," he began cheerfully. "What did the doctor say?"

"He said I'd got to wean him at once."

"Wasn't he getting enough?"

"It isn't Jackie, it's me."

She saw him stiffen as a dog freezes and points. She lifted her head and stared at him with leaden eyes.

"I'm going to have another baby."

He took an impulsive step towards her but the look in her eyes stopped him.

"Are you sure?"

"The doctor'd know, wouldn't he? D'you think I'd say it if it wasn't true?"

"How long?" he muttered. He reproached himself for the thought that had first leaped into his mind. The expense. Ally wouldn't want to go to the District Hospital. She'd expect to go to Nurse Carter's like she had for the others—Nurse Carter, the terror of husbands, genial on one side of her face, and on the other teaching young wives their rights, opening their eyes to all their grievances; the flimsy weatherboard cottage where every word spoken was heard by all, whorl of female gossip, small deep pit of man's humiliation. Not only Nurse Carter. The doctor. Ally didn't know, but he wasn't paid for Jackie yet. That would have to be settled at once in common decency. And help. Towards the end she couldn't be expected to look after the house and the children. They would have to get someone in who could take charge while she was away . . . and extras. And Ally would want some cash to spend, to spend, to spend. His brain hammered painfully. He didn't have to enumerate his other commitments to himself, they were there like stones fixed in his brain. The interest on the mortgage, the payments on the plant, the account at the store, the difficult hiatus between disbursements and payments. . . . He had thought of all this first, because that was the way his mind was becoming rutted. It was his part. There was her part, worse than his. If each of them only thought of himself they'd never get through. He realised that he had asked her a question and she hadn't answered him. She was staring at him as if she were reading his thoughts. He was shocked again at the black resentment that he saw in her face. There had been flares of temper between them often enough — they were both quick tempered — but not the heavy oily swell of this undeclared quarrel. Every quarrel they had ever had, every hardship she had suffered, every wish unfulfilled, every disappointment, besides this new burden, and a hurt he did not know of, were piled against him. And he *was* the guilty party. His attitude had made things worse, for it was at once an admission and an opposition. He had not given a word nor a gesture of tenderness, the tenderness that was still in his heart for her, only overlaid by cares and anxieties. He wanted to break through.

"Ally. . . ."

In the pause she had accumulated the venom to answer him.

"Nearly two months." She spoke slowly, as if she had planned what she would say, and it had long passed from impulse to conviction, as if she now had the right to indict him. "We've been married just over five years and I've got three children and another one coming. What sort of a life is that for a woman? D'you expect it to go on? I could have ten children by the time I'm thirty and all you'd think about would be paying for them and having them work for you later on. What about me? I'd be an old woman if I wasn't dead." Her voice rose.

"Good God, woman, you're not going to have ten children."

"Who's to stop me? You? If you go on having your way in everything—You're right, I'm not going to have ten children, not living like this. It's no sort of a life even without having babies all the time. What do you think the last five years have been for me, living in this filthy, little hole? You wouldn't know, because you never think of me. But I'll tell you now."

His temper was rising, rasped more by the note in her voice than by what she said. He was willing to admit things hadn't been altogether bright for her, for either of them, but she needn't make a meal of it.

He said brutally. "You're working yourself up."

"Am I?" she cried, "Am I? Listen to me for once. I was nineteen when you married me."

"My God," he thought, "My God."

"You were mad to get me, remember? Well, you did. You got me properly. I'd had a good time and plenty of fun — but not after I was married. It stopped dead. You brought me out here. The house wasn't much, you said, we'd do better later. We're no nearer now, we're further away. I couldn't have any nice furniture like other girls have when they marry. We couldn't afford it. All right. Other people can't afford it either, they get it on the hire purchase. You wouldn't hear of it. Anyone would think it was a crime, getting decent furniture; you don't have to be ashamed of on the hire purchase. You get your incubators and I don't know what on the hire purchase."

He made an impatient movement. She forestalled him. "Oh, that's different. They were things *you* wanted. You didn't care what the house looked like, that was *my* place. It didn't matter. We couldn't go to the pictures — not even once a week for certain — because you had to go into market in the morning or you were too tired, because you were too mean to get any help and did all the work on the place yourself. Do you think it was any fun for me having a husband who was always too tired. Then Ruthie was coming and a year later Wanda, and I couldn't go anywhere or do anything or have anything. But I didn't nag you."

She hadn't nagged him, not at first. She'd been as much in love with him as he with her. She'd forgotten. His anger had died down. He hadn't the heart to be angry. It was too pitiful and too futile. She knew how it had been, the struggle they'd shared and would have to go on sharing, but she refused to understand.

He tried to be gentle, to reach her. "We did have something. We were happy together. The children . . ."

"Always the children. When I told you just now you thought at once how much money another one was going to cost you. What do you think it costs me?"

She had him there.

"But when they're born, it's the children all the time. They are more to you than ever I am. You got an idea that Jackie was sick and the Parramatta doctor wasn't good enough. I had to take him in to Sydney. And it wasn't Jackie, it was me. Only you hadn't bothered to notice."

"Don't, Ally. Don't, old girl." He had got to be patient, it was the only thing he could do. She was overwrought and beside herself. It would pass.

"Looks like I've got a life sentence. Four kids and no money."

"Things will be better. We're not broke, Ally, we're keeping up."

She looked at him with cold fire. "We haven't any money, not that we can spend. And the only thing that we're keeping up that I know of is payments. You're not working for yourself, you're working for your creditors, the mortgage and plant and all. They've got a lien on your wife and children as well as on the land and house and everything. They've got a finger in everything we call ours and they have to be satisfied first. Maybe if you're good you'll be let have a little something later—when you're old. Things won't be any better, Harry. Not in my time. Because you are a mug. I was a mug too, not to see it. Now I do. You've always been a mug. You were a mug to go to the war and let the chaps that stayed behind get in front of you. You came back and sank your gratuity in this place—so that someone would have a nice little investment. We could of had a good time with that money. Then we'd have had something. Not now. Wait. When's the good time coming? You know bloody well it's never coming."

She hadn't finished yet. "A job would suit you better and it ud suit me better too. Money coming in regular every week, nothing to do but spend it. A job's about your measure. But you think too much of yourself. Want to be your own boss. You are nothing like your own boss here. You're a slave and so am I. The only difference is you seem to like it and I don't."

This was worse than old Mother Carter and her gab.

"Even the way things are, you think you can have luxuries. You and your bloody Co-operative."

"But the Co-op is going to make things better."

"Oh, no, it won't, it won't be let. All it does is give you a chance to swank. You wouldn't have spent so much money on the place if it hadn't been for the Co-op. and you in it up to your neck."

It was true in a way. Because he always advocated scientific methods and the higher standard equipment in the Co-operative he'd felt bound to practise what he preached. It would be best in the end but the sacrifice was now and the end a long way off.

"You don't find the successful people like the Grants in the Co-operative. They put their energy into looking after their own. You're good at fathering kids, but you're not much good at keeping them when you've got them."

His mind blazed under that. "You've never had to go without. Never for a day have we been without necessities. You know I'd cut myself in pieces before any of you went hungry."

She was a little frightened, her eyes shifted with the old, quick flicker of an animal when it means to break out of a trap.

"I been steady, haven't I? You've got nothing against me there." He pressed in on her.

She laughed at him then with a sort of broken jauntiness. "You've been steady. I give you that. You think that's enough. I oughter be grateful. We've had enough to eat and you've been steady." It was like a flame licking out of her. "Steady's not enough. A steady man can make you as miserable as a gay one. Worse. You and your steadiness. You don't know you're born, that's what. Enough to eat. Well, so we ought to have. No one gets any fun out of enough. It begins after that."

The whole thing was becoming unreal again to him. He'd had a long day, no tea. That was real. He'd have to be up at four to go into the market at Parramatta tomorrow. That was real.

His mind strayed back to the war. The times his belly had been sticking to his backbone, times when he'd been perishing and the food had come up stone cold, or there hadn't been any, because Fritz had got the ration party. Times when to lie down and sleep in the mud, even to the thunder of a barrage, would have been the sweetest thing in the world, times when he would have welcomed death itself for the sleep there was in it. He'd sworn then if he ever came back he'd not be ungrateful again for food and sleep, quiet, and a body free from lice. A woman wouldn't know about that.

"If you hadn't enough, you'd know. Plenty haven't."

"I don't care about the people who haven't," she answered passionately. "Plenty have. There's good things in the world, lots of them, and I want a share." She thought of the city, its lights, its amusements, its piled-up plenty. She wanted all the silly things, the things she didn't need, to lord it over them. The people who had them were the victors.

"You've got to wait a bit, Ally," he said it placatingly, as he'd said it often before. This wasn't just a quarrel and he knew it.

"I won't wait."

Their eyes met. She knew she would have to wait. They both knew it. Silence fell. For a long time there had been a loose rubble of discontent in her mind. This day's strain and weariness, the knowledge that another child was coming to rivet her chains, had trampled it hard. It was as if suddenly her unrest and distress had turned from dust, which a fair wind would blow away, to clinker. The incident in the train of which she would never tell anyone and which she would herself forget, had left a wound that would become a scar.

The alarm clock ticked on the shelf above the range, a loud cheap tick. It was time to go round the incubators. Without a word he went out.

When he came back she was sitting just as he had left her. She had not even put away her things. He stirred up the fire, got out cups and saucers, bread and butter, and made tea. He brought a cup to her and put it down by her side. She looked at it mutely and burst into tears.

"I've got to go through with it. I've got to go through with it."

He tried to comfort her, taking her in his arms, but she wouldn't yield or turn to him. At last he persuaded her to drink the tea and to eat some bread and butter. A little colour came back into her cheeks.

He told himself that the worst was over. It was after all just one of those storms one must expect from a woman in her condition. He had already accepted the new situation.

She surprised him by saying in a cool matter of fact voice. "We don't have to stay here. We could sell the place. Maybe the Grants would buy it. We could go to the city and you could get a job. Arnie could get you one like his, driving a lorry. You'd have the basic wage, perhaps a bit more."

"We can talk about that another time." He'd had enough for one day. He'd got to get some sleep before he went to the market tomorrow. She saw his face harden and her own sank back into the ugly lines of its obstinacy. Neither spoke again. He got up, carried the cups to the sink, wound the clock, and went into the bedroom. She remained where she was in a sulky dream. He undressed the baby and sponged him, put on his nightgown. The little chap hardly stirred. He was tired all right. The man undressed himself and without washing got into bed. He heard Ally moving about in the kitchen, but before she came in he was asleep.

.      .      .      .      .      .

It was almost dark, the premature darkness of a stormy sky, when Harry Munster brought the truck, piled with his furniture, to the kerb outside his new home. It had been a long day on the road, coming from Old Toongabbie by the Great Western Highway and the Parramatta Road, those great culverts draining into the city, to the steep little gut of a street in Darlinghurst. He had had some trouble on the way with the engine, delaying him beyond his expectations. Ally had come in by train in the morning with Ruthie and Jackie. She shouldn't be carrying Jackie now, he was far too heavy for her, but there had been no other way to manage. He'd put her into the train and her sister-in-law, Arnie's wife, had promised to meet her at Central. Ruthie at four was a sensible little thing, already more a help than a responsibility, with the eldest child's premature grasp of reality. Wanda, Harry had brought with him in the truck. She had been wildly excited and full of chatter. He had humoured her all day, bought her penny icecream cones and chocolate bars at their numerous stops and let her take fizzy drinks, triumphantly and noisily, through a straw into her unaccustomed stomach. He let her stand on the seat beside him, holding her securely with his left arm to look at the new world. Her little cheeks grew scarlet. She knew that she felt like a little queen and lorded it very happily. She was three years old. He was ready to spoil her out of a dim sense of guilt. He was taking her away from a world he believed to be safe, however hard, into one he didn't trust. The bright prizes of the city awoke his countryman's distrust. Poor little kid, let her be happy when she got the chance. He owed her something. His heart dragged with an obscure pity and a heavy tenderness. More obscurely still, he was sorry for himself, and the day alone with the child, so dependent and, in her little demanding way, so loving, had comforted him. But it ended badly. Emotion and strange foods had had their way with her. She had grown tired and sick, had cried and vomited, and at last, tired, dirty, sticky, miserable, had fallen asleep against his side and so, tired himself, he had held her and still found a weary joy in having her there.

As they turned into what was to be their street the storm broke. First, in the heavy calm, slow drops made large dark circles on the asphalt. Then came a gust, the rush of rain and wind sounded like a procession in the narrow street, a procession that became a rabble. The light changed sharply from grey to steel, a cold wet breath, and then rain and wind, turning the corner, poured down the street in a torrent of air and water, every surface darkened with wet, white flapping of a newspaper before the rain bore it down, a white curtain flapping from a window, a white curl of water in the gutters, pedestrians like leaves, the solitary tree straining at its roots, leaves cast up, fixed buildings seeming to stir and flicker in the downrush of the rain.

Harry could only disentangle Wanda and run with her into the house. The child began to cry with fear of the storm. Ally met them, heavy and querulous. She'd been waiting for hours, whatever had he been doing, and look at the state Wanda was in; there wasn't any electric light because the Council wouldn't connect them until they paid a deposit, the place was filthy, and she couldn't do a thing about it even if she was fit to, because the brooms and buckets were on the truck, she was dead tired, Jacky had been playing up, she didn't know what had got into him, he was asleep now, and for God's sake, don't wake him up. Chris was still there and it was a good thing she was, what with Jackie nearly screaming himself into fits and not so much as a chair to sit down on and Harry taking his time on the road till she began to think there'd been an accident. Chris, Arnie's wife, came forward in the midst of this interior downpour, shook hands with Harry, vaguely muttering "What oh" and retired again. She was a phlegmatic girl, wholesome looking and willing enough to do anything she was asked. She was of passive rather than active assistance.

The Munsters had the upper floor of a terrace house, two rooms, one behind the other, a latticed-in balcony in front where the two little girls would sleep and a latticed-in balcony at the back which served as a kitchen. The rooms would always be dark because they depended for natural light on the two balconies which were now both screened. They were now as dark as night. Ally had bought a couple of candles from the corner shop and they burned in their guttering wax with a wan yellow light. There was a box lent by the lady downstairs, so that Ally could sit down; the remains or beginnings of a meal, a cut loaf, butter in its paper, a large tin of sardines, lay on the kitchen sink, and Jackie slept on a coat spread in a corner, a handkerchief under his head. There was a girl in the attic above, an ovenlike room with a surprised gabled window poking out of the slates, a family downstairs, and an old age pensioner tucked away at the back.

Harry levered up one of the candles and went to look at Jackie. The child was a bad colour, and breathing rather hoarsely with his mouth open. The relief of the city doctor's reassurances had quite worn off and Harry was again oppressed by a foreboding that the little boy was really ill. These screaming fits, were they temper, as his mother said, or were they pain? He was a year old now but backward. He had not begun to walk and wasn't lively or happy as a baby should be. Ally said it was his teeth. She didn't worry. Lots of babies had difficult babyhoods and grew up none the worse. It was just another trial for their mothers. All Harry's fears rose up in him now. He told himself it was the light, veering and flickering in the empty room. Ally stood watching him, her grotesque shadow thrown on the wall. He looked up at her from where he knelt on the floor. Their eyes met as they rarely met now. She said nothing, but he was laid open to her jeering silence. Her burdened body was a reproach to him, the sickly child was a reproach to him. There was no need for words. The strain and weariness of the day, the savourless weight of the change they had made, had for the moment stripped them in one another's eyes. This was the communication they had with one another. Her eyes were alive in her sick, sullen face. They asked a question he could not answer. "A bob both ways," he thought. Whichever way things went for them, well or badly, she'd have her cut. She meant to have all there was to be got, and if there was nothing, then she could still feed her resentment. Nothing dismayed her, she was invulnerable, and that was the measure of her power and their estrangement. They had this grudge against one another but they could never express it. When it broke out in the pustules of a quarrel it could only be in terms they both understood—a quarrel in the accents of other people's quarrels, the debased small change of hostility that passed as meaningless as pennies through hands greedy for all that money cannot buy. There was no quarrel tonight. Harry got awkwardly to his feet and put down the candle. He wanted to get into the open air. This room was like a bad taste in his mouth.

He went downstairs and stood on the oblong of iron-railed verandah beside the gas box, looking at the rain. It was still falling heavily but with less conviction. The storm was passing. The stormy twilight was like a bruise. This wasn't like the open air. Houses and streets crowded in, acres of them, square miles of them, as far as the mind could reach. The sky itself was cut into a narrow thoroughfare between buildings. People were standing on verandahs and balconies staring at the rain. Unseen they were looking out from opaque curtained windows in the dark caves of houses. No one greeted him nor did he greet anyone. Maybe they were curious about him or maybe there were too many coming and going for them to notice. He had the feeling that the rules were different here and that at any moment he would blunder into someone else's world. It made him feel inferior and angry. Probably this strip of verandah belonged behind that window—mean-looking, tight-shut window. The rain didn't mean anything here. It never reached the ground at all, it ran down gutters and into concrete pipes and away, something to be got rid of as soon as possible. It was waste. Under the asphalt the earth was dry and barren. He didn't like it. It made him feel bad. It wasn't anything to do with him, of course, and he'd get over it. He couldn't unload the furniture until it stopped raining. It'd be dark. He could manage by himself, there were only a few sticks. The thought that one of those lounging men might offer to help filled him with embarrassment.

Behind him in the house Wanda was crying. Her mother was washing the grime and stickiness of the day off her, ungently, at the sink. The child cried because everything was strange. Ally slapped her and she stopped. Ruthie came and stood by her father, holding to his trouser leg. He twisted a finger in her hair. They hadn't anything to say to one another. They just looked at the rain. It beat him where the children would play. Not in the slip of backyard at the back among the garbage tins. Out in the road. They'd have to learn they couldn't go where they liked. There wasn't any place for them and they'd have to learn it. He hadn't liked this place, looked like a slum to him. Agent was quite shocked when he said so. Not a slum rent anyhow. It wasn't easy to get a place. This would have to do until they could look round them. Wait till Ally could look for herself. They'd shake down. Bit hard to get used to after the country. Funny, didn't know he'd liked the country. Always said it was a lousy life, poultry farming. Everyone did. Still . . .

The rain was stopping. Chris came downstairs. She'd have to be getting along as soon as it stopped, she said. It was late. Arnie went to market if his tea wasn't ready. She tittered as she did when sex was referred to, however remotely. She'd be along tomorrow to see how they were settling in. She gave Harry a nerveless hand, and he noticed that she had a strong cottony smell. "Goodbye, love." She kissed Ruthie, who was shy, stepped into the dwindling rain. Harry went down and began to unknot the rope which held the tarpaulin. Tomorrow would be Sunday. He'd have to drive the truck back to Toongabbie and hand her over to the man he'd sold her to, and come back by train. After he'd finished paying for her there'd just be enough for his fare. Maybe he'd take Ruthie. Get her out in the open for the day. Ally would say he wasn't to be trusted after the way he'd brought Wanda home. Monday, he'd see about the job. Arnie said it would be all right. Arnie always said that. Plenty of jobs going just now. Don't go pulling the returned soldier, though.

He carried up a kerosene case packed with crockery.

"Bring up a bed, can't you?" said Ally, "I got ter put the children somewhere." Wanda had fallen asleep in a corner and Jackie was whimpering.

The dismembered beds were underneath. He got Jackie's cot out first and was carrying it upstairs when he heard the screams. They broke out suddenly and they weren't like a baby's cries at all. He rushed up stairs. Ally had just picked Jackie up. He was bent backwards in her arms, screaming, his face bluish and distorted, in a fit or a convulsion. She could barely hold him. Harry took him. He had the poor man's instinct to run with him to the nearest doctor or hospital, but it was still raining, and he did not know where to find either. His fear of the strange world was stronger. The woman from downstairs was already at the door.

"Is she took bad?"

"No, it's the baby."

She would help. Better to leave Jackie with them to do what they could while he got a doctor. He knew it was urgent, they all did. The air itself changed. He plunged downstairs. The hoarse screams followed him. He ran towards William Street. All these people— there must be a doctor near. He caught a passer-by by the shoulder and gasped out his enquiry. The man gaped at him oafishly and he let him go, ran on, turned up the hill. A river of traffic flowed in the great thoroughfare, a blaze of light and noise. He cannoned into an old man, repeated his enquiry. The old man took his time. "Dr. Jones will be the nearest, over the road and straight along Darlinghurst Road, not the first one, that's Victoria Street, the second one. On the left, straight on, you'll see the red lamp . . ."

He jumped into the river, cars hooted, brakes screamed, a tram clanged very near him, he thought in an unheeded flash, "What would they do if I was run over?" but he was on the other bank, crossing another road, battling against a leisurely stream of people, lights, noise. There were many red lights. There was a chemist's.

A chemist would know. Then he saw the square red lamp with Dr Jones in white letters. It looked calm and steady, rebuking. It was a big building, trees in front, a car at the kerb. He ran up the steps. The doctor's name was printed on a door, a bell marked Night Bell. He rang it. A stocky, middle-aged man opened it.

"The doctor in?"

"I'm the doctor. This isn't my consulting hours."

"The baby's taken bad, please come."

The doctor sized him up, unperturbed. "You should have gone to the hospital," he said.

"I don't know where it is. We only moved in tonight."

"You could telephone the ambulance. That's what they are for."

Harry shook off the entangling argument. "Please come. I think he's dying." An idea crossed his mind. He thrust his hand into his pocket and brought out two crumpled pound notes. "I can pay."

The doctor seemed offended. "Wait here," he said, and went back into his rooms. Harry didn't know if he were coming or not, whether to wait or look for some one else. He heard an altercation going on, a woman's voice, the doctor's answering brusquely as he had spoken to him. At least the door wasn't shut. After what seemed an interminable time the doctor came out with a bag.

"Look sharp," he said, "Where do we go? I've an engagement."

They got into the car outside. Harry gave the address. The doctor grunted. It was nearly eight o'clock and the theatre traffic was at its peak, shining cars in a long fluent stream under the lights. Harry saw now that the doctor was in evening dress.

The upstairs room seemed full of women. The fat woman from downstairs was in charge. She was putting Jackie into a hot bath rigged on the kerosene box. His little body was rigid between her hands. He wasn't screaming now but breathing in choking gasps. There was no mistaking the look on his face, it was one common to all in extremis.

"Are you the mother?" the doctor asked.

"It's her, poor soul."

The doctor drove them all out except Ally and the fat woman. Ally was collapsed in a chair someone had brought in, a swollen frightened look on her face. The fat woman held a candle in each hand to give the doctor light as he laid Jackie in the cot and began his examination. Harry stood by the door. The doctor took his time.

He wasn't doing anything. It was quiet. Harry even heard the whining of the trams in William Street. The doctor's shirt front was splashed with water, his face expressionless, only intent.

The fat woman screamed, "He's going, doctor." He told her harshly to be quiet. There was a pause. He could not see what the doctor was doing. The wavering light danced on the wall. Harry clenched his fists.

The doctor touched him on the arm. There wasn't anywhere for them to talk but down on the street. The other room was dark and Wanda asleep on the floor. Ruthie had woken up and come in, her eyes big with fright, but silent. Ally was crying hysterically and the fat woman was soothing her. It was about half-past eight.

They were down in the street standing by the doctor's car. The rain was over and the pavements were dry. There was the partly unloaded truck. The doctor was explaining something. He could not give a certificate because he could not state with any certainty the cause of death. There would have to be a post-mortem, an inquest. He'd get in touch with the authorities. Jackie would have to be taken away, it emerged. Harry rebelled. The doctor was dry and matter of fact. It had to be. He didn't like the business. He'd had an engagement. Well. He hoped he'd made it clear.

"This is bad for your wife in her present condition. She shouldn't be left. Can you get her mother or some one responsible? Keep her quiet."

Ally would be all right. The doctor started his car. It took itself off neatly and suavely, turned the corner and disappeared. Harry stood on the kerb.

A policeman with an open notebook had to speak to him twice.

"That your truck?"

"Yes."

"Can't leave it here like that, you know. Been standing a couple of hours, obstructing the traffic. I'll have to book you if you don't get busy."

Harry balled his fists. "You get to hell," he shouted. "Me bloody kid's dead, ain't that enough?"

"Now Dig, now, none of that," said the policeman, kind but admonitory.

Harry Munster drove his lorry into a little side street and pulled
up. Twelve o'clock. He generally did better for himself than this,
worked it out so that he could have his lunch in a bit of a park
somewhere. He'd look forward all the morning to sitting on a
patch of dusty grass under a tree, smelling the droughty smell of
the earth, soaking up the sun, thinking of nothing for a bit, private
to himself. When it was over he'd feel disappointed. Being pleased
or disappointed, or liking a bit of green weren't things he'd admit.
They were the things that got pushed to the wall, didn't belong to
the standing and status of lorry drivers. Sometimes he'd pull up at
one of the beaches. Might be nice in summer but it wasn't so good
in winter, you get the winds, and the sea, unless the day was very
bright, made you feel blue. It went on dragging and dragging at the
earth, night and day. You'd think it hated the earth where everything
grew. Some day, in a million years perhaps, it would get it all back.
He'd look at the sea and think, "What the hell," but not in a
comfortable sort of way. Something that never stopped, was never
still or silent, soft water that beat rocks into sand, ground sand with
sand, dead but moving, lifeless but hungry, moved by nothing but its
own mindless compulsion. It gave Harry the willies. It didn't grow
anything but fish. People said, "You poor fish." It mightn't be so
different from living on the land after all. If you listened hard enough
you could hear the beat, beat, beat, wherever you were, in Martin
Place or Alice Springs or on the top of Mount Kosciusko. Life got
you, made sand of you. Or was it death got you? Life or Death?
Death only happened once, a pit that opened suddenly at your feet,
a long black crack in the earth. No one else saw it, only you; they
went ahead as if it were not there and you fell headlong. Or you
walked through the interlacing shadows that a big tree casts on a
sunny day—the others went safely through, but to you the shadows
clung, about your feet, wrapping your legs, binding your arms to your
body, not shadows but barbed wire, not cool but red hot, strung up
on the barbed wire in no man's land till you died. If you weren't
alive you couldn't die, being alive was the main difficulty. Trapped
in being alive with no way out but dying. Poor fish. He'd seen too
much of fish lately. Fish and chips. Easy sort of dinner but not much
for a man to come home to. He couldn't blame Ally, the way she
was, for taking things easy. But she leaned too heavily on the fish
and chips. He'd swear the man round the corner hadn't changed his

fat once since they'd come to Carnation Street. You could smell it across the road. The ancestral fat, he'd called it, but Ally didn't smile. She just thought he was slinging off at her. Maybe things would be different now, maybe not.

On wet days he didn't bring tucker but went to a cheap joint—a place in a side street, always full of taxi drivers and other lorry men. All men, and all in transport of one sort or another. Funny that. Meat pie with as much Worcestershire as you liked to use and a dollop of potato, size of a threepenny icecream, sausage and mash, hamburger, tomato or onions a penny extra, stewed fruit and custard or a wedge of tart, tea and return. Stacks of bread ready cut on the tables. Whether you had a bob or a one-and-sixpenny feed, they filled you up just the same. Everything easy, men talking, different from a pub. All right for a change, but it went against the grain to buy food when he could eat at home or take it with him. Harry always had to sit near the door to keep an eye on the waggon. He was always scared someone would pinch a case off it. They docked you if that happened. Other firms generally put a boy on the lorries to give a hand and keep guard. Mullangar's were too mean. Mullangar's Miracle Marts. Meanest firm in the city, that's why you could always get a job there, forever changing their drivers. Arnie stuck. He seemed to be on the inside running, in with the store boss, anyway he could always work things to his liking. A couple of days a week he'd get home to lunch and Chris would cook him steak and onions with an egg on top. He'd gone home today taking the message to Chris. Harry was perfectly willing to believe Chris was a good sort without liking her. Arnie always spoke of her with a wink and a smacking of the lips as if she were the Queen of Sheba. Maybe she was the sort of woman that was a lot better when you were married to her than when you weren't. Some were like that, most were just the other way. Arnie generally managed to be satisfied with what he'd got, showed what a clever fellow he was to pick a winner any time. Could have been a commercial traveller, Arnie could. Harry often thought he'd like a dog with him to mind the lorry, a black and tan, good barker but companionable. Good old Spark, he'd be the one, but he wouldn't take to the life after the country. He hoped the Grants were treating him proper. He wouldn't be able to have a dog because there'd be nowhere to put him at night. Couldn't have him up with them, couldn't or

wouldn't tie him up in the backyard. . . . He didn't want a boy.
A man had to be alone sometimes.

When he finished up round about lunch time at the store, he'd
have his tucker there, sitting with the others on the kerb in the lane
at the back, leaning up against the wall, munching and talking,
throwing crusts to a stray dog, encouraging it but not wanting it.
Harry never said much. When he'd finished eating he sat forward,
forearms resting on bent knees, hands hanging between them, head
down, half asleep in the sun, listening to talk that went nowhere—
dogs, S.P., women, engines, boasting, and anecdotes, half dissolved
in rambling, slangy speech. Not much of a bunch. All right. They
liked Harry all right, thought him a decent, quiet chap. One of the
blokes in the store had a two-up school, a bright spot in the drift.
Made Harry think of the army. He'd join in if they asked him.

Harry worked for a big firm of chain grocery stores. He drove one
of the lorries and his work took him all over the city and suburbs;
from the wharves to the depot, from the depot to the branches,
from factories and canneries back to the store. It was heavy work,
loading and unloading, the constant alertness of the road. At first he
had been bewildered finding his way; now, after two months, he
knew most of the places he'd be likely to go to. There were six
lorries on the road, they could do with a couple more. Often you had
an extra trip on to the day's work. The first man in at the end of
the day job. Harry hadn't been wise to this at first, now he was. The
store boss said old Mullanger was next thing to a millionaire. He
seemed proud of it, thought they all ought to be proud of it, too.
Harry couldn't have said whether he liked his job or not. It was a
job, he was getting used to it and coming to think that way. Only
now and then, when he thought of going on and on and nothing
in particular coming of it, he felt a knocking in his head. He didn't
think much unless something happened to upset the protective
routine he'd made himself. Like today. Then a knock or a jolt
to his mind and the thoughts flowed like blood.

The lane would have to do today. He wouldn't be in anyone's
way, it was a cul-de-sac between a blank wall and a row of narrow
backyards belonging to a dilapidated terrace. The wall shielded him
from the cold wind and the sun struck back warmly at him from
the wall. Christ, he was tired. He'd an ache in his solar plexus.
Yesterday was a heavy day, to and from the wharves all day. He'd

been up all night or most of it. Round about midnight Ally and
Mrs Blan had decided it was the real thing and he'd taken her along
to the hospital. They'd been slow enough admitting her and she'd
had awful pains in the waiting room and he'd sweated nearly as
much as she had. The place was like a great factory. There wasn't
anyone you could ask anything. The sister said he could wait if he
liked. He'd have preferred Nurse Carter's. She might be an old
cow, but she wasn't an institution. He felt he was shut in by
high glassy walls on which he could make no impression. He'd felt
worse about this one than about any of the others. He'd been anxious
before but he hadn't felt it was his *fault*. Ally hadn't either. He
remembered his blaze of pride and joy when Jackie was born. My
son. A proper fool. Maybe Jackie couldn't have lived. He'd been sick
nearly all his short life. But Harry didn't believe that. He remembered
him leaping in his arms, kicking against him with his little feet,
strong and full of life. Jackie never ought to have died. Bright's
disease, they'd said it was. His kidneys. A little fellow like that.
It wasn't right. They should have been able to do something. Ally
had taken him to the Children's Hospital and the doctor had hardly
looked at him. Said he was all right, to take him home and put
him on the bottle. If he'd found out then what was the matter he
could have been saved. He knew it. He'd told Dr Jones and Dr
Jones had put him off. You couldn't get satisfaction anywhere. There
were the hospitals—you could go there and get the best attention
for nothing. That's what they said. A specialist the rich'd pay guineas
to see. But if he didn't bother, you were no better off. He didn't
know the doctor's name or where he was now. He couldn't prove
anything. And if he could, what would be the good, the boy was
dead. The inquest. The coroner's perfunctory sympathy. . . . Well, a
coroner had that sort of thing happening all the time, you couldn't
expect him to take it much to heart. The whole thing wound up
to every one's satisfaction; only took ten minutes. Best clothes.
Feeling guilty and angry and helpless and miserable. Going home
when it was over—to Ally. Jackie's death hadn't made any difference
in Ally or their life together. She'd cried a lot but he hadn't felt
she really cared.

He'd waited three hours at the hospital. Then a different nurse
had come to tell him the baby was born, a boy, and Ally was doing
well. He hadn't felt sure they'd got it right. In this place they might

have mixed Ally up with some one else. She went away and left him. He didn't know what to do. He waited another hour and they let him see Ally. All she wanted to tell him was that they hadn't given her chloroform. They only gave it for first babies or complications. He took it that she blamed him.

Another boy. Well, seemingly you didn't throw up your hat for joy. You went down on your knees and asked for forgiveness. You asked the hospital to forgive you for being such a nuisance, and the kid's mother to forgive you for all the pain and no chloroform. Most of all he ought to ask the baby's forgiveness. Poor little beggar. Ally wanted to call him after her father, Benjamin. Ben. Ben was a good name. Benny. Something wanted to stir in his heart but he wouldn't let it. He wasn't going to be taken in that way again.

He took out his packet of sandwiches. The wind had dried them through the paper and the bread was curling back from the slabs of cheese. His dry mouth would hardly receive them. He unscrewed the top of his vacuum flask and swilled down some tea. One and six-pence at the bargain basement. A vacuum flask for one-and-six. Ally thought that it was one of the wonders of the world, that to be able to get it ought to resign him to leaving the poultry farm for the city. The way he worked it out was, with all the wonders of science and inventions and progress and mass production, we ought to be getting everything cheap and plenty. To make big eyes when some little thing slipped through to us—that wasn't sense. It wasn't the right way to behave. Bobbing and pulling a forelock, new style. Flimsy things they were, and a good profit on the one-and-six, he'd be bound.

Harry felt better for the tea out of the one-and-sixpenny vacuum flask. Mrs Blan was looking after the children. Jackie's death had given Ally a good start with the neighbours. Mrs Blan, the fat woman who lived downstairs, had been kind. Wherever anything happened there you found Mrs Blan. It wasn't all kindness and it wasn't all curiosity. You might say it was a sense of life. First Jackie and then the new one had held her interest. Mrs Blan had been a mother to Ally. He was grateful. Chris would be over this afternoon to get Wanda. She had promised to take her while Ally was in hospital. Ruthie would be all right with Mrs Blan. Ruthie was never any trouble, he was sometimes afraid she'd be put upon. He'd have to look out for Ruthie. Wanda was the taking one, she'd be able to look after herself better than Ruthie, you could see that even

at three. She ran rings round Ruthie now, not because Ruthie was
stupid. She was willing to give, that was all. Best little kid in the
world. Soon she'd have to go to school. Five years old in August.
School. Something else you got for nothing. Fine. The picture of
children teeming out from the asphalt playground of a school in
the street, a mob of children with raucous voices, children mass
produced in the big hospitals, herd educated, stamped with a
meaningless pattern. . . . He'd been to a little bush school himself,
ten or a dozen children, one teacher. The other thing alarmed him.
He didn't know why. He was afraid of the institution or the mass,
of letting a creature as tender as a child go so soon and so utterly
into the world, delivering it over to forces he could not control or
understand, to the indifference that he believed to have killed
Jackie. The city. You couldn't trust it. You had to hold out against
the world. But you couldn't. We were all in it together. (His tired
mind grappled with its thought, trying to drag it out of his tired
brain into the light. Sometimes a man thought more and more
clearly when he was tired, really tired, all the barricades knocked
down, because he could not resist thinking—like children being born
in the night when resistance was low.) You'd got to live in the
world. A little farm up at Toongabbie, scratching like hell to keep
going, wasn't the way out. It was only the way out for you, but
maybe it wasn't. It was a little island of sand and the sea had got
at it. It crumbled under you. It had crumbled under him. Everywhere it was crumbling under people and they were giving up and
coming into the city. They couldn't live in a tiny world and they
were trying to live in a big one. Out of hand. Refusing wasn't enough.
Not enough to stall. It drove you into that, but you couldn't stay
there either. It's not "These are my kids." You couldn't draw the
line. All of them or none of them. You gave up your kids or you
made things better for all the kids. No good being thrown higgledy
piggledy into the world, like scraps into the pigs' trough. Got to
work together. If you're all going together, every one responsible,
being many didn't matter. It was strength. Mess into pattern. How
did you begin. The good old Co-op. That's part of it but not enough,
of course. Not enough protest in it. You saw Co-operatives getting
sucked in, doing this and that because it was expedient as things
were and then waking up to find themselves a part of the system
they'd set out to break. The strong thing pulls the weak thing. But

everything's weak to begin with—like babies. Except us. Us is everybody. What we've got to find is a sticking point. It doesn't much matter where. Shout, mates, all together, "Stop that." Let every one go to their bosses, whoever they are and whatever they do, on one day and say, "We won't work unless the miners get a fortnight's holiday on full pay every year." Every one strike for it except the miners. Let the housewives in every constituency go in a body to their member and say, "We want a decent deal for the girls in the textile industry." Let the rural workers and the wharfies say, "No more raw material sent overseas until the Indian coolies are freed from slavery." . . Say it and stick to it. We could just about do anything all together, but who's to start? Not me. I've three kids and a wife. I've got to keep her even if I don't cut any ice with her now. Maybe things will be better now the baby's come. Maybe they won't. Maybe it's going on like this always. Women are tough, give 'em a grievance and they can stick to it till death do them part. The good old army. It wasn't a bad life, take it all in all. You did what you were told, no responsibility, never had to live more than a minute at a time, take what you could get and it was jolly well yours, the man next to you was your mate, you went the same way, were all bits in some sort of design or thought you were. Perhaps you weren't. Bloke in the pub who'd had a few started saying the war was a bloody swindle. Pub was full, round about 6 o'clock, lot of Diggers there. They roared like hell at him. He felt like roaring himself. It was their war and they'd not much beside. They'd have thrown him out. Chap wasn't afraid of them, sort of look on him; you knew he'd had his issue of everything and wouldn't ever be scared of anything again. Nobody could do anything to a man like that. Must a' been pretty clear for a mob of angry men to see it. "Passchaendale," he said, and held up his two arms for all to see. He hadn't any hands. Great voice he had on him above the din. Might have been a sergeant-major. Men who've been soldiers will obey a voice like that. He had as much right to tell them as they had to tell him. "Bloody murder," he said. "What's generals but bosses?" he said. "War's big business," he said. "Poor sods," he said, "Don't you fight no more wars unless you make 'em," he said. "You're a bloody revolutionary," yelled a little pipsqueak. There was a roar then. The bar man was ready to do some chucking out, but he didn't rightly know who. He and Timmy Andrews had gone out then, they reckoned it wasn't their fight. Timmy said: "How do you suppose he lifted his pot with his mits gone?" Timmy had been right through without a scratch. Never talked about the war, but he did that day. He could tell some, too. What if the bloke from Passchaendale was right? You had to cut back a long way before you came to the end of rottenness and found something that would stand by you.

No more kids, he'd got that straight.

Harry sat collapsed over his wheel, the hard rim pressed against his hard lean ribs. Ally was right, he was a mug. What she didn't get was that he couldn't have been anything else, hadn't any choice. The smart alecs were mugs too, only they hadn't dropped to it. Time he was getting on. He threw his greasy lunch paper into the lane and started his engine.

.  .  .  .  .  .  .  .

"That's the first phase." Knarf laid his hand on the pile of sheets he had scaled off as he read.

"So." Ord was still more interested in the writer than in the book. Knarf was gathering confidence, his mind had drawn together in firm and cleanly lines, had tautened. He was still anxious to forestall comment, to get the book before Ord in something of its proper shape, wishing it were a picture or a statue that could be seen in its entirety at once. It had shape and mass but they could be seen only in retrospect, and he was still afraid that the parts would betray it. At first his own words had been like chaff to him, but gradually they had awakened the sap that had produced them. He had begun reading badly, the rhythm of his voice cutting across the rhythm of his prose. Now the words were at home in his mouth. He would be able to shape it, smaller but in the same image, condensing and telling it in place of reading it, keeping it whole but reducing its size.

Ord said rather heavily, "You did well to choose the antique form of the novel. It was the typical form of the period; large, rich, confused, intricate, it needs an elastic, free, inclusive form. Strange how form sculptures to period, have you noticed? Of course you have. Those times were efflorescent, these are astringent; we use the more deeply channelled and succint forms. Writers to-day seem intent on imparting a sense of definition, of something still and completed.

The novel is the organ of becoming, the voice of a world in flux. You know, the thing that most reassures me that you've got inside your period is the ease with which you're using the form. Not imitation. I recognise that, but a story in terms of itself."

Ord's getting old, Knarf thought. Prosy. The lecturette has entered into his soul. He looked at Ord sideways, with humour and irritation. Solid piece of human carving. Time could not get at him from without, so it was attacking from within.

Ord thought, the way we say things is so much more significant than what we say. The forms betray us. In times of struggle and becoming, the words are released, the forms break of their own inadequacy. Literature ceases to be an art with canons, it becomes a hungry mouth. The novel was a mouth, sucking avidly at life. A Protean form for an age out of control. The twentieth century, a time of riot. The nineteenth piled up riches, opened doors on eternity, Progress, Speculation, Education. The concept of Freedom proliferating like yeast. The democratisation of appetite. The right to want. The twentieth became its desperate legatee. How to get "have" to "want." The disastrous answer, Competition. The old hierarchic idea carrying over into the new age. Christ and all his angels, the congregation of the saints, Christ's vicar on earth, the Fathers of the Church, the power to bind and to loose, the suppliant people, the humble and contrite hearts. All this, translated into the new order, masters and men, haves and have nots. The disastrous will to pour new materials into old moulds. Mediaeval thinking rested on the inequality of men. On that basis there was order, method, theoretic if not actual. The temporal world followed the spiritual in its hierarchic pattern. Aberrations did not shake the basic concept. The whole structure was kept in place by spiritual mandate. Then came the change, comparable to breaking of the atom. The change-over from a poor world to rich world. Call it, if you like, after one of its nodules, the Industrial Revolution. Plenty, enormous plenty. Some to have, some not to have. It would no longer work because the prize was different. Men had venerated without coveting the martyr's crown. The chosen of God must suffer, but not the chosen of Mammon. With them it was being, not having. The enforcement of the hierarchical idea on a basis of having instead of being. At first there was a high proportion of automatic consent, carried over on the time lag. The Golden Age of Capitalism. The workman paid to his employer the meed of respect that he had once paid the feudal lord who had protected him. But the employer did not protect. The natural basis of the relationship was swept away. The substitution of a desirable earthly prize for a (on the whole undesirable) heavenly prize sharpened men's consciousness. One element of the social ensemble suffered elephantiasis. Competition. The veneer of fair play, the shibboleth that competition afforded protection from within itself. Competitive manufacture led to the production of ever better and cheaper articles. Competitive breadwinning led to the undercutting of standards by the men themselves. Competitive manufacture decreased, replaced by combination and monopoly. A value on improvement. Competitive breadwinning continued, despite the partial barrier of Trade Unions and State action. The perfect trap, Man in his own trap, villains and victims. But mass villains, mass victims, the safety catch of intention swept away. Competitive society was not a machine operated scientifically, to be started or stopped at will, intellectually conceived and intentionally perpetuated. Rather, it was a force of nature, an organism, a jungle that could only be cleared away by an ice age. Perhaps. Rising against it an awakened mass consciousness. The race between the thing in possession and the will to change it. Never was change so deeply rooted or more conscious. When the basis of life was power or spirit there was inequality. When it is a matter of money inequality becomes unreasonable. If few can give, all can possess. To be rich required no ability. Even the dullest had to perceive that there was no moral sanction for wealth. The slow destruction of consent. Refusal versus Power. Out of the untenable situation a new way of life being born but, as ever, altered and flawed by the circumstances of its birth. The enormous clash and upheaval was reflected in chaotic literature. The surge of novels—what was that but an attempt to get the chaos of circumstances into some sort of shape, using every method of attack, every ingenuity. A natural organic reaction.

There must be something in this book of Knarf's to set him off like that, into generalisations, the romanticism of the scientist, secret debauchery of the tied and regulated mind. This man, Harry Munster, he's the eternal *homo tragicus*, man caught in a trap and knowing it, futile awareness, false dawn of rebellion. There must be many like that before there can be any action, inevitable wastage.

The straw that shows how the tide flows has no influence on the tide. Little Man, Everyman. Dust in history. Dust like stars, stars like dust. He does not matter, but if he does not matter, nothing matters. He is Man. Man throwing down a greasy paper in a back lane.

"Go on," he said, raising his chin from his breast, looking, not at Knarf, but beyond him to the new world. The light swung at him. The pause had lasted perhaps for the space of a dozen breaths.

Knarf was not waiting for Ord. He had paused for his own reasons, to pick up some mysterious beat. He began talking, carrying on the story, in the smooth voice men sometimes use when they are telling something that they know very well indeed, as if they read it off the air, and the words they used for it were the only possible words.

1925, the year Benny was born, was a pretty good year for everybody. So were the next three years. It was a boom. Trade throve, confidence flourished, employment was easy to get. There was enough prosperity for some of it to seep down into the back streets. It flowed in the veins of the city like spring or love, it came out of the taps with the beer. It affected men like the first pleasant stages of drink and women like an aphrodisiac. All were affected so no one noticed it. The times were normal, progress was a road running straight and fair into infinity. Why shouldn't it go on if people believed in it? Prosperity in one place made prosperity in another. You earned and spent. Your spendings were another man's earnings, and he in turn spent, and so it went on, the beneficent circle, the maypole dance. Building went ahead furiously. The skyline of the city was changing. From the hill of William Street the horizon bristled with cranes. Taxis multiplied. Month by month, traffic was heavier and a Main Road Board began to overhaul communication, rooting up old roads and laying down better ones. Commercial travellers came into their own, insurance agents went about their business and drew pleasure as well as profit from arithmetic. Go-getters, large and small, kept harvest home. Hire purchase stretched its roots in sympathetic soil. The community could afford to be gulled and to enjoy it. There was an easy way round rainy days and responsibility circulated as comfortably as prosperity.

The Munsters stayed in Carnation Street. It had been a temporary expedient, a camping place while they looked round for something better, but it became a permanency. It suited Ally. It wasn't a house, so it didn't make a house's claim on her. Living in rooms might be a come down, but it let you out. You lived as other roomers did. Without effort she sloughed off all her housewifely traditions. She rarely cleaned the place, at first because the coming child gave her the right to take things easily, and she was minded to take up that right to the full, afterwards because she had got out of the way of it. The rooms were dark and a bit of dust didn't show. Besides, people didn't drop in here, you met them in the street, standing in the doorway, at the little corner grocery, in the paper shop. Except on rare occasions you didn't see the inside of their homes, an iron shutter of privacy was drawn down over them. Each built about herself a world of her own choosing and it was accepted at face value. No oriental could outdo them in the art of saving face. Why strive arduously for the reality when the illusion was so easily achieved? You had only to say and to keep on saying, "I'm that particular, dear. I wouldn't put a thing in my mouth unless I knew where it came from," or "I must have things just so, I'm funny that way," and you were an immaculate housekeeper. No one was ever short of money, she just "ran out of change." So inconvenient to have all one's money in five-pound notes. They could haggle over halfpennies "for the principle of the thing." Of their husbands they talked with the utmost freedom except on subjects touching their own pride. To complain of them, their importunity, their jealousy, their general lowness, was a mark of sophistication. There was an elegant reason for everything. They knew the truth about one another and would, at the right seasons, discuss it very freely, but not with the party concerned. Politeness demanded unlimited credulity. It was given and received. If Ally must play this game with her neighbours, it was folly to throw away all it offered in ease and negligence. It came easily. She was adaptable. She saw her home as her neighbours, similarly placed, saw theirs. They were over-crowded but, she said comfortably, they were going to take the attic room for the little girls when they were a little older or when it fell vacant. If things became unbearable, one could always move. One complained of noise and neighbours and landlord and was always on the point of leaving as a protest, and so, maintaining a high standard, one was never actually put to the trouble and expense of going elsewhere.

In the two months between Jackie's death and the birth of Ben, Ally spent a lot of time thinking about the good time she would have to make up for all she'd been through, as soon as she was free of her burden. Time and again, violent fits of weeping came upon her. Whether it was on account of Jackie or herself she was never clear. Mrs Blan was copious in her sympathy and her exhortations. Of Jackie she and Harry did not talk. Ally had a vague wretched feeling that some blame attached to her because she had never believed that the child was seriously ill. Harry had never reproached her, but she believed that the reproach existed in his mind. She saw in it the reason for his blank silent grief. He would not share his grief with her and she would not share hers with him. She was quick to change doubt of herself for resentment against him, for that was easier to bear. Deep in her heart she was unhappy, but she did not intend to go on being unhappy. Not for any man. She was young, she'd had a bad time, now she was going to see to it that she was recompensed. The thought that she was one of life's creditors sustained her; in the light of it, whatever she did was justified.

Like Harry, Ally hoped that the baby's birth would make a change in their relationship. She was ready to yield but not to retreat. She was willing to be swept off her feet. It was one of those occasions that no hero of fiction would fail to turn to advantage. Harry didn't drop to it. Besides, the opportunity for a grand reconciliation scene did not present itself. The hospital ward was no place for it. He was stiff and awkward when he came to see her, and felt himself at a disadvantage. When, at the end of ten days, she was ready to leave the hospital, he managed to call for her in the truck as he was returning to the depot. That might have been the moment of emotional reconciliation, but he had time only to carry the baby and her case upstairs and leave her. When he returned late, Ally was tired and querulous. Chris had brought Wanda back. There was no time or energy for scenes. It was not enough that he cheerfully set to work to get a meal for them and then put the two little girls to bed. The next morning it was early to work and the next evening it was the same. Their life ground on. Ally was avid for emotion. Harry was too tired to give it, too unperceiving to know what was wanted. He saw that her eyes were still hard, her mouth still sulky, and he knew that the comfortable argument, "It was just her condition," did not hold. He was confused. He was tired. He had always worked hard, but now the strain was falling in an unaccustomed place. There was no relief in his home. He supposed that most people's marriages

went phut sooner or later. He'd heard men speak of their wives with
latent hostility often enough. Jackie's death had shaken his confidence
in life as neither the war nor his own struggles and defeats ever had.
He continued to miss the little boy, and his heart bled secretly, without
his knowledge. A bitter realisation that this was how things were
and always would be, that he'd been a mut to expect anything better,
began to form, like a slow accretion of limestone, at the root of
his mind.

Ally did not stand still. She set to work to exploit her world after
her own fashion. They had a capital of about £60, what was left
of the money from the sale of the farm, the truck, and the stock,
after their debts were settled. This had been broken into for Jackie's
funeral. There was still over £40 left. The money was banked in
Ally's name and she began to draw on it. She bought, on time payment, a bedroom suite in fumed oak and a wireless set. Harry knew
nothing about them till he came home one Friday night and found
them there. Ally was in a state of nervous excitement, gay with fright.
Harry said they must be returned at once. Ally was determined to
keep them.

She had already shown them to Mrs Blan and boasted of them to
other neighbours. She could not retreat. Besides, she had convinced
herself that it was only what she should have had when she married.
They quarrelled. No woman could have fought more fiercely for her
young. He recognised that this was the same quarrel that they had
had on the night Ally had first determined to leave the farm. He
realised that it would always be the same quarrel endlessly repeated.
She wore him down. He said at last she could have them, but she
must keep the payments up out of the money he gave her weekly.
He'd let the firm take them back sooner than pay for them out of
his share of the family budget. She accused him of spite, and declared
that all she wanted was to make their home a decent place for him
and the children. He asked then why didn't she keep it clean, and
their voices rose. When Ally gave the baby his night feed he was
sick and she accused Harry of upsetting her and poisoning her milk.
Speechless with rage at this last mean advantage he returned to the
balcony to spend what was left of the night with Ruthie and Wanda.
He found Ruthie, awakened by the quarrel, crying silently, her head
buried in the pillow and her little bottom raised in the air, a grotesque
and pathetic attitude reminiscent of the ostrich. His anger died. He

was contrite. He took the child in his arms and, murmuring in a low voice so that Ally should not hear, comforted her. Reassured, she nestled against him and fell asleep, the episode becoming in her mind only the vague trace of a bad dream. He gently pushed the sleeping Wanda to the wall and, with Ruth still in his arms, lay down to snatch some uneasy sleep. He quieted his distracted nerves with the thought that tomorrow he must drive a heavy lorry through traffic all day. Whatever happened he was determined that the children should not be sacrificed.

Nothing more was said about the furniture, but when Ally came home late on Saturday she found the house reorganised. Harry had taken the discarded old double bed down to the Furniture Mart and exchanged it for a divan bed. This he had set up in the living-room. The little girls were to sleep there and he had made up his bed on the balcony. Ally protested that she would not have the living-room cluttered up. He told her shortly that it was only for a time, he would take the attic room for them as soon as they were old enough to sleep alone. They would keep the other pieces to furnish it. Their living space was more congested than ever. Ally had meant to realise on the old bedroom furniture and use the money — it would not have been more than a few shillings. She looked on it as her property. However, she said nothing. She was disturbed by Harry's departure. She told herself cynically that he wouldn't be able to keep it up and then she'd teach him a lesson. But he showed no change of mind, he took her at her word and she hated him for it. All right, she thought, if he doesn't want me, there are others that will. She took to using lipstick and got a permanent wave on time payment. But she went no further with that.

Having the fumed oak bedroom suite, Ally took no care of it. She let the children climb over it, put down cups of hot tea on the polished wood, spilled medicine on the washstand and did not trouble to wipe it up. The shoddiness soon appeared, but that neither surprised nor troubled her. Possession was all she cared about. The payments were a grim struggle. Once she was in such straits for money that she went through her husband's pockets and took a pound note that she found there. She didn't feel anything when she did it and later helped him to search for it without a tremor. He did not suspect her. She justified herself, "I wouldn't have to do it if he weren't so mean." She wondered how he came to have a pound note like that and began to suspect that he had more money than he told her. It made her very angry. Nevertheless that pound note kept coming into her mind in the way that indigestible food repeats. She did not do it again.

Her only means of saving was on the food bill. The meals grew obviously scanty and inferior. Harry protested. She told him that prices were going up and she couldn't manage on what he gave her. He worked overtime, servicing the trucks, and gave her another fifteen shillings a week. When the woman from the corner grocery store waylaid him and told him his wife owed her six pounds and she wanted it, he was furious. In the quarrel that followed Ally thought he was going to strike her and hoped he would. She had an answer for everything he said and stood before him, defiant and provocative. He thought with disgust that she looked like a tart. It turned his anger from hot to cold. He paid off the debt week by week. Ally and Mrs Blan started a feud against the corner shop and the whole street listened to their slanders.

There were other things. Mrs Blan initiated Ally into the pleasures of S.P. betting. It was illegal and Sol Morris in the newspaper shop arranged it for them on the telephone. They bet in small sums, sixpences and occasionally shillings. Sometimes Ally won and sometimes she lost. The small trickle of excitement went on all the time. It was like an itch, but an itch that she soon could not do without. The races were reported over the air and Ally and Mrs Blan could hang over her wireless set waiting with febrile eagerness to know if they had picked a winner. It filled the days, supplied an interest. The wireless, Ally felt, justified itself. It was almost a business investment.

It was a capricious instrument, but could generally be relied on to fill the place with noise. Ally liked it on all the time. She got so that she felt lost without it. The syrupy music used to make her come over all sentimental. Using it a lot gave her a vague sense of triumphing over the dealer who sold it to her. There was a lot of money still owing on it. Benny was quite inured to its noise and could sleep through massed bands. He sometimes woke up and cried when it was turned off.

Ruthie was five and could go to school now. Ally got the authorities to take Wanda too, saying they were twins, Wanda being tall and rather forward. This left her freer. She could go to cheap morning sessions of the pictures with Chris, or spend hours window shopping and making trifling purchases. She had an encyclopaedic knowledge of all the bargain basements. Chris was quite lively when you knew her well and had a fund of salacious stories, perpetually renewed by Arnie, which she imparted to Ally. Ally took good care that Chris shouldn't know about herself and Harry. Nobody knew about that.

Sometimes, at odd moments when she wasn't amusing herself, Ally had a curious feeling rather like homesickness. She vaguely wanted "things to be different", even "like they used to be." She felt sorry for herself then. She saw her life as threadbare and shoddy. She even felt shoddy herself. But she fought against such weakness and stamped it down.

She and Harry had very little to say to each other. They rarely quarrelled. Often they were quite pleasant to each other in a detached sort of way. But nothing was changed. One day he asked her how much money was still owing on the furniture, and when she told him gave it to her. He thought he had cleared up the whole thing and that now they were even.

Ally used some of the money to pay back a loan to Mrs Blan, with the rest she cleared the debt on the bedroom suite. They still owed money on the wireless. She reflected that Harry must have won the money gambling. She began to get an ice chest on time payment. Why not? They needed it and things seemed pretty flush with Harry.

Harry got used to seeing the children playing in the street. At first he corrected them for the words they used, but, after a while, it didn't seem any good, all the children were the same. When Benny was a year old, his father took him to sleep out on the verandah with him. He said it would be good for him to have more air, but he liked having him there. He was a healthy, cheerful baby with a wide, friendly grin. Harry no longer watched him uneasily for signs of disease. Ally was fond enough of the child, but left him a good deal to Ruthie and was pleased that Harry should take him at night.

"Harry makes a fool of himself over the kids," she told Mrs Blan.

"Well, I must say it's nice when they take notice of someone beside themselves," that lady countered amiably.

Harry stuck at his job. Arnie was storeman now and they did not get on very well together. There had never been much sympathy between them, and they had disagreed on the matter of joining the Transport Union. Harry, the former zealot of the Co-operative movement, had joined and had succeeded in persuading the other men to join. They had all been non-unionists when they were taken on, though the question had not been raised and nothing indicated that their employer objected. Only Arnie stood out. He argued that he hadn't anything against the Union, and if he worked in a big place he'd join, but when there were only six of them it was better not. Harry felt only contempt for this point of view and showed it openly. He had an independent way of condemning anything he thought was a lapse from principle, calculated to annoy people who did not agree with him. Arnie grinned nastily, quite unperturbed. They'd see who laughed last. Harry wasn't exactly smart. When the storeman's job fell vacant then, Arnie got it. He was then in a position to punish Harry. Harry found himself getting the heavier jobs, though Arnie remained outwardly good-tempered and he could never be quite sure whether this was intention or chance.

Harry had plenty of pals, did a bit of pubbing, went now and then to a fight with Timmy Andrews, gambled as much as the other men. Life looked reasonably safe. He had an affair with a girl called Elsie Todd, who was employed at one of the chain of stores. It didn't last long and he came to detest her so much that he thought of looking for another job, but she got the sack before he'd made up his mind. He didn't speak of the war or of the farm at Toongabbie, except on the rare occasions when he had had too much to drink. He didn't think about anything much. He no longer expected much from life and thought they were getting on well enough. But in his heart he was discontented. And so was Ally. Both waited, as most men wait all their days, dumbly and uncomprehendingly, for an exterior force to fuse their lives into coherence.

.        .        .        .        .        .        .        .        .

"You see," said Knarf, "I am only keeping now to the main thread, the Munsters are no more than the dominant in a large pattern which I try to keep simultaneously alive. It includes the Blans downstairs, the old-age pensioner Joe, Rita, the girl in the attic, all the other inhabitants of the short street, the Hughes, the Nelsons, Bert Cassidy, the roomers at No. 7, the people who come and go, the children playing on the pavement, Mrs Buchan at the corner shop, the people who go to the paper shop to bet, even down to the passers-by in the street, regular and casual, the messenger boys at the post-office. A patch of fibrous, nervous tissue lifted off the pelt of the city, and other tissues clinging to it, the lorry drivers, men in pubs, Elsie Todd, the girl in the Marrickville shop . . . not described, written flatly, as I've been doing it, but in action."

Ord nodded. "Simultaneous assault. Co-operation of the reader, the broken circuit, raw material of pattern, commentary by juxtaposition."

"Exactly."

"Exactly," Ord echoed to himself. "Now we have the professional writer, the man on the rostrum." He felt a homely affection for the man he knew so well. Confidence ebbed and flowed in him like a blush on a maiden's cheek. He had his moments of transparent confidence; confidence to him was a sort of exaltation. It never hardened into assurance. That was why he was, perhaps, a great man. He had still the bared quick of his imagination when most of us were turning to wood.

"I've wanted to make again that lost world — a magma in which few, I think, were at home. Man's creation had gone past him, he was bound on a mechanic wheel and the wheel was due to plunge downward, carrying him with it. All were sated and none satisfied. Civilisation was loaded with an insufferable burden, the wrong sort of plenty. The shoddy replica of everything the heart can desire in the bargain basement. The simulacrum of every human emotion on sale in the cinema. Man's greed enlarged out of all proportion by constant stimulus. The swollen belly of an undernourished child. Competition from being a means become an end. Man building his life in repetitive images from bargain sale to war, from competitive breadwinning to competitive nationalism. Man, shamed and impotent, making sacrifice to the pitiful god of luck, ikon of the hopeless. Gambling, astrology, necromancy, quacks, faith healers, fortune tellers. Magic in daylight, enchantment at bargain rates, old charms in new wrappings, the new heaven and the new earth in trial packets, monster offer for ten days only, no obligation. The city of steel and concrete, of polished and impervious bankfronts, of packed concrete roads and everlasting pavements, mechanic, mechanised, controlled, product of reason and science, dependent in its working, not on mother wit of man, but on specialised knowledge, formalised knowledge, the secret code of the gasfitter, the closed corporation of the electrician, the higher arithmetic — abracadabra to you and me — of the constructional engineer, the apostolic knowledge of the loftier sanitation. Science and technology, uncomprehended, wear the same face as astrology and magic.

The city making men in its image, conditioning their characters as well as their daily lives."

"Economic determinism."

"That was one of the barren phrases of the twentieth century. It never explained more than half the process. Reaction to, reaction against, acquiescence and revolt, moulding by conditions and to conditions, the inevitable thrust against conditions. Increase reason and you strengthen magic, drive men into a mass, and everywhere the cracks of separatism widen. Man's mastery increases man's dependence — press the button and the elevator works, pull the lever and the engine functions, turn the knob and music flows, the pressure of the foot on the accelerator gives speed. So easy that a child can do it, so difficult only the initiated can grasp why. The haves and the have-nots, and the cross division, the initiated and the uninitiated, tribes within the people, languages within the language, differences coming to the surface in speech. On one hand standardising, centralising, pooling; on the other, the assertion everywhere in speech variation, of the existence of peculiar peoples — thieves' argot in the underworld, technical jargon of the great guilds, each its dialect, gibberish of the racecourse, cant of the politician, journalese, party patter, slang both snobbish and anti-snobbish. . . ."

"Phantasmagoria."

Knarf picked up a sheet as if at random and began to read.

Benny's first articulate memory was of the iron railings that fenced in the narrow strip of verandah outside Mrs Blan's window from the street. He had forced his head between them and it had stuck. He remembered this very clearly; in a flare of pain and fright he had found himself staring into a different street, dark, blood-red, awful, a place that didn't exist. His screams had terrified him into panic, his screams or what he saw. He didn't know what he had seen. "Black," he said, "red." He couldn't formulate the idea that he had poked his head out of the real world into an unreal world and found himself caught. It was quite beyond him to say that behind the familiar was the unfamiliar, that the world, even the most commonplace and solid manifestations of it, had Another Face, and that the way to it was so simple that you never found it but might slip into it in an unguarded moment. Whatever happened was as much a part of experience, as genuine an experience, for all that it was undeveloped, as a fleck of protoplasm is a part of the living series. He could say,

"I got my head stuck," and the rest closed in behind the statement, incommunicable, a *true* nightmare. No one else remembered the incident. In vain Wanda, with her exasperating common sense, declared that it couldn't have happened, the rails were too close together, even a little baby could not get his head between them. She offered to show him with Mrs Blan's daughter's baby, then on the premises. His obstinacy defeated Wanda. The only other argument she could think of was biting him. Benny knew it had happened.

Other fragments of the first years persisted, but so trodden down by time as to be barely decipherable. Till the end of his life any sudden joy evoked the almost dissolved memory of hearing on a still summer afternoon in the deserted street a canary singing from a cage hung in the window of the house opposite. There was another image that became one of the worn coins of his mind, a thunder of light and movement. It might have been the vestigial memory of a cavalry charge or of Niagara Falls, but in reality it was the traffic in William Street. Ruth would take him sometimes after dark on an excursion to the corner of the street, and they would stand stolidly thrilled, mindlessly absorbed, watching the cars stream down the hill to the city. They were capable of standing for hours, mesmerised by the glory of it, all the grander because it had been dinned into them that to step off the footpath was to die. Vaguely he remembered the backyard full of garbage tins, grey washing, castor oil plant, and a smell of cats, as a place of horror where his father had forbidden him to go, and he remembered Old Joe, the pensioner, as the Bad Man, to whom his mother threatened to give him when he was naughty. He had fled howling from the ferocity of two men fighting in a laneway, to be slapped by his mother and then by Wanda for wetting his pants. He had scrambled with other children for fragments when the ice man had dropped a block of ice on the kerb, and when he had thrown his piece away, "Burny, burny," they had laughed at him jeeringly with voices of big sparrows. He had memories of being taken to places he could not name where everything was big, big, big. Big meant more than big, it meant bright, exciting, strange. Perhaps these places were the Botanic Gardens, the Domain, the waterfront. He could not identify them later, they were right off the map. Although the scenes of his infancy became the commonplaces of his boyhood, the rational vision of a later period did not seep back into these memories of memories of a lost time. They carried the print of an emotional outlook which he later outgrew, and so their colouration set them apart.

His father was in his mind inseparable from the lorry he drove, although he saw his father daily and the lorry only occasionally. It was the lorry he adored. When Harry brought it to the door, as he did sometimes, Benny would swarm up into the cabin, violently resist the efforts of any other little boy to follow him, and from his vantage ground survey the street with consummate pride. He fingered the gadgets on the dashboard with reverential joy, sniffed up the petrol fumes, the grime and oiliness with delight. The dry smell of the groceries at the back he found intriguing too. His father's efforts to describe the Store resulted in an impression of Aladdin's Cave.

It was Ruthie who was his friend and companion. "You can trust Ruthie," their mother used to say, "but she is not bright like Wanda." Wanda was sharp as a pin, and she had a head on her, she could work points with anyone. Ruthie, who was very sensible in the house, showed backward at school, probably because she had never got over being afraid. She was content to make a companion of the baby. She would talk to him for hours, telling him "stories," an almost meaning-less jumble of words in which she expressed the obscure megalomania of childhood, a sort of poetry that, skirting her inadequate mind, gave her emotions and dreams the relief they craved. Benny listened charmed, as if for him too it had an intimate meaning, moving his head in time with her gestures. She stopped doing it before he was old enough to laugh at her, but continued to dream in the safe privacy of her own mind. Once she said to him, "We had another little brother but he died," a statement which at first baffled and then angered him. She refused to tell him any more.

At an undefined moment Benny changed from a baby into a little boy.

.    .    .    .    .    .    .    .    .    .    .

Knarf looked up, eyes morose, brows drawn down, staring unseeing into the horizon washed with light. "We can't know what happens in the mind of a child. We change, and memory changes with us. The history of memory. No one ever wrote that, did they? Let it lie in the mind and the simplest fact undergoes change. We agree to accept a common coin. The young child has not agreed to this convention. His world, once he has left it, is further from his reach than the stars."

The book that had been so near them a moment ago receded, shrank, became no more than a fleck on the horizon — a story about the irretrievably lost world of an imaginary child, four hundred years dead. It took confidence to write.

Knarf went on talking, his palms pressed down on the manuscript in an awkward and unconscious gesture of determination, like a man, following a difficult path, who fears to call on either memory or judgment lest they interfere with instinct.

"By the time Benny was four in June 1929, a new alembic had been thrown into their lives. The Depression had begun.

The first cold warning drops had fallen in 1928. It was the year of maximum confidence, the year that the Duke of York had opened Parliament in the white building like a bride cake, at Canberra, the costly brand-new capital. On the floor of a tranquil valley, almost encircled by the blue wall of the Australian Alps, across the brown and silver paddocks watered by the Molonglo, architects with compass and set square had laid down the design for a city. It was to be the perfect modern capital, rootless, blameless, minutely regulated, of a partyless, unsectarian beauty. Roads were laid down, columns of exotic trees marched in, government offices, white and classical, standardised houses for standard public servants, were built. It was a shame that human beings should live there at all, it was a shame that, living there, they should remain so terribly human instead of taking the hint from their surroundings and becoming high-minded and peaceful. At the opening of that first federal parliament in the new capital, no expense was spared, a king's son performed the opening ceremony, a world-famous prima donna sang "Advance Australia," rootless flowers bloomed in garden beds, huge sums were spent on transport and on putting hotels into commission for a day. An advertisement could hardly have been more beautifully and sumptuously executed. And yet Australia was not impressed, people grinned a shade sardonically, noted vulgarly what everything cost and didn't refuse to foot the bill. Times were good and the rich life stream did not flow through Canberra.

A few began to cry warnings, a crash was coming. The tempo of life did not slacken for that. There was nothing anyone could do to prevent it. Stop spending? Save? At this headlong speed, that would only precipitate trouble. Australia was in fact quite helpless, because, despite Canberra, despite the illusions of independence, despite the confidence of success and merit it advertised, she was bound with chains of gold to the world overseas. A debtor country and exporting country, she felt the least tremor in overseas markets. It took only a murmur of disquiet, amplified by the sounding board of the overlarge national debt, to bring the Australian pound tumbling down. World prices of wheat and wool fell steeply. The national income fell with them. The effect was felt in every quarter. Unemployment figures rose steeply. Confidence wavered and broke. The ice age was beginning. Paralysis crept by back channels through the city. Men sought to save themselves by retrenchment, frightened people stopped buying, canny people took advantage of fear to lower their costs by reducing staff and wages, strong concerns mopped up weak and grew stronger. There were bankruptcies, real and strategic, and men were cast on the streets, amalgamations were formed and half the staffs dismissed; men were out on half time and families plunged below the minimum wage; men replaced by boys at half the money, boys sacked at twenty-one without prospect of employment; the standard of living sagging lower and lower. The weakest went first and being without reserves were in dire want at once.

It was happening very quickly. It showed on the face of the city — more men about on week days, lounging on the corners, clustered outside the newspaper offices where the advertisement sheets were pasted up, hawking unwanted goods to housewives who began to fear them, sleeping in parks and in caves of the foreshore. Traffic lessened. Children came barefoot to school and compassionate teachers discovered they were hungry and fed them, till the thing got too big for them and they gave up in despair.

People moved from houses into rooms and then whole families into one room and still could not pay their rent. The tax on the community for hospitals grew. Misery began to show like a bruise.

Trouble came to Carnation Street, just off the main thoroughfare. First one man and then another fell out of work and could not get back. They were ashamed. They made the best of it, tried this shift and that, moved away and were lost. Mr Blan lost his job. He was a skilled man, a machinist, he had been at the same job and earned good money for years, but he was over sixty. Mrs Blan came up to tell Ally on the Saturday morning. Her face was grey, her cheeks hanging after a sleepless night. Her comfortable, platitudinous good humour was gone. She knew what unemployment meant, she'd been there before. She could pick out the difference between times that were really bad and a passing slump. She knew that her man was too old. She burst into tears. Ally was profoundly shocked, it was as if a public monument had dissolved before her eyes. She felt scared for herself, felt danger like a cold wind. She tried to comfort Mrs. Blan with a sort of cheerful platitude that Mrs Blan had often used to her. But the old woman only turned heavily away. "I thought I'd tell you," she said and stumped down again. Ally was first shocked and then resentful, as if the Blans had brought an infection into the house. Afterwards her heart smote her, because Mrs Blan had been very kind to her, but she didn't know what to do or say, because she thought it was a very delicate matter.

Old Blan didn't think so. Instead of going off at the usual time every morning to look for work, as some of the other men did, hoping to find it before their state was revealed, and storekeeper and landlord descended upon them, he sat on his little strip of verandah, smoking his pipe for all to see. When neighbours hailed him he told them bluntly, "I've been paid off, the shop's closing down. Bin there ten years, too," adding cheerfully enough, "Ma'll be getting the Old Age Pension in three months and in three years I'll be getting it. Then we'll be set." He gave in to it at once, just like that, and some of the neighbours said he ought to be ashamed, he wasn't that old, there was plenty of work in him still. He gave in and yet he didn't give in either. He was the first man to face what they were all up against. He knew it was hopeless to go looking for work, the way things were, but he didn't panic and he didn't pretend. It had its effect on the street. He didn't blench either when his daughter came back home a fortnight later with her two children and a couple of battered suitcases. Her husband had lost his job and, as they had fallen behind with payments for the furniture, it had been seized. She couldn't stay in an empty house of which the rent was in arrears. Her husband had carried the suitcases as far as the corner and then had left her, too ashamed to come to her father's door. He'd been rather a smart guy and the neighbours still remembered the wedding. They didn't know that the old man too had lost his job. The girl learned of it in person from her mother in the first five minutes. Mrs Blan was not so much angry as overwhelmed and made no effort to conceal her distress at this new disaster. The old man said shortly, "Glad's welcome, and you tell Art not to be a fool, it's not his fault."

Harry Munster wasn't worrying about his job. Mullangar's Miracle Marts were prospering. People who had never patronised them before now became regular customers. The goods were cheap, but no credit given. Also a shrewd business man had better chances than ever of buying goods cheaply from bankrupt houses and small manufacturers, only too glad to sell their products for what they could get. Harry reckoned that so long as they were busy he wasn't in any danger of being sacked. What was happening all round him didn't worry him much. It was a staggering blow when, opening his pay envelope early in January 1930, he found his notice of dismissal. The envelopes came down to the store from the office and Arnie handed them out. Harry had been the last to come in from a trip to Bondi. Arnie had waited back to give him his money; he had been unwontedly genial, and they had stood talking a couple of minutes, more friendly than usual. After putting his truck away Harry opened the envelope. In the ordinary course of events he would have carried it home as it was, but he was short today and wanted the price of a drink. He stood beside the truck, his body stiffened, his attitude like a pointing dog. He crumpled the paper and walked back to the store. Arnie was locking the door into the street, a deserted street of flat-faced warehouses, blank walls, and asphalt pavements.

"Do you know anything about this?"

Arnie grinned, the same cheerful grin of a few minutes ago.

Harry repeated, "Do you know anything about this?" He was holding out his pay envelope. They both saw that his hand trembled.

"I don't open your pay envelope," Arnie said, grinning more broadly.

"You do know then, you bugger."

"Hold on, you're not the only one."

"How do you mean?"

"You've all got the sack, see? The six of you. Mr Mullangar's decided to reduce wages, but he didn't want any nastiness about it, see? So he's making a clean sweep and getting men as'll be glad of the job. Unionists make trouble when they get cuts and he don't want trouble. Get it?"

"You dirty bastard." Harry crashed his fist into Arnie's face. Arnie staggered but did not fall. Swearing and milling, they made at one another. Neither had any science, but Arnie was soft and Harry was lean and hard. The driver of a passing lorry stopped and leaned out to watch; a youth, two little boys with a billy cart, and an old man gathered from nowhere. The air sang with fury. Another blow landed heavily on Arnie's face, Harry only just saved himself from falling as the other went down. Arnie didn't attempt to get up. He looked at Harry and Harry looked at him. Harry turned abruptly away and went. His own face was bloody, but he didn't notice. He'd wiped something out. That grin. He wanted a drink. It was six and the pubs were shut, but he knew where to go. Beer wasn't strong enough. He hadn't the confidence to call for whisky. He asked for rum. He hadn't drunk rum since he was in the army. Going over the top. Between his first and his second he did a little thinking. He couldn't go back and do his last week. Not after this. Clean finish. May as well happen quickly as slowly. All the same in a month's time, whether he had one more pay or not. Between his second and his third, he thought with distaste of telling Ally; he wouldn't tell her, not yet, he'd get used to the idea himself first, make some plans. He'd harden himself up before he took the lash of her reproaches. He had another drink. He didn't like this place, not enough people here. The stuff wasn't any good either, had no effect. He'd knock Ally out, too, if she complained. That was the answer. He hadn't thought of it before, but it'd worked with Arnie. By God, it had. He felt better, more cheerful. Some men he knew came in. He joined them and stood beers all round. Soon he was putting them down in fine style. He felt good. They wanted to know what he was celebrating. He laughed at that one. One of his mates solemnly dipped a handkerchief in some spilt beer and washed the blood off his face. The publican told them that if they couldn't be quieter, he'd clear them out, he didn't want the cops down on him. He might give the Sergeant a case of whisky now and then, but you couldn't expect him to stand a riot. They went on drinking. Harry felt bad again when the noise dropped. He thought it was tough when a man didn't get any help at home. Ally. No more his wife than the lamp post. A kept woman. He laughed. Wrong sort of laugh. Mouth full of bitter saliva. The kids were all right, but they were growing up like little savages. What could he do? He seemed to see a crack open before him. It wasn't the future that sickened him, it was the past. He'd goddam do something about it. "What we want's another war," he said, "mop up the whole bloody lot."

"Plenty of jobs in wartime."

"Yeah, getting shot."

He had another drink and felt better. Told the story of his fight with Arnie, as if it had been seven rounds in the stadium. They cheered him. He put them down steadily. Sometimes the crack was there, sometimes it wasn't. In a moment of lucidity he thought, "Chris will tell Ally."

It was not till eleven o'clock that he left. He'd spent his pay, he was taking nothing home. The pub he'd been at was in Ultimo, not far from the store. It was a long way home. He wavered into Harris Street and turned towards the railway. He had the wide street to himself. He passed small factories, some of them boarded up, the others, at this hour, just as dead; dirty corner shops with a few odd-ments in the windows, halfpenny confectionery, penny exercise books, small goods. . . . Walls, "Billstickers will be prosecuted", premises of some large works with the inevitable notice on the gate, "No Hands Wanted", dark breaks in drab walls that were laneways, terraces dark and mute, crouched down in the hot sick night, standing siege; squares of feeble yellow light here and there to mark where a woman tended a sick child, a man lay ill, or a family still toiled at piece work; street lamps, light doled out by prudence; gleaming tramlines along which every now and then a tram rocketed, carrying people home from the pictures, having no connection with the streets through which they passed. Harry stumbled through the dead smell of hot asphalt, a taint of refuse, a whiff from a butcher's, the lingering odour from a fish and chips joint. He turned aside to vomit, vomited his very soul out, and went slowly on. He had to sit down to rest, fell into a dream. He felt the pavement with his hands, "Hard," he thought, "City streets are hard." It seemed a very sapient reflection. There was no reason why he should get up but he did, walked on, past the Tech-nical School and the Technological Museum, smelled the vegetable markets, Friday's markets, the smell could not escape in the hot air. He came out into George Street. This was the living world again. Some shops were still open, there were fruit barrows in Railway Square, lights, traffic. He gathered himself to cross the wide open space of the square, stood looking up at the station tower, a dizzy column against the dark blue of the night sky, holding up the round lighted face of the clock, soaring, beautiful. He was no longer drunk, he could see it, impersonal, uncaring, beautiful. It made him giddy. He skirted the station; trees in Belmore Park, men lying under them sleeping, like dead men. He followed Elizabeth Street for a block, then turned up Albion Street. Now he was in the dead world again, the stricken city, more terrible than any desert. Here he would walk looking for work, here men came in ever greater numbers for ever lessening work. Parched walls, cliff-like shadows, sickly patches of impenetrative light, smell of dust, thin, dry, deserted smell. Life had receded, here were the shards. This was the city, not the bright open spaces where the shops and idle crowds were, here were the roots from which that leafage grew. Battle or plague might have passed through. This thing, this Depression, was only another aspect of battle and plague. It was war and disease.

Harry Munster went from hollow street to hollow street, looking about him as a countryman or old soldier might, for pickings, and seeing none, seeing them as they were in the beaten down transparency of his mood, untroubled by any hope. Today wasn't only today. Like a sickness it had been coming on for a long time. "I didn't take it lying down," he told himself, "I let that dirty little bugger have it." He hadn't taken it lying down, he'd knocked Arnie's head off and then he'd gone out and got drunk like a man. His steps slowed to a halt. He'd beaten up someone who wasn't to blame even if he was a filthy little twirp, and he'd spent all he had boozing up so that he could be sick in the gutter. That's what the protest amounted to. He grinned with no special bitterness.

He turned into Bourke Street and swung down into more populated misery. The huddled houses gave out heat like the bodies of animals. Here people were waiting, driven in, and driven in by want, waiting for what came next. By God, how patient they were. He'd not had one day out of work yet. Taylor Square was wide and empty, everything tucked away under the eye of the courthouse. He doubled up Liverpool Street into Forbes Street, a more discreet world. Trees, a few dusty trees. In Clapton Place one side fell away, there was open space, a sudden enlargement. Here was a triangle of vacant land, a cliff overhanging the city. Beyond a black fringe of Port Jackson figs was a panorama of the harbour, blue as silk in the daytime, now dark, dusted with lights. Cooler air flowed through the gap and fanned against the faces of the houses, each a honeycomb of flats, rooms, apartments, people living like cave dwellers of New Mexico, like rock animals on a precipice, like insects in cells. Another corner and another, the sky cut again into a deep narrow river with a thousand islands, then the short steep channel of a street running into the great artery of William Street. With slow steps Harry Munster came to his own door.

. . . . . . . . . .

"He feels it," thought Ord, "Damn me, if he doesn't feel this, the cool, slippery beggar." Ord almost fell to wondering what Knarf would have been like if he had lived four hundred years sooner. Would events have broken the remoteness out of him, would he have given deeds not words? Knarf, battling, competitive? Whatever man has been, every man can be. That was one of the things Knarf said.

But the tight voice went on with its narrative, only the movement of his hands showed that a phase had ended and another phase had begun.

. . . . . . . . . . .

The narrow house was packed with life. In summer it had the effect of overflowing, of boiling with sound and movement. You thought of its inner partitions in a state of flux, its wall bending outwards. In the winter it shrank and congealed, drew in itself for warmth. The cold searching westerlies took it straight in the face, chapping the very stove. The cold fug indoors seemed better than the wind-lashed sunshine, even to the children, in the second winter of the depression.

Rita had gone from the attic room and a young couple with a baby had taken her place. The girl had a job as a waitress. That kept them. The man looked after the baby. At first they seemed quite happy, you could hear them laughing together after she came home from work. Pa Blan liked to stand at the foot of the stairs to hear her sing to the baby. He went all soft and his women folk laughed at him. But as weeks went by, the girl's voice got shriller, there were quarrels and silence. Every night you could hear her upbraiding her husband because he hadn't kept the place tidy or washed the child. Glad and her mother looked at one another and nodded, they knew. It wasn't natural and even if they meant to be different it got them, sure as sure. The husband was a pleasant boy, very talkative. He'd meet Mrs Blan out at the clothes lines as he was hanging out the baby's naps, and he used to try to explain things. "Honest, I don't know what comes over me, Mrs Blan. I get laying on the bed and I forget. I just don't seem able to do things, and Hilda gets that wild." He hadn't had a job for two years, they wouldn't have got married but for the baby.

Downstairs at the Blans, things had changed and changed again. At first Pa Blan had had things well in hand. He'd been the one to keep calm. He had stood between Gladys and her mother when Mrs Blan had given vent to what was more nerves and alarm than ill nature. He had kept things going smoothly between the two women by an indomitable display of cheerfulness. By refusing to allow quarrels and reproaches, or even lamentations, he stopped the rot in his own household. He smoked his pipe on his verandah and drew his unemployment pay from the union in conscious rectitude. He won a victory over the landlord which reverberated through the street, sending his agent away with half the rent. To refuse part-payment as they usually did, was — it appeared — illegal, and Pa Blan knew it. However, when Gladys got work, office cleaning, and brought money home, a subtle rearrangement took place. Gladys lost her meekness, mother and daughter clove together, and Pa became of no account. They took their revenge on him for the restraint he had put on their legitimate feelings. About that time his unemployment pay stopped. Artie had not reappeared, and from being pitiful he became villainous. Mrs Blan's early prognostications proved true, he had deserted Gladys. When this was beyond concealment, Gladys let herself go in vilifying him to all and sundry. Mrs Blan took heart and showed a little of her old spirit. She had sagged under the first assault of hard times, because she felt it took from her her place of leading lady in the street and clipped at their root the small generosities with which she had queened it. In time their life settled into a jagged rhythm, not insupportable. When Pa got his old-age pension and his stock rose accordingly, it looked as if they could go on indefinitely, in hand to mouth fashion, but still surviving. Their position was stabilised, if poor.

Upstairs, at the Munsters', circumstances were more uncertain, at once more hopeful and more precarious. Harry was forty and in good physical condition. He could still hope to get a job, but there was nothing immediately coming in, except the child welfare allowance of five shillings a week for each of the two younger children. Harry's union didn't carry any unemployment benefits. Ally took the news that he was out of work fairly well, she was far more angry with him for getting drunk. They had one of their quarrels that was still the same old quarrel, beginning with the grudge that she had been only nineteen when he married her, and slowly enlarging itself with the tale of all she had suffered since. She always succeeded in making him feel guilty, but she never quite broke his self-control. Now the household was subjected to a day-to-day strain, a tourniquet slowly tightening. Their quarrels were a thing apart. There were other short desperate colloquies between them that cut deeper, in which they spoke to one another, not as warring husband and wife, but rather as two people driven by necessity out of their individual beings and becoming the antiphony of one distress.

"How much is there left?"

"Only a shilling."

"What am I to do?"

"How do you expect me to know?"

"Where shall we go?"

"Stay here, we have nowhere to go."

"We must . . ."

"We can't . . ."

"Where are you going?"

"Nowhere."

Ally entreated him, "Take anything, Harry, any job at all, just to tide us over."

He answered, mocking but gently, "Even anything is something."

These colloquies went on in thousands of homes. All that people had to say to one another boiled down to a couple of sentences. They hissed like a lash in silence. Children did not have to hear the words, they knew the lash.

Ally talked of looking for work herself, but she was paralysed by the sudden unscalable vastness of the world as she saw it. She did not know how to look for work, had no ideas about it, though in a vague way, where Harry was concerned, she assumed that the will would be enough. Gladys might have shown her how to go about it, but Gladys was not disposed to be helpful. Office cleaning was overcrowded as it was. If you were so much as off sick for one day someone always had a friend ready to shove into your place. Ally only talked and threw the idea at Harry now and then. Knowing that she did not mean business, he only grinned at her sardonically. Yet she was willing if only Harry had taken her at her word and helped her.

There were times now when Harry, lying on the balcony bed so near the unsleeping noises of the street, the pattern of the lattice cast by the street light motionless on the wall, night after night without quiet or darkness, longed to be reconciled to Ally. He wanted to go back to her whatever she was or whatever she thought of him. In her and the children his life had its only continuity. Things were too bad now for the quarrels that had separated them to matter any longer. There was comfort they could give one another and it cost nothing. She would have taken him back without a word, because she was lonely and afraid and they could have been, like so many couples, enemies by day and friends in the night, a truce, a refuge kept secret for its own protection. He did not put his fortune to the test. Bitter doubt, doubt of himself as much as of her, came too quickly after the impulse. Letting himself in for God knows what sort of rebuff and castigation, a funny sort of man to come crawling back when he had nothing. He should have found a way to put things straight between them when times were good. It would have been easy then, now it was too late. Afterwards, when exhaustion had conquered him—and it gave him a sort of sour satisfaction to beat down his needs, saying wryly to himself, "After all, I'm still a man"—afterwards he thought of the children. Wouldn't have been much of a world for Jackie. Benny looked like doing better. Benny was a tiger. Four children instead of three, 15/- a week instead of 10/-. . . . There was little enough to calculate, but the whole night often passed before his mind could find a patch of peace to sleep in.

The house slept badly. The girl upstairs, too tired to sleep, her young husband restless because he had no exercise and no interest in the day, Pa Blan awake with a pain, Mrs Blan waking to lumber out and get him tea, to scold and cosset him, the children for ever wakened by the cold or the stuffy heat, the unrest of their stomachs, or the dark tides of the house, Harry and Ally lying awake, playing anxiety's eternal game of the thimble and the pea.

Only the old age pensioner on the ground floor, Joe, was unaffected by the times. His "income" went on as usual. He didn't notice what was happening about him, he was getting very old, mumbled a lot to himself, but rarely spoke to anyone. If you spoke to him he'd answer straightly enough, and his room still showed the vestiges of an old sailor's neatness. He sat in the sun, cutting his plug with trembling hands, chewing it with loosely wagging, bristly chin, staring fixedly at the little girls. He'd fitted well enough into a prosperous world. He'd been a "poor old chap" on the bottom rung of charity, the women had given him oddments from time to time and looked after him if he were ill. In a sagging world he was a death's head. An eddy of resentment broke against him for his small security. The women began to fear him and hunt him away from their children.

Harry Munster began a systematic search for work. He went the rounds of places he knew and drew a blank everywhere. He bought a newspaper and studied the advertisements as he drank a cup of tea in the kitchen before Ally was up, marking the possible ones with a stub of pencil. The addresses were scattered over the city and suburbs; he had no money to spend on fares, so he set out at once. Everything depended on his first choice. It he chose the most likely sounding, a couple of hundred men would be there before him; if he chose the least likely, it turned out a dud, a trick advertisement, or an agency. Sometimes he tried to placate fate by going to the farthest and most difficult to reach. All with no result. He had, after a while, to give up this method of hunting for a job; it exhausted not only his body but his spirit too much. Worse, it wore out his boots.

Next he tried a very simple and dogged plan. He went into the industrial area, which he had so prophetically traversed on the night of his dismissal, and going from shop to factory to store, disregarding notices on gates and even vigilant gatemen, asked for work. It was generally a courteous, often a regretful, refusal. Sometimes he was thrown out. As his heart sank he became belligerent. Often he ate nothing all day, and tramped home muttering, his brain going round and round, looking for someone to fight. He came to this much quicker than you would expect, but even one day is a long time when it is filled with refusals. His feet blistered, his body, which had been hard and handsome, grew slack very quickly. Anxiety is like an acid sweat which eats the tissues. Many other men were on the same mission; they did not join forces—they were competitors, enemies; there was no brotherhood between them yet. Nor did any of them fraternise with men eating their lunches in laneways outside factories in operation. These feared and hated them too.

This also was too expensive a way to look for work, for nothing came in whilst he looked, and his only stock-in-trade, his vitality, was running out fast. It was not the physical effort, it was the shock of throwing himself over and over against an impenetrable wall.

On Saturday, walking home at midday, he decided that he could no longer follow this plan. The few pounds he had had put away without Ally's knowledge were gone. He must find a way to earn something immediately. A job was out of the question; it must be odd jobs. He was so pale when he came in that even Ally noticed it and was alarmed. He went and lay on his bed without a word. She brought him a cup of tea and a slice of bread, but he did not open his eyes. She wanted to comfort him, and if they had been alone she might have tried to break her long silence with something gentle. But they were not alone; the children were there—not only their own, but the two from downstairs. They stood watching, uncomfortably wondering what had happened. She left the food beside him.

He lay in bed all Sunday, and on Monday he went down to the wharves. He saw at once that that was useless. Wherever they were taking on men to unload a ship there were hundreds offering; the first essential was to be known to the stevedores.

Next he tried hawking his labour from house to house in the suburbs. Here he did a little better—found someone who wanted wood chopped, some gardening or other job, quite often he was offered a cup of tea or even a meal. He never learned to pitch a tale, and that was a disappointment to the would-be charitable who like to hear something for their money. Doors were slammed in his face and dogs set on him. He had always got on well with dogs; now, he discovered that they had a strong sense of property and he was outside the pale. He learnt about suburbs, how it was useless to go among big houses, for here he saw only servants who had nothing to give and no sympathy to squander. Poor districts were also barren, but there were streets of comfortable small houses where he was likely to pick up something, people who had no regular gardener because a casual was cheaper. Even here now he was likely to see the master of the house at home in his shirt-sleeves, to be told, "No good, digger, I'm in the same boat as you are," or men, not so friendly, who drove him away as a bird of ill omen, a pre-vision of what they might themselves come to. He fell in with the usual issue of cranks who thought he would have time to stay and listen to their pet theory. At one house an elderly bearded man in spectacles came to the door. He heard him out, did not answer his request for work, but said:

"Did you know that this depression is caused by over-production? There is plenty of everything and plenty of machinery to make more. You have nothing. You are many. I am not a man of action myself. Think it over." And he shut the door again.

Of all the rum coves, thought Harry, and stared back at the tight-lipped, single-fronted villa. One of these reds.

The worst of this sort of thing was that you began each day no better off than the day before. Each day was harder to begin. He sickened intolerably of the whole thing. Never before had he been entirely without place in the world. Once he had been a man who owned a farm, a free man. That made him more difficult of adjustment, and yet he clung to the thought. His pride, his amateur status. He would still go on believing in the form of society that had rejected him. He could still retain that. It was easier to believe that the fault was in himself—and thousands of others—than that society had to be changed. He could still say, no matter what he lacked, "I'm no red."

The odd-job scheme came to a standstill. He couldn't scrape up enough odd jobs to make any sort of living for his family. After a month he still had nothing. It was getting worse because everybody was getting poorer. He went to the Returned Soldiers'. They put his name down. They did their best to place members. He was behind in his subscriptions. The man at the ledger just smiled. That didn't matter. Pity he hadn't been in sooner; there was a long waiting list. All they could do at present was to set him up with a hawker's licence and pack. It was quite a complicated business, but the clerk had it all worked out. There was a living in it. The outlay had to be paid back, of course.

Harry took it on. At first he felt almost jaunty. It was something tangible, something on his hands. "Like a commercial traveller," he told himself, and "On the road again." Ally took it very badly. "A hawker," she said, "A hawker."

"You said, 'Take anything,'" he pointed out.

Then they quarrelled and, because he was feeling a little more hopeful, it was a worse quarrel than usual and they were less careful.

The catch about hawking was that so many were on to it, and they all had the same goods. Disgusted housewives told him that he was the third or fourth man that morning, and shut the door in anger at imposition on their good nature. Or they looked at everything and decided that there was nothing that they wanted. A line that went off like hot cakes—and that some enterprising fellow ahead of him seemed to be toting—was little enamel plaques for screwing into gate posts, bearing the legend "Hawkers not admitted." They sprang up everywhere. They filled him with blind rage. What right had people to put those things on their gate posts? It was free to anyone to go up and ring the doorbell. At last, to relieve himself, he took a stone and battered a whole line of them. It was dusk in an empty street. He felt better till he realised that they were property. He could be arrested. He sweated.

A hawker's pack was not the spiritual protection he had hoped. Other people didn't look upon it as a visible means of support, they thought it an excuse for not working. Old ladies, in particular, took him to task for not working, "a big strong man like you." They bought from cripples, but not from men who should be doing a man's work. It was wonderful the people who had not heard of the depression. One householder refused to buy, but said sweetly, "I will give you something," and brought back a tract, "The Lord will Provide." He did not investigate to see what it was that the Lord provided. This was offset by an intoxicated lady who gave him a double whisky and soda.

In all his shifts and efforts Harry had followed in the well-trodden tracks of other men. They believed that they were thinking for themselves, fending for themselves, making a choice. They had no choice. Circumstances canalised them. They went the way they must, like sheep to the dip. They responded to different pressures by trying now this, now that, not one in a hundred broke free. They did not realise that they were a horde and could be an army.

Harry made sales; not many, but some. Day by day he brought home a few shillings, and they went at once on necessities, his gross takings, not only the margin of profit. He knew it was happening, gambled on a run of luck that would let him pull up. The day came when he had a depleted pack, no money, and no means of replenishing his stock in trade or of paying the money he owed. His heart sickened. This was disgrace. He'd got so that he didn't mind owing the rent, or money to tradesmen, but to steal money from the Returned Soldiers', his own mates—that was different. He remembered how decent the clerk had been to him, how grateful he'd felt. Out of a fog this had burst on him. He must do something. He had a nerve storm. No one recognised it, but that was what it was. His whole world was sucked dry. There was no money to be picked up anywhere, no one he could borrow from, nothing even to steal. The fantastic idea of going to see Arnie presented itself, of asking him, almost the only man he still knew in a good job, for money. He would have done it if he had thought there was the least chance of success. He reckoned the sum he owed at thirty bob, little enough, but as impossible to reach as the moon. Even if he begged in the street he wouldn't get a tithe of it. You couldn't expect people to give in proportion to the effort it cost him to ask.

There was nothing to sell. Even as he thought that, his eye fell on the wireless set. By God, that ought to fetch two quid at the Jew's. He began to force it from its moorings. Ally was beside him screeching.

"Harry, what are you doing?"

"I'm taking this bit of junk to the Jew's."

"You can't. It's mine."

"My money paid for it. Stand away."

"I won't. You're not to touch it."

"I'm going to touch it."

"No."

"The infernal thing has never been anything but a curse to us with its everlasting din." He was glad it had to be the wireless set. He'd always hated it. It cluttered up the place and they'd little enough room.

"Harry, you're not to take it."

"Stand away, Ally."

"I won't."

They were both angry.

"Are you mad?"

"Do I have to be mad to want to keep some sticks of furniture in the house?"

"We've got past luxuries, didn't you know?"

"We won't have a bite to eat if you don't get yourself a job."

"You know all about that."

"Arnie could keep his job. Why couldn't you? Oh, yes, I know all about that."

"Stand out of the way," he told her savagely.

"You don't keep me. You can't order me about. If anyone keeps me it's the children."

He caught her by the shoulder and thrust her away. She sprang back and struck him on the side of the head.

He seized her, propelled her violently across the room, almost threw her into the bedroom and slammed the door. She fell shrieking across the bed. He heaved the cabinet on to his shoulders and carried it down the stairs. The whole house watched him go. They accurately connected Ally's screams with the rape of her once famous wireless set.

Ally stayed in her room and continued to cry loudly. She was angry, but not as angry as Harry. She had not the courage to tell him that they still owed £2 on the wireless. He had given her the money and she had spent it on something else. She feared what would happen, but she feared Harry more. Mrs Blan came to comfort her. Benny padded cheerfully downstairs to teach the other little boys how to play Mummies and Daddies, an interesting version founded on what he had seen.

Harry eventually returned, stone cold, with five shillings in his pocket. Radios were a drug on the market; this one old and battered. He threw it in front of Ally. "There you are," he said.

There was now only one thing to do. The day he went down to apply for the dole had no significance at all. He thought, "I'll feel this tomorrow." But for the time being he had given up feeling anything.

After that there was a pause. Harry had given up striving for the moment. He went to the Returned Soldiers' and took what was left in his pack. He saw the same clerk. The man looked sick and wasn't as friendly as he had been. Harry returned the goods and explained, in what seemed to be the middle of a large silence, that he hadn't any money. The clerk didn't seem surprised. He reached for a form already printed and told Harry to fill it in. It was a sort of I.O.U. acknowledging the debt. Instead of being comforted by the evident commonness of the occurrence, Harry was humiliated by the way his shame had been taken for granted. When the clerk had checked his address, he went away. He salved his hurt by determining to pay at any cost.

He gave up buying tobacco. Benny collected cigarette ends for him. He was between five and six now, going to school. After school he'd run about the streets gathering butts as he might have been running in paddocks gathering mushrooms. There were others at it, but Benny was quick and shrewd. He knew the streets round his home were not much good, because everyone smoked their fags to the last gasp, but in the tree-lined streets beyond the Cross life was still lived generously. He never came back empty-handed. It was a secret between father and son. Together, out of sight, they went over the booty. Benny knew where he'd found each one, his interest was minute and joyful. Carefully disentangling the clean from the dirty, they piled the good tobacco on to a cigarette paper. Harry spread, rolled, and gummed it. Benny watched his deft fingers as if they were a Punch and Judy show at the least. Then he must see it smoked down to the last shred. Benny had a grand contempt for people who threw away their fags while there was yet some good in them. It was a ritual and a bond. The child's eagerness took away the sting from what they were doing and gave the occasion, so often repeated, a savour of its own. Money saved on tobacco never reached the sinking fund. It evaporated in mid air. Harry put the debt out of his mind, but it remained, a small, distinct sore when all else was calloused.

Harry saw more of his son now than ever he had been able to before. He got the boy away from the street whenever possible; took him to the Domain, to the Botanic Gardens, to Hyde Park. They lay on their stomachs on the dry grass, and Harry initiated his son into the art of running a poultry farm. He sketched one out on a patch of bare, sandy ground down by the Blind Institution. Here we'll grow fodder crops, there are the pens; we'll put the incubator sheds here; that's the house; in the paddock behind there is a cow and a horse— the children to ride to school on the horse; there's a breakwind of loquat trees, a small orchard, beehives; don't let's forget the pig; pigs aren't dirty, not if you treat them right. It was a good game; Benny didn't tire of it. "I'm going to have a farm when I grow up," he announced. "You mightn't be asked what you'll have or won't have," his father thought.

Perhaps because of these games, or because his energy flowed again after a brief rest, Harry determined to try his chances in the country. At home the situation was a slow exasperation. The episode of the wireless cabinet had left a trace of shame on his mind, and Ally owed it to her dignity not to forgive him. It was an impasse, passed over into stalemate.

His weary nerves wanted to escape for a time from the constant domestic abrasion. Deeper than any of these reasons, he had an impulse to escape from the city, the doomed city, closing in on him, crushing him slowly to death, beating him into its pavements, where the ceaseless footsteps passed. That image really did haunt his mind, of a man, himself, sinking still sentient into the macadam. A city paved with men. Standing at the corner of William Street, watching the traffic stream up the hill at dusk on a winter's night, the cars like Frankensteins of the jungle, robot animals of unvarying, mindless, mechanical ferocity, coming from prey and going to prey, the tender sky fenced by the hard serrations of the city's skyline, the living, changing earth sealed beneath the insentient and unchanging concrete, he felt himself grow unreal along with the things he cared for, came to feel that he no longer existed for anyone about him, but turning, not to stone, but to concrete, the grey, dead, false stone. He looked at the passers-by in the light-streaked dusk, and it seemed to him that, however much they differed, they were alike too, always the same face, hungry and afraid. Not the people in the cars—wax images in hurtling glass cages—they were a different breed, safe. But the People. The People. Once they were individuals, now they were masses. They had the same fear, but in different degrees. The man with a job feared to lose it, feared the man without who might take it away from him, undersell him. The man without a job feared and hated till he exhausted his capacity to fear and became sludge. The race was between sludge of despair and hatred, everywhere less hatred and more sludge. The people do not know whom to hate. Someone must tell them. Who must tell them and what? You could see the change everywhere. In the good times men had counted their strength, taken the credit to themselves. The wheel had turned and dragged them down, not accident that could be retrieved, but the working of a force beyond their conception as well as beyond their control. They suffered, not from deprivation only, but from impotence, driven from their own strength and manhood, a mortal wound if they could not retrieve it in protest. What protest? Taxi drivers who had been jaunty, easy, the most democratic in the world, gone haggard and taciturn, hunting fares in their hunting cabs; girls who had been pert gone shabby; men and women who were solid grown worn and suspicious; live wires sagged; commercial travellers, their certainty worn thin and shabby, scarcely wide enough to cover their despair; the hill steeper than it used to be. Faces in the street. Pa Blan used to quote that, Pa Blan talking of the 'nineties, the great days of militant labour, era of progress. Isn't today born of yesterday? What was wrong with the great days that today is no better, but worse? What was the good of all those little bulwarks, those walls made of pebbles, if this can happen? What's the good of the basic wage if you don't get any wage at all? Doesn't it only divide the people now at last? Some, the strongest and cleverest of them, separated out and bought off? What safeguards have we? Old man's talk, old Pa Blan's talk, sick to death with a cancer in his stomach and he didn't know, talking of how fine things used to be when he was a young man, and the world being made. What world? This world. No recognition in any face. Night now. The two ends of darkness resting on nothing. The city whirring with its own momentum, a strange machine for devouring men.

Harry stood on the corner watching the flow of traffic in the culvert of the great street as Benny and Ruthie had stood, hypnotised. Thoughts moved under the surface of his mind—a decision that was not so much of the brain as a slow flowering of the blood—he made up his mind to get out, to leave the dole provision for Ally and the children, and to try his luck in the country. A man could live off the country somehow, but not off the paved streets. He'd walk out with nothing and make his way in a world he knew. He did not know this world. It was drying up; men everywhere were doing a perish, caught in a trap. You couldn't do anything with a machine when it broke down, but out in the bush there was always something to try. A man wasn't a grain of dust there, he could manage for himself somehow. He would go tomorrow, there was nothing to keep him. Ally and the children would be better without him, they would have his food and his room. He'd go where the earth was still alive and make another place for them, come back and get them. Hundreds were feeling the same urge, turning over the same argument. Harry walked home feeling more nearly happy than he had for months.

Ally had her own troubles which she bore furtively. She was as deeply involved in financial troubles as any government. The sudden cessation of the family income had thrown her down a precipice. Buying had been her passion, buying for its own sake. Not only did she get clothes and furniture to which she persuaded herself she had a transcendental right, but she got them in an involved and sophisticated way that appealed to her imagination. She savoured in turn the blandishments of salesmen, their spoken and written persuasions, the, to her, almost heroical sums involved, the signing of a contract as momentous as a document of state, the arrival of the goods, possession, the gambling excitement of raising the instalments, the juggling of the domestic finances. It was all right while there was something to juggle. She tended her set of hire purchases, cash orders, and lay-bys as if they were a garden, encouraging now one sickly plant, now another. She flattered herself by living dangerously, would not have felt happy or believed she was getting the most out of life, if she had not been surrounded by these enterprises. To stop, to draw in her horns, would have been to let her courage down. Suddenly there was no money and she was afraid.

She remembered the papers she had signed without understanding. She did not know to what she was bound, or what would happen to her. The lay-bys—coats for the little girls, a bedspread, a tea set, a scooter for Benny's Christmas—dropped away silently, she did not go back. She lost them without regret, with relief almost. No one knew of them. She would not expose herself by returning to the shop to find out if she could recover any of the money she had paid. They were gone. The ice-chest, for which she had been paying for three years, was the next to go. After much correspondence, which so alarmed and numbed her that she could not even attempt to answer it, the plain van, whose purpose by this time was as obvious to the neighbourhood as a fire engine's, came and took it away.

More tormenting were the cash orders with which she had bought her winter coat, a wristlet watch, and a roll of linoleum. She could only wait for something to happen. First there were letters. Her mind shut against them in panic and she could not understand. Then a debt collector came. He was a young man for whom this job was a last desperate resource. He lacked the easy geniality of the hardened. He too was frightened, frightened of losing his job if he didn't succeed in collecting the money. He blustered and threatened, Ally quailed, and the neighbours took note. At last he went away without the money because there was none. The company threatened proceedings. Ally went to a dingy office in town, waited two hours, and saw an ugly little man who knew she wasn't worth a blandishment, or indeed any form of politeness. He agreed in the end to take back the watch for a third of its agreed price, and to consolidate the rest of the debt for six months. She signed another paper. There was apparently a fee for collecting debts which she could not pay, and so it must be added to the original debt. There was a fee for the new contract and a first instalment of interest on the new debt due at once. All these had to be funded. The ugly little man looked very glum. You would have thought he was going to starve.

The wireless set was the greatest source of anguish, because it no longer existed. The debt was insecured. To have sold it was probably criminal. That she had any rights in the matter never occurred to Ally. She did not tell Harry that she owed the money because she knew he could not pay it, and she would have to endure his reproaches for nothing. Once she scraped up the interest, paid it, and breathed again. It had come out of money allotted for food.

Ally's struggle was secret and desperate. All about ner the struggle for existence was going on, it was the one struggle to the one end, more often unaccomplished. People continued to exist, but not as a result of their efforts, rather by grace of a social system that, having made waste products of them, yet lacked the decision to despatch them utterly. A sentiment persisted. a sentiment that would not let them die, though, with a show of righteousness even, it would take from them everything that might make life worth living. Life itself was given back as a charity. The system was deified. Those who were destroyed by it were brought down by an act of God. Comparatively few realised that their struggle for existence was indistinguishable from the neighbours', that it was the same struggle. They put an individual connotation upon it, to some it was one thing, to some another. To keep a job, to get a job, to pay the rent, to educate a child, to keep up appearances. . . . They chose a sticking point and braced themselves upon it. They clung to property rights in the struggle for existence. The symbol Ally put upon it—*her* struggle—was this phantasmagoria of her debts. Its amazing unreality of a nightmare, while it frightened her, yet fed her sense of drama. It was the dark side of what she had once found bright, and in a vague unconscious way it reassured her of the brightness. She acquiesced. Wretched, she fought for luxuries not necessities, preferred face to food, nightmare to tragedy. . . . She had no scruples, but there was no field on which to exercise her unscrupulousness.

Ally gave no confidences. But Mrs Blan was not deceived. She observed everything and she thought Ally a fool. She did not know when the game was up. She had no sense at all. Mrs Blan had her second wind. She was militant. Militancy was the thing she had chosen to save from the wreck.

In six months Harry was back again, walking up the street late one afternoon with a slow steady step, with the same dogged persistence that had carried him the last fifty miles and that he dared not slacken. Pa Blan met him in the hall. The old man, his skin a greyish yellow, was shrunken almost beyond recognition. Each knew what ailed the other. Ally found Harry sitting in the kitchen, his tattered boots beside him. He had nothing to say about the six months of his absence, nothing to say about anything. He had not brought anything back with him. Ally dared ask no questions, there was something alarming about him, about his feverish eyes and the rank smell of his body. Mrs Blan elucidated later. "He's been doing a perish. I've seen 'em before." She looked hard at Ally. "Starving," she said, and walked away.

Harry knew now that he was one of the unemployed.

.        .        .        .        .        .        .        .        .

This, thought Ord, is only a frieze cut out of a relief map. Knarf was gathering speed, the words came cleanly and easily off his tongue, as they do when the mind works freely.

.        .        .        .        .        .        .        .        .

It was 1935 before Harry was in regular work again. In all he was five years unemployed. They were the years of his education. He went on relief work, road building, Two weeks on, three weeks off. For the two weeks he received the basic wage, and it must stretch over the three weeks of idleness. Ally did not manage badly, the children got, not as much as they wanted, but enough. The work at first was torture. He had gone soft in mind and body. His hands blistered, his sinews ached, his veins felt like bursting, a sick unwillingness dragged him down. The work too was discouraging, it had no vitality. Sometimes they were put to shifting sand, sometimes to building an unnecessary road. They never saw a project through because it was policy to break and constantly re-group the mobs of men. Always they were given work far from their homes, generally in camps outside settled areas. The gangers were men in continuous work, not unemployed like the men under them. That separated them as surely as anything could. The men sent them were raw material—men out of condition, unused to manual labour, irritated by an ingrained suspicion that they were being exploited, or else utterly indifferent. The works were financed by a special tax on wages, so that every pay day the man in employment saw the hand of the workless in his pay envelope. Worthy citizens never lacked pen and paper to write to the newspapers about the ingratitude of the relief worker, the dole who didn't want work, and the working class women who went to the pictures and bought tinned asparagus.

The whole experiment of relief work was hedged about with difficulties. Organised Labour watched anxiously lest standards—the last poor crumbling standards—be brought down by the use of the unemployed. The unemployed must not rob the employed of their jobs. They might not be put on productive work for the economy was already overproduced. There were jobs of national importance to be done, work on the water supply, but men were not put on it. A big scheme would co-ordinate the workers into a force, give coherence to the unemployed. They must be scattered. The waste product must be given waste jobs, their uselessness underlined, they must not be allowed to upset the system that had created them. Society was secretly afraid. When the depression was at its worst there were over half a million unemployed. From their misery and frustration arose a miasma that spread through the community. Let them work, said the righteous, hard work will cleanse them. It wasn't the kind that cleansed. It did not rehabilitate.

But it brought men together, men without women and without possessions, in wayside camps. A living ferment began in the stagnation. Camps varied, jobs varied, mobs of men varied. Sometimes there was a haphazard conjunction that turned out well. There was one on the South Coast, building a tourist road through the mountains out from Kiama, that stuck in Harry Munster's mind. They arrived in Kiama by night, segregated in carriages tacked on to the ordinary train, and were transhipped at once into waiting lorries. There were six lorries loaded to capacity, men and bundles. They set out at once on the curling road to the west. It was a dark night with stars, the air, clear, cold, and with a sort of echoing brightness even in the dark. Ahead was the opaque wall of the mountains against the stars; the road ran dimly white, with grass at the edges, showing under the headlamps like giant eyelashes. On either side was a feeling of space, open country with fugitive dark shapes, trees like black plumes, camellias, little wooden houses fast asleep, cabbage tree palms, sentinels of vanished jungle in the quiet paddocks, faint curve of a hill, white-washed bridge in a timbered dip. . . . The men in the first lorry began to sing. The wind carried it back to the following lorries, and, like a fire lit by flying sparks, they each began to sing. Many of the men had been in the army, so it was soon the old songs they were singing—"Pack Up Your Troubles", "It's a Long, Long Trail", "Mademoiselle from Armentieres", and "Tipperary". They all thundered in on "Tipperary". It flamed like a comet through the night. In the sleeping farms men roused and their hearts turned over in their breasts with a nameless longing. Women heard and drew their safety closer. Some did not wake, but the sound drew a dream across their minds. A few thought, "Unemployed," and felt a whiff of envy and reproach.

Beside Harry, a man with a great bass voice trolled it out. Jammed together as they were, Harry could feel the easy resonance of his big hard body. This was Peter Hally, his mate on the job. Australian born, an old soldier at twenty, veteran of Villers Bret, the Somme, and Mont St. Quentin, he had come through without a scratch and with the sense that he owed nothing and his life was his own. He was that thousandth man who is free. He turned sailor to see the world, left his ships as lightly as he joined them, turned his hand to many other trades, but never for long, did as he pleased, and lived off the world at large. The depression had caught him in Australia and stopped his wanderings. He was waiting for it to pass over, and he was still living off the world. At thirty-five he was in his way a philosopher. He had looked about him, he knew the shape of things. Harry hadn't had a cobber since Timmy Andrews—he'd no idea where Timmy was now. Peter was his cobber for the fortnight they worked side by side, slept in the same bark hut, and ate off identical tin plates at the trestle table of their mess. Peter's was the first integrated mind Harry had met. Peter talked. He also acted. After two days he had the incompetent cook sent back to the gang and found a man who knew something about it and got him duly elected. He herded a deputation of the whole gang to the ganger to ask for better living conditions, took him by surprise, and got a half-day to put the huts in order.

"I always got to clean up a camp when I go to it," Peter explained. "There's two sorts of circs, the kind you can change and the kind you can't. The thing is not to get them mixed."

Peter had a crude and trenchant outlook on the world about him. He preached the class war.

"You bin through the war?" he asked Harry.

"Yeh, four years of it."

"D'you reckon you'd recognise another war if you saw one?"

"I oughter."

"Yes, you oughter, and if this isn't a proper one I'll eat my mattock. They're winning it hands down."

"I didn't think anyone was winning the depression. The bosses are getting it in the neck too," said Harry heavily.

"Maybe the little bosses are, but there are big bosses further back. They're the ones that are winning it. Finance capital."

"You mean the depression was engineered."

"It didn't have to be. It's a natural feature of the capitalist system. There are some, the real big fellows, who take advantage of it. They're your natural enemies, only most of you poor buggers don't know it. They count on your not dropping to it. Being good boys, see?"

There was a look in Harry's eye that showed he did not see, and Peter went on to explain with a pleased sort of unctuous patience.

"It's this way. The capitalist system gets itself into knots now and then. Sort of indigestion. Overproduced. Something has to go and it's the weak link that busts. That weak link has always been labour. Men have to eat and so have women and kids. Hunger gets you mighty quick. *They* can last a long time. Besides, labour can be relied on to break up under pressure and fight among themselves. Fight like hyenas for jobs. You've seen 'em. You can't blame them. It's human. It's the last sort of pressure men can bear, and it falls on the greatest number. The bigger the group the more weak spots there'll be. The way to get round these depressions when they come along would be to lower profits, raise wages, and peg prices. Up would go consumption, you'd take up the slack of over-production and there we'd be on an even keel again, now d'you see?"

"Yes," said Harry, "it's the profits that ought to give way, but it's labour that has to."

"You've got it. In booms labour gets strong, demands this and that, up go wages. Along comes a depression, all the pride and fight's taken out of us. We're grateful to be let live. They don't have to fight us, we fight each other. Labour's knocked out, or pretty near. That's an advantage to them, isn't it? The unions stand firm, maybe. There's the basic wage. That's the law. But the men, poor cows, are ready to let the bosses out. Take less money and sign a paper to say they're getting the basic wage, work broken time, do any damn thing to keep their jobs, even to shedding tears twice a day over the sufferings of the poor dear boss who has to make do with only two cars instead of three. Another thing, a depression gets rid of a lot of bosses, the weak ones. The strong ones survive. You wake up at the end of the bad dream and find Father Christmas has given you a lot of monopolies. Competition for the working man, monopoly for the bosses. A nice world, I don't think. Monopolies are so strong with all their interests spread about, and their powers of life and death over thousands of working people, that they bloody well control the government. Don't matter to me personally, I never walked into the parlour, but you're getting badly boxed, comrade."

This was Harry's first intellectual adventure. He found the mechanics of his world absorbing. Peter Hally's logic took his mind by storm. Peter talked with an attractive swagger; when his argument was under way his speech sloughed off much of its natural colloquialism and showed its bookish origins. He liked an audience and a disciple gratified his vanity. He put his best foot foremost. Harry did not know how much of the theory was the fruit of Peter's own perspicacity, how much he'd picked up from books. He gave Peter the benefit of every doubt and Peter accepted it. Peter's vitality was a ferment in the camp. Men heard at his lips the great words "solidarity", "Comrade", and some they fired. Yet it was a matter of inverted pride with him that he did not practise what he preached. None of it was his affair. He wasn't a wage plug, he was on the other side of that steel ring. He persuaded them of that, even though they saw him caught like themselves. He was full of object lessons but without execution. When the gang had to stand aside to let cars pass on their half-made road, Peter turned aside and spat. "Not that I mind the buggers," he explained, "it's the principle."

In the second week Peter was often absent from the camp in the evenings. In the solitary cottage down the road lived a mother and daughter. The father was away on relief work elsewhere. He'd been a timber getter. As far as the camp was concerned, the woman and girl had been as shy as wallabies. Peter became a nightly visitor. Comment in the camp was loud and bawdy. Peter himself listened to it with pleasure. No one knew whether he went for the mother or the daughter, but it was generally believed that he got what he went for. When the six lorries took the gang back to Kiama, Peter went in high spirits, without any apparent regrets. It was Harry who looked with homesick eyes at the good green dairy lands, mellowed in the long shadows and tawny sunlight of late afternoon. In the train Peter told him many tales of his cosmopolitan experience of women. Among so many no one particular woman could matter very much. Harry lost a lot of it in the din of the loose-jointed train.

He didn't see Peter again, but he went on thinking and observing what went on around him. In his quiet way he added to it. Sometimes he passed on the gospel he had received. He discovered a whole literature on the subject, thumbed copies of Tom Paine's *Rights of Man*, of Ingersoll, and of Winwood Reade, left over from last century, political tracts from the two tons of I.W.W. literature brought to Australia in the 'twenties, copies of *The Worker*, old and more recent Marxist pamphlets, Douglas Credit manifestos, other literary fragments, badly printed on poor woolly paper with an air haggard but indomitable. He dropped them all into his mind like oddments into a *bouillabaisse* and ruminated upon them. He discovered a fraternity, a confluence like an underground river, and he heard a good deal of talk that formerly had passed him by. The Revolution rose like an exotic star in his mind. He had heroic moments when he felt the world rising under him, men's minds consolidating and finding direction, and times of cold clear-sightedness when he saw that men wanted to be led back, not forward. Everywhere it was being said there was change in the air, but there was no change. There was a ground swell but no tidal wave. He realised that he was not himself a revolutionary or a leader. His heart sickened and the ferment in his mind staled. He began with renewed despair to long for a job, to rest in that job, and think no more of bright unattainable futures and the long hard pull of social reconstruction. The sense, when he was on relief work, of being herded with misfits and unemployables, galled him, and the stagnant period between tours of work exacerbated his nerves. The flame that Peter Hally had lit was dying fast.

Anzac Day 1935 fell in a period when he was off work. Some blind desire to dip himself again in the fountain of his youth, immerse himself once more in the comradeship that had almost dried up, and only achieved a forced and artificial flow on set occasions, determined him to go to the dawn service at the Cenotaph. He rose in the dark cold April morning, dressed himself without a light lest he should waken Ally. He put on his old military overcoat, the material stiff and shrunken. In all the years since the war he had had no other coat. He let himself out quietly, and set off down the hill. His feet rang on the asphalt. The air was cold and wet like air at the bottom of a well. He felt he had surprised the street lamps in their all-night vigil. As he tramped down the hill towards the city, other figures sprang up everywhere. They were behind him and before, they came out of every cross street and seemed to spring from the pavement. They were like the ghostly figures of Menin Gate, converging on the barren city. Special trams and trains were bringing them in from the suburbs. Men were arriving from the country after travelling all night. They gathered in the great vestibule of Central Station and streamed down the hill between the balustrade and the unawakened trees of Belmore Park. A few wore old uniforms, but most were in the clothes they wore every day, yet they had for this hour assumed the look of soldiers again. There was an unconscious rhythm about them, a sense of pent energy, the scattered and dissipated drawn together again on some common core, blood returned to the heart. Some years only a few came, then the fever would take them and there would be crowds of them. There were a lot of diggers marching this year. They were middle-aged men, some of them already old men. Some had grown fat and lost their soldierliness. Many were worn and shaking, stripped of their pride, all were changed from what they had been in their youth, when uniform, discipline, and the enforced sharing of their lives had given them a common likeness. It was hard to believe that these were the men of whom Masefield had said:

"They were the finest body of young men ever brought together in modern times. For physical beauty and nobility of bearing they surpassed any men I have ever seen; they walked and looked like the kings in old poems, and reminded me of the line in Shakespeare:

'Baited like eagles having lately bathed.' "

The Anzacs. And yet . . . . . .

Harry Munster stood in Martin Place, the centre of the city. The buildings rose austere and dark. The Cenotaph was piled with flowers, their scent hung in the still air. There was a great crowd. People filled the pavements and thronged the steps of the post-office. There were many women. Some had come for the sake of emotion, others on pilgrimage, tying themselves to a memory, year after year, by this rite, lest they forget; women who had "given" their sons and husbands, women who would so gladly have given them had they had them. Men there for the same reasons, old men who had lost their sons, young men who had never seen their fathers. They were very quiet, waiting, strung tight. "The cauldron," thought Harry, "the closed vessel. A revolution might begin here."

Police kept the cordon, impassive, their ribbons on their breasts. The V.C.'s made a guard of honour for the governor. They looked undistinguished, men from anywhere. Perhaps their hour had come and gone, the bravest of the brave, and life required no more of them. The archbishop was visible in his white lawn, ready to speak the too solemn words. The buglers were standing beside the Cenotaph, ready. Moment by moment the crowd's dread of the bugles wound tighter and tighter. Emotion ran from heart to heart, unimpeded. The air grew stiff, difficult to breathe. Sixty thousand dead. Sixty thousand dead. Now the indifference of the living to the dead was broken. Now in this moment. The iron door had opened. The dead could come back and no one know, the closed heart was broken and ichor flowed like the blood of sacrifice into the trench. Out of the smoking trench. . . . The crowd was denser, the silence denser, waiting, suffocating, for the dawn and the intolerable bugles. Harry looked about him. He expected to see some young faces, but they seemed to be all middle-aged or old—a countryman, weatherbeaten, far-sighted, resistant, a short fat man, a buffoon, tragic under the farce he dared not relinquish; men guttered like candles, men grown slack, grown hard, sharpened, dulled, steadied by some unpredictable maturity, lost in some unrecorded battle. All came back for something. Youth? Death? Companionship? The cleansing moment? The long, pale face of the man beside him twitched painfully. Their eyes met. They had never seen each other before, they met now. The bugles took them unawares. The Last Post. The piercing, passionless lament, defiant in its clarity and steadiness, defying the emotion of the crowd, sealing down the dead. The wave lifted the crowd up, up.

Its great crest curled but did not break. The bugles ceased, the wave fell dark and slow; men and women felt it leave them, dragging their hearts. You cannot hold the sea with your hands; salt and black it fell away from the dawn, drained into the streets on a long sigh. The service ended in the softness of shallow water. In the bleak light every face was grey. The crowd fell apart.

"Come and have a drink," said the man beside Harry Munster.

The piece of pasteboard worked where everything else had failed. From the general office Harry was sent to the superintendent of the garage. A girl left her typewriter to show him the way. The superintendent was a man in a white collar, it was that sort of joint. He received Harry, business-like, unsmiling, as if everything were already arranged, took down his name and address, looked at his old licence, which was without endorsement, told him to renew it at the police station, gave him the fee, and told him to report for duty at 8 a.m. the following Monday, award wages. The ease and naturalness of the whole business abashed Harry. He felt unnerved, sweat broke out on his temples and behind his knees. He walked out into an enormous gulf of light. He was a man in a job again, a driver for Margaret and Hurst, Importers. He felt a bewildering impulse to weep. Obscurely he dreaded going home to Ally with the news, dreaded the emotion he felt and his inability to share it with her.

Olaf Ramsay, who had worked this miracle, was not given to quixotry, he was too shy to be impulsive, but occasionally some act of faith got through. When it did, he pegged it. He accepted it into his life, honoured it as his bank would honour his cheque. It was perhaps his way of holding the last remnants of his youth's idealism. He had come back from the war with a shot through his right lung. He had been able to take his time recovering, and then he had gone straight into a partnership in his father's business, a well-entrenched firm of accountants. The depression had wrung his heart, but it had not ruined him. His brain had not been wrung at all. It was an act of God. He would not dismiss any of his employees, even though they sat idle all day. He gave generously to soup kitchens and the like, and his wife complained that he was ruining his health. In his home it never occurred to him to be anything but a perfect gentleman. Family life was set in aspic. Of his three children, the eldest was a girl, Paula. He saw in her a replica of his own sensibility and sighed. When they decided to send her to a finishing school he felt he was throwing her to the ravening crows, but it had to be done. He had few friends, but a great many people thought well of him. He had influence and it was something he took for granted, like service. Noblesse oblige. He had given Harry the piece of pasteboard and telephoned Jonathan Hurst to make sure something came of it.

The new job was anguish. Harry had been five years out of work. He had changed more than he knew. Now that he came to measure himself against the old job he felt the difference. He had lost his driver's nerve. The traffic. The traffic frightened him. He saw it as a whole, as a torrent. Coming out from a side street on to a main road, he would stop and try to gather himself for the plunge. His legs turned to wood, a blind confusion descended on his brain, so that he could not remember the traffic regulations. Policemen shouted at him, other drivers cursed him. He tried making detours, keeping to back streets, but this took more time and more petrol. He was hauled over the coals for it. It was a well-run garage. In two days he was haggard and worn; even in bed at night his hands did not stop trembling. He was frightened and tired, he yawned all day. On the 5th of May what he dreaded happened. He was coming up the Bayswater road with an empty lorry, the traffic was heavy, there was a bend in the road and an on-coming tram. A sense of nightmare descended on him. A car hooted and tried to pass him. He pulled the wheel over, and, with a nervous jolt, rammed down the accelerator. The lorry leaped forward across the road, narrowly missing the tram and crashing into a stationary car. He stopped crossways on in the narrow road, the traffic piling up into a jam. The police arrived, the owner of the car arrived, a clamour of tram bells and motor horns broke out. Harry was paralysed. At last, with a policeman standing on the running-board telling him what to do, he successfully backed the lorry across the road and down a side street. The radiator was dented, that was all. The bodywork of the car was crumpled. No one was injured. Harry thought he was going to be arrested, but the policeman contented himself with taking particulars.

"Thought your steering gear had snapped," he said. He looked puzzled. "You all right?"

"Yes."

"You'll hear about this." The policeman went away, but Harry could not move. He had grazed his arm and the pain was out of all proportion to the slightness of his hurt. It blinded him. He went on sitting in the cabin. The policeman came back.

"Suffering from shock?"

Harry nodded.

"I'll get the ambulance for you."

Harry shook his head. "I'm all right. Where'll I find a phone?" The policeman told him where there was a public phone. "You got to move that lorry."

"Yes."

He reported to the garage and an emergency driver was sent out. Harry walked home. He knew his job had come to an end. He looked so terrible that Ally retired to consult with Mrs Blan. Harry had what would have been, could he have afforded it, a nervous breakdown. He could not keep his food down, he could not sleep.

On Sunday, when he was lying unshaven on his balcony bed, Olaf Ramsay came to see him. They sat and talked for a long time. It was a relief to Harry that Ramsay accepted the situation, knew it was inevitable, and indulged in no platitudes. The nervous sensitive man brought peace into the house. Harry would not have to go back to Margaret and Hurst's. Ramsay had brought his week's wages. He wrote out a report of the accident from Harry's statement. The insurance would take care of the damage. There would be no action. The incident was closed. He produced another visiting card, a job in a big shop this time. Harry was to go when he felt able, to see the staff manager. There would be something, he'd prepare the way. Did Harry object to a uniform? Harry didn't object. They sat on talking about the war, the only thing they shared. Harry thought that Olaf Ramsay was a very fine gentleman.

A week later Harry was driving a lift at Morgan's, the palace of concrete and steel that catered for every need and whim of woman. His thin worn face looked strange above the snappy uniform. On his breast he wore his service ribbons. The firm advertised that it gave preference to returned soldiers. All its lifts were driven by veterans, every commissionaire a decorated hero. Harry's one dread was lest he forget the list of departments he must recite at each floor.

"Pulling a handle all day. You ought to be able to do that," Ally said.

It was a job. He had crept like a half-drowned dog out of the water on to dry land again and lay there panting. It was chance that rescued him—another man's sentiment. He had caught Olaf Ramsay's eye at dawn beside the Cenotaph on Anzac Day. He was lucky. This was a gift from a man more fortunately placed than himself. It solved nothing, altered nothing. He was too tired to care.

Ben was ten years old when his father found permanent work. He didn't remember a time when Harry had not been unemployed, and looked on a father out of work as one of the normal phenomena of existence. It was the same with the fathers of most of the boys he ran about with. He was of an age to take anything that happened beyond his own little circle of activity for granted. A small incident penetrated the safeguards of his childish state, and gave him a glimpse of something that, beyond his capacity to understand, disturbed him deeply. It was the day he began to sell newspapers at the Cross after school. He got home late after the evening rush, about a quarter-past seven, and came bounding up the stairs to get his tea. He landed into the middle of a family row. He knew it was a row by the edge on his mother's voice, and the quick way she was talking, like a tram going down hill, before he heard any of the words. His father was sitting at the kitchen table, a plate with the remains of meat and vegetables on it pushed away from him. His mother was leaning towards him, her palms pressed on the table. Ruthie, in that defensive way of hers, was standing against the wall.

"If you can't come for your meals at the proper time, you don't think I'm going to keep them for you, do you? That's Ben's dinner. The kid's working now and he's got to eat. Where d'you think I'm going to get him a meal? Tell me that. Can't I go out for five minutes without this happening?"

Ben saw what had happened. His father had come home late, found the flat empty and a plate of dinner keeping warm in the oven. He'd thought it was meant for him and he'd eaten it. Now mum was going to market. He was no account any more because he hadn't a job. They saw Ben in the doorway. There was dead silence. The child looked from his mother's face, ugly and distorted with anger, to Ruth's, pale with misery, to his father's. Harry said heavily, "Looks like I've eaten your dinner, son." Ben felt guilty, wicked, ashamed. He didn't want his dinner. He wanted to get away as fast as he could, he was choking. He turned and fled, he raced down the stairs and out into the street. He had the dodging speed of the gamin. His bare feet were neat and quick on the pavement. He turned the

corner into William Street and made off down the hill. He wasn't
going anywhere, he was just expending a lot of energy. He reached
the bottom of the hill by the Palladium, the floodlit T. and G.
building hung like a great wedding cake in the sky from him. Ben
jay-crossed the intersection and entered Cook Park. The grass was
cold under his bare feet, the trees and bushes had a dead blackness,
as if they got no rest. Now he walked slowly, idling along College
Street, round the curve, past the entrance to St. James's Station. It
was winter but not very cold, and he was hot from running. He
paused for a moment in front of the station, watching a newsboy's
activity in the thin stream of traffic. In the square the old queen
stood on her pedestal, extended sceptre pointing implacably downwards. Thumbs down. Ben had no idea who she was and it didn't
occur to him to wonder. Macquarie Street, wide and purposeful,
appeared to have withdrawn into dignity for the night. The wind
came up from the water. The Domain beyond was black with Port
Jackson figs and winter. Ben began to feel depressed, barefoot, and
hungry. He drifted on to Elizabeth Street. The world was awake
again. Things felt big here. Above the dark forbidding jumble of the
Supreme Court rose the green spire of St. James, bathed in its own
phosphorescent moonlight. A super cinema glittered with white
lights, the eight o'clock audience was streaming in. Next to it a
great department store, built of luminous compartments against the
dark blue sky, offered a long sequence of brightly lit caves, shimmering
behind plate glass, advance news of spring. Facades soared in light,
coloured taxis, beads on an abacus, slid to and fro. Hyde Park, like
the open side of a box of toys, lay to one side.

This wasn't Ben's world. He knew where he was, and not far
from home either, but he was a stranger. He knew tacitly that he
did not belong here and he rarely came, so that tonight there was
a trace of strangeness and wonder about it all. He had no intention
of going home. He was no longer thinking about the reason of his
departure but his intention stood firm. He had never been in the
park by night. He felt time give a big leap and realised that it must
be very late. So much the better. He followed a path which brought
him to the Archibald Fountain. It was playing in the winter night,
lighted from beneath the water. He liked the tortoises, the bull
interested him, and he observed it minutely, the deer he thought
sissy. He walked round observing and identifying the cigarette packets

and other flotsam in the basin, until whiffs of cold spray repulsed him and he walked away up the long straight path that ended in the pale shape of the Memorial screened by one large dark tree, like a cut-out. He trotted towards it, it was somewhere to go. When he arrived, the building was shut, its smooth bronze doors like closed eyelids. The shallow rectangular lake lay like a mirror in front of the building, bordered by poplars. It was lonely now, though the busy street was only a few yards away, very quiet, very still, a dome with four walls. There was enough light in the air to see it well. Ben's heart beat heavily. He stood looking up at the frieze of stone figures high against the sky. He saw a massive brooding figure. The colossus sat, looking straight before him, his stone arms resting on his stone knees, a soldier after battle, accoutred, his battle dress a rough swaddling on his tired limbs, an infantryman in a slouch hat, hard, lean, far-sighted, one who had covered great distances, a man worn down to bedrock, an immortal ghost in stone.

Ben knew the name of this building. It was the Anzac Memorial. His father was an Anzac. His heart swelled with pride. He felt a little giddy with looking upwards, so he sat down on the steps. Suddenly he was tired and weak, and odd thoughts, that he could not hold, churned in his mind. A man was coming towards him down the long straight path. It seemed to Ben quite natural that his father should come to him. It solved the problem of going home which was beginning to press on him.

They walked back through the park. Ben took his father's hand. It was night and they were alone. At the bottom of William Street there was a coffee and hotdog stall. Harry stopped. "Better have a bite," he said. "Manage two, son?"

"Yes, dad."

Harry bought him a cup of coffee and two hot dogs, yellow sausages split and laid between two halves of a roll. The vendor expertly flicked a dusting of pepper and salt over the recumbent sausages, spattered them with worcestershire, slammed-to the rolls and shoved them across his little counter. With a flourish he poured coffee from a big aluminium teapot into an enamel mug. The coffee was a curious purple colour, very sweet and flecked with tea leaves. Ben drank hungrily. It was good, a marvellous exotic beverage. Over the mug's rim his eyes took in the compact little stall—the oblong oil stove where the sausages floated in boiling water, ready to be speared and served, the two big teapots of coffee and tea, keeping warm, the neat stack of torpedo-shaped rolls, the bottles of sauce, the pepper and salt sifter, the long slender blue knife with a horn handle, the fat stall keeper in his white apron, who filled the whole interior, a counter in front of him and a hood of striped canvas tenting him and his wares from the wind. A snail's shell was not tighter or more shipshape. Himself between the stumpy shafts, the vendor would draw it home at the end of the long night. Ben looked and marvelled at the little paradise. He sniffed the smell of hot wet sausage, the coffee ran into his stomach, good and comforting. His thin little body swelled with contentment. He watched his father count out the pennies, his father's hand in the light of the flare slowly spilling pennies on to the counter. He remembered then what he had forgotten, that he had money, his paper money. Everything was all right. He bit into a hot dog, the roll had a leathery freshness, the sausage spurted in his mouth. He almost choked in the gush of saliva. He pushed the other hot dog along the counter.

"You have it, dad."

"No, son, I've had my dinner."

They grinned at one another.

Ben finished his coffee and they moved off. They walked slowly up the hill as he munched. He was as conscious now of the money in his pocket as if it were a volcano. At their own corner he pulled it out.

"Here you are, dad." He tried to force the handful of coppers into his father's pocket.

"Give it to your mother, Benny." Harry's hand closed for a minute over the small hard paw.

They went into the house together.

Benny must have been just nine then because not until his ninth birthday would Harry let him sell papers. It had long been his ambition, but his father had been adamant. Younger boys did it, and for the past two years Old Rumpty, who had the corner stand at the Cross, had been willing to take Ben on. He could see he'd be the quickest of the lot. He liked his grin, too, the quick sharing grin in his quick dark eyes. Old Rumpty lived in a cloud of auxiliaries. He was lame, indefinitely old, dressed in seedy clothes so old and so habituated to him that no one could imagine him ever renewing them or even taking them off. He sat all day on an up-ended kerosene box, its open side turned to the shopfront. It was his bank and larder. The placards advertising the news he sold leaned beside him against the same wall, his magazines and weekly papers were deployed on the footpath. He sat there all day and far into the night, seeing the last of the theatre traffic go home. At intervals he was revived with glasses of milky tea laced with rum. He had a lieutenant, a raucous, incommunicative man in his thirties, called Lefty, who might or might not be his son. Lefty had no personality, and personality counts in the paper-selling business. Early in the morning when the dailies were in the streets Rumpty had a few boys selling them, but in the afternoon, after school, he had a whole fleet of them serving the crowds returning from work, boarding the laden trams, darting through the traffic to sell to cars momentarily halted by the traffic cop, scaling off papers with dexterous fingers on the corners, thrusting them under laden arms, gathering in the coppers, shouting scraps of news that, with repetition lost meaning and shape and became strange cries in the hubbub, perpetually active on their bare feet, often in danger, rarely caught.

One of the starving poets of the Cross, disciple of the new mechanic beauty, seeing old things in guise of new and the new in terms of the old, weaving the world together with simile and image, thought of the newsboys as seagulls, strident voices crying storm, quick light bodies graceful in the heavy traffic, erratic and light, hard predatory eyes, swooping on pennies wherever they saw them in the crowd. The streets were channels scored by traffic through the honey-combed infested rock of dwellings. Cars were the giant, ensharded beetles, trams the green of drab myopic lizards, double-decker buses the megatheria of the future's pre-history. Metallic flowers of sound on terraces of asphalt, air vocal with ten thousand radio sets, primordial ooze of civilization. Armour of macadam on the earth, armour of light on the night, armour of unreality on the brain, and tough armour of romance on the human heart.

The policeman stood at the top of the hill where the five highways converged. He locked the traffic, as if it were a river, with a gesture. He opened the sea for pedestrians to pass over. Unscathed in the very middle, he turned with slow authoritative movements from side to side, a tall man in white helmet and white gloves, not only commanding but creating the tides. But it was Old Rumpty who really held the baton. He alone knew the whole symphony by heart.

He sat on his box and conducted it from beginning to end, six days a week. Only he had the detachment. Policemen came on duty and went off duty; Old Rumpty stayed. He saw the workers drawn in from the peninsula of South Head to the city in the morning, a rising wave from seven o'clock to its crest at ten to nine, a steep drop, the smaller following wave of shoppers in the mid-morning, ladies who did not buy papers, the small returning wave in the afternoon, the grand crescendo of the workers' return, five to seven in the evening, theatre traffic, seven-thirty to eight, its return in the hard brilliance of the night between eleven o'clock and midnight. Old Rumpty didn't work himself. He organized. His regulars came up to him, bought papers and exchanged greetings and reflections. Lefty, standing out on the pavement, caught the casual passer-by. In the peak hours of the evening he threw out his net of boys. Rumour said he was fabulously rich.

Old Rumpty couldn't read. He had an enormous contempt for those who could, but in slack times he liked to have a boy squat beside him and tell him the news out of the papers. He could then pour his contempt upon it. He was a martinet with his lads and considered himself responsible for their education. Language he would not tolerate. Dishonesty he winnowed out with a terrible perspicacity. Some boys he singled out for special training. To them he opened the vials of his wisdom. Ben was always a favourite. Ben read him the afternoon headlines and absorbed in return his comments, gaining a brief, racy slant on events. He also gave Ben the much sought-after privilege of delivering papers to the nearby shops. This meant perquisites. Italian fruiterers would give him an apple or an orange, rubbing it first on their sleeves to give the gift a personal touch. The Greek fishmonger would silently hand him a bright yellow fillet of flathead or a handful of hot chips. The delicatessen girls would slip him a pie or a sausage or a titbit from the sandwich counter. In the hotel one of the barmaids, a resplendent girl with vivid complexion and a diamond star in her hair, leaning on the counter like the blessed damozel, would give him a swig of Tom and Jerry or Coffee Royal on a wet day. The inconsequent kindness of people was great. Ben could always rely on picking up his dinner like this. There was generally more than he could eat, and he ran round with odd bulges in his jersey or the blouse of his shirt. He brought home contributions to the larder.

To Ben, selling papers was all profit. He enjoyed it enormously but it wasn't his only pleasure. He was the young hunter of the city. The city was his playground and a rich mine of sensations and profit. William Street was his galaxy. He early learned to know all the different makes of cars and to argue their merits. He window-shopped through the plate glass of the motor sales rooms that lined both sides of the street. He got his thrills scaling trams, chased by irate guards, or tearing down the hill among the traffic in his billy cart to the imminent danger of his life. Where or how he got the billy cart—a box on wheels, two strands of string for steering-gear—no one knew. He may have traded for it, found, or straight out pinched it. He didn't seem to know. All the boys had billy carts. It was Ben's principal means of prosecuting his business. Profit was everywhere. He knew where ashes were given away, where broken boxes and bits of wood could be picked up and sold again, dirt cheap but at enormous profit, for firing. Now and then he got away with a billy cart of coal from the railhead at Darling Harbour, a long trek by back streets, but worth it. He could always allay his lust for ha-penny confectionery by collecting newspapers for sale to the butcher, or bottles garnered out of dust boxes. The competition, especially for bottles, was enormous, but Ben was spry. He picked up oddments in the very gutters, cigarette butts and cigarette cards—till they were stopped—matchboxes, fruit with only a spot of badness on it, an occasional coin.

He was not really precociously shrewd. He was cheerful and open handed, but he was very much alive, and in his world living and the main chance were very closely connected. School, to which he went perforce, was an interruption to the main business of living. He bore with it stoically and presented an invincible indifference to his teachers that successfully thwarted all their efforts to impart to him anything beyond reading, writing, and the elements of arithmetic. He wasn't dull, his mind was simply turned away. The things he was taught in school had nothing to do with his daily life, the teachers were creatures from a different world whose humanity he barely recognised. He thought Ruth, who took her lessons seriously and had a painful and desolating adoration for one of her teachers, a poor mug. Wanda was more of his way of thinking, but vanity prompted her to work occasionally and to "suck up" to her class mistress while she laughed at and parodied her before her class mates.

Ben ran about with small boys, especially Tony Nelson, who was a little older and, even then, an active purposeful lad, and joined heartily in the various sports of plaguing cranky old men, ringing door bells in respectable neighbourhoods distant from home, chalking rude words and even ruder drawings on walls, gambling in kind, running round in packs looking for men in hard-hitter hats or with beards and yelling "ziff" or "beaver" every time they scored. He liked also to make excursions alone or with Tony down to Woolloomooloo Bay to see the ships and the sailors, to hang round the salty old pubs getting, had they only known it, a taste of life. They enjoyed the commotion of a departing liner, they loved a fight but saw few in the open swept area of the docks. They would go anywhere to a fire, taking their billycarts in the hope of loot. When a monster tide and storm broke down the embankments at Rose Bay, submerged tram-lines, and wrecked pleasure craft on the road, Ben made posthaste to the scene. He paused to wonder at the gardens, the great bastions of flats, thousands of windows looking unblinking into the harbour, the spaciousness of everything. Police and salvage teams were at work. Ben stood for a time watching. More and more he became aware that there was nothing for him here under the stare of all those windows. It wasn't his world, he felt small and exposed. He turned about and began to trudge the long way back, pulling his billy cart. He was more at home on his own hill, matted with dwellings, its rounded shoulder turned to the Bay, its terraces, old stone cottages, cut-throat alleys, steep streets, breakneck steps, its crown of light and noise.

.    .    .    .    .    .    .    .    .    .

Knarf and Ord knew that hill. They had often climbed to the top through the long grass and the plantations of young trees. There was a road, but they did not use it, preferring to scramble up the rough hillside. It was sunny and quiet in the afternoon. Few people came there, perhaps because a lingering sense of ruin and sadness abode there. There was rubbish in the grass, ridges faintly discernible still, where the streets had run, blocks of stone with tooling on them, fragments of slate and tile, rust-eaten fragments of iron worked to some almost obliterated antique pattern. It was too stony, too encumbered to be fertile, and yet none of that detritus was of any value or any interest. It had the melancholy of places once living, now dead, laid waste, without dignity. The plovers flew low over the shaggy ground where they nested, uttering their despairing cries. The bush had not come back willingly. The hill had had to be trenched and eucalypts planted to take away the appearance of waste land, even of a rubbish heap. The old broken world did not give it up without a struggle. Port Jackson figs had sown themselves and you could lie upon the grass, your head pillowed on nameless stone, and look up at the blue sky or down at the blue water, through the labyrinth of their black-green leaves. Ord was not sure in this moment which was further in time, the dead hill or the living hill. It had had its night of fire mounting to heaven, when its life guttered away. Ord felt that Knarf and he leaned now upon some aerial sill with the old world poured out beneath them. What they saw was the world rolling up like a scroll.

"The nineteen thirties," said Knarf. "That was the fateful decade."

"The last chance before the cataclysm. The graveyard of lost causes."

"Those were the years when the margin between cause and effect in the international and social field narrowed to vanishing point— one of the really tragic periods of history, in a way more tragic than what came after, because there was an appearance of choice about it. It was so full of endeavour and so empty of imagination."

"Today, we have neither energy nor imagination. The average citizen does nothing towards shaping his world."

Knarf answered almost absentmindedly, "We hang like a drop of water, pendulous over an abyss. The really curious thing about the nineteen thirties is that the world was never before, perhaps never since, so aware. The decade began in the depths of the Depression, something calculated to stir the social forces as even the first world war had not done, an object lesson brought into almost every home, certainly every working-class home. If ever event brought indictment against a social system, the Depression brought one against capitalism. Here and there an agitator, bolder and clearer than the rest, said to the people: 'You are hungry because the world is too rich. There is food to be eaten and work to be done, but the food must rot and the work go undone because to "give" you either would upset the economy based on profit.' It was set out more completely in books that instructed the intellectuals and provided them with ammunition in the battle of wits, but went no further. It was proved up to the hilt by the very reasoning on which men claimed to base the whole fabric of their living. But nothing happened. Here and there a little fire was lighted in some receptive mind. There was, maybe, a deep inarticulate murmur in the masses, lifting blindly towards no envisaged goal. But for the most part the people crouched down and waited for the fury to pass, as if it were a storm or some other 'act of God.' The whole great lower middle class plumped for a continuance of things as they were.

"You can't blame the people. Organized protest? That would have been treated as rebellion. The State would have put down a protest against the social system as if it were an act of disloyalty to the State. Men were suffering enough. The sickness was in their hearts, crumbling them. They weren't quite desperate enough. To fight, men must have something to fight for or nothing to lose. The people here and then were in between. The time for protest and reconstruction is the good times. If the workers in days of prosperity, fit and well fed, their skills in demand, their homes intact behind them, had taken up the cause of social justice, they could have cracked the system open and would have brought in some form of working socialism.

"But it didn't happen. It won't ever happen. Men aren't reasonable. They prefer a familiar disaster to an unknown remedy. In the years of depression the people obeyed the shibboleths, like the snake, the flute, or the rats the pipe. Men lived by slogans—'Prosperity round the corner,' 'Equality of sacrifice,' when interest rates were cut as make-weight against the cessation of wages; ex-millionaires committing suicide as well as unemployed breadwinners; the trail of depression bargains from bankrupt estates to business men's luncheons, potato pie, slush and oddments, sixpence; the hobby of economising for those who could afford it, the virtue of spending that made every purchase a charity. And the economists with frantic manipulations did pull things together and set the machine going again without radical change. The patient was convalescent, rather tremulous and transparent and inclined to be imaginative, but none the less convinced that the worst was over. The unemployed returns still made an alarming fever chart, but fewer and fewer watched it. Enough people were satisfied to weight down the situation and make things safe. That's how the decade went, everyone a little upset, ready to catch at remedies, anxious to be reassured in their complacency or a little conscience stricken. Their resistance down."

Ord dashed cold water in the face of all this eloquence.

"What about Russia?"

"In Russia the miracle happened. In 1917 the people had reached the point of creative desperation. There was a programme to meet the emergency. There was a man to implement the programme. A people not long emerged from serfdom could be relied on to respond to the voice of authority. The great unwieldy mass turned on the small point of Marxism, Communism, Bolshevism, Leninism, whatever you like to call it. The socialist state, antique pattern, was created. Hopelessly unscientific, as we know socialism, but there in germ. Another object lesson. The rest of the world bristled against it in suspicion. Obscured between libel and legend, but there, a new conception in practical politics, working like leaven in the unresponsive world mind.

"The basis of change is not law or logic but human psychology. That's the rock on which Communism split. It postulated a law and tried to nail human nature to it. We were talking about the 'thirties."

"The community had had a searching experience. It came through it to face rapidly maturing event. In 1933 Adolf Hitler raised himself to power in Germany. Buffoon into conqueror. The world underestimated him and overestimated humanity. He took the lid off."

"He didn't invent the garbage. He only took the lid off. A homely gesture."

"Everybody laughed. The world looked on unconvinced, put cotton wool in its ears. The British supported the Hitler regime as a bulwark against Communist Russia. In 1931 the China incident had begun in earnest, a slow sporadic war. The West took little notice. Sentiment favoured the Chinese, policy the Japanese. England at one time closed the Burma Road, cutting off help from the struggling Chinese people. Civil War in Spain, the church and vested interests rising against a moderate socialist government, duly elected. Again sentiment was with the Spanish Government, the International Brigade was its expression. The world was watching tragedy like a stage play. Pens plied with power and passion. The British Government's non-intervention policy favoured the insurgents, a valve that cut off aid from the government but allowed Germany and Italy to send troops and equipment to the insurgents, to win their war against the gallant Spanish people. It was socialism's war and everywhere men stood by and saw it lost. The shutter of silence came down on conquered Spain, decently to veil heaven knows what depths of oppression and suffering. The spotlight of attention passed to other crises. Italians in Abyssinia. Young men prating of the beauty of destruction. Public sentiment was again with the attacked. It led to nothing but ineffective sanctions and the white rape of Ethiopia. The growing power of Germany. Pogroms. The Anschluss, bloodily bloodless. Sudetenland. The hysteria of Munich. Adoration of an umbrella. Czecho-slovakia. The chance of a Russian alliance against the Nazis muffed. The Russo-German non-aggression pact. Poland. The whole slow conflagration, so incredible that no one believed what they knew to be true. Never were people so aware, so powerless to act. It was a decade of books. Books poured from the presses, prodigal of information, focussing attention on the present. Eye witnesses' accounts. Books of foreign correspondents who had had it straight from the horse's mouth. Left Book Clubs. Pamphlets. Penguins and Pelicans. Men talking. Men listening. Everything predicted. Hitler writing a book *Mein Kampf* telling the world what he would do, how he would do it. Then doing it. Dealing in lies, rhodomontade, moral indignation, every sort of transparent chicanery, and bringing it off. The whole impulse of the decade expending itself in books. Scandals and crises following so fast on one another's heels that each erased the effects of the last. Men lived with printed horrors until they became calloused. So many sticking points but none of them stuck. So much propaganda that people learned not to listen, or, listening, to discount.

"It was the brief day of the intellectual, the orgy of ideologies. Democracy fighting a rearguard action. Liberals calling on precedent. Realism a cloak for every violent and opportunist expedient. Idealism repairing the lost complacency. Never did the demand for peace stand higher than in the turbid 'thirties. Peace by conference, peace by disarmament, peace through emotion, miraculous peace. Most of those who made the noise thought they could get peace without changing anything else, holding tight to their nationalism and their competitive living. But there were some who knew that there could be no peace without social change, national and international, not idealists, hard, practical men who consciously chose the most difficult way, the way of peace in all its implications. I think I know how they looked at things. It was this. Every man has in varying degrees the possibilities of all men, and each has a margin of action within himself, but that margin was in practice very much reduced by circumstance for all men. Men are inevitably conditioned by the world they live in. Now the salient feature of that world of the twentieth century—and for many years before—was competition. Whether they willed it or not, men lived by profit. From this basis of competitive living, there followed a series of reactions of which war was one. The system gave rise to fiercer, more frequent wars, leading on to war, total and continuous, and the death of civilisation. War was not an isolated phenomenon but a logical consequence. These men of the Peace Party, these nuclear men, saw man the only half conscious victim of a vicious circle. At some point the circle must be broken. They chose war as the point of attack, chose it with a sort of cold steadfast logic. To war with its sufferings and destruction, there was less consent. The misery implicit in the series was more obvious here. Peace was still a word to conjure with, and around it clung the remnants and tatters of a religion that claimed to worship the Prince of Peace who counselled men to love their enemies, to do good to them that do despitefully use you, and to turn the other cheek. Great things can be asked of men when half measures fail. War proved the quixotry of common men, their willingness to die with matchless courage for a cause not their own, to endure and die for a shibboleth, for a sentiment, for a flamboyant lie, for a man they had never seen, a liberty they had never enjoyed, a world they never owned. Might not this heartbreaking valour be turned to another use if it were equally quixotic, mad, and out of reach. If men could be induced to refrain from fighting with the same courage with which they fought, if they could say, and it would not be more preposterous, All men are brothers instead of Dulce et decorum est pro patria mori. . . . This handful preached total peace in the midst of total war. They cried, voices in the wilderness, Lay down your arms. The man you kill is no different from yourself, no better, no worse. It is better that he destroy you than that you destroy him. Stop war by refusing to fight it. No army could stand against a people that would not fight, that said, 'We are brothers, and death, yours or mine, will not solve anything.' If there must be bloodshed, let it be the fruitful blood of martyrs and not the blood of men slain in battle which rises again in new wars. A people who steadfastly refused to fight could not be defeated, but they must be willing to make sacrifices greater even than the soldier's. These men refused war and they preached a new sort of resistance. They attacked the system at its most vulnerable place when life was driven in extremes, they allied themselves with every progressive movement; their hand was in co-operative movements making their slow headway against competition, they joined in every little group that laboured for the public good, they saluted Russia, the socialist fatherland, they forsook no danger and no toil. All they asked was to work for life and not for death.

"If anyone had the right of it in those mad troubled years, I think they had." Knarf's chin was sunk on his breast, he looked unseeing away and away. His voice grew slower and deeper.

"They were beaten. Habit and unreason and the loud voices were too many for them. They were overwhelmed, and the tragic farce went on. But they pegged an idea, they kept something alive in their doomed generation, an aspect of humanity, if you like; by their thought and their action they kept it as an ingredient of life, for a later flowering. A wall against the darkness built of dust, and every grain a man's life. Men learn, I think, by destroying their saviours. Perhaps there is no other way. You know how it is when something is very much on your mind—evidence gathers like filings round a magnet. I discovered a passage in an old book, one of the few chance preserved from this very decade, but written about a time further from the nineteen thirties than they are from us.

" 'Prophecies are never worth anything,' said the Essene. . . . "Prophecies do not count, he who receives them counts. . . . For there have been many who recognised the Sign and received the Word."

"And you know what befell them?"

"I do, for there were many, and none was the first. There was, for instance, a certain Agis, he was King in Laconia. This man Agis had heard from his tutor that once there had been an age of Justice and common property which is called the Golden Age, and this he meant to re-awaken. His aristocrats and the wealthy naturally objected to this, but the King gave away his riches to the people and brought back the ancient laws."

"And what happened to him?" asked Spartacus.

"He was hanged. Then there was a man by the name of Jambulos, who went on a long sea voyage to a friend. In the middle of the ocean they found an island on which the Golden Age is alive to this day. The natives of his island were called Panchees, and, because of their just mode of living, they are of truly wonderful body. They share property, food, shelter, and share their women too, so that no man may know his children. In this manner they not only avoid pride of property, but the haughtiness of blood as well. So, in order to do away with a good example, the wealthy in Jambulos's country killed him, peace and blessing to his memory—and now no one knows where the Panchee island is . . ."*

Ord had never heard Knarf speak in the old tongue before, though he knew he had a book knowledge of it. It had a curious evanescent beauty that he had not realised, the whole system of linkage and cadence poetic rather than logical.

"He goes back and back," said Knarf, "world beyond world. It is as if one man can travel such a short distance in all his life he is only in focus for a moment. Life takes that moment and then discards him. Often he does not know. We live our whole lives with all their dust and heat"—Ord grinned, smoothing his mouth with his hand—"and only one function is chosen for the pattern, the rest rejected. If we give something it is all we can expect, our time goes over. It is like a Turkish funeral. I read about that too in an old book. The coffin was carried out of the house into the street, there were no bearers, no procession as was usual, but men passing in the streets lent their shoulders as a pious duty, carried it a few yards and then relinquished their place to another, and so the journey was made. So endeavour passed from hand to unknown hand, without reward, none following all the way, few seeing or foreseeing the end. . . ."

Knarf was silent so long that Ord said, "What are you thinking, Knarf?"

He answered churlishly, "Nothing," looked up at the sun which was already high, and ruffled a pile of papers with his fingers. "I can't read you all this. The best I can do is to pick out the voices here and there. . . .

"Here's a bit about the Domain, the Dom, on a Sunday."

.        .        .        .        .        .        .        .

Sunday was the empty day. The street as a whole spent it in an atmosphere of unmade beds, scratch meals, the luxuriant Sunday

---

*From Arthur Koestler's *The Gladiators 1939.* Cape, pp. 94 sqq.

press, a torpid day with a renascence about dark when the young of both sexes put on its best and sallied into the streets, the parks, the waterfront, looking for adventure. To Harry it was about as congenial as a furred tongue. The tepid slackness reminded him of his workless years, and the last remnant of the farmer in him was affronted by the shapeless days. However tired he was, he liked to get out. On warm Sundays he and Ben usually went to one of the beaches. With a lunch of thick slices of bread and slabs of cold meat, to be supplemented on the spot with bananas and ginger pop, and their bathers rolled in a towel, they boarded a tram before the crowds and were carried through quiet streets to Bondi, Bronte, or Maroubra. Bubbles of excitement broke in the little boy's throat when he saw the dark blue line of the sea against the pale blue of the sky. No sooner had they arrived on the almost empty beach than Ben wanted to eat the lunch. They changed into their bathers without going into the surf sheds, if they could manage it. The child ran about the beach, trailing seaweed after him, kicking up the shallow water, enjoying his own energy. After a quick dip Harry generally lay on the sand, letting the sun soak into his body and his weariness soak into the sand. He fell into a drowse. More and more people collected, family groups with babies and hampers and striped umbrellas, schools of young people, the girls smart in waterproof make-up, the men oiled for suntan, couples lying side by side in drowsy contented intimacy, solitaries like himself, caring for nothing but the hour and the sun. From time to time Harry would lift his head and look about him, the laughing water, the clear sky, the throng. He knew it wasn't real. When his eyes had found Ben he let his head down again, drew in a deep breath, the smell of the sand, the tang of seaweed. Only Ben was real. He had generally picked up a gang of other children. All children were on a level in bathing suits. Watching Ben among the others Harry felt pride of himself and of the boy. Ben was brown and quick and full of life. He'd got the boy through the bad years of the depression unmarked. The beach was so packed you could hardly see the sand for legs and arms. No one cared. No one owned the beach. Whatever they did in other places, here they were willing to share. Gregariousness came naturally and hampered no one. Again and again Ben came back, asking for a penny because he was hungry, and Harry always gave it to him. Then there was the return at sundown in the crowded

tram, shoulders stiff with sunburn, sand between their toes, Ben's
nose peeling, his lips salty when he licked them, his eyes sliding
sideways with good weariness, both of them softly drunk with sun
and light. . . .

Other Sundays when the weather wasn't right for the beach, or
when Harry had been cleaned out by some extra expense and had not
the money for their fares and food, he and Ben generally went down
in the afternoon to the Dom. The trees made a hollow square, dark
spreading Port Jackson figs, indigenous. On its north side behind
its stone wall, the Botanic Gardens, lawns and flower beds, trees,
aviaries, kiosks, barred with paths, dotted with statuary, flowed down
to the bright water of Farm Cove. On the east the columned sand-
stone facade of the Art Gallery showed through the trees. Across
the square were the Mitchell Library, the arcaded backs of Macquarie
Street buildings, the honey coloured truncated towers of St. Mary's,
and sweeping round, the long climb of William Street up to King's
Cross, bristling with its stalagmites of brick and concrete.

The grass of the square was shaggy, worn by many feet, littered
with leaves and the round brown figs. Overhead the blue sky arched,
pigeons wheeled, and the flag fluttered from the Art Gallery. Under
the figs and on the grass of the people's common a large crowd
collected, clotted in groups, tight at the core, fringing to indifference
on the outskirts. It was the impromptu public forum, the black
market of ideas. The crowd was mostly seedy, largely men. They
came out of a sort of catholic mental curiosity, they picked over the
ideas laid out, looking half the time for stimulus rather than reason;
some came to refresh themselves at the font of their own peculiar
convictions; others, with open mind—open at both ends—drifted
from group to group, seeking conviction, hoping to find ready-made
a panacea, an elixir, a drug. A burning question or a burning cause
could bring this drift together into a formidable and impassioned
crowd. On the beaches nobody cared, here they at least wanted to
care, and some cared with an eccentric violence.

The rostra varied from soap boxes to step-ladder platforms,
according to the strength of the body to which the speaker belonged.
Men stood on the ground and began to talk, without audience, went
on steadily until a small knot collected round them. If they had
anything to say, or said it with sufficient assurance, the knot became
a crowd, grew and spread. The crowds and knots, Harry noticed, were

roughly circular, not fan shaped as you'd expect. High voices of women, the inevitable bearers of collection boxes and sheaves of pamphlets, wove in and out. Police mingled with the crowd, detached, contemptuous, officially cognisant of all that took place.

The Salvation Army prayed stertorously, offered up testimony of salvation full of rich mundane detail, sang racy hymns to brass band accompaniment.

A man who ran a small grocery business during the week, but lived for Sundays, mounted a kitchen chair in the interests of Douglas Credit.

Next door, a stocky man had his own individual message to which few listened. Its interest was still remote.

"D'you know what the British Government ought to do? If you don't, I do. It ought to scotch this man Hitler. For why? Because he's right. Not because he's wrong, mind you, but because he's right. He's on to something. We can't afford to have him doing the right thing in Germany, making them strong. A bit of Nazism would do us good, but we don't want them done good to, we can't afford it, see? So what I say is scotch Hitler while there's still time." (Laughter.)

There was an old man with a weak quavering voice and hollow cheeks who had preached salvation by diet for twenty years. He talked rankly and intimately of man's interior economy, and, like a banner planted beside him, he had a large diagram of the intestines looking like a jungle of red and blue snakes. He was mystical and religious. He always had an audience, for such things attracted people, but his heart was heavy because he had no disciple to carry on after he was dead, and his unique system would be lost to man. He neither sought nor made any profit, what he did was done for love of humanity.

There was a variety of religious fanatics, one-man shows. Among them was one who regularly worked himself into such a fury that he foamed at the mouth and performed strange contortions. The people watched him as if he were a Punch and Judy show, their faces bland and cruel. A rationalist, a steady unemotional man, maintained his ground, Sunday after Sunday, and reasoned with a small group able to appreciate the fine logic of his dialectic. British Israelites talked of the Pyramids and juggled figures like coloured balls, and astrologers talked of the stars and prophecies, but kept their prophecies under a caul, precious and exciting in vagueness. Fish-faced, the audiences gathered round them. They were comforted. Man's destiny was written in the stars, unalterable. Why all the fuss and anxiety to change the unchangeable? For Man, fate was fixed, but for the individual there were backways and secret passages, On this day he might invest his savings with profit, on that make a journey with safety; he had only to pick the right day for everything and he would have good luck always beside him, and that right day could be chosen by the stars with mathematical precision. Public irresponsibility and private safety. Eureka! Mankind is saved.

One small group had brought a deal table with them. Leaflets and pamphlets were set out on it, a jug of water and a thick tumbler. The pedantic touch raised a grin. A man said to Harry with a thrust of his thumb, "He's got to have a counter before he can sell ideas." There was a young squarish man, not remarkable but very obstinate in a quiet way when you came to look at him closely, the others were younger still, two boys and two girls. They might be students, a rather self-conscious turn-out, shabby middle-class, faintly clerical. They were only just breaking into the Dom. They had a sign up, a strip of calico between two stakes driven into the ground. It read "Peace Party." People streamed by, few paused. Peace was either something they took for granted, a condition that would stay put without any particular effort on their part, or something already destroyed, now war had begun in Spain, an anachronism, a tramelling husk to be cast away. "Bloody parsons," they said. "Bloody reactionaries," "Poor bloody cows."

There were some of their own people there, some strays, some curious. The squarish man did the talking. He wasn't an orator, but he stuck to it. Bowmaker was his name—not a very fortunate one in the circumstances, his friends called him Bowie. He drove in his arguments methodically as if they were nails. He didn't forget that most heads were wood. His satellites stood behind him and didn't know exactly what to do. Later they could distribute leaflets and sell pamphlets. Now they could only stand. In what attitude? The militarists had bagged all the best ones. It would hardly do to stand to attention or with folded arms and immobile faces. Nor must they slouch, droop, or wilt, cast their eyes down or up, fold their hands.

Paula Ramsay was in the audience because one of the girls in the group by the table, Katherine, was a friend and Paula had promised to come. She had not told her mother where she was going because her mother would have tried to stop her, nor had she told her father because he would probably have come with her. Although she liked being with him most times, there were some, especially if she were going to face a new experience, when she wanted to be alone. It left her free to see with her own eyes. When she was with people, especially the few who mattered to her, her mind was never free of emotional entanglements. This afternoon her awareness was like a bubble, complete, floating, carrying a reflection of the whole scene on its shining sides. She saw the dark figs, the grass pale under the gusty wind, the people, dark in knots, clusters, whorls, small crowds, the pale spring sky with thin wind-driven clouds, flicker of leaves and signs, the music of the band broken by the wind flapping like a great banner floating over their heads. She saw Katherine tugging in the smirk at the corners of her mouth, and watched Bowie boring his small, neat, hole in the raving darkness of the world.

Paula stood beside Harry Munster. He saw a girl, young, delicate, austere, in a dark blue coat and small close-fitting hat.

A man began heckling, a note of exasperation, like the whine of thin steel released, sounded in his voice.

"All very nice, mister," he said, "but it won't work. Not in this world, it won't. We won't get anything if we don't fight for it, and we won't keep anything if we don't fight either. If you tell people they can sit down on their tails and think lovely thoughts, you're just leading them up the garden. 'Tisn't practical. We've always fought and we'll go on fighting."

Bowie paused and looked at him through his spectacles.

"Are you the man," he asked in his mildest voice, "who caught a cold three winters running and thought he was under a moral obligation to go on catching colds till he died of pneumonia?"

He got his laugh.

"There you go," shouted the man, "We're not talking about colds."

A new Bowie whipped into view. "You're quite right, we're not. We're talking about survival. You say peace isn't practical, that war is the means of survival. You're old enough to remember the last war, perhaps you fought in it. Have you any idea what it cost? I can't tell you the whole cost, nobody knows. It cost the world fifteen million dead and six million men living but totally incapacitated. That's fighting men alone. Civilian casualties and victims of malnutrition are extra. Out of a population of six million, Australia alone lost sixty thousand killed and a hundred and sixty-eight thousand wounded and sick, all men in their heyday, fighting fit. The same small population has paid something like £530,000,000 for the war already, and it's not nearly paid for. The war was fought to preserve our way of life. Well, on the figures of the National Debt, every citizen owes £39 for the war and £17 for public works and other purposes. Like all wars this one was followed by plague. This time it was attributed to a neutral—Spanish Influenza. Four million died of it in India alone. We had it. You remember. As a delayed result of the war, or if you like, of the same factors that caused the war, we had the Depression. No one knows what toll that took in life, health, sanity, happiness. You say war's practical and it must go on. I say war is the most ruinous and unpractical method of reconstruction. It destroys the very basis of our life, lowers physical standards, curtails liberty, sows the seed of the next war. . . ."

Harry walked away. He'd come out for a Sunday afternoon stroll, not for this. Pretty tough, he thought. There's a war. They tell you in the papers and churches and everywhere else that it's a just and holy war, and it's your duty to go and fight. You go, you stick four years of it, a lot of blokes get knocked, it's bloody hell about a quarter of the time, and a colossal bore the rest. You come home, and twenty years after some bright chap discovers it was all a mistake. It wasn't worth it. You shouldn't ever have fought.

Harry strode across the Dom looking for Ben, who had slipped away in search of more lively entertainment. He had kept a trace of his military carriage, the body of a disciplined man. Now pride had come back to his body, facing up to the threat. He looked about him. All these people peddling salvation of one kind or another, people accepting, believing, clinging. Yet all the faces, when you looked close, were troubled. Anxiety and strain worked secretly on them. If it didn't get them in the day, it caught them in sleep. Everywhere the stamp of distress was under the skin. Would a happy and victorious people bear this imprint? . . . For the first time the realization broke on him that not only had he himself met bad luck and frustration, not only had his class been weakened and driven back, but that the whole world was sick, and from prostration it was turning to catastrophe. All the preparation it had for that impending doom was a multitude of conflicting voices.

No go, the Yogi man,
No go, Blavatsky,
What we want's a roll of notes
A bit of skirt and a taxi.

## December 1936

Early December, and the store was already decked for Christmas. Green wreaths on the pillars, and in them candles with steady cardboard flames, streamers of coloured paper, clusters of balloons straining to the ceiling, miniature Christmas trees of wire and chenille in miniature tubs, and, special feature as advertised, huge cut-outs on the walls of the main shopping hall, depicting scenes from "Christmas Round the World." At the end opposite the lifts was the largest and loveliest "Bethlehem," a golden-haired baby leaping from his tranquil mother's arms between sheaves of reverent men and angels. Layettes on the third floor. Above the lifts, it was balanced by a comic scene, "Christmas in the Cannibal Isles," in which our sable brethren dined hilariously on missionary. Everything for the Christmas party, Ground Floor. In between, you could see "Santa Claus in Scandinavia," Toys, Fifth Floor. Hungarian dancing Czardis round a tree. Dirndls 8/11, Second Floor. And so on. The difficulties of Christmas traffic were increased by those who stopped to gape at these masterpieces. Merchandise, packaged and displayed with élan, loaded the tables and fixtures. A profiteer's dream of Goblin Market. Xanadu with a price ticket. A sort of corporate vision of wealth and plenty from which each comer carried away a token, a sprig broken off the universal Christmas. Christmas orgy measured out and charged. If you stood on the stairs above and looked at it with eyes unfocused, it had a bright fluttering gaiety and something else, deep sunk in it, like an old lava stain on smiling country, the ineradicable folk quality of the fair.

If you spent your days there, all day and every day, it was different. Outside it was hot. Summer. The streets were like tarnished brass, smoke in the sunshine, fume of distant bushfires drifting into the city. Inside, the cooling plant could not cope with the heat of many bodies. The glass of the showcases was warm to the touch from the display of lights. The air was thick with scents and dusts and human exhalations. The escalators carried a constant frieze of customers up and down from floor to floor like marionettes in a shooting gallery, but the pressure on the lifts was unrelieved. Twenty lifts in a row. Call them elevators, it's more refined. Harry took his gilded cage to the sixth floor, stopping at each floor, chanting his piece. Stand back in the elevator, please. Mind the door, please. First Floor, Ready-made Costumes, Maids' Wear, Boots and Shoes, Ladies' Boudoir on your right, Telephones on your left. Going up. Mind the door, please. Madam. . . .

At first he used to be afraid that he wouldn't remember which departments were on each floor, that his mind would jamb or his tongue fail. Then he had got used to it. Now, the second Christmas, he knew them so well that he was afraid of forgetting them again. His mind panicked now and then out of sheer fatigue and boredom. "It's not a hard job," said Ally. "No, it's the sort of job they give crocks."

From the sixth floor he went to the Restaurant de luxe on the eighth floor and then to the Popular Restaurant called the Hasty Tasty on the ninth. He brought the people from the restaurants direct to the ground floor. Ten lifts did this, ten lifts went through to the restaurants and stopped at all floors coming down. When Harry thought of the twenty lifts all working but never getting into line, and the twenty liftdrivers gabbling their piece all the time, opening the doors and closing the doors, starting the lift, stopping the lift, repeating it over and over, he felt a little crazy. But he was a little crazy now, anyway. When he tried to work out how many trips they all made between them every day, and how many words each must say on each journey and multiply that by twenty . . . he got a light feeling in his head as if his brain were like a clenched fist. One day trod on the heels of the next. He tried to work out how many times he had taken the lift up altogether, but there were so many factors to take into account that he could never be sure he had got it right. It worried him and he struggled against it. Christmas was the worst. The lifts were full from nine in the morning till the shop closed. It was hot. He thought of the people who came to the shop as a special sort of people whom you did not find anywhere else. He hated them. They were mostly women. He was aware of recurring faces but he neither noticed nor cared. These shrewish women, smartly dressed, they'd spike your guns; fat opulent women who moved slowly and took up a lot of room, superbly unconscious, talking loudly; tailored women who pushed; fluffy women who asked idiot questions and didn't know whether they would go up or down. Most of all he hated the big bosoms. He took them up and he brought them down, load after load of self-satisfied big bosoms. They puffed scent and powder at him, the smell of armpits and rubber corsets, and a smell like candles that he could not identify. Another thing, they moved slowly, they paused half in, half out, of the lift, they stood in the middle and wouldn't let people in or out, they took their time. He spent all the time shoving big bosoms along, which was hard work because, of course, he must not ever on any account touch a passenger. They didn't mind touching him. They lolloped against him, nudged him with parcels, trod unconcerned on his feet. His brain was hard and tumescent with prolonged exasperation.

He was tempted to let the lift drop right through from the eighth floor to the basement. He could do it, release everything, pull up the lever, not slowly and smoothly as he had been taught, but wrench it over suddenly. The eighth floor, not the ninth. He didn't mind about the Hasty Tasties so much, he'd catch the over-fed ones from the Dining Room de luxe. Drop them all. Woosh. There'd just be time to see their faces change.

He heard them talking. He never heard all they had to say because they got out of the elevator, only fragments of scoldings, gushings, grumblings, scandals, the weather, the bargains, bridge, the news. It made a crazy pattern, broken and meaningless, rubbing a jagged edge against his mind.

This December they had something to talk about, a royal abdication. Edward the Eighth was leaving the throne to marry the woman he loved. What a plum. What a scoop for the papers. What a real life story in high places. They were picking it over with the other Christmas bargains.

"It's nothing new. When I was in England last year I heard . . ."

"Why not? If it meant an American Alliance I should say it was all to the good. Times have changed, you know."

"It isn't as if they'd have any children. Didn't you know. . . ."

"I'll always be loyal to the Prince of Wales. He's my King." Shining blue eyes, vague pleasant memories of a king over the water, Roundheads and Cavaliers, or was it the Wars of the Roses?

"His father would turn in his grave, he was so moral."

"Third mate on an American tramp . . ."

"The whole thing is rigged. Edward was too democratic, that was the whole trouble. Baldwin . . ."

"And the Archbishop of Canterbury. They do say he's Queen Victoria's natural son. It it's true that accounts for a lot . . ."

"We're not being told the truth."

"The people ought to rise . . ."

Harry took them up and brought them down. God damn, he thought, what does it matter? Let him go, let him stay, it won't make any difference. Gives the big bosoms a thrill, that's all. They treat themselves to it like they treat themselves to a slap-up feed. Who pays for Kings and all their fancies? "Stand well back in the lift, please, ladies. Going up . . ."

Mrs Blan had a wireless now. She said to all and sundry. "Come and listen." She was giving an Abdication Party. The bandsman and Gladys poured out the beer. The bandsman was Mrs Blan's lodger. Glad had brought him home one night and he had stayed ever since. People talked about it, but not loudly out of consideration for Mrs Blan. But whatever it was, with a man in the house and Glad's wages and Mrs Blan's O.A.P., things were quite prosperous there these days.

Harry didn't go in. He stood out on the passage in his socks and he heard all he wanted to hear.

The disembodied weary voice.

"But you must believe me when I tell you that I have found it impossible to carry the heavy burden of responsibility and discharge my duties as King as I would wish to do without the help and support of the woman I love. . . . I now quit altogether public affairs and lay down my burden. . . ."

A lonely voice going out over the world, the traffic of the ether stilled for a moment to allow it to be heard for the last time. The moment of valediction before he stepped out of the spotlight into nothing, even this moment dragged down by weariness. The loneliest man in the world—but even that distinction would pass presently in the slow choking commonplace of his every-day life, of the super man about town, spending a fortune on telephone calls and being reprimanded for it. Ever since he was born he had been swaddled in legend. He had had a constant flow of the most skilled publicity in the world. The Empire and the world had been reassured of him, he had been reassured of himself. Prince Charming. The mask had been held to his face so long that it had grown into the flesh. Now he behaves like Prince Charming off his own bat, so to speak, and his masters wouldn't have it. They turned off the limelight and put the legend into reverse. They said, in effect, "We made you a Prince, now you can stand on your own feet of clay and try your hand at being a man. You're fixed."

"Poor little bugger," thought Harry. "He didn't mean to live his life this way. No one does. Things happen and you can't stop them." He thought, too, leaning against the wall in the half-lit passage, the shadow of an aspidistra in the flickering wind gesticulating inanely behind him, that his own life hadn't gone to plan. He hadn't been able to do any of the things he'd meant to do. He'd got things he wanted sometimes, the place at Toongabbie, Ally . . . , and then they'd slipped out of his hands again. Funny sort of world when no one lives the life he meant to live. He didn't know anyone who did. Not for long. The Prince of Wales couldn't. Perhaps Mr Baldwin did. That wasn't any consolation. Not much. Lot of bother keeping the world going just for that.

All for love and the world well lost. They'd kept him on advertising pap all his life and now he was trying a new brand. Poor mug. Love was a fairy tale told so often that people believed it. There was sex but not love. It wasn't enough. It left you empty and disappointed. It only lasted a little while, a relief, but you wanted something to go on. A safe private place in your life where you could refit. No bloody goddam love. He'd find out. The boy who put the Buck in Buckingham Palace. No love. Cheated. No such thing as love. Not between men and women anyway. You loved your children, but that couldn't amount to much. You never got to know them, they were changing all the time. And they were going the other way. They were on the escalator going up, you were on the escalator going down. You passed one another, that was all. Couldn't stop the escalators, didn't know where the control switch was, probably wasn't one. . . . Men invented things and then couldn't get them. Trapped in being men. Better to be an animal. Even animals in a cage, they got fed. Going up, Stand back in the elevator, please. First Floor. Ready-made Costumes, Boots and Shoes. Ladies' Boudoir on your right, Telephones on your left. . . .

A fierce pain shot through the woolly fog of his melancholy. He smashed his fist against the faded green plaster. The shabby aspidistra struggled with the wind as if it were trying to leave its pot. Magnified in the sickly light the man, the plant, and their shadows filled the cramped hall.

Mrs Blan's voice, rich with beer and unction, saying, "No good crying over spilt milk. Fill up your glasses and drink to the new king. He never did take my fancy like his brother, but there's the queen and the two little loves of princesses. A family does give a bit of human interest."

Ally set down her glass half-emptied. Beer wasn't a lady-like drink. It kept you running outside. If Mrs Blan knew what was what, she'd have had a bottle of port for the ladies, money being no object. She looked at the bandsman. He had an arm round Glad's shoulders. Shameless. Glad wasn't any better than Mrs Simpson, if you asked her. Mrs Simpson was forty-two. Ally was only thirty-five. But then Mrs Simpson hadn't had four children and a hard life and a cranky husband. Or if one of her husbands had got cranky she gave him the sack. Harry was cranky enough. Wouldn't come down tonight, said he had sore feet from standing on them all day in the heat. Like a bear with mumps, he was. Anyone would think he was the only one who had anything to bear. Never gave a thought to the sort of life she led or how she felt about coming down in the world. When she married him they'd had a place of their own, they'd been somebody. They weren't anybody now. They'd come to this wretched hole just while they looked round for something better, and here they were, stuck fast after eleven years. Harry used to be a lorry driver, that was man's work anyway, now he drove a lift and she knew, if he didn't, that he'd never do anything else. The children were growing up all anyhow. Harry spoilt them. They could have been listening to the King's speech on their own radio if he hadn't sold it for five bob out of spite. . . .

"Hey," shouted the bandsman almost in her ear, "Hey, drink up, Mrs Munster. Can't have you going to sleep. Take uncle's advice, never go into a trance at a party. Anything might happen." Ally's eyes slewed round. Glad had gone out of the room. The bandsman surreptitiously pinched her leg. As Mrs Blan said, he was a real good one at making a party go.

Chris paused to listen to the re-broadcast. She had been addressing Christmas cards on the round table under the light. She performed this duty to society early, to oblige the post-office and because she liked to get the cards before they were picked over. If you paid twopence or threepence for a card, you wanted the best that twopence or threepence could buy. Arnie lay on the chesterfield, his collarless shirt unbuttoned for the heat. He had put on weight and he looked soft and smooth, lazy but ready to give advice on any subject, good-natured when it was the same price. The room bulged with plush and oleographs. It smelt of newness. In one corner a marble statue held aloft a lamp.

"Well," said Chris disapprovingly, "I don't know why he had to do that. He was the king and she wasn't anybody." Chris evidently thought it wasteful and foolish to make all that fuss over something that would have been arranged quietly and no one the worse. "There's been a lot of money laid out on the coronation." Chris had developed a good deal, too, in the opposite direction to Arnie. Her character which had once seemed neutral was obviously strong. Colourlessness had been her version of youth and inexperience. Now she knew how many beans made five and it showed in her face. She added, as one driving in an extra nail, "That would only be a recording."

She turned the wireless down to a low mutter and returned to her job. Arnie watched her; indolent himself, he had no objection to an active wife, quite the contrary.

"Who do you think I saw today?"

Arnie made an indeterminate noise.

"Harry Munster. He's driving a lift at Morgan's."

"Did he see you?"

"No. I took another lift. He looked very aged."

"Harry wasn't a bad cove, taking him all round," said Arnie, forgivingly. "Only he never got the hang of things. The sort that goes to the bottom, lots like him."

"What I can't stand is ingratitude."

"Oh, that," said Arnie easily. "You had a bit of a go to with Ally and evened things up, didn't you?"

"We passed a few remarks." After a pause she added, "Ally's your only sister, after all."

"All right," he said. "Send them a card if you want, a twopenny one."

Chris drew out the biggest card, embossed forget-me-nots and silver bells. A Merry Christmas and a Prosperous New Year, a sixpenny one. They could afford to be magnanimous. The Munsters had gone down and they had come up. No harm in Ally knowing they were prosperous. Full of airs, she used to be. And they *were* prosperous. Chris wasn't one to sit idle. She'd gone into business on her own account. She ran a servants' registry office, a lucrative affair that didn't require much outlay to begin with. All she'd done was to hire two rooms in a decent-looking terrace house between Woollahra and Paddington and put two sets of advertisements in the newspapers, one in the Situations Vacant listing a number of attractive but fictitious jobs and the other in the Situations Wanted, offering able-bodied, intelligent, refined, but equally fictitious girls for hire. Both brought bites, and the resultant hauls could be made to cancel out. She soon got going. Girls were hard to get, you could charge both parties a fee. They were always changing jobs. Chris liked the work. She made a steady income. Arnie, too, made more than his wages. They lived in comfort and they were putting by. They were agreed that raising children was a thankless job and they had no intention of being mugs. Theirs was a happy marriage of almost perfect accord.

"Where'll I address it?"

"I dunno. Try the old address. Maybe it'll find them."

"Are you living where you're living now or have you moved away?" warbled Arnie, from some long forgotten musical comedy.

"I feel we've done the right thing, Arnie. Forgive and forget. That's the Christmas spirit."

"Oh, yeah," he was still playful.

"Have a heart," said Elsie Todd. "Give us something a bit more cheerful." She turned the knob of her radio, but from the next station the same sad, weary voice met her. She turned it off. She was miserable enough without that. What had he to grizzle about, he'd be all right whatever happened? The cessation of sound in the room was like the sudden dropping of a high wind. The narrow airless room, the pile of dirty crockery, the unmade divan bed, the litter of loaded ashtrays, soiled clothes, cosmetics, were suddenly dumped at Elsie's feet. "For Christ's sake," she said.

"I don't understand you, Paula."

"I know, Mummy. I'm sorry. Couldn't you just—take my word for it?"

Mrs Ramsay made it a rule never to lose her temper, but this argument had been going on for more than an hour and they were getting nowhere. Paula was such an odd child, obscure and persistent in her ideas. This last idea didn't make sense.

"What is it I must take your word for? Oh, my dear, it isn't as simple as that. You have more liberty than most girls of your age. You do what you like with your time. You have everything you could possibly want. Too much, perhaps that's the trouble. If you wanted to take up some sort of work, I'd understand that and I'd help you whatever it was. But this idea of going away, to do what? Nothing apparently. If you must do nothing you had better do it here. You're only nineteen and I am still responsible for you. You may think that is old-fashioned, but it's a fact."

Paula had to explain. You had to go on explaining even when it was useless. Mummie loved explanations. "In Tibet," she said, "boys go into a monastery for a couple of years, just as they grow up. To steady their minds. To think things out."

Mrs Ramsay despaired also. "Paula, you can't mean that. Oh, yes, it's true for all I know. But for you. My dear, the whole idea is thoroughly morbid. Of course, you are at a morbid age. No one is more anxious than I am to think things out sanely and coolly. A monastery isn't the place to cope with the modern world. I've often asked you would you take an interest in affairs. You could come with me to meetings. The house is packed with books. You won't get anywhere shutting yourself up and thinking. You don't know anything to begin with."

"I want to be alone."

Didn't she get that from some actress? Mrs Ramsay seemed to have heard it before. One of the hank-of-hair school?

"There's nothing in being alone. If you go to Timbuctoo you won't be any different." Had some ism got hold of the girl? Paula was secretive. She glanced at the young troubled face. A queer streak in her. Like Olaf. He had a queer involved way of getting at the simple things. Thank goodness the boys were straightforward, healthy young barbarians. If one of them had to be queer it was better that it should be Paula. Her ideas were harmless enough, so long as she wasn't allowed to put any of them into practice and perhaps ruin her life. Anyone could get hold of Paula, thought her mother, who had never succeeded in getting a satisfactory grip on her herself. "Be quite frank with me, Paula," she urged.

"I'm not holding anything back, mother. Truly. It's quite simple. I just want to live by myself for a while. I've got——" How could she describe that tangle of ideas, budding, immature, that must have time and silence to flower, that need in her for loneliness, like the need for a drink of cold water?—"things to think out. Not concrete things, big things." No good. It sounded foolish even to her own ears, but it was there, a brick was not more tangible. "It's just something private and special to me. Different people want different things."

Mrs Ramsay sighed. It would be a good thing to get Paula married, that would stop these fancies. It was like struggling with a phantom in the dark. "We'll have to talk of this another time. You know this idea of leaving home will wound your father."

"I don't think so." Paula was utterly exhausted and nothing gained.

"Turn on the wireless, dear. It's time for the King's broadcast. We ought to listen, it's an historic occasion."

The Grants on their farm at Toongabbie meant to listen in, at least it had been one of the reasons Norah gave for hurrying home when Edith pressed them to stay to tea. Old Grant hadn't thought a wireless necessary so Edith didn't have one. Norah wanted to get home. She was all bottled up in her quiet way, but driving back with Kathleen wedged between them and little Vic asleep in her arms, all she said was she supposed Edith would buy herself a radio now. She fed the children and got them to bed in a gritty silence. Jim went out and found himself some jobs. She was waiting for him in the kitchen when he came back. Everything was quiet except the clock among the canisters on the mantle over the range. It ticked so loudly that it seemed to dance on its little metal legs. Jim thought "now." Norah had been thinking, the air was heavy with her thoughts.

"I don't mind for myself, Jim, it's you and the children. I don't like to see you made a fool of after all your work. It's not a nice thing to say about your father, but he was just the meanest man in these parts, and that's saying something. I shouldn't wonder if he did it to spite me because I wouldn't live the way he and Edith lived. I wanted something better for my children and I slaved to get it.

Now he's got even with me. I don't grudge Edith the big place. She looked after him and put up with heaven knows what. But Ted. You don't even know where he is, do you? I was only a girl when you married me. I'd always been taken care of at home, but I soon learned what hard work was. I thought it was for ourselves. I'm not blaming you, Jim, it isn't your fault. You always kowtowed to the old man. Another man would have seen that everything was tied up properly—for his children's sake, if for nothing else. There's such a thing as being too easy going. Now we've all got to pay for it, that's all. What I'm asking myself now is, what are you going to do when Ted comes? One thing, I'm not going to have him here. There's the children. I wouldn't have you hard like your father, Jim, but there's the other extreme, and if you don't look after the children, I have to . . ."

Jim stared at his big work-coarsened hands. He couldn't meet his wife's eyes. He felt wretched and guilty because he wasn't angry, because he didn't hate his father—or Ted. He thought things would work out all right only he'd never get Norah to see it.

"You don't have to hurry away, love," said Mrs Castles. "Come in and have a cupatea. The kettle's on the boil. I thought you'd be passing through and I was on the lookout for you." A lot of Mrs Castles' time was spent in looking out for and ensnaring the neighbours who passed her door. The house stood in the middle of a barren paddock, half a mile from the main road, but a short cut carried farmers from further out past the door. That short cut was Mrs Castles' lifetime. She had finally retired from childbearing and grown very stout. She didn't go out twice in the year, but was none the less alive for that. Everything came to her.

"D'jer hear the news? You'll laugh when I tell you. Old Grant's will. He's left the big place to Edith, lock, stock, and barrel. Nothing surprising in that. I'll say she was a good daughter to him, whatever we may think of her among ourselves. She'll run it the same way he did. She's a chip off the old block, all right. Shouldn't wonder if she got married now. It's a dandy place and not a penny owing on it either. Like to call herself Mrs, Edith would, forty if she's a day. But that's not what I was going to tell you. He left the rest, the place Jim's on and a bit of land in Parramatta, to be equally divided between Jim and Ted. You could of knocked me down with me own pot stick. Every one thought Jim would get it. That Norah thought so from the day she married him, thought they'd be set when the old man went. Ted was a nice enough boy. You wouldn't remember him, hasn't been seen hereabouts for a long time. Must be twelve years. Before Jim married, Old Grant bought that place from Harry Munster and put Jim on it. It's about twelve years since the Munsters left. Ted lit out just before that. Couldn't stand his father's domineering ways. Drank a bit. The old man was temperance so that riled him. They had a row one moonlight night outside the barn. The MacDougalls could hear the noise, but they couldn't make out what was said. Ted came round and said goodbye next day.

" 'Nothing to keep me here,' he said. We all thought the old man had finished with him. He always preferred Ted to Jim. Jim hadn't enough spirit for him. Sort of gentle, Jim is. He took on a bit in a quiet way when Ted went off. Always uster tag round after Ted when they were youngsters. Now maybe Ted'll come back, or maybe he won't come back, he'll just want his half share and Jim'll have to sell. Can you beat it? Made the will after he got sick. Maybe he lay there, thinking about Ted and wishing things had been different, maybe Edith got at him. She didn't like Norah. Bit high flown, which Edith isn't, whatever else she may be. Maybe it was a bit of deviltry he thought out for himself, just to show Jim his power didn't stop when they buried him. The best cup's still in the pot."

Ma Castles cackled jubilantly. "We bin here twenty-five years, and we've seen a lot of changes. You'd wonder how we stuck."

People did wonder. A few barren paddocks, mortgaged to the limit, a little dilatory cultivation, some scrawny fowls, didn't seem sufficient reason. She survived, not through any skill or capacity, but from sheer inability to worry. They didn't want much and they didn't worry about anything. There was always tea in the pot, corned beef in the safe, and pumpkins on the roof of the shed. The youngsters brought in a bit. Foreclosures and evictions were unpopular, the banks only resorted to them when it was worthwhile. To turn people so long established in the neighbourhood, so loquacious and so shameless as the Castles, off their almost useless land would be more trouble than it was worth. "It's the poor hardworking sods like Harry Munster that have to go, ain't it, pa?" Pa, who rarely spoke and never worked, though apparently hale, nodded in complacent agreement. "You're right, Ma. Work and worry shortens your life."

"Pa'll live to be a hundred. Funny thing, our Arch is a regular hustler. Got himself a good job in the city, but now he wants to go for an airman. 'Why do you want to go for a sojer?' I said to him. 'An airman's not a sojer,' he said. 'I want to have a future,' he said. Funny idea of a future putting yourself in the way of getting killed. He's got a young lady. Works in a milk bar in the city. I said 'Bring her home for Christmas, son.' Do her good to see a cow. She could try her hand at milking. Terrible artificial life they lead in the city..."

"Spain," said the man in the train. Arch Castles tried to catch what he said. The carriages were clanking over a culvert and he lost it. The conversation bobbed against his ear. He picked it up again, in and out of hearing. "The beginning of another European war... Nothing more certain... the spark has fallen... war of the idealogies... non-intervention... It isn't a policy, it's wilful blindness... The democracies can't afford to let Spain go... a window on the Mediterranean... Never a clearer case... will of the people... They ask for aeroplanes and we give them a stone... David... Goliath..."

"The romantic margin of war has been cut down. Equipment isn't any good without courage, and courage is no good without equipment. You think we can stand aside, neither send help nor allow it to reach the Spanish Government, and the courage of the Spanish people will still win our war."

"Russia..."

"Look at the map... Russia's fought one battle for Socialism. Must she fight all?... You decry her and expect her to perform miracles in the one breath."

"War..."

"Nothing more certain. Italy has ninety thousand men under arms, and her industrial system won't absorb them. She can't afford to have them unemployed."

Spain... Russia... War. How the word Russia jerked at people's attention.

"War," Arch thought. "There's going to be war." Christmas Eve. The crowded train. Going home. He looked at the people about him, tired, laden, laying aside the Christmas spirit for an hour. He looked at the dust-laden, half-empty country. At one end of the journey lay his home, dilapidated, inert, his garrulous mother, his lethargic father, his swarm of brothers and sisters. Didn't amount to much, the whole lot of them, he thought with rueful affection. At the other end of the railway line was his job in the post-office, his digs—not bad for the money—his girl, pretty, soft, stupid. He guessed he was in love with her, he knew that if he married her, as he wanted to do, it would be the end of him. What a dumbbell a railway line is, with a knob of lead at each end. War. The word rocketed through his mind. Bust up the whole show and begin again. He'd go into the air force if they'd take him and get a front seat. Step out of his old life into the blue uniform. He'd book his place in the new world that was coming, early. Not a pigeonhole in a post-office, but the whole sky. He saw a fountain of fire on a dark sky, beautiful and harmless as fireworks.

"Spain . . . Russia . . . Hitler . . . Democracy . . . War . . ."

Summer. A thick sky and a coppery sun. The thermometer in the colonnade of the post-office mounting steadily in the heavy hours of the afternoon. Smell of smoke in the city streets, blowing in from bushfires in the west. Tang of burning gum leaves, reminding the people that this was a frontier city. Not a mechanism whirring by and for itself, but the outpost of a great hinterland from which it drew its life.

1937. Harry took the elevator up and brought it down. Up . . . down. Hauling Big Bosoms from one place to another. They got out of the cage and he stayed in it.

Two ladies met in a puff of warm air, smelling of furs and violets.

"Oh, Mrs Ramsay, this is fortunate. I was going to telephone you. I've a drawing-room meeting next Wednesday. Such an interesting man, just back from Spain . . . the inside story. I do hope you'll come."

The name caught Harry's ear. He looked up. A middle-aged woman well preserved, preserved in lacquer, dripping with pearls and furs. The girl beside her was the one he had seen in the Domain, young and austere. He did not know he had remembered her, but he recognised her at once.

"So kind of you. You know my daughter, Paula, don't you? I'll come if I possibly can, but my husband's ill. . . It may not be anything serious, but I just can't plan ahead."

"Mummie," said the girl, "You're blocking the doorway."

Ally said, if he complained or came back obviously tired, or was boiling with rage after one of the Tuesday pep talks, "Why don't you ask Mr Ramsay for another job? He's got plenty to hand round." He couldn't do that. Whenever they met—and they did meet sometimes, for whenever Ramsay came into the building for a Board meeting he always sought out Harry afterwards, and when he came off duty they had a drink together. Once he had even, to Harry's chagrin, asked the managing director to release him from duty, and it had been done—whenever they met, and Ramsay asked how the job was going, he said "Fine." He couldn't quite make Ramsay out, and he had an uncomfortable feeling that their relationship depended on his having done him a good turn. Olaf Ramsay was a lonely sort of man, he'd read a lot and thought a lot, but never done anything —not since the war. He lived in a world he did not believe in and he had caught its ghostliness. He made money and deprecated it, yet never would have had the courage to live without it. He had power of a sort—and flouted it with carefully chosen caprice. Against the world he made, he called up an antidote, the lonely man's fiction of brotherhood. He looked back with nostalgia to the war, for then barriers had been swept away. The army was a brotherhood. Many things he forgot. He himself, Harry thought, was an experiment in brotherhood. Even while he resented it, he pitied, saw the man's sincerity, his painful delicacy of mind, his defeated and defeating awareness. Secretly Olaf longed for a world in extremis, for then circumstances would break the barriers for him and give the moment stature. There was no power in himself to create the thing he longed for, or to carry him to those heights where alone he could breathe. Harry felt all this, not as a judgment, but as a malaise in their relationship. It wasn't that they had nothing in common. It was that Olaf Ramsay wanted too much in common. Harry wasn't used to people lonelier than himself. They made him uncomfortable. He was better at bearing things for himself than for other people.

Meanwhile it was Tuesday. Every Tuesday a bunch of the staff had to stay back for half an hour and listen to the staff manager. It fell to Harry's lot every fourth Tuesday. The manager didn't actually call the roll, but you were on your honour to attend. No coercion, but if you didn't go someone was sure to notice and conclude that you weren't interested in your work, and there was no place for people who weren't interested, as the staff manager often pointed

out. It was all very reciprocal and matey. You gave half an hour at
the end of a long day, but then so did the staff manager. The firm
gave the use of the Welfare Hall and the lighting. Each session
was drawn from all over the building—salesmen and sales girls, clerks
from the office, cooks and waitresses, cleaners and shop walkers, heads
of departments and the messengers—a fine democratic turnout and
no respecting of persons. The manager gave a pep talk, manly and
humorous, the muscular Christianity of big business, all about loyalty
and esprit de corps and playing the game—the bosses' game, of
course. Sometimes, he'd slip in a few sour ones, letting you know
where you got off if you didn't want to get on. His accent was so
good that a lot of them couldn't understand what he said. After the
pep talk there was a Pat on the Back. The Pat on the Back was an
honour given for some special service, some more than ordinary
devotion to duty, or some fine moral action that had come to the
notice of the benevolent management. The citation was read and the
recipient called up to the dais. If a man, the manager slapped him
heartily on the back, if a girl he shook hands, bowing gallantly. Everyone applauded. Last month, it had been a girl called Gwen Leslie.
She was a runner in the main shopping hall. She didn't serve people
yet, she fetched and carried and stood about ready to do as she was
bid. It seemed that a rich old lady had dropped a pound note out
of her handbag and Gwen had followed her with it into the street,
and had stopped her chauffeur as he was driving off, to return it. The
old lady, much impressed by such honesty in the lower orders, had
written to the management. Gwen, who was pale and fair, not more
than eighteen years old, had blushed a painful scarlet and dragged
herself to the dais with miserable reluctance. Harry had been sorry
for the kid, nice kid but hungry looking. He had known just how she
felt, rebellious anger that people should think honesty remarkable
in her. He'd thought of speaking to her afterwards, but had decided
to leave her alone. Well, she'd had her dose, they wouldn't pick on
her again. He didn't think they'd pick on him, he had no
intention of doing anything especially praiseworthy.

Olaf Ramsay lay propped up in his bed. He did not as yet feel
very ill, but he knew that that would come. The early stages of fever
lent brilliance and mobility to his mind. He felt that at any minute,
by an effort of the will or the imagination, he would be able to

slough the discomfort that was gathered like a crust over the living fire of his mind and body. A nurse was already installed, and the familiar room stripped for action. It was as if they were trying to get ahead of his illness, forestall it; as it increased, and he knew it would, there science would be waiting for it. His room was like a hospital room already, it had a new clean bright airiness. He was the only infected spot in it. A hard sharp line was drawn round his illness. It made him feel like a bit of decaying flotsam cast up on an alien shore. His wife and the nurse spoke to one another with brisk hearty cheerfulness, clean antiseptic words, meant for him, but he didn't bother to listen. He did not heard Paula come in, but she was standing at the foot of the bed, her eyes enormous. When he smiled at her, he realised that his lips were swollen and stiff. The doctor came in late, with elaborate casualness. The nurse let loose the light. The doctor looked large and black in its watery whiteness, it was like a big pump coming into the room and sucking up the air. Pneumonia wasn't what it used to be, the doctor said, they'd a short way with it now. He went away. Nothing more was likely to happen. The gulf of the night opened. A thick black malaise spread over the patient's spirit. The nurse brought a tray. On the tray was a glass of water and a large pill, sitting in the exact middle of a small plate. Why did she have to do that? She could have shaken it out of the bottle into his hand just as easily. He was unreasonably irritated. If he had felt equal to the disturbance, he would have refused to have anything to do with it. "Nurse," he said. "Sister," said his wife. So they were in league now, were they? "Go to sleep now," said the sister in a cajoling voice.

He could feel his temperature going up, like a great key turning. He didn't want to be ill now. He had so much to do, so much was happening or just going to happen in the world. Perhaps it was a good thing he was laid up for a few days, it would give him time to think things out, and up here on the mountain top he could see quite well. He knew a lot about it but somehow he'd never. . . He'd read most of the books his wife gave him, and a lot more he'd chosen for himself. He knew all about it really, all the bits and pieces, but he'd never had a chance to put them together. Once he'd got it straight he wouldn't let it get mixed again. First there's us— England and the Empire. We want the Balance of Power, the status quo and Business as Usual. Europe divided up into nice little countries that pay their interest regularly, respect British passports. Versailles had a shot at it but it didn't work out. Wouldn't stay put. Only got 8/7 for the pound in Budapest. The Englishman found out he wasn't popular, too. That hurt. Like the man who took the cure for halitosis and then found he was unpopular anyway. That's torn it. Mistake to laugh. Everything's all right if you keep to the rules. Laughing's out of bounds. Like running up a red hot staircase in your bare feet. France, what did she want? Damned if he knew. One half of France afraid of the other half—the revolutionary half. Falling birthrate. Wanted to live up to her own legend but didn't know which one. M. Blum. The Croix de Guerre, The Legion of Honour. The Foreign Legion. Germany wanted living room. She'd invested so much in Hitler she couldn't stop. And he couldn't stop. The Great Have-nots and the Cross with its toes turned in. Scandinavia wanted Peace. Switzerland wanted tourists, and consumptives. Italy wanted the Mediterranean. So did we. The road to India. She'd gone hungry from the conference table at Versailles. After four centuries the Czechs were so delighted to be keeping house again they didn't want anything else. All the little fellows want is to be left alone. Balkans like a marble cake, an angry marble cake, all the people mixed together. Russia. She stood for danger and they were all afraid of her. All the governments had had a cut at her when she was down. Just like animals turning on an injured one, fearing blood and the lure of blood. She'd survived and was knocking on the door with a red hammer. She didn't owe anything to any one. It wasn't all as simple as that. All these nations bound together in the same continent and all at different stages of development. Russia somewhere in the future. Germany landed four-square on today. England trying with all her might to get back into the nineteenth century. The return to the womb. The Balkans still in the age of brigandage. What a mess. And Europe only the beginning of it. African hotch potch. South American patchwork. Indian ferment. Japan a hornet's nest on the yellow cheeks of China. Treasure islands lying about all over the Pacific, tempting and vulnerable. Australia, remote and thinly manned, with her immigration policy a drawn sword lying between her and Asia. Crowded Asia, empty Australia. Where was the logic? A sort of elaborate madness.

Now war was coming to stir the cauldron. War of the ideologies. Democracy, dictatorship, Bolshevism. Triangle. Treskilion. No one knew what democracy was. The word was a bag into which anything could be stuffed. The will of the people. But minorities were always right, they said. And what was the will of the people? Public opinion? The newspapers thought they made public opinion. If so, we had government by the Press. Heaven forbid. Or it came out of the propaganda machine like sausages. That would be government by government—a terrible inbreeding circle. There must be something else. Democracy meant the even spread of power. It was power that debased men. In every heart blackness, and power let it loose. That's the virtue of democracy. It spreads the power, safeguards it, lets it out in small packets, no one allowed to be irresponsible. Democracy could cogitate and plan, but what about implementing its decisions. To implement, you need power. That's the catch. Responsibility without power. Dictatorship, that's power without responsibility. Power without people. Bolshevism is power and the people. Dictatorship of the Proletariat.

They're only words. If words are really mightier than swords, why war? Not mightier than tanks, planes, and bombs. *They* have the last word. If they are only words, what do we fight for? To fight. All this pother just to rationalise an old habit. Too hot to fight. Amazing where people got the energy.

If you did fight, what would you fight for? Just to keep things as they were? No good, no good, no good. To make a new world? But we haven't decided what new world yet. Such a large choice of things that didn't exist, worse than Christmas shopping. Liberty? Another pig in a poke. Paula thought there was such a thing. She had her own little secret store. He hoped she'd keep it. Fight for Paula? Not justified, whatever I might feel. There's going to be a war, so there must be a reason for it. A new sort of war perhaps, fought for the Common Man, Everyman, the Man in the Street? It was his turn, he'd never had a war fought for him yet. Trouble was to find him. No one would own up to being the Common Man. Plenty of Unknown Soldiers. Suppose there would be another crop now. Rather pleasant. You'd lie there, anonymous, in a marble tomb, fulfilled, quiet, no more bother about being yourself, remembered and forgotten. Lucky devil. Not the Common Man, though—he had to be alive. If you could find this man and ask him what he wanted . . . Harry. Harry Munster. He was Everyman. He'd known it the first time he'd seen him. At the dawn service on Anzac Day. Dark, worn face, tragic, uncomplaining. Nothing special, just a man. Fought for four years, came back, had a little place somewhere, lost it, lost his job, out of work for five years, three children and another who died, glad of a job now on the basic wage, driving a lift. He was the whole of a man. All that expenditure of courage, patience, fidelity, to win that. The gentleness of human dignity. There in thousands of them, getting a dusty answer and not giving ground. Treated like cogwheels, and living like men. It was there in the people, but you didn't often notice it. That man's face against a background of bugles. Everyman. Like meeting Jesus at a railway station. Time a war was fought for men like that. What a mess. What a mess the world was in. We die and don't know why. The wrong people die. It can't go on. I'll have to see some one in authority.

"Have you an appointment?"

"No, but it's very urgent business."

"It's after business hours, you know."

"All the really important business is done after hours. I'm on the board of five companies."

"In that case I think the head of the firm will see you."

In black letters on the ground glass panel of the inner door was the legend, "God, Son, and Ghost. Please enter."

Olaf Ramsay's first feeling was one of relief. God was obviously an Englishman, in fact, resembled Mr H. G. Wells, and everything about his office was reassuringly normal and commonplace. It was just like his own office.

"What can I do for you?"

"I wanted to see you about the state of the world."

"Oh, yes. There's some talk of reconstruction, isn't there?"

"You must know that things are in a very bad way indeed."

"No, no, no. Not worse than usual."

"I assure you, the whole world is in a turmoil. It's unprecedented."

"I remember someone saying that same thing to me—Belisarius, I think it must have been—at the time of the fall of the Roman Empire. He was sitting in that chair where you're sitting, and he seemed very upset and overwrought. But you see, it wasn't the end." God checked himself, and bending forward enquired courteously, "But perhaps you have a suggestion to make, a plan?"

"No. I thought perhaps you'd do something about it."

"I'm afraid I hardly see my way at present. I used to try direct action occasionally. The Flood, you remember. But the results were very disappointing. I gave it up. After all, the world is only a subsidiary, a hobby, you might say. I don't expect a profit. I'm interested to see what happens."

"You mean Free Will?"

God pursed his lips. "That's what it's usually called on the prospectus. It's a doubtful asset."

"You're still running the show, aren't you?" Olaf Ramsay had a sudden sickening suspicion that the world was running itself, had been abandoned to its own devices.

"Yes, yes, I've still a controlling interest. I'll be frank with you, Mr Ramsay. The situation is perfectly simple. I've laid down one plain ruling and I'm leaving it at that."

"What's that?"

"The Law of Cause and Effect. Oh, yes, I know most people don't believe in it. They think there is another way round. But there isn't."

"You speak as if the situation were reasonable. That's just the trouble, it isn't."

"Speaking as a good democrat . . ."

"I'm very relieved that you are on our side."

God bowed. "Speaking as a good dictator . . ."

"But you said democrat."

"Did I? Well, it amounts to the same thing."

"Really?"

"Yes. You see, I abide by the will of my people, so I'm a democrat, and since they've plumped for dictators I'm a dictator. I shouldn't be a democrat if I weren't."

A terrible suspicion crossed Olaf Ramsay's mind that God after all might be an Irishman. He certainly had a look of Bernard Shaw. He felt discouraged. "It's confusing, very confusing," he muttered.

"Yes. I get confused, too." God agreed placidly.

"Oh, *no*." The cry was wrung from Olaf Ramsay. If God couldn't keep a clear head, who could? God seemed to read his thoughts.

"But you made me in your image, didn't you?" he asked mildly.

"I think it was the other way. I'm sure it was."

"It doesn't really matter."

They fell silent. God was toying with a paperweight. Olaf Ramsay gathered himself together. "I really wanted to speak to you about a friend of mine. His name is Harry Munster, but he's really the Common Man. You know, he's a very decent chap, and he hasn't had a fair deal. He's the one who always gets stung."

"I am no respecter of persons."

"But he's the Common Man."

"It cuts both ways."

"He's had a raw deal. In wars and depressions and every other bloody thing, he's always the first to suffer and the last to recover. He carried the burden. He's good to the core." That ought to appeal to God.

God shook his head sadly. "Good. That's a word I'm always hearing. Every one means something different by it. It's my personal belief that it's a fiction." He looked kindly at Olaf Ramsay. "I'm sorry I can't do anything for your friend. The historic moment has not come. I'm afraid you're rather disappointed in me. You didn't think I'd be a rational being, did you?"

Olaf could only mutter, "It's so hot in here."

"The windows are stuck," said God simply, "I can't get them open."

Olaf saw then that there were heavy locks and bolts on them. They'd probably been magic casements once, before God outgrew that sort of thing. It would need a locksmith now to get them open. God is Love and Love laughs at locksmiths. No, no, that wasn't God, that was the Crusades. Girdles of Chastity. Phew. Might have put my foot in it there. Never, he thought, had his mind worked so fast or so cogently. He'd have to go, it was so hot.

"Thank you for calling," said God.

Olaf Ramsay saw that God was, after all, the image of Winston Churchill, but he had a Hitler moustache, and in his hand he grasped an umbrella. God wouldn't do anything, because, after all, he was the image of our thought, the leader we chose.

"I must do something," he thought. "I can't be idle here while the world goes to ruin."

The sister pressed him back on his pillows. "Now," she said soothingly, "you must lie still." She put a hand to the back of his head and held a glass to his lips. As the cold liquid flowed into his mouth, the room, unfamiliarly familiar with dim light flowing

upwards from a shaded source on the floor, the hangings pulled back
from the open windows, shot back into his consciousness like a
scene on a revolving stage.

.     .      .      .      .       .        .       .      .

Knarf turned many pages quickly. "I can't read you all this," he
said.

"By the way, what have you called this book."

"Little World Left Behind."

Like a stone buried in sand, Ord half remembered the words from
a different context. "That isn't yours, is it?"

"It's a translation. I lifted it from the ancients." Knarf repeated
it in the original English.

"Henry Lawson."

" 'There were the same old selections—about as far off as ever
from becoming freeholds—shoved back among the barren ridges;
dusty little patches in the scrub, full of stones and stumps, and called
farms, deserted every few years and tackled again by some little dried
up family, or some old hatter, and then given best once more . . .
the same number of stumps on the wheat paddocks, the same broken
fences and tumbledown huts and yards, and the same weak, sleepy
attempt made every season to scratch up the ground and raise a
crop. . . .' He wrote it about the place where he was born, you know,
in the west. Eurunderee."

"He knew his world was sick and dying."

"His genius grew in that barren soil and fed on it all his life."

"He was bitter and angry, as men who live at the end of the
cycle must be."

"No man ever had greater love for his own people. He lived in
a dawn too. The beginning and the end were so close together. He
was part of them both in the little world he never left behind."

"Yes," said Ord, "that'll do." He felt the book rush in upon its
title like blood upon the heart. Upon this it steadied and stood.

"Time is getting on," said Knarf.

"I'm hungry," said Ord. "Early breakfast."

Knarf took no notice. "Olaf died of his pneumonia. Pity I can't
read it now. I did it rather well, I think. Lin had pneumonia three
years ago. You remember. Before he died, Olaf Ramsay added a

codicil to his will. His daughter Paula he released from her mother's guardianship by giving her immediate control of the income he had willed to her. It was his way of securing her liberty. To Harry Munster he left £200. All the days of his manhood he had been possessed by millennial longings. For every one he had desired happiness. He loved liberty. He wanted peace in the world. Peace without socialism. He was an idealist. He had fought in the war from the highest motives. To end war. For Democracy. To make the world fit for heroes and children. These did not prove to be the fruit of war. He had never found another opportunity for intervention. At the end, in his own way, he poured his trickle as libation to his gods, Liberty and the Common Man.

"There's a piece here. Men talking in the dark. It doesn't matter who they are. Just voices. I'll read that and it will have to suffice for 1937."

.    .    .    .    .    .    .    .    .

Dusk and a salty wind off the sea. They had dragged deck chairs out on to the little lawn facing the sea. The great dark mass of the flats rose behind them. The sea glimmered. "Wine-dark," somebody said. Its voice mingled with everything that was said or done. On the left, and much lower, was the long wide curve of the beach, pale to the dark water on which the line of breakers showed sharply white. The beach was empty and had an air of utter loneliness, cut off by its palisade of pine trees. The weather had turned warm, it was not hot enough for people to be bathing or lying on the beach at this hour, but warm enough to bring the summer visitors. Manly was alive. The dusk was full of footsteps and voices, snatches of music from open windows. Lights clustered brilliantly where the Corso cut across the isthmus, spangled behind the pine trees on the Esplanade. Here in the quiet streets above the beach, the dusk was patched with squares of pale gold as lights were switched on, perforating the big blocks of flats which rose like bastions one behind the other up the hill and along the cliff's edge. The men had been in the open air all day and a state of comradeship was established between them.

"Communal living," one said, indicating the ramparts of the flats with the glowing end of his cigarette, "with soundproof walls."

"It doesn't mean communal thinking."

"If people live together long enough, forced by circumstance to share, the communal spirit must grow up."

"People who live in houses are more friendly than people who live in flats. For real neighbourliness you've got to go to the country, where the next homestead is ten miles away. Brotherliness is in inverse ratio to propinquity."

"Do slums, tenements, breed brotherly love? These flats are only the slum idea adapted for the well-to-do."

"The sort of sharing that is forced on people in flats only breeds competition. It lacks the first essential of communal living."

"What's that?'

"Responsibility. The flat dweller hires everything ready made. The landlord carries the liability. It's escapist living."

"Why shouldn't the poor devils escape while they can? Grand target, they'd make, wouldn't they? All these great, big, complacent, probably shoddy blocks of flats, staring trustingly out to sea. Bricks don't stand up to bombs a bit well."

"D'you think there'll be war?"

"Of course there'll be war. Abyssinia, Spain, China, Hitler's Germany, anti-Semitism, the revolutionary ferment . . . the scroll's rolling up."

"There isn't a will to war or we'd have had it months ago, years ago. When Alexander of Jugoslavia was assassinated, for instance. Europe would blow up only the powder's damp."

"America doesn't want war. She's the sheet anchor."

"It'll come."

"We've had twenty years to build up safeguards against just this. We haven't done a thing, or rather we've done all the wrong things. There's been peace talk but nothing done. The only result has been to let down the people's morale. The public has never been so well informed on the international situation before. We see what's coming and we just sit here helpless, dumb, waiting for it."

"Not dumb."

"There's still a hope. Collective security."

"Who's going to collect? America won't. She's isolationist. It-can't-happen-here-and-you-all-can-bloody-well-take-care-of-yourselves.    England won't. A lot of people in England might want it but the great British public doesn't. If it did it wouldn't tolerate its present government. France might have, but she can't. England's got a lien on her.

The little fellows are all tied up. Alliance with Russia is the logical answer to Hitler, but it's not going to happen."

"What then?"

"Maybe we'll muddle through, maybe we won't."

"What'll happen if we don't?"

"Life goes on."

"That's not good enough. Life isn't going to save us if we can't save ourselves. She'd as soon have rabbits."

"Bowie has the answer. What shall we do to be saved, Bowie?"

People jabbed these questions at you. "Don't fight—and get on with the job that has to be done sooner or later, war or peace."

"What do you mean?"

"Internal reconstruction. If we ever stop being romantic and idealistic long enough to think clearly, we've got to face the fact that if there's war it's our fault because we've created or tolerated the circumstances, domestic and international, that make war inevitable."

"If you ask me, the stage things have got to now, we'll have to fight another war and win it, to get the chance to reconstruct."

"We said that last time, then we used up all our energy on the war and hadn't any left for reconstruction, or we got so sold on the war we thought we'd done everything when we'd won it."

"Wars make wars. Look at history. Chain smoking in a big way."

"What's reconstruction, anyway? If we had some sort of clear idea of it we might do it."

As no one seemed disposed to answer, Bowmaker said, "As I conceive it, it is the substitution of practical socialism for this monopoly capitalism, using not one sovereign means but every available means, working through historic channels for preference. The Labour Party."

"Fellow travellers?"

"Yes, if you like, but it would not be a matter of using the Labour Party for ends not its own, it would have to be a genuine co-operation. Socialism is the policy of the Labour Party—subject to the Law of Detours. Then the fostering of co-operative efforts of all kinds—men and women working in small groups in their own world, the municipality, the extension of local government, the pinning down of responsibility. There is no finer education for any man than to be responsible to his neighbours. The Council should be the seedplot of government."

Someone was restless, this seemed to be developing into a lecture. "A war," he said, "might be all to the good, smash up everything and begin again."

"Smashing doesn't put men in the right temper for reconstructing."

One said, "It's not wars that will get us in the end. It's the long-range factors. The falling birth rate. . . ."

"Soil erosion and the desiccation of the country, the march of the desert. Who knows or cares what happens, out there? We cut down the trees and clear the scrub, grass grows, we bring the sheep and the rabbits and they eat the grass. In a dry spell they dig out the roots of the grass and ringbark the trees that are left. The rains come and channel the naked earth, scar it with crevices. The heat dries the earth to powder, the wind carries it away. No exhalation rises to refill the clouds. The wind and the dust scarify the country. The seed reserve is exhausted, dried out, blown away. The future dies. Man and beast are driven from the far western runs, the Birdsville Track is deserted, sand covers the deserted homestead, rivers silt up, the bore water is giving out, silence and death come like a tide. . . ."

"Cry havoc! They'll cancel out, won't they? The desert will get us but then there won't be any one here, the bottom will have fallen right out of the birth rate."

"War will get us first."

"The Pit and the Pendulum."

"Christ, you're a cheery lot."

"How did we get round to this?"

"Someone said 'war'."

"It all hangs together, doesn't it? Competition makes greed, greed strips the country and won't wait to rehabilitate it. War is competition raised to the nth. Threatened people don't breed."

There was a pause. The voice of the sea seemed to grow louder. They were all aware of it, thinking their own thoughts. It was continuity, eternal continuity in a world they would change.

Bowmaker began to speak as if he had picked up the beat.

"If we're going to survive, we must break the vicious circle. The only answer to war is not to fight. No creative decisions come out of war. No reasonable gain, only death, misery, pain, destruction. War makes the brotherhood of man a mock and postpones indefinitely that internationalism which alone would solve those questions over which wars are fought. The idea has been to stop wars abroad, but a better idea is to stop them at home. The people must say 'No' and back up their refusal with steadfast courage. If we refused to condone social injustice, if we refused to accept war, they would wither away."

"The senators of Rome, when the barbarians entered the city, put on their togas, sat in the forum and waited. The barbarians, recovering from their momentary surprise, killed them to a man."

"They were only a handful. If the citizens of Rome had followed their example the barbarian would not have had an easy victory. An army is made up of men, it cannot fight without the stimulus of opposition or the more terrible incitement of fear. Can you imagine an army that went on killing people who met them without arms and without fear? There is enormous power in passive resistance. It takes courage, but there's no lack of courage in the world if only it can be convinced."

A man sat up suddenly, sharply eager. "You're not on the soap-box now, Bowie. Do you really believe that?"

"Yes."

"Would you apply it here, in this country, if we were invaded, if the Japs came?"

"Yes."

"Even if the world would have nothing to do with it, if war came, if the whole world willed it and you and your kind were treated as traitors, would you still hold to that?"

"Yes."

There was a pause. Then the steady voice went on: "Greed and competition and violence haven't worked, have they? For the few but not for the many. They're in our blood—in mine as surely as in anyone else's. But a different sort of world has been conceived. A long time ago. Always there have been some to believe in it and to work for it. Kept alive from generation to generation. Kept in the world. It might take a terrific effort in the future just to do that. It's what will fall on us and we know it. Even that's worth doing, worth dying for, if it comes to that. Changes come so slowly. Like a range of mountains raised out of grains of sand fused together, every grain a living man. That's how it is, to believe something and keep it alive till it becomes a power, a deciding factor, at last a commonplace, taken for granted and no more thought of."

Silence. No one had anything to say. Each brooded uncomfortably in his own heart, resentful. Beside this bleak and distant creed, war itself seemed homely and comfortable. They wanted to go away and forget. The sea was a lament now, a forlorn eternal voice crying in the darkness for some indelible grief. The voice of the land came to them, faint but reassuring, the purr of cars climbing the hill, the footfalls of young people going out to their pleasures, fragments of music shaken from high windows like crumbs from a cloth. Lights pinned together the curtains of the night. To have a lighted window in a towering facade, to buy and pay for beauty, safety, cleanliness, warmth . . . to share amusements with a hundred thousand others, to reassure yourself with artifice and gadget at every turn—that was to be safe and to be human.

## 1938

The big shop where Harry Munster worked had its calendar. Christmas was its peak, the grand festival of trade. The Christmas holidays found most of the employees too sodden with fatigue to do anything but sleep and quarrel irritably with their families. A slack week hung between Christmas and New Year. Then the summer sales began. The decorations came down and in their place up went placards advertising bargains. The great store was like a hive. Harry knew something about bees, and, as the hot, exhausting, summer days followed one another, he saw it as an overheated hive in which, the comb breaking down, bees, wax, and honey flow together in sticky destruction. The fan in the roof of the elevator buzzed all day, but it could not keep the cage cool. Its even whirr, brushing hour after hour upon his boredom, produced an intolerable sleepiness. Inside his uniform, buttoned tightly to the neck, sweat trickled down his body. Bulging, heated bodies surrounded him. He felt they might coalesce into one solid lump. He'd turn the fire hose on them.

One morning he saw that Gwen Leslie was in charge of a half-price table in front of his elevator. Evidently she'd had promotion. She wasn't a runner any longer, she had a table. Later she'd be sent to a department. He thought again that she was a nice little girl. Not hard and pert like most of them, but nice. She looked very small in her close-fitting black dress. Maybe she wasn't very strong. Every time the lift came down he had a look at her. She smiled at customers as if she liked them. Towards the end of the day he saw her begin to droop. "Poor kid's tuckered out," he thought, "It's standing all day." Every now and then he felt the standing himself, even now. He looked with understanding at her cheap high-heeled slippers. He was glad Ruthie wasn't on her feet all day. She worked in the shop too, now, but in the Mail Order Department. Ruthie had got her Intermediate Certificate in a Commercial High School. He'd kept her a year longer at school than he had to, so that she could. Ally had thought it waste, but it meant that she could sit addressing catalogue covers, or putting accounts into their envelopes all day long, instead of standing in the heat of the shop. The shop was so big, he hardly ever saw Ruthie at work. She might just as well be employed somewhere else. But he'd been able to make it easier for her just at first. Nervous she was, at first, hardly able to eat her food.

Wanda had left school too, and had got herself a job. Wanda was sixteen. She had a job with a fashionable milliner as messenger girl. He hadn't any time for that sort of thing, but Wanda had, all the time there was. He'd rather see her doing a job of work, but he couldn't talk. She'd be the first to turn on him and say, "What about yourself?" Wanda was a smart girl, but she wasn't good in the home like Ruthie. Maybe she needed looking after too, but in a different way. He remembered the day he'd brought her down from Toongabbie on the old truck. Bright as paint she'd been when they set out, sitting up like a little queen and chattering all the time, but she'd been a poor little draggled thing by the time he got her home. That had been his fault. He guessed it would still be his fault if she came to grief now. But it wasn't easy to look after Wanda. She didn't want it, thought she could take care of herself. But she was only a kid. He felt guilty about her, because she wanted to be apprenticed to the milliner, said they'd take her at half the premium because she was smart, and he had the £200 Olaf Ramsay had left him put away and no one knew of it. If Ally and Wanda knew of it they'd be after it like a couple of gulls. He meant to hang on to it. It was a little piece of security. It meant that later on he'd be able to give Ben a start. Life wouldn't down him while he had £200. Nevertheless, he felt mean. He let Wanda think there wasn't any money. She was in a dead-end job, poor kid, and she'd soon be feeling it. He didn't want to see her fine feathers down in the dust, but he just wasn't giving up any of that money, not to put into a posh milliner's pocket.

He caught Gwen Leslie's eye and smiled. She smiled back. Friendly, no coquetry in it. In the dead flat plain of monotony in which he was marooned, he felt a small green blade of interest quicken.

After the sale came stocktaking. The staff had to work back in relays and one of the lifts was kept working. The night Gwen was kept back Harry was on the lift. As he carried her up and down to the office, they talked. The shop was a much more friendly place without customers. It didn't occur to either of them that they had not spoken before. Both were poor hands at the sort of badinage the situation demanded, but they went through with it with shy inept clumsiness. It was the right approach, last vestige of the ancient rite of flight and capture, itself a token of the basic war of the sexes, the image of conflict set up in the moment of coming together to round out the truth.

As they worked, a storm broke. In the big building they heard it only remotely. In the half-empty dressing-rooms, conspicuously quiet because usually so full of noise, they became conscious of rain beating on the black windows. Harry changed slowly. It was after ten, so late that there was no need to hurry. It had been a long day. Looking back at the morning was like a giant looking at his toes. Now at the tired end of the day a sense of well being had come upon him. He sluiced his head in a wash basin and sleeked down his wet hair in front of the mirror. Plenty of hair, no going bald, he thought with mild satisfaction. Bit of a treat not to have to hurry and not to have to climb over other people to get to the tap or the glass. Harry was the last man in. One of the caretakers was waiting to turn out the lights. He chiacked Harry and absentmindedly Harry chiacked him back. He let himself into his lift and dropped it down between the dark floors. "Passenger this time," he thought. He let her swoop down with a sense of power in being the only thing moving in the big pile. The main shopping hall, draped in covers, looked like a graveyard. A night watchman checked him out. It was raining hard, the storm was returning on its circular path. A girl was standing in the doorway, pressed against the wall, her face a disconsolate little moon in the darkness. "Hullo," he said, "What's up?" It was Gwen. No matter who it had been he would not have left her there, so obviously distressed.

"I'm afraid of the storm. I know it's silly, but I've always been scared. They shut up the dressing-room, I couldn't stay any longer."

"It'll soon be over," he reassured her. "Tell you what we'll do. We'll scoot along to the little coffee shop and have a hot drink. You're tuckered out and I could do with it. I'll talk and you won't notice the storm."

"I oughter get home," she wavered.

"A quarter of an hour won't make any difference." He knew she'd come. He took her arm, feeling it thin and young through her flimsy frock, and they ran together the thirty yards to the coffee shop. The way was under cover, only the flying spray of the rain reached them. The shop smelt strongly of coffee, it was steamy and quiet, the seat backs were high like old-fashioned pews, giving an illusion of privacy even in the cramped space. They sat opposite one another, the wooden flap table with its bakelite sugar bowl, salt and pepper, and menu between them. She really was frightened, he knew by her pallor and the darkness of her eyes. Tendrils of hair were plastered on her forehead, not by the rain but by the heat. Poor little kid. At first she would agree only to have a cup of coffee, but he finally cajoled her into a ham sandwich and an ice-cream. He had some money in his pocket. He felt good. She was hungry. As she ate the colour came back into her cheeks. She talked easily and freely about herself, with a childish confidence in his interest. Her father was dead and her mother married again. There wasn't room for her at home, she said matter of factly. She was on her own. A ghost of pride moved in her voice. She roomed with two other girls. Shirley's mother was a friend of her gran's, they fixed it for her. Shirley used to work at Wentworthville, but that wasn't any good to her, so she came to town. She was in the hairdressing. She earned good money, but she didn't want to spend it all on lodging. Beryl did manicure at the same place. She had the most gorgeous red hair. They both had boy friends.

"Have you got a boy friend?"

She temporized. "Not a steady," she said.

He knew by her eyes that she hadn't. Maybe she didn't take the eye, nothing bold about her, but she was an appealing little thing. Sweet, he thought. Young enough to be my own kid, he added.

They had a big room, nice, she said it was. Opened on to a balcony. A terrace house in Paddington. She gave him the address. He hoped the other two didn't put upon Gwen because she was the youngest. He saw how it was. They each paid a third of the rent and fed themselves. The other two had "good money" and put it on their backs, had their fun out, and only used the place to sleep in and get up their clothes. Most of the cleaning and tidying would fall on Gwen because she wouldn't have anything else to do. She'd have her dinner at the "Welfare," and for the rest "do" on tea and bread and butter. After she'd paid her third of the rent, her fares and the things a girl had to have, she'd have her work cut out to keep afloat without going out. It'd be lonely. Friends were one of the things she wouldn't be able to afford. He realised that this was quite a party for her. They forgot the weather. They sat in their pew for three-quarters of an hour and didn't know where the time went. Extra cup of coffee, no charge. It was eleven o'clock when they came out into the street again. The storm had gone, the pavements were drying off, it felt late.

"I'll see you home," Harry said, "and then I can walk back to my place." It wasn't gallantry that spoke, but the responsible belief that a little thing like that shouldn't be about alone at this hour.

The Cross, people said, was more like Montparnasse than ever with the foreigners about. The refugees. The Italian fruit vendors and Greek and Cypriote fishmongers had long ago sunk into the pattern and become part of it. This was a new infiltration, a medley of people from Central Europe, from Germany, Poland, Spain, where the old life was breaking down, persecuted people, many of them Jews. They congregated at the Cross. They began to leaven its life. You could pick them out on the pavements, different clothes, a different air, striking noses, black hair. Their quick-firing speech or their rich heavy tones caught the ear acclimatised to the Australian drawl and twang. Their shops began to appear, little shops with an air, chic. Delicatessen with sharp-flavoured new goods, patisserie with elaborate torte and gateaux, fatal lure to the obese, dress shops that were different, gloves and handbags with a continental flair. All these people had legends. They were persecuted. They were all famous surgeons, musicians, professors, actors, bankers, archdukes, princelings. They were a nine days' wonder. But the nine days passed. As long as they were a sideshow and a sensation, it was all right, but it turned out they were human beings. They must live off the country. A chemical change took place. The cry went up they were taking work from Australians, they competed. Their doctors were not allowed to practise, but the others could not be prevented from trading. They had faults. They were ungrateful. At first they were embarrassingly thankful to be in such a beautiful peaceful land, but later they forgot to be humble. They asserted themselves. You saw them walking about as if they owned the place, going in and out of shops as bold as brass. They hung together, too, preferring one another to their native-born neighbours. They were different. When anything happened, a crime wave perhaps, it was blamed on the foreigners. Their hardships even were a black mark against them. Men and women who had been through the depression did not see why foreigners should grumble. They mistrusted those who had money and feared those who hadn't, the one could compete, the other undersell. . . . Some landlords refused to let rooms to foreigners and arrogated virtue to themselves. Placards began to appear in shop windows: "These goods were made by Australians in Australian-owned factories." They were not easy sharers, the Australians. Competition had entered into their hearts, but why not, it was into the already competitive world that these strangers were pushing? They too were competitive.

As for the refugees, they felt their foreignness like another skin. They must exploit it and they must apologise for it. New ways emphasised in them their old ways. They had suffered and that made them fearful and yet more than ever determined to survive. Both in assertion and abnegation they ran counter to the sardonic Australian temperament, suspicious and humorous. When the refugees told their stories of persecution, internment camps, escape, they met either the avarice for sensation or an immovable incredulity. After a time they began to feel like hollow men, having lost the past and not yet grasped the future. An intangible resistance rose against them.

The attic room above the Munsters was let now to a white-haired old Jew from Vienna. His presence brought old Joe back to life, anger and hostility sharpened his dulled wits, for this man was a rival. He went about muttering "foreign trash" and committing pograms in his imagination. The Viennese, whom they called Mr Isaac, though this only faintly resembled his name, had little communication with his neighbours because his English was sketchy. When they had anything to say to him they usually shouted or talked pidgin. He acquiesced politely. His manners were beautiful and he was wont to express his friendliness in smiles and bows. If it hadn't been for these friendly manifestations Mrs Blan, Ally, and the street generally would have dismissed him as "harmless." Whenever he passed them in the laundry or the passage, he bowed from the waist, not once but three or four times, smiling deprecatingly. It gave them, they said, the jitters. They didn't know what they were expected to do about it, so it made them fell awkward. To feel awkward was much the same as being snubbed.

"Poor old coot," said Mrs Blan. "Sometimes I'm that sorry for him. But you never know with foreigners."

"That you don't," agreed Mrs Nelson, "never tells you anything, does he? I'm not one to poke my nose into other people's affairs but it's natural to talk, and when a man goes round as mum as that, it makes you think, doesn't it? They were saying down at the shop he used to be a banker, worth millions before Hitler took his bank from him."

"It's not true. He was a bookseller. He had a shop in the Grab 'em."

"How do you know?"

"I asked him. I said to myself 'It's better to know.' It took me half the morning to find out, but he twigged what I was after in the end."

"He told you. But it mightn't be true. He could just as well have made it up, couldn't he?"

"He always seems friendly—in his funny way," said Ally weakly.

"He's deep," said Mrs Nelson. "Took you half the morning to get that out of him. These bankers are pretty bright in the top story. You've got to get up early in the morning if you want to put one over them."

"But he wasn't a banker."

"So he says. And how do we know it was Hitler drove him out. He might have had another reason."

"The rent collector says he pays regular, no fuss."

"And where does he get the money from?"

"I don't know."

"There, you see. No visible means of support but pays his rent regular. A bit more natural if it weren't so regular, that's what I think."

"There's nothing much in his room. I was passing, the door was open, so I couldn't help seeing in."

"He might be lying low."

"He looks that harmless."

"Well, all I can say is that when there's a murder mystery, it's always the harmless-looking one that did it."

This argument seemed cogent to all three ladies. They nodded sagely. "You don't mean to say . . ." Ally began, a cold fear moving at the bottom of her mind. Under the same roof. . . . She'd always had a funny feeling about Mr Isaac.

"I don't mean to say anything. Just this. Keep your eyes peeled, Mrs Blan. Foreigners are Foreigners."

"I do, Mrs Nelson."

"You don't know a thing about him. Not really. Would you say he had a job, now?"

"He goes out three days a week at half-past nine sharp, all brushed up, but the rest of the time he stays in. Not a sound out of him."

"My Tony saw him getting into a posh car down at the bottom of the hill."

"Well, I never."

"There he is now," said Ally.

The three ladies peered through the curtains of Mrs Blan's front room. He saw them, halted, removed his hat and bowed three times.

"He's home early today," said Ally, when his slow footfalls had died away on the stairs.

"What do you think of that?" asked Mrs Blan meaningfully.

"No flies on him," Mrs Nelson agreed.

Harry and Timmy Andrews breasted up to the bar. It was nearly six o'clock and the place was a chaos of men putting them down in a hurry. The pubs closed at six. It wasn't often Harry was in time for a drink. For the sixth or seventh time Timmy smote him between the shoulders and bellowed loudly, "Fancy meeting you, old son, after donkey's years." Timmy had been in the pub some time, fortifying himself against closing time. Harry was tired and couldn't rake up much surprise or enthusiasm. A lot had happened to him since the last time he'd seen Timmy, the day they were both sacked from Mullangars. He agreed, however, that the world was a damn bloody small place. They had a beer together for old time's sake. The extra ballast seemed to right Timmy.

"How's things?" he asked.

Harry told him.

"I got a cow of a job, too," said Timmy. "Me and the missus are caretaking a block of flats at the Cross. Posh flats. Well, near posh. The money's not so bad, it's the life. Always cleaning up after bloody foreigners. The place is crawling with them, crawling." He kicked the brass rail in sombre disgust. Men reached across him for their pots.

"What's wrong with them?" Harry asked.

"They got the wrong social outlook, that's what I can't stick."

"How do you know?"

"Stands to reason. Couldn't get here without money, and if they got money, they got the wrong social outlook."

Harry's mind was on something else. He answered mildly, "We've got one in our house. Poor old pot, lives on tuppence a week by the look of him. Couldn't offer him a fill of tobacco, though. Not that kind."

'I know. He'd have the wrong social outlook, too. All have. It's an invasion."

"This is better than the depresh." Harry tried to comfort him.

"We've all got into port somewhere," Timmy agreed. "Any old bloody port. You hauling fat women up to overeat themselves and then hauling them down again. Me clearing up after bloody foreigners. If it wasn't for the perks I'd quit tomorrow. I'd better be thankful, had I?" A brief truculence flared up in him and then subsided. "Any old port's better than no port. But there's going to be a war and we'll all be blown out again."

"Nuts," said Harry.

In the autumn Harry was made controller. He didn't drive an elevator any more, he walked up and down in front of the lifts, controlling the traffic, seeing that no lift was overcrowded, answering questions. He wore the same uniform with a cap, such as a lieutenant in the army wears, added, and "Controller" in metal letters on his chest above his ribbons. It was an advancement and meant another ten shillings a week. He told Ally it was five and gave her three. The change bore hardly on him at first, he had to adjust himself. Let out of the cage, he felt extraordinarily exposed. He wanted the bars again. And it wasn't the same thing all the time, he had to learn to think a bit. He wondered if wearing the cap all day would make him bald. He thought about his age now, and when he had a haircut he told the barber to cut it close on the temples to get rid of the grey hair.

Being controller soon gave him a sense of greater freedom. A hundred times a day he passed Gwen's table. They smiled covertly at one another. Sometimes, in the morning when business was slack, he could stand and talk to her. He looked forward to it. Her eyes told him that she did too. He took her out a few times to the pictures. It was easy enough to tell Ally that he was working back. Then, of course, she expected a cut out of the overtime. It had to be juggled. He would have liked to take Gwen out more often but held back. She didn't have much of a time. She hadn't a boy. It wasn't as if he were spoiling her chances with someone else. They were so happy together, like a pair of kids instead of just one. It wasn't doing her any harm to give her a bit of fun. She didn't seem to want to know about him, he'd told her he was married, just in case she got ideas. He'd added, "Ally and me don't get along, so we've just agreed not to." That didn't explain things but it would do. Now that he didn't care any more, he could look back and see the whole business with Ally like a spreading black bruise under the skin. Losing Ally had done something to him, because she was his wife. A front tooth knocked out. It had happened so casually. If he'd had sense he could have stopped it. There hadn't been enough quarrel between them at any one moment that he couldn't have made it up. But the moments had added up. It was the times they were not quarrelling that made making up the quarrels impossible. It was his fault. Ally was a poor thing now, nothing to her on account of letting a lot of fool women get hold of her. If they could make up Ally's mind for her, well, so could he, if he'd cared enough at the time. You're more likely to be right if you do the giving. When he thought of making things up with Ally now, though, everything turned to wood. No good trying to explain all that to Gwen.

She nodded her head gravely. She knew all about that sort of thing, took it for granted that most people didn't get on after they were married, but it didn't touch her personally. He wondered sometimes if she really were a child in mind, at twenty. He didn't know. She was so natural, a clear simplicity about her, accepting things as they were. Quiet, shy, but natural, not embarrassed by her own shyness. Didn't pretend, not about anything. Funny little kid. Steady, a little marvel. Innocent. Oh God, he'd not harm her, no thought of that. It didn't seem as if he'd ever been quite at home with anyone before.

Harry was full of energy. He hadn't felt like that for years. It made him restless. There was nothing to do at home. A few fidgetty minutes after he had eaten his tea, he'd go out again for a walk.

"You're on your feet all day. What do you want to walk for?" Ally asked. She didn't expect an answer. It was just to say something.

He walked without object. Sometimes he went down Forbes Street between the lines of terrace houses to the bay, to look at the dark water, the liners with illuminated funnels in their berths, the span of the bridge phosphorescent green in the darkness. He liked the space, the damp cold air from far away. He returned, his feet clanking on the cold pavement, striding freely, feeling tall and vital, between the quiet houses and furtive lanes. "Sounds as if the hill was hollow," he thought. Other times he went up the hill, through the Cross, and into the quiet streets beyond, tree-lined, leisured, running down to dark gardens by the water. The sky was like black ice, the stars hung low. In the clear cold, even the soaring buildings had a brittle look, pavements were clenched to greater density, lights crackled without sound, lights piled up in shops, golden, rosy; warm air flowed out of restaurants on to the pavement, as the Amazon drives a fresh water wedge into the ocean. All edges were sharp, even the edges of light; only the traffic flowed suavely. The cold air went to Harry's head. It touched him on the temples, the cheek bones, the lips.

Sometimes Ruthie went with him on these walks. Wanda never would. Every minute she could snatch she was off down to the roller skating at the Palais. Ben had to be driven to his homework. Every night it was the same.

"Aw, Dad, what's it matter? I'm leaving school soon."

In a year he would be fourteen. He didn't see much of Ben and that little was often troubled by argument. The boy didn't want to do anything but play or run barefoot round the Cross selling papers. Harry was beginning to be troubled about him—not the boy himself, he was a good kid—but his future. He'd have to think what to do with him, and it would be uphill work if the boy himself had no ambition and no aptitudes. He didn't want to see Ben go into a dead-end job and get sucked down into the great morass of unskilled labour. Maybe he could apprentice him to the engineering, if he'd study. Hard on a boy working all day and going to Tech. at night, years of it. Unless Ben changed, he knew he wouldn't stick it. What then? Keep him at school to get his Intermediate? Might as well try that on a colt. Ben wasn't hard to manage, a good kid, just not a scholar, and he'd wriggle out of it every time with a grin. This worry in Harry's mind spoilt the relationship between father and son. Harry thought with remorse that Ben was more friendly to him than he to Ben.

.   .   .   .   .   .   .   .   .

"Ren," Ord thought. "Knarf is bound up in Ren and doesn't know it. Even the names. I didn't think of it before."

.   .   .   .   .   .   .   .   .

It was Ruthie who went with him, in her brown beret and the brown coat with astrachan trimming that she'd outgrown. They didn't talk much, but they were companionable. There was a new tenderness as well as a new strength in Harry, both more conscious than the strength of his youth had been, or the tenderness he had always borne his children and other young helpless things. He would pause at the shops with Ruth, interested in what attracted a girl. Together they looked at hats, scarves, vanity bags, a bracelet of silver filigree set with green stones. He surprised a rapt look in Ruth's eyes.

"I didn't know you liked all this stuff," he said. Unlike Wanda, Ruth didn't use cosmetics or make any attempt at smartness.

"What's the good? I can't have them."

That was the difference. Wanda would take what she could get and Ruth wouldn't.

"Maybe some day you'll have all you want."

There was the same wistful inflection in both their voices. She smiled at him and slipped her hand into his arm.

Sometimes, before he pulled himself up, Harry let his mind run on giving Gwen all the things Ruth wanted.

They moved from the lighted cave of one shop window to another, the worn man with a vestige of military carriage still in his bearing and the shabby girl with the dreaming eyes. Their feet wove a nameless pattern with many other feet, like the pattern of raindrops on the pavement, coalescing and obliterating one another. Crazy pattern, but perhaps with some basic significance.

"Wunderbar," exclaimed the little man, standing transfixed before the reckless plenty of a confectioner's window, where mountains of chocolates offered themselves in abandon to the public appetite.

"Ach," said his companion, bending to scrutinise them through his thick glasses, "They are only wood."

The first man was relieved. It was too much, and too much is to tempt providence.

The other said sadly, "There is so much and so little valued." The ostentatious plenty made them feel, as they were, exiles.

Paula Ramsay was on her way home. Of the many thousand cells, piled side by side and one on top of the other, one was hers. A room with a view, soundproofed, air-conditioned, with hot water service, refrigeration, built-in radio, telephone, wall-to-wall carpets, rubbish chute. Its plate glass windows looked out over a great avalanche of dwellings to the blue of the harbour, the low-lying green of Rushcutters Bay, the hammer head of Darling Point with its dress circle mansions and flats. A peak view. At noon, it had the hard sophistication of a fashionable resort; at dusk, it melted and blended into a soft and pregnant beauty; at night it was a broadcast of stars. Paula had her freedom wrapped in cellophane, the shining and expensive loneliness that she had wanted. She hadn't known that she had wanted it shining and expensive, but that was how she had seen it and that was what she had. She had it and now she found she had nothing to put in it. The vacuum was prepared, swept, and garnished, but the obstinate buds of her mind refused to flower in it. She had expected something to happen, something like love but not love, because she was afraid of love. Nothing had happened. She would not make allowances for the shock that was still echoing through her nerves—the shock of her father's death, the shock of her break with her mother. Masked by her grief, she had hardly noticed the break at the time. Her gentleness had been steeled by an impregnable obstinacy. Her father had left her money so that she could go away and lead her own life. She would go. At once. His death was her sorrow, hers only. She hugged the thought that she alone had understood him. She hated her mother's competent mourning. When her mother had begged her to wait, at least for three months, had leant her head on her hands and cried, Paula had been repelled and become more fixed than ever in her resolve. Her mother had helped her to move. They had said the right things to each other. "If you want me, I'm here," and, "Come whenever you feel inclined." Nothing vulgar or unnecessary, but a break. Paula decided, an irretrievable break. It began to trouble her despite herself, like a deep splinter beginning to fester. She felt young, helpless. She told herself she wanted her father and wept wildly, face downwards on her expensive bedspread. Almost anyone would have done. Life had taken her at her word and she bore it a grudge.

Now, standing in the delicatessen buying eggs, butter, something easy in a tin, she felt utterly desolate. The thought of cooking herself a meal underlined her loneliness. She could eat in a restaurant, of course, but she knew all the standardised foods, and was heartily sick of them. She wanted to surprise herself with something very nice to eat, cook it herself, but it didn't work. Liming the twig in sight of the bird. With falling heart she bought eggs, butter, a tin of boneless chicken tamale. She didn't know what that might be. It was imported, expensive, it might be *the* lovely thing to eat that sometimes you tried to imagine. Afterwards she would read, but she didn't really enjoy the books that she liked to see herself reading. Waiting for her parcel to be wrapped, she thought of this and that she might do, but the boredom of loneliness shrivelled everything. The shopkeeper handed her the package with a little bow. The gnadige fraulein who spent money almost without looking. At the door she met the wall of cold air.

Two air force trainees were swinging along in their long blue coats. "A little bit of all right."

Arch Castles agreed. "Not bad. Looks as if she hadn't much go," but he was not really interested. He was spending his few days' leave with Don, and Don's idea of sport was to tramp through the winter dark, giving the girls the once over. Arch suspected that that was as far as Don had got. At a safe distance he was knowledgeable enough, but when it came to speaking to a strange girl he had seen Don blush to the roots of his fair hair. Arch felt much older than Don though they were the same age. Don was class, good at his job and keen, but he didn't know much. Not about girls. Don had no more money than he had, his pay, but he came out of a different world. He'd gone straight from school into camp. His were the sort of people who kept a boy at school till he was eighteen even if they were poor. Don was in the air force because he wanted to be, not because it was a way of escape from something else. The same uniform covered them both. Arch had done what he had planned, stepped out of his past into the uniform. Walking like this at a loose end in the evening, was the time Arch was most apt to think about Ruby. They'd picked one another up, easy as snap your fingers. He'd been fond of Ruby and she'd been fond of him. She'd have replaced him by now, got another chap long ago. She was a good girl, but it was easy come, easy go, with her. Pretty, plump, ready to drop, like a fruit heavy, ripe, but without a spot on it. Laughed. Incurably silly—innocent. Cried a lot when he said he had to go into camp and wouldn't be seeing her. Cried, but took it for granted it had to be like that. Really, he'd gone into the air force because of Ruby, because if he'd married her it would have been the dead finish for him. Perhaps she'd really been his girl though, and he'd never find another one like her. He hadn't wanted to find one at all so far. What he'd done had left its scar. The memory of Ruby made this one look thin and pale.

"Thoroughbred," Don said.

Arch agreed. The girl coming out of the delicatessen was a thoroughbred. Thoroughbreds were an acquired taste. Both boys looked after her. Paula looked back but not at them.

She had seen the man before. He was as thin as a scarecrow. He wore a Norfolk jacket buttoned up to his neck to conceal the absence of shirt. He stood in front of the window bulging with food. He might stand there for an hour, looking. His lips just moved. There was no madness in his face. It was aristocratic, reserved, he held himself with dignity, a man to whom it would be impossible to offer any help.

He was like a lost and starving dog whom no one will take in because he still wears a collar.

The delicatessen was invaded by a motley crowd, a little wave of people, all seedy, with Elsie Todd borne triumphantly on its crest. They were not the sort of customers the shopkeeper liked to see. Elsie had had several drinks in quick succession. The fumes were mingling with the confusion in her brain, but she was happy. She was on top of the world, she had a firm grip on that anyway. She had difficulty in focusing her mind. Never before had she been able to buy whatever she liked.

"Yes, Madam?" said the shopkeeper, patiently.

Elsie beamed on him. "I want . . ." she began. "Well, I'll have some cheese."

Elsie's satellites laughed. They consisted of every one who had happened to be at home in the residential where she lived when the good news came. They had rallied round her then and hadn't left her since.

On the cheese Elsie stuck. Her eyes ranged the laden shelves in an agony of greed and indecision.

"The lady's just won the lottery," a sandy loquacious man began to explain. "She wants to celebrate."

"Yes," Elsie broke out, released. "£5000, isn't it a scream? You could have knocked me down with an eyelash. A nice young fellow comes out to tell me. Caught me proper without me corsets on, just taking a laydown before I got dressed. 'What are your reactions, Mrs Todd?' says he. 'Oh,' I say, 'Oh, I'm all of a heap. It'll be time enough to see about reactions when I'm dressed.' 'And what are you going to do with the money?' says he. 'Have a good time,' says I. 'It's what I've always wanted, a good time, but somehow I've never got round to it. Isn't it a caution?'" The shopkeeper continued to look stony. "There you are, look for yourself. It's in the paper. I collect tomorrow." She waved an evening paper and a crumpled lottery ticket before his eyes. He looked. It was true enough. This woman was worth £5000. He thawed.

"Get a move on, Else," the sandy man adjured.

"Get some ham, love," a fat woman suggested. "It's real tasty for a foundation."

"I'll have a ham," Elsie said grandly to the shopkeeper. "And you needn't worry, I'll pay you cash. See that?" She flourished a handful of notes. "Mr Bernstein came over as soon as he heard and offered me a loan. Thoughtful, I call it."

"Come on, Else. We don't want to be here all night," the sandy man urged. He was the self-appointed master of ceremonies. "If you don't see what you want here, there's plenty more shops."

Elsie began to buy in earnest. She stood there in the shop and pointed to anything that took her fancy. She bought luxuries she had never tasted before, she bought foods whose names even she had never heard. The pile on the counter grew and grew. She was happy, everyone was happy, including the shopkeeper. The thing had developed into a party. Everyone made suggestions and she took them all. Every now and then she interrupted herself with some solemn reflection, rolling her good luck on her tongue.

"Who'd a thought of this happening to me? There's times lately when I was so low I wouldn't of minded going out to it, and here I am rolling." Then she dropped into a reminiscent mood. "What do you think? Just as I was coming along here, I saw a chap I used to know. Nice chap he was too. Harry. Didn't look too prosperous, poor Harry. Always remembered him."

"Gee, you got a good memory, Mrs Todd."

"Shame on you, Fred. You've no call to talk like that. I'd of stopped and spoke to him and asked him to come along, but he had a girl with him. I never speak to a chap when he has a girl with him. You never know."

"You're white, Else, old girl."

"Maybe I'll see him again when he's alone. I'd like to do something for him."

"Come *on*, Else."

At last they had about as much as they could carry. The shopkeeper began to add up the bill.

"I'll look after your interests, Else," said the sandy man. "What about a commission, mate," he said to the shopkeeper, "I introduced the customer."

Elsie handed over the money in a grand way to the sandy man. "You're me business manager, Andy," she said.

She moved to leave the shop. The cold air wrought a chemical change in her blood. For a moment she stood wavering. She saw the man without a shirt. He was still gazing into the window, oblivious of everything, his lips moving. Tears came into Elsie's eyes. He was hungry. He wasn't like her. She fumbled at her bag, but Andy had the money. Out of the bag in her arms she took a large jar of caviare. She stepped up to him, holding it out.

"Please," she said, "you have it. I've lots. It's all right." She put it in his hands, closing his fingers round it as if he were a child.

"There," she said.

*Spring 1938*

It was spring. The trees in Victoria Street were coming into leaf again. Florists' windows were packed with flowers. There were early strawberries from Queensland, and last spring's hats from Paris, and winds carried pollen instead of dust. It was Spring and people felt vaguely that they ought to do something about it, but hardly anyone knew what. The trees in Victoria Street were fortunate, it was all arranged for them.

The starving poet of King's Cross—who was also a well-paid public servant—walked in the evening through the streets. The sap was stirring in his veins, too. He felt the poetry start from him like sweat. His mind opened and yielded to some secret pressure. He was reassured that youth was not quite over. He did not hanker for brown paddocks and blue hills. He preferred works of art, and the Cross, which he loved, was a work of art. He saw the hill as a black wave with a crest of fire; God had made the hill and man had set the fire upon it. Coloured fire. Vivid, acrid, neon lights, coloured taxis, red two-decker buses swinging down Wylde St., striped awnings, fruit, flowers, buckets of marigolds out on the pavements, gee-gaws, and women's clothes. Necessities looked like luxuries here. Even bread. A window full of bread, beautiful, fantastic, full of sex appeal. It was bread that became the body of God in the token sacrifice. But not these breads, they were pagan, sophisticated, adult. Civilization was nature into image. Higher and higher the edifice of bright unreality built out over the gulf. A fantasia on given themes. Man climbing up out of black depths of nature into his bright eyrie of civilization, getting used to its unreality, making it his reality. I'll write an epic, he thought, an epic in blank verse and the theme shall be Man in search of civilization. Man the creative, who could not acquiesce. Sometimes he had acquiesced. The aborigines had found a way of life through acquiescence, a way of life adjusted to circumstance and the country. Perpetual life, it would have gone on without variation into eternity, but for the accident of the white man's coming. Because he was perfectly adjusted, the aborigine could not resist the white man. Sealed to one way of life, a life so concrete, so definite, so circumscribed, that it could be shattered like a plate. That was only an episode. Discontent, maladjustment, was the plastic in man's life. Trial and error on a large scale. The civilization of the mind. Greece had tried that. Content without form. The civilization of method. Roman law and Roman organization. But that had held no rich content of poetry and philosophy. Try God. The Middle Ages did but the cult became professionalised, too narrow a basis, too many left outside discontented. The beginning of gangsterdom. The emphasis passed from spiritual to temporal power. For God read power. Power is expensive. For power read money. The means to power becoming the end of power. The search for money created the machine. So the machine is civilization. The lovely, exciting, mechanic world. The hegemony of the expert, the most impersonal power the world had ever known. The virtue of the machine was its wide range. International and classless. He looked about him. This strange blossoming. It wasn't entirely new because nothing was ever entirely new, only new manifestations of the old themes. What race memories were there here? Was this the new jungle? Labyrinthine life. Neon lights for flowers, traffic instead of rivers flowing in the narrow gulches of streets, synthetic barbarism of jazz and swing on tap in every cave-like flat. The old things sharpened and dramatised, synthetised, canned, bottled, injected. The folk mind of the people accepting the machine and building with it. Folk patterns in a mechanised world. Curious, immense. But doomed. Perhaps doomed. There would be war sooner or later, and what would war do, using the material of the new civilization, destroying machines by machines, neutralising them, cancelling them out. Violence will be the spanner in the machine. There is bound to be change. I stand now upon the peak of the doomed world. It is doom that makes the lights so bright, that heightens the tempo. The fiery crest shines because we see it against the overhanging night. Somewhere, far away, probably in Europe, a fatal moment will come, a shot will be fired that is not like any of the other shots, one man too many will be killed, one more slogan lie upon the laden scale and bear it down. The unseen distant root of this bright mechanic beauty will be touched and the secret withering begin.

This epic. This new Paradise Lost. The skyscraper of modern poetry. The dance of words. He walked like a prophet and his spirit was lifted up.

In his heart the poet knew that this was the spring working in him. He rejoiced that he could still feel the spring, and it reassured him that he was still a poet. It is good when the mind wells with great images. It puts the world between your hands. They don't have to be true. Another spring.

That spring, Harry and Gwen acquired the habit of walking part of the way home together. They were within sight of one another

all day. That had been good at first. Each had developed all sorts
of little mannerisms for the benefit of the other. Soon the limitations
of the situation began to irk them. Harry grew irritable and did not
know why. Without overt arrangement they began to meet after
work, not at the store's entrance, of course, but some distance up the
street, drifting together in the flood of peak hour traffic, crossing
the park in the anonymity of the dusk. Small particles in a great
mass, they felt themselves alone and secure. In Oxford Street he
would put her into her tram and climb his own hill on foot by a
zigzag of small streets. They talked very little because, for the things
that would have suited their mood, they had no words. Harry did
not ask himself what Gwen thought or how she felt. He was content
that she was willing to walk with him in the dusk. The secret honey
was sweet on his tongue.

One night Gwen had something to say. All the way across the
park he could feel it struggling in her. At the tram stop she let a
crowded tram go by. They stood, one still spot, waiting, in the swirl
of traffic. At last she got it out. Would he come to tea on Saturday;
Shirley and Beryl would be out. Would he come at half-past five?
He said he would. Half-past five, on the tick. He helped her into the
tram, half lifting her.

"Cheerio, Gwen."

"So long, Harry."

She smiled back at him, radiant, as the tram moved away.

On the way Harry bought a bunch of flowers for her. Wrapped
by the florist into a tissue paper bludgeon, they made him ill at
ease. He seriously thought of putting them down somewhere and
walking away quickly. "Looks as if I were going courting," he thought,
to reassure himself of his own blameless intentions. They had looked
so pretty and so natural in the window. To have a dozen counted
out and rolled up in mauve tissue paper, secured with a pin, was a
different matter.

He knew the house, though he had never been in it. It stood
in a terrace, there was a terrace opposite. They were stone terraces
with slate roofs, verandahs and a balcony rail of fancy ironwork,
which showed they were old. In the older parts of Sydney there
were thousands of houses built on the same plan. The doorstep was
blacked and the knocker polished, a respectable place. There was a
big doorknob of topaz glass and a narrow pane in each side of the
door, ruby red with a white convolvulus design.

The landlady let him in. Her eye went straight to the bunch of flowers, as he knew it would. Her eye was not unbenevolent. She didn't care to see a young girl moping round without a boy friend, it wasn't natural. This one was a bit old, but then, once you'd got one boy friend it was generally easy enough to get another. She told him to go upstairs, the front room.

Harry knocked. Gwen's voice, with a squeak in it, said "Come in." After the dark landing the room was very light. Gwen took his hand. "Oh, Harry."

He couldn't speak. He saw how she had decked the room for him. She had bought flowers and put them about. Everything was carefully arranged. The table was set as if for a party, with cakes and sugar-coated biscuits, ham, fruit salad, cream. She must have spent all her money on it. She shouldn't have done that. His throat swelled painfully. He looked at Gwen standing there in her new frock, waiting for him to say how pleased he was. He couldn't say it. She was looking at him, a mask had fallen from her face. He saw it clear, shining. He knew. If her face hadn't told him, the room would have. He was taken unawares after all. They both were. He put the flowers down carefully on the bed.

"That's Beryl's bed," she said.

They took a couple of tranced steps toward each other. She was in his arms. His arms fitted close about her. Strong wings were beating, closer, closer in the silence. She lifted her head and tried to say, "I love you, Harry," but his mouth fastened on hers. All the world drew slowly into the vortex of the kiss. This had been coming for months. Now it had come. They were engulfed in Now. There was no time but now. He gathered her up and carried her across the room. They might have been alone in the world. She was his love, he hers.

Harry could not sleep that night, his mind a hotch potch of triumph and remorse. He didn't want to sleep because he felt so good. The knots in his flesh that had become like the knots in hardwood had gone. Gone for the moment. He felt young. But his sober mind told him he had no right to feel like that. That Gwen was a child and he. . . . But Gwen wasn't a child. She'd been the steady one. Innocent, sure. They had been caught by life, and because she was the clearer stuff it shone through her most brightly. Without fear, without regret. Her face pale, her eyes luminous with tenderness, cajoling him to come and eat the party, as if he were the child who must be reassured, clinging to him at last, exhausted, fierce, as if she must protect him. The thought twisted in his mind, "It's not only today. Today was perfect. But we can't leave it at that." Today had been a sort of superb accident. They'd had their miracle, they'd have to be reasonable. He'd have to be reasonable. It wasn't going to be easy. Even if he didn't have difficulties with himself, he'd have them with Gwen. My little love. He could not think of their coming together as commonplace. It had happened. It mattered. He rubbed his hand over his springing beard. Trapped. Ally, the children, Gwen. Ten shillings up on the basic wage. Men had affairs with girls every day. It didn't signify. They got off scot free. But if you loved the girl, then you were for it. The fat was in the fire. They'd both have to pay. He didn't know what. That was the devil. His mind turned and twisted in a dark labyrinth. Like a star in darkness, he thought of Olaf Ramsay's £200. He had money, and money meant some sort of security for Gwen. A barricade, a flimsy barricade, but still something to hang on to. You needed money for love and he had money. His mind eased. Triumph began to seep back into his mind.

At first Harry was too preoccupied with his own affairs to realise the crisis. Suddenly he felt it as one feels a thunderstorm. There was a state of suspension in the shop. People stopped buying. They were waiting. The whole world was waiting. The brink of war. Hitler was threatening Czechoslovakia. France had guaranteed the integrity of the Czech state. England was bound to France, the Empire would follow England, the little nations had everything to fear between the millstones. . . . The whole world was in the dragnet. The crisis swelled like a great bubble, unbelievable. Newspapers sold as they hadn't sold since the last war. Benny, wildly excited as if the crisis were his own personal achievement, dashed hither and thither, peeling papers off his bundle, snapping up the pennies. The leather money pouch was like a millstone round his neck.

Old Rumpty sat hunched in his shabby overcoat and held his parliament. "Ugh," he said, "we better fight the buggers and have done."

Voices of men talking everywhere.

"There won't be war. Last time finance capital wanted war, this time it doesn't suit their book. So it won't happen."

"England isn't prepared. The War Office is in a frightful stew."

"Time someone taught Hitler."

"If they want to fight in Europe it hasn't anything to do with us."

"A scrap would clear the air."

"There's worse things than war."

"If it hadn't been for that disarmament foolery he never would have dared."

"The last war will be a pup to this one—if it comes."

"The safest place will be the army. Hitler's bombers don't stick to military targets."

"Isn't civilian morale a military target?"

"If Hitler goes to war he'll have a revolution in Germany. The German people don't want war."

"A war every twenty years. . . ."

"If the working classes refused to fight, there wouldn't be a war."

"Poor bloody working class, have they got to do everything? What about some of the knowalls stopping the war?"

"We should have put the light out in Germany last time. Now we've got to do it all over."

Lord Runciman went to Czechoslovakia with his golf clubs, Mr Chamberlain went to Munich with his umbrella. The bubble burst. Peace in our time. A dove produced miraculously out of a top hat. Some one said, "What about the Czechs?" Some one said, "Dishonour." Some one said, incomprehensibly, "Canossa." But the voices weren't heard. Every one wanted to be reassured and relieved. They were. They all ate it like porridge with a spoon. It had all been like an advertising stunt, effective but unreal. Confidence is everything. The way was open for a record Christmas.

## 1939

The unease began again. It was obvious to everyone that the nettle danger had only reproduced according to its kind. There always seemed to be a crisis coming up like a blind boil. People tried to get rid of the malaise by saying to themselves, secretly, "Even if there is a war, it won't come here." They comforted themselves, "War bumps up the prices of primary products." But they weren't comforted. Out of the morass a new star rose. Make an alliance with Russia, and Germany would be sewn up. People began to have more kindly thoughts of Russia. The bear would pull the chestnuts out of the fire, and he'd be pleased to. We'd recompense him by taking him back into the comity of nations. As every one had been so disagreeable and unhelpful to him in the past, that ought to flatter him enormously.

People hoped. They did not trouble to be logical. They just hoped. They felt that by hoping they built a wall round themselves. The negotiations between the diplomats fluctuated. Hope was tied to a kite and the wind veered now this way, now that. Two sections of the community wanted a Russian alliance. The Left, with its spearhead in the Communist Party, stood for the Popular Front and Collective Security. The Right wanted an uncontaminating diplomatic and military alliance, hoping by means of it to draw the war east instead of west. Most people stood dumbly, hoping or trying to believe that a war wouldn't affect them personally.

The situation worked like dust into the minds of even those people who took no interest in politics and didn't read the papers. It was in the air.

There were more quarrels in the street than there used to be. Ally and Mrs Blan fell out about Russia, of which neither knew anything. Mrs Blan accepted the views of the bandsman who, perhaps from playing *God Save the King* so often, was a rabid imperialist and described a Russian pact as "trafficking with Beelzebub." Ally imbibed her opinions from a taxi-driver, an international brigader from Spain, Sid Warren, who lived at Mrs Nelson's. Mrs Blan was the shrewder fighter.

"We don't want to be beholden to the Russkies. We can do our own fighting as well and better, like we've always done. Just tell me this, who won the war in Spain, Russia or Italy? If they can't beat the Itics they're no good. And another thing. Men who live promiscuous like they do can't fight. Fine ideas they'd put into our boys' heads."

Even those who disagreed with him, like Mrs Blan, were rather proud to have an international brigader in the street. Someone who had been somewhere and done something. Sid Warren was a lean hard man, with a sardonic eye. He would talk to the boys, Ben, Tony Nelson, and the others, when he wouldn't talk to anyone else. He'd listen to the rambling political arguments of the pub and the street corner with an ugly wry smile. He spat eloquently. "You don't know you're born." He was reputed to have a way with the girls. He'd chiack them, but they'd always come back for more. Wanda had the pertest tongue in the street and she'd score off him. Ruth didn't. No one ever noticed her in the noisy group that often gathered round his cab where he parked it at the kerb. But sometimes, if he passed her as they were both going home to their tea, he'd give her a lift, which was more than he did for most.

Mrs Blan and Ally came together again on the subject of Mr Isaac, who was nearer home and therefore much more important. From being too quiet, Mr Isaac had become too noisy. He wasn't noisy personally, but by proxy. He developed the habit of entertaining his friends. Sometimes they weren't even his friends, just people he'd met, foreign Jews like himself, who were down on their luck. He asked them in to sleep. Sometimes there were five or six people camped in his little room; once a whole family, father, mother, and three children were there for nearly a week. The woman scolded her children at the top of her voice in German. They tramped up and down stairs at all hours. The baby cried and cried. The baby's washing was draped over the banisters. All the water they used must be drawn from a tap on the landing outside the Munsters' door, and, worse still, they must share the same lavatory. Ally accused them of using too much water and of being dirty. When she found a bug crawling up the wall, it was too much. She attributed it immediately to the family upstairs. She scooped it up in a piece of paper and took it down to show Mrs Blan.

Together they waited for Mr Isaac and bailed him up on the stairs. Mrs Blan was spokeswoman.

"Mr Isaac," she said, "there's three adults and three children, that makes six, living in your room, it ain't decent and it ain't healthy, and it never was intended. What's more, it can't go on. Just take a look at that."

She offered him the bug in its paper. He peered at it through his thick glasses.

"Ah, a boog," he said mildly.

"Yes, and it's those people and their dirty ways that brought it. You got to send them away, Mr Isaac. We won't stand for it."

"But," he protested, "but you do not understand. They have nutting, nowhere to go, if I send them away, what will they do? They haf no place. What is a boog to that?"

Mrs Blan and Ally exchanged a look. That was foreigners for you.

"This ain't a slum, Mr Isaac."

"Please?"

"This ain't Germany. We don't want to be nasty, but I tell you straight, if you don't send them away and get cleaned up, I'll speak to the agent. He won't have the place turned into a dosshouse."

"But the poor people," pleaded Mr Isaac, tears in his eyes, "One little boog, what is that when people are in trouble?"

"It's not only the bug. It's lots of things. They go or we speak to the agent. He comes tomorrow."

"I am disgrace."

"You're right, it's a disgrace. I'm glad you've seen it that way at last."

The family departed the next morning. Mrs Blan watched them go, her arms folded, her eyes hard. "You got to fight if you want to keep decent," she told the bandsman.

"Go it, ma," he said.

Harry heard of all this but took little notice. His mind was preoccupied. Day by day his passion for Gwen grew, it approached the word from which he shrank—the word "love." She was new life, escape, a miracle when he had thought himself beyond miracles. He gave her a tenderness such as not even his children had evoked in him. And she loved him in a way past counterfeiting, a way that amazed and humbled him. Yet, like a cotton back to satin, there was always the reproach in his mind. He was wronging her, not in the conventional sense perhaps, but at her age she wanted a future and he had none to give. She asked nothing and yet demanded everything. He was staggered by her single mindedness and intimidated by his power to hurt her. They could snatch only moments together. She agreed that he could not desert his wife and children, that they had first claim on him, yet she became more and more reckless. He reasoned with her and she pleaded her love. He persisted and she abandoned herself to tears. Always he was the cautious one. It always fell to him to say no, to counsel prudence. It hurt him that it had to be so. It hurt them both. He marvelled at her emotional strength. She was capable of loving twenty-four hours a day, and he was not. He had his sagging moments of doubt. He was rarely at peace. He began to wonder uncomfortably if anyone at the shop had come to suspect them. If anyone guessed, the story would go the rounds and a harsh chemical would be thrown into their idyll. It would become a vulgar incident like hundreds of others. A man who had lived in an overcrowded area for years knew the value of that thin precarious wall of secrecy. Gwen wanted to show him off as her "boy." It touched and alarmed him that she should feel like that. Poor kid, she missed a lot through him. All their meetings were snatched. Like all poor lovers in the city, they suffered because they had nowhere to go, no place of their own, no privacy, no security. Gwen took him to her room sometimes, when the other girls were out. He didn't like the arrangement. He was too much aware of the others. He had met Shirley and Beryl once, and so they had become real to him. Beryl, with her red hair and heavy mouth, was good humoured in a thick-skinned way. Her humour might have passed over Gwen's head, but now, he suspected, she would be more vulnerable to it and might become its target. Beryl was twenty-two, she looked at men with frank appraisal. She had never been caught by her emotions, and thought the whole business of love a racy game, and the first duty of woman to keep her end up. Her sensuousness was still satisfied by sparring. Shirley was a different proposition. In her late twenties, she was already overripe—not her body, but her heart perhaps. Her looks were negative, but she knew how to handle them. Thin, flat-chested, with fair straight hair, pale eyes, and a thin pale mouth, she had determination, strength, and a sort of thin hard courage. Over her whipcord mouth she painted another, a scarlet cupid's bow, her hair, tinted golden, was sculptured in the latest mode. It looked rather like a wig in its odd isolated perfection. She imparted a peach glow to her cheeks. But her eyes were greedy. They asked the same question of every man. There was an edge to the question. She had a boy friend. She could always get a boy friend, but none of them ever lost his head for her or wanted to marry her. She had a scale of failure and success. Not to be married before thirty was failure. While she remained coldly experimental, she wanted the boy to lose his head. She was more afraid of losing face than of losing her immortal soul. As a child she had been greedy for life, for love, for everything, and now, while she was still young, she seemed to have shot past it. Unhappy, unsatisfied, she could seek neither remedy nor friendship, because with whomever she was she must be first, the leader, the ruler. Gwen thought she was wonderful.

Beryl was selfish without being competitive. And so they managed the difficult business of living together. That Harry disliked Shirley was a bit of grit in his relations with Gwen. Gwen had to defend her. Harry always felt her malign influence in the room. He couldn't have analysed his feeling. It was there. That greedy and frustrated people were dangerous. There was a malign feminine world, a pool of discontents, a treasury of bruised vanity, constantly recruited. Women as women, rather than individuals, had a grievance, a mass grievance, a mass hostility, a mass frustration. Of this black legend Shirley was an initiate, so Harry, as a man and Gwen's lover, must fear her. None of which made the least sense, either to himself or to Gwen, and could not be explained.

. . . . . . . . . .

"This peculiar and sinister female . . ." Ord interrupted.

"She is neither peculiar nor sinister," Knarf asserted pedantically. "She is merely one of those unfortunate women who are women only and not human beings. They are quite common."

"You may be right," Ord agreed cautiously. "I've always felt, too, that there is a sort of femaleness . . ."

"Woman is the complement of man, and sometimes, by the law of recoils, she becomes the complement of her own complementariness."

Ord grinned broadly. The husk of Knarf's sententiousness also split in a wide grin.

"What I was going to ask is," said Ord, "Is Shirley the little girl in the train with the fat mother and aunt who saw Ally beat Jackie before Ben was born?"

"Yes."

"Well, how in the name of fortune do you expect the ordinary reader to remember that?"

"I don't. It isn't important. If they do remember, that's all right; if they don't, that's all right too. It's this way. There are many characters in this book, they recur and recur. It saves me inventing new people all the time. Even if the reader can't place them, they are sure to have left a trace in his mind from their last appearance. Most of the time it isn't important who they are, they are people talking, acting, living. They are the background. They are the universal texture of living. It's as if I pushed my oar into the mesh of a submerged net and dragged it to the surface. Life's an endless reticulation. I'm not aiming at a pattern. A pattern is jejune and naive."

"How do you know the reader is going to play your game? He'll probably run round in circles looking for the plot and feel disgruntled because he doesn't find it."

Knarf passed his hand across his forehead. "He probably will. I cannot postulate the reader. I'm not responsible for him. He is not my business."

"But the reader is your business. What is the good of going to all this trouble, compiling this mountain of words, if you are going to retire into some writers' cult where they can't follow you? Like going to a party and sitting it out in the lavatory. And why should you choose the very moment when you are using a pattern to tell me you scorn it? Something on both ways, as the ancients used to say?"

This was no new contention between them. Knarf assumed the patient expression of a man determined to pursue an argument to the bitter end. It was, he knew, his indefensible stigmatisation of pattern as jejune, which even to his own ears rang false, and not the main contention that had aroused Ord.

"You," he said, "as historian and archæologist, unearth a heap of rubble. Every shard is, I agree, for the sake of argument, authentic, but the whole is still a heap of rubble, and as such remains the preserve of historians and archæologists. To replace its original significance you must reconstruct. You can do so in a brick-by-brick disquisition that no one, except another archæologist, looking for stones to throw at you, is likely to read. Communication is not necessarily achieved by being meticulously accurate."

"It is not achieved by being inaccurate or by device and manipulation."

"I didn't say so. You contend that there is only one legitimate approach, and that that is through the canons of exact scholarship. I contend that imaginative reconstruction is equally valid, and, as a means of communication, more potent. It is a method of shaping chaos so that it becomes assimilable to the human mind. Fiction does not claim to be anything but a vestment, an image or a fantasia on a given theme. As such, it is as genuine a means of communication as, shall we say, an equation, there being three sides to communication, the infallible, irrefragable truth, which, as far as history is concerned, is out of reach, the conditioned recipient, the conditioned purveyor. . . ."

"Stop," said Ord, flapping his hands as if to ward off a swarm of insects. "I make an innocent comment and you deluge me with your platitudinous sophistries. My friend, when you leave your own domain your mind becomes pure clag to the bottom."

"Your mind is full of basic confusions—you confuse insult with argument, and the canons of historical research with the canons of fiction, you ignore the subjective element of truth. For the sake of clarity, and to get the desired effect economically, I use and reuse the same characters instead of creating new ones. You say I rely too much on coincidence, that life does not break in that repetitive pattern, I am falsifying it."

"I do not remember saying that, I don't object to that particular device—I think it is a humane one. If I challenged anything, it was your general attitude to your raw material—let us say fact, not truth—something for you to play with and twist to suit yourself, and towards which you then have assumed an attitude of intolerable proprietorship."

Knarf looked up quickly. "I've had to do a lot of that, and not in the way you suggest. I've had to do it. Not here, but further on, I've manipulated time. I've pressed events closer together than they actually were. Something had to go, and time was the expendable. The phase I wanted ran to more than the lifetime of my characters. To keep time extended meant to break every link of interest and emotion that I had forged, to break the image that focussed the whole period. Can't you see the leakage of power that would result if I started off a new generation two-thirds of the way through the book? If I used this form it was incumbent on me to make it cogent. At this distance, time has dwindled, it is a colourless substance. To telescope it makes little actual difference, since history has already discarded great swathes of it. To spin out time which contains no new element is not to increase but to decrease verisimilitude. The angle of vision has to be taken into account—just as the sculptor, carving statues for a plinth, must allow for the angle of vision."

"What have you done?"

"I've taken a pleat in time. I have kept events to the order of events, but I have brought them closer to one another. The uneasy years between World Wars II and III, since they yielded little except uncertainty, I have dwindled down. They were one and the same war divided into two parts by a truce and a reshuffling. The pestilence was later than I set it, the fall of the City, about twenty years later. I have, I admit, crystallised the turbidity, I have given sharper outline to events that are in doubt. The bombing of Sydney, for instance, that's wrapped in obscurity—nobody knows now what happened on that night. Some accounts say that the city was shelled from the sea, others that shipping was attacked within the harbour with great loss of life, others that the bombing was from the air. I could only use one version, so I took the version that seemed, after all, the most likely."

"Sorry for the red herring. What happened to Shirley?"

"Oh, she married her cousin."   .

"The boy on the train?"

.    .    .    .    .    .    .    .    .    .

"Yes. She came in one Saturday when Beryl and Gwen were both at home and told them. She stood in the centre of the room, swinging her hat, and brought it out. She'd always rather made fun of this cousin to them. They stopped in the middle of what they were doing and stared at her.

"We used to fight awfully when we were kids," she said, "but I'm used to him. It's better than fighting with someone you don't know. Mum and Auntie Tib want it. He's doing quite well so I guess I'll be all right. I'm fed to the teeth with this life."

She had never been so close to sincerity. It left the other girls speechless. They felt the huge gulf between themselves and Shirley. A week later she gave up her job and went home to get ready for her wedding. The room was too expensive for Beryl and Gwen. Beryl got a chance of going in with another girl from the beauty parlour where she worked, and so in a week the rootless little establishment was broken up and Gwen was looking for a room. She got one, the sort of room a girl earning her money did get, in one of the crowded areas off Taylor Square. She was excited about having a place of her own. "Our home" she called it to Harry. She asked him to come to tea the second night she was there, and strained every nerve to make the occasion a success, but it fell flat. The room was cramped and sordid; a big building next door shut out the daylight. The block was infused with a rank life from which Gwen shrank. Harry was

repelled by the place and could not disguise his feelings. He wanted
something better for Gwen. He wanted to give it to her but could
not. He might have drawn on the £200 and helped her with the
rent, but it was their sheet anchor. He said nothing, but he felt
gloomy. When he had gone Gwen was overcome with horror and
flung herself crying on her rumpled bed. She hated the place, she
hated Harry even, she wanted to be safe and happy. She caught a
glimpse of her smudgy romance and felt utterly lost and alone. It
was a mood, and though robust it passed. The next morning, when
she saw Harry in his uniform coming towards her, her heart smote
her. She loved him. She'd give up everything for him. Shaken, she
crept back into her dream. Her demands upon him grew. Against
reason, his heart betrayed him. She was his second dawn. They had
their moments of happiness, snatched, ecstatic. Very few people,
Harry knew, had as much as that.

The inevitable thing happened. He was waiting for Gwen one
evening in a doorway a few yards up the street from the store entrance.
It was raining and the pavements were crowded. He was reminded
of their first evening, the night of the storm. He saw Gwen coming
towards him, hurrying, her face flushed and happy. A couple of paces
behind her he saw Ruth. Gwen came straight to him, slipped her
hand into his arm and looked up at him with an unmistakable
gesture. He stiffened as he always did in a moment of crisis. He knew
that Ruth had read the little scene. She went past them without
slackening her pace. He saw her borne away in the crowd. He must
go after her. That necessity overrode all other considerations.

"I can't stay tonight, Gwen . . . have to get home."

She wanted to argue, he cut her short and left her.

He caught sight of Ruth again at the corner of King Street. She
did not try to board the crowded trams, but turned her face up the
hill into the rain. She was walking fast, head down. The collar of
her old coat was turned up against the rain.

"Ruthie."

She ducked away from him to avoid a string of umbrellas.

"Ruthie, stop."

She kept on. He was beside her now and could hear her panting.
He tried to take her arm, but she shrugged it out of his grasp.

"You've got to listen," he said harshly. He didn't know what he
was going to say to her. They had turned to the ascent of the William

Street hill, and her pace slackened, whether because she was tiring or out of willingness to listen to him, he didn't know.

"So it's true what they've been saying in the dressing-room." She might have been sobbing or only panting.

"Not the way they've said it. You don't understand."

"Yes, I do."

She started off again, faster. Girls always sided with their mothers, it was only natural. A moment ago he had wanted to shake her, now he didn't. He thought instead of the many times they had walked together, looking in shop windows or idling with the crowd along the tree-lined streets, of the companionship they had had. He'd spoilt that now, she was hating him. He thought of Ben, too, what a decent little nipper he had always been and how he used to collect cigarette ends for him in the bad days of the depression. He'd got out of touch with Ben too. And there was the £200. Wanda could have been apprenticed. They could all have had a good time with the money, and then if things had busted up they'd at least have had something. He thought of Jackie and the way he'd been let down, he could only think of his death like that. His children had had a raw deal, he'd not done much for them. All he'd had to give them, £200 and his attention, he'd given elsewhere. His heart was raw under the thought.

Ruth was thinking too of the evenings she had spent with her father. It had been nice. He hadn't known what she was thinking, but it had helped, being with him, and now the scorching thought ran through her mind that he hadn't been with her at all, he'd been thinking all the time of that girl.

Harry wanted desperately to save something. He began again.

"When you're older, Ruth . . ."

She wouldn't have that one. She cut him short.

"I'm not going to tell, if that's what you're scared of." He wanted to say, "I'm not. It's you I'm thinking about. I love you too, Ruth. You're precious to me. I haven't really forgotten you. It's different, and I want you to try to forgive me." That was what he wanted to say, but it was impossible. He couldn't get it out.

"Look here. D'you think it's been all roses for me? I want to get something out of life. You'll find out about that."

That was the wrong thing. They were turning into their street now. It was too late. She walked into the house, head up, in front of him. Ally didn't seem to notice anything, Wanda was in too much of a hurry, and Ben wasn't in yet. The evening meal wasn't more taciturn than usual. Once Ruth glanced covertly from her father to her mother. *That* didn't worry her, it didn't seem to matter. She knew well enough how it was between them. It was something else that left her with a sense of shock, hurt and angry, something to do with herself. It wasn't fair. He'd had his turn. Now it was hers, but—he had and she hadn't. It was a sort of betrayal, an unnatural competition between the generations. He wasn't her father at all, he was a man, just any man. In their crowded rooms, with the rain pouring outside, she had no escape. Once she looked at Harry. "He was happy and I've made him miserable," she thought, Thoughts she did not recognise turned and turned in her mind. Ruth went to bed and lay awake. She felt herself a battleground of unknown forces. She yielded, gave herself up, cried silently into her pillow until her whole body felt sodden. Then she lay quiet, exhausted, a door seemed to open in her mind. "It isn't all over at once," she thought. Life gave you other chances.

Harry refused to think. His spirit revolted against the whole situation. He went obstinately to sleep. He dreamed that a great hand came down out of the sky and began picking up buildings and dropping them into a bucket. People swarmed out like ants. With a coarse and homely gesture the hand wiped the edge of the bucket. Harry woke. He felt as if he had been asleep for a very long time and that while he slept something had happened. The rain had stopped, the street light burned indefatigable and meaningless, all-seeing, naught-comprehending, municipal eyes. Christ, he thought, the end of the world wouldn't look much different. Holding his alarm clock so that the light of the street lamp fell on its face, he read the time, twenty-five minutes past two. His dream oppressed him. The casualness of the big hand smearing the edge of the bucket took away all hope and dignity. There was going to be war. Let it come. Let it wipe out the whole bleeding lot, all the cramped and crowded houses in the narrow streets, the big shiny places and the walled gardens, the shop and the elevator and the big bosoms. It could take the lot and after the first shock no one would be any worse off. He looked at Ben sleeping in the other stretcher, the unmoving light fell across him in a broad band but he slept tranquilly. If it went out he'd probably waken. If you took Benny into the country he'd be miserable, he wouldn't know what to do with himself. He wanted to leave school but he didn't want a job, wanted to sell papers, foot-loose, end up like old Rumpty. Old Rumpty was big business in a very small way. That's what Ben wanted. Give him anything there was and he wouldn't know what to do with it, he'd only muck it up and waste it. What would come to the world if that was the only way for most boys to grow up? You're getting old, he said to himself. He lay down, turned his back on the light, hunched himself under the sheets and at least pretended to sleep. To Ben, opening one eye, he looked like a craggy bulwark, always there. Ben went to sleep again.

The year climbed out of winter. The winds came in August. The country was very dry. There had been a drought on the catchment area for five years and now there was talk of water restrictions in the city. People shrugged and blamed the government. They thought of it as a political rather than a natural phenomenon. There was a catch in it somewhere, a bit of political dirty work.

"I'll use all the water I want," said Mrs Nelson, "I've a right to it and I'll use it. They charge you water rates and then say don't use the water. It's like their impertinence." Nearly everyone agreed with her.

The drought would have occupied more attention if it had not been for the international situation. Austria and Czechoslovakia had fallen, bloodily bloodless, to Hitler. Now the spotlight was on Poland. The Russian alliance had dangled out of reach. The people watched the situation wax and wane. To them it was a gigantic game of chance, a world roulette. If the Russian alliance didn't come off it was bad luck, a gamble that didn't come off. They watched tensely to see where the hammer would fall. The effort of facing the logic of events was beyond them. Their minds, for the most part, were as helpless as their bodies in the face of impending catastrophe.

"There's not going to be war," the bandsman declared. "Don't you believe it. Hitler's not such a mug he'd go to war for Poland. Bluff's his game."

"Sure we'll have war," said Sid Warren, leaning on the bar, "but it won't be the right sort of war. When a pair of gangsters start fighting no one gets anything. When I fight I want to fight for something."

"Ah," said Timmy Andrews, who had palled up with him, "We got to dispose of the Nazis first, get rid of them and then we can have the Revolution."

"Got your hands full, ain't yer?" said the barman with a grin.

"I don't want to get popped off in an imperialist war before I get round to the Revolution."

"Got to take your luck, Siddy boy. I'm over age, but you're just nice, just like they want 'em." The barman winked at Sid.

Arch said to Don in the mess, "It looks like a show this time. And we're going to have a front seat."

"On top of the world, old man." And he began to whistle "All God's Chillun got Wings."

Paula listened to Bowmaker talking. War and Peace. War didn't solve anything, war was all evil. Peace was the world's first necessity, to refuse war the greatest moral triumph. If the people . . . the people had nothing to gain by war. . . . Women who knew the value of life because they bore the children. . . . The Prince of Peace. . . . If one made sacrifices for peace comparable to the sacrifices of war. . . .

Her heart swelled. The world in extremis and a sovereign cause, large enough to be worth any sacrifice. She was sure it was what she was looking for. After the meeting she waited for the speaker, her eyes shining. "Bowie," she said, "give me something to do. I'm free and I'm ready to do anything for the cause. I'd die for it if that was the only way."

She waited. He looked at her steadily, the dogged gaze of the tired man. "Are you even willing to learn?" he asked.

Everything went on the same, fear and uncertainty mixed subtly with daily life. It came to the surface in irritation. Faster and faster Ben's feet beat on the pavement of the Cross, getting rid of the Final Extras. "We'll sell plenty of papers if there's a war, won't we?" he said to Rumpty. "There've been wars before," said Rumpty, "and there'll be wars again, but I don't know but what a good murder doesn't get an edition off faster. The public has the fun without the responsibility."

The news reached the streets as the crowds were going to the theatres. Everything was as usual, and then the first placard, the first reading of headlines. From every corner where papers were sold, silence spread. Everyone stood still. Through the silence came the sound of bare feet running and the strident voices of the newsboys, "Poland Invaded," "War." The wireless was pouring out the same story in thousands of houses, flats, and rooms. A city full of people stopped to listen. It was something you could feel, like the stopping of a great heart. After the first shock they went about their business and pleasure. The picture theatres filled. The war was still fifteen thousand miles away, but it had come. This was the third of September 1939.

# SYMPOSIUM

Lin gathered together her anger till it was as hard and compact as a stone in her hand. Knarf had made no attempt to come down and greet his guests. All the morning he had been in his pavilion with Ord, talking, talking, as if this were an ordinary day and he had no responsibilities. Now the meal could wait no longer and she would go up and tell him. She was ashamed that everyone should know how he behaved. Sfax and a dark middle-aged man were crossing the square now. That would be Oran. Someone had waylaid them, but they would be here any moment now. Lin mounted the stairs. She didn't hear voices. They were both in the pavilion, not even talking, Ord sunk down in his chair, his thick hands on his knees, his jaw thrust out, looking, as he looked in moments of intense speculation, morose and obstinate. Knarf was sitting at the table, one hand shading his face, the other resting on a pile of manuscript. There were papers strewn round his feet.

She said, without any pretence at greeting, "Your friends are here, Knarf. You know I cannot entertain them. And the meal is ready." If Ord were such a close friend she could speak plainly before him.

They both stood up and Knarf said quietly, "I'm sorry, Lin. I meant to come down early but I forgot the time."

Ord was pretending to take her part, as he often did, standing up smiling. "He's a terrible man, Lin. None of us would put up with him if he weren't a genius. I must apologise, too. I looked for you when I came in, but I could not find you."

"I was busy."

"Of course. I brought a few things from the farm. As there was no one about I put them down in the courtyard."

"Thank you."

She crossed to the parapet to see if Sfax and Oran were still in the square. They were, standing in the sun, the centre of a little group. It would be a chance to get Oran to take an interest in Ren. But that wouldn't occur to Knarf, and she didn't know how to set about it herself. It was a lovely day, she hadn't had a chance even to look at it till now. People were picnicking on the river bank. There must be a couple of thousand people in the Centre. It was murmuring like a drowsy beehive in the sun.

The two men were waiting for her to precede them down the stairs. There was no stone in her hand now. It had melted and she was unarmed. She had been abrupt and awkward. They made her feel like that, but it wasn't her true self. She wondered if it were true what Ord said about Knarf. You couldn't tell with Ord; if he mocked when he was most serious, he also said what he really meant sometimes as if it were a jest. She wouldn't dislike him so much if he didn't confuse her. If it were true, if this book of Knarf's were really important, then all her sacrifice would not have been in vain.

Under an awning a long table had been laid in the courtyard, and Knarf paused to look at it with a quick sense of pleasure. There is something basic in the beauty of food. There were baskets of deep brown varnished rolls, some sweet and some savoury, flavoured with the good bitter herbs of the countryside. There were cheeses, white, brown, pale yellow, marbled green; platters of poultry, whole birds, steamed and roasted, wrapped in lettuce leaves and so tender that they would fall apart easily in the fingers; shelled eggs in a bed of dark green cress; bowls of dark honey in the comb, tasting of gum blossoms; thin crisp cakes tasting of ginger and cinnamon; black grapes; pyramids of persimmons, translucent with ripeness; wine in transparent cups; a beaker of milk sweetened with honey for the children. He wanted to tell Lin how good it was, but she was no longer beside him. He crossed the waiting courtyard to the vestibule where the guests were assembled. Oran and Sfax had joined them and there was a hum of conversation. Ren was going from guest to guest with a brass bowl of hot water and the long ceremonial towel over his arm. He looked very young and serious as he passed from guest to guest, performing his duty with grave courtesy. They touched the water with their fingertips and touched the towel. There was no purpose in it, but it was pleasant to watch Ren. He made of it not a perfunctory custom but a ritual, not because his mind subscribed to it, but because in all his contacts with people he was friendly and generous. The washing of hands was probably the vestige of some ancient sacrament, and a trace of its sincerity survived, running underground and yet informing the action, when a boy like Ren was its minister. When life was lived simply, it fell naturally into the folds of ritual. Knarf was still wrapped in the world of his book, so that the scene about him was like a picture, framed in time, more discrete than the action about us usually appears. It made him feel powerful, lonely, and more like an actor than a participant. For a second or two nobody noticed him, standing in the doorway. Then Sfax, assured and smiling, came towards him, bringing Oran, the important guest, to his host.

The guests willingly filed into the courtyard and took their places without ceremony at the table. There were seventeen in all, twelve men and five women. The conversation which had begun in the anteroom scarcely suffered a break. It had already developed a tempo, because the occasion had focussed men's minds and because all these people, except Oran and Sfax, were accustomed to meeting one another and talking interminably. Their minds were adjusted and discussion was a pleasure to them, like eating. It was a game of chance with set moves, but also a game of chance in which they risked themselves in small stakes. If the afternoon's vote had been their first interest, they had gone beyond it into the wide country of speculation and philosophic enquiry.

An old man, Avik, with a long thin neck, bright eyes in a weathered face, indefatigable, kindly, inordinately fond of talking, was making a leisurely sweep through history, as he gathered on to his plate, with an almost equal concentration, all the food he proposed to eat during the meal. It was selected, like his ideas, with pleasure, care, and moderation, and also with a civilised forethought and fullness which did not chance disappointment.

"During historical times," he was saying, "man has made four great conquests. Each arose out of what you might call a ferment of the composite human will, a slow process and natural only in the secondary sense."

He paused, weighing in his hand a persimmon, heavy with its saturated ripeness, as if it were a world. "The natural law is inevitable, and, if you know all the factors, completely predictable. Into this plain process man has brought a variable, an unreliable ferment, his will, intention, or whatever you like to call it. Will must have begun first as a sport or aberration, a minute flaw gradually enlarged until it became a factor in the whole process, and, this is the point, an unreasonable, variable, imponderable factor. Will was undoubtedly a perversion by which the human organism slipped out of mesh with its environment."

Oran, with slightly raised eyebrows, helped himself resignedly to food. In the provinces, he thought . . .

"That it *could* happen was its justification. That it *did* happen is the nexus by which it is joined to primal law. You see, tangential yet joined. The calf with two heads from whom a whole herd descended. Man has invented his own sense of direction. Slowly and blindly he gropes his way along it, instead of, like the rabbit, going the broad and, for the rabbit, inevitable way of nature. Man has introduced elasticity, and by his will he has made himself a destiny, and a great many tribulations that are not in nature. He has imported something into life and, being there, its results are slowly working themselves out. The immense cumbersomeness of man's way of life is part of it, the mass of fallible machinery that he requires to live at all, the huge and terrible superstructure that he has built upon his primary needs which might, without the intervention of his will, have been so easily satisfied, all part of the same process."

"You promised us history," said Ord, "but you unfairly keep us floundering in prehistoric chaos where we cannot even reach you to confound you. What were the four conquests? I cannot bear the suspense." Everyone laughed.

"I am coming to that," replied the old man amiably. "There is no knowledge without patience, and to state a thesis without at least indicating its logical basis is a barbarism insulting to civilised company. I was merely pointing out—a truism, I know—that man is capable of conquest, whereas the far more successful and better adjusted ant is not, because he has introduced an ingredient peculiarly his own into the scheme of the natural law. This aberration, once started and logical in its illogic, created a new set of divergent circumstances, and, out of the same quality, man has sought to dominate them."

A girl with a thin intelligent face said, "We have created an illusion and have left the solid earth to live in it. Enclosed in our fairy tale, we invent magic to combat fact and sometimes we succeed. Is that it, Avik?"

He beamed at her. "You put it with your usual acumen and grace, Illil, but you are a romantic. That is only natural, for you are young and still in the poet phase. Eight hundred years ago a poet, usually called the Bard, from which I deduce that he was not a single man but a composite of folk phenomena, said the same thing. 'We are such stuff as dreams are made on. . . .' But I digress. It would be more scientific to say we live, not in the natural world, but in an approximation, a tilted world of our own invention, yet real because it has become an ingredient in our evolution. It is our natural environment, though not *the* natural environment. It is real because operative. To keep in touch with our environment the whole scale of our values is approximate." He looked round hopefully, like a conjurer who has produced a rabbit.

"The salt, Avik," said Ren, passing it to him.

"The conquests?" asked Ord. "Are we coming to them? I like a little action."

"Yes, yes. Having created himself a world, man has had a long uphill struggle to make it habitable. Having made artificial conditions, he has had to counter them, and he has gradually, in a slow, puzzle-headed way, worked out a way of living. There have been four great steps. First the substitution of indirect for direct action, that is, the raising of life from an individual to a consciously communal basis, co-operation, delegated power, law and laws."

"The displacement of violence in private life," interposed a red-faced man of about fifty, who looked as if he wanted to get out and push.

"The *approximate* displacement, the birth of a concept and its partial application. If man has a will to control, he also has a will to be controlled. Secondly, the conquest of scarcity. The first victory was very slow, subjective, and partial, the second, which came in the nineteenth century, was rapid, objective, and complete. Interference with the natural law of survival made this revolution a crucial necessity. It was the next step in front of man and he took it. He decreed a higher survival rate than nature, so he had to provide for the survivors. A phenomenal technical development answered the question. By the twentieth century humanity was in a position to feed, clothe, house, and generally maintain itself. It was safe, or it could have been safe. Material plenty was achieved."

"That," said a quiet man, "was the very moment when the old world started in earnest to disintegrate."

"Certainly," said Avik, "and I'll tell you why."

"I know why," said the quiet man.

"It was a time of collision between two worlds—the natural world and the one humanity was making for itself. Scarcity was conquered, but the law of the wild continued, the natural law of Survive-who-can. In the natural world there was health in competition. It eliminated the unfit. Well, that's one view of it. Now it became a terrible and abnormal thing. It tapped new sources of power, and it subjugated rather than eliminated. Competition and its doctrine of profit ravaged the world. It seized the benefits of man's invention and turned them into power. The world became charged with such social power as never before."

"Now you're coming to a place where I can follow you," said Ord.

"Competition was quite a mild and self-cancelling thing beside monopoly."

"Monopoly was competition on another plane," said the quiet man. "The units were larger, that is all, the armed few against the unarmed many, class against class and nation against nation."

"You're right," said Ord, "a sort of inflammation that spread to every part of the body politic,"

"It wasn't anything new," said Knarf, "but something that had always been there, abnormally produced."

"All the forms of competition co-existed, fed by the discoveries that should have released the world," said the quiet man, seeming quieter than ever. "All against all, as well as the pitting of gigantic interests against one another. All under the triumphant sign of the Double Cross."

"Competition, distortion, violence, war, total war, civil war, exhaustion, blackout." Illil spoke in a sort of litany.

"We are all historians today," said Ord, laughing at her. "I am still waiting for the triumph of man." He looked at Knarf, but Knarf was not to be drawn. He had no wish to enter the discussion which seemed to him stilted and academic, a red herring drawn across the trail of his preoccupation.

The quiet man said, "Those days had stature." There was a faint vibration in his voice. "A world foaming itself away in despair, a black epic of death, a synthesis in confusion. Last stands for their own sake. Nine men out of every ten fanatics."

"And we bred from the tenth, the onlooker. Today, a world full of onlookers."

"A phantasmagoria."

"Hell to live in."

"It was all so long ago," said a woman's voice, quite clearly, at the other end of the table.

"Then the reaction—the impetus spent, everything spent. The morning after death on the grand scale, with nothing to eat and the props covered in dust. The population melted down to half, didn't it? And the birth rate fell and fell until at last life found its sticking point."

"Men no longer resisted life, they reached a dead level of apathy."

"The only people who had anything to offer were the technicians and scientists, the remnants of them."

"And therefore they were the only ones with any driving will to live in them."

"The cold pale dawn of the Age of Reason."

"Not reason, Science."

"If there's any difference, I don't see it," said Sfax.

"Politics were anathema. The theory of the economic state. The slogan 'Butter and Peace.' The deification of facts and food."

"And so," said the red-faced man, "there began a new cycle of power."

Avik had vainly struggled to get back into his own argument.

"As I was saying . . ." he began.

The tension of the party relaxed, people began to talk quietly in little groups. Lin thought, "How they talk—and how they eat." The table, which a quarter of an hour ago had been a beautiful set piece, was now plundered and untidy. She was not one of those women who win a sense of fulfilment from feeding people. She was irritated by the wreck of her handiwork. In particular Oran's hands offended her as they fumbled, dark, hairy, and coarse, among the lettuce leaves, tearing apart, without even looking at them, the delicate white flesh and frail, almost transparent, bones of a chicken. A rat on the table would not have been uglier or less appreciative. She stifled the thought. Oran was an important man, and if they played their cards well today he might be willing to do something for Ren next year, get him into one of the more favoured branches of work from which he would be much more likely to progress into the permanent service later. Everyone knew that, despite the tests, these things went by favour. Only it was something you couldn't prove. Clever boys might be set digging irrigation trenches and kept at it through their whole compulsory social service, far from the schools and all the advantages that would help them to make the grade at the end of the service, while dolts went into the Technical Bureau as cadets straight away. If you protested, you were rebuked for seeking favours where none was given. If you still persisted, you might in the end get an interview with the Director of Vocations, and he would have your son's test card brought to you out of the files, so that you might satisfy yourself that he had been scientifically graded to his work, but all you would see would be a string of figures, quite incomprehensible. The official stylus would point, "You see there is a deficiency here. . . . Certain temperamental idiosyncrasies. . . . We have, of course, to take the medical chart into consideration also. . . . Believe me your son is best where he is, best for himself and for society . . . thousands of young people pass through our hands every year, the rules must be rigidly applied and only scientific considerations can be admitted. . . . All work is equally useful and honourable. He will have another chance later."

Later was too late. It was an anxious time for mothers when children set out in the world, everything depended on favour or chance. Lin didn't believe in scientific measurement. Patronage was something she did understand. She didn't suppose it was right but it worked. It had to work for Ren, nothing mattered so long as he got his chance. Her will, woody and acrid, infused her mind with obstinacy. Oran could have hands like rats, and legs like a goat for the matter of that; he was influential and his coming here must be turned to advantage for Ren. Knarf should be paying him more attention. But Knarf was preoccupied, taciturn. He could be so different, charming and brilliant, if only he would exert himself. But he never did when there was any advantage in it. He was the most infuriating man in the world. Lin looked from her husband to her son, from her son to her husband, and wondered, with bitter curiosity, what she really felt about them. For years she had told herself that she loved Knarf, and sometimes even now, when she saw him suddenly—his grave sensitive face, his unexpected friendly smile, his gentle reassuring hands—her heart turned to water. But her love for him had been a blind alley, leading neither to joy nor to tragedy, only to a dull beating imprisoned pain. They never came close to one another, in their lives or in Ren. Then she had told herself that she hated him, but that led nowhere either, was just as impotent. Now she didn't know. As for Ren, if she didn't love her son, she had nothing at all. Love was battling for the loved one, and not caring what happened to anyone else. No good battling for Knarf, he didn't want any help, ever, in any way. If Knarf weren't going to speak to Oran about Ren, she would. The thought stiffened her limbs with nervousness and dragged at the corners of her mouth. She hoped Ren would do something to distinguish himself today. She doubted if the man would notice his intelligence, seriousness, and young charm unless he were jogged into it.

Avik was winding his long argument to a close. He had dealt with his last two conquests of man, distribution—"the equitable organization and distribution of the fruits of production"—and the establishment of world peace through the world federation of economic non-national states "each composed of a number of cells or communes," the two movements interdependent and coexistent.

"Thank you, Avik," said Ord, "now we have the millennium."

"No," said Ren sharply.

"What do you lack?" asked Oran, pausing to stare at the boy.

"Liberty." The word was like a catalyst.

"The boy's right. Avik's last two conquests arose out of exhaustion. They have never been consolidated in public will."

"They can't be consolidated without liberty. Without that they are only imposed from without, they aren't a part of us at all," said Ren, speaking very quietly but with bright eyes.

The quiet man said, "Society has reached, or is quickly reaching, a state of saturation. The machine dominates society and can do nothing but repeat itself. The individual has more leisure than he can utilise. Like anything that ceases to be useful it is now a menace. It drags us down, as unemployment did once, it unfits men for living. Whenever the material side of life outstrips the spiritual, there is trouble. We're in a dead end now."

Illil said, and it was obvious that she was one of Ren's allies, "Circumstance has concentrated power in the hands of a few. The ruling class is in theory recruited from the whole population, but in reality it becomes more and more a closed body. Power is having the effect upon its holders that it always had. It becomes an end in itself and a source of tyranny." She stopped, a little breathless.

Ren beat lightly upon the table, his face alight.

"The power must be diluted before it destroys us," he said. "It can be diluted by the will of the people speaking through a council. The machines can't cater for the whole of life. There is a side in us all that is being stifled. Many of us not only want, but need, fuller and more responsible lives. It's the beginning of liberty to be able to say so and to have the right to work to that end. But liberty," he said faltering, coming down suddenly from his soapbox, "isn't just something useful. It's bigger than that. It's like vitamins in our food. Something we need to be healthy. Lots of young people think like that."

Oran was smiling and nodding his head, not in agreement, but rather as if he were noting all that was being said. He was the darkest man in the room and he seemed the biggest. Like a dark stroke on a bright canvas, like an obelisk in a sunny field, thought Knarf.

"Liberty," said a man who had not spoken before, "is something that never has existed and never will. The idea of it is a sort of recurrent fever to which mankind is prone. It's a pipe to carry off his vain aspirations, something he uses to fool himself when he is too lazy to use his brains. I'll tell you something, young man, this phantom liberty never comes alone, it has a partner, violence. Look at history. When men raise the cry of Liberty, they are always ready to fight for it. That's logical. Loose, heady thinking leads to loose heady action, which is a substitute for logical thinking and rational planning, the easy way drives out the hard way, and only the hard way, our way, is any good in the long run. Liberty is poetry, and it intoxicates worse than wine."

"Youth is the time of poetry," said Avik, beaming fatuously. Oil on troubled waters, applied with the medicine dropper.

"Nobody wants violence," cried Ren. "It's something we've outgrown. Forever."

"It's not a matter of wanting, it's cause and effect. Certain types of thinking lead to certain types of action. No human trait is ever lost, it is only submerged by circumstances. Change the circumstance again and the old attributes will crop up. Isn't that what you say, Knarf? That every man has the qualities of all men, and that it is only environment and circumstance that develop some and suppress others? Individually and communally we are still capable of repeating everything that has happened in the past. Nothing is outgrown forever."

"Yes, it is what I believe, and so this troubler, Liberty, is not outgrown, and it is something which cannot be destroyed and will come again and again, until it is fulfilled and built into life. Nor can I believe it will of itself lead to any recrudescence of violence. This time it will occur in a new context. Also I think if you look more closely at history, you will see that liberty and violence are not linked together, but that if they occur often in the same period, it is because violence is invoked against liberty. It is oppression and violence that hunt in couples. What is will always fear what is not. It is fear that makes violence and the present always fears the future."

The red-faced man was waiting his opportunity. "The greatest forward step humanity has ever taken was the renunciation of ' violence. But, as I pointed out before, it occurred through exhaustion and has never been consolidated by will. We are no longer exhausted, speaking in world terms. So we approach again the danger zone."

Knarf thought, "Bude does not know which side he is on. He believes thinking is safe." Aloud he said:

"In a period of world exhaustion a shift of power took place. At first its action was benevolent because it was doing a job of work and had an objective outside itself. As it reached accomplishment it became its own objective, power for the maintenance of power, the present embattled against the future, the glorification of the status quo."

Ren was quick to follow on. "The status quo is only a fiction. It's a door slammed in the face of life. It's a sort of violence to try to make life stand still."

"It isn't true," said Illil, "that we have got rid of violence. Violence isn't only wounding and killing people. It can just as well be the ruthless use of power in any context and by any means. We've got it here and now. Ask in the workshops, look and listen in the factories. I've done three years of my compulsory social service. I know. We are kept in a prison of glass. None of us dares have a will of our own, or protest when we catch a glimpse of how corrupt things really are. We'd lose our chance of making the grade and getting into the ruling class if we did. If we do make the grade, well, we go over to them. If they weren't sure, we wouldn't make it. And if we don't—well, after eight years of holding our tongues, we go on holding them. We have to, to save face. Slow, cold, scientific violence."

"So," thought Oran. "So," and he turned his slow heavy regard from the girl, to Ren, to Knarf. They were the ones who mattered here. The others were—just packing. The girl would probably find her own level, they usually did, they flared up and then, when they got a man and a child or two, they fizzled out. The boy was of an age, and in a position to be disciplined, imperceptibly but no less surely. Not much could be done with Knarf except perhaps through the boy, but these middle-aged writers weren't usually formidable. Security had usually tamed them by that time. A trashy lot, but still he wasn't quite satisfied. If there was smoke in an outlying province like the 10th Commune, there was probably fire in some of the big Centres. He caught, or thought he caught, a vibration swelling under the words. Rebellion was a very curious thing, unreasonable, and this was just the sort of fodder it grew on. What the girl said was true enough, though she played a melodramatic light on it. There were constant manipulations and adjustments; you couldn't have scientific management of human beings without it. If you admitted the system you'd have to admit that. But these romantics thought they could have one without the other, a Utopia of incompatibles. If there were unrest there would be an answer to it. Somewhere in the vast labyrinth of the system there was always an answer. The romanticism that made people dangerous also made them vulnerable. Oran did not question his own loyalties; he never had, for he was an integral part of the system he administered and it of him. His ability did not waste itself in questioning or his will in doubt. He fitted his world so well that there was no seam between them. All this talk was only curious to him, but he realised it might be dangerous, and if it were, he was justified in any ruthlessness. He did not even have to think that, it was in his blood. He was not touched by any personal considerations at all, and neither Illil's epicene youth, Ren's bright charm, nor Knarf's fame in the world of letters, moved him. They were not even secondary considerations. He was here to make a test and he would make it calmly and carefully, as he might apply a thermometer to a bubbling liquid to ascertain its temperature. This boy and his friends in the movement probably thought they were making history, Sfax probably thought his gadget was going to change the face of the world. All these old fogies had come along like good citizens to register their votes. They were all a bit above themselves, slopping over with pomposity, because nothing ever happened in their quiet musty lives. None of them knew that this great occasion was nothing more than a little test conducted by the Technical Bureau for its own scientific reasons. He didn't believe that there was any public opinion. Today might yield some concrete data. It at least brought opinions to the surface. He was here to evaluate them. Marvellous how impenetrable people's vanity was, even to common sense. If Oran ever had any doubts at all, it was about the value of these people for whom so much was done. The great bright shining machine which he served with such pleasure in its mechanical efficiency had, as its avowed object, to keep alive and in comfort this soft-witted trash. The machine was for itself and whatever impeded it must go. If its own ultimate aim impeded it that must go.

Oran meant to sift a little deeper while he was about it. Looking at Ren, he began with a heavy irony he took no trouble to disguise.

"I'm a scientist and therefore ignorant. What is Liberty?"

Ren answered, remembering the morning, " 'Liberty therefore cannot help being a courage to resist the demands of power at some point that is deemed decisive, and, because of this, liberty also is an inescapable doctrine of contingent anarchy. . . . Where there is respect for reason there also is respect for freedom, and only respect for freedom can give final beauty to men's lives.' That isn't mine. A man in the old times, called Laski, said it."

Illil said, "Liberty is the right to direct or misdirect our own lives."

Knarf said, "Liberty is the plastic which prevents life from becoming a strait jacket."

Ord said, in his flat metallic voice, surprising everyone, "Liberty is the right to go on seeking the unattainable which is man's manifest destiny."

"A galaxy of epigrams," said Oran. There was a perverse smell about the whole thing, anything that gave rise to decadent phrase mongering was wrong at the root. "What do you say it is, Sfax?"

Sfax laughed uneasily. "I'm a technician. I only deal in facts."

"So," said Oran.

There was danger in the courtyard, not immediate but none the less real. It had come in like a ground mist, it was at their knees and rising higher. Everyone was aware of it, sharply or as a nebulous unease. Knarf thought quickly, "This man is dangerous. If Ren convinces him that there is something in this movement of his there will be trouble. It will strike softly and we won't see whence it comes. The damage is probably done now. Even if Oran doesn't think much of what has been said, and nothing very notable has been said, he'll smell the feeling there is behind it. It's bad tactics, Ren ought to have let Oran think the movement was negligible until at least they had some firm ground under their feet. But you couldn't expect that from a boy like Ren. Come to that, I threw the game away for the pleasure of standing by him. If it had come to playing tactics, we could never have been a match for Oran. He isn't bothering now, but he could outmanoeuvre us all if he wanted to. Tactics and gadgets aren't any good in the long run. The run might be so much longer than any of our lives. . . . Sfax sees how things are and he has scuttled back to safety. He won't come to any harm. He's today's ideal young man. He's clever enough to be useful, clever in the right way, shrewd enough to be careful and not bright enough to be dangerous. The Technical Bureau has a nose for young men like that. They only let in enough real brains to carry on the inner junta. Oran's one of the real brains. The rest are men like Sfax is going to be. Specialised brains, no imagination, specialised stupidity. A thousand times tougher than the old demagogic politicians could ever have been."

Knarf saw in a flash that Ren was committed for life to the course he had taken. Today had committed him to it, young as he was. Unjustly, unjustly. And he himself had not had the wit to save him from it. If Ren didn't go on with his movement, no matter what happened, become a leader of it in the face of any danger, he would have nothing. He could not expect a full life from the system now. A nineteen-year-old boy from a frontier commune was such a negligible quantity that he'd be brushed aside on a suspicion far fainter than today's showing. No redress. Ren must give up altogether or take the hard way. He had stood by Ren today, but it had been only a gesture, and a harmful one. Knarf had no illusions about the help he could give his son in the future. At forty-seven he could not make himself over miraculously into a fighter. Ren would have only himself and his comrades to depend on. Unless, perhaps, the book he had just written worked on people's imaginations, leavened them, and so, circuitously, made a track in the wilderness for Ren's feet. This was the very beginning of something. He wouldn't see the end of it, neither would Ren. The movement was nothing but a nebula yet, it would have to be hardened and shaped, it would take its long toll of sacrifices, and Ren would be one. Like a green field in the distance, Knarf saw the life his son might have had but for something which might have been, but now could not be, a transient youthful enthusiasm. His heart twisted with tenderness and pity. He looked across at Lin. The distress and anxiety she felt did not show in her face, only an intent expression. Bell without tongue.

The conversation had become an examination. Oran was harrying the boy, but Ren, although his colour was high, was not giving any ground. It might be a probe or it might be an attempt at intimidation and an effort to strip him of his arguments, discredit him in his own eyes, and so purge him of his nonsense.

Ren, of course, took the bait. He obviously thought that he had some chance of convincing this man; that, by answering him freely and honestly, he was benefiting the movement. Even his anger was generous, open, and trusting. Ord was watching him with kind sceptical eyes. Ren, he knew, was looking at the world with the eyes of a well-treated child. He believed that he only had to be reasonable and that people would be convinced, that they wanted the best for everyone. He was taken in by the thing he was blindly setting out to combat. Knarf wasn't much better. Thousands of people were like that because of the safe and glossy surface of life. That fair seeming was more effective than any propaganda. There was no nursery for rebels. The historic function of the movement would be to force from power an education in tactics. It must first bring out into the open that thing which it was going to fight. He had the same thought as Knarf. This is a beginning. He looked at Ren and in his mind measured the distance between the boy and a stone figure, the Brooding Anzac, that had been exhumed seven years ago out of the debris of the old city of Sydney, and that from the first time of seeing had been an integral part of his imagination. That distance was the via dolorosa between a world becalmed and a world in extremis. Must it come to that again before man could take another step in his evolutionary journey? Or was this evolution a circle like the natural circles of night and day, summer and winter, a tilted circle with part of the rim always dipped down towards darkness? Fatalists don't fight.

"What," Oran asked, "would you do with Liberty?"

"It is not a commodity. It is one of the means of life."

"You would do nothing with it? You would just possess it?"

"All men would share it."

"But it has no use?"

"It is a necessity."

"At present, however, the world is without it?"

"The spark never goes out. It is in our hearts, but it is being slowly blotted out of the visible world. The world must be brought into line with those needs again."

"Again? So we had it once?"

"In a few places and at a few times, men had liberty. In every age they have fought for it."

"It is necessary to fight for this liberty?"

"I should have said 'strive'."

"There is an old proverb, 'It is better to be going somewhere than to arrive.' It has been the fashion in every other era to strive for this unattained liberty, and so we must strive too. It is the tradition. There is something in our hearts that demands it just as a tickling in the throat demands a cough. Now perhaps I am beginning to understand you."

"No, sir, I do not think so."

Oran looked directly at Ren for a second before he spoke. "It is a mystic cult, then, and I am too old or too debauched by power to understand it."

Ren's hands clenched. "If you want to mock me, you have all the advantage."

Oran made a gesture as if he brushed away an obstacle, neither friendly nor angry. Sfax stood up. "If you will excuse me, I still have a lot of work to do." He addressed himself to Oran, not to Lin or Knarf.

"Since you are contributing nothing to this symposium," said Oran, "I am sure your host will excuse you."

Sfax jerked a little bow and turning on his heel went out. Ren's eyes followed him involuntarily. Oran turned again to Ren.

"I am giving you every opportunity to explain yourself. That is what you want, isn't it? That's why you have been canvassing the commune for the last two months instead of attending to your studies. Isn't it?"

So Oran knew that.

An old man who had come with Bude said in an aside to a neighbour, "He came to our farm. I was having my afternoon nap, but he talked to my wife, all of two hours it must have been. A great talker and very beautifully expressed, so she said, but what it was all about she had no idea. It wasn't anything she had heard before, so, while she understood it all right as long as he was talking, as soon

as he stopped she forgot it all. But she liked the boy. She liked everything about him, the way he smiled, the way his hair grew, the way
he ate up her cakes. Said he'd be just right for our Avda, and how
nice it would be if we could get Avda fixed up with someone before
she went to her compulsory social service, it steadied a girl, after
that you never knew." He gave a high senile titter. "I said I didn't
know that I wanted a son-in-law who talked so much and maybe he
had ideas into the bargain. But she said it was just boy's talk and
nothing to worry about. But I don't know. Looks to me as if he
really were bitten with something. Don't know how the sheep would
take to it, very conservative, they are." He tittered again as if he
had said something very witty.

But his companion knew there was sense in it too. She was a
large capable woman of the ruminative type, Bude's wife. She took
a practical view. "If the young people liked one another, and why
shouldn't they, it could be arranged very nicely. You've a farm and
that makes everything easier. If your own boy makes the grade, and
his mother was telling me only the other day how clever he is now,
you'll be wanting someone else on the place. You could adopt Ren,
couldn't you? Knarf has not a foot of land or anything else to hand
on to him. It would be a wonderful chance for the boy. Ren's a
good boy, he knows what's right, and if you fixed up an adoption
for the sake of the farm, he wouldn't look anywhere else for a wife."
She glowed with selfless pleasure. "You'd get value from Ren, he'd
be so grateful. He's the kind who would feel it most if he had no
place to go after his service. Avda's a sweet girl. As you say, you
never know when they go off to the Centres without anything
arranged. . . ."

The old man had turned peevish. "Don't rush me. Don't rush me.
All you women are the same."

The woman took no notice. "They wouldn't have any trouble
with the Health Department," she said flatteringly.

"Of course not. No one in our family's ever been refused a licence
to marry. Not that I know of."

"Nor ours either."

"Let's be practical," said Oran, "for after all it is only the practical
side of affairs that can concern me. What will liberty do for us if
we attain it?"

"It will make for general happiness."

"I have never yet met anyone who knew what happiness is. I do not know myself nor even if I am happy. It is something I have not time to think about."

"I would rather say fulfilment."

"But that is an entirely personal matter. The State—and the State is the only channel of public action—has nothing to do with that. It can only assure that every citizen will have security and an adequate share of the necessities. For the State to do more would be unjustified. It would mean interference in private life, the importation of controversial matter into a scientifically organized plan, and would end in disruption. You have not explained to me what liberty is. That is not your fault. Liberty is x, the unknown. No ten people will ever agree about it. Bring it into the fully rational field of state activities and you will at once have chaos. There was only one thing really wrong with the Old Days every one has been talking about. That was muddle. Loose ideas mixed with facts, no cohesion or co-ordination. because everyone thought and acted from unstable premises, and of course the results were confused and unexpected. Nobody could cope with them. Now the state is reduced to a few rational functions. It is in the hands of men of science recruited from the whole population, according to merit, scientifically assessed. Playing with ideas has become a marginal activity. Everyone, except the poor hard-worked devils in the Technical Bureau, has ample leisure for indulging in it. As a private activity I have nothing against it. It's not my business. It *is* my business, in collaboration with my colleagues, to keep society functioning along tried and tested lines, and not to endanger everybody's means of existence."

"The good life is more than the sum of facilities." Ren might not be able to cope with the argument, but his inner conviction still held.

"The good life! *This* is the good life. You have known no other. But I assure you life could be very different. If in the palmy days of liberty men could have had the life you have they would have thought it the millennium. It's so good, if you only knew it, that it makes these substitute ideas, such as liberty, unnecessary. It is the substance, that is the shadow. Fall in love with liberty if you want to, it is you who will have to marry her, not the state. But you have some other scheme for implementing this idea. You are not content with admiring liberty, are you? You want to take steps to bring it about in some more tangible form?"

Ren said doggedly, "You know what proposal is to be put to the commune this afternoon."

"Yes. The formation of an auxiliary non-technical council to put the case for the man-in-the-street when the Technical Bureau has to make public decisions."

"That is the first step."

"Only the first?"

"Yes. In itself it is nothing."

"So I thought."

"Public opinion cannot learn to function without functioning."

"You are suggesting as an improvement that unrelated opinion should be brought into specialised fields?"

"It is a fiction that government is specialised. A government of human beings by human beings cannot be. When you reduce the governed and the governing to two equations you get an idea which does not tally with fact."

Ren's getting a hold on things, thought Knarf. He isn't beaten. That no one had sought to interrupt this long duel was a product of Oran's natural force and authority.

"Government no longer tries to cover the whole human field. It has selected its proper province, material welfare. Everything else is controversial."

"So is that. It is an artificial restriction that prevents its being being overtly so."

"You make statements that are incapable of proof. In effect, you say that you have something better than reason to offer."

"You claim to have cornered reason."

"I, personally, claim nothing."

"There is a factor called public opinion."

"That remains to be proved."

"It will be proved this afternoon."

"It is never safe to assume the result of an experiment before you make it. This afternoon's test should be very interesting."

"There is a good deal of unrest and dissatisfaction. That must have some sort of answer."

"You assume that the answer would be to make government as muddled and unscientific as are the minds of the dissatisfied. You talk of this imponderable thing, public opinion, but your aim is to measure it scientifically. Is that consistent?"

"It is not an important point. The movement will use the means to its hand."

Oran raised his heavy brows. "I might almost take that as a threat," but he said it lightly. The probe was over. It was as if a high wind had dropped suddenly. There was no longer any sense of danger in the courtyard, and no one could quite believe or remember that it had been there. General conversation began again, over-casually. Knarf stood up, everyone else rose, the meal was over and they were anxious to leave the untidy table. Only Ren sat on staring at his clenched fists, preoccupied and troubled. He was thinking, not of Oran, but of Sfax.

# AFTERNOON

Knarf mounted the stairs to the roof with relief. Ord was at his heels. The house beneath them was like a cast-off garment. With the self-centred impatience of the sensitive, Knarf was escaping from what had just happened. Already he was in full flight from its implications. It was always like that. When anything had affected him deeply, his first impulse was to shake it off, or to smother it down as if it were a pain, and this was not any deep depravity or even a form of cowardice, but only a gesture of self-protection. He could not come to grips with any situation until he had got rid of the initial shock, reinforced his mind against all its by-products and cleared its too tender surface. He retreated, and these retreats were naturally misunderstood and had given him a name, with most of the people who knew him best, of being cold, insensitive, self-centred. Knarf knew that Lin wished to speak to him and that his guests would think his departure strange and slighting, but just the same he was impelled to go. He meant to carry out the programme he had planned, and to spend the afternoon as he had spent the morning, on the outline of his book, struggling, more for his own sake than for Ord's, to bring it into a last perspective. Ord called it "The return to the womb." He admired the grand manner in which Knarf swept out of his responsibilities. "You always look noble and grave and dignified when you are behaving badly," he mocked.

As they stepped on to the roof the great tide of midday light caught them, and the airy space all round them lifted them as if it were a wave. Light flattened the hills and beat down the colours, you had to shield your eyes from its brilliance to see the deep endless blue of the sky. Buildings, trees, contours, were reduced to their simplest terms, without shadows; the distances seemed to float with a natural buoyancy. The sun was hot but with the soft cadenced warmth of autumn. The stone parapet was warm under their hands and felt alive. Everything was alive and sentient, the air tasted of sap and grass.

"World without end," said Ord.

Knarf did not want to say anything. He was looking, not at the hills, but into the square. The scene had a new ingredient and an unexpected one. Whilst they had been at lunch a company of the Civil Guard had arrived and were now being dismissed by their officer. They looked like mechanical figures with their set movements in the lazy little square. They were not often seen in the Tenth Commune. "Why do you suppose they are here?" he asked.

"Pomp and circumstance," Ord answered lightly, but Knarf was not satisfied. He looked at the soldiers with brooding eyes. They were attracting so little attention that they might almost be a figment of his imagination or an externalisation of his vague fears.

There was a little knot of activity where Sfax and several cadets were working on the apparatus, watched by a group of children who, understanding nothing, were still fascinated by the pattern of movement and the mystery of its intention. Ren was not there but Oran was, looking fore-shortened, dark, and clumsy.

"He's a tough customer," said Ord, "Sort of type you get in a society where there's too little variety. Result of inbred ideas. Tighter and harder all the time. Always seeing less and seeing it clearer. It's a pity Ren had to run up against him. He'll probably get plenty of proof that he's right, only it won't be tangible."

"Yes," said Knarf.

"They'll fight like fury if they find they are losing their hold, they won't stop at anything. Makes me wonder if it's worth while, disturbing them. That's because I'm either getting old or have what I want anyway." Ord could feel his words hitting a blank wall. "You can't change human nature, Knarf," he said, offering the cliché as if it were an attempt at consolation.

Knarf said, wearily, "You don't have to. All men are all things. Circumstances can bring pretty well anything out of any man. Change circumstances and you change men." This was one of his mind's own platitudes. He believed it, disbelieved it, believed it again. It was a basic truth, opening up an immense complication which left his imagination harassed and jaded. The complexity of the human range, the multiple branching of the few basic traits founded in that instinctive life that, being the product of common necessity, was shared by all men, the creatures of their necessities, constituted the fate and the hope of the human race. A million years and more of accretion had produced a baffling diversity out of a root similarity,

creating a reticulation of character, progressive and retrogressive. The
science of living consisted of playing this vast instrument to advantage.
There was an answer to the human problem, for there must be, in
the vast resources at man's disposal, a concatenation of circumstances
that would in all essentials favour man's growth and progress. The
Elixir of Life, the philosopher's stone, Utopia. Chance in its endless
kaleidoscope had never out of its resources matched circumstances in
which man could be at home and disentangled death from life.
Chance never could throw up the right answer. That left the fallible
tools of mind and imagination which, encumbered by adverse circumstance, could never come into full focus. The half-evolved must ever
live in an approximation. The sliding answer lay somewhere in the
middle register of the everlasting phase rule—Utopia was a scientific
possibility. Somewhere, across impenetrable marshes, the Right Answer
marched parallel to the struggling column of humanity. Knarf felt
his brain stuffed with an infinity of silken threads inextricably tangled.
His thoughts struggled in a blind maze, silk drawn through sandpaper.
Hope corroded the tender flesh of the brain. Were the arts a false
answer, descriptive, not creative? They pierced more or less deeply
into what was, but did not break through into what might be. They
prepared the ground for living by illuminating the status quo, but
did not penetrate into the field of living itself, brought in self-
consciousness but no new ingredient. The artist was in a forward
position, a few steps nearer the ultimate stone wall, no less palpable
for being unreal. Ren thought he had found a panacea, the narrow-
ness of his attack would defeat him. Knarf thought he could outflank
the problem and was going down in a welter of eclecticism. . . .

Ord turned his back to the parapet, leaned on the warm stone,
and, lifting his face to the sky and the blaze of the sun, stared into
the unfathomable blue between narrowed lids. You said something
commonplace to Knarf and he went off into one of his brown studies.
He was as remote as if—as if he were lost in the mythical maze of
Crete. This affair of Ren's didn't seem to be worrying him, but there
was something else, over the horizon. It was one of those moments
when the thoughts in his mind seemed to change the molecular
structure of his body. Here was a man looking out from a fortress
on a world he had not seen before yet had always known existed.
Here was a man deserted by confidence, defeated by vision, isolated
for a moment in himself, cut off on some crumbling mound in a

chimerical marsh and knowing it, the flesh turned alien on his bones. . . . And all for nothing, a chance word, or a chance thought, standing in the sun on a warm autumn day, in the safest world humanity had ever known. Knarf and his cross currents. And this book he had written, so unlike anything else he had ever written, or that anyone had written for a couple of hundred years at least. It stood up like a silo on the western plains. It was going to trouble and perplex and anger people, and make trouble for Knarf. It was so real that it might burst right open the whole mild convention of modern writing, even touch the bedded-down imagination of a slothful generation. Queer that all that passion and despair should have banked up in Knarf when his outward life gave no sign of it, queerer that he should pour it into the vessel of something past. Perhaps the clue lay in something he had said more than once and evidently believed. "Nothing passes, we carry with us all that there has ever been."

Knarf, as if he had received an awaited signal, walked towards the pavilion. Ord followed him. Knarf picked up a bundle of manuscript and began to turn the pages, not reading it, but rather touching it with his fingers as if it were a bas relief. They would finish the book. The long interruption dwindled to a slit, a mere crack in the face of the day.

.    .    .    .    .    .    .    .    .

"War," said Knarf, "war. In a moment, almost between breaths, a change began that would influence the life of almost every living man, the beginning of the last great wave. I know, I know, that day to day, year to year, event and event are bound together by iron bands of logic. The past is cause, the future its effect, and an irrefragable law joins them. There are no fissures in history, no north-west passages to hell or heaven, but there are moments when, out of saturation, coalescence, the whole brew of factors, change precipitates. It is, I suppose, possible scientifically to ascertain the exact moment when a tide turns. That moment of pause when the spring night 'drew one cold breath,'* the people going to their pleasures suddenly halted, a world with the lights on gone suddenly

---

* From Gerald Gould: *Compensation.*

hollow, bare feet on the pavement, shrill voices, excited but uncaring, crying the news—that moment was historic. It may have been the nearest thing to a miracle—men's minds bristled with the realization of their hour. They were hardened to crises, for years they had expected this till it had become like death, something that would surely happen tomorrow or next month or in a year, but not today. It was today. Men's thoughts crystallised upon a point."

Ord didn't say, as he would certainly have said at any other time, "You are elevating a local and fortuitous occurrence into an historic moment. You're indulging yourself at the expense of the truth." This was part of the book, it had its own sort of truth, he admitted that. He didn't want to break the circle of a creative mood to which he had for once been admitted.

.    .    .    .    .    .    .    .    .

Communities, as well as individuals, have a trick of turning away from their moments of realization. They see, and then go to great trouble to disprove their own vision. From its beginning the war sagged away. Poland fell in a matter of days. Her skies were darkened with planes, in spearhead after spearhead the armoured divisions thrust across her plains from east and west. Only Warsaw held for several weeks, an heroic stand, hopeless from the beginning, an upthrust of human courage, its reason in itself rather than in any cause or tactic. Warsaw fell. German and Russian invaders, pledged to mutual non-aggression, met on the plains and halted. The waiting world hoped for a clash. There was only yet another partition of Poland, and in the British Commonwealth opinion hung hesitant, whether to rejoice that Germany had been forestalled at her own game, or to turn the firehose of their moral indignation equally on Russia. Those who took a high moral stand on the war had no alternative but to condemn Russia, however useful her action might have been. Stalin feared Hitler, people said. Hitler feared Stalin, they said. The whole thing was a plot cooked up between them when they signed the pact, they said. Stalin, they said, wants Germany and England to cancel one another out, then he will swoop down on the west. They prayed that Germany and Russia might cancel one another out and so to an honourable victory without fighting.

The black curtain fell on Poland. From under the curtain only rumour, like trickling blood, escaped. Starvation, disease, the massacre of Jews, labour battalions pressed for Germany, destruction, despair. Only the Quakers, God's jackals, went in, a few very determined men with food and clothing, medicines and cod liver oil. Undismayed, because they believed in God, calm, because they had His work to do, they ministered to as many as they could reach. In the black chaos they fixed a token of man's other side.

"Are they the guiltless men?" the professor asked, half ironically.

Bowie shook his head. He said quite briskly, "Philanthropy, even at its noblest, isn't enough. Hell, I take off my hat to them. All of that, but you can't baulk the logic of it. They are treating symptoms and doing nothing about the prime cause. Your Quaker, by and large, is a good business man. Honest as the day, of course. He accepts the whole competitive profit system as honest. The bed's clean, but he doesn't look under it. He doesn't fight, but he condones the system that makes wars. He's content with the most limited sort of personal cleanliness."

The professor cast a quizzical sidelong glance at Paula. "You have all the answers, Bowie, but you are too much of a purist to get anywhere. Man at his best is only half baked. His world has got to match him. You can't successfully apply absolute standards to half-evolved creatures. From any group of individuals you won't get all the ingredients of perfection. We can only hope that all the bits and pieces will eventually fit into a roughly satisfactory pattern. Your Quaker is at least doing something positive and creative. You calmly demand all of him."

A flame was stirred in Paula. "I'd like to be a Quaker. Only I don't believe in God, so I don't suppose they'd have me. It must be so splendid to see a job in front of you and do it, at no matter what cost. To—just walk into the midst of it all and begin helping people, the sick and the wounded and the children, never thinking of yourself, just helping and helping, till maybe you die on your feet." Colour burned in her cheeks, her eyes were dark stars. She saw it so clearly. The black icebound street, the one lighted doorway, the queue of wretched, starving, furtive people, the girl in the plain grey frock ladling out the hot soup, cutting generous slices of the black bread, never too tired or too busy to listen to the pitiful stories, to soothe a crying child or find comfort for a distracted woman. At the end of the day, "But you've eaten nothing yourself." "No, they needed it more than I." The tears came into her eyes. She was tired of words.

"Ah," the professor shook his finger at her, "that's not at all the right attitude, is it, Bowie? You'd like to make all sorts of personal sacrifices to save yourself the trouble of thinking. If you were working yourself to death for the poor and oppressed you'd be doing your bit, wouldn't you? You wouldn't have to think, you wouldn't be plagued by doubts. You'd buy peace and certainty with good works. Now that's just the spirit in which people accept wars. Wars save them the trouble of thinking. It's easier to be brave and die. You see, Paula, it's dangerous to trust your emotions. Hasn't Bowie brought you up better than that?"

"You don't practise what you preach, professor." Bowie answered for her, rather stiffly. Why couldn't he leave the girl alone? And what was he getting at? Why couldn't people be allowed to work together without all these insinuations? The poor old prof was the last word in ineffective intellectuals.

The professor looked puckish, seemed pleased with himself for drawing blood. Paula detested him. She didn't quite know where she was. This thing that she was working for, the new order of the Peace Party, slipped out of her reach every now and then. While Bowie talked it would be clear and solid and she would feel comfortably convinced. Then it would slide away, become unreal, nebulous, unpractical, and she would feel uneasy and unmoored again. She did so want to be absolutely certain. She might have to make great sacrifices, even of her life, and she wanted to be certain. To belong to a Peace Party in war time was surely a dangerous thing. But no move had been made against them. Was it because they didn't after all matter?

"Well, we're all human anyway," thought the professor. An intellectual like Bowie was fair game in any camp.

After the brief episode of Poland the war sagged. "Poland will rise again," said the Right, but it wasn't possible or expedient to do anything about it at the moment. "The Poles were a reactionary people, anyway," said the Left. "Their constitution . . . their history . . ." The Democracies cut Poland's losses. The Democracies marked time. Left, Right, Left, Right. The French stood to arms on the Maginot Line. The radio poured out rationalisations. Polite voices whittled away the German strength, proved that they wouldn't fight, couldn't fight, hadn't enough petrol, hadn't enough officers. Sit tight behind the Maginot Line and let them break on it. The greatest problem was to keep the troops amused. Ersatz army songs full of boasting. 1914. 1914. 1914. The bloodless war, the sitzkrieg. It's a phoney war. Unreal.

At sea the war was real enough. Men in merchant ships running the gauntlet of the Atlantic with food and munitions for England, voyage after voyage, till the submarines or the bombers got them; men in submarines bearing the strain of danger, the abrasion of confinement and close quarters. Silence, uncertainty, endurance long drawn out, the law of the wild on the seas.

Life went on the same in Sydney. It looked the same. Khaki began gradually to mix with the crowds in the streets. Prices began to rise. Ally fought every halfpenny with the woman at the shop. Her mind ran with dark suspicions. "It's the Jews," said Mrs Blan with conviction. Ally liked spending money, but not on necessities, and this drain of pennies and halfpennies threatened her dearly-prized indulgences. It was the line where she fought. She had learned to put up stoically enough with major discomforts, their crowded living quarters, the general tenor of their lives, but she must go to the pictures two or three times a week, lay her sixpenny bets, munch sweets and other titbits out of crumpled paper bags. She no longer believed that she could retrieve her fortunes at S.P. betting, the romance had been snuffed out of it, but she had come to need the constant dribble of excitement that it provided. At table she ate little, but in between meals was always running out for threepennorth of this or a quarter of that, snacks, sweet or greasy, of what took her fancy. On these things, the luxuries of her life, the sensuousness of her nature, torn from its proper root, became fixed. She was not yet forty, but she had put on weight and her complexion had thickened. It didn't occur to her that this was not inevitable. All about her, women on their marriage gave up all attempts to conserve their looks, or if they did not they were suspect. Decent women settled down. Ally was "decent." When she noticed, as she did sometimes in unguarded moments, the deterioration in herself she blamed Harry. Harry had kept something she had lost; she was dimly aware of that and resented it. It was unfair. It was his fault that they were where they were, stuck fast, with him in a dead-end job and doing nothing at all but strut round in a uniform. He could have done better if he had cashed in on Mr Ramsay. Something perverse in Harry, and they all had to suffer for it. Now Mr Ramsay was dead and couldn't do any more for him. Harry hadn't any right to wear better than she did. His face was worn and lined, carried the imprint of pain, but not of defeat. He had been defeated, but he'd got out of it, forgotten, for instance, the bad time he'd given them all, being out of work so long. His body was lean and compact, his carriage good. She couldn't get at him. The thing Ally resented most, though she did not name it to herself, was his dignity. That was the wall between them, the thing she had never been quite able to break. She had noticed a change in him recently, and sensed a new flow of vitality. She was not one to ask many questions, even of herself, because she had her infallibility to maintain. She knew Harry through and through. Sometimes now she surprised a look that might have been happiness in his eyes, and spontaneous anger welled in her heart. She made no effort to trace it, and even in her heart did not admit the possibility of Gwen. Their relations, after a long period of indifference, worsened.

Ruth saw it and she felt as if a hand clenched round her heart. She knew that her father and the girl from the half-price counter, only two or three years older than herself, were lovers. She found this not so much shocking as disconcerting, a little frightening, as if something she had always believed to be steady and fixed had slipped out of place. Under this there was something else, a pity for Harry as tender as flesh stripped of its skin. Her resentment had been short-lived and had been replaced by a new feeling of kinship, a shared vulnerability too tender to be explored even in her own mind. If she could love a man much older than herself, Harry might love a girl. Understanding budded in her. People were driven. She knew that. And there were secret springs. When you found one you must drink. She wanted to be friends with her father, but now, when there was more understanding, it was more difficult. The thought of meeting Gwen or speaking to her filled Ruth with unconquerable shyness.

For her mother Ruth held no brief. Ally had forfeited. Hard and clear now, her daughter's mind registered that. Sordid living had pared away her natural child affection for her mother. Her young asceticism was revolted by Ally's slackness and self-indulgence. The greasy and sticky paper bags into which her mother's hand was always wandering made her sick with disgust. She felt the injustice of their miserable, ill-cared-for home and must fasten the blame on someone. She blamed her mother as Ally had blamed Harry.

As for Wanda, her home was to her like a shabby, dirty old dress that she would be ashamed to be seen in. At every opportunity she tore it off and hid it from herself. She had long made up her mind that she would leave home as soon as she could support herself. She had given up hope of an apprenticeship to the millinery trade and instead was concentrating her energies on getting a job in the showroom of the fashionable milliner's where she was still messenger girl. To this end she modelled herself on the other saleswomen, their refined accent, their artificial smiles, their patter. Often she was sent to wait on the senior saleswoman, fetching, carrying, and standing in attendance. She learned a lot and quickly. The family wouldn't have known her, polite and willing and refined. The day she got the job she meant to leave home. Not the very day perhaps, but the first payday after. She was to be seen more often in the streets these days, going about with the young people she had recently shunned, paying her way with the sharpness of her tongue, hanging round Sid Warren's taxi, leading the badinage against the boys who gathered there too. At home she was short and nonchalant. Ally complained of her. With Ruth she had little in common, so little that they didn't even quarrel. Harry was troubled in his conscience about her. He wondered sometimes if perhaps Wanda had it in her to "go to the bad." If she did, it would be because there was something wrong with the world he had provided for his children. He'd remember what a taking little kid she'd been, clever and affectionate. If she'd got what she wanted, the apprenticeship, that after all he could have given her, she wouldn't have been wild like this.

To this household, grain by grain, the war added its sand. There was more money about, because unemployment was falling through enlistments and war production, but the Munsters were getting poorer. Their income was fixed in a world of rising prices. Every one in the house felt the tightening strain. Ally didn't take much notice of the war. She was confident it could never touch her. She didn't even read the war news, the only things that interested her in the newspapers were the accidents, crimes, and divorces. Mrs Blan, on the other hand, took a proprietary interest in the war and was a great authority on it. Glad got into munitions right away and wasn't living at home any longer, she said she had to be near her work.

That was as it may be, the neighbours said. The children remained with their grandmother. Glad paid well for their keep. "Glad ain't mean," Mrs Blan pointed out to everyone, rather defensively. And the bandsman stayed behind too. He was the apple of Mrs Blan's eye. She took far more trouble for him than she ever had for her old man. He knew when he was well off. He was at heart a placid cat of a man who had come to value the mother's spoiling above the daughter's charms. So Mrs Blan got him. He used to read the papers to her, annotating the news freely while she washed up. When he could find any support, however shaky, for optimism in the news, he expatiated on the glories of the British Empire and the inevitability of victory. Whenever he could find none, he would say, sadly but heroically, "I'll have to enlist, ma, the Empire is in danger. I'll have to enlist." And she would say, terribly concerned, "Don't do anything in a hurry, Alby, maybe it's only rumours and it'll all be denied in tomorrow's paper, wait a bit." He waited and they forgot that particular bit of sad news. Mrs Blan really had a deep-rooted conviction that this war was a newspaper stunt. "The last war," she'd say, "that *was* a war. Mowed down like cattle, they were."

Ben felt the restlessness of it all. He'd had his fourteenth birthday in June 1939, but he was still at school.

"You'll stay at school, son," Harry said, "till I get you a job."

"I got a job, dad," he protested, "Rumpty'll take me on full time. Lefty's going for a soldier."

"Selling papers doesn't lead to anything. You'll want something better than that. If you haven't a trade you don't get anywhere."

"Aw, what's the good, dad? I'll be going to the war. Reckon they'll take me in two years."

"Reckon they won't. You can't go without my permission till you're twenty-one. This war's not going to last seven years."

"Gee, dad, you're hard."

Harry was sorry to have to head the boy off in everything he wanted, to leave school, to sell papers, to go to the war. Ben took the pause for an opening. "If I left school now and Rumpty took me on full time, he'd give me ten bob a week, and I'd get threepence hapenny a dozen, same as I do now. That'd be more than two quid a week. I wouldn't get that in a job, would I?" His eyes were bright as an animal's. It was his conception of freedom he was fighting for, Harry realised, freedom and mobility in an iron world.

He said heavily, "I want you to do better than your father, Ben."

The boy was quick to respond to the inflection. "You done all right, dad, honest you have."

The reassurance cut Harry like a whip, but there was no guile in Ben's eager trusting eyes, no criticism.

Harry asked at a venture, "How'd you like to be raising chickens on a farm?"

"Gee, dad." Ben's consternation made Harry laugh.

"You don't have to. Only it's probably what you would have been doing if I hadn't come to the city before you were born. It was largely because of you we came."

"Cripes, I wouldn't like the country, it's too slow."

"Isn't there anything besides selling papers you'd like to do?"

"I dunno. Don't know anything as quick as papers. There's motor-cars. I wouldn't mind much mucking round with them. Sid Warren let me help when he took down his engine." Sid was an owner-driver and vetted his own machine. "I'd like that."

"Like Tony?"

Tony Nelson was sixteen and apprenticed to the motor trade. He'd been on a bowser for two years, and now he was working at a big garage at the Cross. Tony was the best boy in the street, everyone thought so: big, strong, steady, didn't belong to any push. Despite two years' difference in age, the two boys had been cobbers till Tony, beginning to work, had gone beyond Ben's range. If Ben sticks to Tony, Harry thought, he won't come to harm.

Ben brightened now. "That ud be good oh." Then his face clouded. "They don't pay much and they want a lot of money to apprentice you. Papers don't cost anything."

"Don't worry about that, son. I can fix it. I'll go to the garage where Tony works and see if they'll take you on."

He had £200. That would cover any premium they could possibly ask, and Ben would have a living on his hands. He wouldn't go down into the dump of unskilled labour. The boy would be all right. A door seemed to have opened ahead of him.

Six weeks later Ben started work at the garage. There had been no vacancy for another apprentice, but they were willing in the growing shortage of labour to employ him at a fair wage. He fitted in easily. He and Tony were cobbers again. Sometimes after work Ben helped old Rumpty out, coming back to the old job like a veteran.

It was something, Harry thought, to get a little bit of your world tied up.

The Russo-Finnish war was dragged like a red herring across the international situation. The ideological confusion was worse confounded. "Aggression, barefaced aggression," cried the Right. "Self-defence," declared the Left; "look at Leningrad up near the border, exposed to attack. Russia must protect herself." "Finland's a democracy, we are fighting for democracy, so her cause is ours," asserted the Right. "Oh yeah," said the Left, "What price Mannerheim?" "Idealism," said the Right. "Realism," said the Left. Allied help did not reach Finland any more than it had reached Poland. In Germany the question was even more barbed. It was a matter of choosing between a quasi ally and a potential ally. Germany acquiesced in the defeat of Finland, albeit with pious regrets, confident that the rage and humiliation generated in Finland would make of her a jumping-off place, a beaten iron head, for a German attack on Russia. In the meantime, thousands of men, Finns and Russians, died on the Karelian Isthmus and in the swamps of Lake Ladoga, in the thick forests and on the snowy plains. Alive, these men had not differed greatly from one another, they were men and brave, they were conscripts; dead, they did not differ at all.

The Finnish war, the ideological confusion and its stirring up of enmity between Left and Right, had its consequences. The Government, perceiving a cleavage, proceeded, under cover of the State of War, to sew it together in their own way. Parliament passed the National Security Act. It looked short and meek enough in the statute book, pages of dry legal jargon, but it severed at its root that democratic principle of government for which the war was, presumably, being fought.

"Then they made a cult of short hair and spent ten times as much at the hairdresser as ever they used to. This is one of the arguments that go round and round and never come to an end. We still don't know why the Australians in the twentieth century were so curiously unreasonable. If time were an hourglass and could be stood the other way up, they'd probably think we were curiously unreasonable. It's in the nature of man to be unreasonable and to conceal it from himself."

"Reason's no more than a cork on the dark tide of man's instinct. We don't act out of reason, or only partly, but we persistently judge our past and other man's present according to the canons of reason. That's why judgement is almost always wrong. Come off it, Knarf, and get on with your story."

It was a hot Sunday in January 1940. The street lay gasping. The bandsman downstairs was practising a tiddley bit, over and over, on his trumpet. It sounded incredibly desolate, and like a fish out of water. Ally lay on her bed reading. Harry, Wanda, and Ben had dispersed immediately dinner was over on their own occasions. Ruth was restless. The dinner dishes were still stacked in a greasy pile on the sink. It was Wanda's turn to wash up, but she had gone out, and for once Ruth didn't intend to do it. She couldn't make up her mind about the afternoon. The house was insufferable, all the greasy emptiness in the world seemed stacked up in it. There was nothing to stop her from going out, but if she dressed and went out it would only underline the fact that she had nowhere special to go and no one to go with. An insuperable sense of disappointment was on her, like a headache or a malaise. There was a boy at the office who wanted to take her out, and Tony Nelson would have liked the chance, but they wouldn't do. She was a year older than Tony anyway. Lonely and uncertain, she put a veneer of awkward aloofness over her vulnerability. She "kept herself to herself," and then she felt disappointed.

Finally Ruth got dressed. She put on a printed cotton frock, white scattered with small posies in bright clear colours, a green velvet ribbon round the waist. Wanda had cut it out and fitted it for her. Wanda was clever and, over clothes, friendly. She had trimmed the big white hat too. The trimming consisted of a bow of the same green velvet. At first Ruth had thought it looked poor to have nothing but a piece of ribbon on a hat, and a big hat too. But Wanda said it was right, "distangy," she said. When Wanda helped you things had to be done her way. Now Ruth liked the hat, felt good in it.

She bent close to the small mirror and made up her face. It was a cheap mirror with a wavering tinny surface and the light was merciless. It generally sent Ruth out feeling depressed. She saw a pale face, straight fair hair, high cheek bones and knobby forehead, a pale sensitive mouth, and grey eyes. Wanda said, "If you've got to be plain it's best to be plain your way. You can *do* something with your face, it hasn't a mind of its own." Ruth was learning to do something. She pencilled in her eyebrows, rubbed a little Glamour Girl rouge into her cheeks, applied Conquistadora lipstick, and finally dusted her face with April Bloom powder. It was as if she had dragged a new face out of the mirror's shallows, she felt reassured. Though each preparation she used had its own strong individual perfume, she added a dab behind each ear of Wanda's Tropic Night scent.

Only on the stairs did Ruth remember that she still had nowhere to go, and the sense of disappointment rose again. There was these days an unacknowledged ache deep in her mind, the battleground where her spirit struggled against circumstances over which she had no power. Given the chance, it spread and enveloped her whole outlook, masquerading as pain or disappointment or anger. It was flooding her now, taking advantage of the unimportant circumstance that she had nowhere to go on a hot Sunday afternoon.

She stood on the little verandah, no more than a platform, at the top of the steps, bounded by an iron railing, trying to make up her mind. The street was empty, but someone might be looking from a window. She wanted to rush back, throw herself down on the bed and cry her heart out. But for that she must have privacy and there was none. Tears were as much a luxury as champagne. She was never alone, wholly, completely alone, and that, though she did not know it, was something she also craved. Union or solitude, and she had neither.

As she stood irresolute, not thinking but letting the two impulses fight it out in her, the Nelsons' door opened and Sid Warren came out. Ruth stiffened. He looked up and down the street. It was still empty. He saw her and began slowly to cross the street, stopping half way to let a car pass. Ruth had an impulse to walk quickly away as if unaware of his intention to speak to her, but a stronger impulse to wait.

"Hullo, Ruth."

"Hullo."

"You look cool." He eyed her with a sort of amused detachment. She didn't answer. "Got a date?"

"No. Just going for a walk."

The amusement deepened in his eyes. "I'm going down to the Dom. Care to come?"

She hesitated the moment she owed herself. "I don't mind."

They walked down to William Street, crossed and continued down the hill. Sid crossed behind her to take the outside place. Ruth thought in sudden gratitude and joy, "Sid's a gentleman." She put an inordinate value on the small action, it was something to be treasured. It turned her mood completely. She was happy, carried herself proudly. She looked at Sid, who was not looking at her. As he walked, he looked about him in a casual but alert way, as a man who had till recently been a soldier in a guerrilla band might still have the habit of looking, automatically noting the disposition of the terrain, the cover, the opportunities for escape.

There was no moment when he did not have an air of readiness, as if he were never quite off his guard, and as if he did not take the city, as most people did, as a place of cut and dried safety wherein man's hour-to-hour survival had been handed over to the proper authorities. His face was burnt brown, his hair dark and thick, his eyes dark and lively. His hands and his eyes were the only quick things about him. His mouth was sardonic, his carriage slouching and casual. There was speed in him but he didn't waste it, kept it in reserve. Not more than thirty, he was one of those men whose physical characteristics set early and do not change till remote old age suddenly crumples them—if, that is, old age ever gets the chance.

Ruth hadn't anything to say. Sid talked about fishing rather as if he were talking to himself. It would have been a good day for fishing, but he had been up almost all night with the cab, and he'd have to take her out again about five. No one wanted cabs before five on a Sunday, but after that they wanted them bad. Ruth was puzzled by Sid's attitude to his cab, the way he often seemed to grudge taking it out, the time he gave himself off when he could be making money. It wasn't that Ruth herself was inordinately attached to money or the idea of money, but she recognised that it was that sort of world. People went after money when and where and how they could. It was holy and sacred. But sometimes Sid's cab would stand in the gutter outside Nelsons' all day and no one knew where Sid was, or he'd bring it back at the peak hour because he said he "was fed up for today." When he first came back from Spain a reporter had come to interview him. "What's your sport, Mr Warren?" he asked. "Fishing and revolution," said Sid.

Often on a Sunday morning he went fishing with a rod and line on one of the beaches. He brought back fish too, a marvel to the children of the street, who never thought beyond salmon tins and fish and chip shops. Sometimes he took Ben with him, only to report with cheerful disgust that he'd never make a fisherman. He was too lively.

There was a big crowd in the Domain and a sense of ferment. Even Ruth was aware of it, like the impingement of a dramatic current on her skin. Sid looked from group to group. "Want to see what they are up to?" he asked. "Same old thing, same old thing, these coves never learn. They get an idea and think they're set for life." He stayed longest with a cluster round a squarish young man.

"Aggression," the man was saying, "is a symptom, not a cause. The so-called aggressor nations are the have-not nations. There will and must be aggression whilst there is inequality of opportunity, and so long as the people of the world are fenced off from one another by borders and boundaries. Under the present system the nations are units of competition. . . ."

Ruth wasn't listening. She was looking at the girl standing a little behind the speaker. "Pretty," she thought. "If I looked like that. . . . Her hat's plain, too. She's smart."

The speaker was on another tack now. "Under the National Security Act any man's liberty can be taken from him, any society can be declared illegal, their machinery confiscated, any newspaper or journal silenced, and these things can be done under cloak of secrecy. Liberty is become a perquisite for supporters of the Government. When you surrender another man's liberties you surrender your own. Liberty ceases to exist. The National Security Act is a typical wartime measure. It makes legal the destruction of all those liberties and safeguards we have won with such effort after so long a time. It isn't legality that has the last word, however. It is public opinion. If each one of us stood by other people's rights as we stand by our own, the Act would become a dead letter. . . ."

To oppose an Act of Parliament seemed utterly remote to Ruth, like trying to stop an express train with your hands. Again her mind wandered, but not far—to the man beside her. He had a world she knew nothing about. She could see it by his intent expression now.

"Peace," the speaker was saying, "Peace . . . there will be no peace while these things are tolerated. If war recurs every twenty years our world will founder. Peace, not war, is the first necessity of survival, human survival. Peace is not a miracle attained by prayer. It is a matter for sustained and cogent effort. . . ."

Ruth was jerked back by Sid's voice beside her.

"What about Collective Security?"

"It didn't collect."

Sid's voice overrode the little scatter of laughter. "D'you know why?"

"Yes. Largely because the people who control public opinion by and large feared Communism far more than they feared war. Any horse from that stable was suspect."

"What about your party?"

"My party's willing to play fellow travellers. But Collective Security wasn't a Peace move. It was a bit of political hygiene. Preventive not curative. It was still hanging round the neck of the Latin tag, 'If you wish peace, prepare for war.'"

Paula Ramsay, from her vantage point just behind Bowie, looked at the man who had interjected. She saw a hard wedge-shaped face, at least he was not a fish like most of the audience. If you put your finger in a goldfish bowl the goggle-eyed carp gathered round and you felt their soft aimless mouths vainly occulate your skin. The people who came to listen were like that. Whatever you said didn't hook on. Paula wasn't listening to the short duel. Bowie had learned to "handle" people, he turned the tables on interjectors. But that wasn't the best way to do it, Paula thought, it was sucking up to the fishes and snubbing the few who really wanted to know. You didn't persuade people by getting the better of them. Perhaps Bowie, under all his assurance, was afraid of being heckled. He could be. She had taken him rather uncritically. Anyhow, you couldn't expect anyone to see round himself all the time. *Stop* fishing in honey, she entreated herself. Yes, there he was leaving the group, the wedge-faced man, and the fair girl was going with him. You could use people like that for a chock. It wouldn't give way. Almost everything gave way.

Sid and Ruth walked across the grass. "That cove has got something," said Sid, "but he's not going to do anything about it. He talks ideas and not practical politics. People'll agree with him and disagree with him and it won't matter either way."

"What's to be done about the National Security Act?" asked Ruth, hoping she sounded knowledgeable, but giving the impression that she expected the Act to run out and snap at her heels any moment.

Sid grinned at her. "There's nothing wrong with the National Security Act, except that the wrong crowd has got hold of it. You can't shape anything without power. The National Security Act is a power switch. The Liberals are squeamish about it. *That's* all they've got left, squeamishness."

He was steering her towards a very large group, tight at the core, fringing out loosely at the edges. At the centre was a bright new flag emblazoned with hammer and sickle, and a short man, bald as an egg, mounted on a stepladder.

From a distance his words were inaudible and he looked a ridiculous little mannikin, something of a Punch and Judy show, turning to this side and that, raising his clenched fist and bringing it down on his open palm, but some centrifugal force was holding the crowd.

"Let's see what the comrades are up to," he said.

They could not penetrate beyond the edge of the crowd. Ruth could not hear very well, and, unaccustomed, she could not pick up the trend of the argument in the middle. Stray words and phrases reached her. "Realism," "The Socialist Fatherland," "Imperialist war," "Fight between gangsters." She could sense an electric sizzle in the air and feel the movement of the people, not the fidgetiness of the uninterested, but a deeper unconscious rhythm, as if they swayed to an accepted beat. Every now and again there was a growl of applause and a flickering cross current of dissent. Here and there police stood in the crowd, unmoved, foursquare, with blank official faces, subtly insulting to enthusiasm

Something was happening away to the right, shouting and confusion. Straining upwards on her toes, Ruth could see that a wedge of khaki was driving into the flank of the crowd. Jostling broke out everywhere. The cauldron, long on the bubble, had begun to boil. Some were backing away from the disturbance, others surging towards it. Ruth looked up at Sid. The casualness had left his face, it was alert, set in a half grin. He was ably pushing himself towards the khaki infiltration. Ruth followed close behind in the wake he opened. Soon she was separated from him but still in the same jet of activity. A line was being forced, arms linked in cordon, swinging forward against the soldiers. Ruth was in it, so were other women. She linked arms with a boy and a man. People were banked behind her, she moved with their momentum rather than her own, felt their excitement flare through her. The police moved in on the focal point of the disturbance.

The speaker continued undeterred, his only reaction a greater outward ferocity of gesture, till an arm reached up to pull him down. He tried to fight back from his precarious perch, toppled and fell down from sight. A big private took his place, stood swaying a moment as if in amazement, while a hail of hoots, cheers, and catcalls broke out. A falsetto yelled, "Speech, Speech." A roar went up. The man made a slow semi-circular movement with his arm.

"Cobbers," he began and stopped. A blue arm shot up and hauled him down. There was a struggle and the stepladder collapsed. A police whistle slit across the din. For a moment things looked ugly, as if a three-cornered battle between the Party supporters, the soldiers, and the police were breaking out. The military police arrived. Discipline began to tell, the discipline of the police, trained for such an emergency, upon the crowd, and the discipline of habit upon the soldiers. The crowd broke and scattered, leaving a handful of prisoners, combatants from both sides, in the hands of the police. The speaker was bleeding from a gash on the head, the stepladder had fallen on him; and another man lay on the grass, an ambulance officer kneeling beside him.

Sid became aware of Ruth again. "Jeese," he said, "You were in it all right."

Dumb with shock and exaltation, Ruth nodded. One sleeve was torn out of her dress, her hat gone.

"Are you hurt, kid?"

"No. I was in the push." She showed him how she'd linked arms.

"Good for you," he said. He looked round, found her hat, rather battered, on the grass near them, and gave it to her. "Not so chippy as it used to be," he commented jocularly, then looked at her keenly as she stood automatically straightening the brim. "Know what it was all about?" Ruth shook her head.

"But you went in just the same."

She gave him a wavering smile. Oddly she wanted to cry.

Sid drew her hand through his arm. "That's the spirit," he said. "It's better to fight first and think after, than to think first and never fight at all. You've had enough for one day. We're going home. Don't feel like being arrested today, do you?"

Ruth giggled.

They walked back slowly. The Sunday crowd was draining away. The shadows were lengthening, the sunlight, impregnated with dust and smoke, glowed apricot on the facades of William Street.

"That wasn't anything," Sid assured her. "Didn't mean a thing. Some of the boys got excited and began throwing their weight about. Got a vested interest in the uniforms they wear. It's their war and if anyone says hard things they get wild. It'll make a bit of a stir because things like that don't happen here, and, of course, everyone's going to sympathize with the boys in uniform. It may come in very handy to the men up aloft, an excuse to come down on the Party and shut it up. The cops took up a couple of soldier boys, they'll get C.B. probably. That'll make it fair, see? Impartial justice. But they won't close down the army because a few privates cut up rough."

Sid fell silent, exploring the possibilities. Ruth hadn't been listening anyway, she had been sorting things out in her own way. Sid had dropped her arm before they began to climb the hill. Just before they turned their own corner, she said, "My father is an Anzac."

He didn't trouble to find out whether she were accounting for her fighting blood or ranging herself on the other side.

They stopped at Ruth's door. "What'll your mum say about your dress?"

"I'll get it off before she sees it. It's only the stitching gone. I can mend it."

He grinned at her. "Looks like I can't take a girl for a stroll on Sunday afternoon without getting her into trouble. So long, Ruth."

After the rumpus the crowd melted away out of the Domain like water off a duck's back. No one had any audience left. The speakers packed up and went away. Bowie said he'd see Paula home. He always did anyway, but he used to say it as if it were just this time.

"It doesn't happen to us," he said. He meant the fight.

"Do you want it to?" She was laughing at him.

"No," he answered gravely. "No, I don't. But it is a sign of life."

He stopped and looked back. Pigeons whirling in the blue sky, the trees and the city, the air itself, powdered with gold dust.

"We are right," he said doubtfully. "It's the only way. The hardest and the best."

"Yes, Bowie," she answered, too smoothly. "Peace is the only thing worth fighting for." She didn't want to be shown his feet of clay.

She wanted to be sure herself. If his confidence weakened hers would come tumbling down.

He sighed and looked at her. Dark and sweet. Tenebreuse. The word affected him sharply, drew his feeling into focus, sharpened a pain he only felt sometimes, but more often now.

"Really, Bowie," she said, "You needn't come. You've another meeting tonight. I'm not going."

Whether the disturbance in the Domain had anything to do with it or not, the Communist Party was shortly after declared illegal under the National Security Act. The members went to earth, the party documents went up in smoke, the Anvil Bookshop was closed down and its stock confiscated. Apart from these things, the main drive was against the written word. *Mein Kampf* was still available in libraries and bookshops, but the works of Marx and Lenin were suspect. Subversive literature was hounded down with effects so comic that the drive eventually defeated itself.

Sid Warren's room was raided for subversive literature in the early days of the hunt, an occasion long remembered with delight in the street. Politics ran hot in those gutters sometimes, but Sid was popular, Sid was a Spanish veteran, so everyone, whatever their political colour, sided with him against the police, even Mrs Blan's bandsman.

It was Ben who first saw the policemen going into Nelsons' at nine o'clock one evening. He shouted the news up the stairs. By the time he crossed the road, things were in full swing. The light was up in Sid's room, the two policemen were stooping over the bookcase, and Sid himself, come in for a bite between the flow and ebb of theatre traffic, was leaning against the wall smoking. Nothing but the exaggerated casualness of his attitude and the outward thrust of his lower lip betrayed the unusualness of the occasion. Sid had quite a lot of books. Before he went to Spain he'd had some idea of getting himself an education. Mrs Nelson was in the room bustling about. As soon as she saw Ben she came over and opened the window.

"Come right in, Ben," she invited cordially.

"You stay out, boy," snapped the sergeant.

"You can see all right from there, can't you Benny?" said Mrs Nelson, sweetly.

The sergeant told her to be so kind as to leave the room.

"My husband here is the lessee of these premises."

"That's right," agreed Mr Nelson from the doorway.

"You're hindering us in the discharge of our duties, madam."

"Oh, is that so? Why didn't you tell me before? I wouldn't do that, sergeant. I'll go."

She joined Mr Nelson in the doorway, standing scrupulously in their own legally-hired passage. Tony craned his head round the door frame. The police went on stolidly with their job.

"What cheer, Ben?"

"Hullo, Tony."

"Two cops."

"What they looking for?"

"Seditious literature."

"Gee, that's bad."

"I'll say it is."

"Have they found any?"

"That pile."

"Gee!"

"They got the atlas."

"Oo, can't you look in an atlas now?"

"Not if there's a map of Russia in it."

"Cops got to be educated men these days," Mrs Nelson put in admiringly. "Used to be common Irish when I was a girl, but it's different now."

The red-headed constable was heard to snort.

"I read some of those books," Tony confided to Ben.

"Cripes, they'll put you in the jug."

"Maybe they will."

"Now then," said the sergeant, "now then. You're the householder here, clear those people off the premises."

"It's only the neighbours, Sarge. I can't turn them out of the street, now can I? I haven't any authority." Mr Nelson tugged mildly at his walrus moustache.

"It's like this, officer," said Mrs Nelson, all smiles. "The neighbours always drop in to see us of an evening. We're that popular. Don't mind them." Practically everyone in the street had collected outside the window.

The police had finished with the bookcase.

"There's a box of books under the bed, officer," said Sid, winking at Ben.

"I'm coming to that."

A box was indeed hauled out and its contents tipped upon the floor. They were a tattered collection of children's books, fairy tales, and what not. The sergeant scattered them with an angry hand.

"Shame!" cried the bandsman in a rich voice, as if he had seen a child assaulted.

"Don't be too hard on them," said Mrs Nelson, oilier than ever. "They're only doing their duty. They've got to live, haven't they? They got wives and little ones at home just like anyone else. It's tough for them to have to do things like this against their own class and all."

"Hear, hear," murmured the chorus.

"That Rose Nelson's having the time of her life," Mrs Blan remarked to Ally. "Regular show off, she is."

"You haven't taken up the flooring boards, officer," Sid suggested.

The police began pulling out drawers and rummaging in their contents.

"My," came a falsetto from the street. "Look at Siddy's winter woollies."

One drawer yielded a package, which, undone, revealed a box containing an enormous pair of feminine bloomers.

"What they all laughing at, mother?" enquired Mr Nelson.

"Must be something up the street, pop."

"That ud be it, mother."

Voices floated in from the street. "Isn't he a caution?" "I'm sorry our Barbara's missing this. Rare one for a laugh, she is."

The police looked round to see what else duty required of them. They were not very happy. For grown men, and very big men at that, to be watched while they rummaged among underclothes was embarrassing.

"There's a wardrobe," Sid encouraged. Suspecting a trap they let the wardrobe go.

"You got enough to hang him there, haven't you?" asked Tony, pointing to the heap of books they had stacked to take away.

"None of your lip, son."

"Shut up, Tony," shrilled Ben. "You've got yourself in bad already."

The constable gave Sid a receipt for his property and in a dead silence the Law took its departure.

Everybody waited until the car drove away.

It had been a good entertainment. The crowd began to break up.

Someone hailed Sid, "Did yer lose much, Siddie?"

"No," he drawled, "they took all the books with red covers, that's all, and an atlas and a Bible in Yiddish which I borrowed from old Isaac for the purpose. Thought they'd got something that time, probably a code for blowing up the British Empire. Not enough evidence there to drown a kitten."

People began to drift home. Ben ran off whooping to tell Old Rumpty.

One said to another, "He had a lot of books and pamphlets, you know, the kind they're after. I've seen them. What did he do with them?"

"Search me. No flies on Sid."

Stout old Mrs Flannagan came up, wheezing and laughing. "Gimme back me pants, there's a dear good boy, tomorrow's me day for changing."

There was a sequel to the incident. Next evening Ruth was in the kitchen washing up; Wanda went into the room they shared and opened a box in which Ruth kept her personal oddments with a view to borrowing a scarf. It was a large hatbox that Wanda had herself given to Ruth. It lived under Ruth's bed, and was the nearest thing to a private receptacle that she had. The box was heavy. Under a layer of odds and ends Wanda discovered that it was full of books and pamphlets. Ruth must have heard her. She came in with the dishcloth in her hand.

"What are you doing?" she almost shouted. But she had seen. A dark flush of anger spread over her fair skin. "You went to my box," she cried.

"So that's where they were. It was you." Wanda's face was dark with venom.

Ally came in. "What's the row about?" She caught Wanda's arm and her eyes fell on the books half strewn on the floor. "What have you got there?"

"It's Ruth," cried Wanda. "Those are Sid Warren's books. The ones the police are after."

"Yes, they are, and you hadn't any right to go to my box."

"You wouldn't care if you hadn't something to hide."

"I haven't anything to hide."

"He wouldn't have given those to just anyone. Besides, you went for a walk with him and you came back with your dress torn. Don't think I don't know what that means."

"You dirty little beast," Ruth flung the sopping dishcloth in her sister's face. Wanda screamed with rage.

Ally caught each by a shoulder and held them by the sheer weight of her bulk. "Stop it," she said. "Stop it, both of you."

Ruth began to tremble with the shock of what she had done. "Be quiet," said Ally, "and tell me what it's about."

"She hid those books for Sid Warren."

"What does it matter to you if I did?"

"You'd do anything for him wouldn't you?"

"No, I wouldn't. But you've made it pretty plain that you'd like to."

Ally did not care about a little thing like jealousy. "Take those books back at once, Ruthie. Do you want the police here? Give them back or I'll burn them. I thought you were a decent girl. Taking up with Sid Warren! He's a red and old enough to be your father."

"He isn't."

"Isn't what?"

"Old."

"I'll talk to you later. You've got to take those books back now." Ally had always quoted Sid against Mrs Blan's bandsman, and she had enjoyed the discomfiture of the police last night as much as anyone, but her mind had begun to swing. If he was going to bring the police into the street, if what he said or did was against the law, the less decent people had to do with him the better. She had a deep-rooted prejudice against being mixed up in anything.

Ruth was obstinate. "No one'll look here," she said. "What would Sid do with them?"

"That's his business, not yours. Let him bury them."

"You can't dig a hole in the asphalt."

"I'll talk to your father."

Wanda's anger sank into unforgiving sullenness. Ruth was sly, Ruth had been quicker than she, Wanda, who was the smartest girl in the street. He liked Ruth best.

Ally tackled Harry when he came in late at night.

"Ruthie's taken up with Sid Warren. She's got his books here that the police were looking for, and she won't take them back. You got to speak to her. Sid Warren's no good to her. The next thing we'll know, she'll be in trouble. I haven't been respectable all these years to have that happen to me. You got to speak to her."

Harry found talking to Ruth very difficult in prospect. To begin with, there was nowhere private where they could talk, and besides there was that unresolved, unspoken confidence between them sapping the parental authority.

He called her on to the balcony. Sitting on his bed, he took her hand awkwardly, held it in both his.

"Your mother wants me to talk to you," he said.

She gave him a clear look, and waited.

"About Sid Warren and those books."

"I can't just take them back. I said I'd mind them."

"They can't stay where they are, either." The thought formed in both their minds. "Not now that Wanda knows." "It would be safer if he found another place."

Ruth said almost inaudibly, "Yes."

"Would you like me to see him about it?"

"No, I will."

"What about Sid?"

She raised her face in one of those gestures of candour natural to her, so that the light from the street lamp fell full on it. "I haven't anything to be ashamed of, Dad."

"I know that, my dear. But——" embarrassment thickened painfully between them. "You are sort of fond of him aren't you."

She turned from the light as if she would hide her face in the darkness. "Sort of."

"I don't know how it is," he blundered on, still holding her hands against which her body dragged; "but I don't want you to get hurt, Ruthie. Men are sometimes thoughtless. They'll let you do all the giving."

She came to him now, let him pull her round.

"It's all right, Daddie," she said, a little breathlessly, as if she were laughing. "I haven't. I won't. He thinks I'm just a good kid, that's all."

Harry wasn't satisfied, but he knew he couldn't go any further now. Ruth felt it too. She withdrew her hand and walked quickly into the dark room behind them. Harry stayed, looking out at the houses across the street, but seeing nothing. Himself, Gwen, Ruth. Oh hell. Softly, with the lilt of strong emotion, he began to swear as he had not sworn since he was in the army, words like an unconscious incantation, smooth and natural, for all their ugliness, as the springing of natural sap. He could do nothing but beat frantically in the web that held him, unable to free himself from his own nature, from the ceaseless entanglement of lives not his own, and conditions to which he did not consent, unable to reach others caught like himself.

The web of a thousand million flies.

Paula Ramsay, coming home from a meeting, alone through the tree-lined streets, aware of a warm sibilance in the air, of lovers walking hand in hand; lifting her head to see a square of golden light high up in a dark building, feeling her heart touched, but touched to nothing; saying "Why am I not in love? What is wrong with me?" asking herself coldly, calculatingly, "Would Bowie do?" and knowing he would not; knowing only a miracle is any good.

Bowie walking from the same meeting in another direction, that word "tenebreuse" still working in his mind, a small flint upon which each passing hour left its accretions; seeing his square shadow on the pavement and realising how unlike himself this emotion was, how unlike his outward seeming all that he cared for, fought for, hoped for, was; knowing himself the prosaic champion of lost causes.

Mrs Ramsay looking up from a letter she was writing because of the silence in the house, feeling in the void the cold seepage of her loneliness, figuring things out. Her husband was dead, her daughter had left home, her sons were at boarding school. She had not loved Olaf, she had meant to, but she hadn't. He had been her husband and she had been his faithful competent wife, the convention had been fulfilled. Paula she had neither understood nor loved, but her going had robbed her of a daughter—or the simulacrum of a daughter. Her boys, being the normal healthy animals of her boast, had no need of her, the convention to which she subscribed reduced her to a figment in their lives. She had been bereaved and abandoned, and she felt it in her arid heart, in the terms of her glacial world, just as deeply as a passionate woman might have felt it in her emotions.

Arch Castles was flying his bomber over the sea, dark, cold, in the northern winter. Behind him was the mess where you talked of engines, of women, and other technicalities, and never mentioned death though death was their business. Death was with him now in the plane—his or the other fellow's—but the same death. It was more important than anything else, more real. The very effort not to acknowledge it stripped his mind of its natural armour in these lonely hours. Death wasn't an emotion or a thought. It was reality. It was not so much something that happened as a presence already there, beside him, a cause rather than an effect—the thing his training didn't cover. He understood something now. Competitive living had become competitive dying. The understanding hazed away in the mess, on leave, in the din and danger of the anti-aircraft barrage, but it came back again on night flight. In the great black emptiness it stood up like a pillar of fire. Death was his offsider there in the plane. He knew death though he had never seen any of the men he must have killed. Havoc was only a rose of fire and smoke. You didn't even bomb a target, you only "pranged" it.

It was Shirley's wedding night. She stood among the hire purchase furniture of her new bedroom, surrounded by her luggage. Geoff was putting the car away. She could hear the sounds he made impaled on the country silence. She could see through the window the swathes the car lights cut in the darkness as he backed it into the shed. She held her hat in her hand, blue straw, thinly pert, sharply gay. "A ball of style," Auntie Tib said with an air of indulgent censoriousness you couldn't do anything about. Shirley saw them—Auntie Tib and Mum sitting side by side, bulging identically in their electric blue dresses, Mum holding her little basket of red roses and frangipani on her sliding satin lap. Year by year those two grew more alike, and the self complacence each felt extended to the other. They had planned this marriage between them and now they were satisfied. It had really been their night, sitting side by side, high and solid because they had put on most of their weight round their hips and haunches, receiving the neighbours' congratulations over the heads of the bride and groom. Auntie Tib liked the marriage because it meant that Geoff would get Mum's place when Mum died, because he wouldn't be marrying a stranger, but someone she could manage and because, for all Shirley's flighty ways, going off to the city and all, she was a known quantity. Besides, now that Geoff was a married man people wouldn't say he ought to enlist. She had heard a plangent voice saying, not meant for her, "Geoff finds it easier to get married than to go to war." Mum had been all for the marriage because it got her (Shirley) fixed. She had been "flighty," but now it would be the same for her as it had been for her mother. Babies and work on the farm and the all-seeing eye of the neighbours. She probably would have a baby before the year was out. *That* could happen to her without her wanting it or willing it. All the things now would happen to her without her willing or wanting them. She was caught—in the machine called Life. Geoff was right. She'd fight with him but she liked him too. No, she didn't like him, not really, but she wanted him. There was a good hard chunkiness about Geoff that attracted her. And he'd been bothering her to marry him for a long time. He liked her all right, but he wouldn't want to marry her if there wasn't something else in it. Always, since she had grown up, she had longed for a fairy tale, but it had to be a true fairy tale. It had budded in her like her budding womanhood. She had only known the stale commercial name for it. Romance. She had taken the word of the cinema, the novel, the women's journals, for it. She had been enchanted and beguiled by the very name of it, and she had gone out to look for it. She'd tried the substitutes but they weren't any good. If she could have had the expensive illusions, they might have worked, but the cheap ones didn't. The glamour peeled off, the brocade showed its cotton back. The vessel was empty, marked "Made in Japan." So she had sickened and turned in her malaise to the thing from which she had fled, telling herself it was "real." She knew now, all at once, that it was no more "real" than the other. Her marriage satisfied, not her, but the greed and maternal ferocity of two old women. They were all looking for some sort of dividend—Auntie Tib, Mum, Geoff, herself—something on the side. The marriage itself was hollow, only a means. None of them would get what they wanted, and in a few years it wouldn't matter. Shirley accepted the immutability of her new state, just as she had accepted the fairy tale at its face value. Nature had put out two baits. It had caught her with the second. If only she hadn't had to know, if only she could have been in love with Geoff, or he with her, if only there had been enough glamour of any sort to float them along. . . .

Geoff stood in the doorway. She faced him, pale and wide-eyed, across her new luggage, her hat on the floor at her feet.

Chris and Arnie let the wireless run. When they came home in the evening they switched it on just as they switched on the light. They took whatever came, unless it happened to be classical music. That was a bit too thick, so then one or other would turn it to another station and accept its wares until it too offended. The blare filled all the available space in their overstuffed living-room, so that to one coming in from the comparative quiet it seemed a solid mass of furniture, light, and sound. It didn't trouble them, they rarely listened and could talk, read the newspaper, or make up their accounts without hindrance. It was companionable. It kept their world firmly packed in comfortable sawdust. If they did not happen to have anything else to do they could listen. This night there had been a vaudeville entertainment and they had listened. They like the jokes, and Arnie could sing a comic song with the best of them, so it came near home, so to speak. It put them into such an expansive mood that when it was over they went on listening. The vaudeville was followed by a talk on reconstruction and the sort of world the world might hope to be after the war was won. They heard the beginning of it quite by accident. An assured voice was saying, "Only the most thoughtless and romantic can imagine that life can ever return to its pre-war tempo. Change is inevitable, radical change, and it is for us to see that the change is for the better and not for the worse. One thing is certain. Our present economic system must be revised, the whole mechanism of profit must be overhauled and possibly scrapped. There will be sacrifices for all in the world that is coming. Be assured, privilege and parasitism must go. . . ." Arnie strode over and switched the wireless off. In the ensuing silence, a cold wind seemed to blow between them. The world and its troubled waters suited them. Freedom to fish in them was all they asked.

"A bloody red," said Arnie.

So many things could happen while a man cursed himself and his world. Every night there was a Passover and a slaying of the first born.

The war went its way, growing like an organic thing. Looking back, you knew it had begun not now, but long ago, in China, in Spain, in Abyssinia, in Austria, and Czecho-Slovakia, in Albania, in Jewry. . . . War was diffused through every country. Men were tortured, slowly and covertly by unemployment, malnutrition, frustration, maladjustment, or sharply and openly by pogrom, torture, concentration camp, by social instead of economic humiliation; men were fighting, not with the simplicity of destructive weapons, but with the confusion of words and ideas and the blunt pressures of authority and economic stress, with slogans and theories that were never wholly right and never wholly wrong; their hearts were calloused with horror, their reason seduced with argument, their confidence undermined by their own propaganda, their morale disrupted by hope and fear. It was a relief to cast all this away, or rather to blanket it, for the simplicity of war, and yet the war began with the people, on one side at least, already staled and weary, at the end of their first wind. The democracies could rely only on the dead weight of their wealth, the mechanic power of their defences, the resurrected habits of twenty-five years ago. Imaginatively they were exhausted, dispersed. In Germany, whatever else happened, the people were drawn into one steel-hard phalanx, not undone with false hopes but beaten hard with despair, chan-nelled, and concentrated. All the initiative was with the enemy. After the Polish campaign the war hung heavy and slow. For months the blackout took a higher toll of life than the war. Prophets lifted their voices, warning men against their own complacency. That complacence was the mask of spiritual exhaustion and imaginative sterility. The torpor was all on one side.

Suddenly, the thing opened another freshet of growth. The German armies overran Holland and Denmark and invaded Norway. The garnered peace of the north was ruptured like tissue paper. The optimists said, "Hitler has walked into the jaws of the Navy." There was fighting in the fiords, in the Skaggerak and Kattegat, and at Narvik the battle for Norway was lost. The black shutter came down over northern Europe. In England the Government fell and war came into the kitchens, for there was no more Danish butter and bacon and eggs, no more cheese from Holland.

There was another pause, shorter this time. England darned over the rents in her self esteem. Then came the drive east into Belgium, south into France. The Maginot Line was turned. Divided, uncertain, France wavered under the impact. The King of the Belgians surrendered at the head of his army, knowing help would not come and believing that he must save his people, better sooner than later. The very fabric of France broke in confusion. Villages in the German path emptied on to the roads, refugees hampered the army and were mown down. No one knew what to do, no one had the resolution to deal with that flood of helpless humanity. It was as if the very cells of the nation's body were breaking down in decay. It was not the refugees however that ruined France; they were only the symptom of a deeper ill. From top to bottom nothing held. In vain were premiers shuffled, commanders changed. In vain did France appeal to America— sentiment could not be harnessed to reality. With unconscious superb bathos, England offered France the shelter of the union and was rejected. On her southern flank Italy came into the war, looking for easy spoils. Paris, bombed once, was declared an open city. France had fallen, it remained only to capitulate. The British Expeditionary Force, fighting alone now, outmanœuvred, out-equipped, out-numbered, was rolled up and driven into the sea at Dunkirk.

Now at last, the imagination of the English people stirred. They saw a clear and simple issue and they rose to it. Their shattered army, their men, were across the Channel on the shell-torn beach of Dunkirk, the arc of fire closing in on them. This was no policy, no abstraction, no specialised service. Every available man, young boys, and old men in every craft that would float, went out and, working with the Navy, under fire, in calm and fog, they brought their men home. Dunkirk was the first victory. A people's victory.

It had nothing to do with war or fighting, the people had risen at last, to save not to destroy. Dunkirk pegged the war for the moment.

There was another pause and that was strange. Germany had everything to gain by pushing on immediately to the invasion of England. England was laid open, her army disorganised, her battlegear lost, but the push did not come at once. It was as if the war had a life of its own, a life apart from German initiative; it moved like an organism, not like a machine. It had rhythm. It spent itself and must pause before a new effort. In August and September came the blitzkrieg that should have been prelude to invasion and was not. England weathered the blitzkrieg. Again it was the people's victory, the organized will to live. The invasion fleet was broken before it set sail. "Never have so many owed so much to so few." Churchill was Prime Minister. He looked like a bulldog, he was eloquent, he was of the blood of the great Duke of Marlborough. He was the Great Slogan, the very figurehead of the unconscious conspiracy to believe that advertisement was worth, and propaganda fact, that the gestures of power were in very truth power. People were only too glad to believe in Winston Churcill and to lay on him the burden.

For Australia, the war was still over the sea and far away. The A.I.F. was in Palestine. Presently it was fighting in the First Libyan campaign, rolling up Graziani's great army, from Sidi Barrani to Benghazi, sending back its horde of prisoners, collecting its souvenirs, domesticating the desert, looting Italian champagne, swimming in the Mediterranean. That was not all. Casualty lists began to come home.

Again the war broke loose, pouring down the Danube into the Balkans, submerging the conflict already in progress between Italy and Greece. Despite ominous murmurs of a German army gathering in the desert, the victorious Libyan army was brought to Greece. In the mountains and passes of Greece, at Thermopylae itself, the Diggers fought, ill-equipped and without air protection. They were trapped and driven into the sea. It was a black Easter in Australia. Under a sky that rained bombs the Navy brought the Army, as many as could get away, to Crete, and there it made another stand, without air support, without anti-aircraft guns, against an enemy that dropped fantastically from the skies and against the shattering assaults of dive-bombers to which they had no answer. Once more the Navy evacuated them, at heavy cost, to Alexandria in Egypt. Now there were casualty lists without victory. Even the Libyan victories were gone, for the phantom army had come out of the desert with tanks and bombers, and taken the coast again from Benghazi to Hellfire Pass. Except Tobruk.

Again the pause, when it seemed as if the Germans must move from Crete to Cyprus, from Cyprus to Syria, and so to the oil of Persia. But the blow did not fall. England, moving carefully under a diplomatic umbrella,

invaded Syria and took it from France without declaration of war. The
A.I.F. was there too.

The world waited for the new blow that would dissipate the complacence
of the democracies that sprouted again in every pause. It came, not
through Turkey, not through Spain to Gibraltar, not even an invasion of
England, but an assault on Russia. From the White Sea to the Black Sea,
Germany, Roumania, and Finland moved against the Soviet in the most
gigantic battle strategy the world had ever known. That was in the autumn
of 1941. The Russian armies gave ground, scorching the earth as they left it,
burning crops, wrecking bridges, laying waste the land, destroying their
great dam on the Dnieper, one of the world's wonders, one of the symbols
of their own creed and triumph. They retreated but they did not yield, till in
winter they turned and drove the invader back, four hundred miles, five
hundred miles, over the same scorched earth with enormous casualties.

In that same winter the fourth Libyan campaign began and at first went
well, and then not so well. Now the whole world was criss-crossed with fire.
War in the air over England, British bombers over Germany, sea war in the
Atlantic, the Hood lost, the Bismarck lost, the long fight of the convoys
bringing food and munitions to England; in the Mediterranean; as far away
as the River Plate; the land war in Russia, China, Africa; conquered people
fighting secretly and stubbornly all over Europe; guerrilla bands in the
mountains of Jugo-Slavia, Free Frenchmen dismembering France's
colonial Empire; Spain, Portugal, Sweden, Turkey, Eire, uneasily neutral;
the A.I.F. in Malaya learning jungle warfare lest the Japanese in their
incredible folly should join their partners of the Axis. . . . Snow storm of
leaflets, high wind of propaganda.

There had been three winters of war now, it had imposed its pattern on
millions of lives. The armies, great hordes of men taken from the normal
context of their lives, and, by that change, both disciplined and freed, were
become new social entities. They built their legends and their folklore.
They had their songs and stories, rough, genuine, coming up out of the
substance of their lives. Of the present, they were also legendary, the
ancient primitive background of life, stifled by civilisation, was reinforced
and allowed to flower again. Everywhere, men were doing the incredible;
men, enduring incredible perils and hardships in open boats and surviving;
men cut off in the desert trekking two hundred miles to their own lines,
finding their water in the radiators of abandoned trucks, in the water bottles
of dead soldiers, in the enemy camps; men adrift everywhere in strange
places, fending for themselves, domesticating danger, finding ways to live;

Diggers throwing pennies to dignitaries come to welcome them; Diggers stoning their own airmen in bitterness of heart after Crete, the ancient token of revenge. Since the dinosaurs perished from the earth, the like of those battles had not been seen. Soldiers floated down from the sky, sailors lived under the sea. Mechanics became fabulous, science a grim fairly tale. Engines of death, ships and planes, had folk names—Tribal cruisers, Kittyhawks, Hurricanes, Spitfires. . . .

The strange old-new life of the armies seeped back to the people at home, altering too the minds of those who waited. The lives of civilians were regimented. They learned the value of bread. They formed new habits. They learned new tempos and rhythms of work. In danger they went back to mother earth. They shared fear and emotion. A clarification was taking place in the confusion of men's thinking, sides took more distinct shape, the crisscross faded, the main divisions deepened. The Right must call Russia ally, however unpalatable the word, the Left must support the war, for the Socialist fatherland was at stake. So some of the fissures were closed for the time being, and war become more real, peace more remote.

In Australia war was more than an echo, it was a vibration under foot.

.     .     .     .     .     .     .     .     .

Knarf paused and looked across at Ord, something more than thought struggling in his eyes. "I can see the pattern of those days clearly enough, an iron framework laid down on the soft tissues of life, and within that framework, like tender, necessary, human breath in an iron lung, life springing anew, under the name of adjustment, repeating its ancient design. Beyond this again I see an enormous sweep of event, not mechanic, not planned, but the logical outcome of the vast aggregate of human planning. Beyond its authors' control, probably beyond their apprehension. We can see it because the astringent of time has simplified and stilled it. World events in the making must be like a mountain range in the making. Only after centuries is the outline plain and set. The turmoil of the rock is stilled, the heaving strata fixed. One is as logical a process as the other, as fore-ordained by the law of cause and effect, as much in ease at one moment as at another." Knarf stopped and frowned.

"Plenty of heaving strata in mind," Ord thought, watching him, waiting to see how he would extricate himself from his own thoughts.

Knarf turned back from the involved conception of a becoming that was yet at any given moment in esse, to the firmer ground of his argument.

"The immense sweep of event in the twentieth century was, must have been, quite broken loose from human planning. Ideologies, strategies, tactics were only ingredients. There was a flow, majestic and in a way rhythmic, for which man himself was not responsible. He made war but war also happened to him. The world was undoubtedly out of control. But event was not, of course, in the wider sense, arbitrary or unreasonable. The basic logic after which man's reasoning is imperfectly modelled was in control of it. I can see all that well enough, the shape, the flow, the middle register of which the politicians and leaders and generals had a precarious hold, and the overtones and undertones, but it is like a hard still pattern. I cannot clear my mind of the knowledge that it is all something that has· happened, something accomplished, finished. That's why I fail. I can't get back to the emotion of that time. Think what it must have been—men living amongst events raised to the nth, a world a hundred times bigger in all its implications than ours. The sort of world they lived in must have warmed to feverish life every emotion of which man is capable. All the rest can be re-imagined. But not emotion. That is lost."

Ord stirred himself. "Aren't you treating emotion as if it were an arithmetical progression? It isn't, you know. Your argument about control applies to emotion. If the mind did not apprehend the mass of event, neither would emotions. Actually people may have felt less and less acutely than they do in our plainer simpler days. They were overwhelmed by a world out of control. Their lives were as self-contained as veins, their emotions channelled."

Knarf seemed to have lost interest again. He was turning the pages of his manuscript. The general having become untenable, he was in flight to the particular.

.    .    .    .    .    .    .    .

Harry watched the war from what might be called the disadvantage point of the main shopping hall at Morgan's. He saw it, of course, in a distorting mirror, a war in little, a war in shoddy. He was a unit in the great business-as-usual front. The great store adjusted itself to war conditions. The management urged its young men to enlist. It did not make up the difference between their military pay and their salaries—that would be making free with other peoples' money—but it did follow the policy of employing their wives if suitable. Once employed, it encouraged them to look on their service as war work. The whole shop was intensely co-operative in the war effort. Every man and girl could do his or her bit, by selling more wool for soldiers' socks, more trousseaux for brides (10% reduction if the 'groom were in the Forces), more layettes for war babies, packing more parcels for men at the Front, keeping up other women's morale with more cosmetics, indirectly brightening the lives of countless soldiers by selling more hats and dresses, furs and undies, by contributing regularly via the store to war charities and fighting funds, by attributing all hardships and inequalities to war conditions and not grumbling. Old men didn't retire, they kept on working, girls at girls' wages did the work of men. The store was busier than ever. There was a new magic formula that pepped up the vitality of sales in every department. "There is going to be a shortage of this, madam, we have no new supplies coming in." Every salesman and woman availed himself of it because the management believed in competitive selling. They pitted sales record against sales record, and, of course, the assistant who had the best record got on and those who had poor records didn't. Merit must be rewarded. When labour was plentiful the girl who "didn't make her book" was dismissed when, periodically, the department retrenched. It was like a weekly examination to be passed, a source of misery and anxiety. That was lifted now. It was a dumb girl who could not "make her book" when everyone wanted to spend. Goods were better than money. Merchandise was solid, you could see it and use it, but money was only a fiction, and one day its value might disappear, and then, where would you be? So people, chiefly women, bought and bought and bought. They liked it, the management liked it— for, apparently, they still preferred cash to merchandise—it made the assistants feel safe and it filled the shop with a good rich smell of prosperity that reassured everyone who came into its lively air-conditioned atmosphere. One customer incited another to buy. And wasn't everything a bargain when you thought how expensive things were going to be? A rise in prices didn't quench the buyers' ardour, rather did it stimulate it, because it went to prove that there would be further increases later. Therefore it was better to buy now. Now went on and on, elastic Now.

Customers like co-operating, too. They were rarely disagreeable when they were asked to take an inferior article at a greatly enhanced price. It was the War. Most of them were quite ready to carry their own parcels or buy their own paper and string. Customers and management suffered together, quite pleasantly and even dramatically. Life was dramatized, a box-office profit accrued. The staff got the backwash and that was something, even if they were always tired, must do without holidays, and fell more readily a prey to colds and minor ailments.

Harry could see all this, and it provoked him to bitterness. It was not quite clear to him against whom he should be bitter. He naturally felt that the management was the villain, because after all they got the profits, and it was a simple reliable rule that if you tracked down the profits you found the villain. But it was always pointed out that the management too was caught in the war machine. If people wanted to buy, why shouldn't they sell? Did he want the shop to close its doors? Well, no, he didn't. And all the profits, or nearly all, were taken away in taxation, and if there weren't any profits, then all the poor widow women who had invested their mites in the business would be thrown on the state. And the shop did keep a couple of thousand homes going, and a great human responsibility to survive in an uncertain world was laid on the management because of the dependent shareholders and the two thousand homes. The manager, too, was just a man on a salary like himself—only it was rather a different salary. In the end, Harry got confused and supposed it was society that was to blame. That was an unsatisfactory answer. The bitterness persisted, like a thin sour taste in his mouth. It might have been a hangover from the last war, a soldier's resentment against civilians. It might be that he recognised anew the futility of his job.

Sometimes he felt that he was having a good look at the world for the first time. There were the same crowds, always in and out of the store, the lifts were as full of big bosoms as ever. No one was getting thin on the war. He didn't want them to, he just noticed that they didn't. It was just the same, but not quite the same. You could smell the news, whether it was good or bad, in the shop. The atmosphere was never quite even and prosaic. Sometimes it got very tight. Because there was a war people thought they had more right to let their emotions go in public. They had more emotions to release. So many had the same emotions, and that gave them confidence. Perhaps it didn't go very deep, but there it was, a shimmer. It didn't really ball up into a force you could use. There was a lot of co-operative effort about, but that, on the whole, was only superficial. New societies were continually being formed to help the war effort. The assembly rooms upstairs were continually let to one or another, the personnel was always changing, always quarrelling. The big bosoms were in it up to the neck, and Harry hadn't any faith in the big bosoms.

When you looked round the shop it seemed piled high as ever with merchandise, but when you looked closer, it wasn't the same merchandise. There were more tawdry things that people didn't need and fewer that they did. Hollowness was creeping in. Like food that filled without satisfying. Gradually it began to seem to Harry that he wasn't looking at reality but at a facade, not a facade to anything, but just a facade over nothing, and it was as if people weren't villains or victims, they were dupes, and things were changing without anyone giving them leave or being responsible.

Gwen had not yet been sent to a department. She was still at the half-price table. She tried but she didn't get on. She still looked very childish and rather helpless. It was just as if no one noticed her and she had been forgotten in the big staff. There did not seem any reason why she should be remembered. By dint of always giving satisfaction, being unfailingly polite, smiling her shy sweet smile, perennially sincere, she escaped. As the cost of living rose, she found it more and more difficult to live. The first time she got into difficulties, Harry, seeing she was miserable, forced her to tell him the reason. Shamed and wretched, she accepted a loan. Soon it came about that he helped her every week, two or three shillings. She took it with a tender sadness. When she did not need any help she was gay about it, as if she were giving him a little present. The arrangement, from wounding her sensitiveness, became a source of happiness. He knew that the way she looked at it, though neither of them said so, was that, but for him, she would be rooming with another girl, and so her expenses would be less. It was quite reasonable that he should help. To leave the arrangement indefinite and irregular saved face.

It was difficult for Harry to find the money, but, because he had concealed his increase in wages, he was able to manage it, cutting down his smoking and giving up the beers he occasionally had on his way home. If he went home with Gwen he didn't want the beers anyway, but he spent more than that on their dinner. It made him think that Gwen ought to have someone to look after her "properly," and feel curiously and unreasonably guilty. It seemed to him that her youth gave her all the rights in their relationship. When he said to her, "You ought to have someone younger than me," she had smothered the words with kisses, as if she feared to lose him, feared that the slow force of age would separate them and she would be left alone.

So they went on. He had for her the glamour, not easily worn out, of a mind more integrated than her own. He reassured her in a dozen ways, not least by showing her consistently a picture of herself that flattered her. She was romantic and tenacious. Having believed—as she must to justify herself—that she loved, she would not and dared not relinquish the belief. It was her one foothold in Arcady. For his part, Harry clung helplessly to an idyll, knowing its tenuousness, knowing all about it, still seeing it as a gift, an unexpected reinforcement of his hungry spirit. There was a genuine tenderness on both sides. They were always kind to one another, not like young lovers. His body, still hard, still straight, satisfied her. Hers, womanly for all its fugitive girlishness, could enchant him. Sometimes, just sometimes, she seemed very remote as Ally never had in the days when they were lovers, and he did not know if the remoteness were in her or in himself. The change, when it came, seemed at first no more than a flicker, a change of light, a passing shadow, that hardened into something real.

To many 1941 had seemed a year of fate. On the calendar it rose like one of those waves that in a storm at sea hump themselves upon the horizon. There is the ship, one point in the great troubled circle of the horizon, there is the culminating danger moving on its path, plotted as surely as a star's orbit. There is the whole wide ocean, the ship would seem to have infinite opportunity of escape from that one danger, but she is in its path. While it is distant it seems small and those who talk of it are prophets. They are not so much prophets as mathematicians.

In the economic alignment of the world, the have-not nations against the haves, it was inevitable that sooner or later Japan must join the battle. She was surrounded by treasure-bearing islands with absentee owners, and was as much a victim of nature as would be the hungry dingo in a lambing paddock. In the race for armaments, observers thought, Japan would reach her optimum moment for attack somewhere in 1941; that moment would be the highest peak in her own armament and preparedness before the strength of America began to gain on her. The storm broke on the night of the 7th-8th of December 1941. Japan attacked on a wide front from the American base at Pearl Harbour in Hawaii to Hong Kong on the coast of China. A shock ran round the world, an hour had struck. The attack was a surprise. Nations cannot really prepare for that which they hope will be averted. America was caught napping. Britain was caught unprepared. The battle of the Pacific had begun. In three months Hong Kong had fallen, and with it the whole fabric of British tradition in the Far East; Malaya was invaded and taken; Singapore, the great island fortress, surrendered; the Dutch East Indies were attacked; Burma was invaded and the Burma Road threatened. Two capital ships, the Prince of Wales and the Repulse, were lost in one action, and the Japanese possessed the sky and the seas. It was a brilliant and precise campaign, moving from objective to objective with unwavering military logic. It was war waged, not on strong points, but on vital links—to cut lines of communication, to destroy or capture air bases, to seize oil fields and storage. When this was done the strong points could be bypassed or became useless through attrition.

Australia knew the reality of danger at last, saw her bulwarks stripped. The covering fleet had gone, impregnable Singapore had gone, the strategy on which she relied had broken down, American help was still little more than imposing figures on paper, the last shield, the Indies, was in peril. She had lost an army in Libya, Greece, and Crete, she lost a second army in Malaya; her men and armaments had gone abroad and now she must face the storm. She was vulnerable and laid open, and there was the White Australia policy to add savour to the conflict. For the first time, and perhaps in theory only, Australia became a Commonwealth. The Government, organising all resources in the face of danger, assumed control of manpower, industry, finance, pegged wages, pegged profits, pegged interest, drew in to itself and for the common use the wealth of the country.

The flying voices asked, "Is this Socialism or is it Fascism?" No one knew what it might turn out to be. They asked, "Why is it that these changes which amount to revolution can be made only in the face of a war which nullifies all good that might accrue, and not when their logical consequences might have made war an anachronism?" And other voices answered triumphantly, "This is no time for argument, discussion, theory. All that is past. Now we act." Somehow men must find powers of organisation such as they had never used before. It was not enough that wealth should flow into the treasury, that everyone should work; the power must be implemented, the work co-ordinated, the whole means must be focused on its end.

The people waited to be led, it was easier to trust than to doubt. They clung to their habits for reassurance, but the situation was brought home to them in scarcities, in air-raid precautions, in blacked-out cities, in the changing face of their daily lives. Realisation gradually penetrated people's minds and was made over according to their natures. As ever, it was the mature who carried the burden of the world. Everyone, whether they knew it or not, was a little heightened, a little dramatized, posed against a new backcloth. Panic went like a shiver through the community and passed. Life went on and people lived it.

It was the day of the first full-dress Australia-wide black-out test. The shop was just opening. Harry paused by Gwen's table.

"Ready for the black-out?" he asked her. One thing was as good to say as another.

She shook her head. "Could you come out tonight, Harry?" she asked in a low voice, pleading. She looked pinched, he thought, and a little desperate.

Whatever she had asked, he would have answered the urgency of her voice.

"Yes, of course. Go straight home and I'll follow you." They no longer met in the street near the shop, they had come to accept a technique of secrecy, to be sensible and accept the chill that that involved. They rarely spoke to one another when on duty. Harry's uniform, from being a precarious cover for snatched words and glances, had become a barrier, a formality between them. He no longer had to guard himself against the temptation to look at her.

Now he walked away and exchanged a few words with other girls standing at their tables and counters. "Harry," they called him, "Miss," he said. "Now, Mr Munster, leave my young ladies alone. Get to work, girls," rolling up the idle moment like a strip of carpet.

"That's a madam," thought Harry, returning to his lifts, scooping up and despatching the first hesitant customers. He wasn't busy yet. Through the distant door he could see the yellow sunlight in the street. His mind turned to Gwen. Something had been wrong for two or three weeks now. He tried to pin it down, but like a shadow it evaded him. He'd seen very little of her. That was easy to explain. Two nights a week he was kept back for instruction in fire fighting, another night she had to go to a first-aid class. They'd both been tired, driven, they'd let the time go by, he as much as she. She hadn't wanted any money, either. He had asked her, "How's the budget?" and she had just shaken her head. That mightn't mean anything, but it stuck in his mind that it did. A grain or two of evidence refused to melt his mind. A girl in the handkerchiefs had given a birthday party. It must have been a couple of months ago. Gwen had gone and she'd met a soldier boy there. Cliff. Cliff something or other. Down from the country. He'd made a hit with her, or she'd been sorry for him because he was lonely. She'd talked about him. And then she'd stopped talking. Just that. She'd had a lot to say about this boy and then she'd shut up. Maybe he'd fallen for her. Maybe she'd fallen for him. Maybe he'd just gone away and she'd forgotten him. Perhaps she was just tired now and suffering from war jitters. But that wasn't how she looked. Harry stood still and stiff, obstructing traffic, disregarding the customers and the lifts awaiting his signal. He knew what it was. He'd seen that look on Gwen's face, half happy, half sad, vulnerable, tremulous, faintly ecstatic. He had seen it there before in their early days together. The look of a girl in love, diaphanous, transient. You saw it and you lost it, you couldn't be sure, but he was sure. She was in love with her soldier boy and she was worried—about him. Tonight. Tonight she was going to try to say something. He'd have to make it easy. He didn't know what he thought or felt. Only that look of Gwen's, that she wore now for someone else, stirred him, made him feel again as he used to feel when it was for him

He came to himself with a jerk. There was a big crowd this morning and it had tied itself into knots round him. The lift men were grinning. The only fun they got was in seeing someone go off the rails now and then. The madam at the stocking counter was staring at him. The supervisor wasn't down on him yet. He got it straightened out. Looking across at Gwen he saw only the back of her neck, childish and vulnerable. If I were a rich man, he thought, and free, I could marry her, and give her everything. But I'd still be twenty years older. It was more than twenty years. He didn't worry about details. Passing her he said softly, "I'll bring the eats tonight."

She gave him a quick smile, agreeing as if she wanted to please him.

He bought some ham, tomatoes, a tin of peaches, a tin of cream concentrate, a bottle of cheap wine. He was determined that they would eat handsomely. Situations were often improved by eating. It was a gesture of tenderness too. He remembered the little feast she had made for him the first time. That seemed a long time ago.

It was late when he arrived. She was waiting for him, the table set, an air of shamed expectancy transmitted from herself to the room. When she saw what he had brought, her eyes filled with tears. They ate slowly, each pretending for the other to enjoy the feast more thàn they did. Despite everything, the wine worked on them, a little colour came to Gwen's cheeks. They washed up and then it seemed as if the evening had run into a blank wall. Harry didn't guess nor suspect now, he knew. The shadow had become as solid as the walls that surrounded them. He wanted to make it easy for her but he did not know how. He felt her gathering nervousness.

"Why doesn't it begin?" she cried at last.

He had forgotten the blackout, Yes. That was what they were waiting for the signal, the solvent. He looked at the one window.

"You haven't any blackout."

"We'll turn out the light. It's only for an hour."

"It might be every night too. I'll come out one evening and fix it for you."

"Oh, I'll manage. It doesn't matter."

"You can't be alone in the dark."

"Who cares?" He hadn't heard that high note of recklessness in her before.

"I won't come if you don't want me to."

"I didn't say I didn't want you to, only that it doesn't matter."

"It comes to the same thing."

"Don't, Harry."

She seemed frightened because they had come too near to what was in her mind. He put his hand over hers. She neither accepted it nor rejected it. Presently she got up and moved about the room.

The alert took them by surprise. It wailed and swooped, filling the air with a clamour of disaster, a ferocious mechanic lamentation. Harry snapped off the light. They stood still, darkness congealed round them. He could just see Gwen standing against the paler square of the window. He crossed to her and with his arm about her drew her to the open window. The sirens seemed to be focused on them.

"It's dark," she said.

"Of course."

The building next door was a black crag against the cloudy moonlit sky, the street below them was a gulch of darkness. It was strange, changed, foreign. The sirens stopped abruptly. Silence congealed on darkness. Harry felt her trembling and his arms closed tightly about her.

"It's only a test. We'll have the lights back in an hour." He spoke soothingly.

"It might happen—really." It was as if this pretending made a channel along which reality could flow.

"It might. But it wouldn't be nearly as bad as you'd expect. The things that happen to everybody all at once never are. We'd all be in it together, so we'd find a way out. It wouldn't be like having trouble alone." He knew the fallacy of his words. It would probably be much worse than anything she could imagine, or that he could remember from the last war. He talked on, explaining away the danger. It didn't matter what he said. She was not really listening. It was his voice and his arms that reassured her. She had always been afraid, he remembered, of thunderstorms. He felt the panic dying out of her, leaving her changed, washed up and helpless in his arms. He wanted her to sit down, but she would not leave the window. The roar of traffic was stilled. Perhaps it was that, rather than the darkness, that made the night so ghostly and menacing. Harry waited. He felt more sure now. If the unnatural darkness and quiet cut them off from the world that had always been so much with them, it cut them off together, held them in a confidence that might be transitory but was real while it lasted. He knew that under cover of the darkness they would be able to say things that would be too difficult in the light. He wasn't in any hurry.

He didn't know how long they stood like that, time flowed at a different pace under new conditions. He knew he had conveyed to her something of the quiet tenderness that was in his heart for her.

"You're nice, Harry," she said at last, as if it were the end of a long train of thought. She rubbed her cheek softly against his shirt. He passed his hand over her hair and rested it on the back of her neck, the white, vulnerable, childish neck that always had power to move him.

"Something you got to tell me, isn't there, Gwennie?" He could feel her stiffen, emotion knotting in her again.

"Its about that boy, isn't it?" He caught the name as it was disappearing out of his mind. "Cliff."

"You know?" There was relief and accusation in her voice. "There isn't anything to know, only . . ."

"I don't know, I just guessed how it might be. You've got sort of fond of one another, haven't you?"

She caught her breath. "Oh, Harry."

"It's like that, is it?"

"I couldn't help it, truly I couldn't. He's a soldier and . . ." she gulped. "Poor kid."

"I didn't want to hurt you, Harry. I wouldn't have seen him any more, but he's going away." Her misery overwhelmed her. "He's a soldier. He could get killed, easy as anything. I couldn't . . ." She was appealing to him.

"Of course, you couldn't."

"You been good to me, Harry, I didn't know how to tell you."

"Shut up," he said roughly. "You don't have to worry, we're not bound."

She wasn't deceived. "I feel mean, but I can't help it."

"You don't have to."

"I don't want to spoil your life." She'd got that out of a book, but she meant it too.

"I'm a lot older than you. I knew this'd got to happen, see. I can take it."

She felt him grin. She was relieved. Yes, she thought, it had got to happen. That's how Cliff felt too. They belonged.

"Yes," she said softly and slowly.

"What's he going to do?"

She was puzzled. "He's got to go where he's sent. Any time now."

"I mean about you."

"We're—sort of engaged. Only what's the good?" Poor kid. The war. What was the good of their planning, they were helpless.

"He'll come back. Most of 'em come back, you know. I did."

"That's what he says. Oh, Harry, he's . . ." Poor funny kid. She wanted to tell him about her boy. She only remembered just in time. She didn't want to hurt him. He knew with a pang that nothing that had been between them really mattered. It had all been blown away.

"Tell me," he said.

She did tell him, a jumble of details like the treasures in a small boy's pocket. He felt her growing flushed and happy as she talked. He knew that she had that indefinable look. She fell silent at last, he felt trouble in her again.

"Harry, he . . ."

He knew what she was going to say.

"Harry, Cliff doesn't know . . . about us."

"He hasn't got to know."

She was thinking herself a woman with a past.

"I haven't hurt you, have I? Or done you any harm?"

"No, Harry."

"Well, it doesn't matter, does it?" He was trying to say, only it was too difficult. "You're going to him, enriched not impoverished, a woman not a girl. He'll want a woman."

She said slowly, again, "You been good to me, Harry."

"You've been good to me too, Gwen."

That seemed final. She didn't draw out of his arms. He held her. There was an interval of darkness.

"Harry."

"Yes."

"I'm frightened."

"It's all right. It may never happen. Probably won't." He thought she meant the war.

"It has happened. It'll go on happening. We're helpless. All of us." He rocked her gently in his arms.

"So you know that, do you?" He wasn't speaking to her but over her head to himself.

"Please, Harry, don't leave me alone. Because of Cliff . . . He's going away and I . . . I can't be alone, I'm frightened."

"No, Gwen, no. I'll stay around."

"You do understand? It's all . . . so dreadful . . . like . . . being lost in the dark." She was sobbing wildly. Poor kid, she'd been trying to cope with it all, the war and being alone, afraid of him and afraid for him and heaven knows what. He comforted her. It was a relief to comfort someone, the only thing that could be a relief.

The prolonged steady note of the All Clear sounded. Lights leapt in windows and in the streets. The world was familiar again, dropping back into its old slot. Harry could see Gwen's face in the light reflected from the opposite wall, like a pale drowned face floating in water.

Slipping out of the building half an hour later, Harry looked about him consideringly. He thought for the first time of the war potential of this place. This crowded hill above the city, this great tangle of bricks and mortar, so much of it jerrybuilt. Warrens. Old houses, encrusted with balconies, temporary partitions, bric-a-brac, lumber of all sorts. Inflammable. The back lanes, culs-de-sac—what a shambles it would be, what a trap, if the bombs began to fall. Imagine fire in those crowded streets. And panic, the logical retribution of the sordid greedy herding. And the unconsolidated people. Thousands of them, living alone in single rooms, without families, without friends, without resources. A few bombs and the whole fabric would break down and gutter down the hill into the slums below. Gwen might well feel the terribly anonymous loneliness of her state.

A wry smile twisted his lips as he walked away. The young asked for plenty. She wanted her soldier boy and him, asked him to stay on as second best because she was afraid of the dark. He'd never come so near to loving her. She should have every bloody thing he could give her. He'd be Santa Claus.

Bowie, Paula, and the Professor were working in Paula's flat on party business, a committee of three. The Professor was more disposed to talk than to work. Paula didn't consider him much of an asset. Sometimes she let her intolerance show through her perfunctory good manners. The Professor only cocked a quizzical eye at her. "Ah, youth, youth," he said with an inflection that implied something damaging. When the alert sounded, Paula jumped up and hooked the three-ply blackout shutters over the windows. She had only to close the doors and they were in a tight light-proof box.

"Efficiency," said Bowie.

"She got a highly-paid expert in to do it all, didn't you, Paula?"

"We pay for other services, why not for blackout?"

"You don't profit by the opportunity the times offer to prepare yourself for the return to cave dwelling?"

"Don't I work, don't I slave?" She continued to jab viciously at the typewriter with one finger and a frown. The Professor chuckled.

The siren wore itself out. It was quiet and stuffy. They worked in silence. Compressed light and silence—they all felt it.

"Damn," said Bowie, throwing down his pencil, "we can't stay here. Let's go out."

It was intolerable to be shut up when the world outside was changed. They felt as much entombed in their patch of hemmed-in light as if they were in a tunnel.

"Claustrophobia," said the Professor, briskly banging his books together.

They set out along Darlinghurst Road, arms linked, Paula in the middle. She could feel the professor's brittle sprightliness. A young man would not have been more active, but the whole quality of his activity would have been different. Paula was ever so slightly repelled. She liked the old to stay old. She knew too, for all his dry mockery, some of his display was put on for her. Even if she disliked it, it was so much current and she used it. On the other side she felt Bowie's controlled and even strength. She was aware of it as a slow vortex into which she might be drawn. She was afraid that some day the need for spiritual safety might drive her to Bowie, and she didn't want safety or, rather, she didn't want to want it. It would be capitulation and betrayal of the carefully built up self she hoped to become. To marry Bowie, or even to love him, would be the end of adventure. If you accepted him you took something so definite and so steady that you'd be moored for ever. She wanted Bowie behind her, but not beside her. His self-control was like a cage and she'd be on the inside of the cage if she married Bowie. He hadn't asked her, but she knew she could. Bowie had grown up very young—on the outside. He was an old young man. Inside he was maturing slowly. Like a cut that heals from the outside. Bowie and his soapbox. Bowie and his Cause. Bowie was a natural haven in a stormy world. She was too young for havens. She wanted to believe and be free. Perhaps you couldn't have it both ways. She wanted to be sure. The thought of Bowie standing by waiting—for all the world as if she were a wreck or a potential wreck—made her wild sometimes. Not now. Not tonight. Bowie's arm was a good arm to hold in a blackout.

There was a full moon, but clouds were scudding over it. Its direct light was fitful, but the world was pervaded by a faint luminance. The professor spread his handkerchief over his chest, tucking it in like a bib, to give himself substance in a world of shadows, he said. It was easy enough to avoid running into people, but at first they could not walk fast because the darkness seemed to tangle their feet, the ordinary balance between sight and pace was upset. It was short-range walking instead of long-range walking, and the natural confidence of the pedestrian was impaired. A little pulse of excitement beat in Paula's brain.

She said, "Everything looks bigger." There was a close drawn purposefulness about the Cross. She hadn't felt it there before. And something else. She struggled to define it. There were cliffs of darkness and chasms of shadow, here and there the moonlight picked out a facade in sharp clarity, unexpected outlines showed against the sky. Not only was so much rubbed out in darkness, but other unrealised aspects were emphasised.

"I know what it is," said Paula, "the incidence of light and shadow is quite different. It's strange, it's new, it's marvellous."

"Every day the light paints a new city, but we've got the convention of what it looks like so stuck in the mud of our imaginations that we don't see it. We live in a mirage and don't know it. It takes something unusual to shock our eyes open. We live in a flux and a mirage."

"There are thousands of cities here, everyone has one to himself."

"When you make the idea too mystical it blows away altogether, like a cobweb.

"There's a solid core of bricks and stone, but in itself it is meaningless. Over it the city of the imagination is laid, layer upon layer. We build it out of ourselves as the bees build their comb."

"So if it is destroyed, it won't matter."

"There are, there must be, a few things worth saving. I don't really know what they are, I can only postulate them, but several human beings, a few pictures, perhaps a torn sheet of paper here and there, with a few verses written on them, a letter, a bowl. . . . Things on which life has left its fingerprints. I collect, *objets d'art, objets de vertu.* The collections aren't valuable though they are worth money. I look on them as dragnets. They might catch something, just one thing with life's fingerprints on it. The trouble is I don't trust myself to know so I have to keep a lot of things. If the city were bombed no one would think of saving the valuable things. All the wrong things would be saved."

"The G.P.O., for instance."

"The quick, the pulse would be buried under the debris. It would be forgotten because no one had recognised it."

"What would you save, Bowie?"

"The youngest child I could find, because there'd be a chance he might be a Shakespeare or a Beethoven."

"What would you save, Paula?"

"A powder box that I have. It belonged to my great great grandmother, it's beautiful and sophisticated and I love it. I know what it is, it would never turn out to be anything else, a Bluebeard or a Ned Kelly."

They laughed.

"And you, Professor?"

"Myself."

They had come to the Cross itself, the nexus at the top of the hill.

"Isn't Sydney nice when it stops shouting?" said Paula. "All lights are so noisy."

"Listen," said Bowie.

They stood still. There were many on the streets, very quiet; they heard no voices, just footfalls like leaves blown over asphalt, a melancholy autumnal sound that impressed them with a moving pointless significance.

The William Street hill swooped down into darkness, with a new precipitancy. The trams were stopped, dark and empty, slotting the lines like a message in morse. A few cars moved with hooded lights, cigarettes glowed like stars.

"Come on," said Paula. Down the hill they went, three abreast, not hampered by the darkness now.

"I'd like to sing," said Paula, "only," she added sadly, "I haven't any voice."

"It doesn't matter," said the Professor, "we're all anonymous tonight, you wouldn't have to claim your voice in the morning."

Maliciously she made the pace fast for him. She could hear him panting, but he didn't give in. The little park beside the Blind Institute appeared to stretch away into infinity, pale luminous grass and spreading mythical trees. There may have been people there but it looked deserted and quiet.

"If we went through there," said Paula, "we'd come to the well at the world's end. Or we mightn't and I couldn't bear knowing for certain it wasn't there."

St. Mary's was a dramatic mass of shadow.

"I know," said Paula, "let's go to the Anzac Memorial. I must see it in a blackout."

They humoured her, making for the park.

"The Anzac buffet will be roaring with soldiers."

"We won't let them get you."

They passed the Archibald fountain. The moon was out. The statuary looked dark and flat as cutouts, composing like a fake photograph. Ahead they saw the white dome of the Memorial with the dark tree espaliered against it. There were many people in the park. The thought came to Paula that life was drawing in upon this one point, that this moment mattered. Her heart beat heavily. It was moments like these that she needed, they fed her. She broke free. Unconsciously she withdrew her hand from the professor's arm.

He said, "There ought to be a seat somewhere here. Only the young should make pilgrimages. The old know only too well what they will find. Run away, my children, run away."

He stepped on to the grass and almost immediately dissolved into the shadows. The broken moonlight gave only an illusion of light, the colour of a dissolving pearl.

Paula laughed. She was not going to look for him or pretend she minded his going. She slipped her hand down Bowie's arm into his hand and began walking very quickly. He wanted her alone, he wanted to talk to her, but her mood came between him and what he wanted to say. It was nearly always like that. It was useless breaking through her moods. If he did, what he had to say misfired.

When they had skirted the lake, oblong and shallow as a mirror, Paula stopped suddenly.

"There," she said, "that's what I wanted to see." From where they stood one of the great figures on the memorial jutted against the sky. Its solid outline was clear.

"That's the stake driven through all this shifting mess."

"Courage?" he said experimentally.

"More than courage. Man with courage. Endurance. Being sure. Not bluffed, not sidetracked. He's a man not a soldier."

"Man and soldier."

"He might just as well be a workman."

"Only there wouldn't have been any memorial."

"He's real."

"Everything that exists is equally real, we just add the emphasis to suit ourselves. He isn't real, he's only a token for reality. One man's conception. You can't," he went on doggedly, "make a work of art the basis of a philosophy because it is the product of a philosophy. It's a deduction not a premise."

Paula moved restlessly. "You do take me up so, I meant he's a realist in the best sense of the word. He *knows*."

Bowie was cradling her slender hand in both his. With whatever she said the touch of her hand mingled. She seemed quite unconscious that he was holding her hand.

"What does he know?" Bowie asked softly.

"I'm a realist, too, Bowie, in the last resort. I know that life is a sword painted on my breast."

"What's a romantic, then?"

"Someone who expects a north-west passage. You're a romantic, Bowie."

"Am I?"

"Yes. You think you can bypass reality with commonsense."

He had to chuckle. Paula drew her hand from him and started to walk away. He followed her. He thought she was cross, but she wasn't. She only said soberly.

"We can't stay here. It's all right to come and look, but we can't keep it, it goes stale." That disarmed him.

Presently she said, "It seems a long time since we heard the sirens. The hour must be nearly over. Don't let's be caught here."

When she reached William Street she said, "I'm tired and we forgot to look for the professor."

"There's nothing to do but walk."

After a pause she said, "I wonder if I'd be frightened."

"If this were real and not make-believe?"

"Yes. I try to get it straight in my mind so that I won't be frightened, but then I find I'm making up a story about how it didn't happen to me. It's always a story with a happy ending. I'm always somewhere else when the bombs fall or the walls are thick enough or I have a marvellous escape of some sort. That doesn't help really. I don't quite believe in it."

"Nobody does. We can't really prepare till it happens."

"I put it to myself. We bore it with complacency when other people were bombed—Spain, for instance. It's up to us to bear it when it's us. I tie myself up to that, do you think that will hold?"

"I don't think you'd be frightened—not specially, that is."

"Don't you?" she asked eagerly.

Paula was so much her natural self again that Bowie thought he could talk to her about his own troubles.

"Paula," he began. Just then the All Clear sounded, high and persistent, cutting off speech. Lights sprang up, the spare illumination of the brownout.

"It all looks dirty and ordinary again," said Paula. "Having the lights on again has made me ever so much tireder."

They walked in silence. Others like themselves were drifting home. The show was over.

Paula surprised him by saying after an interval, "Aren't you likely to be called up soon?"

"Yes, the notice came today."

"Oh."

"I'm in a reserved occupation."

"It's all right then?" Paula knew that Bowie had a good job "in the government." She took it for granted that her friends had good jobs, and hadn't enquired very far into Bowie's.

He said slowly, "It isn't all right at all. I'm thinking of throwing up my job, if it isn't too late, and doing something I can feel is useful."

"Have you any money outside your job?"

"No."

"You're just being romantic, Bowie."

"I don't think so."

"It would be self-indulgent and do no one any good. Could you do more if you were starving?"

He had to grin. "I shouldn't starve."

"What would you do?"

"I don't know yet."

"There, you see." She sounded relieved. They had reached her doorway. "I'll go straight up, Bowie. I'm dead tired. Mind if I don't ask you in tonight?"

"Of course not, Paula. Goodnight."

"Goodnight. Thanks, Bowie."

He walked away and Paula waited for the lift. "He might have seen me into the lift," she thought. Perhaps she'd disappointed him in some way. She didn't want to think that, and put the idea away as absurd, but it stuck like a grain of dust in the sensitive substance of her consciousness. She had lifted, lifted, and he had pulled her down. Now the whole incident seemed thin and theatrical. She was depressed and resentful. She and Bowie would never get on. Besides she didn't want it to happen like this. Slowly. Drearily. If this were all she'd be cheated. Love should come sweeping on great wings, splendid, making the world anew. She sailed up in the lift.

Bowie walked away with grinding steps. Everything went all right till he asked something of Paula, even if it were only her attention for five minutes. Then he met a blank wall. In the days that were coming, men would have to put aside their private lives. He'd messed things anyway. He'd hung on to safety too long. . . .

The professor found a seat and sat upon it gratefully. There was a dark lump at the other end that must be somebody. The professor stretched out his legs, tilted back his head and looked at the sky. Well, the blackout gave them the sky back.

"What do *you* make of it all?"

"I'm a stranger here, myself," the professor answered.

Timmy Andrews cackled, "Aren't we all?"

The professor, hoping he'd met someone with the grace to be a little insane, said, "It's rather like putting our heads under the blanket."

"The Golden Calf with its head in the sand."

"The Golden Calf?"

"Sydney, the great city. It wouldn't hurt us if we lost Sydney, it isn't our city, you know. The people don't own a stone of it. If it wasn't for defending places like these, golden calves, we'd be more enthusiastic about the war."

"You mean, if we could make up our minds they didn't matter, we'd be less defensive and more offensive?"

"You get me. D'you know what we ought to do?"

"I wish I did."

"Government oughter conscript every man and woman, young and old, sane and insane, and put 'em to work on soldiers' pay. No one to have a bean more than that. Cost of living 'ud come down to meet it. No one 'ud be suspicious of anyone else then—thinking they were making a pile out of the war. They'd work for love. The less men get the harder they work. Give' em next to nothing and they'd slave their guts out. Hasn't it been proved all the world over? Turning the capitalist system on the capitalist system. I would laugh."

Mrs Ramsay spent the alert sitting very upright knitting in her scrupulously blacked out drawing-room. She was alone in the house, for Betty, the only maid left, had gone out, all excitement, with her boy, to enjoy the blackout. Mrs Ramsay suspected that "boy" in this instance was a generic term. There was always a boy, sometimes in uniform, sometimes not. It was a matter into which she did not enquire. If Betty were not lazy she would have gone into munitions before. As it was, Betty's laziness must be not only condoned but fostered, her boys must be overlooked. Shamefacedly, Mrs Ramsay did most of the work herself. Otherwise she would be quite alone in this big house on the crest of Vaucluse, with its great view over the harbour and ocean. Most of it was shut up. No one would want to live there now, she could not sell, let, or even give it away. Like a whale it was, stranded in the great panorama. The view, once something valuable, purchased at great price, was now a menace. She inhabited a target. Looking out day by day she was amazed that nothing changed. It was incredibly lovely—the complex gemlike beauty of the harbour, the unbroken dark blue sweep of the ocean to the horizon, the soigné pictorial foreground. Mrs Ramsay had a dull fear that all her possessions would meet the same fate as the view, her money become valueless. She would be marooned.

She had done everything. The house was an arsenal of sand-buckets, shovels, rakes, stirrup pumps. . . . But she knew that in a crisis she would not be able to use them. It was even more certain that Betty would not either. Mrs Ramsay worked ceaselessly. One day a week at the auxiliary, one day packing parcels for the boys at the front, one day rolling bandages, one day at the Anzac Buffet, innumerable meetings in between. In every spare moment she knitted, a barricade of khaki wool between herself and disaster. As a contribution to morale she continued to live in the house on the heights. Nearly everything she did was to set an example to *les autres*. She did not succeed in encouraging herself.

Above all she was tired. She had no confidence. Victory was only a word like any other—defaced words slipping past her mind in an endless stream. So long as the war didn't come *here*. So long as she wasn't mixed up in a lot of mess and frightfulness that she couldn't cope with. If only it would stop. Stop. She didn't know how people got the energy to fight. It must stop before the boys were old enough to be taken for the army. John was sixteen. Sixteen and a half. If only peace would come before everything was spoiled. She did her bit keeping up appearances, but underneath she was deathly tired.

The two fat sisters, sat, each in her rocker, on the farm house verandah. Moonlight cast the dark shadow of the sagging vine on the white wall, it whitened the grass, gleamed on the galvanised iron roof of the shed, and thinned out into a tenuous mist, suggesting an infinity of emptiness. Through the open french windows behind them, out of the dark cavern of the room, the wireless poured cheer-up music.

"It's like the old days when ma came here first. Not a light, nothing but bush," one said.

"We're safe enough here."

"Prices keep up, and they will too."

"People'll buy food, whatever happens."

"Geoff won't be called up, he's in primary production."

"Shirl's expecting. She'll be looked after."

"I don't see we have to bother. We're doing our bit, keeping the place going."

The tranquil air was warm as milk. The wireless cut sharp bright stencils of sound in it. The knock knock of the rockers on the uneven boards of the verandah punctuated the music.

Chris said, "These blackouts . . . I've been thinking, Arnie. We ought to have a burglar alarm."

"I've been thinking that too. There's an old one at the store. It's gone wrong. I'll put a new one in and bring it home and mend it. It'll do fine."

"Better do it tomorrow."

"Right."

Ever since they had taken their money out of the bank and put it in the safe that Arnie had built into the cupboard, Chris had been as conscious of it as a woman of her unborn child. Truly she carried her money under her heart.

Ally complained bitterly to Mrs Blan. "Here we are in the blackout, anything might happen, and Harry out as usual. You'd think he'd stay home on a night like this."

"I guess they want him at the shop," said Mrs Blan vaguely.

"I don't see why. His place is with his family. Would you believe it, Mrs Blan, he didn't so much as put up the blackout paper? He just put a roll down on the table and said, 'There's the paper, mother, and there's the tacks,' and off he went."

"Did you put it up?"

"I did not. Blackout's a man's job."

Mrs Blan sighed. "I put ours up, but there, when you're widowed, you got to learn. I coulda asked Alby, but he was that tired I hadn't the heart. They work them so hard you wouldn't believe. My old man was all for his home— you couldn't get him to go out. He was a good husband if ever there was one. And he was taken. You don't know, praise God, what that means."

Ally thought Mrs Blan leaned rather too hard on her widowhood. She went off on a new tack. "Ruthie's out too. *I* don't know where she is. It's hard enough looking after girls without blackouts. If we are going to have them regularly—well, I don't know. Wanda's over at Nelsons'. I do know where she is for a wonder."

"Where's Ben?"

"Ben's never home. I don't know what Harry was thinking of, putting him in a garage. With the petrol shortage he might have known there wouldn't be any future in it. Now they've taken him for transport. He's doing a man's work and he won't be seventeen till next June."

"He seems happy enough."

"That's Ben all over. He's that easy to please. Says when he's seventeen he's going to be a driver. He could do it now only he's under age. You'd never get young Ben shut up, wants to get out on the roads, going places. He and Tony stick together."

"Tony's a good boy."

"Tony's all right, but Ben's too young to be working like he does. I never know when he'll be home. Harry's nearly as bad."

"Well you've got him, dear. When he's gone you'll know the difference. I'll put on the kettle and we'll have some tea. Somehow I don't seem able to settle to anything with this blackout. D'you know I think Heffron and all those like ordering people around and telling everyone, 'Do this, do that.' Got to earn their money, I suppose, and believe me they get enough. Alby says it's all stuff and nonsense. The Japs won't come here. We're safe as houses." She dropped her voice conspiratorially. "It's all a racket."

Ally nodded. "I shouldn't wonder."

They stood almost touching one another, rigid like chunks of rock. They had never been really alone together before, and now they seemed to have the whole world to themselves. It was only the strip of park beside the Blind Institute, but it seemed like the country.

"It isn't any good," he said roughly. "You've got to understand. I'm not free to marry you."

"You've . . ."

"No. I never was such a damn bloody fool. I've work to do and I couldn't do it if I had a wife and kids. That finishes a man, gets him scared, puts him in wrong."

"I wouldn't be like that."

"I didn't say you would, only that you wouldn't get the chance."

"The Revolution?" Ruth said softly.

"You've got it."

"You don't have to marry me."

"You make it hard for yourself, don't you?" he said, a little more gently.

Involuntarily, she moved towards him. "Not so hard as if . . ." she broke off. He knew what she meant. "I can be hard too," she told him.

"You wouldn't come first, you know. I'd go straight ahead as if you didn't exist."

"I know," she said stonily.

"This war's going on. It's going to change. In one form or another it will come here. We'll all be swept up. I wouldn't be able to look after you, or even think of you. I'd have to be free."

"I know."

"You're not like that, really," he accused her. "You're not rough and tough. It's just a show you're putting on to get your own way. You mightn't know it but it is. All women are the same."

She understood his anger for what it was. She had felt his need. Shaken, she was still reinforced. She couldn't tell him that she wanted this hard difficult love. It was a part of the world opening before them. It was her charter of equality. She accepted it. It was he who was clinging to tradition, gone rotten, from the world he thought he had abandoned. She didn't speak or move.

"You're not my kind of woman. You're not even in the Party. You don't understand a thing about it. You'd get the kicks without the faith."

"I'd learn."

"Oh, would you? We don't recruit members that way."

She flared at that. "Why don't you get a girl in the Party then?"

"They're too fierce and scrawny."

He felt a little sob that might have been laughter. The sap of their emotions was flowing soft and warm between them again.

"Don't you want me then, Sid?"

"I was a fool ever to lay a finger on you."

"Don't you?"

"You know I do. That's the whole goddam bloody point." In the moonlight he could see the look in her face of white exhausted ecstasy as she swayed towards him. The long shiver that ran through her body was a part also of him.

Old Rumpty sat in his usual place at the Cross, hunched on his stool, in his frayed and greasy brown overcoat. He was the same, but the world had changed about him. It was dark. No one bought papers. No one spoke to him. All his boys had left him. Lefty was gone too but that was long ago. Lefty was in the army. Old Rumpty couldn't move, he was chained to the spot. For one thing he never went home at this time, for another he didn't feel sure that he'd find his way home, he wasn't sure that home was still in its old place. For a little while he went on croaking the news, but his voice, with no one listening, alarmed him. He drew into himself, sat as still as a soapstone bird, his hands clasped tightly over the tin boxful of pennies. People saw the piles of white papers beside him but they could not see him. They blundered past. He heard nothing but footsteps, no clang of trams, no honking of cars, no voices. The world he knew was gone. He was alone. Night had come. The sun wouldn't rise. He still lived but life itself was dead. Others died decently before the end of things, he'd outlived the world. The news had never meant a thing to him. But this did. Now he knew. He was afraid. Afraid.

The night of the nation-wide blackout was, as it were, the first crucible. War and the imminence of war breached the wall of every mind. If men were still concerned with themselves alone, it was with themselves in a world at war. It could not be denied or forgotten. Life flowed in different channels. More and more of the young men were called up, women flowed into industry, old men went back to work. Work became an anodyne and an intoxicant; in work men sought and found a release from the burden of responsibility. All night men and women watched on roofs, fire spotters, and the stars in the empty sky passed over them. They manned the first aid posts and the N.E.S. establishments. They slept in dugouts beside telephones to be ready. By day they went on with their work. They made all the gestures of readiness, but they were not ready. They couldn't believe, even while they feared, that the attack would ever come.

The face of the city was changed. Mounds of raw tan-coloured soil weathered and paled in the parks where the slit trenches were dug. Sandbags and scaffolding cluttered the narrow pavements, facades were masked in brickwork, plateglass was plastered against the shattering blast of bombs. The traffic had changed, army trucks and camouflaged waggons, few private cars, monstrous growths of producer-gas installations, or strange ballooning sacks of coal gas on the cars, crowded trams and trains. The crowds in the street were changed. Everywhere uniforms, men and women, air force, navy, A.I.F., militia, American marines, soldiers, and airmen. The outer shell of war, but not war—not yet.

Beyond the city, too, life had changed. The exodus to the country, women with young children, old people, people with the jitters, living unaccustomed lives, disgruntled, bored, wondering if they need have come, if they should return, asking themselves why they had come, finding life had to be lived day by day. Dull in the country, and was it really safe?

Couldn't they be cut off? Feud grew between country and town, and with it rumour. Ten thousand evacuees in Katoomba, all of them women, all of them on the golf course. In the country towns beyond the mountains the police were measuring the cubic capacity of every house. "You can take so many evacuees." Evacuees ranked with a plague of grasshoppers or an outbreak of pleuro.

The summer carnival on the beaches was over. They were wired and patrolled, forbidden, out of bounds. The long Pacific rollers broke on untrodden sand again. The moon silhouetted not lovers but tinhatted soldiers on guard. The coastal scrub masked camps, where the trainees practised counter-invasion tactics and the snouts of guns poked up out of the sand dunes. But still long stretches of the lonely seaboard ached empty and vulnerable on the map. A boom stretched across the entrance of the harbour. The brilliance of the metropolitan night was gone. Black and blind, the coast faced the sea. Only sometimes a rod of blue light from a searchlight measured the immensity of the sky.

The threat of war was accepted, a part of daily life. The child said, cheerful and matter-of-fact, "Daddy, can I have a scooter for my birthday, if I'm alive?"

Singapore fell. That was the second crucible. For days, weeks even, it had been inevitable, but the official voices had gone on talking of the last man and the last gun, of fighting for every inch, of backs to the wall, of Gibraltar and Tobruk, and the people had gone on hoping for a miracle. There was no miracle. The great naval base that had cost sixty million pounds had been in use for one week, was lost in eight days. It had not been equipped, and it had not been reinforced. Too little and too late. The way was opened to the Netherlands East Indies, to the Indian Ocean, to Burma, to India, to Australia. The keystone was kicked out. And seventeen thousand Australians, her prime shock troops, were lost with it—those that were not dead in that last useless stand. The sacrifice, the pouring out of life and treasure had been for nothing, a sacrifice to the incompetence and complacence of the High Command. In one stroke Australia found herself bereft of her army and laid open to attack. It went deeper that that. It was the betrayal of sons and lovers, the volunteer army of a small people, every man chosen. It was the breaking down of an ancient confidence, the denouement of a system. The record of courage was source of bitterness, not pride. It had been spent for that. The Imperial Dream died at Singapore, and the hoarse salutary cry of an angry people, not to be soothed by eloquence, not to be stopped by promises, rose to the sky.

Life changed again, a chemical change, in men's minds, a different tension, more real, more natural this time, sardonic, distrustful, in place of that indulgent and romantic mood that had existed before Singapore.

The flying voices said: "When Singapore goes, Australia goes."

"It's the Netherlands Indies Japan wants, not us."

"It's India. She'll by-pass Australia. . . . If she cuts our communications she'll be able to deal with us later."

"It may be today or tomorrow."

"America . . . work it out for yourself on a piece of paper . . . look at the map. Japan can't *last* . . . America."

The Japanese took Rabaul, they raided Port Moresby, they took Timor, they raided Darwin. It was like a shock in the blood to know that the physical peace of this earth, after one hundred and fifty years, was broken.

The Professor balanced his teacup. He belonged to the generation of cup balancers. He knew it himself. Young men were less expert and more assured. They either refused teacups altogether or they put them down anywhere and everywhere, regardless of safety, human or ceramic. Mrs Ramsay saw him standing there momentarily isolated, looking quizzical and pleased. She wanted to talk to him, her mind was full of painful questions, like a pincushion stuck full of pins. Although she had dutifully read all the publications of the Left Book Club, she had never found really satisfying categorical answers. There were a lot of people, she feared the professor might be snapped up before she could get to him. It surprised Mrs Ramsay that there should be tea parties at all, these days, but there were, and if everyone wore uniform and was in a hurry, it was all right. This was one of those strange lacunae of peace and normality in a tormented world, when people were grateful and happy in momentary tranquillity.

"Ah, Professor," she touched his arm.

He hardly knew her without her make-up. The sacrifices some women made for the war effort! Under her smile she was haggard.

"You're tired, Mrs Ramsay."

She was grateful to him. He knew a place where they could sit, a little balcony behind that curtain. They went out and found two iron chairs and a breeze with a slight chill in it off the harbour.

"I wanted to talk to you. Not tea party talk."

"We've sacrificed that to the war effort. It shows how sensible we are at bottom."

"It's about the war. Things are worse than we're told, aren't they?"

"Yes," he said, "probably. In a way we're told, but people don't grasp it."

She looked at him with pale hungry eyes. "Why don't we do better? We're losing this war. You know, I wouldn't dare say that to anyone else. Why is it? We've the resources and our men are brave. No one doubts that. Is it leadership? Do we need a Leader? We all hoped Churchill was the man. Where is the Leader?"

"I think it goes deeper than that—or perhaps it doesn't. If we were willing to trust one man, a Leader, and let him run this war, we wouldn't be a democracy any more, would we?"

"You mean democracies can't wage successful war? No democracy can win a war and remain a democracy?"

"I mean that only a socialist or a fascist state can wage war competently. It's only the Fascists and Russia who are waging war competently, isn't it?"

She gave doubtful assent. She evidently thought, "We'd come round to it some day when we got going."

"It isn't the fault of democracy so much as of what democracy condones. The side that admits the profit element into its war effort puts itself at a disadvantage, naturally. It's a drain on every effort and every contribution. It has to be fed. Big Business takes its cut, and, believe me, that cut amounts to something. Besides, competitive profiteering drives out every other motive including patriotism. Men give their only sons but not their profits. Abraham was willing to sacrifice Isaac, but he was a hard man when it came to flocks and herds. Again, the very presence of that leakage, and all men know of it, weakens morale. There's a doubt in people's hearts. For whom, for what, are we making our sacrifice?"

Mrs Ramsay smiled faintly, as if the Professor had just taken King Charles' head out of his pocket. "Would Socialism solve everything?" she asked, as if she were humouring him.

"Socialism is only a stopgap, a means to an end. It is not in itself a millennium. The function of socialism is to put a stopper on competition, competitive living, and its natural result in competitive dying. A sort of historical chock. Socialism will not solve everything. There are evils inherent in socialism that humanity will have to overcome, just as, if we are going to survive, we shall have to break through the evils of the present system. Socialism will break down the major evils of this system and provide an improved environment for the majority of people. Out of the response to that improvement the future must come."

"You are looking very much into the future. We've to win the war first."

"Win it or lose it."

"You mustn't say that."

"The two things might not be so different."

"I hoped you would say something helpful, to cheer me up."

"And haven't I?"

"You've taken even socialism away from me."

"But you never were a socialist."

She smiled wanly.

"Oh, I see, you wanted to put something on both ways."

"I've come to the point now when I would accept even socialism if I believed it would help. Anything would be better than this war."

She thought she saw sympathy in his bird-like eye, knew there was seriousness beneath his bantering.

"I've upset you. You feel as a religious person might feel on learning there's no devil."

She laughed now more naturally. "You're too clever, Professor. You put me in the wrong without saying anything."

"I meant to say something. Socialism isn't a panacea and it isn't enough. There is no solution of world problems or rather, of the problem of living in the world, but I believe that there is a working hypothesis and that it lies in a paradox. In a word, that we must always work in opposite directions in order to attain a balanced result. What I mean is this. Internationalism is a natural corollary of socialism. National Socialism is an obvious contradiction in terms, a fiction as monstrous as the 'pure Nordic race.' Socialism is in its essence international, the Brotherhood of Man. A vast expansion of responsibility, a pooling of humanity. A delightful but unwieldy concept, full, in its implementation, of dangers, the primrose path to bureaucracy. The bureaucracy and the masses, a world-wide state socialism. Horrible, Mrs Ramsay, horrible. An end not to be striven for except in conjunction with its opposite—the division of government among the people. Group government with responsibility sheeted home to the individual. Men responsible to their neighbours, co-operating in small bunches for local welfare. All benefits to be the result of co-operation, not a bestowal. Everyone working, not only in some industry or other, not merely for his daily bread, but at the construction of life. Our existence must be widened and narrowed. We must have socialism and co-operation, internationalism and local government. You see?" he eked out his words with gestures that had long become stereotyped in him.

Mrs Ramsay saw that he was a dreamer. One expected it of professors. But it wasn't helpful.

"But what are we to do now?" she asked him resolutely.

"The best we can. Foch said, 'In war you do what you can'."

"I am doing what I can."

"You're all right then."

In the pause that followed it was evident that the conversation was dead. Neither wanted to go back into the crowded room.

Presently Mrs Ramsay said tentatively, "You see Paula, don't you?"

"Paula is in a very flourishing way."

"Do you really think so?"

· "She is like a young vine. Whatever she touches she twines round, and whatever she twines round she uses to pull herself up. She's a delicate creature."

"The life she leads, all this independence. You don't think she is any the worse for it?"

"She isn't coming to any harm. She is getting her experience without paying for it. That's what every mother wants for her daughter, isn't it?"

Mrs Ramsay could only sigh, "She's very young."

The Professor patted her hand. The little wind slid over them, cold under the summer warmth, reminding them that they were old. To be old was a protection. The world had passed to the young.

While the tea party went its immemorial way under a thin wartime veneer, Bowie was hanging on a strap in a crowded eastbound tram. The tram was a mass of humanity. From a distance it appeared to bristle. The conductor had a hard job collecting fares. He had to climb over the passengers to do it. Most of them had parcels, all but the bulkiest articles had to be carried home now, some of them had children, all of them wanted to go on living their private lives, which at the moment meant to read their newspapers. With one hand Bowie folded his paper into an oblong and manoeuvred it between the shoulder blades of the man in front. A youngish man beside him, puffing breath tinctured with alcohol down his neck, read it over his shoulder.

"British retreat to a new line in Burma," he read. "Rangoon threatened," "Japanese submarine shells Californian coast." He couldn't contain himself. "When we get going we'll wipe them out, the dirty yellow-bellies, we'll show the yellow scum what's what." He looked round belligerently. No one responded. He prodded Bowie. "What do you say, mate? Australia's white and she's not going to sit down and let the dirty yellow buggers have everything their own way, even if the bloody English do."

"Shame." A red face that might have belonged to the bloody English was momentarily thrust into the discussion.

"It isn't a matter of colour," said Bowie, abandoning himself to one more argument. "What colour are the Germans? And what about the Chinese?"

"Oh, isn't it?" said the man truculently. He turned to the car in general. "Do you want the Japs here because they are the same colour as the Chinks? Do you? Here's a bloke that does."

A spare woman, her tongue sharpened by many a matrimonial fracas, said, "If those are your opinions, young man, why aren't you in khaki?"

"Come off it, ma. I'm in a reserved occupation."

"Oh, are you? From all I can see a girl could do anything you can do, or an old man. Anyway, I'll give you this." She opened her handbag and handed him a white feather.

Some people near by laughed.

"And here's one for you." She handed another feather to Bowie with an expression of imperturbable venom. "I don't let them get away with it," she told her neighbour, "whoever they are. I had two boys in Singapore. The Almighty Himself doesn't know where they are now." A spasm passed over her face, "I'll shame the slackers," she said.

The woman beside her said, "My youngest's there too. I wouldn't want any mother. . . . Twenty last July. Always happy. Curly, we used to call him." She began rummaging among her parcels like a small volcano, for her handkerchief.

Bowie held his white feather and thought, in a surge of pity and despair, "Oh, God, how patient they are. All they do is this. Why do they put up with wars?"

The other man wasn't taking it that way. He threw the feather on the floor and turned angrily on Bowie. "I've seen you before," he shouted in a voice for everyone to hear. "I've seen you in the Dom talking against the war. That's a fact, ain't it?"

"Yes," said Bowie. He turned to the wiry little woman. "Do you think the destruction of young men is a good way to settle international quarrels?"

"I wanter see the Japs smashed. Our boys are gone. That's all we can do. Smash 'em."

"You're right, mister," the tearful woman said. "Curly hadn't anything to do with their quarrels. Just a bright friendly kid, that's all he was."

The spare woman was white hot. "If your Curly hadn't more spirit than you've got, he'd be a mighty poor soldier. He'd be ashamed to hear you."

"Now, missus," said an old working man, sitting opposite, "Don't you speak like that to a poor body in trouble. Don't mind her, ma."

The first man wasn't going to be put off. His face was about three inches from Bowie's. "He talks against the war. He's a fifth columnist, that's what he is. He's the kind that will get us beat."

"We're not going to be beaten." It was the voice that had said shame.

"He's a pacifist, ask him." People at the far end of the tramcar were craning their necks.

"Fares," said the conductor, phlegmatically elbowing his way along the corridor, "Fares, please."

"Now," thought Bowie, "Now." This wasn't a platform or a pamphlet, it was a bit of living. He must put what he thought in a nutshell. This was an audience, he must speak. "The Jap isn't the real enemy. He's a man like any other. The system of the present world forces him into war as it does us. We're fighting for the system not for our country." He knew, even as he spoke, that he had missed his target, gone past.

"He's a Bolshie, too," said the man triumphantly.

"The Bolshies are our best ally," the working man reminded him. "The Bolshies can fight." That got a laugh, and the tension relaxed for no particular reason.

"Talk not deeds," said the little woman with a snort and a toss. "I wish I was a man."

"You're quite safe, ma."

Bowie and the working man got out at the next stop. They walked together by mutual consent.

"You're right about the system," the old man said heavily. "It makes the wars and we fight them. But I don't know. I wouldn't like to see the Japs here. What 'ud happen to the unions? What 'ud happen to the standard of living? The whole labour movement would go before you could say Jack Robinson. I'm a labour man. I been a labour man for fifty years. What do you mean, you're against the war? D'you want us to give in and let the Japs walk over us? Just like that? Don't seem reasonable to me."

"It isn't just like that. Peace has to be prepared the same as war has to be. It isn't only a matter of laying down arms. People are always saying that to me, as if they expected to see me pull a miracle out of my hat by the ears. We hadn't much to begin this war with, we've seen the results of unpreparedness. We've even less to begin a peace with. Such an act would cost us very dear, but I believe not so dearly as the war. A negotiated peace now, whatever we could get, and then a long hard unresting attack on the causes of war—the root causes, in competition and profit, a joining up throughout the world of all the people who want a genuine new order. Socialism from below. We do get co-operation for war—why can't we get it for peace?"

"Struth," said the man, "you wouldn't get that bunch in the tram to co-operate would you?"

"You might, if you could get the idea into their heads. The labour movement would be the foundation."

"I get you," said the man, "but there wouldn't be many that would. Free speech, I say, live and let live. But you better look out, mister, saying things like that."

"Does it matter?" Bowie asked wearily.

"Does what matter?"

"Looking out for my skin, when skins are going ten a penny."

"I say, win the bloody war, and then have a go at the chaps at home."

"It's going to be very expensive winning this war. I don't mean only men and money, but energy as well. A drained and exhausted nation can't build a new world. Capital is looking to the home front while we're fighting. We'd better too, and not wait till after."

"You're right there, mister."

They walked in silence for half a block. The old workman stopped on the corner. "I go down here, so I'll say so long. I always did like a bit of intellectual conversation. Good night."

"Good night."


Ruth drew her brows together in the effort of understanding. "I don't understand, Sid. Are you against the war or do you support it?"

"There are two wars," he explained. "They are messed up together at present, but they'll separate out later. I support one war and not the other."

"She's scared of not understanding," he thought, amused and touched. "Who'd have thought I'd take to wet nursing girls?"

"I'm for Russia and against the Germans and the Japs, because they are fascists, and against the British Empire and America because they are constructively pro-fascist. Before the U.S.S.R. came in, it was a war between gangsters. I didn't support it. Now Russia is in, it's different. If Germany and Britain knock one another out, that's all to the good for the socialist fatherland, and brings the revolution in the west so much the nearer. So I support the war. Russia's got to survive and will survive. If America sends tanks so much the better. She only sends tanks because she thinks Russia's fighting her battle. Russia isn't. The wily old gentleman in

Downing Street knows that, but he's caught in a cleft stick. He hasn't any Frenchmen to fight for him this time. He's watching and he hasn't given up hope of turning everything to the advantage of his class, sooner or later. He and Stalin are playing much the same game, but I'm backing Stalin to win it. This business of China and India coming together is part of the other war. The war against the Empire—only to save its bacon the Empire is pretending to sponsor it. If the oriental peoples unite, not under the aegis of the British Empire—well, that's the beginning of the end of things as they are, isn't it? It's a great big wonderful war and there's plenty of room in it for everyone to fight for the world he hopes to see."

"But if we win the war. . . ."

"We won't—at least, not a fine cock-a-doodle victory, followed by a professors' peace, telling all the naughty boys where they get off. The day for that has gone."

"What is going to happen?"

"The war's going on, it won't stop till you can't tell the difference between the war and revolution. Then we'll be getting somewhere and we'll throw in the reserves."

Her mind translated: Then you'll be fighting. She blenched from his hard unremitting certainty. It bruised her mind. Much of their time together— snatched and in short lengths—was spent like this, Sid packing Ruth's mind with his own beliefs. "I can't let up," he once said to her, "I've got to eat and breathe the revolution. It's a full time job." Out of his hard intellectual plane, his need of her would rise suddenly as a whirlwind. It was not her idea of love, it affronted her and laid waste, but she found the strength to face it and to snatch joy from it. She grew into his life. She was content with that. Silence and discipline beat her love to an enduring hardness. She might not make a home for Sid and bear his children, that was something outside the orbit he had set himself. She took instead for her hearth and marriage the fanatic world of effort that he had chosen. Though he did not consciously know it, she made his home in it and transposed, in the years that followed, her whole woman's life and expectation into the key of his. She had the strength of the gentle and selfless, content with first things. As for the tenets of Sid's political creed, they became her tenets by a process of natural infiltration.

Knarf, struggling with the great mass of his book, cast into it an explanation, like a handful of salt into a cauldron of broth, to bring out the flavour.

"I have tried," he said, "to build up the pattern of ideas behind the pattern of the event, and rightly a part of it. The agonized groping in the midst of turmoil. Thinking was then a great welter of thought and possibilities, the magma in which the seeds of today were already sprouting. War, whatever it destroyed, fostered the technician and mechanic. With the advance of war that eclipsed every other kind of life, the technician became the only man who felt sure of his worth and who had, in his work, a point of attachment to life accepted by society, endorsed by the will to live. The exhaustion of war finally left only the one type standing. We haven't yet re-achieved the complexity, the plethora of those years that closed an era. A dying world put forth all its strength in a great spate of thinking and seeking. Far too much of this mental and spiritual effort was directed at effect, too little at cause. I think of it as a great tropical vine whose root was cut. It sagged and died and fell, flowers and leaves and fruit. . . ."

For all men's thinking and planning, events took their implacable course with nations and individuals.

.    .    .    .    .    .    .    .    .    .

Ben was in transport. He got his driving licence before he was seventeen and did a man's work. They put him into uniform and he was happy. He had always a surplus of enthusiasm and only wanted something to which to attach it. Now he attached it to the internal combustion engine. His world that had been poor in possibilities was now rich. Able-bodied boys were at a premium. Ben was maturing fast, not only because he was wanted, but because all his fellows were wanted too. His slice of the world was going well, and he didn't look beyond it. It was a world of trucks and loads and journeys. He had pride in it. His mates called him Munt, the earthy name that would be his till the end and that in time ahead he would make almost legendary.

Wanda went into munitions. The high pay attracted her. Her ambition to be a milliner or a server in a fashionable milliner's shop was blown out. She no longer cared twopence for any of that. Her short and sudden blooming was over. No one had noticed it, and now she was changed, hardened and coarsened. She knew too that that would also pass unnoticed, that what had happened to her and would happen mattered to no one but herself and very little even to her. She worked in a rough shop and soon found that she could be as loud mouthed as any of the others there. That was one kind of success. She was quick, and at piece work she made big money. She spent it with a swaggering recklessness. She picked up with men, often soldiers or sailors off ships, who had much less than she, for which she held them in contempt. She did not bring any of her prosperity home. She had nothing to do with Ruth, the core of bitterness between them remained unexpressed and unresolved. When she met Sid she gave him the rough edge of her tongue, in effect challenging him, "If you're tough I'm tougher." He treated her much as he would have treated a puppy worrying his shoe lace. He never bothered to understand women.

Ally went on as usual. She defied the war, and, come what might, she meant to get her share of everything there was. In a small way she hoarded food, not for the family, but for herself. The more the public were asked to conserve water, the more she used her tap. For sensation value in the newspapers she found the war far inferior to a good murder or divorce. She put on weight steadily, and when she could get at Harry she nagged him.

Cliff was sent to Darwin and Gwen fretted. Love had sapped her courage. She turned to Harry, and her demands on him were greater than ever before. After a time, out of fatalism, loneliness, and the need he had created in her, she was ready to resume their former relationship, but Harry very gently, and without words, refused. That was over.

He did not tell her that, after Cliff had been sent north, in a dull sort of loathing to himself and his job, and a blind pity for youth, he had himself gone down to the recruiting office in Martin Place one lunch hour and offered himself. When he was called up for medical examination the doctor turned him down. He felt irrationally humiliated and told no one. When he saw the petty shifts that were used to induce men to enlist, the stunts in Martin Place, the posters with pretty girls and cheap slogans, he was sickened. In these days, when he heard the valour of the A.I.F. praised, his heart was black with anger, especially when the speaker's intent was to flatter the public and smother their criticism. That courage, which meant men's lives, limbs, liberty, had been used to make up for their lack of equipment and support. It had been used as if it were dross. Men or women who had not suffered the onslaught had no right to boast of that betrayed valour. The soldier in Harry was resurrected. He knew what price had been paid for these brave tales that newspapers printed so glibly, and that formed the stock in trade of the recruit mongers. He knew. The knowledge hammered on his brain. He belonged with them, with the Army, not with the cajoled civilians. He remembered and he looked forward. Only the present was hollow.

On the evening when even the optimists admitted that Java must fall, had to all practical purposes fallen, Batavia gone, Sourabaya gone, and the rich lowlands inundated, every port sealed against the help that had not and would not have come, Harry walked home, head down, oblivious of the evening crowds about him. He might have been alone on a black mountain at the world's end.

His mind tugged at the bitter knot—the betrayal of the Indies. We betrayed the Dutch. The Dutch used up their navy and aircraft fighting for us in Malaya, trusting us, us and America, to send them reinforcements in time. We didn't. All that came were the rats of Singapore. Singapore was lost in the distilleries of Scotland—that's what they said. Singapore went and Java "was slipping away"—that's what the paper said. Only it wasn't an easy death. The Dutch, with the handful of British, Australians, Americans, were trapped in the mountains. No way out. Full of hatred for their own. It wasn't inefficiency really. Deeper than that. The sort of rot that got at people's minds when they thought money could buy everything, when they'd ruled subject people at home and abroad. . . . People who'd found an easy way to live. Short-cut living. No reason, no natural right under it. Minds built on slogans and tags and national advertising. People who thought they were the sort of people they said they were and that the world would be whatever they said it was. People who said "Britannia rules the waves" and "Britons never, never shall be slaves," not even on the dole. The ruling class couldn't talk about being free while they made slaves of their own fellow-countrymen, and not expect the crack to come. It would open out and they'd fall down it. It had opened and he hoped a lot had fallen down it. They'd be surprised. They'd stuck a reality on a myth, and expected the myth to stand, and of course it hadn't. After all the big ones they'd swallowed, to say Singapore was impregnable when it wasn't even a fortress was only a little one. To say that sort of thing was inefficiency was all wrong and made you think a bit of weeding out and screwing up would put it right. It wouldn't and it didn't. It was a damn sight bigger and deeper than inefficiency. It wasn't especially British either. It was logic not nationality. The British people were all right. Look at Dunkirk. The only thing wrong with them was that they could take it. They'd been taking it for centuries. It had made them physically a C3 nation. It had given them the dole and the means test and malnutrition and a lot of other things. Out of all that had come the somnambulists of Singapore, the fine words and the bloody tragedy. The dying was real enough, the wounds and the prisons were real. The same dream of a spoiled people was betraying the Dutch. The Dutch didn't belong in Java. It wasn't really theirs. It belonged to the Javanese. If there *was* any belonging, which there wasn't. The Dutch had taken the

Indies and made a profit on them, now the Japs had taken them from the Dutch and we were dishonoured. No one was dishonoured for letting the Dutch take Java from the Javanese because that wasn't anybody's business. No, you couldn't get out that way. What it boiled down to was people getting killed and wounded and trapped. A bloody business, all right. Us next. They say people are waking up. Waking up to what? They find the world's getting too hot for the profit dream and they want to fix it so that it will be safe for finance again. The bloody swine. But that's wrong too, it isn't people, it's an idea. Talking guilty men puts us off the scent. Bank slanging is only a witch hunt. Here we were looking for what we were fighting for with the invader at the garden gate. All he knew was they'd all been betrayed, the Aussies and the Tommies and the Dutch, and the "brave native soldiers," and the Japs too, for that matter. All fighting for what they'd never had and weren't going to get. All being let down in the same big swindle. What price "dishonour" in the face of all that?

Timmy said moral indignation wasn't any good, just a bit more wool for the eyes of fools. What Harry felt wasn't moral indignation. It was plain black rage. Maybe you could get angry even if you lived in Russia. No right and no wrong, only the logic of events and circumstances. That took the hatches off all right. Boiled down, it meant everything you chose to do was right because *you* interpreted the logic of events and circumstance. God didn't come down and point out what was necessary and what wasn't. You decided yourself and you decided in your own favour. It was all punk, saying there wasn't any right or wrong, only expediency. The way Harry worked it out was this. There was a sort of natural basic right and wrong, ways of acting that made the work more or less valuable. The system built up its own code of right and wrong, which had nothing to do with the natural one but didn't disprove it. Men aren't sticks and stones. They don't just want things to happen to them. They act and their acts are part of the circumstances of their lives. Well, if they take all the pegs out and say, "Anything I do is perfectly all right if it's against my enemies," they're going to make themselves a pretty bad set of circumstances. If "realism" meant any sort of shift or expedient, it contradicted that "dialectical materialism" that Timmy talked about. Actions being circumstances, wouldn't bloodiness make bloodiness? Oh, you say the other fellow was bloody first, so I've got to be bloody, and so it would go on for ever. Got to be broken somewhere. If you've got a war the logical thing is to make it as bloody and vicious as possible. All right, you'd get just as much bred up to war and convinced of its rightness as the profit mongers by turning everything to profit have got themselves convinced that it's holy and sacred and mustn't be touched. Mind-conditioning, that's what they called it.

Harry gave a barking little laugh that turned people's heads towards him. "That's my smoke screen," he thought. He beat out his thoughts with his feet as he tramped up the hill. He did all his thinking in the streets. Where else could he do it? Not in his overcrowded home, not at his job.

It seemed as if the war might pass to the north, flaring through the Indies into the Indian Ocean to the doubtful bastion of India itself, or that Russia might save the Allies again if Siberia and not Australia became the target. The northern spring of 1942 began to loom on the world's imagination as a great upflaring of violence that had come to have about it the awful and intimidating majesty of a force of nature. The violence was accepted as inevitable as the spring.

The Americans swarmed in the cities. There was something nonchalant even about their army waggons. When for half a day one of their trucks stood outside the "Australia" people stopped in the street to look at it with a kind of veneration. It was strange and a little heroical that a battered, camouflaged, American army waggon should be standing, defiant of traffic regulations, outside an expensive hotel, in a narrow street. It made the hotel seem a trifle provincial. The popular imagination clung to the Americans. They hadn't been defeated. Pearl Harbour was only a trifle, ridden down by event, talked away. Washington fed the hope of an exhausted world with estimates and production figures, deep draughts of them, making victory a mathematical certainty.

The American legend grew. They were pouring men and planes and munitions into the country. The troop trains went north, engine to tail, night and day. The Americans did everything for themselves, unloaded their ships, assembled their planes, cut secret aerodromes in the bush, secret runways down to the sea where the great steel eagles waited for the invader. Everything was done with miraculous speed and efficiency. They were rolling in money too. N.C.O.'s occupied the best suites in the best hotels. They bought up everything of value as soon as it appeared in the market. They hired all the taxis, they filled all the theatres, they never went without tobacco, and they never went short of girls. All the Australians had to do was to stand by and gape. The American legend was the hope substitute of the hour. The sight of the Americans in the street gave the Australians a sense of themselves—the handful who garrisoned a continent and fought over half the world.

The Professor said, "When I look at the American soldiers I'm persuaded that there is an Australian type. It isn't scientifically possible, not in a hundred and fifty years, but it's there."

Timmy Andrews looked round the pub. It was full of men in uniform, Diggers and buddies, mostly buddies, and a sprinkling of gobs. Timmy was at the prophetic stage and he felt lonely in a large way. He waved his pot grandly. He drank to the American army. Pink faces swam before his eyes. From his innermost mind he produced these words. "Dairy-fed pork."

"Wot's the great idea?" asked the Digger over whom he'd sloshed his beer.

Timmy stared at him, the leathery desert-tanned face. A slow grin of infinite satisfaction split his face. "Smoked mutton hams," he said.

"Pore bloke's got delusions of grandeur," the Digger explained to his mate.

Timmy drank to his own perspicacity. His Adam's apple bobbed up and down like a cork. The idea floated away from him on the tide, but he knew that he had been very clever and that was enough.

Stories went round. They had to do with the enormous potency of the American soldier. The matrons talked about it behind their daughters' backs. The Americans were like a cloud of grasshoppers devouring the green and tender virgins of the land, and, because there certainly were not enough virgins to go round, many others beside. The girls rippled with it. The lieutenant who asked his host in the middle of dinner where he could get a woman for the night went the rounds in both circles. So did the young captain who, on being introduced to a pretty girl, excused himself for a moment, and on returning triumphantly, informed her that he'd been able to engage them a room for the night. There was scarcely a woman who was not at least theoretically seduced.

This was only a variant, a domestication if you like, of the legend of their industrial productivity. It didn't endear them to the A.I.F. They felt what, twenty years before, the poilu had felt when the better-paid Australian Diggers had invaded the French villages, crowded the estaminets and bought up their sweethearts. The poison seeped back into the civil population. The legend, which was one more sick fancy of a people at war, crumbled from within before it was despatched from without. People began to say, "The problem after the war will be getting rid of the Yanks." The rage of the have-nots against the haves burned in thousands of hearts.

One Sunday when the big picture show in Market Street was filling with service men and their girls, a Digger saw his quondam girl clinging to the arm of an American sailor. He had had a few drinks and had no girl. The gob's face was fair, frank, and fatuous. The Digger, his repressions suddenly released, landed a punch in it. The girl screamed high above the normal tumult. Oblivious of the crowd the two began to fight. Other sailors leaped to the assistance of their mate. Every Digger in sight dropped his girl and made for the combat zone on the good old principle of one in, all in. Doughboys joined the gobs. The vestibule was a seething mass of angry males and frightened strident girls. Police whistles flashed through the uproar. News of the affray spread to those already within the theatre, and they began to surge out. American naval patrols, their truncheons swinging from their wrists, waded in. Diggers, whose democratic hearts had for weeks been outraged by their parade of naked force in the city streets, now set upon them with a will. There was no doubt as to their enormous zest. Everything that could be torn loose in the vestibule was torn loose, and used as a weapon of offence or defence. The street outside was soon blocked with a huge crowd. The fight seemed to be acting like a magnet upon the whole city. Servicemen on leave with nothing to do and nowhere to go hailed it with enthusiasm. A colonel or two and some other superior officers tried in vain to control the men. They could not make themselves heard. The chief of police thought it was not his pigeon. It was not until the military police arrived in force, and the fire brigade ordered out, that tear bombs and hoses broke up the mob. A dozen or so men were left unconscious on the ground, several badly hurt. Some arrests were made, but the majority of the combatants made off through the half-dark streets. Next day the press threw in its weight with the home team, publishing highly facetious accounts of the fracas. Respectable and law-abiding citizens chuckled over it, and everyone, rather mysteriously, felt better. They had avenged their own romanticism. The Americans had no organ of publicity and were not consulted about their feelings. High officials on both sides poured soothing syrup on the troubled waters. The manager of the theatre sent a long and circumstantial bill to American headquarters. History does not relate what success he had.

In the Australian towns, particularly the great coastal cities, people continued to live under the pressure of fear. The pressure varied, sometimes attack seemed imminent, at other times the likelihood appeared to decrease. Now one argument, now another, usurped the public imagination. When fear receded the leaders and politicians must bring it back, for it was a powerful lever to advance the war effort. When it increased beyond a certain point it became dangerous to morale, and the people must be soothed by reassurances of final victory. The pause was something to be filled, the uncertainty crippled effort. Life apart from the war began to wither. People doubted its validity. It was, however, quite useless for the leaders to inveigh against the pleasures of the people. They flocked to the race courses, the dogs, the picture theatres. They needed the diversion and would have it even to the brink of invasion.

Daily life was more regimented. Every man and woman up to sixty must register. Commodities were rationed. Scarcities were taken at first as temporary inconveniences, but they were not, they were part of the change over, not accidents but logical consequences. People thought that life was becoming irregular and out of gear. It was not, it was being regularised and geared. Now every person was a docketed commodity and must carry his identification card.

Rabaul was occupied, Port Moresby was raided, Darwin was raided. The public mind adjusted itself to that. Suddenly, with the magnified force of an expected shock, the Japanese struck again on the mainland. A pearling town on the nor'west was raided. First a wave of planes came over and dropped bombs, then a force landed from the sea, small, but more than enough to take the parched dilapidated little town. It just crunched together like a handful of dry twigs. It was deserted when the landing party arrived. The blacks had melted into the distance. The whites, having a little warning, had stacked their valuables, that is all the beer and whisky in the pubs, on to the few remaining trucks and had departed into the spinifex. What remained was only a shell. Although the remains of meals still littered tables, clothes hung in cupboards, and fires smouldered in stoves, the place might have been empty for a dozen years. It was parched, bleached, sanded into a state of timeless emptiness. There was nothing to loot. The wealth that had flowed in from the pearlers had always promptly flowed out again. In any case, civilization could not hold in that terrain. Red sand blew down the main street, the yellow grey spinifex spread like an all-covering sea into the distance. Only an old goat, dignified and inane, met them and brayed in their faces. He might have been the place spirit. They shot the goat and wrecked the telegraph office. That didn't seem to make much difference. There was something about the torrid little hole that made the war seem pompous and absurd.

The inhabitants, two score of them, mostly male, were getting gloriously drunk on the beer they had saved. Being saved, it was now everybody's beer. They knew they were safe and didn't worry. In the cloudless sky they could see the enemy's planes circling over the settlement. Presently, coming up from the south, they saw a wedge of Australian fighters. "Well,

I'm jiggered," they said. "Who'd have thought it?" They laid bets on the resulting dogfight. The bombers made off with the fighters in pursuit, but one didn't get away. It turned slowly over and dived with smoke streaming from it. It seemed to be almost over their heads. They watched it open-mouthed. It wasn't even real. As the plane hit the ground, a couple of hundred yards away, it burst into flames, a man burning like a flambeau freed himself and staggered a few steps and collapsed into a little mound of fire beside the sheet of orange flame rising from the grey spinifex into the blue sky. For a sobered second the watchers stood at gaze.

"Look what the buggers done."

The spinifex was on fire. They had a hard struggle to save the trucks and the beer.

"It woulda been better to leave the buggers alone," they said.

The next morning, having sent out scouts who reported the settlement deserted, they returned home.

When Sydney heard of the raid, "No casualties, no military damage," a faint sigh of relief went up. It was to be the west not the east coast. The nor-west was very far away. The point of the raid was obscure. The Japanese may have hoped to catch the pearling fleet. However, the luggers were well away. Its significance seemed clear. Java, still holding out, had been by-passed.

In London, the event, occurring in a lull, received banner headlines. "Australia Attacked. Invasion Attempt on North-West Australia."

As Arch came into the mess there was silence and a flutter of newspapers. That was unusual, the boys weren't interested in the war news, they didn't read the papers. They had their own bit of the war to hold down, that was enough. They had no faith in the rest of it, no spiritual energy to spare. When they were off duty they had as good a time as they could, stretching out the thin and shrunken hours to cover themselves, or they slept.

Their squadron was going on duty in half an hour. They were all there, slumped round the mess in little groups reading the papers. They had been together now for months, they'd had losses and closed up their ranks. They had come, strangely, to look alike, young and worn to a common brotherhood of strain and fortitude and effort. They were men forced by their calling to take up all their possibilities of courage and endurance. Now, too, they shared another emotion, stronger and deeper than anything of which they thought themselves still capable.

They said nothing, didn't even swear. This thing, although expected, had come as a sudden stroke upon their tightened nerves. They hid their emotion from one another in silence. It was broken in a way that tore them open. A boy who came from a farm in the Riverina began to talk as if to himself, biting at his forefinger between words.

"It can't happen there," he said, and added as if it were a reason, "it's such defenceless country, old and quiet and easily hurt. There are the brown paddocks and out beyond them a ridge with blue trees on it and away and away pale blue mountains just one shade darker than the sky. There's the homestead on the little hill, the tanks and the windmill and the pepper trees. The light comes flooding down and then the darkness floods down. Any amount of earth and light and air, and smells of hot grass. The water in the dam is like a blue eye in a brown face and the new iron roof on the shearing shed is like a silver fire. You hear the earth ticking and there's nothing in the sky but a crow. . . ."

Arch felt his throat harden. He thought of the way the night came down on the plains round Toongabbie, empty and still, without fear, without urgency. . . .

The squadron leader, red-headed, tough, twenty-four years old, stood up.

"We've got to go home, boys."

"And take our buses with us."

"We're veterans, we'd be the nucleus."

"We can't stay here, there's plenty here."

"They've hardly a feather to fly with at home."

"We've got to go home and go quick. Any way we can get."

They all thought the same thing. "We're Australians, we don't belong here. We're exiles and we've never been anything else here. We're suffocating for air and light and space and silence. Australia."

The order came to go to the briefing room. The boy who had spoken first said the second unforgivable thing.

"Tough luck if any of us get stonkered tonight."

They had believed for that moment that they would go home. By the sheer force of their will and need, they believed they would work the miracle, but the source of power was too distant and the walls of discipline too strong. The hour was like a fountain when an unseen hand switched off the water.

Sydney relaxed a little in her steel armour. The danger, she thought, she wanted to think, was going the other way. No danger is quite real by *my* danger. It is something in the newspaper.

There were many who still believed that the war, the real war, could be fought in Europe and that Europe was still Australia's bulwark. The password in everyone's mouth was "The Second Front." The United Nations were hoarding their might and would attack across the Channel, through Belgium, through Norway, or strike up through the Balkans to join Russians, and everywhere a people, waiting to be liberated, would rally to them and bless the beneficent bombs as they fell on their occupied cities. Or better still, they would sweep the enemy from North Africa into the Mediterranean, Mare Nostrum—let them drink it then—and then strike up through Italy, carrying the treacherous and cowardly Italians before them impaled on their bayonets (serve the Dagoes right) into Germany. Or the Second Front might be in the air, a thousand bombers over Germany every night, laying her in ruins town by town, acre by acre, "softening her up," as the phrase went, in dust and fire paying back the score of London and Coventry and Liverpool, of Cardiff and Hull and Southampton, of the anonymous towns "in East Anglia" or "on the north-east coast," and avenging all the casualties down to the "rabbit in the field" a hundred thousand fold. The Second Front would come in the Spring. The concept blazed like a comet across the dark skies. The war would surely have its grand romantic denouement when Spring came. They had said it last Spring, they said it again this Spring. Like Dante creating Hell for his enemies, the mass imagination dreamed of Armageddon. The rites of Spring. There had always been blood upon the Spring. Without knowing it, man cried upon the ancient sacrifice, the blood sacrifice to purge them of the guilt and blunders and humiliations of the war. Atonement, catharsis, and the death of all evil would be consummated on the smoking altars of bombed cities, and then would come peace and reconstruction, the Four Freedoms, Security from the Cradle to the Grave, N.R.P.A., and the Atlantic Charter made flesh.

Everywhere men's imaginations quickened, and here and there some private jet rose high into the air. The starving poet of King's Cross was touched to poetry. He had played so long at being a poet and now he was caught in it. He conceived and proceeded to bear his "Spring Symphony." It was not so much an epic—as a towering image of the world in conflict, of man and the mystic vine whose fruit is Life and Death. It was the black mass of the Spring, the anguish of renewal when the unfurling bud was the signal for death, when the soft winds reopened the stench of last year's dead, and the lovers' moon led the way to destruction, when the rising sap, the terrible inevitability of spring, filled every heart with fear, when love died in hunger, when beauty was destroyed at its source in the eye, when everything the heart treasured was buried under the weight of metal, when every hopeful flower that broke the sod was a candle for a lost generation. And in this maze of life and death men moved in age-old images, Petrouchka, the defeated who must rise again, the Wandering Jew and the Flying Dutchman, immortal man in search of his death; the Scapegoat, the Thief, and the Man on the Cross; the youngest prince who must be the hero whatever befalls, Leda and her swan, Hecate and Cybele. . . .

He wrote it without rhyme and often without reason, for reason had little to do with most of it, and he wrote it in a strange medley of styles, sometimes labyrinthine, curling and intricate like a vine, sometimes in short clear lyrics like translucent fruit among dark foliage: other passages like meteorites, cold after fusion, others obscure as the blind words of a forgotten language engraved on obsidian. Sometimes he wrote with a simplicity that was shocking in its innocence, and sometimes he caught in the delicate mirror of poetry the metallic echoes of worlds in conflict. He had never heard guns (for the path of glory is reserved for strong arches and his feet were ingloriously flat), but his imagination knew them and could catch and hold their metre.

He became in his own way demoniac and possessed by his own poetry. He no longer read the news, he no longer cared. He was quite apart. He was exalted and everything he saw now wore a changed and significant aspect— a tree against the evening sky, the face of a woman in the street, a moving shadow or a flying beam. The purple bloom of asphalt after rain, a broken sentence heard in passing, the first star, an odour he could not name, were so many catalysts to his thought. The texture of a stone or the mystery of a patch of bare earth could hold his mind in secret brooding. Everything contributed to and fertilised the thought in it.

The poetry spurted in him: day and night it tormented him. His pockets were full of scraps of paper on which he had written the ideas and images that came to him. He got up in the night to write down the ideas that would not let him sleep, and fell asleep at last slumped over the table, his unshaven face buried in his arms. His wife picked up crazy fragments of poetry lying on the floor. She discovered strange images written on the telephone pad and even fragments of blank verse scrawled on the landlord's wall beside the connubial bed. She could make nothing of them and hated them as if they were bugs. But she secretly respected them too, as if they were magic. Nothing could have made the man to whom she had been married for fifteen years seem more like a stranger than this unaccountable burst of poetry, just when he should have been settling down to snug middle age. He had always been a poet. Poetry had been like a cat in the house, not useful, a pet; now, it was as if the tame cat had suddenly become a tiger. She feared and hated her husband for it as if he had gone mad.

He grew constipated and mangy. He fell out of his exaltation, but he had invested too much in his symphony to retreat. He was its Laocoon. He was like a man suffering from pressure sickness for whom there was no decompression chamber. So consumed was he that he lost his world and came to live only in his conception. In moments of exhaustion he glimpsed it again, like a haggard unshaven prisoner looking through a barred window upon the unconcerned world he had left for ever. . . . In current events he had lost all interest.

.    .    .    .    .    .    .    .    .

Knarf lifted his eyes: "The world in the years of fury," he said. It was as if he gathered up all his puppets with one sweep of his hand, leaving the great stage bare.

Ord grinned. "You want the whole world now."

"Any story, if you let it spread, covers the whole world. It was a much smaller world then, so much more helpless, no watertight bulkheads. It was swept from end to end with the tumult of its disease. Men were in bondage then in a way that few can even conceive now. Unplanned living. Behind the law of cause and effect itself, only a blind inconsequence, so that every one was subject to forces he willed as little as he controlled. They lived in a world they did not make. We at least make our world. Or do we? I suppose they thought they made theirs. Only at this distance we can see how utterly out of hand it was. That's why I can't even tell the story of Harry and Ben without having it spread over the world. It took the world to make their story. There's no logical place to draw the line. It is like an enormous jigsaw puzzle, I've fitted together a little corner of it, but that has *no* meaning unless I at least sort out the other pieces and arrange them so as to indicate the completed pattern, however cursorily."

Ord asked gravely, "Do you know there aren't above a dozen people who would understand you when you say that. I only know by chance and the skin of my teeth that jigsaw puzzles were a fashionable craze four centuries ago and now are one with crosswords and diabolo. Is it true that you have given up this world for that one?"

"A man can know only one thing." Have I, Knarf asked himself, become one of a galaxy of stone figures long since dust? Imprisoned? Did I stop for ever in the moment when I saw the Brooding Anzac for the first time and imagined that my mind had touched uncovered life?

"Tell me," Ord said, speaking more gently than usual, "what the world looked like in the years of fury. I've handled the fragments of the puzzle often enough but I haven't put them together."

"The whole world was sick. The war was not an accident but the expression of a deep and terrible distemper, erupting from within. Two thousand miles of war in Russia. Crazy pattern of disease and famine and war in China. Abstract war in the desert. Lurking war in the jungle. Smoke and dust of bombed cities like scattered pustules on the stricken body. The unsafe skies. The dark seas where ships went stealthily seeking cover under the naked skies where there was none, and only those that carried the sick and wounded under the Red Cross went white and lit like pleasure cruisers.

"In men's minds was the shadow of the things they did. War and the knowledge of war and the acceptance of war penetrated every activity and every thought. There was at last no corner left in any man's mind where he could escape it. The microcosm of the individual reflected the macrocosm of society—as if you held mirror to mirror and the exchange image repeated itself to infinity.

"People could not hate the enemy without also hating one another, so that within society the cracks widened and competition hardened and increased, competitive living, competitive loving, competitive suffering and death. Out of their blind rage, irritation, discomfort, the people fashioned schisms. There was hatred between the United Nations, the plutocracies feared and hated Soviet Russia, Russia returned it with a warrior hate. China was bitter, she was neglected and left to die by her rich allies, excluded from their councils, the Fighting French had an inferiority complex and all the world knew it. Had not France 'let us down'? Glaze it as they might with smooth words, there was dislike and distrust between Britain and the United States. The gibe that England fought her wars with other people's armies and kept her own to bludgeon the peace rankled like a fish hook. They said here that 'the Yanks couldn't fight' and that when the war was over the next job would be to drive out the Americans. Within the British Commonwealth of Nations old hostilities deepened and proliferated. India burned upon the pyre of her wrongs. British power in the East showed itself a rotten fabric. Behind, beneath the actual war there was a latent war. The Left feared America as much as the Right feared Russia.

"It was no different within each community. The cleavage of class became deeper, the army became a state within the state, competition for dwindling resources and supplies devoured the mind of the people like a plague. Propaganda spread suspicion, in every mind was the irritated knowledge 'I am being got at.' In every move of the government, in every rumour, scare, event even, the citizen looked for the catch. He knew the news was being manipulated, his amusements adulterated, his consciousness raided from all the points of the compass. He must suspect everything, but, even so, propaganda found its way under his guard and conditioned him. He could not draw himself clear of it, and that, more than anything else, warped and embittered him.

"That, and the ever-increasing difficulty of daily life, the labyrinth of regulations and prohibitions, the scarcities, artificial and real. The hunting age was come again and men and women in cities must forage for their food.

"The amenities were drying up. The system that had created, for profit, an unexampled state of comfort and luxury now, by its natural progression into war, cancelled them out again, and all the appetites they had created were denied. If you could have taken an aerial view of society in those days it would have looked like country under drought, the arid earth grown hard and fissured, eroded and blown away. Cracks opened in a pattern of destruction where no weakness had shown. The sweep of events like desert wind carrying sand excoriated the denuded surface, iron hard, iron barren, yet vulnerable."

Knarf looked into the distance over the coloured band of cultivation, over the river to the country beyond. He had seen the great inverted miracle of the dry spell worked upon that undefended earth, and it had become one of the master images of his mind just as the Brooding Anzac had. In some odd way they were connected like strophe and antistrophe, question and answer, the filament of their relationship so fine that any explanation must break it. That country had the look of eternity in good years or bad. When it was in good heart you could only believe that it was inexhaustible; under drought you could not believe that it would ever live again. It was absolute, it went beyond eternity because it cast eternity like a vestment. . . .

In his metaphor of stricken society in the terms of the drought-stricken earth, Knarf had tried to tap this deep feeling he had of the earth and its immutable mutability. He saw he had failed. The image veered in his mind. He saw instead something of which he had heard, a story that had taken root in the landscape, of how in the old days when drought had come to the overstocked land, the cattle had stood and died of thirst in the waterless paddocks, just stood like painted animals in the pale brown and purple of the withered landscape, unmoving for days, in a trance, until they died and fell. Not one scapegoat driven out in the wilderness to die for the people's sins, but herds. It was like them that society foundered. The sacrifice of the scapegoat was not a counter to Nature but a yielding, an act moulded in the curve of law, a repetitive sacrifice. It was the nemesis of the overstocked paddocks and of the mis-run world. To ask too much is to get too little, greed, and after greed the immolation. And greed had been so dear to men that they died for it. Other men's greed. . . .

Knarf half expected, like a lash on his uncovered mind, one of Ord's gibes, "If you must be an artist, why set up as a thinker?" or that tag he had unearthed from somewhere in the past, "Analogy isn't proof," but Ord said nothing, only followed his eyes over the river and far away.

Knarf took a deep breath. "There was a season of hope. Victories in Russia, in Italy, in the air and on sea. Men talked of reconstruction and "winning the peace," and wrangled about the world to come and a meting out of punishment for war guilt. Danger was rolled back, precautions relaxed, and with the passing of danger, the reason of much that people were forced still to do seemed to perish, the coherence went out of life. Victories, but not victory, and the time was so long. The painted cloth of hope and confidence tore under the strain and beneath it were new vistas of war uglier still than the original conflict.

The war in the Pacific went on and on, it was a slow moving war, clogged by water and great distances. Both sides were fighting a holding war, so a holding war it was. Japan had already acquired a huge and rich empire, the United Nations had their urgent preoccupations in Europe, their transport difficulties, their shortages of raw materials. The action became like the grinding of two great wheels, rim against rim,—where they ground blood flowed, but the hub of each turned in comparative safety. Time was neutral. China was encircled—Russia's neutrality on the north, Britain's impotence on the west, Japan crushing steadily in from east and south. Her voice went begging through the world to the courts of her allies who boasted their wealth and strength.

The enemy, the Japanese, remained to the Australians a mythical people, as alien as robots, as inexplicable. There was no understanding of them as human beings. They were hermetically sealed in their world, the Australians in theirs. There was only war between them. It was like a war against monkeys, criminal monkeys. There was no understanding, so it became a purely mechanic war, hatred itself was mechanic. The enemy was an ape with no feeling, only vice. There was no genuine comprehension anywhere of what the Jap felt, of the inferiority that mixed with his pride, of the insatiable anger that his victories, even the conquest of a great empire, had not been able to quench, the blazing grudge he nursed against the complacent cities of White Australia, the desire in him, stronger than the desire of victory, to smash that complacent superiority, the willingness to pay a disproportionate price for such satisfaction. That willingness was the unpredictable factor, the unrecognized danger spot. No one dreamed, for instance, how big a price the Japanese might be willing to pay for the satisfaction of raiding Sydney. Actually, the reality of danger did not decrease in the same proportion as its feasibility.

A new power entered the Pacific war, fighting against both sides. A very minor incident had enormous consequences. An American destroyer, homeward bound for refitting, fell in with a Jap destroyer in waters where she did not expect to find one. The visibility was bad and the two ships were quite close before they discovered one another. To the long experienced eye of the American captain there was something a little queer about the Jap even at first sight. He could not have said what it was, it was one of those things that disappear as soon as you give them thought, but whatever it was it was his eye, more knowledgeable than his brain missed some normal sign of life about the ship and was suspicious.

The American opened fire, the Jap replied, but her shooting was weak and erratic. In a quarter of an hour the Jap was sinking and obviously hadn't more than a few minutes to live. She didn't behave like a normal ship in her circumstances even now, or rather the crew didn't. Only a couple of boats were seen to put off and they were nearly empty. The American captain was thoroughly puzzled and, instead of shooting down the life boats as had now become the custom on both sides, ordered some of the survivors to be taken aboard for questioning. Had there been a mutiny and mass desertion? Were they starving? Whatever it was he very much wanted to know and disliked the thought of mystery going unresolved to the bottom of the Pacific. The sailors brought seven men aboard but there was no officer among them and no one in the American ship could understand Japanese. The survivors were emaciated and morose, inscrutably Japanese. They were, by the look of them, starving but they refused to eat. This was attributed to the pigheaded, suicidal nature of the Jap. The American crew, in high spirits at the prospect of going home, ragged the wretched creatures unmercifully, and authority indulgently shut its eyes. It was not till a couple of days later that it became apparent that the prisoners were not starving but sick. On the third day the terrible nature of their disease revealed itself. The naval surgeon bluntly advised the captain to throw them overboard at once. An agonizing conflict began in the captain's mind. He had been nurtured on tales of heroism and in the romantic tradition—some of it still stuck. Although he could shoot down survivors in the water with a grim sense of duty, once he had taken them aboard he felt differently about them, his conscience was involved. In the end, after listening to the surgeon and to his own heart, he decided to keep and succour the dying Japanese.

He sealed them into their quarters and fumigated the ship. Many of the crew had already been in contact with them, some had each day to go into the prison with water and later a fatigue party had roughly to parcel up the dead and commit them to the sea. Mercifully they were all dead before the destroyer made port. The captain did everything that common sense and the naval surgeon could suggest, and when the destroyer berthed there were no signs of disease in the crew. The surgeon had not been able to name the disease and was reprimanded by his superior for not bringing at least one body home so that the sickness could be identified. He smiled grimly.

A month later, when the destroyer was almost ready for sea again, the first signs that she had not got off scot free began to show. Man after man fell sick with an unknown and terrible malady. Barely two percent of them recovered, it took from ten days to a fortnight to kill. The naval surgeon died and so did the captain.

The ship's company had been scattered far and wide on leave, and presently with an awful inevitability the disease showed itself here and there through the length of the west coast. Thousands had been infected before it was even suspected and they in turn infected thousands of others. No one knew its nature, how it was transmitted or how to treat it. It raged among the workmen of the shipyard where the destroyer had been fitted. Those who were not ill struck and fled the place in terror. They carried death into other shipyards.

The black filaments spread down the coast and inland. The long period of incubation made it impossible to control. Charlatans throve on quack remedies and safeguards. Many fell ill out of the terror, many fled east before they could be stopped and took the infection with them. The disease flourished in the virgin soil as white men's diseases had always flourished among the Pacific islanders.

It soon became clear that Japan was also infected, that the thing was in their crowded cities, and not only Japanese were dying but the contagion was spreading among the army of occupation. The plague had originated in China, the result of prolonged mass starvation, of a soil saturated with death, a civilisation broken down by war. The pirates had carried it through the islands into Japan. It was stamping them out and they were dragging their conquerors down with them. America could only appeal frantically to China to send doctors who had some knowledge of the plague to help her fight it.

Australia felt the vibration of panic. To her armies in the field the command went out "Take no prisoners." Land assaults almost ceased, there was no desire to take any position that had been held by the Japanese for fear lest it was infected, but the additional strength of a new hatred went into the air attacks. The enemy was doubly feared now, a superstitious horror entered into the people. Panic did not show openly but it lurked in a sultry atmosphere like the calm that preludes a cyclone. Rumours twisted underfoot like snakes in the grass. The plague, they said, was in the northern armies and the truth was being kept from the people. Everywhere people were saying, cynically, suspiciously, "We're not being told."

.    .    .    .    .    .    .    .    .

It was Saturday, and for once it felt like Saturday because Ben had the day off. He was hanging round the flat when Harry got home. He'd blued his money so that he couldn't go anywhere and Tony Nelson was working. The waste of good time stuck in his throat. When Harry suggested that they go for a surf, he jumped at it. It was a hot day, one of the late hot days with autumn in the air, a rounded pendant ripeness as of fruit ready to fall. Even in the city there was a taste of fermentation in the air. The sunlight was thick hot yellow syrup.

There was a small section of the beach still left for surfers between the barbed wire entanglements. It wasn't the same. You knew that a limit had been set to all good things. The barbed wire was detritus now, snarled and rusted. No one believed in danger any more. For a time it had given coherence to life, then it had passed, not officially perhaps but it no longer existed as an imaginative fact, and life had fallen apart into a tangle of wasted money and effort, the jagged and patternless dump of wire. "Looks silly," Ben said.

Even when they lay on the sand, looking up at the endless blue of the sky or out to sea, they were aware of a net drawn in till it was nearly closed. The cloudless sky was an impenetrable curtain, its candour illusory. A ship, Harry thought, could stand off out of sight and under cover of that innocent sky, shell the city into dust. He did not believe in any ship. It was an idle thought, a little wave breaking without trace in his brain.

The sun burned their salty bodies, but not fiercely. There was a slow powdering of gold on the blue of the sea. It was calm, with a slow cradling movement of deep waters. Harry and Ben felt constrained. They knew they were in a fast changing world, that because of their different ages the changes must carry them apart further and further. Almost for the first time the thought of their relationship to one another was in the forefront of both minds. I am father. I am son. We have something to say to one another now. Each was embarrassed by the pressure of the demand to which he was too inarticulate to yield. The valediction, if such it was, remained unspoken. When they talked it was in little freshets. The main topic was Ben's new camouflaged truck. That it was camouflaged filled him with innocent bravado. She was a beautiful truck, the road flowed like oil under her. He could talk for hours about her, but he didn't. Even that subject dried up. They returned with the burden of a confidence beyond expression upon their hearts.

The street, when they came back to it in the later afternoon, had a desultory look. Everyone who could go out had gone. Over its dinginess was thrown a rich pattern of sunlight and shadow, blooming it, even if only with dust. In the flat, Wanda, who was going on shift, stood by the kitchen table, eating her hasty self-inflicted tea. Ruth was sitting on Ben's bed to get the last light, sewing. Ally was down with Mrs Blan. Harry went to the safe to forage. Except for Sunday's dinner there were no set meals at the weekend. They helped themselves to whatever there was and, if they didn't like it, went out and bought something. The safe now was crammed with plates and saucers, each containing some fragment of leftover food thrust in, one on top of the other; butter, jam, and gravy were smeared on the green gauze of the safe, a sour and ugly smell rose from it. From the bottom shelf Harry disgustedly yanked out a couple of sausages covered in bluish mould. All Ally had to do was to keep the place decent, and she didn't do it. The safe hadn't been cleaned out for a week. Ruth used to keep things fairly right, but now her interest had moved away from home. A wretched home it had been for the children. Harry fished two shillings out of his pocket and gave it to Ben.

"Go out and get yourself some tea," he said.

"Right oh, dad. Then I'll go up and see old Rumpty."

He took the situation cheerfully and for granted. Harry hoped he'd get a proper meal but forebore to give him any advice. Ben was doing a man's work, but he hadn't changed much since he was a little boy. He was as frank and friendly, as natural. Somehow or other he seemed to have missed the awkward age. Ben's all right, he thought, we haven't been able to hurt Ben.

While the light lasted Harry lay on his bed and read. When it got dark there was nowhere to go but into the kitchen or out into the street, so he stayed where he was and watched the moon rise. It was a full moon. large and yellow. "A bush moon," Harry called it, and it set him off thinking about his life as a youngster in the bush and of the farm he had left at Toongabbie. It seemed for the moment nearer than the street outside. When the moon was half way up the sky he went to bed. He heard Ally moving about in her room speaking to Ruth. Ben wasn't in yet, he'd probably spent half his tea money on the pictures.

It must have been half-past ten when the sirens sounded the alert. People heard them and paused. They didn't believe it was true. Their impulse was to turn on their house lights, to pop their heads out of the windows and scan the sky, or simply take no notice. It wasn't real, they didn't believe it. They were angry and tried to push it away. It wasn't even the right time for anything to happen. At dusk or deep in the night but not at ten thirty, which was no time at all on a Saturday night.

Immediately on top of the alarm came the roaring of planes and the bursting of bombs. Harry knew that sound. This was the real thing. He plunged out of the bed and began to drag on his trousers. The few lights in the streets had gone dead. The city lay open to attack, encrusted round its gleaming waters under the full moon. A warden's car roared up the steep pinch from William Street and a stentorian voice yelled to a shocked and inquisitive householder, "Put out that light." People were running out into the streets. The nearest shelter was to have been in the basement of the post-office on the corner, but it was Saturday night, the building was deserted, the doors locked. They ran back into their houses. The explosions were nearer. A blaze sprang up somewhere down near the wharves in Woolloomooloo. The bicker of anti-aircraft began and the flak was falling not far away.

Ruth was gathering up clothes for herself and Ally. Harry brought them both downstairs. The safest place was in the little back hall and under the stairs. Mrs Blan was already there, squatting grotesquely under a kitchen table on top of which by a supreme effort she had piled her mattress. She was amazed and very pleased with herself for acting according to plan.

Harry went out to the verandah to turn off the gas. New fires he saw had started and the noise was more intense. He seemed to be in the quiet centre of a circle of tumult. When he went back from opening the windows the bandsman was in charge and everyone in the house gathered together except Mr Isaac. Harry raced up to his attic. He couldn't make himself heard above the din, but, feeling his way in the dark, he found the old man sitting upright in his hard chair. So cold and rigid was he to the touch that for a second Harry thought he had died of shock, but the gnarled hands came up to grip his. With his lips to the old man's temples he said, "You must come downstairs at once."

Isaac's voice came thin and calm through the noise.

"No, no. I will stay here, I've run enough," and "No more."

"It's dangerous."

"So is everything else."

Harry picked him up and carried him down the stairs. Old Isaac ceased to resist. He bowed himself to that too. His body was light and brittle as dead leaves, but he wasn't frightened. Harry knew the feel of frightened flesh. At the foot of the stairs he put the old man down.

"I got to go out," he said. "Keep them together. Don't let them get frightened."

The old man nodded, the eyes that met Harry's were full, beautiful, and entirely human. Harry knew he was leaving a man behind him who would be equal to any spiritual strain that might be put upon him, the stronger and steadier because he no longer had any personal concern in the outcome. They said in the street that he was mad. His sanity took short cuts, that was all. Harry told him what he thought they should do if the raid got nearer. Mr Isaac nodded. Now his nose had been turned in another direction he would follow it. The din was less now, the first wave had gone over.

Harry stepped out on the verandah and pulled the door to behind him. He remembered he had no key. It didn't matter. His mind was clear, every detail showing up in it with unnatural clarity and speed. His mind was cut free of its desperation: for him, for everyone, he believed, the issue was narrowed down to survival point. The raid had lasted so far not more than ten minutes, fires were blazing down by the wharves, in the city, and there was one quite near—it might be in Taylor Square. Their glare made the full moon look lonely and nacreous. The drone of planes was audible, and, Harry thought, increasing. It wasn't over yet. A curious elation possessed him. The civil world in which he had failed was crashing down. He was not frightened. He'd been a soldier and survived far worse than that. With an ounce of luck you didn't get killed or hurt in that sort of thing. It would give him the willies to be cooped up waiting, but in the open he felt like one who triumphantly rode the tempest. His duty was to go as quickly as possible to the store. His firefighter's badge, which was with his identity card in his trousers' pocket, would take him through the streets. However, he had no intention of going to the shop. It could burn for him. Tomorrow didn't exist. The flare in the direction of Paddington and the increasing noise decided him. Gwen. He had a vision of that congested and inflammable area. Gwen alone. Gwen frightened by thunder storms. He hadn't any faith in her power to take care of herself. He thought Ben would be all right. It was to Gwen that his instinct and his steps turned.

He turned to the left and skirted the shoulder of the hill. On the vacant land in Clapton Place the Port Jackson figs showed black against a red sky. He tried to locate the fires. One was near the shop. It might be the shop. The city had a gaunt blackness between firelight and moonlight. Columns of black smoke stood up against the luminous sky. "We're getting it," he thought, "Christ, we're getting it." He could feel a deep vibration under his feet. The streets he traversed at first were quite dead, life crouched down and waiting. He passed a few tin-hatted patrolling wardens. When he came to Taylor Square it was different. Half of it was ablaze. Fire engines, hose, and demolition squads at work filled the open spaces. All the surrounding streets were strewn with fragments of glass. Men were working with herculean speed and efficiency. "It's working," Harry thought.

Despite the efforts of wardens a crowd had collected. The police were too busy to disperse them. To some people it was still a show.

Harry made a detour. Above in the moon-dazzled sky R.A.A.F. fighters were going into action against the enemy. A flaming plane, like an apocryphal comet, streamed headlong throught the sky. There was a smell of—what—cordite? in the air, mixed with smoke and the odour of civilization breaking down, ruptured drains, ruptured gasmains. The noise, which was immense again, seemed to come at him in flying walls of sound through which he passed. Metal rain was beating on the dry city.

It was a new world—no, not a new world, the new world unmasked. Harry still had the feeling of intrepidity, almost of elation, that had come upon him when he first stepped out into the raid. He'd find Gwen and put her in a safe place, then he'd be free and he'd join one of the rescue parties. The energy of years was released in him.

Harry heard a bomb wail towards him. He flung himself down in the gutter, protecting his head with his arms. The crash came and earth heaved under him. "Not so near," he thought, and "I got to get through." He jumped up and started to run, bent low as if he were running along a trench. Another crash came and the blast threw him down, spreadeagled on the road. It was a minute before he stirred, got to his knees and then to his feet. His chin was wet with blood, but he felt nothing—only the sky was red with whirling black stars, and the ground rose steeply under his feet. He was running up the slope at Gaba Tepe, carrying his equipment, his lungs bursting, the surf of the Turkish fire just ahead of him; he was caught by their own barrage in the crumbling French village out of Bouchevenes, stumbling blind and suffocated towards a shelter that had gone; he was running through a blasted and hopeless city, a man without a job. It was a long, long journey, but it could have been only a matter of seconds before he saw the wall bulging out towards him, tried to push back the curtain of blood from his burst lungs and run, only to falter and go down in the great smoke of rubble; the sliding, breaking, vanishing world.

Long after the raiding planes had gone and the sky was quiet, a fragment of the Anzac Memorial still stood swaying precariously. One brooding resolute figure still looked down at the chaos of the shrine. It had received a direct hit. The formal mirror lake was burst and spilled, the dark, old tree, so often threatened, that from a distance had seemed to be espaliered on the pale stone, was a splintered stump. The bronze doors were torn out, the boy crucified on the sword and the mourning women were rubble, the golden stars were dust, like the men they commemorated. Because the Memorial was built on hollow ground, the debris was carried through into the railway excavation beneath. Only that one corner remained, a great splinter of stone carrying its figure, steadfast and undismayed. It stood until the early morning when a vibration, perhaps the thundering of fire engines along William Street, brought it crashing down. A last plume of dust rose into the air.

It was Sunday morning. There was dew on the railings because it was autumn. The milk was delivered as usual, the newspaper came with a stop press account of the night's raid, on the front page in red ink. It had lasted a little more than an hour, forty planes had been over Sydney, twelve had been shot down. The damage was comparatively slight. Some bombs had fallen on the docks at Woolloomooloo "doing little damage but starting fires in a thickly populated area," others had hit Taylor Square and the labyrinth of streets beyond, a falling plane had started a big fire in Five Ways. A direct hit had been scored on the Anzac Memorial. "Repeated vicious attacks had been made against the Memorial as the symbol of the nation's courage and heroic sacrifice." All the fires were under control by dawn, casualties were thought to be small, military damage to be slight, as the aircraft when pursued had jettisoned their bombs at random. Simultaneous raids had been made on Newcastle and Port Kembla. The raiding planes had come from an aircraft-carrier. Incredibly, foolhardily, it had slipped down through the open Pacific for the satisfaction of striking once at the arrogant white city. That was worth death. And the long shot had succeeded. "Units of the Navy were in hot pursuit." At the end the public was assured that the "raid had not been heavy," but that it had "whipped the fighting morale of the people to white heat."

"Not heavy?" Ally echoed disgustedly, "What more do they want?" She had the jitters this morning and it aroused her febrile rage to hear minimized in this way the ordeal she had been through, crouched half the night under a table with Mrs Blan and the old loony from upstairs, never knowing but that any minute might be the last. Wanda, who had just come in full of ginger from her experiences at the munition works, sat at the table talking with a vivacity she rarely wasted on the home circle, while Ruth prepared breakfast. Ben stood in the doorway listening, a little chagrined. He had been in the pictures when the alert sounded and the audience had been marshalled into a near by shelter and, except for N.E.S. workers and those with fire fighters' badges, were not allowed to leave till six in the morning. All he'd heard of the raid was "an outsize thunderstorm and a dozen women having hysterics."

Ruth spread the cloth and put out the plates. "If Mr Isaac's awake I'll bring him down to breakfast," she said. She felt stretched with fatigue and the night's strain. But she was relieved, too, a small voice said in her brain, "If that's all I can stand it." She'd looked out and seen Sid's taxi safe outside the Nelsons'. Mr Isaac was asleep, lying on his bed fully dressed. He looked small, brown, childish, vulnerable. "But he was fine last night," Ruth thought as she stepped softly away from the open door.

"It's no good waiting for your father," said Ally, "they'll probably give him breakfast at the shop. They think they own him down there. If I were a man I wouldn't leave my family to shift for themselves in an air raid, not for all the shops in Kingdom Come."

"Stow it, mum," said Ben. He'd discovered a brave new world in which jobs were all suddenly raised to an heroic level. He and his father had something in common.

Ally would not have let that pass. This was a subject on which she always had a lot to say, but at that moment a current of wind from the landing whisked the newspaper over the butter.

"That's the front door," she said, peeling it off. "Go and see who it is, Ruthie."

It was Mrs Blan who opened the front door, closed this morning, contrary to custom, as a protest against the world's insecurity and the cold wind. Also contrary to custom, a policeman was on the step. Mrs Blan contented herself with opening the door only a few inches. There was a low official murmur.

"Christ," said Mrs Blan in a high bleat and let the door fly wide. She turned and saw Ruth on the landing above. "It's for your mum," she called, and in her agitation lumbered up a few stairs, making grotesque beckoning signs with her arm as if she were about to bowl.

"Mother," called Ruth, and ran down stairs.

In an instant, in a second, the house was full of the presage of bad news, its ordinary sounds suspended, listening tense.

It was Ruth who ran over to Nelsons and waked Sid, lying asleep in his clothes just as he had fallen across the bed half an hour before, after a strenuous night with the rescue gangs down at the 'Loo. When he realised what she wanted he got up at once and went out to the taxi. There was no great hurry, but she thought there was. The neighbours, Mrs Blan and Mrs Nelson, the bandsman, and several others, hoisted Ally in. To every one she said hoarsely, "I got to go and identify him." They nodded with dumb and awful comprehension. Ruth got in beside her mother. As the taxi drove away Mrs Blan wagged her head at the group on the kerb. "It's hard for a woman to lose her man even if they didn't get on so well." Wanda and Ben walked back into the house with hanging heads. They felt as if their world had been stripped off them, as the near blast of a bomb strips off your clothes. When Mrs Blan yelled to them to come in for a cup of tea they bolted up the stairs, jostling one another.

Arrived at Paddington Police Station, where the cells were being used as an impromptu morgue, it was Ruth who said to the policeman in charge, "Will I do?"

"What relation?" he asked.

"Daughter."

"Over twenty-one."

"Yes."

He looked at the dazed heap that was Ally. "Yes, you'll do." He led the way. Sid followed close behind Ruth. The policeman consulted a list, slowly, laboriously. "Here he is," he said. He wasn't abrupt or harsh, but there were so many of them, the next of kin had been coming for the last hour, not to mention those who were looking for missing friends. When it was a wholesale order you'd got to be official. This girl wasn't going to give any trouble. He'd got so that he could tell at a glance the ones who would throw hysterics.

"It's a pity we got to put them in quod," he said awkwardly, trying to soften what he knew must be looked on as an insult to the dead. "Couldn't be helped. Everything knocked endways." Shouldn't wonder if things aren't a sight rougher than this before we're done, he thought to himself.

Trestles had been set up in the cells, on the trestles, boards, and on the boards the covered mounds of the bodies, three to a cell. On each coverlet were pinned a label and an identity card, face down. The policeman picked up the identity card and lifted back the piece of canvas that they had to use as a sheet. He held the card like a watch timing them.

Sid's hand tightened like a clamp on Ruth's shoulder. She saw her father. She had never really looked at him before. He had changed but not greatly: the dead go on changing as the living do but much faster. The acquiescence of death had not come yet. His face was bleak and haggard, with a look of arrested struggle. The cuts and bruises didn't mean anything, he was whole under them. His hands. She saw them for the first time, but she knew they had managed to hold her world together somehow or other. Safe, empty. "He got hurt plenty," she thought. She didn't mean what had happened last night. "He was hurt so bad there was nothing for them to do but kill him." Them. She indicated the whole world. "If you hurt people enough, you got to kill them." It broke her heart open. He was Ben too. And Sid. And—the twisting pain forced the last name out of her mind—and Jesus. She did not know that she was seeing Harry as Olaf Ramsay had seen him in the dawn light at the cenotaph—as Everyman. She tried to turn away.

"Do you identify the deceased?"

"Yes. He is my father. Harry Munster."

"Thanks. The officer at the desk will tell you the arrangements."

They went down the corridor again. It had taken only two minutes. Their policeman spoke to the man at the desk, nodded, went away. There was something to sign. Ruth thought of it as a receipt for her father. Sid found out the arrangements.

They hoisted Ally into the taxi and drove her home, where she was received into a warm bath of neighbourly sympathy, tea, and tears.

Later Ruth standing white and tearless beside Sid, asked him suddenly, "Did you read the card?"

He knew what she meant—the card on Harry's coverlet. He nodded.

"What did it say?"

"It gave the cause of death."

She looked at him.

"Rupture of the lungs from shell blast. Skull splintered by flying debris."

"They made a good job of it while they were about it. Anything else?"

"Only where he was picked up." He named a street in Paddington that was new to her.

"Where's that?"

He told her. In the harsh unresolved pause he saw her eyes slew down the street.

"He wouldn't go that way to the shop, would he?"

"No. What is it, Ruth?"

"Nothing. It's all right. I better go in to mum."

"She don't know what's hit her yet."

Ruth smiled at him, a smile that had the thin sharp edge her voice had had when she said, "They made a good job of it."

"Look here, kid. . . ."

"Thanks, Sid."

She turned and walked up the steps into the house. Her brittle shoulders looked like iron. "Poor Harry," he thought, "poor bloody sap. What did they have to go and pick on him for?"

In the afternoon telephones were working again and Ruth was able to get Gwen Leslie's address. She found the place on Sid's road map. She found the other street, too, the one now blocked with debris. She understood.

"Can I take you anywhere?" Sid asked.

She shook her head. This was a new Ruth who took what she needed from him and no more, but took it as a sort of right. She was following some single track. His heart ached for her.

Ruth went to Gwen. She found her sick and shaken after the night of fear, crouching in her room. It was difficult to tell her. The words were square in Ruth's mouth. At first Gwen wouldn't or didn't understand, and burst into a tornado of weeping. Ruth, frozen at first, realised with something like relief that this was a grief that could be comforted. She took Gwen in her arms, cradled and soothed her till Gwen turned and clung to her as a clinging plant, thrown to earth by a storm, will begin to twine again about anything that comes within reach, knowing not its support, but only the need to cling and pull itself upward again. Ruth calmed her at last, found cups and saucers—there were two, one for him, one for her, she thought—made them both some tea. Then she got from Gwen the name of friends to whom she could go, helped her pack, found out that the conveyance she would need was running, and packed her off.

"Oh, Ruth, you're wonderful," said Gwen, beginning to cry again. "I had no idea you were so wonderful. I wish I'd never . . ."

Ruth shut her up. She just stood waiting for the tram, holding her case, her eyes slowly filling with tears.

The last broken sentence stuck like a splinter in Ruth's mind. One thing she hadn't told Gwen, that Harry had been coming to her when he was killed. She had two reasons. She didn't want to add remorse to Gwen's grief, nor want her to make a trophy of it.

When the neighbours had gone and she was alone, realization reached Ally through the voluminous folds of shock and consolation. The years had made her prematurely numb, but there was still a quick of feeling, like a bright cinder in ashes, hidden in her heart, and this had touched it. All day she had felt shock, malaise, and almost insupportable pressure, "the burden of grief." For all its outward seeming, it had been a day of self restraint. Her body ached in every cell with the effort, blind and unreckoned, to assume her widow's grief to the liking of her neighbours. She had wanted and with passion, not Harry's return, but the return of the easy life before his death, before the raid, before the war, when she could lie all day on an unmade bed reading, with a good conscience. A world, she thought now, without reproach and without pressure, making no demands. She'd got it, despite Harry, despite every one: it had been to her like his savings to a miser. Going to the pictures, placing sixpenny bets, eating titbits from crumpled paper bags, made up for her the last remnant of the glory of life for which her youth had sought, and, being despoiled of it, she had never found a new objective. The remnant was in a way her life's savings. It was being taken from her. The world wasn't safe any more. In the last twenty-four hours it had become rabidly unsafe. Even the landmarks were going. She was hardly herself any more, just a widow in a crumbling world. That was what she had mourned, unknowingly, yet recognizing a lack in herself.

Now a secret spring was touched and a long closed shutter flew up. For the first time she thought of Harry. Harry had gone. He'd been her husband. She remembered with trembling incredulity that she had loved him. She ought to love him again now that he was dead. A faint ghost stirred in her breast. Harry. She remembered his arms round her, his proud laughing face, his energy, his hands. He was happy, she thought still with wonder. He had something once. Where did it go? A new fountain of tears opened in her. She reproached herself bitterly because she had not had the courage to see him after he was dead. That seemed the last pathos of their miserable story.

Ally wept till she was exhausted. Swollen and nerveless, she was still in an inverted way triumphant, as if after many barren years her spirit had given birth. But she could not leave it at that, the tears oozed from her eyes. Pity for Harry became pity for herself. She'd had a raw deal always, and now this. She was young still, only in her forties, but what future was there for her? To self pity there succeeded in natural order an emptiness, a craving. Ally diagnosed it as hunger. She'd had next to nothing. Emptiness was a pain in her vitals. But could a widow of barely a day rise in the middle of the night and eat a meal? The very query like an obstacle in her mind made her angry. She remembered a stick of chocolate dropped hastily into a drawer and temporarily forgotten. The thought began to tickle in her mind, her mouth watered. She must retrieve the chocolate, it would steady her. She wanted it more than anything in the world. She put one foot out of bed. The house was a concentric whirl of darkness. Carefully, so that the bed would not creak, she slid off it and stood up. It did creak, a sudden sharp wail from the strained springs. Ally felt giddy from much emotion. She swayed across to the chest, her bare feet making a rubbery sound on the linoleum. She eased open the drawer and began to rummage feverishly.

Ruth, lying awake, had heard every sound. She came in now with a candle. Ally paused, her face a mask of suspicion. Was the girl spying on her? "What is it?" Ruth asked.

"I'm getting a handkerchief," said Ally crossly.

Ruth put the candle down where the light could not show in the blackout and sat on the end of the bed, resting against the foot in an attitude of profound exhaustion. Ally's hand closed on the chocolate, she wrapped it in a handkerchief and carried it back to the bed, thrusting it far under the pillow. Ruth watched her with unseeing eyes. It was intolerable, lying alone with her thoughts on this endless night, but she had recognised long ago, philosophically, that nothing was to be expected from her mother. They looked at one another now almost curiously. Ally remembered that this fair sagging girl was the child of their first year of love, hers and Harry's. That didn't mean a thing.

Ruth said unexpectedly, "I can remember the farm——" She said it with a broken wistfulness, as if she spoke of heaven.

"So can I," said Ally, in a hard wry voice.

Ruth saw herself very small, following her father and his lantern out to the incubators to see the new chickens, being lifted up, held in one arm on her father's hip while he worked.

The pain spread like a blot. Ally said at last, "You got to go to work in the morning, Ruth. You better get some sleep now. I feel that done. I'm going to try."

Ruth blew out the candle. She went back into her bed and lay there. She felt as if the flesh were dropping off her bones, and still misery, like a sword, like something hard, sharp, completely objective, turned and turned in her.

Ally scrambled under the pillow for her fragment of chocolate.

In England that year the winter continued far into the spring. It was as if the earth, so laden with death, were too discouraged to mime its resurrection. The war news was not bad. It was good, but there was much weariness, the raid on Sydney had filled only a paragraph or two in the press, and that was days ago. It was sunk in the great welter of war already. It had had little military significance. Only to Australians serving overseas, it had wrenched away the little security that they had sheltered in their hearts. It worked in them.

Archie Castles stood with the others beside an open grave, men in uniform, dark strokes on the pale lustreless day. The wind blew their long service overcoats about their legs. Only the coats moved, the men were standing as still as lead. They had smartened themselves up for this ceremony of death. In their uniforms they looked alike, man repeated against the cold neutral background of the winter day. They alone were animate against the sealed winter earth and the passionless wind. They had come to bury Everyman. They had carried the coffin draped with the pale blue airforce flag from the church to the grave. The padre had walked at the front in his billowing surplice, reading aloud the prayers for the dead according to the Anglican ritual, his voice strong, insistent, impersonal. The wind had carried the prayers like a banner, stripping them of meaning.

They were the Australians. They stood close together. They were burying one of their own. He had come down over the Channel, the sea had had him for a week and then he had been cast up, one more dark wrack of flotsam on the shingle. Now he was screwed down decently in his coffin, being given Christian burial, all loss, all sacrifice made good with honour, the debt paid in spurious funerary coin, decent amends for the irremediable.

For whom was the consolation, the living or the dead? Were they laying food and weapons, corn and wine and the body of his dog, on the dead boy's grave that he might have sustenance, company, honour, on his dark journey, the ghostly powers of this world giving him his passport through the ghostly powers of the next to his reward? They were too late, he had gone like a beggar to the sea. Everything decent and in order where nothing was decent and everything out of order. The young, the brave, the skilled, cancelled one another out, and the dead were recompensed with honour. He asked for life and they gave him a chrysophase. He was dead without begetting a child, killed in the effort to kill, dead in the glamour of a courage to which life had a right, not death. So they spoke over him the terrible, beautiful, smug words of a ritual no one believed. "I am the Resurrection and the Life." It was part of the great Mumbo Jumbo, the advertisements wherein a girl's smile enticed you to buy toothpaste, the recruiting poster, Caesar to his army on the eve of battle, poets who glorify war, politicians who cozen their constituents in all sincerity, the ironic detachment of the man who sees through it. Would any man believe in heaven when the skies had been his battlefield, or that God noted the fall of a sparrow when men were dying in thousands in the face of His omnipotence?

The frost-bound English earth was forced open to take the dead boy. The old tombstones of men who had died in bed leaned clannishly together. He was an alien here. He had been born to a continent, he had run his race in the skies, he had died in the sea, and now they shut him in this cell of frozen earth. When the spring came it would be just as alien. It would bring all the wrong flowers, the too soft winds, the sapless sun. Pushing up daisies. Christ, it made you sick. That was the last straw—to push up daisies in an old gray sleepy place like this, to take the boys and find nothing better for them to do than to push daisies in a country churchyard. God. God. God.

The men stood close together but each was divided from each. The cold wind froze the flesh of their faces until each felt his skin fitted upon him like a metal mask. Under the mask they were alive, but nothing passed between them. If it hadn't been for the bough of wattle, this would have been just one more. You take it as a parade and you don't think more than you have to, because you've got to go on, haven't you? And it's no good thinking, the contingency is provided for and you leave it at that. You even think, "Well, anyhow, we got him back," and you get a bit tougher. The wattle tore the whole thing wide open. It blazed in the grey lifeless day. You could smell it, the scent pulled at your knees. You remembered how it was at home, the golden patina winding through the bush, the avenue of trees blazing gold, heavy-laden with powdery flowers tarnishing to bronze. This came out of a hothouse and you called it mimosa. It was precious, costly, only for the privileged. In one man's mind a little string of words ran round and round like a clockwork mouse. He'd forgotten where he'd heard them, they didn't seem to mean anything, but there they were. "Riding into Lichtenberg, riding in the rain."

Some woman had done it. Like all regimented men they despised women. Individually they might want women and love a woman, but as a mob they feared women. You didn't talk of women in the mess. When men live for dangerous work they live monastically, sustaining the cohesion between themselves and their work. Women have no part, they must be held off. They must be taken lightly or romantically, stowed away in a ritual, or they burst things open and your spirit leaked away. A woman would be like a hole in the petrol tank. They didn't understand the conventions of a man's life, the conventions that held things together while his strength was filling the channels of the job. They sent wattle to a dead Australian airman. They did the unforgivable thing. They turned the screw too tight.

Pain forced its way through Archie's flesh. Like a bullet. All that he had suffered in mind, in body, in strained nerves, was present in him, and this moment transfixed them like a bayonet in the vital flesh. I am here and my knife is here. The two moments have met. He didn't know if the others felt like that too. He was alone in the iron day, the cell of air.

By a great effort he lifted his eyes and looked at the sky. No clouds, only a clear watery greyness, forever scoured by the invisible wind. One speck moved, so far and high you could not hear the engines or know whether it was "ours" or "theirs." One of the natural fauna of the skies, like a mosquito larva in a tank. Archie didn't look at it as a pilot looks, but as a child looks. He was slipping, wasn't he?

He remembered the night flight when for the first time he felt death beside him at the controls, the time at the pictures when he didn't want the girl he could have had because his heart was sick, and he had felt disappointment and resentment; the day in the mess when the papers had run the banner headline "Australia Invaded," and Blue had said, "We got to go home and go quick. Any way we can." Now they ran together into one breach. They and other unnoticed moments. Moments he had lived down, put away, but that never really died or left him.

The goddam bloody wattle, he wanted to stamp it into the earth, the cold, wet, foreign earth. It had no right to change him, no right to strip him naked. It drew a sword across his heart. No sentiment, only a sharp pain, a pain incredibly naked and real. In the last conscious second of the fatal spin, in the moment when the flames covered him or the hot bullet got him, or when his nerve broke like an over-strained rope, parting strand by strand, the pilot's brain clicked, "This is it." Always that flash of recognition, the knowledge that the thing long awaited had come. The spirit can be shorn away by a thought sharper than a bayonet. The one sure thing was that the moment would come, death within death, the moment before the crash. It wasn't the crash you thought of, but the split second when you saw it leap at you, the echo before the event. It came, it always came, one way or another. Either you stuck it and went out on mission after mission till you were killed. Or you didn't stick it and the mainspring broke. Whichever way it was, your fate stood beside you like a visible presence. The Bridegroom. The Master of the House.

In the still core of his passion Archie thought, "This is it."

He recognised it but he could not name it. It wasn't a sentiment. It wasn't homesickness—though that is not just a pale malady, but can be a cause of death, a fatal haemorrhage of the spirit. It wasn't "home," a cosy little word like that nor the bleached shack perched on its barren land where he was born; nor the stony life out of which he had dragged himself for this; nor the sum of the happiness he had ever hoped for; nor the inarticulate legend of his people. No soft memories that a man might cradle in his hands, no souvenir of happiness or ease. No halcyon. It is not for these things that men will to live nor for them that they break the illusions binding them to death. Men will die for their ease and live for their bitter pain.

A branch of wattle is nothing in itself—"The hired bugler." And the cause can be consumed by the effect, as the match that lights the fire perishes in it. It is true only that a man's life may swing many times to its crisis and away again and that at last some trifle will decide the scale. No act, however tangential, is a sport but has roots as true and deep as any conformity. This man, Archie Castles, held year after year in the vice of a discipline, member of a small close group in a ravelling world, specialised to a purpose, his life and thought in every detail guarded to that end of highly skilled killing, given a legend, given a decor, given a code, the blue prints of a morale, had slowly disentangled himself. Imagination had begun to work like a yeast in him long ago, realisation of his own part in the world's phantasmagoria had been pressing up through all the superimposed layers of routines, technicalities, and fatigues, and he had moved from acceptance to question, from question to a new tangential certainty. By learning his job, by surviving, by going on, he had reached the top of his grade. He was an ace, with ribbons on the breast of his tunic. And his life had reached saturation point. There had been another young man in another war, nurtured in the grand tradition, the bravest of the brave, whose name Archie had not even heard, who had taken this path before him. Siegfried Sassoon. He had turned, braver still in the height of the struggle, and had tried with his bare hands to stop history. Such men are sparks turned off the great wheel in its velocity and sent out into the unending space.

It was part of the fantasy of the times that so bizarre a thing as a branch of golden wattle in full bloom in an English churchyard on a winter's day, should mark the culmination of a long process of rebellion or liberation in Archie. Since his will to end his way of life must take on some form, he gave to it, too, the bizarre and arbitrary decision, "I will go home." Neither the cold northern sea nor the cold northern earth should have his body. But that was only a rationalisation. The springs of action in him were deeper than the will to live. It was the immature working out of a man's maturity in a distorted world.

The world to which Archie was returning "from the grave" was in the trough. After years of war the people were in a black and bitter temper, or rather, its passive equivalent, a sullen and suspicious lethargy. They had been forced through too many emotions, natural and induced, now they suspected everyone, their leaders and their allies most of all. They thought less of the enemy and more of the war. It was the medium in which they lived and on which they lived. The economic security of every man and woman had come to depend directly or indirectly on the war. It was their means of livelihood, it was their norm, for all they were so utterly weary of it. A world not at war was already inconceivable to most people. The war mixed with everything. It was in their food, in their pay envelopes, in their pockets, in their sleep. Neither pleasure nor drink nor love could keep it out. It worked under the horny armour of indifference. It demanded progressively more. Strain and overwork took secret as well as open toll. Scarcity begot scarcity and as regulations multiplied, supplies dwindled, and ordinary daily life became a fantastic obstacle race or a living game of snakes and ladders. Permits, priorities, coupons, quotas, queues, and when you got to the counter at last with all your papers stamped and ready, the commodity was sold out. Even black markets were dying of attrition and in their extremity became fantastic. For the time being there was no emotion in the people but resentment. Gambling was much increased and exaggerated, but it was savourless since nothing had value. Crimes of violence were frequent but meaningless, merely explosions of rage against society, the number of delinquent children was alarming because they had caught the contagion. Every sexual restraint was relaxed. What did it matter, here today and gone tomorrow? Morale was low, and yet the people were not at breaking point. They were too lifeless to break. They could not conceive of anything else but going on. The war had become a habit.

King's Cross, the pulse of the city, beat erratically. The streets were fuller than ever because people were too restless to stay in their homes, and because shopping, even for necessities, was a slow tedious business, hunting commodities from shop to shop. The crowds on the footpaths were coagulated by queues. There were many empty shops with boarded windows, all were thinly stocked and had a harassed air. The people, too, who thronged the streets had a different look, anxious, sullen, apathetic. It was as if behind their ordinary faces another face, furtive, pinched, looked out, and however the originals differed, there was a strong resemblance between all the peering faces. Only here and there was there still a complacent face, some one who had worked himself into a little pocket of security and whose imagination, as if it were a gland, had ceased to work.

The city was, as ever, tidal. In the mornings the crowd flowed to the workshops, factories, and offices. In the evenings they flowed to the modern catacombs in which they dwelt. Four times a day the picture shows sucked in large crowds. Here the old values were evergreen, and what had once passed for realism was now a heroic dream, a fairy story into which tired minds escaped. At the hours when news was broadcast, a pause like the shadow of a cloud ran over the community. In homes people clustered round the radio. In public houses where the loud speakers blared like strong lights, men paused with their pots raised. In the streets they suddenly clotted to listen, like flies on a greasy spot. They listened from habit, they listened out of a vague faith in miracles, they listened because they had no alternative. Regularly, eight times a day, news bulletins were poured over the city. News and propaganda were one and the same thing. The newspapers were in the conspiracy too. There was no way round. The smooth voices of the announcers, the smooth exhortations of the editors, the slick rationalizations of the foreign correspondents, were all the walls that the world had. But nothing could stop the secret dark leakage of rumour. The bright facile sphere of words was itself being carried away on a tide of which as yet few were aware.

It was anybody's world. A few determined men who knew where they were going, whose minds were integrated and adamant, could possess it. It did not matter what their doctrine was, it was the force to create it that mattered. A saint or a dictator could have snatched it, it was ripe to the strong and ready hand. Australia was cut off from the world more completely than she had been for a century or more. To the north was the great semicircle of enemy-held islands. Europe was silent, communication with England and America was almost entirely in official hands. No travellers came, no letters passed except through the needle eye of officialdom, she was insulated from whatever ferments there were in the outside world. But there was, still latent but continually growing, a rebellion as individual as the upsurge of the 'nineties, against the very premises of society. There were men with two-edged strength, belief and disbelief, belief that had passed over into their blood, passion that had saturated their minds. They saw clearly, not necessarily the truth, but something. They had accepted as axioms that men could not change until their circumstances had changed, that wars could continue to grow while their roots in the social system were left, that exploitation would continue while the means for it existed. They were neither idealists nor romantics. Some at least of them knew that it was never the men who pushed back the night who brought the dawn.

They were only a handful and they did not seek to be many, not yet at least. They didn't want the enthusiast, the doctrine taster, the easily led. The overladen times were working with them, going rotten. The time would come when a few men, steeled for their purpose, would upset them. After that they'd be on the winning side and could take their numbers with the check of weight on their loyalty. It was still too difficult to be loyal for the leaders to trust many.

Sid Warren was one of the few. He'd learned something long ago in Spain, and the years had hardened his mind and his courage. He was one of those who took what offered but was not beholden to it or influenced by it. His mind and will followed a secret undeviating course and left no trail. He had an instinct for men, the few who would serve, he picked them up here and there, sometimes in unlikely places and they in turn became the nuclei of small tight hard groups, working in the great amorphous mass of public opinion, cutting a trend. They weren't in a hurry. Their time would come and they would recognize it. They reversed the demagoguery and ballyhoo of their age. An idea can stand so still in the mind that it is invisible and yet colour every thought, so they, working with their subterranean steadiness, without press or machinery, escaped the clumsy tangle of repressive legislation, the censorship, the heresy hunts.

It was to this world, flaccid, discontented, yet veined with an unrecognised strength and purpose, that Archie returned.

.    .    .    .    .    .    .    .    .

Knarf broke off and lifting his eyes smiled at Ord, that quick, gay, self-comprehending smile, from which the mask of his middle age seemed to slip away. "The story of that journey is a tour de force. I have written it with great élan. It is almost a book in itself. I won't read it to you. It depresses me. A tour de force is always wrong. A state within a state. A patch of self-consciousness. It never works and yet you're always taken in. You sit at your own feet. . . . Really the book needed it, it's an astringent drawing it together, tightening its large loose structure into one single taut strand. I'll skip it all. How, by a ruse, he took off from an English aerodrome one misty morning in a long-distance bomber loaded with petrol, how he made his first landing at Gibraltar and bluffed his way through . . . the world had reached such a state of fantasy then, as it always does under pressure, that anything was possible, and those young airmen were demigods, they could do no wrong, the garlanded sacrifices, the one chosen to die, honoured and fêted. . . . I've written that first part in the style of the adventure romance of the day, objective, superficial, full of shifts and devices and moments of suspense, with a trace of satire on the mania for secrecy, pompous, labyrinthine, incestuous, in which the Services were then invested, and by which Archie was profiting . . . how he made his second landing at the base of an Australian squadron in North Africa to find that the news of his desertion had outstripped him and that there was an order for his arrest; how the squadron sped him on his way with cynical glee, the first pulse of that disruptive rage against authority that was beginning to move even in the strong points of authority . . . how he began his desert flight knowing there was no retreat, that he had left his last foothold in the old world and was incalculably far from home, that shifts and devices out of comedy romance would not help him any more, that he had come clean through the world of fantasy into reality—here the whole tempo of the narrative changes, adagio after scherzo; it becomes subjective, with a wide lucidity like the sky, a moment of pure living, half triumph, half realisation—how he slept one night utterly exhausted beside his plane with the desert for a cradle and half the starry sky for a canopy; how his mind raced between exaltation and exhaustion; how he fought with primitive nature, and, in the world's most modern machine, went back a thousand years to the most primitive struggle for existence, with petrol not bread as the staff of life; how he ceased to be himself and became journeying man; how he lost all sense of why he made this flight and kept only the endurance to make it; how the war grew infinitely small and inconsequent; how, as the end of his journey approached, he felt the drag once more of gravity (he was a man who had been, as it were, driven by a meteoric accident off the periphery of one world to be sucked at last into another) . . . here the narrative leaves him and picks up the echo in Australia, the despatch that a newspaper correspondent as a move in his eternal battle with the censors pirated through, the banner headlines, "Castles in the Air," the stir that ran through the jaded imagination of the populace, the elevation of the outlaw, opinion suddenly embattled on an unimportant issue, the perfect stunt, the synthetic excitement with its element of rebellion and escape, the unsuspected audience hourly growing, awaiting his arrival, the rumours, the whipping up of emotion, the corroboree . . .; how he left the sky and, half delirious with exhaustion and endurance, landed on the airfield at Mascot; how the ravening people fell on him, mobbed him, photographed him, pressed on him there and then incongruous gifts, demanded his autograph, and almost killed him; how he went willy nilly through a barrage of receptions, command performances, acts and motions, a phantasmagoria of kleig lights, voices talking nonsense, hands taking and giving without reason, that the appetite of a democratic people for vicarious achievement might be satisfied; how he became again hero and sacrifice in a context, different but no less fantastic; how all he had done and endured and thought was filched from him until it had no meaning; how one day a train, whistling as it went to tell the world that it carried the hero of the hour, took him to Toongabbie, and a press car transported him over the rough road and across the brown and barren paddock to meet once more, in a little perched house, his embarrassed but flattered family. . . . Epic into stunt. All the way from the grave to the cradle.

"You see?" said Knarf, suddenly rounding on Ord.

"What about the story?" Ord asked. "It seems to have bogged down in world history. Did it ever get out again?"

"The story goes on, but as the book rises to its crisis it shifts into the major theme of the whole community. It is people in a context and the context grows more and more important. They are only little fishes in a maelstrom."

"I'm fond of fish," said Ord , obstinately, determined to get Knarf off his high horse. "What happened to that poor fish, Ally?"

. . . . . . . . .

Ally wasn't so much a fish as a limpet. She clung till there was nothing to cling to. She felt Harry's death very much, not in any sharp thrust of grief, but in a dullness, loneliness, emptiness, that she resented. It was like the end of expectation. The circumstances of her widowhood cast a little pale glory on her, but it didn't last long. The street found a new interest. Tony Nelson was decorated for gallantry. Everyone had known Tony and everyone shared in the honour and glory. Almost, you might say, the gutters ran for a week with rich unction of their melancholy pride. Of course, the war had been going on a long time and decorations were as common as blackberries, but blackberries didn't grow in Carnation Street. This had happened to Them. The news came so long after Tony's death that there seemed little connection. When Mrs Nelson had "got her telegram," as they put it, the event hadn't made much stir. There were a lot of telegrams about just then, there had been a push in the north, and death wasn't quite real to the street without a body. Mrs Nelson herself was "wonderful" and "bore up." She hadn't had an allotment and Tony was never one for writing letters, so his death didn't make much visible difference. She'd feel it later when the boys came home on leave. She didn't have to feel it just yet, she was only numb. No one really felt it as much as Ben and he wasn't saying anything. One of the boys had told him just as he was putting the lorry to bed one night. He'd stayed fiddling with the engine till the others had gone, and then he'd climbed back into the cab and sat there in the half light, among the silent megatherium shapes, in the smell of grease and petrol, while his mind grew heavier and heavier with thoughts. He knew how alive Tony had been. He had wanted to go with him. At last he put his head down on the steering wheel and cried, as he hadn't cried since he was a child, since the time his father had eaten his dinner and Ally had gone crook about it and he had run away and his heart had burst right open, as he would not cry again ever again in his life, for that was the unmarked end of his youth. Afterwards he'd been ashamed, and if the others talked of Tony Ben walked away. Tony was just another soldier who had stopped one.

The medal was different. It stood up out of the ruck and called for endless comment. It was a miracle—as if the hire purchase people had let you off an instalment.

"The King himself," marvelled Mrs Blan, "who'd have thought His Majesty would ever hear of anyone from this street?" The bandsman had left his mark on Mrs Blan. "If it was going to be someone I'm glad it was your Tony," she added magnanimously. She had, without any effort, grasped the principle that all decorations were fortuitous.

"You're lucky in Tony," said Mrs Cassidy, and she said it not bitterly but flatteringly. Her own boy was in the V.D. camp, poor sod.

"My nephew, that's my brother Herb's boy, was recommended," said Mrs Buchan from the shop, "but it never come to nothing. You wouldn't believe the jealousy and nastiness there is among the high up ones. And they don't like giving nothing to the poor lads that are still alive, that's what it amounts to."

Mrs Blan introduced a more hopeful note. "There's sure to be something with it, Mrs Nelson. Of course They wouldn't say so on the paper, They're always so reserved about money, but there's sure to be a pension, or if it isn't a pension it'll be a present, something substantial, I say. And not too much either after all poor Tony did for his country. His Majesty would never give you an Empty Honour."

Mrs Nelson had to go to Government House for the investiture. She was so nervous that for two days before she couldn't keep anything on her stomach, and at the actual moment was too flurried to notice anything. In retrospect all was made good. The memory of the great day became pure gold.

Tony's medal proved an Empty Honour, but on the whole Mrs Nelson preferred it that way. "I wasn't looking for anything," she said. After all she had given Tony and didn't expect the king or anyone else to pay for him. She was hurt that Ben Munster, who used to think so much of Tony, didn't even come to see the medal.

.        .        .        .        .        .        .        .        .

"You were telling me what happened to the Munsters," Ord reminded Knarf patiently.

"Yes, yes, very well."

.        .        .        .        .        .        .        .        .

The family went on living in the old rooms, not because any of them wanted to, they would gladly have separated now, but because in the housing shortage it would have been impossible to find anywhere else to live. Ben and the girls were earning good money and they all threw in to keep the place going. Ally whined and went her slatternly way. They took no notice of either her whining or her slatternliness, they were both "just mum's way." Only Ben now and then had twinges of conscience and made a half-hearted and vain attempt to do something for his mother.

It was not until Harry had been dead several months that Ally found his savings bank passbook, with the credit of £200, under the newspaper lining of the drawer where he kept his underclothes, the only place he had been able to find to hide it. She had stared at it for five minutes before the enormity of her discovery dawned on her. She couldn't bear it alone. She had to go down to Mrs Blan. Mrs Blan too was thunderstruck.

"Well, I never," she said, "You could knock me down, you could, that's £200. . . ."

"Where ever do you suppose he got it?" asked Ally. "Why we never had £200, not all at once, all the time we were married. I can't imagine."

"Perhaps he won a lottery and never told you."

"Wouldn't that be in the papers?"

"Not all the little prizes wouldn't be. Maybe he won several little prizes."

"No, it was all put in together and never touched."

"Maybe he was lucky at the dogs."

"He didn't go to the dogs."

"That's all you know. There was something he didn't tell you, wasn't there?"

"All those years I slaved for him and he had £200, and never told me."

"That's men all over."

"Look at all the time it was lying there. He wasn't even spending it."

"That's funny, ain't it?"

"I just don't know what to think."

"I always say, you can't trust a quiet man, you never know what they are up to. My old man, now, he couldn't deceive a child unborn. I knew everything about him and there wasn't much to know either."

Ally wished acutely that she had not told Mrs Blan. All the excitement of finding the money was poisoned by the mystery of its origin. It was worse than if she'd found that he was keeping another woman. Perhaps he had, if he had so much money to spare. It was only because they couldn't afford anything else that men ever kept straight. The £200 might be only a part of what he had had. He might have been doing all sorts of things and she didn't know. There she was at home, scrimping and saving, and he just rolling in money. He'd made a proper fool of her. Had he stolen it? Even she couldn't quite believe that. Perhaps he'd been saving it for something. Yes, he's been saving it because he meant to go away and leave her. Well, she'd seen him dead first. That night she couldn't sleep, her mind was on fire with painful conjecture, her suspicions made a bed of thorns. She and Harry weren't done with one another yet. "He did it to spite me," she thought, "to keep me out of what I had a right to share in, any way. All the things I could a done with £200; made the place nice and had some decent clothes so that the children could be proud of me, and I could have gone about and lived a normal life." The sticky tears of self pity began to flow. She had the money now. If only she hadn't told Mrs Blan. If only no one knew it wouldn't matter so much. She went down first thing in the morning to Mrs Blan.

"You won't tell anyone, will you?" she pleaded.

"Have I ever betrayed a confidence?" asked Mrs Blan, drawing herself up.

Ally lacked the courage to say, "Yes, many times," and Mrs Blan thawed again, for she was really interested. She wanted to know what Ally was going to do with the money. Ally hadn't got as far as that. "I haven't got it yet," she said, voicing a dark suspicion that during the sleepless night had been adding to her troubles. "How do I go about getting it, Mrs Blan?"

"Now you're asking me." She put on her spectacles and looked judicially at the passbook. "Did Harry make a will?"

"No, not that anyone ever found. We didn't really look. You see. . . ."

"Ah," said Mrs Blan, not without triumph. "You'll have to be careful or the government will take it before you know where you are. That's what they do when a man dies intestate, and as likely as not they'll fine you for concealing it. You'll have to be very careful."

"But. . . ."

"And there's the children. They'll be wanting a share, won't they? That is, if there is anything to share when all is said and done."

Backwards and forwards they went over the whole thorny business, abstractedly drinking cups of tea, coupons or no coupons. Mrs Blan threw herself wholeheartedly into the problem. To every suggestion that Ally made she replied, "Do it if you want to, Ally, it's your money, but if you're not careful you'll lose it that way."

To the ferment in Ally's blood was added a new poison, distrust of her children. They neglected her now, soon they'd rob her. The law, she found out, would give them two-thirds, and her one-third. If that wasn't robbery. She'd have to get it without letting them know and without letting the government know. She would have forged Harry's signature if she hadn't been too frightened. "It *is* my money and only Harry could take me to law, and he's dead, so what would be the harm?" But she had the sense to know there probably would be, if not harm, trouble. She must find another way. She could think of nothing else, she became ill with worrying, but worst of all was the fear that the children, especially Wanda, would get to know. Wanda was as sharp as a needle where self interest was concerned.

"Don't breathe a word to Wanda," Ally begged Mrs Blan again and again.

"As if I would," said Mrs Blan. She was wholeheartedly on Ally's side. Not that she had anything against Ruth, Wanda, and Ben. If they had come to her with a complaint against their mother, she would, as likely as not, have sided with them. It was the way she was built.

Ally as usual could see nothing but herself, but there were changes going on about her. The microcosm of the street was slowly foundering in the macrocosm of the sick world. Big wages were being earned in the street now, there was no unemployment, but not in the worst days of the depression had things gone so badly. Everyone was on edge with war strain, and with the short supplies, the black markets, the privileges, wangled and boasted, the bitter competition, suspicion was universal and quarrelling constant. Men and women earning good money after years of leanness and denial wanted to enjoy it, and could think of no terms of enjoyment except buying things, and everywhere in this they were thwarted. The little shop on the corner became a veritable cauldron of bitterness. Every customer suspected Mrs Buchan of favouring some one else, disbelieving her when she said she could not get supplies, accused their neighbours of being forestallers, and poisoned the air with complaints. She, poor woman, complained ceaselessly also, whether her customers would listen or no, for she found it very hard that just when she could do a good trade she hadn't the goods to sell, and that while others were making a good thing out of the war, she found it more than ever difficult to make a living.

The young, under the threat of war, wanted a good time while there was any good time left, and their greed in nine cases out of ten defeated itself, and even in their good times they couldn't trust one another. There was in pleasure and in love the same cut-throat competition that there was in getting and spending, and here time itself took a hand and must be cheated before he could cheat them.

The times did not bear so hardly on Ruth and Ben, Ruth because she was anchored on Sid. She knew Sid wasn't going to marry her, but they had an understanding, and she would rather have that with Sid than a marriage with someone else. Other bonds grew up between them. Ruth no longer rebelled against Sid's ideas, or, giving them lip service, thought of them as a sickness that would pass. Now things that he had said to her in the past began to bear fruit. In the light of private disaster, she had seen, as behind a thin curtain suddenly illuminated, the wasteful vicious world, the tragic absurdity, the price of competition being exacted now in life as it had been in happiness. First, she had seen in the depression the sacrifice of Everyman's happiness to the system, and then in the war a further demand on Everyman's life. Having seen it and felt it, she was welded to such a picture of its redress as Sid could give her. They were bound together in their interests. She loved him and he found her more to his taste and less disruptive of his life than he had ever expected a woman to be. Curiously, she was more sure of Sid now that she accepted the limitations of their union and recognised, with hard pride that hurt her still, the honesty of his attitude to her. She grew thin and strained, working by day in a munitions factory, doing yeoman service in the Movement till far into the night, and being at Sid's call whenever he needed her. Often her wages kept them both, but neither of them thought anything of that. . . .

Ben too had his work, which absorbed most of his energy and imposed its discipline. He was a transport driver, and so in a reserved occupation, not to be enlisted. Most of the time was spent on the roads, bringing in food to the city. He must do the major part of his own loading and unloading, and, because the garages were so shorthanded, service his own vehicle. He was strong, he could stand the work and the long hours, and he liked its rhythm, its coherence, and the responsibility. His self respect had grown strong on it and so he lived, for a young man of his time, a hermit's existence, not much contaminated by the city's fever. He was one of those Sid had marked down to be one of his lieutenants. Sid often gave him something to think about, and yes, he guessed Sid was right, only just now he hadn't much time, he was worried about the carburettor. Cripes, yes, Sid could count on him.

Wanda hadn't any anchor.

.    .    .    .    .    .    .    .

"You were always hard on Wanda," Ord interrupted. "Why?"

"As God said to Olaf Ramsay, 'There's only the law of cause and effect.'

"Those were hard times to live in, a phase of civilisation was dying, and those who could not or would not create the new world must take the print of their times. Wanda was a girl, like thousands of others, in a city full of soldiers. She had the cheek and independence of a sparrow and about as much chance of taking care of herself. Gwen was another girl in a city full of soldiers, less able to take care of herself. Nature makes them in hundreds, you might say, trial patterns, and is just as ready to scrap them. After Harry's death, Gwen just drifted. She couldn't bear to be alone, and there was no one permanent in her life. That's how it happened. Cliff was eighteen months in New Guinea, neither could convey much to the other in their letters, their feeling for one another was not a matter of words, and so it starved and fell away. Gwen couldn't remember what he looked like, and for Cliff, Gwen had just sunk back into mass of Girl. When he came back on leave he meant to look Gwen up, of course he did, but not right away. They hadn't been lovers before he went away, it had all been very high and romantic, but that wasn't what he wanted now, not straight off, not before he'd had a good time. The thought of being tied up with a girl who perhaps wouldn't give him a good time herself and crooled his pitch with other girls chafed him. Gwen had just become for him an uncomfortable feeling. He knew he'd changed a good deal, it never occurred to him that she might have changed too. Gwen had changed a lot from the shy sensitive child Harry had known, but somehow or other it wasn't in the direction of maturing. She stayed immature and coarsened, pitifully, helplessly, as the only protection she could find for herself. Now that her first youth had gone, she tried to make up the leeway with lipstick and mascara till her soft prettiness was overlaid; her manner too had become overlaid by false shrillness. They were her maladroit efforts to play a part in the shining world she longed for. It was like that that Cliff saw her when they met face to face in a penny bazaar. Cliff's new girl was hanging on his arm, and Gwen was hanging on the arm of her current boy. They must have suffered some shock in seeing one another, for Gwen burst into hysterical reproaches, and Cliff, who was half drunk, shook off his girl and offered to lay Gwen's escort cold. The proprietor wasn't going to have any of that and drove them off his premises. Cliff's girl got him away, and that was the last he and Gwen saw of each other. That night Gwen let herself get drunk for the first time. She found that after all it made things much easier."

.  .  .  .  .  .  .  .  .

"What about the other two, Paula and Bowie?" Ord asked, hoping perhaps for something more cheerful.

.  .  .  .  .  .  .  .  .

Bowie spent the better part of two years in gaol for conscientious objection to military service. He was called up in his age group for the army and refused to take the oath. After a long and rather unnerving pause he was summonsed and tried before a magistrate. He conducted his own case and made a good, reasoned, but not impassioned plea. He had no thought of saving himself but only of using, according to plan, this public opportunity of airing his views. He was reported, but only in his own party rag; there, the saved read his words with some edification. He was not proud of his effort for his words tasted wooden in his mouth. He laboured under the disability of having come from an extremely respectable family. No fanaticism could make him feel at home in the dock, nor would his emotions agree with his intelligence that this was only another rostrum and that what guilt there was lay with his judges. The mundane atmosphere of the court, where everything was stale, worn, ugly and mean, and where crime of every sort was commonplace, sapped his strength. His arguments had as much effect as straws against armour. They weren't in the same category of event. He wasn't being judged on a point of reason—that was decided—it was his sincerity that was at the bar. Of that he might well have convinced the magistrate had he been convincible. Then he would have been sent not to prison but to work in a forestry camp. But he didn't. Bowie got three months.

He left the dock feeling defeated, not so much by the sentence, though, despite himself, the scathing comments of the magistrate were a shock to him, as by his failure to strike an effective blow before he descended into impotence. When he tried to explain this sense of belittling and frustration to the Professor later, when he met him in one of the brief interludes between sentences, the Professor smiled dryly. "What did you expect it to be like?" he asked, "Clive of India indicted before the Lords?"

Gaol shocked him too. It wasn't an idea any more, it was a fact. The knowledge that he was shut up pressed intolerably upon his mind. He thought: "I'd be less free if I were in the army, my mind is as free as ever it was," but he was not deceived. Freedom was so shrunk in the world that men called having a bare chance freedom: while they had that they were, through growing habit, satisfied that they were free. In prison there wasn't for the time being any chance. Life was stilled. The cooler, they called it. Subtly it took the fight out of a man by insulating his existence.

Bowie tried to fix his mind on Paula as a star, a talisman, but there was no certainty there. He was troubled, as men in prison are, by the importunity of his sex. In the world, even if a man had no lover, as Bowie had none, his nature is fed by a hundred stimuli that are also minor satisfactions. He feeds on the laden air, on scent and sound and sight of woman, on contacts, steady and fleeting, that have no overt sex significance. Now he was deprived of this and took from his own needs a battering that hurt, and, again because of his ingrained respectability, humiliated him. To these episodes, out of some dim impulse of self protection, knowing that she had nothing for him and never would have, and that to feed his needs upon her image would only trap him more cruelly, he never linked his thoughts of Paula. So Paula remained a bloodless figment.

It wounded him that gaol was so undramatic. He looked at his fellow criminals and with a few exceptions they did not seem very wicked, just creatures who should never have been born. He felt that they and even the warders had contempt for him because he wasn't properly speaking a criminal at all, but only a conchie.

He thought of John Bunyan but decided that Bedford Gaol must have been different. In this dry living there was no becoming. Out of his leisure he could not fashion anything.

When Bowie was released that first time, his friends gave him a welcome back party. There was a lot of muscular christianity about it, awkward jokes, clumsy kindness, embarrassment, curiosity. "What was gaol really like?" They tried to treat him like a hero—they wanted a hero, why couldn't he be heroic and play up to them?—or they tried to laugh it off. He thought he'd lost touch. *They* hadn't been to gaol, they could only think of it in terms of what it wasn't.

Of course he hadn't a job and he hadn't much money. When he set about getting one, he ran foul of Manpower. Manpower wouldn't give him a job unless he had his clearance from the Army authorities, no one could employ him without the consent of Manpower. It was quite automatic. For a second time he refused to take the oath, and after a pause of what looked like forgetfulness, he was tried and recommitted. This time he got six months. While waiting for his trial he found himself in a fix. He soon had no money and no place to go. He went to Paula. She received him pitifully. She always indulged herself in a matter of pity. He was now her private martyr. She made up in pity what she lacked in passion. It wasn't the same thing. Passion doesn't make for righteousness and pity does. She gave him a shakedown in her flat and treated him as if he had been ill. She was solicitous and unattainable. Bowie was deeply humiliated and lacked the ruthlessness to deal with her.

He went back to prison and all the time he was there he worried about what he should do when he came out, and each time he came out the world seemed to have matured to a frightening degree. For him the social procession moved in violent jolts. His mild precepts no longer held, his arguments were chaff. But it didn't really occur to him to give in. He realised that what he did was ineffective, but his whole nature cried out that to give way would be even worse. The line he held now was within himself. He called it the first line of resistance, it was really the last.

The second time he came out of prison he avoided his friends. It was quite easy for they all seemed to be dispersed now. He met by accident in the street a man who had once belonged to the group. The man began to explain, at once hurriedly and distressfully, why he was in uniform. The brief encounter left Bowie exhausted. Tears pricked oddly behind his eyes as he walked up a street that no longer looked familiar. It was William Street, lined now with empty shops. He was hungry at the time, and that might have had something to do with it. That he was about again leaked out. Paula sought him out, took him back to her flat. He was amazed to find that things were much as usual there. There was butter on the table, sugar, fruit, meat, even tobacco, and occasionally some wine. She did not say how she got these things. She tried in her own immaterial way to seduce him with them, but it seemed to him that he could no longer taste. Something had happened to his tongue and palate. He didn't even want the luxuries with which she so happily and tenderly plied him. She was disappointed. He didn't realise that "pity is the voluptuous mother of love." He imagined that he was at a disadvantage and did not take his opportunity; Paula felt a dull shock of disappointment and frustration.

It was in Paula's flat, the night before he stood his third trial, that Bowie met Archie Castles, then at the height of his fame. He saw, what others were unwilling to see, that Archie was a man with the life half eaten out of him, a man like himself, at the crossroads, a man who had taken heroic means to reassure himself and was still unassured. The old fire leaped up in Bowie in a last spurt for this stranger. They talked far into the night of a world that might be different, and the reorientation of values that would follow the acceptance of peace as a dynamic principle. Paula brought them relays of coffee. They scarcely noticed, though it was very clever of her to have the coffee at all these days, very generous to expend it on them. After a bare two hours of sleep Bowie got dressed for his trial. He felt neither hope nor apprehension. He knew what he would say and what would happen. The fire was out.

It was the same as before. Bowie went back to prison for six months. After that when he came out he successfully avoided his friends. Paula did not seek him out. The fourth time he found himself completely trapped. Not only could he get no work at all without a military clearance, he could get no ration coupons either, and without them he could not eat. If there had been the strength of leadership in him, he would then have found plenty to follow him. There was discontent and despair and restlessness enough. But he hadn't the strength or the élan, he could only bend his head and blindly, obstinately, pursue the difficult path of his own personal salvation. His mind and his whole life had crystallised round a negative.

This time the authorities did not bother to try him, nor was he offered free board and lodging in gaol. He was dumped in a labour battalion with a great many other derelicts, gaolbirds, mental defectives—all those who were misfits, who weren't useful for anything better, who had lost the race. They were the labour reserve. Gangs were sent wherever they were needed, to load and unload ships, repair roads, harvest crops, scavenge the streets. They didn't work well, but they worked and were kept at it. They lived in camps and were mass fed. They never stayed anywhere long and the gangs were continually broken up so that you never knew who your mate would be. They were rootless men in whom the very individuality was effaced. The few old stones that were left in Sydney must have thought that convict days had come again. They didn't go manacled, it wasn't necessary, the whole community was chained and barred. They were not dangerous men. Bowie was one of them. The juggernaut of the people's faith had run him down. He did not know that he had handed on the torch, the days trampled him, he had energy for nothing, over and above his extorted toil, but for keeping alive. He was lost in the mass.

Paula, in proportion as she gave less, was less vulnerable. She still kept her belief in a private life and individual salvation. She was sure, at the bottom of her heart, that her little world would survive, like a glass marble in an avalanche. Her mind could be convinced, her emotions swayed, to a cause, but tucked away behind them, concealed from herself even, was the naive assurance that whatever she and her friends might do to change the world, there were forces, cleverer still, that would keep her income flowing towards her and her consequent independence intact. She could talk eloquently and passionately about the war, but still it wasn't her war, her grief, her responsibility. She kept her sleekness, her sweetness, her bloom of gentle gaiety, that enchanted all her new friends. She continued to look for her private paradise, and, behind the sweetness, to stand aloof. With the tightening situation she had accepted her obligation to work and joined the

V.A.D.'s. The blue uniform suited her, and, as she washed up in a hospital kitchen in half cold water, she thought This is Reality. She did not wash up for long, the commandant discovered that she had other talents. The commandant was also a friend of Mrs Ramsay. Paula became "attached" to the commandant, as an aide or social secretary or something indefinite. She was a show piece. She used to say to her friends, with that shining look they knew so well, "It isn't the work, it's the camaraderie. I'm not helping the war, but its victims." Living was easier; she had a servicewoman's privileges added to those she had been able to acquire and keep for herself, and once you were "inside" there was a lessening of responsibility, an illusion that everything was under control. She saw how it was that people just couldn't imagine that there had to be a change, and she smiled.

It was at a big rally of the women's services that she had met Archie Castles. It was when he was at the height of his popularity, bound helpless on the wheel of fame. He was the guest of honour. The V.A.'s were being given their helping of the burnt offering. Paula had been contemptuous of the whole business, a typical newspaper stunt, she thought, or possibly arranged higher up to boost morale or the current war loan. When she saw Archie, he was not what she had expected, much older, worn by pain and endurance and an insatiable weariness. Her heart was moved by compassion and she thought, "He's real and he's caught in this ghastly trap. He tried to free himself, or to come and save us, and we not only didn't understand, we took it from him."

He said, "I think we've met somewhere before," and was embarrassed by the banality of his words, but Paula answered gravely, accepting them, "Yes, somewhere, it might have been just passing in the street a long time ago." Their eyes met, and it seemed to Archie that it was a long time since anyone had met his gaze. People had only looked at him or stared.

Paula said, "This is terrible for you. If you want to escape at any time I've a flat at King's Cross. Look . . ." She wrote the address on a slip of paper. "There it is. You'd be safe there." They couldn't afford to misunderstand each other.

"Do you mean that?"

"Yes, of course."

"I'll come." He put the scrap of paper into the breast pocket of his tunic.

She waited tensely for him through two evenings. On the third he came and it seemed quite natural and easy. He came in out of the darkened streets like a fugitive. The light-filled room was barred against the whole world. She saw again the exhaustion and disillusionment scored on his face, but they smiled at one another with human confidence.

"I can give you dinner tomorrow if you can come."

He couldn't. He was on show. But he came the evening after and they were suddenly very gay, getting a meal together. She broke the precious precious eggs, three of them, and made an omelette. They ate in the kitchenette, practically out of the pan because, she solemnly assured him, that was the only way to eat omelettes. Afterwards they talked, and he told her about himself, what his home had been like, why he had joined the air force, and what it was like flying in the war, the fear and then the certainty, the sense of imminence, the sense of victory, the taut pattern of technical efficiency, the rhythm of a life in which every thought and action was directed at one end, the beauty of death and destruction seen from a distance, trees and fountains of smoke and dust, flowers and petals of flame, the sky like a carnival with tracer bullets. . . . What happened under the blasts you didn't see, but you joked about it, and when you shot down one of the enemy's planes you joked about that and did the victory roll coming home. It was a fine sight, a great flaring comet falling down the sky, and it wasn't you. He told her how he'd gone through all that as if it were a cloudbank and come out on the other side. He told her about the first pinhole in his mind's protection. He'd taken a girl to the pictures "for the usual reason, because it was dark." It was a flying picture with all the usual thrills and victories and handsome young actors in flying suits. It was all so shoddy and unreal that he'd caught a glimpse through it of the unreality in himself and in all of them. They had to make it unreal so that they could bear it, just as the picture was making it unreal for the audience so that they could bear the reality, "a sort of double ricochet, you see." He'd seen the faces of the audience in the dim radiance from the screen, row after row of intent white blobs sucking in the soothing syrup. "It was a circus for them, it was horrible, I can't tell you how horrible it was, the repetition of the same greedy look on every face. They couldn't help it, it was the war. It was human nature, and we couldn't help being their clowns either. It wasn't only that they wouldn't face what might happen to them in air operations, they wouldn't face what doing the bombing meant. Being murderers and hiring murderers if it came to that." But he had seen it, it had gone crashing into his brain. "My hand turned to iron on the girl's flesh and she knew it." He told her about the night in the mess when the papers ran their banner headlines "Australia Invaded," and the whole squadron was ready to desert. He told her about the bough of wattle. She knew that it was good for him to open the dams of his mind, and she not only listened but received it into her mind. When he left, after midnight, she might have said, "Don't go," but she didn't.

For two days he didn't come. There was a faint feverish film over those days. On the third he came in late, after Paula had given him up. In the pause the thing between them had grown immeasurably. She brought him coffee and they sat smoking, divided by half the room. There was nothing to say, but in every thought, movement, glance, there was fullness and significance. He put down his cup, rattling in its saucer with a sound phenomenonally loud, and came across the room to her. She stood up to meet him. The air tightened round them. It was charged. "This is it," thought Paula, and slowly raised her arms.

In the first light of the morning his body took shape in the bed. Raising herself carefully so as not to disturb him, Paula looked down on him. In the faint light he was cadaverous. His naked body lay as undefended as the dead, his legs and arms dark sticks, surrendered, his ribs cliff like, his belly a hollow between the pelvic bones, his face moulded to the skull with deep eye sockets, bony brow and jaw, the flesh drawn back from the big nose. Like a broken man. Who was he? What was he? Pieta? . . . But he slept as he had not slept for months in profound release. She had given him that. Tears of love and tenderness, pride, and shock of her experience, flowed down her cheeks and were a sensuous relief. It seemed as if her spirit were being born at last—in a caul.

Like a supernatural watercourse with flowering banks in a desert their love took its way through the dark arid days. It was Paula's private salvation, for Archie it was one of nature's feints of preservation, a token gesture towards life when the spirit is driven to its boundaries.

They spent every moment they could snatch together, but their love did not run smoothly. Sometimes they were exorbitantly happy, sometimes Archie was plunged in despondency, his war neurosis heavy upon him, and Paula found herself shut out. Those moments were the more shattering as she had fallen into the fatuous self-congratulation of a mature woman who has taken her first lover. When they were separated she fell into the habit of writing her thoughts about their love and life together in a journal. One day, thinking his interest in this would be as great as her own, she gave it to Archie to read, and while he read it she watched him, a look of delicate fine-drawn greed on her face. He shut the book and put it aside. His eyes were angry. "If we all thought so much nothing would ever be done," he said. He took her in his arms and crushed her till she was breathless and the greed in her eyes was open, then he thrust her away, still angry, and walked out.

The outside world provided obstacles too. Archie was irked and chafed by the position in which he found himself, and one of the circumstances that made it more than ever difficult for him to break out of it was that he had no money. As a deserter he got no pay, he was fêted and lionised, but there was no money in it and this left him helpless to break free. The government was in a quandary over him, he told Paula with bitter mirth. He was a deserter but they dared not arrest him, not so long as he was the people's idol. "As soon as they stop making a fool of me I'll be penniless and in gaol, so I'd better hang on to fame as long as possible, it's my only protection." Or they could have him certified, or send him to hospital with a nervous breakdown, or some such face-saving stunt, and then deal with him quietly afterwards. His inactivity and uselessness exacerbated him. He had not come twelve thousand miles to be useless and a laughing stock.

"What do you really want to do?" Paula asked him after one of these outbursts. "Really, at the bottom of your heart."

He sat staring at his hands for a long time, and then he said slowly, "I want to stop this war. I want to show people that they don't have to commit suicide. I want to tell them all men are brothers. That's why I came back. I thought my own people might listen."

It was soon after this that Archie met Bowie in one of his spells out of prison. They talked together, and Bowie was for a little while like his old self.

For Paula, love was enough.

But love, sacred nor profane, could not hold the sweep of events. After a long and costly indecision in Europe, while thousands upon thousands died on both sides and famine took its stealthier toll, Germany had broken under assault from the East and West, the aerial hammering of her cities, war exhaustion, and internal turmoil.

It was difficult to decipher at close range whether the capitulation were a military collapse or an uprising from within, a return to sanity, a loosing of new madness, a revolution, a victory or a defeat. So often had the optimists declared that Germany was on the brink of defeat, and so often had they been wrong, that the news that fighting had stopped in Russia broke on the world at large as a complete surprise. Germany Beaten, ran the monster headlines. Capitulation on the Russian Front. Armies Fraternise. (I don't like that bit about the armies fraternising, the sapient said, one to another.) There was nothing about England and America. The people didn't worry about details. This was victory, this was peace. No sooner did the news come through than everyone downed tools, streamed out of the factories and workshops without changing from their work clothes; here and there in excess of excitement men sabotaged the machines to which they had so long been slaves, countless whistles and sirens smote the sky, infidels broke into churches and rang the bells, tumultuous discordant chimes, housewives ran out into the street with dinner bells, staid people were as curiously gymnastic as if they had been caught in an explosion. Blackout blinds were torn down and with the coming of dusk every available light blared forth. What a night it would have been for an air raid, if any had come. The city was like a brazier and piled high its own fuel. A government official, infected by the occasion, unwisely released large stocks of liquor.

Good will was born again. Wireless announcers wept at the microphone. The starving poet of King's Cross passionately embraced his wife from whom he had been long estranged. And many other curious and unlikely phenomena occurred. King's Cross excelled itself. Young and old came forth to dance in the streets. Such motor cars as had braved the streets were overturned in sheer exuberance. Shops were broken into and their contents distributed as largesse to the crowd. In its freakishness the mob chose as its mascot Elsie Todd, the ageing prostitute who had won the lottery and graduated as an identity of the Cross by her fantastic fickle generosity, carrying her about the streets shoulder high, plying her with strange drinks. In the flaring lights, bedizened in her finery, she did look like some barbaric idol being carried in procession. It was her apotheosis. She screamed with laughter and delight and as she became drunk, sang bawdy songs and responded in kind to obscene witticisms. When she became quarrelsome, yelled abuse, and wanted to fight, the mob thought her funnier than ever and plied her with more drink. At last she became inarticulate and purple in the face and collapsed into a helpless mass. Her captors, tired of her by then and in no very good shape themselves, for it was about four in the morning, dumped her in a doorway and left her. There she lay and there she died at an undetermined moment before the street cleaners came in the dismal soberness of a new day.

The next day Sydney was filthy and dishevelled, and looked not unlike a city that had been sacked. There were a number of deaths as a result of the celebration, the casualty wards worked overtime and about 40 per cent of the workers were absent from their employment. Authority tried to drive home the lesson "We are still at war." The following weeks and months were laden with disappointment. There wasn't any definite peace. Russia said in effect to the United Nations "This is our victory. If you want one, go and get it." Murmurings against Russia never silent, grew louder, especially in

America. The British Navy did not stream into the Pacific to end the stalemate of the Japanese war and destroy Japan, as most people hoped it would. It stood by for new storms in the cyclonic calm of Europe.

Doubt was in every heart again, unease. Material conditions were in no way relieved, still the scarcities, the queues, the discontents and inconveniences. The threat of invasion persisted and the more terrible and secret fear of plague. Stories of its ravages in America leaked through persistently, and for this reason fear of America and of all contact with America grew and grew, and out of fear came dislike and out of dislike suspicion, mounting to hatred. As open war broke down, the latent war declared itself openly. The news that Hitler had hanged himself in Berchtesgarten scarcely raised a cheer. He, after all, was not the enemy, the enemy was everywhere.

In Europe the situation clarified a little. Russia's victory was seen to be as much political as military. Military defeat had been only a precipitant. Germany, goaded and despairing, had swung Left again. Communism was sweeping the country, irresistible. The United Nations were still at war with Germany but Russia, in the face of her most solemn undertakings, had made a separate peace. The two countries were not only at peace now, they were allies. America blazed with fury. The banner headline ran hot. "We are betrayed." "The dirty Bolshies" said the man in the street.

In England the propaganda was more subtle because there was a more powerful and organised Left to be considered. "Alas," murmured the propaganda machine, "the Russian victory has not shortened the war but prolonged it. Now that the two nations are at peace raw material is flowing from inexhaustible Russia into Germany. The cunning of the German has triumphed again, she has hoodwinked the brave but stupid Russian bear. Germany hates England and only England: by a change of front she has got rid of the enemy on her east flank so that she can concentrate all her force against England." A war weary people had been mulcted of their victorious peace by Russia. Their danger was greater than ever. They must fight on. Closely guarded figures, of sinkings in the Atlantic, of raids on England, were revealed with dramatic suddenness. Food rations were curtailed. A weary and exasperated people grew bitter. They were so tired of the war that they were ready to believe anything. A persistent story went round that Russian planes were taking part in raids on England. It was officially denied in such careful terms that suspicion struck deeper roots. There were those who could swear that they had seen a dead Russian in a crashed bomber, and others that they had heard prisoners talking Russian.

News of a peace move by Japan leaked out. She had acquired a great and rich empire, in her southward drive she had reached saturation point. She could say with truth that she had no designs on Australia. Her assaults on Australia had arisen out of her fear that America would use Australia as a base against her. If that fear were removed, not only would Japan cease to have any aggressive intentions but the very root of them would be removed. Japan's danger was from the north, from Russia. Whoever menaced Japan was her enemy. She recognised no other enemies. That was reasonable. It was obvious that, relieved of the Pacific war, Japan would attack Russia in Siberia. Japan was ready to promise self-government to all the Asiatic people in her sphere of influence, she was willing to give the British Commonwealth of Nations rights of trade. What did England want but trade? Not the responsibility of backward colonies, not subject peoples unfitted by nature to partake of her glorious liberty. Liberalism lifted its head long enough to agree with the principle of national self determination in the east. Japan would co-operate with Britain and even with America in keeping the peace in the Pacific. It was Russia who was to be feared, who broke the peace, not perhaps by open acts of aggression but by the far more insidious policy of political penetration. Wasn't China's fall due, when you looked at it honestly, to Russia? It was Russian influence that made China a menace to Japan and caused the Sino-Japanese war, and it was the disruption within China, again due to Russia, that made it possible for a small poorly endowed country like Japan to conquer her? Look at Germany whiteanted. It will be France next and France is only just across the Channel.

"Good old Axis propaganda" said the Professor, "but the insidious part is that there's something in it."

"Quite, quite" said his colleagues.

The Japs were human beings after all. They'd been staunch little allies in the last war. The tales about their frightfulness were only propaganda. Lot of it in the last war too, all debunked later. Fake photographs, that sort of thing. It was those bunglers at the Peace of Versailles that upset them. We'd do better this time. A rational peace.

"Playing the Yellow Bellies off against the Soviet, England'd rather see the Japs get us than the coms get hold of France. Sure she would." said Timmy Andrews.

Are we going to bear malice for ever because of Pearl Harbour?

"The cocky bastards" said the man in the train, "Didn't do them any harm to be taken down a peg or two."

Peace with Japan and the status quo. Thing as they used to be.

"Good old days or bad old days. You knew where you were any how. You were sure of the O.A.P. any way."

Seventeen thousand Australian prisoners in Japanese hands.

"For God's sake let the boys come home. They'll be old men at this rate before we see them again."

The temper of the people was remoulded. In vain did the enlightened struggle against the miasma of propaganda. It worked. The human mind is so much more susceptible to suspicion and hatred than to reason. Its faiths are old slow growths, an epoch or so behind its circumstances. So it was that men accepted the social monstrosity of the industrial revolution because they were still faithful to feudalism, and now they accepted the social monstrosities of the finance-capital age because they were still led along by belief in beneficent competition and the open road from log cabin to White House. They faced the need for Internationalism (co-operate or perish) with their nationalistic emotions at high pressure. The gulf between Right and Left widened and deepened. The Right had one great lure, the slogan of "things as they used to be." The Left, having a lengthening political history behind it, was acquiring a sentiment and a tradition which would not be fully operative until outmoded. The lag was almost entirely in favour of the Right. But there was another factor to be reckoned with, a rogue force, the recoil. Wound too tightly, the "sovereign will" might spring away at a tangent. That, the fact and the threat, worked for the Left. Left and Right were themselves arbitrary terms. There was a continuum of finely shaded opinion but in major crises it had to break in two. By conviction, instinct, overt act, men ranged themselves on one side or the other. Reason was for the minority. Too often the debased coin of rationalisation passed for it.

The world had come to a defile. It must pass through the narrows or die of its wars and plagues and its hunger. This was no political artificiality, it was history working down through cause and effect to a diminishing point. The powers were now jockeying for possession of the peace. To seize the peace it was necessary to be willing to go on fighting. For the peace the people must be made and kept envenomed. That was the troubled water that the master fishers needed. To statesmen of the Empire it was above all abhorrent that Russia, having won the victory, should control the peace. It was desirable also that America should once more be left on the beach. So the poison was broadcast and the amazing, the incredible volte face was achieved. Insincerity and the Machievellian mind alone could not have achieved it. Many of the men who spread propaganda believed it, others considered it opportune and believed wholeheartedly in the premises that made it opportune. The untended soil itself spawned hatred and suspicion for that was the nature of the times, the historical crop.

To win the peace it was necessary that the people must still be willing to fight. They needed an Enemy, a focal point of hatred. Hitler was gone, give them the arch renegade, Stalin. Dislike and suspicion of Russia did not have to be created. It had only to be brought back, the spade work had been done before.

Obediently the swing over came, easily and swiftly in America because she was now the greatest Have nation on earth. It grew by infection. Canada followed America. South Africa, despite a vigorous minority, showed that her heart was in the right place. The greatest division of opinion was in England itself and in Australia, gravity of the mass pulled heavily.

An armistice with Japan was declared. It was acclaimed but doubt mixed noticeably in the rejoicings, doubt and fear. The people wanted peace, but what was under the white cloth? They did not know, they feared, they doubted. The seventeen thousand did not come back. They were hostages for the armistice now. There were plenty who said in utter weariness and disillusion "We've done enough, poured out our blood and resources. We won't play the power game any more. The little peoples always lose. We'll live to ourselves. Better for all." But they put their heads in bags.

Strain was not lessened but increased, the difficulties of daily life, which had after all the last word in forming opinion, grew worse. Australia had her own difficulties. The armies returned from the north and brought unrest. Tough and independent, the men were restless and discontented with the world they found; they could not endure all the rules and regulations and prohibitions. They were a state within the state and they infected the mass of people. Getting them into employment was no easy matter. Out of employment they were a menace.

Australia was not as docile as her sister nations because her armies had been trained not in discipline but in initiative for jungle fighting. They brought their initiative home, the commando spirit. The population was small and so more easily swayed by the troops. There was too a leak in the Right. Industry had made an enormous war effort and in the process had developed amazingly. This development, envisaged with alarm by industry overseas as a post-war rival, had been hamstrung by bonds and contracts, designed to force Australia back at the end of the war to the role of a customer. As the time approached local industry was unwilling to give up its power and its profits. It flew to patriotism. As the possibility of war with Russia loomed nearer, a secessionist movement began in Australia. It too was not new but a revival. It centred in the hard Left, the people's party of which Sid Warner was the last hard inner kernel: it drew to itself the discontented army, "If we're going to fight any more, it will bloody well be for ourselves", a minority of the Right which thought it could start its own empire at home; and to it clung the vague soft Left, all those who were weary of war, who had wanted a better world, who had patent recipes for one and no chance to try them in existing circumstances.

One of the conditions of the Pacific armistice had been the withdrawal of the American army from Australia. This suited England who, mistrusting her financial rival, feared lest the Americans might remain in Australia as bailiffs. It suited popular opinion in Australia. It suited the American soldiers themselves who had become stale and longed inordinately to return home and go on with their lives. The romantic element, always strong in America, was clamouring "Give us back our boys." So they went and Downing Street smiled behind its hand at another political defeat for the Yanks. Their departure released the political brake in Australia.

There was a Labour Government in office, but as usual the margin of political power was with the monied interests. Nevertheless the situation was precarious. There were explosive elements. Britain would not forgive or condone any secession, there were elements within that felt strong against it too. If it came to an issue there might well be civil war. The government was for compromise, the extreme Right and extreme Left were tugging in opposite directions. The mass of the people had become emotionally unmoored and might turn the scale in either direction. Only an open and irretrievable act would show where the line of cleavage came.

The Right were shouting that safety lay only within the Empire, "the old firm." To stay in the Empire meant, obviously now, war with Russia, peace with Japan, the Empire's prospective ally in that war, a war that would have little hope of success without the co-operation of Japan. Japan naturally had the sense to know this and put her price as high as she dared. America dared not be left out.

It was now in this situation that the first of those curious recoils occurred, a fantasy as a meteorite is a fantasy without being outside the law of nature. (Her dilemma was closing in on Australia.) The Pacific was under an interim condominium, Britain, America, Japan, "a non political police force" and with this force the secessionist party was threatened. If, ran the threat under smooth words, Australia tried to leave the British

Commonwealth of Nations, she would be put under international guard. The Secessionists—a large party of mixed motives unlikely to cohere if its objective were achieved—were for calling Britain's bluff on the assumption that she would not dare to call in the Japanese against her own people. They contemplated secession largely through inaction. The Left was for continuing the war against Japan as an ally of Russia. The Right was for remaining within the Empire but acting only as food reservoir or workshop in the war—safety without fighting. The people were bewildered. They wanted things both ways or neither. They had been whipped up too often. No one could raise a gallop now. But suddenly a new enthusiasm broke. The Peace Party, so long a small submerged nonentity, rose suddenly to the surface. It offered Another Way Out, and advanced a plan so simple, so deeply emotional, so patently sincere, that a people, suspicious to saturation point, tired of trying to think, snatched at it. The Party preached what it had always preached. Peace. Internationalism. Socialism. All men are brothers as a basis of practical politics. Men of good intention of every race and colour unite and you will possess the world. Stop fighting and preparing to fight. Seek allies among your enemies. Offer them constructive peace without threats of pressure. The world must be built not on national or political but on moral grounds. There was enough good will in the world to move mountains. It must be organised. The beginning must be made with the simplest, the least contaminated, men. Men must assume goodwill in other men. The only way to kill competition was to refuse to compete. Appeals to greed and self interest, however good the final motive, was only a reinforcement of the forces of destruction. This creed spread like wildfire as a new religion (or a new diet) sometimes did. It was poetic and simple, like the Sermon on the Mount, and it was desperate, as remedy must be in desperate and dissolving times.

The nucleus of the movement was a small group of curiously assorted men. Among them, soon to be the chief of them, was Archie Castles. He had been sidetracked with an instructional job, he had known frustration and despair and this had germinated in his mind. With ardour once again he gave himself to a forlorn hope. He saw himself as one of those who have nothing to lose and so are free to give all. He had survived where so many had perished so that he felt the urgent need to give back the uttermost. It was Bowie who had opened this door. Archie threw himself into the work of creating an organism without organisation as the early Christians had done. From its headquarters in Sydney the message went out to the world. Stop this thing that is destroying us all, make the world new on the widest basis, your own hearth. Refuse to compete, refuse to fight. All men are brothers. It went out to small labour groups, to village co-operatives, to parish priests, to royal and ancient orders, to dart clubs. Never to leaders or bishops or members of parliament. They had had their chance, they hadn't taken it. It went to England, America, China, Russia. It was more difficult to get it to Japan, but most important of all, the whole scheme was vitiated if the appeal did not go equally to the inarticulate worker of Japan. There was no road there unblocked by censorship. The Peace Party decided to send an air mission to Japan to distribute leaflets through country and industrial districts. This was a matter of enormous difficulty. Authority would not and could not be expected to co-operate. It depended entirely, as did all their activities, on good will and the help of friends. The miracle was accomplished. A chain was established, through Australia to New Caledonia, to the Philippines, to China, to Japan itself, depending all the time on individual links, the sort of thing that only faith would attempt. The three planes needed were themselves a matter of faith and providence, but they were forthcoming. Thousands were in this strange secret. Archie Castles was to lead the formation. He had touched the peoples' imagination before, he could do it again. As the date for the experiment approached excitement mounted. "It's barbarous," said the Professor, "just like a revivalist meeting." Detached, he did see something menacing in so pure and unreasoning an enthusiasm. Archie kept his head, he knew how grave and risky a thing he was doing, putting faith to the touch, but he could not make Paula see. She went about shining; she could not or dared not see any danger.

Paula had been like a miracle to Archie . . . at first. To his exhausted nerves she was peace, to his imagination the unexpected prize. His vanity measured her against the four-roomed house perched in the middle of a paddock and the old frail illusion, the jack o' lantern, that had carried him away from home, into the air force, over the sea and back again, seemed at last within his hands. She was so very lovely—everything that a man might dream that a woman could be. Poise, intelligence, grace, gay tenderness, a delicate clear flame of passion. . . . They had their moments, moments of perfectly synchronised passion, lambent unfolding of the spirit mirrored in the flesh; the touch, the glance so weighted with significance of uncatalogued emotions that they shot through the tissue of time and matter like a falling star. Once and again they found a north-west passage, those infinitesimally small cracks in the iron shell of life by which spirit escapes. But they were moments without context. Just as when one night, walking up Martin Place in the blackout, mantle of wartime lovers, they looked up and saw that many search-lights, like the spokes of an enormous wheel, had caught an aeroplane in their hub and rolled with it across the dark ditch of the sky, a shining metal moth pinned on to the night by shafts of light. They had stood, hand in hand, like tranced children, staring at it, incredulously happy in its completed beauty. For Archie, who had raced before those steely beams in hostile skies, aware that death would strike along them, knowing it now as nothing but a spectacle, the beauty bit fiercely in his brain. He saw, as a resurrected soul might see, his former life transfigured into images that, living among them, he could never have apprehended. Oh, but they were not children and the beauty was by chance and not out of the nature of things. The struggle was not over but before them.

So all the moments were seeds that did not sprout and though for a flash they might raise the iron from his brain and heart, as the seed will raise the clod and the stone, they were not enough.

To Archie's first beatitude there had succeeded a new knowledge of frustration. They were separated, he and Paula, by a pane of glass, flawless but unbreakable. She carried her glass case round with her, her show case, as naturally as a snail its shell. There were times when he was helplessly angry with her, helplessly because his anger had no rationale. Paula had offered him no injury. Then he would want to hurt her, to smash his way through, to misuse her so that he was disgusted with himself and with her because his violence woke in her a crude exultation, a greed that mounted with it. Later, with a change of mood, the episode would seem incredible, and he could persuade himself that nothing had happened.

Now at the last Paula had deserted him through her monstrous incomprehension. He told himself with an impatience that was the index of his strained nerves that she was a creature wound in a silk cocoon, a romantic. But wasn't he a romantic too, living not among men but simulacra that turned to stone as he came abreast of them? He had moved perilously from handhold to handhold, taking desperate remedies to shore up his crumbling world. Every time more desperate. The child had turned against the life that bore him, driven in his flight from expedient to expedient; some day reality would overtake him. Tomorrow he would fly to Tokio on a mission that was either supremely important or supremely foolish, that could be both. It was reality and the dream, as night and day complete the circle. If he and those who would follow him could carry this flight far enough, steadfastly enough, it would pass out of the dream into reality. He now was for a moment of time the small hinge on which the future swung. He believed that. Reality was in believing. How could he know if Paula was his dream or he hers, if he carried event or was, equally with Paula, a mote in its slip stream? Weakly he pitied himself as one driven inexorably beyond the boundaries of the known world, seeking the impossible in the impossible.

For the thousands who watched him in those last days he was the simulacrum of a hero, almost a mythical character, the decked sacrifice, one with Isaac, Andromeda, and Iphigenia, the fortunate sacrifice who would placate the gods and live. They put a mask upon his flesh. His mind was little and peevish within the shell of his great undertaking. Looking about him from his fateful eminence he thought himself a man cheated of his memories. Life had not cumulated in him. As he lived it, it had perished and passed, so that he swung forever like a man on a rope's end over an abyss. He felt like a lonely, deprived child because he had nothing to cherish. Not his home, not his childhood, not his first love (Ruby in the exaggeration of her remembered innocence and sweetness, Ruby whom he had cast away, leapt unchanged before his memory, he had forfeited Ruby and no doubt some ugly commonplace marriage had reduced her to the dead level of thousands of other dull, slatternly women long ago. There might have been peace for him in Ruby); not Paula. He blamed Paula overmuch for not being what he demanded that she should be. Eyes that promised everything and gave nothing; he had thought her so sensitive and delicate yet had found her invulnerable in her incomprehension. She was tied to the foundering ship, the old world. He hated her and pitied her, he loved and condemned her, and put upon her the last burthen of his loneliness. They didn't quarrel. There was no time to quarrel and he dared not, at this moment, put his spirit to the expense of quarrelling. Besides, lovers quarrel only when they still have hope of one another. He had none but she must not know it.

The vermin of these thoughts bred within the simulacrum of the hero. But he also stood outside them and knew them for what they were. He knew too that for all the utter blank of loneliness surrounding him on the brink of his adventuring that he was one of millions dispossessed, each in his own way. A sick world separates men, a living healthy world brings them together. The loneliness of the individual is the index of a system's decay. Man's tragedy was made casual and futile. Archie thought of many he had known and the countless others he hadn't known—faces in the street, stamped with lethargy, bearing often the imprint of a suffering and tragedy of which they themselves were not directly aware. He thought of the men who had served with him in the Air Force and how few of his original comrades still lived. Each time one had gone it had appeared like a bit of tough luck, but the chances of survival had been all along so slender that the margin of luck was slender indeed. They were wastage of the system, only a little more obviously so than the myriad other victims. In civil life men and women, buoyed up by the chance of getting through, ignored the casualties all round them. Security was the competitive prize and not the rule. Most perished. It was the law. Perished as they lived and by the act of surviving. "I stand among the dead and what shall be the resurrection?" his fevered brain asked him. He remembered a man back home when he was a child. Harry Munster. He hadn't thought of him for years, but he remembered him now because his life seemed to sum up the life of the common man. He remembered him quite well. A decent sort of bloke he must have been. Archie had ridden in his truck lots of times. He'd been to the war and had a little place at Toongabbie. Everybody liked him, though some of them, like Archie's father, thought he was a fool to work so hard. Up at Harry's place Archie had first got the idea that things didn't have to be like they were in his own home, feckless with a broken back. Harry had shown him things and talked to him about the Co-op. He'd thought the world of Harry, just like a kid does. Then suddenly Harry had sold his place and gone away and no one had seen any of the Munsters for years. Then when the depression was at its worst, his mother had told him, Harry had come back, a scarecrow of a man with hardly a boot to him. Hundreds had been through before him looking for work. There wasn't any work and him being a neighbour once made it worse. You couldn't give him a slice of bread at the back door and you couldn't ask him to sit down at the table seeing how he was and knowing what he was after. It would have made it worse saying no. He didn't get round to asking for work more than the once. He'd just stand and talk about the weather and then the prospects, and perhaps ask how this one or that one was, and then, when he'd smelt out how things were, he'd grin and say, "Well, so long. I'd better be getting along now," and they'd be relieved to see him go. It was every man for himself, and Harry Munster, as Mrs Castles said, had the sense to know it. She didn't know why he hadn't more pride than to come back where he was known in the state he was in. God in Heaven, they'd expected him to be ashamed. No ghosts wanted. That was the last anyone had heard of him until they saw his name in the paper as one of the victims of the air raid. His memory had flared up for a moment before it went out for ever. That had been Harry Munster. The world might be fashioned anew by an immense effort of the spirit of man, but there would be no reparation for Harry and all those who, like him, had been so casually destroyed in the sight of their fellows. No resurrection.

When men came to their last ditch—surely this was it, this final trough at the end of the long disastrous war—they must rise. The tide would lift at last towards the light, Archie cried to the pain and bitterness of his heart, and he would go with it wherever it led and whatever it meant. It reassured and strengthened him to feel himself irrevocably committed, to know that he was free at last of his long complicity with death.

The flight to Japan would take the full concentration of all his physical and spiritual powers, and yet he felt it dwarfed and unimportant against the issues at stake. Out of his own despair he believed in it. Without despair such hope would be impossible.

In the last resort his heart and his resolve were steady.

The planes got off all right. It was not until they were actually away that a feeling of unreality began to creep over Archie. He thought fatalistically, "This is the second time. No man is allowed to repeat himself." His heart or his faith failed him. No one need ever know it, no one ever did, but it might have made a difference, a hair's breadth of difference, but enough.

The expedition came to the worst possible end. It may have been a mistake in judgment, Archie's, the wrong approach, flying too low; it may have been, as the Japanese authorities said afterwards, hasty over-zealous action of the young officer on duty with his battery; or it may have been intended from the first, tacitly connived at, as the punishment for folly that might be dangerous. Flying low over a military post a battery opened fire. One plane was brought down and the crew taken prisoner. One plane turned back and was eventually lost in a storm over the Arafura Sea, flying blind till her petrol was exhausted. Archie flew on and was last seen with smoke pouring from his engine. There was no further reliable information. The Japanese reported belatedly that a burning plane had fallen into the sea off the coast of Japan.

Black disaster had overtaken the expedition, but no one knew its exact terms. Legend persisted long after hope. Archie Castles was a prisoner, being tortured; he was in hiding somewhere in Japan, carrying on his mission; he was marooned on an island. A Dutch plane had seen his signals, but the weather had been too wild to permit the pilot to land. . . . There were progressively weaker demands for a search. Both governments disclaimed responsibility and were determined that what they called "the rash act of a group of fanatics" should not be made the text of an international situation. The enthusiasm that had bred the venture died as suddenly as it arose. The gamble was lost.

Paula never knew at what moment to mourn for Archie. She covered herself with hope as long as possible, and when hope was over it seemed as if the power to grieve had gone out of her. Besides, the problem of personal survival had grown so acute that she had no emotion for anything else.

While the brief drama of the mission to Japan was enacting all parties waited and watched to see if anything came of it, to gauge public opinion, to see how events could be turned to advantage. With failure and the sudden consequent deflation and disintegration of morale the situation changed rapidly and became more ominous.

Daily, almost hourly, the strength ebbed from the elected government and its policy of neutrality with profit was discredited. Australia was being economically bypassed. South America, enriched and strengthened by other peoples' wars, had built up her production till she was not only the rival but the successful rival, the granary and the slaughterhouse for armies. Unannounced economic sanctions were being brought to bear on the small recalcitrant nation. Graziers and industrialists who had been willing tacitly to support neutrality-with-profit while allowing the labour party to bear the opprobium attaching, markedly preferred war with markets to peace without. They swung over to the Right with all the power of propaganda that their money gave them. The A.T.F. which might have supported the government was demobilised and not easy to reassemble. The Right began to raise its own army as it had in times past. There was no dearth of officers and for recruitment they had the advantage of a strong traditional sentiment. The war against Russia was the war for the Empire. The air force which had not been disbanded was strongly for the Right. "We're fighting men, not politicians," they said. "We'll fight any enemy who shows himself, black, red or yellow." Day by day the ranks of the unemployed swelled. "Loyalty," the bosses told them, spelt work, "disloyalty" idleness and starvation.

The Left with its policy of "Fight for Russia and Socialism, here and now" had the support of the great militant trade unions, an underground movement of unknown strength, and the unemployed in whom experience had at last bred hatred and distrust. "Why go overseas to fight," men were saying openly, "when we can do it right here?"

For the moment both sides were willing to maintain the vestigial government in office, their common scapegoat, while they gathered their forces.

Of the capital cities, Melbourne was strongly for the Right, Adelaide less strongly, Perth was staunch for the Left, Brisbane wavered and Sydney, divided, was yet the great stronghold of the militant Left and centre of a powerful underground movement. Canberra had no voice. Canberra was deserted, a city of trees, shuttered down in green murmurings and arboreal silences, life gone to the faintest pulse of a few people living on uncertainty, having nothing to hold them to the place and nowhere else to go. Canberra, the synthetic stronghold of democracy had no longer any being. Like a faint echo of Ankor Wat Canberra lay overthrown by the mild assault of an alien spring; its once clear geometrical lines frayed and over-ridden; the hollow cubes, oblongs, squares of its buildings, dice thrown on the plain, half submerged in a tidal wave of foliage; its ears filled with leaves against its own death sigh. Pearl bushes grew bold, the tulips were rank; wave after wave of flowers rose from the sap of the unpruned roses; roots and the frail clinging fingers of creepers prized open the fabric of the city to rain, wind and silent corrosive dust. Canberra was the first of the Australian cities to fall.

Sydney was the danger point. It was the Right that broke the truce. Assuming the voice of Australia, the Right appealed to the Empire Council against insurgents at home. The response was swift and dramatic. A strong mixed force of "International Police" representing the Pacific Powers, Britain, the Americas, Japan, was landed at Broken Bay and directly threatened Sydney. The Commandant sent an ultimatum to the Prime Minister in Melbourne. Australia would remain within the Commonwealth of Nations. She would act as a supply base in the war against Russia. She would co-operate in act and spirit "in the common undertaking for the common victory." There was no threat, the threat was too obvious to need enunciation. The old hostility between the two cities was turned to cynical advantage. Sydney's fate was left in the hands of her rival. There was no great urgency. Parliament was in recess. The ultimatum did not run out for ten days in order that the House might be convened. The democratic forms were still observed. There was no hurry, Sydney was too valuable a hostage to put the issue in doubt and Sydney was defenceless. There were no men under arms except the air force and it was willing to cooperate. There was no ship of war in Sydney Harbour but out of sight, over the rim of the horizon, were the grey shapes of a fleet waiting like beasts of prey round an imperial rationale. The situation could not have arisen so suddenly without collusion. The place of landing was well chosen, inevitable, because it thrust a wedge between the two centres of resistance, Sydney and Newcastle.

No one wanted bloodshed; it would, in fact, be highly inconvenient. The Powers had been assured that only an authoritative gesture was needed. Nor did the partizans of the Right want to see the destruction of property. The way the occupying force looked on the situation, both officially and in sincerity, was that a small, mangy, criminal minority was threatening the integrity of the Commonwealth, that there was a political deadlock out of which this "un-Australian" minority was making capital and that they, the interveners were acting in the interests of, and according to the will of, the majority; wholesome force wielded righteously, a matter of law and order, essentially unpolitical. So to those among the right-thinking citizens who baulked at the idea of bringing foreign troops, and more particularly the Japanese, into Australia on any pretext or for any reason, the stalwarts of the Right explained beatifically that this was the dawn of the new internationalism and the brotherhood of man, that the enemy within the gates was inspired by foreign influence. One more great effort, one more purge and the world would not only be free but united. They were lulling words upon an iron purpose and they successfully took in those who were already convinced.

Out of what might be called a perfected and vestigial sense of honour (there is only the antique word "honour" for this curious class substitute, this billabong morality, offering a decorative gesture for a fact) out of this freakish sense of honour—while they blandly committed an enormity—the Powers had put in command of the expedition a man of such unblemished integrity that it would never occur to him to doubt or look beyond the sales talk of his masters. Brother should not be sent against brother, but a foreigner, theoretically as impartial as a judge, put to the task. The commandant had only a bookish, hearsay knowledge of conditions and terrain, underrated the city, thought of it as helpless, uncoordinated, indefensible, as indeed it was in a military sense, and he, like a good soldier, took nothing into consideration except the military situation. "Sure, boys, it's a pushover. You're here for a picnic," he told his staff in his breezy, democratic way. The fleet, he thought, could silence Sydney with a few rounds. But the fleet couldn't fire those rounds till he gave the word. He'd snitched priority from under the Admiral's nose and was the Admiral sore? The Admiral, who was, of course, very very Rear, had been heard to say in his bluff sailor fashion that the bastard could bloody well burn his fingers in the wasp's nest for all he'd do to stop him.

If trouble came the commandant expected it from the north. The coal miners might in their militant wrong headedness march against him. He hoped they would, he could then once and for all liberate Australia from the tyranny of these men. He was confident in the overwhelming adequacy of the forces at his command and so having no fear or doubt of his success he had no hatred and was lulled.

Thus the invader, the task force, approached its mission in an antiseptic spirit, sure that only a threat was required, benevolent even, as to a spoilt child, patronizingly above the disputes and disruptions of this handful, zestfully engaged in private quarrels, ready to do its duty and be gone. Only this complacency can explain what happened, the macabre ending to the cynical comedy.

.    .    .    .    .    .    .    .    .

Knarf broke himself out of the mould of his book. He had been speaking into the air like a bard retelling some saga deeply patterned in his mind. Now he was speaking to Ord, almost, you might say, pleading with him, entreating him for credence. "As if," thought Ord, "he had created the world and invented history."

"Now," Knarf was saying, "there comes the second of those strange wild fleers. As the people had turned to light now they swung towards the darkness of violence and destruction. In the ascendency of the Peace Party they had demanded a single concrete sign from heaven, a miracle, where there could only be a slow honest growth. Upon the ancient need of the propitiatory sacrifice they had grafted the ethic of the new advertising stunt. At the first blow they had relinquished the whole scheme and attitude. It had only been a new inflection on an old motif. It passed like a flicker."

"Do you really believe," asked Ord, "that the whole affair of the Peace Party was more than a sick fantasy?"

"I do believe that by accident and for a short time the people held the thread of life between their fingers. Their mistake was that they underrated the sacrifices that such a course demanded. They thought it easy, when it was difficult; that it required only enthusiasm, when it needed the sternest discipline and tenacity."

"They lacked efficient leadership."

"Leadership?" cried Knarf, stung to bitterness. "They had had too much leadership. What is it but the transfer of responsibility from the people to the individual and then, when the transfer is complete, the subtraction of the responsibility. The leader embodies the ancient fetish of the scapegoat inverted. Ideas and not men should lead. Power is everyman's price."

When Ord grinned, teasingly, behind his hand, a thin flush rose on Knarf's cheek bones.

"They were conditioned by their history, vitiated by the cult of leadership, their thoughts so pooled and open to propaganda by the benefits of their civilization that there was no longer any untouched class, any peasantry even, from which regeneration might come."

"Did it ever?" asked Ord. "Did the noble savage ever intervene on behalf of effete civilization?"

But he was hardly listening, he was looking at Knarf with new eyes, thinking of him in a new way. "The vermin of all these thoughts bred in the simulacrum of a hero." Knarf's mind was "little and peevish in the shell of his great undertaking." He arraigned Knarf in his mind, "You put on this tragic mask, you reach back 400 years into history to find this image of disaster to suit yourself. You have nothing to complain of, no tragedy, no mortal struggle. Society gives you everything, feeds you, clothes you, measures out your ration of honour, opens all the doors to you, and you repay society with this peevishness, this gloom, this fleering midnight story." All this is for himself alone and not for society. He is my friend, and I should know him, but I do not. He is unknowable, a perversity. I am a scientist, a lover of exact truth, he is a man of imagination who would cut the thongs of life and bring in chaos again that he may lay night to night in his own heart and be comforted. We have built the world up out of chaos and held it up. He, out of no more than some vague yearning atavism, would bring it down again. Plato knew better, no poets in Utopia, but we in fatuous generosity kept the poets and let them breed. Knarf is a poet, his son is an agitator. So it is that the helpless blind roots work upon the solid foundations. He thought of the discussion at dinner; the long ragged argument, his own part in it. He saw how infirm the mind of man still was, how easily taken in by the nimble imagination. Under his censure Ord too felt sorrowful as if he were also a deprived and lonely child shut out of an unknown kingdom.

Knarf, recoiling from the unspoken rebuff, returned to his book as if to take cover in it. "This is the peroration," he said. "The destruction of the city."

.    .    .    .    .    .    .    .    .

The newspapers published the news neither of the landing nor of the ultimatum. The censor in a panic had shut down on it, but within an hour of the grounding of the first landing barge on the Hawkesbury sand, the rumour had reached the city. It spread like a grass fire, by nightfall it was known everywhere. The city had changed its note, a deep vibration of excitement, anger, fear, ran through it. The people flocked into the streets. Any one who spoke had an audience, everywhere tense faces turned now this way, now that, ears straining, eyes straining into the darkness. Few slept, few smoked, few ate. They were like yarded horses who smell fire. For many it was a night of intense activity.

Every cell of the underground movement met that night. Its headquarters were crowded from dawn to dusk, not only with its own members, but with men from the trade unions, coming and going. The most secret sympathisers came openly that night. The news had acted as a precipitate; all the long smouldering and resentment, the mounting rage against society that the depression, the war, the scarcities, the suspicions and injustices of the last decade had laid up, took form. The people were turning to the underground for a lead. Lethargy was at last, at last, burnt away in hatred.

Sid Warren, facing a meeting of the central committee, knew that the hour had struck. He recognised it and confirmation was written in the faces confronting him. He had waited and now it had come. For this he had banked down his force and strength all these years, for this and to meet this. It was the story of Spain over again. It was the Right that had risen against organised government. The two causes to which he had given his heart coalesced. They were one. He was back in his youth with the strength of his youth.

All he had to say was simple enough. Simple and direct. "We are betrayed. The bloody fascists have called in the Japs and the Yanks. We can't go out and fight. But we can destroy the city. It's Sydney they want. It's rich, it's the key. We've been its slaves. It was never our city until now. Now it is our city, we can seize it and all its fascist works and destroy it. When the invader comes let him find a blazing ruin." It was a policy of scorched earth in the face of overwhelming odds. But he knew, and those facing him knew, that there would be a subjective satisfaction in the blasting of the city that had itself brought them to this pass. The people would respond, the will had fused in them.

This was no improvisation of the moment. Plans to meet each kind of emergency, every possible threat, had been hammered out in the long secret meetings of the past year. Now, they needed only the last adaptations and the signal for action. Time was their chief danger. Each man went from the brief meeting with his appointed job clear before him.

Sid Warren carried the message to the waiting people. If he was flame, everywhere he met tinder. He was speaking the language they knew. He liberated them. The word "destroy" rose through the labyrinth of the city like an exhalation.

When the hard-eyed summer dawn came he led a detachment of the impatient army against the G.P.O. The weary telegraph office was open, the letter-sorters were at work, the night shift drooped at the switchboard. In a quarter of an hour the whole building, that great ganglion of communication, was in the hands of the insurgents. No mails left. The switchboards were destroyed, the telegraph apparatus destroyed, the lines from the broadcasting stations cut. When the army of clerks, operators, letter carriers, drivers, arrived at work, Sid, with his battery of loud speakers, met them on the steps. He told them his simple message. He poured his fire into them and they responded. In the heart of Sydney, in Martin Place, the word "destroy" was shouted aloud. The dissentients were shouted down and lost. Men who had used the machinery of the post-office had the atavistic joy of destroying it.

At suburban exchanges and at the broadcasting stations it was the same. There was no parley, the switchboards and transmitters were destroyed. Sydney was off the air.

Another detachment of the new army had taken Central Railway Station at dawn. No trains left until the new control was established. Men in the railway workshops had risen; armed with their tools, they gladly destroyed what they had made.

Nothing went out from Sydney that day, neither word nor man nor vehicle. She was silent, cut off. The intention of her people would be carried out.

This was a day of intense activity. Commandeered printing presses were hard at work. Vehicles of every kind were seized, so were all the petrol dumps, and set under guard. Everywhere men burst out of their workshops and factories, wrecking them before they left. Everywhere there was chaos, but the chaos was organization. Many of the well-to-do had left the city for fear of a bombardment. Those that were left, hampered by their wives and children and goods were overwhelmed, not so much by numbers as by the concentrated, single-minded fury of their opponents. For them it was a day of painful shocks and surprises.

In the afternoon a great concourse gathered in the Domain, and there

Sid spoke to them. He said the same things over and over. He was tireless and demoniac. His lieutenants spoke to them and they said the same things. We are betrayed. We have nothing to lose. Destroy. The great crowd was lashed to fury. "Destroy" was like a torch in every hand. It filled the city like the smell of burning flesh. Once that mob had met, listened, and dispersed to its tasks, there was no turning back, no possible reprieve for the city.

That night Paula went to bed early seeking in vain a refuge from her fear. But fear went with her and would not be shut out. It came in through her windows like an exhalation from the city. She did not know what there was to dread, not tonight, over and above the cumulated nightmare that had been, it seemed for so long now, the content of everyone's life. Until tonight she had always felt sure at the bottom of her heart that she was immune, that danger was abstract and for other people. Now at last she was not sure. Grief itself was not as unsettling as this. Footsteps beneath her windows sounded differently. They were the feet not of drifting crowds, but of men with a purpose. The hot air was laden with a new note, a deep surge, as of a city changing gear. Earlier, when she had gone out for provisions, it had seemed to her that there were many new faces in the streets—not only new either, but a different kind of people, not the sort she was accustomed to, and this had filled her with alarm, unreasonable but persistent. She had hurried back to the shelter of her own building, but even the familiarity of her rooms had grown thin. Her possessions, that had been plump and satisfied with pride, had grown mean and haggard like furniture at an unfriendly auction sale. She was alone too. Archie dead, Bowie lost and gone, the others who used to drop in for her coffee and cigarettes, the warmth and peace of this soft place, the talk and other vanities of the vanished world, were scattered and absorbed. Not even the Professor was likely to come any more. She had stood outside the change and the world had gone away and left her.

She went to bed as an animal might creep into its hole. She wanted, at last with a blind simplicity, to cover herself and hide in the darkness. Her existence was threatened, the animal in her knew it, and that private entity, that most precious self, which she had brought through many dangers, like those frail glass vessels that survived Pompeii, the grail of her egoism, was in danger. If she sank down into her malaise and submitted herself, surely fear itself would be ashamed and leave her.

The lights still burned in the streets. The motionless oblong of white light still lay on her wall, high up near the ceiling, as it had always done. She fixed her eyes and her mind upon it and lay waiting for she knew not what.

It was after eleven when someone knocked at the outer door of the flat. Paula lay taut, listening. The knocking went on, insistent yet furtive. Paula got up, switched on the lights, put on her dressing-gown, and went to open. By a curious wild flicker of the imagination, she expected to find Archie on the threshold. She opened the door. It was her mother.

Mrs Ramsay came in with the air of one brushing away all Paula's trivialities in the face of reality. She didn't waste words, whatever she determined was at once immutable.

"We'll have to go, Paula. Can you be ready in half an hour?"

To Paula's blank congealed stare, she added impatiently, "The city's in the hands of the mob. Anything might happen. Pull yourself together, Paula. This is no time to be vague. Your brother has arranged everything. We are going to the station. He has the petrol. Everything. Tomorrow it might be impossible to leave. It's difficult now. They are commandeering all cars. But there is so much confusion we can be pretty sure of getting through. Your brother will be here with the car at midnight."

She had always that impersonal manner of speech. It steadied Paula. She felt a great surge of relief. After all, her world was holding. She was safe. She could play at anything she liked and still be safe. There was always a way out.

"You'll have to leave most of this, of course. Heaven knows what will happen to it. Clothes." She was already at the wardrobe. "Jewellery. Anything of real value. The rest will have to take its chance."

Over the packing the situation became natural, easy. The intent faces of the two women were reflected in the mirror. They were mother and daughter, closely akin, stamped out of the same metal. Paula felt obscurely grateful to this woman who had not changed. As they worked they spoke fragmentarily.

"Of course it is only for a time. It can't last. The army will be here in a few days and mop up the situation. The whole thing will collapse when they shoot that man. But things are bound to be bad for a time. All we have to do is to go to the station and live quietly till it blows over. Your brother has the place stocked up with everything we could need. Even if supplies are cut off we'll be all right. What about your jewellery, Paula?"

That had gone. Paula had given it to the cause in the days of her enthusiasm. Mrs Ramsay only shrugged. It wasn't the time to go into all that now.

"I wonder if your father would have been satisfied now. He used to make friends with the oddest people. Lift men and any sort of down-and-outs. Irresponsible. If our class had stood together this couldn't have happened. Hurry, Paula. Have you any tea? Any coffee? Bring it along. Leave everything, but lock up. We don't want to make it easy for them. Now, dear, he'll be waiting."

Paula pulled the door to after them. It clicked shut. She hadn't even the key. There was no returning and she felt nothing. In a side street a powerful car was waiting loaded with petrol for its long journey, lights hooded, ready to slip out of the open city in the darkness. In an hour they would be 40 miles away, by dawn they would be over the mountains and far out on the plains beyond. Escape, only escape mattered.

The next day the fruit of the printing presses was evident. Everywhere placards appeared, announcing immediate, compulsory evacuation of "women, children, the aged and infirm, and all others not required for duty." (The word "duty" fell curiously.) They might take with them food and clothing to a certain weight but no "capital goods." All private or individual attempts at evacuation were banned. At the end were the stern words, "No panic. No competition. All will be saved."

The city and suburbs were divided into districts and each district had its evacuation team. Every able-bodied man was registered for service and every able-bodied woman who volunteered. The rest were issued with cards giving the number of their vehicle, the place and hour of rendezvous. The evacuation would begin at dawn the next day.

All that day buses, ambulances, and heavy lorries rolled away from the city, south and west, carrying the inmates of the hospitals, asylums, homes, and taking the food stocks to depots along the roads. The electric trains were immobilised, but double-engined steam trains with long strings of carriages were put into commission to relieve the congestion of the roads. Men from the "disaffected" areas were set to hard mechanical jobs of loading. They were given no time for protest, no opportunity for sabotage. A hard ruthlessness informed every activity with its own impetus. From time to time there was a crackle of gunfire, a dissenter was eliminated, a rush stopped. It was no one's business. The police, those who hadn't come over, were securely locked in their own cells whence those "who had committed crimes against property" had been liberated.

The ritual of the city was broken. As when the cells of a honeycomb collapse under heat and the incoherent mass flows in confusion to waste, so in its last days was the broken city. It was as terrible to contemplate as a disaster in nature.

In a brief interval, when Ruth persuaded Sid to eat the meal she had procured and cooked, heaven knows how, she could no longer hold back the doubts that rode her exhausted mind.

"Sid," she said, "what is to become of them all?"

He was eating voraciously, abstractedly, staring blankly at the table.

"What?" he said, raising eyes red with sleeplessness in a haggard unshaven face.

"The refugees. What's going to happen to them all? Won't this mean terrible hardship and suffering, not only now but as far ahead as we can look?" The words were treason. She knew it and they were hard and square in her mouth. She had to speak them.

Sid answered her, as he might have answered a stranger who heckled him in a meeting. "What have they ever had but hardship and suffering? And those that haven't, those that have lived on velvet, it's time they began."

"They're so helpless," Ruth whispered.

"It's the slave life that has been forced on them that has made them helpless. There is only one cure for that. They must be forced to remake their own lives, and they will be. It will destroy some, they would have been destroyed anyway, if not quickly, then slowly, first the mind, then the heart, last the body."

He lifted his eyes, there was light in them again. "When the profit motive is taken away," he said, "society will be healthy again, men will work together and help one another, there will be security and happiness."

"You believe that?"

He looked at her for the first time. "Yes," he said quietly.

Ruth took away his empty plate. "In Spain," his voice followed her, "the people were more oppressed than they ever were here. They had nothing yet they made a state. Men are the same everywhere, only circumstances differ."

He must be tough, unflinching. Now they were committed to this course, they were all dependent on unflinching hardness to carry them through, and yet Ruth wanted him to regret a little, fear a little, placate whatever gods there were with a pinch of human uncertainty. How little she understood of the core of things after so long. She could only think of the helplessness of people; it weighed her down. The time for thinking of that had gone. Pity was a tool of the enemy. Dope.

Like a ship running aground Ruth's heart became fixed in despair. Above all things she feared the ruthless idealism that would destroy everything for . . . pie in the sky. No roads in the sky, nothing, and here was the urgent moment. Sid's least decision now had momentous consequences and he was lost in a dream of the distant future. She must think of today, struggle with today, but in front of her eyes there was a vacuum. Today was gone, destroyed like a missing rung in a ladder. She thought of the street where she had grown up and of her mother. Ally's helplessness extinguished any resentment. There was nothing she could do for her, there were no privileges to distribute, and if she brought her here to headquarters she would be worse off, not better. Ruth knew that she would stay beside Sid, and that that would be till the very end. She had not thought of personal danger before; now it rose suddenly in her, fear of the crashing burning city, the panic desire to run away. Fear stiffened her limbs. She stood holding the dirty plate before her, rigid; then it ebbed and she began to move again. Sid must never know that for a moment she had failed him.

In Carnation Street the suspense, the running to and fro, the helpless questioning the ignorant, the rumours, the panics, were ended by the arrival of the evacuation squad. Rapid and staccato as machine-gun fire, the orders were given, the numbered cards distributed. The street was shocked and acquiescent. Only Mrs Blan, the time-honoured leader, expostulated and tried to explain to the youth in a tin hat. "Dry up, Granma," said he, and moved on. She retired with ruffled plumage. The street would obey but the denizens owed it to their self-respect to gather in indignant knots on the pavement and protest to one another as soon as the squad had moved on.

The street was not what it used to be. It made a poor showing. Most of the young people had gone; newcomers were not of the street and took no part in its corporate life. There were not more than two or three children playing on the pavement these days, and they had been dumped on reluctant grandmothers by daughters with other work and other interests. The street was no longer prolific, its fertility had dried up. Of men, too, there were only a few oldsters, helpless creatures of no account according to their wives, who loudly proclaimed their ineptitude. The street was spineless, shabby, dirty, worn out.

Mrs Blan, Mrs Nelson, and Ally held themselves apart as the oldest inhabitants, the aristocracy, the Daughters of the Revolution. They met now in Mrs Blan's room, and as she brewed the inevitable cup of tea-substitute she fumed.

"The young tough," she said, "teaching his grandmother to suck eggs. All done up in fancy dress"—she referred thus witheringly to the tin hat—"If my old man had been alive he wouldn't of dared. Or Alby either." She impartially added the long departed bandsman. "He was a rare one for sticking up for his rights. An Englishman's home is his castle, be it never so humble, he'd say. He'd have given that young pipsqueak a clout he wouldn't have forgotten, speaking to me that way." No one knew whether she was speaking of the late Mr Blan or the bandsman, and it did not matter. The dead and the lost habitually took on the same featureless mask of virtue.

"Oh, well," sighed Mrs Nelson, "looks like it's settled for us whether we like it or not." Mrs Nelson hadn't ever picked up properly since Tony was killed in New Guinea, which Mrs Blan said was odd because when he was alive she hadn't seemed to set any special store by him. She lived on in the old place, but now she had only one room "and keeps it like a pigsty. Poor Ada's bone lazy, that's all that's the matter with her," Mrs Blan always added automatically.

"I've half a mind not to go," said Mrs Blan belligerently. "They can carry me out, that's what they can do."

Neither of the other ladies bit.

"Six pounds weight," Mrs Blan read from her evacuation card, "that's all we can take with us. And who's got scales that will weigh up to six pounds I'd like to know. I'll get even with them. I'll put every stich I've got on me back and *then* I'll carry my six pounds."

"You'll be roasted," said Mrs Nelson in her flat voice.

"I don't care if I am. You don't catch me leaving a stitch behind me."

They fell to discussing their clothes, for what with rationing and inflation, no one had had anything new in a very long time and each garment had a history known to all. The interests of this discussion quite detached their minds for the time being from the main issue.

Mrs Blan threw another small handful of tea-substitute into the pot and filled it up.

"Drink up, girls," she said cheerfully, pouring out the fourth cup all round. "Who knows?"

Ally hadn't been saying much because she had rashly promised that Ben would come and take them all to safety in his truck. Now it looked as if he wasn't coming. She hadn't seen him since the crisis developed. Ben was working twenty hours a day in transport, snatching the food and sleep he must have, whenever and wherever he could, knowing, like Ruth, that there was nothing over and above his duty, that he could offer to his family, that the new discipline began with himself.

Mrs Nelson had not forgotten. Her flat-footed voice trundled into the first pause. "Ruthie'll be coming to take *you* away, I suppose, Mrs Munster."

Ally flushed. "That one," she said, glad at least to let Ruth bear the blame instead of Ben. Ruth's name brought an awkward pause. Everyone knew that Ruth was living with Sid Warren and that she wasn't married to him. Public morality was affronted and every respectable matron had the right to sniff. But when Ruth appeared in the street, they had to admit that she "hadn't made much out of it" and that she didn't look like "one of them." Nor had Ally suffered the common affliction of having "a little bastard dumped on her." Ruth, they conceded, had always been a good kid, but not as smart as Wanda, who had gone the same way. Wanda had "made a proper job of it." The street hadn't seen her for months but they knew. Even if they drew their lips down, they respected Wanda for making a success in the world, "getting out of all this," and thought little of Ruth for getting so little, not even a wedding ring on her work-coarsened hand. Sid's stock had fluctuated in the street. First he had been the hero back from Spain, and then people had begun saying he was no better than a dirty Bolshie; when he fell foul of the police every one had been for Sid, because, of course, no one liked policemen. When times were good in the street and everyone was earning good money, they were patriotic and righteous and ready to think of Sid as a snake they had once nursed in their bosom, but when times were thin and fretful Sid again appeared in the light of a champion. Now that Sid, a local boy, was in power, those that remembered him remembered all they had done for him and actively looked to him for some return. Mrs Nelson was all too ready to go off into a garrulous account of how she used to mend his socks when he was their lodger, finishing on the tearful note, "And he thought the world of my Tony."

Mrs Blan cut her short. "Looks like we'll have to take care of ourselves, no one else is going to. It's my bits and pieces I'm thinking of." She looked round at the old dark shabby furniture with which her room was stuffed. "I saw that young twerp this morning taking an eyeful, I don't trust them. Getting us out so they can loot the place, I shouldn't wonder. They won't find much here. I'll take the hatchet to mine before I go, see if I don't?"

"No dirty Jap or Bolshie's going to get my maple suite," cried Ally, "I'll do it in with my own hands."

"I don't care who gets my bit of junk," said Mrs Nelson, "it isn't worth nothink."

"It's the principle," said Mrs Blan; "don't you leave as much as a pin for them. I may be old but I've got spirit."

"Yes, you have," said Ally.

"I have," reiterated Mrs Blan with dignity.

She began telling them the history of every article in the room, gathering eloquence as she went along . . . "and my old man won that in an art union. 'Here you are, mother,' he said, 'it'll be something to pawn.' A great man for his joke, he was, a good man if ever there was one. And that vawse Alby gave me for my birthday. 'Go along with you,' I said, 'I'm too old to have birthdays.' And he started right in quoting poitry, he was that well educated. And this poor Glad had in her home, she brought it with her when she came back and never took it again, you can see little Freddy's teethmarks in it. . . ."

Her voice rose and fell. Ally was reminded of a wake. Mrs Blan was keening her possessions. It went for them all. They were mildly intoxicated with tea and emotion.

"Ah," sighed Mrs Blan, "we're three poor widows, three poor old helpless widows."

Through all the muffling sentiment Ally felt the thrust. She had never thought of herself as old, had always looked up to Mrs Blan as someone much older than herself. Although she was always sorry for herself she had never thought of herself as old. In her own eyes she had remained a young woman, perennially young, for she was still waiting for something to turn up, waiting for her spring. She could not envisage the injustice of growing old when she'd had nothing, when her whole life had been a disappointment and a betrayal. It couldn't be nearly over, it couldn't be. But she saw her face in the small mirror of Mrs Blan's chiffonnier, the wispy fair hair gone grey, face sagging, anxious, colourless, a dreary old woman's face floating on the glass in the hot, darkish room. Tears more of shock than of grief welled from her eyes.

"Never say die," cried Mrs Blan for her benefit.

"Well, I better git," said Mrs Nelson, heaving herself up. And she nearly added, as she had so many times before, "My old man'll be home soon and he'll go to market if his dinner isn't ready."

None of them grasped the change that was upon them. They went automatically towards it, that was all.

No sooner had she gone than Mrs Nelson poked her head in at the door again, her face a crumpled mask of comical despair.

"What about the O.A.P.?" she asked. "Will we still get it?"

"Sure," said Mrs Blan, "sure. There's got to be a government, hasn't there? And if there's a government there's an O.A.P. Think of the votes."

But she was visibly shaken. The idea that her old age pension might stop had clearly never occurred to her. Even the triumph of driving Mrs Nelson out into the open at last was lost in this new anxiety. Both of them had been collecting the old age pension for years, but Mrs Nelson had never admitted it. On pension days, she'd be peeping out of her window to see when Mrs Blan went to the post-office and not till she was safe home again would Mrs Nelson, shopping basket on arm, venture out. Sometimes to tease her, Mrs Blan would postpone going until almost the last moment, savouring the anxiety of the old lady behind the curtain with complacent malice. The old age pension was the one sure haven. Life without it was unthinkable. Mrs Nelson had dropped a bomb.

Mrs Blan and Ally sat on silent, each thinking her own thoughts. At last Mrs Blan said heavily: "You'll be all right, you've got your £200 . . . unless . . ."

They looked at one another. Ally's eyes widened. "Unless . . ." she thought. If she hadn't found a way to get her £200 when everything was working, she wasn't likely to get it now. She saw that Mrs Blan thought the same. She had lost forever the prestige of her £200.

The day was hot, heavy, weighted down with its colossal task, slow-moving for all its urgency. It was furious, but its fury was calculating. Everything was done in the interests of destruction. The sky was white with heat, a hot wind was rising, the weather was climacteric. Men's minds were climacteric. They lusted after the moment when they could begin to tear down the fabric of a society they hated. Anger, mounting through years of bitterness and frustration, turning at last into this blind alley, achieved a force that swung thousands to its purpose. At last, at last, time was informed with purpose. It was the least common purpose. The one basis on which all the tormented and dispossessed could meet. The destruction of the city fulfilled a poisoned need.

For Sid Warren, and for perhaps a few others, the burning of Sydney was not the blind decision of a lust, it came out of hard reasoning. It was the overthrow of the golden calf. The city was the symbol of greed and profit, every stone of it was tainted; only by its utter overthrow could men free themselves from it, its numbing delights and illusory prizes. It was the logical conclusion of a passionate unified mind. For the moment his power rested on giving the people what they wanted, shaping their chaotic desires, inspiring the toughness to carry them out. Later it would rest on their helplessness. He knew that many must die and many more must suffer, but he believed, with a hard impacted belief, that only so could the tide of history be turned. These last days were pivotal, he believed that they would shake the world with the first grand negation of greed, the act of primary anarchy that must prelude reconstruction, but he was not himself swept away. Hour by tireless hour he hacked his way through the details of problems. He was accessible to all, and many strange fish, the wilfully articulate, came to the surface.

As he walked into his headquarters, an elderly woman waylaid him. She had been waiting with stony patience for hours. Her hair was strained back from her lumpy forehead and pinned in a tight bun at the back of her head. Her features were pinched, small, sour, and obstinate. Her thin body was as hard and purposeful as a gimlet. She was dressed in a clean white blouse, a dark skirt, and a black hat at least ten years old, perched high on her head. She had not abated her style one jot to the emergencies of the times.

*"I know her," said Ord delighted. "She gave Bowie a white feather."*
*"That's the one," said Knarf, equally delighted.*

She stood accusingly in front of Sid and asked, "What are you going to do about the animals?"

"What animals?"

"The animals in the zoo. What's to become of them? It's not their fault we've come to such a pretty pass. They're innocent and I can't say the same for any man."

"She's mad," said one of Sid's companions roughly, but Sid silenced him. "It's a problem," he said. "Have you any solution?"

But she hadn't. She stood there with clenched hands, her face taut with passion. "You took away their liberty, you shut them up in cages, and now you're going to leave them to die. Starving in their cages, devouring one another, going mad, dying slowly. No one caring."

"They will be loosed," he reassured her. "The cages will be opened at the last."

She darted a suspicious glance at him, quick, flickering like an adder, but apparently she was satisfied. "It is not so bad if they have their freedom. Some will be saved. But what will they eat?"

"People," said Sid, with his sudden grin, shouldering past her to the stairs.

Another deputation was on its way. From the University this time. The old men of the professorial staff—the young ones had been combed out long ago—when the news of the city's imminent destruction broke on them, had gathered there like blood returning to the heart, a heart that would now no longer beat. The Chancellor, a man long used to authority, to whom the University was the child of his old age, convened the Senate and it sat for half a day, considering how they could save the University from the day of judgment. The accustomed surroundings and the quiet lulled them. The Challis Professor of History was inclined to take the long view. Moral Philosophy found parallels in the past, lines of thought, beautifully matched, that never met. It was the Dean of the Faculty of Law who galvanized the meeting into life. With the last spurt of his old forensic fire, he outlined the situation and called them to forsake words for action. On them and the action they must now take depended the very existence of their Alma Mater. He depicted with very real emotion the effect that the destruction of the University would have on the whole community. He spoke of dreaming spires, of "that other edifice not built with hands," of dark days ahead when the torch of learning would be more than ever needed. The University was above politics. What had war or revolution to do with old men, old stones, old books, and the intangible tradition of the place. . . . The Chancellor, moved, rose and thanked them. In truth, they must steel themselves. He knew that he spoke for them all as he spoke for himself, when he said that no sacrifice would be too great. . . . But what sacrifice? They would make it, yes, but what could they do? The argument went on, strophe and antistrophe.

The Professor sat back in a pose unconsciously academic, his hands folded in the sleeves of his gown. He knew that they wasted their time. He was the eternal onlooker, apprehending everything, doing nothing. He was complete in the asepsis of detachment. He was even aware of his own mouth curved in an ironic smile, not a new smile for today, but an old one that had long ago moulded his flesh till his face would scarcely be dressed without it. He was collecting this discussion as he had collected many other splendid rarities that only he, with his acid, twisted connoisseurship, would prize. But his mind slipped away from it. He became aware of the quiet outside. It was too quiet, it pressed on the small diamond panes of the windows. Except for themselves the place was quite empty. The University on its hill, with its park, its pleasaunces, its great quadrangle, its trees and monuments, rose like a sunny, silent oasis out of an encircling sea of slums, the streets and lanes and packed houses whence came the strength of this revolt. Turbid and purposeful life flowed round it, leaving it untouched. It was so quiet you could hear time running out like sand.

"He has the power for the moment," said the Chancellor, "and so we must go to this man, Sidney Warren. The eternal must go to the ephemeral. We must be realists, we must not shrink, we must humble ourselves." He took little gulps of breath between his sentences. . . . Everything was done decently and in order. Motions were proposed, seconded, discussed, and voted upon. A plan emerged and would be put into execution at once. It was a very simple expedient to have been so pompously evolved. The Senate in its robes and with its insignia would go in procession to this Attila of the working classes to beg the life of the University. Such voluntary self-humiliation should be a sacrifice big enough to purchase anything. They even felt, while they were still in their enclosed world, as if they were leaving an ample margin. They believed that if the University were spared now, it could live through the stormy and doubtful days ahead like a seed safe in its hard woody shell until conditions were favourable for germination. It would be the seed of a new era and they, the men of learning, by virtue of it would survive.

The Chancellor put on his robes, they were hot and heavy. Over their tattered gowns the professors assumed their hoods like yokes, "gaudy profs in reds and yellows." The Gentleman Bedell was not available—he was a prisoner of war somewhere or other—but the Yeoman Bedell was. They called him from his inconvenient, dark, stony quarters where he was making preparations for flight. He did not want to come, but habit was too strong for him. He obeyed, abandoning his fat invalid wife, her mouth constantly ajar to suck in the thin pap of his reassurance; the trunk into which he had just packed the marble presentation clock wrapped in his winter woollens, his very hope of salvation. He put on his rusty gown, like a verger's, and took his staff of office.

The procession formed. The Parramatta Road was impracticable. It was running a banker with traffic going west. They went by Cleveland Street and Regent Street, and so by back ways down into the city. Everywhere they saw the signs of disintegration, planned and haphazard. In the streets were people, the sort of people they had never seen before. The birds in the bush have their beats; while they seem as free as air, they fly according to pattern. So the people in the city have their beats, conditioned by their work, their circumstances, the grooves of habit in their minds. Now the grooves were broken, categories torn apart, people spilled indiscriminately upon the streets, driven by new strong tides. This Sydney looked like a foreign city, so much of what had been tacitly accepted was already gone.

It was hot and heavy going and it was a long way. The rising wind that was to fan the flames of the city tore at their academics so that they seemed to wade through dust, hot sunlight, and black alpaca. A job lot, thought the Professor. Old men in fancy dress. But he went with them, knowing the futility of it all. It was his world, even if he rejected it. Neither the future nor the truth lay with him, but it didn't lie with the momentary conquerors of the city either. It was put away out of reach, in an abstraction, treasure hidden in a safe deposit, a socialism unsoiled by hands. It could wait, as it had waited through all the centuries.

The procession attracted no attention. People had other preoccupations. Its members had nothing to say to one another, each had his own thoughts, his own reservations. The Professor let his mind swing: the austere quadrangle, four stone walls brimmed with light, students loitering in the arcades, strange creatures, as remote as Renan's cat; the callowness of teachers, and taught, with its pockets of profound learning and its kingfisher flashes of youth; the Fisher Library in the late afternoon, the narrow windows in the high ceiling, one orange, one purple, making coloured threads of light in the tranquillity; the enmities, the solidarity, the ponderous jokes; men growing older indefinitely, dislodged so rarely by death, so tardily by retirement; walking past the Union, the smell of green things growing in the sun, the click of billiard balls—that was leisure; the smell of ether as you passed the laboratories, the museum smell, the book smell, the stone smell—that was detachment; preparation—prepare, go back, prepare again, a cycle so homely, so safe. The Professor recalled one particular morning when there had been a conferring of degrees, this same procession winding into the Great Hall, the same but so different, in its right context there, grave with dignity . . . outside the thick sweet autumn morning, the city lost in mist, the world beginning only a hundred yards away, trees that Corot might have seen, sunshine beating on the old stones till they were warm and receptive; and the carillon pouring out its music, flying aerial music of captive bells, frail, triumphant, crystalline, soaking into the stones till they lived, vibration within reverberation, bevelled sound, world held englobed in music as if it swung, towers and all in a great bubble . . . until a shamed emotion caught at his throat and he thought like any dotard, "Youth, ah Youth. . . ." He could remember that day and his own emotion with irony. How security sanctifies itself!

This was to be a professor, a man of learning: to walk through the city in weariness and discomfort in this very odd procession, to know it is useless and absurd but to do it, to be able at such a time to roll on the tongue the savour of a world as lost as Tyre. The freedom of the human spirit consisted in seeing through all you did and thought. The last feat of civilisation was to destroy your sanctions and, since there is no reality, to live within the most pleasing artificiality.

Soon, he thought, I'll begin to feel; something or other will touch me and it will be real. Like a man who, shovelling away the rubble of a wrecked building, comes on a live wire. The Professor looked about him and it was as if he saw familiar buildings for the first time. They were changed, as if buildings could go gaunt when their accustomed life left them. It was a phenomenon that he would have liked to hold until he was less tired and could examine it. Nothing would wait now. Nothing would stand still, respectfully, to be investigated and tabulated any more.

Headquarters occupied a building that had formerly been an insurance office. It swarmed with activity, an activity so integrated that it showed no break and made no provision for the extraneous. Certainly there was no enquiry office. By dint of speaking to anyone who would listen, the deputation achieved the doubtful privilege of waiting. As they waited, something oozed out of them. As a body they began to fall apart.

People passed in and out, most of them in a hurry, many of them eating. No one else waited. The Professor felt a rather ridiculous surprise. He had thought that the destruction of the city would be something like the fall of the Bastille. Improvisation in a frenzy. It was not. It was like a business undertaking, rough and ready perhaps, but still recognisable. It required typists and telephones, lists and files, heaven knows what. A thought brought the sardonic twist back to the Professor's lips. Would they become so wrapped up in their organization that they wouldn't be able to bring themselves to destroy it and so would spare the city?

At last a man came over to them and with no more than a jerk of the head indicated that they could go into the presence. It was the sort of room they all knew, the grace and proportion that money can buy, the big bland windows of a clear conscience. On the flat desktop a large and detailed map of the city was nailed, on it stood a pannikin of tea and an old cracked plate piled with tomatoes. On the floor around the desk a miscellany of objects had been dumped, a kitbag and a service rifle among them. There was an air of departure in the room.

The man himself sprawled at the desk. The Professor studied him with curiosity. Rough looking. Not tall but broad shouldered, with obstinate lines, thick skull, head you could use for a battering ram, strong square hands. At the other table with the telephone a girl was working. That would be his woman, always beside him, people said. Not what you would expect, fair, as completely without artifice as the man, her face marked as much by discipline as by strain, rather a fine face when you came to look at it, courageous without knowing it. She made the man seem more formidable, suggested in him a greater subtlety than you would at first suspect. No sense of theatre in either of them, no sense of momentous action. Odd—but then, the Professor added to himself, that's only because I don't believe in it as they do. It's as real to them, this business of destroying the city, as bread and meat. He felt events come nearer.

Sid Warren barely changed his position, barely looked up. He didn't offer the delegation seats. Perhaps there wasn't time, perhaps it wasn't a thing that ever occurred to him.

"What do you want?"

The Chancellor began to speak his piece. The words fell thin and dead, they died away like snowflakes in thin air. Places change the complexion of arguments, thought the Professor, not listening to the words but feeling their full impact. The whole scene was dull, neutral, apathetic. They drooped under the fatigue of their long walk and the burden of their academic robes. Sid's fist, crashing down on the table, made them all jump ludicrously. For the first time he turned his face to them, his eyes blazing. He shouted, "You've had your chance. Centuries of it. What does education, your sort of education, mean to anyone but the over-privileged few? It's just another gadget for keeping the common man in his place and letting the silvertails through into the goldrush. You're bloody damn profiteers, just like all the rest. You say the University is part of the common heritage, do you? You've had your chance, why didn't you make it that way? You've been on top, why didn't you make a decent world men could live in, with your wonderful education? You talk about advantages. You've had them. What did you do with them? That's all over now. You're sacked. See? People like you aren't going to have charge of education when there is any. We'll burn down your precious University and everything in it because if we leave it there, or you there, the past will breed again from you. You're not worth that," he made a sudden gesture, expressive and obscene. "Get out. You're just like any other mob of pot-bellied old men now. See how you get on without your bloody privileges. Show us how clever you are."

The Chancellor was halfway to the door, leading out his team with tremulous dignity.

"Get out. Get out. Get out," like a volley of stones.

Down in the street in the hot sun, in the rising wind, their bodies that yesterday had been well fed were papery. At last they believed in the destruction of the city.

Sid sat slumped in his chair, his chin on his breast, in an attitude that might have been profound exhaustion or one of those lacunae of despair in which the bravest and the most hardened are sometimes temporarily lost.

Ruth, her face warmed by tenderness, touched his arm.

"You're tired out, Sid. Why'd you bother to see them? They don't amount to anything."

He raised his head and his bright fierce impersonal glance passed over her. There was such naked ruthless triumph in his face that she recoiled. A shutter had been swung open.

"Not see them? Like hell I'd see them. It's not enough to show 'em. I've got to tell 'em. Bugger them."

He'd had a great moment and she did not even recognize it.

By mutual consent and almost wordlessly the deputation broke up. Each man's mind was now intent on his own affairs. Their corporate life was ended. The Professor at least was not far from his club where he lived. As he walked the couple of blocks, he paused to read the proclamations pasted on the walls. The printing presses had been busy. The streets appeared ticketed as if the buildings were up for auction. Most of them were directions for evacuation. Everywhere were the big No Looting signs. Men and women might carry away with them only "the means of life," food, clothing, and a specified list of "articles of necessity," a scanty list beginning with cooking pots and drinking vessels and ending with perambulators. Nothing of "capital value" was to be taken out. "The Capitalist regime has ended." There was order in it all, and, too, the Professor conceded, a certain idealism. Childish, perhaps, but there.

He was very tired, too tired to take any further interest. He would go into his club and rest. He would relax for an hour, have a drink and something to eat, stretch himself out on one of the cool leather lounges in the high-ceilinged tranquil smoking-room where he had placidly digested so many good dinners. Afterwards he would have to bestir himself. He would go south, not west. His mind ran on old unchanging places, Jamberoo in the valley between mountain and sea, Picton among its smooth hills, Sutton Forest with its old houses and bands of dark fir trees. . . . First he would rest. The city would not sleep again, he thought.

He entered his club. The place was desolate. There was luggage in the vestibule, but the porter was no longer there, no one was there. The club servants had gone. The discreet and tranquil smoking-room was in chaos, hangings torn down, upholstery ripped, an obscene epithet scrawled across the pale wall in what looked like treacle. There was not a bottle left in the bar or a crumb of food in the larder. It had been handed out to the people in the street an hour ago. The Professor went to his room, it was as he had left it that morning, the bed unmade, but his personal belongings untouched. Others had not fared so well. In one room the contents of wardrobe and chest had been torn into strips and piled in the centre of the room and a bottle of hair oil poured on the heap. An effort had even been made to set fire to a pile of books, but they were barely charred. Only long-accumulated malice could account for it. This was the heaviest blow that the Professor had sustained yet. In some vague way he had always thought of the club servants as "loyal", many of them had been there for years. They were "privileged," they were "faithful." "Service" had always been a specialty of the place, "something no money can buy," but only money had bought it. Only that morning breakfast had been served as usual, the same attentions, the same readiness. The rot had set in suddenly. These men, most of them, the Professor was shocked to remember, old men, had realised that there was no longer anything to gain from servility, and their true selves had appeared. How blandly he and his friends had taken it for granted that they were served out of good will. He felt violently repelled, sickeningly humiliated. His detachment was punctured. He had been betrayed on his unsuspecting, unarmoured side, and there was neither answer nor redress.

The Professor went back to his room. There did not seem to be anyone else in the Club. He too wanted to leave the place but could think of nowhere to go. He could not walk the streets, he was too tired. His friends were scattered and he did not imagine that any of them in this crisis would have time for him. His human relations had always been too suave, too detached, to have meaning in any but an ordered world. He was hungry, but there was no prospect of food. He found a few biscuits and put a small piece into his trembling mouth but could eat it only with difficulty. He lay down on his unmade bed. He would rest a little while and then he would go. He would have to go. Go, an intransitive verb. Go. But where? It no longer seemed easy or even possible. He looked at the flecks of light on the ceiling that were the same as ever. Silence pressed like thumbs into his ears but was no longer fine drawn or sheltering. He lay with twitching limbs trying to make of exhaustion a substitute for peace and slowly in the chaos his mind found a straw to grasp. He knew what he would do. After all, was there much worth saving here? He would take a token of the world he had once loved and go. He could not help himself any more, there was nothing to struggle for. Surely the current would carry him.

There was no break between the days, no night. Hatred and excitement acted like strong drugs. Men didn't tire, they didn't sleep. There was so much to do. A city is not sacrificed lightly or easily. It is a specialist's job. It needs fire and dynamite. All sorts of taboos had to be torn down too. People had to learn how to destroy. They learned very quickly. Sid had sent out an order, "No smoke must rise today." On his mind and on the minds of all those who thought at all, the fear that they might be stopped before they had finished their job, pressed, closing them in, driving them to frantic effort. The army might march in, the bombers might fly over, the fleet might bombard them. Their double shield was the invading army's certainty of its own strength, and the will of its masters to save the golden city intact. This wasn't war, this was protective action. Humanity and tolerance were in its mealy mouth.

All through the feverish day and night destruction was being prepared. The University "fell" without any resistance. One man was seen hurrying across the park, but what was one man? No one followed him. A few of the servants were waiting, obsequious to new masters, with the keys. Their help was accepted coldly. This job belonged to troops from the surrounding slums. Their vengeance was quite impersonal. None of them had ever set foot in the precincts before.

In the Fisher Library the furniture was broken up, the panelling ripped down, a bonfire was built in the reading room and books piled upon it. But there were books and more books in the stacks of steel, glass, and stone. "Gorblimey," said the captain. Books were the very devil to burn. In the quadrangle they built another great bonfire, learning at the stake, tomorrow's auto-da-fé, and out of an old gown and mortar board and sundry trifles they made a guy to sit on the top of it. In the Great Hall they built another bonfire with the Joseph tapestry, soaked in kerosene, draped over it. Plaster casts of the wise dead hurtled through diamond panel windows to crash heavily on the flags. In the laboratories they smashed and smashed and smashed apparatus of whose use they had no inkling. The ink-stained desks of the lecture rooms they viewed with approval. They'd burn. The solid stones of the buildings abashed them a little, but a few sticks of dynamite would settle them. They laid their incendiary trails preparing tomorrow's fireworks. Nothing that they destroyed had any meaning for them. It was a festival, an orgy, and as the night drew on the fun grew faster. They broke into the Medical School and into the dissecting rooms and morbid museums, and, discovering there the bodies and specimens, formed themselves into a dancing procession. Carrying arms, legs, and strange, terrible things in bottles, shouting, laughing, swinging torches, they danced in a wild follow-my-leader parade, a new carmagnole, at last laying their grizzly offerings at the foot of the mock god in the quadrangle and pouring the methylated spirits as a libation on the bonfire. Half-grown boys and girls from the slums joined the saturnalia and discovering the long silent carillon, tugged the ropes and thumped the pedals, so that the demoniac jangle of bells was added to the riot, like oil to fire. Of all the shows, the University was the best. There were a number of casualties from flying glass, falling stones, fumes, and corrosives, but no one cared, no one put any brake on the fun.

In other places, the festival was not so spontaneous nor so happy. At the Public Library a few men with no politics but a fanatic love for books tried to defend the building. They had firearms and they knew the intricacies of the building. They lay in the galleries and from prepared positions behind ramparts of books sniped the mob that came in to make a bonfire. They had to be mopped up, one by one. Armed men were chasing one another through the building, firing round the stacks, bolting up and down unexpected staircases, ambushing one another. The crowd withdrew to a safe distance and watched. It was like those half comic, half thrilling chases they were accustomed to see at the movies, the only trouble was that they couldn't see. It all went on inside with no lighting and no camera man. They could only hear the shots, and once, when two men appeared on the roof in a running fight and plunged together to the asphalt below, the crowd uttered a long sigh of absorbed appreciation. It was quite a bloody affair. About twenty men died for the books, and there were several wounded still lying in their little strongholds when the place was finally fired. It availed nothing, of course, only wetted with blood the sacrificial day.

All day the Art Gallery stood open and unattended. People flocked in. It was truly theirs now. For some reason they wanted to see that which was going to be destroyed, just as they would have visited the scene of a murder. But they only stared. At one stage things brightened up. A maniac began slashing the nudes. First he would dance obscenely in front of the picture and then he would slash it very particularly with a butcher's knife. He was terribly serious. The crowd followed him guffawing.

The city was changing fast. In the last furious hours life was rechannelled. As night came on the change was more strongly marked. The electricity supply failed. Under the wasting moon and the hot westerly the skyline showed like a mouthful of broken, blackened teeth. Streets were runnels of darkness, facades nacreous with windows like empty sockets. Flares and torches blazed unnaturally where men still worked. The incidence of light and shadow were utterly changed, building a new fantastic city.

The Botanic Gardens, which for the first time were not closed at sundown, became a grove of Aphrodite. In the darkness of the bushes, on the lawns in the elusive moonlight, lovers sought and found one another. Many had never seen each other by daylight. For this hour they were sufficient to one another, they were nothing but man and woman, they were oblivious of all the other couples. Live and let love. Trees threshed the sky, shadows fleered and struggled on the grass. Up from the earth there came confused and inarticulate cries. The smell of sap and crushed vegetation was carried on the dusty wind. In all the flux only the statues, the fountains, the pagodas, stood firm. It was the black market of love.

Under the black figtrees of the Domain it was the same, and in every park and open space. It was life flaring up in the face of death. There was nothing new under the moon that night in Sydney. The city was reverting to ancient patterns, her people unconsciously bent themselves to old rhythms and were borne, unknowingly, on elemental tides.

In thousands of homes women clung to one another, weeping with fear, shock, grief, hushed their children frightened by the sense of danger in the air, turned over their possessions in a frenzy of doubt and choice, went about the accustomed routine of their lives in a last dumb effort to conceal disaster from themselves. Stubs of candle threw great threatening shadows on walls and played dumb crambo. Old people declared that they would not leave their homes, that nobody could force them, that they would die if necessary, but they would not go. Others were attacked by claustrophobia, feared the old shell that their hopes had already discarded, panted to be on the road and away from the fear and menace of the city. They fretted and worried over everything under the sun, their children, their ailments, their pets, their plants, their diets, their money, their clothes, their chastity, their future, the skeletons in their cupboards, their insurance, their debts, their ration books. The night Troy fell must have been much the same.

Gwen was one of the frightened ones. She crouched in her bed-sitting-room, three floors up in the narrow old terrace house off Taylor Square where she lived. It was not the same room where she had last seen Harry, but it was indistinguishable from it. She was frightened because there was no light, because she was alone. She did not know how it had happened. The situation had rushed at her suddenly like a stereoscopic film. She had waked up and found the world crumbling. Only yesterday it seemed there had been plenty of pals and plenty of parties, now everyone had disappeared. And it was dark. When she struck a match strange shapes leaped out at her. She hadn't known they were in her room. There were unusual noises in the street below, unusual silences. She was cold despite the heat. Being cold frightened her. She'd been drinking and now the drink had left her. Properly washed up. Dumped. There was a bottle of whisky still in the wardrobe. It took her all her resolution to cross the room to get it. She'd forgotten where the furniture was. When she bumped into something her heart nearly choked her. Her own stealthy movements brought her to the edge of open panic. Only a need stronger even than fear sent her looking for the wardrobe. She found it at last, her hands slipped over the cold mirror, fumbled among the stale-smelling garments, found the smooth nuggety bottle. Black market whisky, raw, fierce, mortal. Joe had given it to her. He was drunk, of course. Only time he was generous was when he was drunk. She'd earned it. She felt better now she had the bottle in her hands. She found the washstand quite easily, almost without thinking about it, the jug of water, the glass. She poured out a good stiff one and drank it, shuddering. The room disentangled itself a bit then. She picked out the window, the bed, the cupboard. She had another. It didn't alter the fact that she was alone, deserted. She'd been so good to them too. She wept and spilled some whisky. She tried to make plans but they broke down. For a long time she thought at random, remembered all sorts of things that had happened to her and that she had temporarily forgotten. She was rather happy in a poetic melancholy way, but sorry for herself. She had never had a chance. A rotten deal. Ever since she was a kid, no bigger than. . . . Vaguely she caressed the bottle, holding it like a child in her arms and rocking to and fro. No mother. A motherless girl, alone in the world. Then there was a man. There always was, wasn't there? Harry. Old enough to be her father, and he'd taken advantage of her innocence all right. They were all the same. She only remembered him because he was the first. It was the first that counted, that's what every one said. If it hadn't been for Harry she'd have been a good girl now, she'd have had a husband and children and a house, she wouldn't be alone. But she'd never had a chance. That let her out. She'd had lots of pals, but pals weren't any good. Where was everybody? Now she felt sick and frightened again. A new sort of fear this time. It had no shape, she was part of it herself. Let it cover her. You went in deeper and deeper till you were safe. You crept into the earth. But the earth was a long long way away. Three floors down and then there was the asphalt. Got to hide somewhere, she thought. Air raid. She crawled to the bed dragging the bottle with her. She got under the bed. There was dust, fluff, and an old shoe there. She drank awkwardly, with difficulty, but she managed it. This was better. The world was tight round her again, she had stopped that awful feeling of slipping in a vacuum. Didn't so much matter about being alone because there wasn't room for anyone else, was there? She breathed dust heavily, she snored, then she stopped snoring. She had achieved Nirvana. She was completely out to it. There was no longer fear in the room for there was no consciousness to apprehend it.

In dry hot brains there was no sleep. For men who had only NOW between a stifled past and a nebulous future, there could be no rest nor pause.

There was some looting, although the provisional committee, austere as new revolutionary governments always are, had forbidden it. Men helped themselves to all sorts of queer and useless objects just to reassure themselves that they were getting a dividend out of the new order, out of automatic greed, or just, you might say, for company in the crumbling world. Wine cellars, when they could be found, were cracked open from more rational and immediate motives. Timmy Andrews struck it lucky. He and a couple of cobbers unearthed a very fine well-furnished cellar, and not black market stuff either. They had an idea where to look and they chose a quiet time when competition would be at its lowest ebb. The two cobbers proceeded without art to get drunk on whatever came handy. Not so Timmy. He selected carefully and with no more than an occasional refresher made provision for the future. He sowed the neighbourhood with bottles, finding hiding places for them with the ingenuity of a child. The streets after all were more his home than any house could be, hoardings were as good as walls to him, alleys as private as passages, drains and ditches as good as cupboards.

"Always wanted to have a lot of something," he explained. "Never did. Now I have. Lots and lots and lots. And it's something useful."

It was two o'clock in the morning. The neighbourhood was deserted in favour of activity elsewhere. From the distance there came a low menacing sustained din the like of which rises from no sane or living city, but the environs were quiet as a dead bird. Only the wine merchant's sign creaked in the unremitting wind.

Timmy felt grand. He was at the very top of his form. The revolution had come. He was on the crest of it. As individual and as political man he was fulfilled. He mellowed to the point of making a political speech. It made sense; drunk or sober his views were the same, for they were as much a part of him as his skin and bones. When his sleeping companions did not respond he wiped them off the slate. "The slave mentality," he said loudly and distinctly.

He drank again, a dozen full-throated swallows of living glowing ichor. He had the gift, miraculous, almost unique, of sustaining his drunkenness at the pitch of maximum felicity. He drank like an artist. Only paucity and inferiority of supplies had ever hampered him in the past. Dawn found him still in a state of perfect spiritual and emotional equilibrium. He watched the streets swing into being. He missed something. He reflected. At last he said softly to himself. "No milkman. No trams. No buses. No work. No sleep. No tomorrow. No bourgeois morality. A lot of nothing." He tried to spread his arms wide, but there was a bottle in each hand. He took a drink out of the left-hand bottle. He added softly, incongruously, but not sadly, "I won't be here long but while I am I'll live like a lord." He drank from the right-hand bottle.

This was the day of the great hegira. The pouring forth of the people. It was hard to believe there were so many people in the city, just as it is hard to believe there can be so much blood in a human body when it spurts forth. Thousands had already left, snatching at any foothold on the conveyances that had poured along the western roads in the last few days. But the great bulk remained. The trains went out in steady succession jammed to their roofs, their last journey. By dawn the roads west and south had begun to move. There were all the hitches and troubles usual to such an occasion, people who had lost their evacuation cards and forgotten the number of their vehicle, who failed to arrive or came late, who tried to smuggle out prohibited articles and resisted when these were taken from them and thrown upon the wayside fires that burned for this purpose, children who strayed and got lost, women who fainted and old people who collapsed. All these were dealt with quickly and ruthlessly because that was the only way. The tragic part was that families were being torn apart, the men staying, the women and children going, and in the formless future there was no means of reuniting them. Only a tithe of the refugees realised this. For the most part they went quietly, calmly, making the best of things, helping one another, trusting.

Sometimes they got a laugh. There was the middle-aged woman with a baby and the man with a broken arm, for instance. She was a stout strong woman, but she bent under the weight of the baby swathed in shawls despite the heat. The guard, a family man, didn't like the shape of the baby. He tried to pull aside the shawl. The woman resisted. "Arnie," she yelped.

The man pulled harder, the sagging shawl gave way, a medley of small tins and packets fell to the ground. As he kicked at them, some burst open. They contained money, jewellery, securities. "So that's your little game," shouted the guard. The woman was scarlet with rage, not shame, the man's face had gone a dirty white with apprehension. The crowd laughed, even people who hadn't rightly seen what happened laughed and stood to stare.

"I suppose that's a fake, too," said the guard, roughly tearing the sling from Arnie's arm. But it was genuinely broken, for the safe, the precious safe, that had been their child, had fallen on Arnie's arm as he was levering it out of its niche for burial in a safe place. He screamed with pain and Chris burst into a flood of shrill curses.

"Keep moving," yelled the guard, as two of his offsiders hauled the culprits away. The valuables were scattered by many feet, the jewellery ground into the pavement. None dared pick them up.

"Don't amount to a bunch of curses, not now," an old man muttered, not knowing himself whether he was triumphant or bitter.

All the incidents were not amusing. There was the old man and his book. The people who saw that remembered it afterwards. It smouldered in their minds, they were hurt and ashamed because of it. He was haggard and dirty, but it was easy to imgine that he had not always been like that. As recently as twenty-four hours ago, he might have been a dapper elderly gentleman with polished speech and a tailored suit. He had a large roughly wrapped package held to his chest, no other luggage.

"What you got there?" the guard asked him as he checked his card.

"A book," said the old man.

"A book?" asked the guard, who thought of such things only in connection with the racecourse. "Show it here."

"Not exactly a book, but I thought that is what you'd call it. It's a manuscript." With trembling fingers he opened the package while the man waited impatiently.

For a moment the pages glowed in their gold, vermilion, and blue, between their dusky covers.

"I saved it from the University library," the old man explained.

"Loot," said the guard.

"It's twelfth century. A beautiful example. It's priceless." The old man said in a soft voice as if he spoke of a sleeping child.

"Capital goods," said the guard and tossed the manuscript into the fire where the ancient pages ignited at once.

A hoarse terrible cry rose from the old man as if it were he who burned.

He would have snatched it, burning, out of the flames if he had not been held. He fought for an instant with long vanished strength and went limp. The tears were running down his cheeks. He turned blindly, dumbly, and tried to go back the way he had come.

The guard was after him. "You can't go back. You're evacuated, see? Move along now. Hi," he called to a group with the same number, "take him along."

"Poor old bugger," one said for all, "why couldn't they let him keep it? Wouldn't do no one any harm."

A little hunchback who used to sell him tobacco recognised him. "He's a professor up at the University," he explained.

A girl took the old man's arms. "Come on, pop," she said kindly. "We'll look after you," and so she led him away.

The guard, feeling himself unpopular, shouted truculently to everyone to keep moving.

Mrs Blan, Mrs Nelson, and Ally had got away early. Their bus was bowling through the morning across the littoral plain. The thirty passengers and their bundles had shaken down into some sort of comfort.

"We're still neighbours," said Mrs Blan, with her old rich laugh. She had carried out her threat and piled on every garment she possessed. Her face was crimson and she was like a stove for heat in the seat beside Ally. In vain did Ally dig her with sharp elbows, she never reached the flesh. When she laughed, she wobbled all over Ally in waves of already odorous heat.

Mrs Nelson on the seat behind pushed her large pale face between them. She had at last resolved the problem that had been troubling her. "If government force us to evacuate," she said, "it'll have to look after us, won't it?"

"That's right," agreed Mrs Blan, nodding vigorously. Mrs Nelson sat back and gave herself up to placid contemplation of the scenery, drawn effortlessly past her eyes. She didn't much mind where she was so long as she was "looked after." It was only the thought of fending for herself that flummoxed her.

"I wonder if they've got round to Carnation Street yet," Mrs Blan shouted to Ally above the rattle, when, looking back east from a bend in the road, the pall over Sydney suggested that her fires were already alight.

Ally shook her head. "We only went there temporary," she shouted back, "it never was home."

Fire sprang up simultaneously all over the city and through the suburbs.

From the air it would have looked like the very perfection of pattern bombing. Every area had its squad and its ration of combustible material. In every gang there was at least one expert to direct the work and ensure its effectiveness. It was surprising how many experts in destruction the city could muster—professional wreckers, trained N.E.S. men who had only to invert their knowledge, soldiers who had had experience in scorching the earth, the handful who, in the long brooding hatred, had worked out their own methods. . . . The new disorder had been strong in the fire brigades and they had come over with their tackle, their stores of dynamite, their skills. To them fell the big work of blasting out the rocklike buildings that could not readily be dissolved in fire. It was they who broke into the sealed banks, the smooth invulnerable insurance offices, the other bulwarks of the old world, and reduced them at last to fountains of dust, smoke, and flame, whose core was twisted girders, shattered stone, fallen pillars, and rubble. It was they who broke open the strong heart of the city against which fanaticism with bare hands would have been futile. For labourers Sid Warren gave them the men from the Labour Camps, that conglomeration of beaten and defaced men, the ever multiplying rejects of the crumbling order that had now fallen.

They were a ramshackle lot but they had to serve, and in forcing the work from their degenerate bodies and exhausted minds only strong measures were effective. Not for them the future. The realists of the caucus knew, as the realists of the capitalist regime had known, that these were not the People. They were wastage, there was no road back for them, the only profit was in using what capacity for work was left in them, ruthlessly and at once, cutting their losses for them.

With them came Bowie. There was a little to distinguish him from the others. He was bearded, shaggy, his clothes stiff with dirt and worn to rags, his trousers held up on his bony loins with a length of rope. His eyes were a little wild. But he didn't know it. He didn't view himself critically any longer. Where everyone was rather queer, they looked on him as a bit odd. He didn't have occasion to talk much, but when he did speak it was still with the voice of an educated man. He was too tired to think, but occasionally memories—a lifeless curdlike scud—passed across the mind.

They worked before and after the dynamite, preparing the way for it and then completing its work. Most of them found it oddly comforting to be tearing something down. Bowie didn't. It went against the grain. The original grain of the man was still there. Suddenly, in the middle of the morning, he said to the man working next to him, "We're destroying the city. It's bad to destroy things. It isn't natural. I'm not going to do it." It was a long speech. The man shot him a suspicious sidelong glance and grunted. Bowie threw down his pick and walked away. No one tried to stop him. The foreman wasn't looking. His action had no significance. He might just have been stepping aside for a natural purpose.

He walked straight on. Every now and then he stopped and looked about him. He could feel change in the air, the sick cloud hanging over the city. He came to Parramatta Road and found it running a banker with people going west. Refugees. He joined them. His hands were empty, his pockets were empty. He had nothing at all but the torn caked clothes he wore. It didn't worry him, he didn't even think it strange. For so long now he had been either in prison or the concentration camp where meals, however meagre and rough, were always provided, that to take any thought for his future seemed superfluous. At sunset he was still walking west.

The westerlies blowing a half gale drove on the fires. "The weather is helping us," said Sid Warren. To Ruth, who was still beside him, his calm was terrible and inhuman. Never afterwards could she quite forgive him for it. He never lost his hold on the situation, never deviated into uncertainty or fear. He was as little touched by physical danger as by imaginative horror. He continued to plan and correlate, to receive reports and issue orders, as if it were a government in the ordinary sense that he had set up. As little came into the city in the way of news as left it. From the north there was nothing. The invading force continued to bide its time. The miners appeared to have missed their moment, not to have risen or to have been crushed before they could develop any strength. From the south, like a thin echo, came the news that the men at Port Kembla had risen, sabotaged the plant and marched away, leaving it burning like a lonely volcano by the sea. The government having declared Melbourne an open city was continuing its deliberations on the "terms". Sid, his mind strained to envelop so much, was totally unaware of what was going on in the thoughts of the woman beside him. In the proportions of his world it would only be unimportant.

Ruth knew that Sid would stay till the very last and that she would stay with him. But she was possessed by fear, saturated and interpenetrated by fear and grief, to the last cell of her brain. Her body was frightened by the stench of fire, by the furnace-like heat, the darkness even at noon when the sky was black with smoke and red with volcanic fire, by the choking air. Her mind was overwhelmed by the magnitude of the wreck and the knowledge that it was beyond control. All that was human and normal in her revolted against destruction as destruction, not for the value of what burned but because, however corrupted, it was a shape of human effort, a palimpsest of men's minds.

In her imagination pictures rose and became fixed like barbs in her brain, tormenting her to the outer edge of her endurance. One of these pictures, the most terrible, the most persistent, was of a dog, forgotten, left chained, without water, maddened with fear as the fires came closer and closer, straining at his chain till the blood flowed, howling in a terrible elemental fear when there was none to hear, till at last he was buried living in the burning debris.

There was no night or day. Time had melted and run together in an indistinguishable mass.

It could not have been that day but the next, for Sydney was then far gone, that Sid, wanting to make a survey, had ascended the A.W.A. tower. Ruth went with him. He did not ask her to go, but since she did, he took it for granted that she would endure what he endured without comment.

They climbed higher and higher. The heat was intense. Ruth thought that their clothing would ignite from contact with the fiery air, and the tears that coursed down her cheeks seemed to cut the flesh till they felt like blood flowing from raw wounds.

The guttering city was spread out beneath them, layered to the horizon in smoke and flame. It was immense and unrecognisable. Death and transfiguration. It boiled with smoke, black, grey, brown, white. Here and there, there were great coils of fire where a timber yard was burning, or a paint factory, a chemical works, or a very dry old building. Against brief curtains of flame, gaunt black shells of buildings stood out in relief. As they watched, walls dissolved, facades swayed fantastically and crashed, opening craters of living fire in the smoke, roofs fell in and fountained stars that were red hot metal and incandescent cinders. All that happens in the grate on a winter night was happening here on a panoramic scale.

Macquarie Street burned with great dignity, each building as it were a set piece. Parliament House, so old, so wheezy, made a fine bonfire. The hospital arcaded with red fire was a spectacle people would have walked five miles to see, were there not so many rivals. There was a bushfire in the Botanic Gardens, flying over the grass, climbing the trees, hanging them with leaves of flame, shrivelling in an instant all the little bushes, blackening the statues and leaving them hideously extruded, like corpses, from the scene whose natural beauty they had once been expected to leaven with culture. The bushfire lapped round Government House as water flows round a sand castle.

Down on the water front, wool stores burned with heavy greasy smoke though there was not much wool in them. Fiery particles floated in the water of the harbour. The bridge which had been dynamited hung half-destroyed, leviathan wounded.

Whole streets were obliterated, reduced to black dead ruin. Here and there fire seemed to have died of satiety and little clusters of buildings barely touched were left standing, only the most perishable parts burned away. Trees planted in the streets had lit like candles and burned to the earth: The old Port Jackson figs of the Domain, which had watched the city grow up, were first desiccated and then burned. The dispossessed birds of the city, the sparrows, the pigeons, the doves, the starlings, the ducks, the swans, had risen in clouds at the first breath of fire. Who would have thought there were so many birds in the city? Their cries as they wheeled in the sky were the city's only valediction. The trees that had sheltered them were gone now.

Sid noted the landmarks that yet stood. Greenway's church, St James's, was still unscathed like Shadrach in the fiery furnace. He could see the cupola of Queen Victoria Markets like hard bubbles in the smoke, and the tower of the Town Hall was still in the sky. The clock tower at Central Railway was gone.

Immediately beneath him Martin Place was a cauldron, the post-office full of bright fire like a box with eyes, a bank facade blown right out blocked the George Street end with a mountain of rubble. Jagged, fragmentary, unrecognisable buildings rose out of the smoke and dust of explosions, the cenotaph was overthrown, its sailor and soldier caught in a second holocaust of death, the lillipilli trees—who would remember them?—gone like matchwood.

Ruth stared out over the ruined city and breathed its hot black breath. She was a rag of flesh, no more, alive, able to understand what she saw, still sentient. She had known the strangling tragedy of her home and it had marked her. In her father she had glimpsed the crucifixion of Everyman and it had impacted her will. Now, not only her heart, but her very self, the matrix of her spirit, was broken open by pity and despair—pity for the people who must now be forced to learn, if they could learn, through new sacrifices, who would be relentlessly winnowed till only the strongest and most steadfast were left to be the stones of the new world, despair for herself. There was no road back. The irremediable that the plastic human spirit dreads had come to pass. She still believed that what had been done was the best that could be done, that the road, the only road through, lay that way, that there was courage and hard logic in it. The people were again the scapegoat. By their suffering, the sins—not the sins they had committed, but that, being committed against them, they had condoned— would be atoned. No, it was harder even than that. Suffering was nothing, bought nothing, brought no compensation, it was a byproduct, and even when it destroyed it was of no account in the logic of event. The people would not be purged or saved by suffering, they would only be selected, freed of the weak and the irresolute, reduced at last to a sticking point. For those who died, for those who despaired, for those who suffered too much and were destroyed in their heart or courage by it, there was no redress. No future would give them back what they had lost. They and their pain would be as meaningless as grains of dust. Ruth consented, and, knowing that she consented with her mind and will, she must bear upon her heart the burden of it, be destroyed, having served her turn. Gethsemane is commemorated and the Son of Man did not watch alone. Down through time there has been here and there one who saw in anguish the suffering of Man and his own destruction—humble people who did not know they kept a vigil—a man perhaps, walking up his street in the twilight from his profitless work to his wretched home, while his imagination widened to the knowledge that his world was doomed, and pain and bitterness flowed in him like blood; or a woman, looking down on a burning city, acknowledging it, realising what it would mean to a million people unprepared for change, unintegrated, who must nevertheless bear the wastage to an end they might never accomplish.

Ruth wanted, not hysterically but out of the same hard and bitter logic that had brought her so far, to throw herself down from the tower. The gulf of fiery air drew her, the dead gulf in her own mind drew her. Only the discipline that had become the unrelenting habit of her mind held her back. She had incurred the future. She must go on into it. She knew in her heart that the destroyer could never be the builder. He was conditioned by his role and must in the nature of things be scrapped. If they had not destroyed more than the city their work and all its consequences were in vain. If they had cast down with the stones of the city a social system or a corrupt way of life, then life in its own defence must rid itself of them. This Ruth knew, as the spirit may sometimes teach the brain.

Ruth tried to pick out King's Cross in the wreck, but all was smoke and chaos. She could not pin the spot with any landmark. The spire of St John's must have fallen, the high buildings had altered their shape. Carnation Street would be a tributary of fire flowing down into the river of William Street, or, perhaps, by now only the blackened banks where fire had flowed remained. To look for it, to look back on it, was utterly vain. Blinded, choking, she turned away. The past had fallen in, the future did not exist. There was only this moment that impaled her like a sword.

As the Cross had lived, so it burned, with greater gusto than any other part of the city, as if it were more inflammable, as if the very stones and concrete of its material body from a constant contact with life had lost their hard inanimate surface and become friable. Once the fire had taken hold it was up and away with banners, out of control. The hill became a volcano and streams of fire flowed down its sides to the waterfront. It had majesty and even, while the fire was new and bright, beauty. Its last beauty was the legitimate child of its first beauty, that had been lavish, brilliant, vainglorious, and so thinly laid over shabby ugliness.

The blocks of flats that had been congeries of little boxes, so packed with life that it bulged from the windows and sprouted on to the roofs, became craters of fire, each one burning stormily of itself. The matchwood partitions, the lattices, the tawdry ornaments, the awnings, the paints, the lacquers of hasty smartness, the hangings, the detritus of habitation, the greasy dirt, spread a gargantuan banquet for the flames. There was plenty of marrow fat. The fiery tongues licking into corners and hiding places uncovered and consumed a thousand trumpery secrets. Facades fell out, and the dens and love nests, the tabernacles and the secret places, the abodes of respectability, vice, dirt, and eccentricity of the great rookery were for an instant revealed in section and laid bare, not to curious gaze but to destruction.

The starving poet of King's Cross had left in great haste and fear. When the fire reached his home it found confusion, as if thieves had ransacked the place, everything in disorder, drawers pulled out, the contents spilled and scattered, the papers from his desk littering the floor, doors and windows left open. The hot wind and the breath of the fire preceding it dried everything to tinder and gave a dancing lightness to fabrics and papers before they perished. The closely written sheets of the Spring Symphony, the epic that had cost the poet so much of his heart's blood and that he now no longer valued nor even remembered, since he was brought face to face with what he conceived to be reality, trembled where they lay on the floor. They began to flutter and struggle for life. Some were blown into corners and stayed there flickering ineffectually against the walls, but others rose and eddied, sank, rose again each time higher, like a ballet when the intoxication of the music begins to work, some escaped into the street. The street was utterly deserted, loud with the noise of fire, distant and at hand. It was undestroyed but on the verge of destruction. The whole street seemed about to explode. There was wind but no air, as it might be inside a furnace. The pages were carried along like dry autumn leaves. Some rose above the houses and were consumed by fires in neighbouring streets. Others took fire in mid-air, burned for a second and fell. No word of it escaped.

The narrow lanes and alleys provided admirable draught. It was dry fire. It did not have to fight with columns of water as fires usually do, but went proudly in unbroken conquest. It smelled different. It made terrific heat, windows burst like bubbles. From the continents of flame, islands broke loose and sailed into the sky. Among the terraces of the meanest and most congested parts the fire lost individuality. Their wreckage fused in a vast anonymity. The fires sent the men who had made them scuttling away like ants. Theirs was work that, begun prosaically or in fanatic hatred, ended by overawing them and driving them before it. The gangs broke and fled. Here and there a man, negligent, exhausted, overcome by fumes, or not quick enough, was cut off and perished as surely, and almost as quickly as the frail sheets of paper had. His companions, preoccupied by their own escape, rarely missed him in time to save or even to search for him.

Timmy Andrews, maintaining his beatific state, continued to ride the holocaust. He did towering sums in his head, reckoning the amount of bourgeois property destroyed and the capital value of the city. He announced the results from time to time to the labouring sweating gang beside which he was camped. He had constituted himself a morale department of one. They were, however, too busy to listen to him. They waved to him good-naturedly when he made a speech. Every now and then when they were particularly hard pressed—they were mining a big block of buildings—he would rush in among them and with flailing energy lend a hand till, going limp with exhaustion, he retired again to his vantage place and stoked up with more liquor. Once the man in charge of the gang, young and cold sober, expostulated with him.

"You'll get hurt if you stay round here, mate, we'll be blowing her soon. Better hop it."

Timmy drew himself up in his dignity. "Young man," he said, "I was a revolutionary before you were born or thought of. When you were saluting the bloody flag in the bloody playground I was instructing the masses in the duties of the socialist state."

They liked having him about. When they took a spell he was ready with a joke and a bottle.

"Decent old Toby."

He humanised the situation, though they would not have put it that way.

It was after one of his bursts of energy that Timmy slipped and fell in a world gone black as eternal night. Nobody noticed at the moment, but when the fuses were lit and they were scattering to safety they saw him. His face was purple and congested, his eyes rolled up, his breath coming in uneven jerks. The ganger picked him up and ran with him to safety. They gathered round him, their grimy faces heavy with concern.

"Poor old bugger, he's for it."

"'Ad a stroke, that's wot."

"Ought ter get him to orspital."

"The hell we can."

Someone remembered that there were still ambulance stations and ran to find one, but before the stretcher-bearers could arrive Timmy was gone. The men stood round bareheaded, disconcerted, moved.

"Poor old bugger."

"In the movement all his life."

"One of the old timers."

"Gone before he could say knife."

"What are we gonna do with him?"

"What the bleeding hell did this have to happen to him for?"

"The drink done it."

"No, he busted himself using the pick."

If Timmy could have commented he would have said that it was a good proletarian death. He died for the revolution in the beatitude of strong drink and among his mates.

Others perished less happily.

Gwen awoke. She was lying among the fluff and dust under her bed, the empty whisky bottle on her chest. There was light so it must be day. She shut her eyes and rolled her head, which felt as if it had been battered to a pulp, from side to side. She didn't want to wake up, she didn't want to go on living, she was afraid of everything, even of crawling out from under the bed. But it was suffocating there. She could not breathe and there was a strange noise that she did not recognise, something like a high wind in an open place, battering on her brain. Before she had willed it her body had crept out of its refuge. Everything rocked and reeled, even the light flowed to and fro like a tide. It wasn't daylight and it wasn't electric light. It was red.

"Some hangover," thought Gwen.

She looked out of the window. The window had gone, there was only a hole in the wall. What she saw sent a stiffness of terror through her limbs. It dissolved. Screaming, she rushed from the room and down the stairs. Through her terror she could feel that the house was empty. It was not yet alight, but, dry as tinder, it waited and seemed about to explode.

In the street the buildings opposite were blazing. They were melting in fire and gobbets of burning wood were falling from them to the pavements. She ran to the end of the street to find it blood-red with fire. She ran back. Her mouth was wide open but no cries came, only a hoarse growling. The other end of the street was blocked with ruins. There was no way through. There was a little alley way between two burnings buildings. She ran the gauntlet, but the street beyond was so well alight that she had to return the way she had come. She thought she was on fire and beat at herself with frenzied hands, but it was only the blistering roaring heat that surrounded her. She ran to the house where she lived with some wild idea of taking refuge there, but now it was alight too. She was hemmed in. She ran hither and thither in blind panic. The whole area was deserted, she was quite alone among the burning ruins. They were immense, she was like an ant.

A facade bulged towards her, she saw it coming. Standing there she knew the final madness of terror. The inescapable thing was upon her. She lived for perhaps five minutes more. Then her agony was blotted out.

The ships that waited over the brink of the horizon saw the western sky redden and flare. They sent out scouts who brought back word that the city was burning to the water's edge. News reached the invader in the north.

"Sydney is burning."

The refugees fanning out into the bush carried the story.

"Sydney has gone." Men looked at one another incredulously and in dismay, and thought, "The port. How will we market our produce now? What will we do?" There were others who spat. Hadn't the city always been the enemy of the bush? The city was a vampire and now the vampire was dead. The glare in the sky was visible for hundreds of miles. Not till they had crossed the mountains did the refugees escape it.

No power could save the city now, nothing could put out the fires until everything but blackened stone and twisted metal was consumed. The last men were leaving the guttering city.

Beside the sliprails of her farm near Toongabbie Shirley stood staring up at the sky. She couldn't stay indoors any longer. There was nothing to do there, and there was nothing to do here but stand, stonily staring up at the sky. It was red even in the zenith and the east was shaken by great pulsations. In the unnatural light the shack showed gaunt, black, and starved. On the main road there was a ceaseless rumble of traffic going west. It had been like that for three days. Refugees. She had wondered if she should go with them, put the mountains between herself and whatever was going to happen. But it was too much to ask. She'd never manage with the children and two old women. It was the old ones that were the real trouble. At the bottom of her mind there had lurked the cold still intention to abandon them. She owed them nothing and they'd be no worse off here than on the road, useless as they were. But there was the farm. Her deep instinct was against leaving it. In the drying up of values the land itself had seemed to wither but it still meant food. It was there, she could see it. She couldn't take it with her. For a long time now everything that was done she had done, a hard losing battle, in which she had long ceased to measure effort. Her man was with the armed forces and it was many months since she had heard from him. She had no idea where he was, he might be dead, he might be cut off and not able to get back. She had no feeling for him or about him. She had never loved him, but that no longer mattered. Only survival mattered. It was a long time since she had done any picking and choosing.

The animals were uneasy in a light that was neither night nor day. The cocks crowed. The cow stood at the sliprails and every few minutes she stretched out her neck and bellowed. The wind tore at the pepper tree and carried, she thought, a breath of burning. The very air was infected. It was as if the city was a volcano in eruption.

An old woman came out of the house. "Shirl," she said in a thin whine, "aren't you gonna get tea? Yer auntie's hungry."

"I'll get it when I'm ready. You had a cup of tea not an hour ago."

"I never."

"Yes, you did. You got at it. You and auntie. I saw the cups in the sink, you forgot to wash them."

"Shirl."

"Get along inside, ma."

"All right, Shirl."

The old woman was placating. She turned away. "Bushfires are bad," she said vaguely.

"That's not bushfires, that's Sydney burning."

"Oh my, oh my, it's the Japs again."

"It isn't the Japs, it's the reds this time."

"What do they want to do that for?"

Shirley didn't answer her.

"I don't like it, Shirl," she quavered, suddenly frightened.

"Who do you suppose does? Go inside, ma, and keep auntie quiet."

"I never did know what side the Russians was on, not really. Aren't they on our side any more?"

"They bloody well aren't."

"Keep a clean mouth Shirl."

The daughter's temper flared, her voice rose in an ugly screech.

"Go inside, ma. Go on."

The old woman shambled towards the house. In the uneven light her gnarled body looked as black as burnt wood. She was no longer fat and cushiony. Her flesh had gone with the old smug assurance and by the same process. Her gauntness had the ugliness of the unnatural.

Shirley watched her retreat with morose disgust. Ma hadn't got over losing her farm. She and auntie, they dragged each other down. Useless. And they ate as much as a couple of strong men. Nothing was safe from them. Wherever Shirley hid the little remaining tea, they got at it; cunning wasn't the name for it. Let them have it, it would be worth it to see what they'd do when there was none left. Hanging round her neck like a couple of millstones. Hatred rose in her throat like bile. Let them wait for their tea, let them bloody well wait forever.

She only wanted to stand and look her fill. She did not know that in a dim way the red horizon comforted her. The city from which she was exiled might burn, other men's property might go up in fire. The front of her mind rejected in bitter scorn the criminal folly of destroying property. On that great bonfire was piled everything that meant happiness, all the means of happiness, the things one saw and strove for and had. Let them burn now. The little girl who had once been so eager to begin her life had become a pillar of salt.

At the top of the rise Ben drew his truck off the road and got down. The water in the radiator was boiling. When he unscrewed the cap a plume of steam rose into the air. He'd let her cool off a bit and then he'd fill her up. He climbed the bank, a miniature cliff of red eroded earth, and looked about him. The sky was red, it moved with a scud of smoke. Fire had burned away the stars. The sky was a great reflector, shedding back on the earth the smoky glare of the burning city in a light fitful and strange. Vision itself was reorientated. For a long way Ben could see the road and its moving load of metal, a long trail of luminous smouldering dust, shot with the gleam of lacquer in the glow of yellow headlamps, as if it were some continuous and organic thing, a fabulous python unwinding itself from the ashes of the city. While it moved it was visible. When a vehicle stopped it ceased to exist. His own camouflaged truck a few yards from him was a scarcely discernible dark lump. The paddocks on either side of the road dissolved, featureless, into nothing. There was the noise of engines coming up the hill in gear and that, too, had fused into something continuous. Ben could feel the quiet behind him. Step off the road and it was there. The dust was only a tunnel through clean air.

Presently he fetched a petrol tin of water from the back of the truck and refilled the radiator. She was an old engine and boiled readily. He'd want plenty of water and would he be able to get it? On the crest of the hill, rising from the left side of the road, there seemed, in the elusive light, to be a house, or at any rate some buildings. He might try to refill his tin there. First he lifted the flap of the truck's hood and looked inside. The other man, the guard, was lying asleep on the freight, the sleep of utter exhaustion, his body as relaxed as if the boxes of ammunition on which he lay were a feather bed. He was not much older than Ben, lean and ribby, his face blackened with smoke, his torn caked clothes still sticking to his body. He'd been through it. He looked like a boy from the slums, sickly and tough. Ben hadn't seen him before, he'd jumped on just as Ben was pulling out, and in the first difficult half-hour of crowds and debris he'd still been busy stowing the freight so hastily slung aboard. Then he had fallen asleep. Ben was satisfied.

He walked up the hill through the rough grass laden with dust. It had been ploughed land, he could feel the ridges under the mat of grass. The house was a little wooden box, bleached, with dolicus, black in this light, hanging in an untidy curtain over the verandah. Ben shouted but there was no answer. The place was deserted. It looked utterly desolate and, without being in ruins, ruinous. The inhabitants, infected with panic, might have joined the refugees from the city, or they might longer ago have been squeezed out by the hard times. The little place, ridden down by circumstance, held no trace of those who had left it. Ben found the tanks round the side of the house, but they were both drained dry. He saw the white outbuildings of a poultry run, but nothing moved there. On the eastern slope was a derelict orchard, a wild pattern of burgeoning branches tossing in the wind against the red sky. It was the season, and Ben began to search for fruit. But the refugees had been through and the trees were stripped, the boughs broken. He was bitterly disappointed. He was thirsty with days of smoke and heat. His whole body craved for fruit, for the sweet cleanliness of pulp and juice in his mouth. He had found most of his fruit in the gutter and knew it best as pyramids of crimson, orange green, and yellow, in the shops of the Cross, the stalls and the barrows. The gutters were not as barren as this orchard. He climbed into a tree and began to feel systematically among its dark leaves. At last his hand met an apple. It felt sound and ripe. He sniffed it, its apple smell living and wholesome. Even this small haul allayed the bitterness of his disappointment.

Ben stood eating the apple, looking about him. The drone of the traffic sounded, he thought, a little like a plane. He scanned the sky, but in the baffling light he could see nothing. It was a thought in many minds—what if the enemy bombed the roads, crowded with refugees? It had happened elsewhere, but so far it hadn't happened here. Ben judged that the procession of refugees must be nearly at an end. There were few family parties, women, or children, on the roads in this section. There was hardly anyone on foot. Those who had seen it out to the end were making their prearranged escape. Sid would be leaving Sydney now and Ruth with him. He didn't know where Wanda was, but he wouldn't mind betting she had found someone to look after her. He didn't know where his mother was either, or any of the people in the street, but he wasn't worrying. People managed, he'd noticed, and they were all in this together. For the city, he told himself, he didn't mourn. Not one brick of it had been his, whatever happened next he wouldn't be worse off. The strength and well being of his body were his passport into the new world. There wasn't much he'd learned except to drive and service a truck, and soon, when the petrol gave out, there wouldn't be any trucks. All the better that he didn't bring anything away with him. He'd always find an apple among the leaves.

It came upon him suddenly that there was nothing behind him. The city was no more. The world he had known had perished; he felt but only for a moment a penetrating desolation.

He thought more of the Sydney he had known as a child than of the city of his maturity. He remembered the living streets where he had run selling papers, their bizarre plenty, their gargantuan riches under glass, the sweep of traffic at the peak hours, the great squandering of lights. He thought of them as if they had been paved with gold. There had been plenty even in the lean years then, even in the gutter. The cigarette butts he had gathered for his father—you didn't find them on the footpaths now. He remembered the monument there'd been in Hyde Park, the one that had been potted in the first raid, the night his father was killed. It was magnified in his mind.

Great brooding figure up against the sky—sort of ark it was. Ark of the Covenant—what the hell did that mean? It and his old man had gone west together. He remembered the truck his father used to drive. It was the first thing he could remember. Just for a moment his mind swung back to being the mind of a child, and the acrid smoky air with its choking fumes became the dust of a sidestreet now lost in rubble and the petrol fumes of a long time ago. The pride and the glory of the grocery truck! He saw, he actually saw, again his father's hands on the driving wheel alive and vibrant against his chest. He saw them as he saw his own, sure and steady on the wheel of his truck down there driving out of the burning city. He saw them with the eyes of a child and with his own eyes. He recognised them as his kin. Strong good hands that he couldn't remember, only see. They'd meant security, and out of their insecurity all this had come. They were the hands that had let the world drop because it was beyond their power to hold any longer.

And now what sort of world was it going to be? There'd be fighting, guerrilla bands, the struggle to eat. That would be the least of it all. They'd strive for that without willing it. But there would have to be something more, a new pattern of life would have to be born unless the Australian people were going to live amongst their ruins for ever. The destruction of the city was only a symbol, an act of repudiation of all the city had come to mean, a gesture single in all its complexity, and a solution only in so far as by destroying the accepted mould it forced men to create another.

Ben stood on a hillside in the apochryphal night, eating his apple.

.      .      .      .      .      .      .      .

Ord asked, "Are you going to leave it at that?"

"Yes."

The book had blazed to its end and Ord was shaken out of his ironic self complacency. He was moved and could not trust himself. He scarcely knew the reason of his emotion, whether it came from the book itself, from some train of thought which it had started within himself, or from the pressure of Knarf's personality, exalted in creation, upon him. It had for him the poignancy of prophecy as well as of retrospect. It had been and it would be. Nothing passed and nothing was lost. The love of life and the love of death were interchangeable and the same. Happiness and despair could be nourished at the same fountain. The heart might be as hungry for death as for life and to die was as natural as to be born. In the depth of this mirror he had seen the image of life from a new angle. He had spent a life time studying this period, exhuming it detail by detail, with scientific care, and now he saw it fresh and living in the light of a creative imagination and it was desperate and ugly and sweet and full, in a way the careful, measured life of today was not. Knarf had spoken. In a world of the dumb he had really spoken, in the loneliness that bound them all he had communicated something. Ord knew that when he came to read the book and found it inevitably composed of ordered words building up a rational succession of pictures and concepts, he would lose this impression, be unable to recapture it. Now he could only turn his face away from the light and watch Knarf's hands among his papers, feeling constraint gradually overtake his emotion, petrifying it. He had nothing to say and dreaded the moment when he must speak. He could not praise and he had no criticism to make; whatever he said would be an anticlimax down which they would both ignominiously fall. He shifted his body with the sense that he reinhabited it after an absence and that there had been a break in the continuum of his consciousness, a continuum that had gone on now for years because neither love nor interest were any longer strong enough to break it and from which he had been relieved in the last hour. Knarf, he assured himself, had put on this recital for his own benefit and a listener had been the merest stage property. He felt suddenly, irrationally, annoyed with Knarf.

They simultaneously became aware that something was happening outside; there was a confusion of sound following a high whistling note of which they were now aware in retrospect. Knarf leapt up. He felt a mask falling away from his body. The clock on the wall accused him. It stood at five past four. The vote had been taken and the occasion, of such importance to Ren, had already passed. A few hours ago he had stood beside his son and had felt a half heroical union with him. He had shared in a fateful moment and admired himself for sharing: with his superior vision he had seen where the moment would lead and had felt pity, fear, and even a sort of inverted elation. Then his egoism had closed in again. *This* was the life he fabricated, that in his book was the one he sincerely lived. He had gone over and could not return. Not emotion but the simulacrum of emotion. At the first crisis he had deserted Ren, or, more important, Ren's idea. Shame ploughed his mind, but a voice, like a drop of cold water, warned him that this too was a pose and would pass. His mind had taken its mould and would not leave it again. Ord followed him across the roof and he heard his voice, as a part of the tindery unreality of all things, saying: "Damned silly they must have looked, all standing round self-consciously thinking!"

# NOCTURNE

Ren walked out of the courtyard with his chin up, uncertain, defiant, and rather pleased. He knew that he had been foolish to push the issue with Oran, and he already had some doubts as to how he had acquitted himself, but he was excited by the first blood. He looked to the afternoon's event to make good all deficiencies. If he had lost substance in his argument when he measured it against Oran's entrenched solidity, he had gained it in a sense of added reality in the conflict. And he had allies. His father had stood by him. He was enormously proud of that. Knarf wouldn't have if he hadn't meant it because he was as aloof and sure as someone might be who didn't have to live in the world at all. Illil's support affected him quite differently. He saw in it something brave, lyrical, and beautiful. Even dear old Ord had come out with something unexpected. Altogether Ren was a little exalted. He had so seldom tasted event at first hand before. Only Sfax troubled him. His whole manner, the way he had left the table, was odd and constrained. It made a breach in the wall of their solidarity. He couldn't understand it and was willing not to try—not yet, until he had talked to Sfax.

Sfax was standing alone beside the apparatus. He did not seem to be doing anything, just staring at a little dial. Ren went over and stood beside him.

"If you don't mind, old man," said the inventor, abstractedly, "I'm busy just now."

Ren suspected that the dignity of the occasion would not allow Sfax to be anything but desperately busy until the last moment. It just occurred to Ren to wonder why Sfax bothered so much about play acting when after all he was the real thing. People did sometimes pretend to have what they actually had, but why should Sfax, with his splendid logical mind.

Ren didn't go away, he was too interested in clearing up the shadow of doubt in his mind. He moved round so that he was facing Sfax.

"D'you think I made a mess of things in there?" he asked, half in challenge, half in supplication.

Sfax raised his light eyes. "As a matter of fact, I do. You talked a lot of romantic bilge. If you want to get anywhere you'll have to be a realist."

"But it was true. It's what you believe, isn't it? You agreed in principle, didn't you?"

"There you go again. What if I do believe it, believing isn't knowing. Knowing is the only thing that cuts any ice these days."

"But Sfax. . . ."

"I've got to deal in facts, even if you haven't. Oran's a fact, the social system we live under is a fact. I don't say things couldn't be better. They could. I'm willing to help make them better, within reason. But it isn't reasonable to throw away what we've got till we are in a position to substitute something else that will work. See what I mean? All you'll do with this premature wild talk of yours is to queer your own pitch. Do you think it will help the movement if you involve me and get me chucked out of the technical bureau? I've done more than any one else for the movement. We wouldn't be taking the vote today if it weren't for me. I sometimes think I'm the only practical man in the movement, but get me the sack and I wouldn't cut any more ice than you do."

"Look, Sfax, I . . ."

"Buzz off now, will you? I've got to work if the whole thing isn't going to be a flop." He added in a rather pleasanter tone, "I'm not really blaming you. You meant well and all that, but you were just a bit naive, haven't had much chance to learn wisdom in this funny little backwater. All I ask is that if you want to be indiscreet, leave me out of it. See you later."

Ren walked slowly away. Sfax was probably right. He'd probably been very young and half-baked. There is nothing youth feels more keenly. He put away the unworthy thought that Sfax had been anxious to get rid of him because Oran was approaching.

The problem was what to do now. His duty was obviously to go back to the house and help Lin with the guests. He rather suspected that Knarf would have deserted them by now, he could never stand a lot of people for long. He got tired and let the situation slip out of his hand in the most natural easy way. He'd probably be in his pavilion on the roof now, working or talking to Ord, while Lin fretted and shouldered all the awkwardness he didn't feel. If Knarf could behave like that, so could he. The thought of going back to be chaffed, advised, or treated with the kindly tolerance of middle-aged people was intolerable, not to be borne. Ren's mind was taut with anxiety and excitement. The events of the day had already carried him into unknown territory, and he wanted to consolidate himself before he faced anything new. He would like to have sought out Illil, but lacked the courage. After the one-sided scene with Sfax he was shy of his elders in the movement. It was happier to think of Illil, to dwell on her grace, fire, and courage, in the safety of his own imagination than to risk a possibly damaging contact.

There were three hours to fill. He decided that he would walk out into the hills, in a straight line across country, letting nothing turn him aside, walk for an hour and a half, then turn and walk straight back again. The plan pleased him, it lacked the ineffectualness of just walking, and the return journey at least would have some urgency about it. He set out quickly lest any one stop him. He aimed west, into the emptiest part of the country, he wanted plenty of space. He turned out of the square into the avenue that led to the bridge.

At the bridge head Illil was waiting for him. At least she had the appearance of waiting for him, for as soon as she saw him she jumped up from the stone coping where she had been sitting, looking down into the water, and came to meet him.

"May I come too?" she asked, falling into step beside him with an assurance that he found wholly admirable.

"I'd like you to enormously," he answered so seriously that she had to laugh, "but I'm not going anywhere in particular."

"I want to walk it all down. I knew you would too."

"Did you?" He could not help showing his pleasure. He told her what he had meant to do.

She nodded. "Let's. That's just right. It splits the difference between somewhere and nowhere. We'll see how far we can get."

"It won't be too strenuous for you?" He knew that she had come to the Tenth Commune to recover from an illness though she never mentioned her health.

"I can always do what I want to do."

"You don't mind fences?"

"I don't mind fences." She was over the first, refusing the hand he held out, and scudding across the brown grass of the paddocks.

"We could keep on walking for ever, couldn't we? And never come to the end of this?" There was a faint timbre of excitement in her voice.

"Nearly. Even the fences stop after some miles out and it's all open country."

"I'm not used to such a lot of country all at once. It goes to my head. I like it here so much."

"You're going to stay?"

"A little longer. Do you know the people here have seafaring faces, much more than those who really live on the coast?"

"I wouldn't know because I've lived here always."

"There aren't many people living this side of the river, are there? It's still untouched, the air's unbreathed, virgin air. And the light. You breathe light not air and it turns to images in your blood. . . ."

"Over the river always seems like a different world to me. I suppose it's because my father used to bring me riding here sometimes when I was a small child. I'd sit in front of him on the saddle with his cloak round us both."

"I know. I saw riders coming in this morning with their children before them like that, their heads poking out like kangaroos."

"It's the custom in these parts. There's no better way to see the world. We'd jog along for hours and not say a word. I expect he was thinking something out, or making up his poetry. It never bothered me that he didn't talk. I always had wonderful daydreams, the kind I could never get any other time. I'd lean back against him and feel his heart beating and know I was safe and free." It was quite natural to tell Illil this.

"You went a long way?"

"It seemed a long way. Sometimes we were out all day. We'd have our lunch with us and eat it anywhere, sitting under a gumtree. I'd go to sleep for an hour on father's cloak. What with so much sun and air and getting jogged up and down and an enormous lunch, I couldn't keep awake. I'd drop off listening to Murrumbidgee—that was the old mare, you know. Ord called her that and it was he who gave her to us—cropping the grass beside us. Father never told about my going to sleep because I was rather big then for a midday nap."

"Your father is a very distinguished man." Illil said it in a detached sort of way as if fathers were objects of common interest.

"Yes," Ren agreed, "but I don't know him very well."

Any one else might have laughed, but Illil only nodded. "It's often like that, being related to people makes you self conscious. You're like him, you know."

"To look at?"

"Yes, and inside too, I should think."

"I can't write or anything like that, I do in my mind, but as soon as I pick up a pen I feel dumb and wooden all over."

"I expect that's only an inhibition. But what I feel about you is that you're like your father, but that whatever it is—genius, I suppose it's called—that comes to a head in his writing, is dissolved through you. Genius in solution." She turned and looked at him without slackening pace. She spoke so frankly and with such effulgent maturity that Ren was not at all embarrassed, only delighted.

"Do you really think so?" was all he could say in a pleased tone.

"I wouldn't say so if I didn't think so. I thought you were fine, the way you stood up to Oran today."

"Did you? Did you really, Illil? Sfax thought I'd made a fool of myself."

"I wouldn't worry about that. We won't have Sfax with us long."

"What do you mean?"

"He's ready to retreat. Didn't you notice? There's a look in the eye, you come to recognise it after a time."

"But I've known Sfax all my life, he wouldn't do anything like that. He's so clever, I expect he has just outstripped us all and sees things a bit differently."

"He's clever enough in his own way, a real smarty, but he hasn't any stomach for sacrifice. Don't look so glum, it isn't important. We've used him, that's all. He thinks he's used us. That's the joke."

"I don't understand."

"It would be plain enough if you didn't know him so well. He's only interested in the votometer, we're only the excuse for demonstrating it. He's useful to us. So far we're quits. But he might be dangerous."

Ren muttered unhappily that he didn't believe it.

"You'll have to be tougher than that. You're very romantic, you know." The gay friendly smile was back in her eyes, the hard creature of a moment ago gone. The thought just flicked across Ren's mind: "Does she think I'm a child?"

"That's what Sfax said."

Illil was coughing and Ren would have liked to walk more slowly but she would not. Her mood had changed again. She was no longer hard and ironic or tenderly mature, but was once more the zealot she had shown herself during the argument at midday. She talked about the wrongs of the young, the cold heavy hand of the Technical Bureau crushing out all initiative and setting a single cramping value on existence, of the future when the hard rind of government should be broken through and the reign of liberty begun, the flowering of life and art. She used the word sacrifice over and over again with a hard hot eagerness. She brought to Ren a whiff of the seething world of the big Centre from which she came, of the debating societies and athletic clubs where these ideas propagated, a world even more cut off from general society than the Tenth Commune, inbreeding its ideas, creating its own ferments, mesmerising itself with mysteries and shibboleths, but not progressing beyond itself. In a few months he would have entered into that heady community. Much as he was under Illil's spell at the moment, he still could feel the meretriciousness of the whole programme. Perhaps he measured it against the hills that he had known all his life, and found it lacking in stability. He did see that the things she talked of were not achievement but only its raw materials, the desire for change which would have to be shaped along much wider lines.

Suddenly Illil said: "Let's sit down and look about us. I want to learn this country and remember it always."

He saw that she was very white and guessed that she was tired and would not admit it. They had been walking for nearly an hour. The Centre was still in sight from the top of their little hill, looking small and neat with well-defined edges. They turned their backs on it by common consent and looked out over the timeless landscape to the west. Illil began to cough, burying her face in her knees. Then she lay full length on the grass, her face upturned to the sky. The light had gone out of her, there was nothing vivid left, only the husk of her flesh, pale and brittle under the weals of colour on her cheeks. Her eyes were dark, sick, and anxious.

Big autumn clouds of palest gold were welling up from the horizon and floating up the sky to dissolve in the zenith. Illil watched them as if their slow untouchable progression held some meaning for her. She was unaware of Ren, who knelt beside her, so cradled was she in her own weariness. His heart was wrung with pity and understanding. All her sudden moods had passed away, the successive illusions in which she wrapped herself and so quickly discarded. He had

thought she was beautiful, brilliant, courageous, and mature, and now
he saw with grasping pity that she was none of these things. She was
like the brown earth on which she lay, that first material at the
mercy of changing light, no different from himself except for her
moods, as vulnerable and immature under the patter of maturity, far
less stayed by real conviction than he for all her acquired sapience. A
new strength and tenderness were born in him, emotions that had
little to do with the earlier feelings Illil had evoked in him and which
went beyond Illil and her need. The human spirit does not move
evenly from goal to goal. There is flight and pause, ground gained,
lost again, and then more easily re-won. There are moments when
the change is perceptible and when the future is not only prefigured
but temporarily inhabited. A barrier is broken down and the spirit
says to the mind without shadow of doubt: "This is love . . . maturity
. . . death." For the first time Ren was aware of sympathy, not as
an impulse or as a need within himself, but as a genuine human
contact. Illil had told him nothing, but he knew what ailed her, body
and spirit, not through clairvoyance of love or pity, but in the full
poignancy of imagination. In this intensification of living, everything
in his mind, the day's crisis, the ferment of ideas, awareness of
himself as a social being, the semblance of the future, were all
illuminated. Two figures on a hillside dwarfed by lonely distance, life
simplified to a moment.

Ren lay down beside Illil, his face turned towards her, his cheek
pressed on the grass. He took one of her hands in both his and
held it against his lips. She did not seem to notice, her hand was stiff
and insentient, but after a time he felt the fingers relax in his
steady clasp and curl softly round his own. He knew that the cold
premonition was passing from her heart too. She turned her face
towards him, her eyes were veiled.

"I can feel the earth lifting like a wave under me and carrying me
on. Forever. Do you feel it too?" she asked in a dream.

"Yes," he answered in the same tone to keep whole the bubble
moment. "I feel it too. And I can hear the sheep nibbling the grass."

"But there aren't any sheep."

"There have been sheep here for five hundred years. They eat the
grass paddocks in rotation. You'll always hear them nibbling in these
parts. Like the sea in a shell.

"It's the old mare, Murrumbidgee, you hear."

"I'll never hear that again. It's gone. Forever."

"I wish I were that child asleep in a poet's cloak."

I owe the world something for that, he thought, because I slept on this grass under this sky, wrapped in a poet's cloak. I owe the world everything I have.

There was a little breeze flowing over the hill, cool like shallow water in the sun, stirring their hair as it stirred the grass. "Illil," he said, "let me put my cloak round you. It isn't a poet's but it's warm. You'll be cold."

That broke the spell. With a single swift movement she sat up and snatched her hand out of his.

"So you're going to fuss over me, are you? Treat me like a child or a sick woman who has to be soothed and coddled. I don't need anything like that. I don't want it, do you understand?" Her voice was harsh and shrill, her face sharp between the windblown elf locks of her hair.

"Yes," he said, "I understand." They were both standing up and without touching her he could feel her trembling.

"No, you don't. You don't understand anything. Nothing has ever happened to you."

"We had better start back." The gentleness of his voice robbed the words of their abruptness. He took her arm to steady her and she submitted.

"I'll tell you, then you'll understand." There was a jerkiness in her speech that betrayed the uncertainty under the spirit of fire. Ren thought, "If only she can stop pretending and talk. . . ." Aloud he said, "You can tell me anything, Illil. This is a little bit of time that doesn't count. We're thrown clear."

"You were going to make love to me, weren't you?"

"No, I knew you didn't want me to."

"That's something I don't want ever. I wouldn't forgive you."

"We can be good friends without." He didn't tell her that he had not yet made love to any girl.

Illil walked with her head down for a few moments, her resolve hardening. Then she began in the same hard jerky voice.

"A year ago I applied for a license to marry. It was refused. It's here." She drove her fist against her breast. "I was to go for treatment but I didn't go. As long as I did everything the same as usual it didn't seem true. Then I had a haemorrhage one day at work and they packed me off to a sanatorium, I didn't have any say in it. I didn't belong to myself any more because I was sick. That horrible place. Sick people are criminals, aren't they? You don't know how awful it is with a lot of sick people herded together. It makes your mind sick as well as your body. They don't let you think of anything else. Lots of them liked it. They hated me because I wouldn't let my mind go sick and hide behind my body. Nobody ever hears anything about the sick people and the mad people. There are plenty of them, though, all herded out of sight in nice, scientific, fool-proof prisons, weeded out and kept separate so that they'll die off and the world will get cleaner and cleaner. We've all got the same ancestors, haven't we? So it's no good just cutting out the ones who have a disease that you can put a ticket on."

"What about the man you were going to marry?"

"He used to come to see me in the sanatorium until I stopped him. Do you know, he didn't matter to me much after just the first. I got a new scale of values and he wasn't in it. I won't see him any more. I expect he has been sensible and cut his losses. After the sanatorium I was sent here to finish the cure, a year and no option."

"You'll get better, Illil."

"Lie on the good earth in the sun, breathe in the lovely pure air and you'll get better," she mocked. "You're a romantic in love with the country. You can afford to be. But it's all imagination, it doesn't do anything. It's in there, it's a part of me. They can stop the symptoms and say I'm cured and put one more little stroke on the sheet of statistics, but they *know* I won't ever be cured. You see they won't take down the barbed wire and let me back into life, however much cured I am."

"You won't get a license to marry but no one can stop you doing anything else you want to."

"Yes, all the world's before me, isn't it? I'm just an outlaw. I mustn't have children because one of my lungs is—unorthodox. I could have all the defects of character there are and it wouldn't matter. I don't want to marry any one, I don't want children. But you don't know what it's like to be cast out, no one does till it happens to them. You are outside what everyone else shares or could share. You haven't decided it yourself, it has been decided for you. You're just written off."

"But, Illil. . . ."

"I'm free, though. Free in a way healthy people aren't. I'm not bribed with security the way most people are. Nobody cares about me and I don't care about myself. I mightn't even be going to live, so what does it matter? There's the movement—I can serve it and I will. It's going to devour a lot of people and they'd better be people like me rather than like you. That's where I can be useful."

"Why do you talk like that?"

"Because it's true. We say 'the movement'—it's a nice smooth word, sounds natural and harmless. We ought to say 'the Revolution,' then we'd realise what we were up against. No one, except historians, has talked 'the Revolution' for centuries. It's time we began."

"I don't think so," Ren answered soberly. "When you start using old names like that, you link up with old ideas. Those revolutions in the nineteenth and twentieth centuries didn't achieve much. Like volcanoes, sending up a lot of molten lava that when it cooled turned into slag and pumice. We don't want to hitch ourselves with words on to old failures."

"At that rate 'movement' is just as bad. Haven't you ever heard of Youth Movements?"

"There aren't any words that haven't been spoiled. We live too late. Everything has happened before and happened wrong and the world is full of ruts." A little ripple passed between them. It was true and they didn't believe it. They had steered themselves away from the dangerous ground of a moment ago.

They walked in companionable silence. The hard core of desperation had melted. Ren's mind was full of warm golden thoughts. It was true, he thought, all the sick and disappointed people could come into the movement and work for it. It would give them asylum and turn to usefulness what would have wasted. It was beginning here in the Tenth Commune, a small ripple, and it would go on round the world, swelling to a wave, a great tide, gathering the enormous voice of the people into an overwhelming force till every channel brimmed. All who had suffered and died for liberty in the past would be redeemed and justified. Already he could see himself and Illil as historical figures, moving in a consciousness of great things. Only Sfax should have been with them. He hated himself for not feeling sure of Sfax. How could they do great things if they didn't have faith in one another? It was himself he blamed for letting his faith be shaken, not Sfax for shaking it.

"We're comrades, aren't we, Illil?"

"Yes."

For the second time he took her hand, holding her hot nervous fingers in the steady peace of his. They were coming back in a very different mood from that in which they had set out. He was no longer a boy whom she could dazzle and instruct, nor was she the young amazon of the revolution, fully armed in mind and spirit. Now she was tender and unfolded, perhaps because she had purged her despair and bitterness for the moment in an outbreak, perhaps because she was reassured and comforted by the delicate affinity that had sprung up between them.

Otherwise the return journey was not so easy. Their pace had fallen away until they were going very slowly, but even so Illil seemed to be wading through an invisible tide. Ren began to worry lest they should not be back in time. It might be better to rest now for a little while so that they might make better progress later. She would not, he knew, suggest it. They were on a little rise looking towards the river. Here, the whole scene composed, the Centre white among dark trees, the river in the foreground a sliver of blue water edged by dark liquid shadows and golden willow trees, in the distance a furrow of dark vegetation across the grassy hills, the encircling distance under the unimpeded flow of the autumn light.

"Let's stop here a minute."

They slid down on to the earth and so stayed, leaning against one another as naturally as two young animals.

"That's the old frontier," Ren said, pointing to the river. "This side of the river has never been taken by force. It's been free country always. I like to think that's the real reason why it seems different. I've always thought so and you recognised it at once. Four hundred years ago the Pioneers crossed the river with their flocks. Conquest stopped at the river. They wouldn't stay to be enslaved. They didn't care about anything but their freedom. There wasn't much good country this side; after a few miles it was semi-desert. It couldn't carry the flocks or the men. They didn't go back, they stayed and perished. They were the flower of the old Australian people. This was where they came over."

Illil's eyes were shining. "I didn't know it was here. It's . . . it's the noblest story in the world. They made liberty imperishable by dying for it. They knew, they must have known, how it would end and they never flinched. They drank the toast and broke the cup. The impossible gesture is worth all the reasoning in the world, isn't it? All their laws and books are forgotten, but that story goes on living. A nation that could produce martyrs was great."

"I don't know that they were exactly martyrs."

"Yes, it wouldn't have been as self-conscious as that. They probably thought that there was nothing else to do." She brooded for a moment, then raised her eyes, brilliant with excitement, and fixed them on Ren. "I meant what I said up on the hill, that I was free because I had nothing to lose. In the last resort I could serve the movement . . . with my life. I've thought . . . if things were very bad . . . if we couldn't make people listen or understand . . . that I could . . . throw myself away . . . and that might break a way through to their imagination. I've thought of it just as something held in reserve. There'll be others like me, who care a lot and don't care what happens to them. We could be the spearhead. I dream of that. Of being consumed in glory instead of . . ." She broke off and let her eyes fall, tugging at the sinewy grass with her fingers, fighting her tears.

Ren said, "We mustn't think of things like that till it's forced on us. Do you see, to work, it would have to be forced on us from outside . . . otherwise . . ."

"Otherwise it would just be theatrical."

"I didn't say that, Illil."

"I know, but it's true. It's just something to be held in reserve. I wouldn't have told any one else, but I wanted to tell you. It's the secret at the bottom of my heart. I thought you'd understand."

"I do. I think you're wonderful and brave. I never even hoped I'd find anyone who cared so much about the things I care about. But let's live, Illil, if we possibly can." He couldn't even imagine death in the moment of tranquillity, but the thought was evidently no stranger to her. They sat still, close together, thinking their own thoughts.

"Illil," Ren said at last, "if things get steep and turn ugly . . . they might, you know."

"They are sure to."

"And we are worried and mixed in our minds, let's try to come back here. You can't sit here and look at that and be too unhappy. We'll get back our sense of proportion and be able to go on."

"Yes," she answered on a long breath, "only I won't have to come back. I'll be able to remember."

"It wouldn't be the same. Actually coming back would be something to hang on to."

"We won't ever quite let go of this moment. It will be in us for as long as we live."

After a moment he stood up and pulled her after him. She was rested and they crossed the next paddock at a good speed, but she had difficulty with the fence, and once more her pace flagged. Neither of them could think of anything now except the distance to be covered and time slipping away.

"You'd better go on, Ren. I'll follow."

"No."

"You must be there."

"We'll be in time. It isn't far now."

"Please go on."

"No."

The ground felt spongy under her feet and then it was as if she were wading through it, up to her knees in half fluid earth. I won't give in, I won't cough. She pushed with all her strength against the inert burden of her fatigue. They reached the bridge.

"Gently now," said Ren.

They were half way up the avenue when they heard the whistle of the small siren, warning citizens that it was time to vote. They broke into a run. People were streaming into the square; already it was lined many deep on three sides.

"I'll have to leave you here. I'm to read the motion."

Ren had gone, winding his way as best he could through the densening crowd, he was crossing the open centre, mounting the steps, forcing his lungs to breathe slowly and deeply. Sfax was waiting, red with fury, and thrust the scroll into his hand. "I thought you were going to let us down. You should have been here ten minutes ago."

Ren didn't answer. It was more important to manage his breath. He stood with Oran on the steps, one step above Oran. Oran said a few words, explaining the occasion and the nature of the vote. His deep easy voice scarcely needed the amplifiers; enlarged, it beat against the walls startlingly loud. Ren didn't listen, he was gathering himself, compact and clean, as if for a jump. He felt that the crucial two minutes had come on him suddenly and found him unprepared.

Illil braced her shoulders against the reassuring solidity of the wall behind her. Through succeeding waves of red and black she saw the square afresh. Always the sleepy emptiness, its honey-thick tranquillity, had predominated over every other quality. It had been a cup brimming with peace, a hollow vessel of no importance, filled with sunlight and quiet hours. Now it had been emptied and filled again with the murmur of a crowd, restlessness, people held unwillingly together, like fish in a net, an unannealed moment, an occasion that lacked contact with either its setting or its actors. She saw a world ripple marked by her own distresses. Determination rose in her and drained away again. Now she saw only the bottom of a long sunk landscape from which the tide had drawn away and in which all known landmarks had become changed and strange. She was afraid with a deep physical fear. With dilated eyes she saw it as a large bright picture, detached in space, slowly tilt and slip towards her. She pressed her sweating palms to the wall and her panic sent a message to every cell in her body, Be quiet, be still. If you lie low, do nothing, think nothing, it may pass you by. Exertion and strong emotion had brought her to the brink of disaster. Don't move, don't think, or the blood will come spurting from your lungs. Even a thought can tear the delicate, abraded tissues. Feel nothing, think nothing, be still and let the dangerous blood in your veins grow quiet, second by second build up the dam against death. Shut all the doors and wait. Get rid of all the useless things, vanity, hope, striving, fear itself, and be still and empty. Nothing else can save you. Don't listen, don't look, don't feel, don't move, don't speak, don't think. Only let it pass this time and I'll never be rash again. This is real. Nothing else is so real as this or ever will be. I'm alone, no one can reach me. If any one spoke to me or touched me it would happen. No, no. Breathe slowly and carefully. Again. Your heart is quieter now. Stop that noise, please . . . please . . . please. It might kill me.

Ren's own voice surprised him. It spoke back to him from the amplifiers, not distorted, but strengthened and deepened, so that it was like the voice of a middle-aged man, his future voice. The amplifiers took the words from him, leaving his lips impotent, and spoke them again from a point several yards away. The situation went off with automatic efficiency and he had no sense, as he had expected to have, of fatefulness. With the amplifiers waiting to snatch his words, he had not time to realise within himself their significance. He simply fed a machine with his voice and the machine turned out a finished article that resembled the raw material only at several removes. The first vote had been taken—a snapshot of the public will —before he could gather the situation into his imagination. The pause that followed appeared, because so consciously lived, very long. Ren held his vantage place on the steps. He had time to look about him and assimilate what was happening. It still seemed unreal because, although he had been thinking of this occasion and of all the ideas that lay behind it and of the hopes that streamed ahead of it, it had remained subjective, embedded in a cloudy nebula, wishful but inexact. Now, suddenly, the planning of months was crowded into two minutes of actuality, hope brought to a sticking point, a system that had existed only in mind coralled in fact, impounded, imprisoned, reduced from boundlessness to bounds. This was the test, the revolution, the changeover from the subjective to the objective. It was like a coral atoll that had grown cell by cell in the green silence beneath the water and now by a shifting of the sea's bottom was raised above the surface into the light and wind, an island with the responsibilities of an island and a land destiny. The whole thing in a moment had gone beyond the stage of canvassing, proselytizing, preparing, and had reached the stage of co-operation.

Ren looked at the crowd. He remembered what Illil had said. A seafaring look. Yes, it was there. A longsighted look in the eyes, far seeing, the accustomed dignity of faces turned to the light, even a way of standing that was infiltrated with the consciousness of horsemen and sailors, an indefinable print of distance, a sub-consciousness of space. This people, conscious not of differences from other people but of affinity to this countryside, this landscape—for all the individual differences a likeness ran through them. The crowd was rather solemn. Never before had the whole community been brought together. It was an occasion. They stood rather impassively, waiting. Only among the workers was a smoulder of excitement visible. The others had no particular image of what would or could happen. They waited with grave noncommittal courtesy. On faces he knew well Ren could detect the ceremonial mask. They were taking it seriously, giving the vote their attention. Even the children were standing still. The girls and women were set in the same mould as the men, one compact community.

A word came to Ren from an incredible distance of time. Auto-da-fe. Had it been like that? A square packed with people waiting, with insulated imagination, with grave politeness, well-fed people with the certainty of their own rightness, while something momentous happened. Ren shook off the thought. Why did his mind slip back to the past when it was exactly with the past—all the pasts—that he wanted to have done? The past meant hands held out to drag the future down. Hidden snares in the grass. Beware. Beware.

He could see his mother standing in the doorway of their house as if she had come out rather impatiently and was waiting for it to be over so that she might return to some urgent employment. She was looking straight at him. He could swear she wasn't voting at all, that it found her unprepared. It couldn't be helped, there would always be some losses. Illil he could also see, just where he had left her, leaning against the wall, head down. He imagined her sending out a solid stream of power, voting with all her might and main. Such a fragile little thing, full of spirit. Comrade. Brave comrade. We'll find a way to stick together and go on with the work, shoulder to shoulder, with no thought between us but of the work. Here and there he caught the eye of a boy or girl whose enthusiasm he had enlisted. They signalled to him, but diffidently, because the occasion was turning out much more solemn than they had expected. But nowhere could he see his father or Ord. At first with uneasiness and then with panic he searched for his father. His glance, like a lost dog, ran hither and thither. He might, he told himself, easily miss one man in a crowd of three thousand. Perhaps he had looked straight at Knarf, but his mounting agitation had blinded him. He must be there somewhere, but he knew he was not. The warning signal sounded for the second vote.

The secret anonymous stream of thought invisibly secreted by the crowd was for an instant illuminated, recorded, and made public. The ether waves were tapped for their poor flotsam. This was the first real unedited voice of man. It amounted, we can only suppose, to a few articulate straws on an inarticulate groundswell.

The thin wail entered Illil's consciousness like a probe searching for the weak spot. She shut her mind against it hard and fast, but not too hard. That also was dangerous. Breathe very slowly and don't think at all. She looked at the fingers she had taken from her lips, expecting them to be sticky with blood, but they were not. The bitter taste in her mouth was fear. Presently, when she felt able to move she would go into a house, the nearest, and ask for ice. Lie down and suck ice. That was the proper thing to do. Panic abated a little.

Sfax stood, one hand on a lever, the other holding a stop watch, his face narrow and intent, stripped down to its most fundamental expression. Oran turned ostentatiously to speak behind his hand to the man commanding the company of the civil guard who laughed obsequiously, the only sound, faintly shocking in the hush.

Ren thought: NOW. He tried to force out his will as if it were a jet of water from a hose. He wanted to shout and stamp his feet. Just to think was terribly futile. PUSH. All together. He felt that the situation existed primarily in his own imagination and that by the intensity of his grasp he could sway it single-handed. Click. The exposure was over, a wave of spontaneous movement passed through the crowd. Ren came down the steps and took up a position where he could see the indicators. The golden liquid which registered the Yes votes reached a third of the way up to the top. But it didn't matter, the silver liquid, that stood for No, was considerably lower. The crisis was over. He felt the tension of his skin change all over his body. It had wanted something more sweeping, but a win was a win. This was only a beginning. From the ground he could no longer see Illil. Again the warning signal. This time it was easier to concentrate. Ren didn't take his eye from the golden column. The fluid rose slowly and steadily. When it touched the halfway mark Ren felt a cheer strangle in his throat. The silver was left far behind. The machine clicked, the siren wailed its finale. The vote was over.

A low roar came from the wedge of workers on the north side. On a barked word of command the military guard wheeled to face them. A confusion of voices broke from the main crowd as it swayed in doubt and hesitation. Ren's impulse was to turn to Sfax, to share with him the first moment of triumph. But Oran was standing at the top of the steps, holding up his hand for silence. His great voice boomed, overawing the confused and uncertain murmuring.

"Citizens, you have just recorded your test vote. You were asked if it were your will that a Council of Workers should be formed to

assist the Technical Bureau in the work of government and to represent in its counsels the will of all unorganised sections of the
community. You see the result of your vote before you. Gold is for
the affirmative, silver for the negative, black for indifference. Twenty-
two per cent of those present voted for the motion, sixteen per cent
against it. Sixty-two per cent were indifferent. Citizens, the motion
goes by default. I thank you for your attendance. The meeting is
dismissed."

It was as if an avalanche of stones had hit a quiet pool. The crowd,
so quiet and docile a moment before, broke suddenly in a half a
dozen directions. The supporters of the motion, unwilling to believe
in the terms of their defeat, started by a natural impulse to force
their way towards the steps. Many who had a long way to go and
wanted to be home before nightfall were getting away as quickly as
they could. Those who did not understand what had happened, and
there were a good many, continued to stand stockstill, obstructing the
way. The workers from the irrigation garden, cut off from the main
crowds by the line of soldiers, were being marched back to their
barracks before they could rally from their surprise.

Ren sprang up the steps. He had a mad impulse to turn back the
moment, undo it by force. Oran blocked his way, spun him round
with his hand on his shoulder. It was as if his eyes belonged, not to
the dark heavy face, but to a man cunning and alert who sheltered
behind the impassive facade. Sfax shouting, "Don't let the buggers
near the apparatus." A swirl in the crowd at the foot of the steps.
Ren stood still, Oran's hand on his shoulder, a gesture that appeared
fatherly but bit into his flesh as impersonally as iron. He had had
no plan, only a blind impulse, and that hand persuaded him, despite
himself, of his impotence, and halted him. He saw the disintegrating
crowd, the thin surge of his own partisans, halted as he had been, by
a single line of soldiers drawn round the foot of the steps and the
apparatus. The soldiers stood like wooden men, automata, expressionless and without interest in what was happening, their small deadly
motor guns held ready for action on their hips with a gesture so
identical and studied as to seem not a reality in itself but a ritual
substitute for reality. As such, it was the more horrible, for it showed
force entrenched and reduced from an emotion to a function, robot
violence that would turn aside for no appeal. It was a violent shock
to Ren, for his imagination had never encountered such a thing

before. He had expected opposition but had believed it would be as spontaneous as the attack. A row of armed dolts could make the Movement look innocent to the point of fatuity. He saw the crowd draining away fast, the small number of the adherents exposed in that impotent group halted by the soldiers. On the roof of his home, silhouetted against the sky, he recognised Knarf and Ord. He knew what that meant. He could not see Illil anywhere. Rage that was near tears swelled in him. Here he stood with Oran's hand on his shoulder like a hostage or deserter, behind the fence of armed men. Oran's voice, like a snake sliding from under a stone, said: "You agreed to abide by public opinion, didn't you? There is no public opinion. You have lost your motion through indifference more surely than if a strong vote had been cast against it." Sfax joined them, his face broadened in an uncontrollable smile.

"Not a hitch, sir," he said to Oran. "Less than one-eighth per cent error. Nothing's as satisfactory as a field test."

"Congratulations," said Oran drily.

Sfax plunged into technicalities but he did not get far. Ren broke free, his face scarlet with anger. "You rigged it, Sfax," he cried, "you rigged it." Oran tore them apart as if they were children.

"I didn't rig it," Sfax shouted. "Technicians don't rig things, you sentimental fool."

"You weren't with us at all."

"I wanted the truth, that was all, And I got it. D'you know, sir, I was so interested in the technical aspect I forgot to vote."

"You're a rat." Ren thought in a flash, "Now they'll arrest me. I hope they do."

"Have I got to stand that?" Sfax demanded.

"It won't hurt you," said Oran, and then to Ren, mildly, "You'd better go with your friends."

The square was nearly empty. The uninterested and the fearful had gone. The soldiers had closed round the little knot of objectors and were marching them away, or rather driving them out of the square like children, without even a show of force. Ren saw that Avik was among them and could even feel surprised and touched.

"They will not come to any harm and neither will you, if you are sensible."

Ren turned and walked down the steps. His mouth was full of bitter water. Realisation of failure and humiliation clove through his mind, but already his obstinacy was rallying against it. He wanted to get back among his own people so that they might mend these tears in the fabric of their plans. He no longer knew who were his friends. All his life he had admired and wanted to follow Sfax. He had been, he supposed, a proper mug. But anger could not cure that gash. The knowledge that Knarf, his father, was numbered with the indifferent who had defeated the motion struck even deeper. Behind him, everything to which he had trusted was withered. He was pressed out from his safe childhood into an exposed and doubtful future. The present was no more than a gap, a chasm between what had gone and what had not yet come. So far, realisation only knocked on his mind. He was walking across the familiar square, grown unfamiliar, filled with a new sort of quiet. In front of him his friends were being driven, incredibly, by a bunch of soldiers. Behind him, Sfax and Oran and the strange young man who had been helping Sfax were watching him go with careless interest. Unseen eyes were no doubt watching his discomfort from windows or roofs looking on the square. He was divided from everything he had known by this hour. His pride was scarcely involved at all, the hurt went far deeper, it was like a physical maiming. Shock, anger, pain, bewilderment, were melted into one indivisible distress. He followed the soldiers, intent on sharing whatever it might be that they would do to his friends. The strength of his emotion gave him dignity. He was relieved and yet disappointed that Illil was not in the group. She would not have wished to escape. He wanted her with him so that he might share her courage and conviction. She was right when she said he didn't know anything about the world he would have to live in. Avik, he noticed, had detached himself from the herded group and was walking at a leisurely pace across the square. No one stopped him. They wouldn't bother about an old man like that. Ren was relieved, he didn't want to be responsible for Avik. He did feel in some unco-ordinated way responsible for everything that had happened.

At the far side of the square where the avenue led down to the river, the sergeant in charge halted his detachment. The flock of chickens halted too. Ren, who was on the sergeant's heels, saw that he was not a robot but a man with a cheerful, kindly, weather-beaten face.

"Now, children," he said, using the diminutive in friendly ferocity, "off home with you and don't give me any more trouble today."

A girl of thirteen, who had probably been involved through her curiosity alone, burst into tears. He was genuinely distressed and wanted to comfort her. "It's all right, girlie. I'm not going to hurt you. Old Mug never hurt a fly, did I, boys? I was just taking care of you, see?" He would have put his arm round her shaking shoulders, but a boy, probably her brother, drew her quickly away and defiantly walked her down the avenue still sobbing hysterically.

"Off with you," said the sergeant briskly. The group moved off sheepishly down the avenue, keeping together. A few looked as if they had something to say, but there was no leader. Ren ran after them to ask if anyone had seen Illil. One boy said yes, he had. She had gone into Knarf's house "a long time ago." They didn't want to talk under the eyes of the soldiers and treated Ren almost as if he were a stranger.

When Ren turned back into the square no one questioned or stopped him. At his own door Avik was waiting for him. He overflowed with sweetness and light.

"My dear boy, I am more than sorry that you have been so grievously disappointed. It goes to my heart to see you so defeated. But take an old man's word, Ren, these troubles and disappointments pass. A setback today, a triumph tomorrow, that's the way the world goes and always has. If you can learn from your defeats and not presume upon your victories you'll possess the world. Take the long view, my dear, dear lad. Your friends won't think any the less of you for this little unpleasantness. Did you see me there?"

"Yes, Avik, thank you." It was kindly meant, even if it did work on his nerves like a fret saw.

"There," the old man beamed. "That's all I wanted to say. Just a word of encouragement from age to youth. Go inside now and your mother will give you a good hot drink. That's what you want, a good hot strengthening drink. I'll be going on my way. Just wanted to see you."

"Goodbye, Avik, and thank you again."

Lin was crossing the vestibule.

"Is Illil here, mother?"

"Yes, dear. She came in before the end of the vote. I put her in the sunroom because of the stairs. Oh, Ren, how pale you are. I'm so terribly sorry that the vote went wrong. I voted for you, of course. Oh, I do wish you hadn't gone in for this."

Ren was a little surprised by such an outburst. "It can't be helped," he muttered. "Thanks for voting."

"But, *of course*, Ren."

But it wasn't of course. "Was Illil ill or anything?"

"She's had a turn but really I think it was more fright than anything. She thought she was going to have a haemorrhage, all the symptoms, she said, only she would hardly talk. She's mortally scared, poor girl. Lying there sucking ice."

"I want to see her."

"Well, I suppose you can, but she won't want to talk and you'd better not excite her."

Lin had her hand on the door knob. "Ren, will Oran and Sfax and the others be coming back for supper? It's awkward not knowing."

Ren wanted to laugh, but he knew that if he began he wouldn't be able to stop. "I shouldn't think so," he answered, pulling desperately at the corners of his mouth. "I didn't ask them."

In Lin's eyes there was a look of fixed distress. It had nothing to do with the problems of the kitchen.

Illil was lying with her eyes shut, her face a pale mask of determination. When Ren took her hand she opened her eyes without the least change of expression or movement of her body.

"I'm so sorry," he said gently. "Was the disappointment too much for you, Illil?"

She continued to stare up at him without answering. He remembered what Lin had said—"before the end of the vote."

"You know what happened, don't you?"

She shook her head almost imperceptibly.

"We lost the vote. The black column, right up to the top. 62% didn't vote at all, 16% were against, only 22% were in favour. The soldiers. . . ."

"Don't."

"Illil. . . ."

"Please don't make me talk. You don't know what it's like. If I have another haemorrhage I'll be back where I was six months ago."

"I'm sorry, Illil. I only wanted. . . ."

"Go away."

"Let me stay. I won't talk."

"Go away." Her eyes were shut, she had retired again into her own private struggle.

Ren looked down on her for a moment. She was utterly changed from the comrade of the afternoon, she was barely recognisable even to the outward eye as the same person. He walked out of the room and shut the door behind him. The vestibule was empty. That was fortunate for he had only one wish, to escape, to be alone. He must think and take stock, sort fact from pain.

Ren crossed the square and struck down towards the river, walking fast, looking straight ahead. He held back his thoughts. Now the main thing was to escape, over the river, into the other world. Then there would be plenty of time and space to think.

It was after five o'clock and already dusk was mixing with the air. The sky was a faint lilac. The landscape had changed from its warm autumnal ripeness to a thin wintriness. The horizon was circled with a soft smudge of mist that presently, when the sun dipped a little lower, would turn in the west to a great smouldering sunset barred with purple cloud. The earth struck cold through his thin sandals. He did not follow the same line as he and Illil had taken in the afternoon. The thought of so coming again to that little hill—forever unlike another hill—where they had sat and talked like children sickened him.

Of this night ever afterwards he remembered most sharply the physical sensations—the cold of the earth striking up into his body, the fine thin grass growing brittle with early frost, the beauty of the invading twilight, the night coming up at his back, slowly to overwhelm him, the tall sky, the thin air tingling with stars, the congealing of his flesh.

He walked with no object except to walk, to tread down his own despair. He wanted, with the sick animal movement of his mind, to escape into the anonymous distance, to come home to something intangible, to take refuge in the earth. He had a fantastic nostalgia for something beyond what he knew, for those remote plains of the west where the mirage moved. He wanted to stand on ground that he had never trodden before. He suffered as the young can, but every minute made himself some new toy, called in to his aid every phantom and illusion that man has invented and re-invented a thousand times for the assuagement of his own grief and despair. Driven for the moment out of his own life, or turning wilfully from it, he sought, not in concrete terms, but in their shadowy essence, that Utopia, New Atlantis, Ultima Thule, those Islands of the Blest, that North-West Passage, that fabulous Cathay, and all the other curious destinations of the seafaring imagination from Sinbad to de Quiros. He sought blindly the world beyond the world, turning to it now in the hour of his hunger as naturally as the child to the breast, and setting upon it his own image. That was his deeply sustaining instinct, but he could not recognise it as comfort, only that it gave horizon to his distress and opened up a way beyond, which, because it did not exist, could not easily be refuted. This was the mysterious process in the depth of his mind; in the front of it he continued to struggle as a rational being though one shot up with emotion.

Ren thought, in that shorthand of detached words, broken images, sensory footnotes, that is the familiar use of the mind but not communicable save in translation, "I must sort out what is real from what is illusion. Nearly everything I have taken for granted has proved a myth. The people I thought were real were only simulacra, the real people are unrecognisable. Illil, Sfax, Knarf, all ghosts, people I invented. The people I canvassed, the friends, and neighbours, they weren't real either. I invented people who were interested and willing and who agreed with everything I said. The people I don't know are just as much inventions as those I thought I knew best. If I'm going on I must have a new sort of understanding. Grow it as a crab grows a new claw, if need be. To see event on its own terms, not on mine. I've been a romantic, imagining things and then putting them to the touch and getting a different answer from the one I expected. Can I make myself over into a realist just by turning a page, or must I change every cell in my body? I am not alone. It's only my personal life that has fallen in. There are hundreds, perhaps thousands, in the Movement, and they are nearly all older and more experienced than I am. Let me be a particle in the Movement, carried along by it and trusting it, willing nothing myself. But that is no good. Like a grain of sand I'd sink to the bottom and with all the other inert grains drag down the whole. The entrance fee can only be my whole self. I must have conviction and how can I have it when I'm lost among ghosts? I believe, but believing alone isn't enough. Ideas in the head aren't real unless you do something about them. Belief must put on its image of flesh, it must become concrete in me. That is what I fear. The plunge into reality out of a world of my own dreaming. I must be willing to play the part for which I am suited, not the part I want. Within the Movement I must beat out the new world on the tender flesh of my own mind because every cell in the movement must be secured, must be able to live alone and function individually as well as collectively. But the whole thing might be a chimera too. Does liberty exist without the will to freedom? If no one wants it, does it *exist?* Only twenty-two people in every hundred wanted it today and probably a lot of them had only been persuaded that they wanted it and could just as easily have been persuaded to something else. The dead wall of indifference. We could spend our lives forcing people to have what they don't want and what we can't even define. An urge in the blood, call it "Liberty."

Ren topped a little rise. A very faint light lingered in the west. He could just see what looked like an endless plain without feature stretching before him. The Promised Land. The *tabula rasa* of the future. He stood still, staring straight ahead, as if waiting to pick up the beat that would carry him across some invisible line into the earth's eternity. The tempo of his thought changed. It was like the change from one movement to another in a symphony, not radical but the unfolding of the old theme in a new light. The hard tight scaly buds of his thought began to unfurl and blossom in a melancholy exuberance. He was not alone. All the men who had loved liberty— and died for it in the past—were with him. This very earth was leavened with the dust of the Pioneers. The love of liberty had been something in their blood and bones, not in their brains. It was still in men's blood or the earth would be cold and dead. The Movement would not exist unprompted. It was itself an outward vestment of an inner need. All man's activities were the successive skins of his need, the habitations, for a long or short time, of the spirit. Otherwise they could not be conceived. Liberty—the word was only a core to many cognate meanings—was one of the oldest human themes. After existing comes changing and this word, liberty, was the rallying point for the attack on the desired unknown. The Pioneers had sacrificed existence for it and they had been hard obstinate men, not romantics and sentimentalists. It seemed as if the lure for men was not advantage but sacrifice. The Movement was wrong when it held out little gifts, all it had to do was to ask for sacrifice. To cry out, "Give your lives and your happiness and your peace," and the ancient springs of man's spirit would open again. Some one must give it a new direction.

Ren thought again of what Illil had said about a life to burn. With her it had been only a febrile dream; she would not ever have the courage to carry it through. She had seen a reality even if she had not been able to hold it. If in a crisis there were always some one in the movement ready to drive home the point by the sacrifice of his life there would be an inexhaustible fund of strength. The ritual sacrifice. The sacrament. Not idly had he thought of the auto-da-fe in the square today. It had been an auto-da-fe without the sacrifice —trivial, childish, unable to hold to its end. Only to sacrifice would men give their final allegiance. Something hidden in his own thought frightened and revolted him but he clung to it. It had come to him like an exhalation from the ancient barbaric earth. He walked with it, on and on, holding it steady in his thoughts.

The intoxication of fatigue began to gain on Ren. It was a long time since he had eaten. At luncheon he had barely touched the food. He felt neither specific hunger nor weariness, only lightness and hollowness in his head and chest. Once he caught his foot in a burrow and sprawled full length on the ground. He lay with the sharp cold smell of the earth in his nostrils, the hard breast of the earth against his and a heart greater than his beating beneath him. It took an effort to rise again. He was giddy and a little shaken. Time and direction had slipped away from him. The will to go on and the desire to lie down again on the cold grass were almost evenly balanced.

Ren went on—or back, he didn't know which or trouble to think. The darkness with its thin elusive glaze of starlight was the same whichever way he turned. He was not alone. Somewhere on his left he could hear the rustle that a mob of sheep might make on the frosty grass, and he could smell the reek of animals in poor condition. From every point, now that he had begun to listen, slight sounds came to him, the beat of hooves on grass, the creaking of a saddle, the clink of gear. Far away intermittently he thought he saw the yellow star of a camp fire. He could not see but he could feel people about him, passing on horseback or on foot, in a broken scattered stream to the west, here a group on horseback, driving a few cattle or a flock of sheep, there a sundowner on foot, his bluey slung from his shoulder with the blackened billy hanging from it. When Ren stood still he could hear a fine reticulation of sound from far and near, feet marching without rhythm or beat. The sound acted in place of vision.

He heard the breathing of a horse just beside him and a voice said, "G'day, Digger. Got any tobacco?"

"Good day. No, I don't carry it."

"Thought not. No one does. Wasn't meaning to cadge any. Just thought I'd bloody well like to smell it."

"Going far?"

"Dunno. Think if I get to the salt bush country might be good-oh. If there's any water."

"Come far?"

"Bin on the roads three months."

"Ever want to go back?"

The man spat. "No bloody good back there now. Can't call your arse your own. Thought I'd try my luck further out. The cows aren't going to get my sheep."

"D' you travel at night."

"Got ter. There's a big mob coming up at the back. If I didn't get ter the next waterhole before them it's goodnight to my little lot. Sheep's pretty poor now. Wasn't any water at the last camp."

"Good luck."

"Yeh. Good bloody luck. So long, dig."

Ren stumbled on. His left leg was hurting, he must have injured it when he caught his foot in the burrow, but the pain remained on the edge of his consciousness. It was bad and yet he did not mind it very much. It didn't impede him.

Another voice hailed him.

"Goin' west with us, mate?"

"Yes, going west, all the way, mate."

He walked companionably between two young men, tall, spare, and slouching. He felt immensely friendly towards them and wanted to tell them everything that was in his mind, to talk to them about Liberty and Sacrifice and the Movement.

"The poor little bastard is crazy."

"Yeh," agreed the other young man. "Plenty of hatters about now."

Ren fell further and further behind. The cold was like a ball and chain and his leg was painful. Only dogged determination kept him moving. He walked without aim and the earth felt strange under his feet. In his mind was irrevocable determination.

All through the afternoon fear and exasperation had been banking up in Lin, fear for Ren and exasperation with Knarf. She must speak to Knarf, now—presently would be too late. Was it really too much to expect, the chance to speak to her husband about their son's future? No one would call that interference, would they? She was continually flagellating herself with secret colloquies like this. As soon as Ren went into Illil in the sunroom, Lin, as if a last straw had been added by the boy's pallor, set her mouth and went upstairs to find Knarf. She met him at the head of the stairs.

"Please, Knarf, wait a moment, I want to speak to you." She brought it out explosively.

"Yes, Lin." He turned to her with a patience that always angered her despite herself, because she interpreted it as an effort to put her in the wrong.

"You've got to stop Ren. He's ruining himself with his folly. You saw the attitude Oran took. Ren will get a black mark. He won't make his technical grade. Unless you do something."

"What can I do?"

"Of course you can do something. You've position and influence. You can find Oran now and have a talk with him, while he's still here. Tell him you'll guarantee Ren's future behaviour."

"I couldn't do that, Lin. Ren would never forgive me if I went to Oran behind his back."

"Then talk to Ren first. Only do it now. Don't you see there mightn't be another chance. Get Ren to promise."

"He wouldn't listen to me, and I don't blame him."

"Yes, he would. He has always admired you even if you never took any notice of him."

"I wouldn't be justified."

"You mean, you wouldn't be bothered."

"You're unjust," he spoke with sudden passion. "It's you who undervalue him. Our son has greatness."

"He's too young. He doesn't know what he's doing."

"He must go his own way and if I can I'll go with him."

"I'll go to Oran."

"No, Lin." He moved as if he were going to bar her way. She knew that she would not go in the face of his opposition. She broke into violent weeping, leaning her head against the wall. The unprotected gesture, so much that of a friendless woman or a disappointed child, touched Knarf to impersonal pity. He put his arm awkwardly round her shoulders. Her body was harsh and angular.

She caught her breath painfully, neither shaking him off nor yielding to him. She wouldn't give up trying to explain.

"I, thought the Movement was just a hobby, I didn't know it was dangerous or I'd have tried to stop him before. I thought being with Sfax would protect him, but Sfax won't be in the Movement after today."

"Sfax is yellow, Ren isn't."

Lin made an heroic effort. "Go to him now, Knarf. He's terribly unhappy. I'm afraid. Just do what you can for him."

He wanted to say something to show that he realised her generosity. He tried to reach her but it was too difficult, they had failed one another too often. All he could manage was: "Go and lie down, Lin. You're worn out. I'll come in and tell you afterwards how Ren is."

"He is talking to Illil in the sunroom."

"I'll wait for him. Please go and rest."

Lin, of course, could not lie down and rest. She went to her room, combed her hair, opened and shut doors, walked restlessly up and down, regretting her display of emotion and trying to reconstruct the scene with Knarf on a more satisfactory pattern. She was on springs and could not rest. Besides, there was supper to prepare. Whatever happened, meals had to go on. The girl too was a little fibrous knot of anxiety. She might really be ill, as she thought she was. It was a responsibility and there, too, Ren was involved or might be involved.

When she went downstairs half an hour later, Knarf was standing in the vestibule looking out moodily into the square. He was not surprised to see her and made no comment.

"Ren has not come out yet."

Lin went across to the sunroom and opened the door. The room was in darkness and Illil asked in a faint voice for more ice. Lin turned on the light. Ren was not there.

It was midnight.

Lin said, "It's not *like* Ren."

Knarf stopped in his pacing to and fro. "I don't know what to do."

"I've called up twenty-seven people," Ord said. "None of them knows anything. Can you think of any more possibilities?"

"He was talking to Avik. Do you think he might have gone out there. Perhaps Avik asked him to, he was always fond of Ren."

Knarf dismissed this as a psychological improbability, but Ord said he might as well follow it up.

Nothing came of it except that Avik was very much agitated and asked if Knarf would like him to drive in at once and give his at least moral support.

"God forbid," said Knarf.

Lin asked, "Do you think that Oran has had him arrested?"

The two men looked at each other. "No," said Ord, "he wouldn't be as crude as that, would he?"

"No," echoed Knarf, "that's hardly possible." But they were shaken. A sense of urgency was momentarily growing on Knarf. "That girl might know something."

"Illil said Ren stayed only a moment and said nothing about where he was going."

"Still, she might know where he'd be likely to go. I'll go and ask her."

"She's asleep."

"It can't be helped. You'd better come, Lin."

Knarf tapped on the door of the sunroom and after a moment went in. A night light, relic of Ren's childhood, was burning on a little table, shielded by a book. The small opal globe was like a quick of life in the shadowy room. Illil was lying asleep, propped up on pillows, her face white but tranquil in the dark shadow of her hair. Lin stood on one side of the bed, Knarf on the other. He touched the sleeping girl on the shoulder and her dark eyes opened at once.

"I'm sorry," he said gently, "but we can't find Ren. I want you when you are quite awake to think carefully. You might know something, some kind of clue, that would help us."

"Is it nearly morning?" she asked.

"No, it is half-past twelve. Ren has been gone seven hours."

She lifted her hands in a little startled jerk. "I don't know anything. I told you."

"Yes, I know. Please don't be distressed. There might be something indirectly bearing on it. We would not have disturbed you if he had not been so troubled."

"Yes," she said, "yes, I am trying to think." She pressed her palms against her eyes, concentrating. "There might be something he said yesterday . . . or before."

"Thank God she's an intelligent girl," thought Knarf.

"I think I can remember everything he said today. But none of it seems to fit . . . unless . . . He said he always thought of the land across the river as a different world. If he was very unhappy . . . he might want to go there. He just might. And there was something else. Can you remember where you used to take him riding when he was a child tented in your cloak on the old horse called Murrumbidgee? He talked of that too, and how you used to wrap him in your cloak to sleep on the grass. It seemed to be . . . something very special to him. He might want to get back. Is that any good? I'm afraid it's all I know."

"Thank you," Knarf said, deeply moved.

"It's nothing much to go on," he told Ord, "but I think I'll take a lantern and go across the river to see if I can pick up any trace of him."

Ord didn't make any parade of common sense. "I'll come with you."

"So will I," Lin offered.

She looked ready to drop now, Knarf thought, and would soon be a liability. "Some one will have to stay here," he pointed out. "Ren might come back or news of him. It's harder, I know, to stay than to come, but would you?"

She agreed readily enough and brought them two lanterns, a thick old cloak which Knarf flung over his shoulders, and a flask of spirit.

In the square Ord asked, "Shall I rouse the neighbours and get a search party?"

"No," said Knarf, "it's too small a chance. It's hardly a chance at all but . . ."

"Yes," said Ord, "it's all right for us but not for a hue and cry."

What Knarf was thinking—and Ord knew it—was that if anything were going to happen they were already too late, while if there were a commonplace explanation tomorrow morning would be time enough.

On the bridge Ord again answered Knarf's unspoken thought. "It's not the way a strong swimmer would choose. Ren would never do that."

On the far side they agreed to separate, Ord would go south and Knarf west. If one of them found Ren he would go to the nearest hill and signal with his lantern. The hopeless task of combing that limitless dark landscape oppressed them. Ren might, of course, have gone for a tramp across country, to escape the condolences of his friends on the fiasco of the day, or to think out the new position. If night caught him out there he might easily be lost. It was country to tangle men's minds in the endless pattern of its ridges. But Knarf could not cheer himself with these ramshackle reflections. His heart was heavy with foreboding.

Knarf looked back and saw Ord's lantern bobbing slowly away at an angle, one small impotent point of light in all that darkness. He shouted Ren's name once, but his voice in the stillness shocked him. It seemed to bring the darkness and silence tumbling down on his head. If Ren were within earshot he could not be lost for the lights of the Centre were still plainly visible. If he were within earshot now it was pretty certain he could not hear. He walked ahead in dogged misery straining his eyes without hope. Before he realised it, he was in among a flock of sheep camped for the night. In a panic they streamed away from him across the paddock and he realised how little he could see. The late moon would soon be up, already there was a brightening in the east as of a distant fire. He might as well wait for it. He set down the lantern: it made a coin of light, a small round coin with hard edges, on the right a few blades of grass across its beams had the appearance of magnified eyelashes. Ord's lantern was no longer visible. The lights of the Centre formed a small grid at a magnified distance. Silence pressed thumbs upon his ears, the cold caught at his feet and hands and fitted like a mask upon his face. The thin bright edge of the moon showed above the horizon. It grew while he watched it till it sailed clear, an old haggard moon, frayed on one side as if it had begun not to shrink but to disintegrate. It diffused enough light to drive the stars before it and to spread a stealthy glimmer over the whole landscape.

Knarf picked up the lantern and went on. The light was most deceptive. There was an illusion of clarity which vanished as soon as he tried to descry any object with exactness. Whatever he looked at directly seemed to melt before his eyes, whilst half-seen objects remained clear. Again and again he turned aside to examine a bush, a log, or a boulder which had at a distance the appearance of a human form sitting or lying on the ground. Each time his heart beat suffocatingly. Once he thought he saw Ord's lantern, a point of light far away like a distant campfire.

The treadmill of his thoughts continued all the time, asking himself how much his desertion had mattered to Ren, if he even knew of it, if it were the vote alone that had driven him to whatever desperate course he had taken, if Sfax had anything to do with it, or if there were some other circumstance of which he did not know. . . . Then all the questions of Why would be blotted out by the more urgent problem of Where, the desperate re-turning of every particle of scanty data, the last admission that there was nothing but a flying chance that Ren had crossed the river. That he might have taken sanctuary in this loneliness because of a childish memory was too poignant a thought to be kept in the mind.

Knarf thought dawn must be near, but it was only two o'clock. Last night he had spent in the final revision of his manuscript. Ren and he had watched the dawn from the roof. Ren had been so hopeful. This dawn he would see from some anonymous hillside, Ren lost, the whole secure fabric brought down. It did not enter his mind that there could be any turning back. This was keeping his vigil with Ren.

The ground was rougher, rocks, tussocks of grass, spiny bushes; he was going up a hill with a hard ridge, they recurred again and again in the soft undulating country. He stood on the top, a little out of breath, and looked about him. He held the lantern above his head in a vain effort to see more clearly. Lately he had turned aside less frequently for logs and bushes, perhaps from a subconscious wish to save himself ever renewed disappointment. Now, looking along the ridge he discerned a whitish patch that might possibly be a man lying full length on the ground. He shut his eyes and looked again. Now it appeared like a rock, a grey rock with the moonlight on it, lying in a tangle of grass and bush. But rocks didn't look quite like that, not in this part of the country. He might as well go and look, one way was as good as another now. As he swung the lantern Knarf saw that the ground here was honeycombed with burrows—wombats and bandicoots, just the place for a man on horseback to take a very pretty tumble. He was stuffing his mind with that sort of cotton wool when he realised suddenly that it was not a rock or a log or any other inanimate object. Ren. He was lying full length, his cheek on the ground, and he might have been asleep but for his pallor and the frosty dew wet on his hair and face.

Knarf knelt beside him. "Ren," he called, "Ren," and tried to raise him. The boy uttered a little moan of pain and opened wide anxious eyes to the light of the lantern.

"Ren, it's all right, Ren, I'm here." The boy half smiled, still on the edge of consciousness. Knarf's unconscious tears ran down his cheeks and fell on the boy's breast. "What happened?"

"I don't know," the boy murmured. "A long time ago . . ."

Lifting the lantern Knarf saw the cause of the trouble. Ren's left foot was caught in a burrow and the leg was lying at an unnatural helpless angle. He had pitched forward on to rocks, his fall partly broken by a bush.

"It's your foot, old man. I'll have to release it. It'll probably hurt. Can you hold on?"

"Yes."

Knarf tore away the root-matted earth with his hands, uncovering the foot. Gently and slowly he lifted it aside. He knew at once by the feel of it that the ankle was broken. Ren made no sound, but he was fainting with the pain. Knarf held the flask of spirits to his lips. He gulped, coughed, beat at the ground with his hands, gulped again. The effect was almost instantaneous. Fire ran in all his veins and he was fully conscious. Knarf took a sip himself. Carefully raising Ren he slipped a fold of the heavy cloak between his shoulders and the earth and wrapped it across him. It was voluminous enough to cover him from foot to chin. Then only, facing the direction in which he thought Ord must be, he swung the lantern in long arcs over his head. He could not see an answering glimmer. He could not stand there indefinitely, a human lighthouse, so finding a tree near by, he broke off one of the branches, cleared away the leaves about, and hung the lantern in the fork. It was all he could do. Single-handed it was impossible to move Ren. To carry him over rough ground in the darkness, even if he could have managed it for the distance, would have caused him too much pain. If Ord saw the signal and came one of them could go for help. It was probably a matter of waiting for morning in any case. It might be best to bring a truck even if it meant taking down a few panels of fencing. Ren would be all right till morning.

Knarf eased Ren's head and shoulders till they rested on his knees and spread his own cloak as far as it would go over them both to keep in the warmth of their bodies. The boy was wide awake now, stimulated by the spirits, and his foot, released from pressure, was not unbearably painful so long as he kept still. The worst part was the aching of the cold.

Now that the normal walls of their existence were down, moment by moment a new intimacy sprang up between father and son. Each felt a great relief. Ren wanted to talk, and the darkness and the spirits both made it easier. For a little while they were both floated free of all the obstructions of their lives. It was a shared freedom and the moment was self sufficient.

Ren caught at a strand of memory that tantalised his mind.

"The Pioneers came through here when they retreated in to the desert, didn't they?"

"Yes. That was four hundred years ago."

"They were the flower of the people, weren't they? They couldn't breathe without freedom. They preferred to die. What they did should have driven a stake through liberty to keep it for ever in man's imagination."

Knarf said heavily, "They were those who would not co-operate. They made themselves a dead end, they perished and everything belonging to them perished."

"Except a memory."

"A romantic memory. It was, after all, the easy way."

"Easy?" Ren knew it wasn't easy to die. He had looked in the eyes of death.

"They didn't have to think, only to endure. If you look at history you will see that men have always preferred suffering to thinking."

"It was for liberty."

"Liberty? Oh, yes. They carried it with them like the Ark of the Covenant." Ren wouldn't know what that meant. "Like a totem, a fetish, if you like. In the desert it was so inevitable it ceased to exist."

"Like a 'Breathe More Air' campaign."

"Yes, exactly. It was a gesture that became the whole works."

"You mean gestures aren't enough."

"Not nearly."

"Dying is not enough either?"

"Dying's the wrong end of the stick. The problem is to live every inch of the way."

"Sacrifice is something every one can understand. It's a weapon."

Knarf, without having the key to this conversation, still knew that it was important. He could only strive in this ghostly inquisition to tell the truth as far as he could conceive it.

"Sacrifice for the sake of sacrifice is only another vanity."

"A gesture, like dying?" From a slight movement he knew that Ren was smiling.

"Exactly. People who have made a sacrifice for some end feel that they've bought themselves out of any further effort. Pain's only a by-product: if we can neither seek it as an alibi nor be intimidated by it, but just realise that it is a sort of meaningless irritation, we're . . . well, we're half way to freedom."

Knarf in his heart was humble and said these things, not because he felt he had any right to give judgment but because be believed them. Ren, who was generous, did not grudge him what sounded like assurance.

They were silent for a time. Knarf felt the increased warmth of Ren's body. He thought they might never have such another moment of intimacy and that he had better say what he had to say about this day while the way was still open to him.

"About today, Ren."

He felt a tremor go through the boy as if his injured ankle had been touched.

"Don't fret too much about it. It's only the beginning, you know."

Ren didn't answer. This was going to be uphill work. Knarf began again trying to put into words something that he himself only glimpsed.

"The idea of liberty is very old, it has recurred again and again in man's history. There must be some seeds of it in every one's blood, but overlaid now for a long time. You can revive it, but not, I think, in a hurry. It will have to be a slow organic growth. You can only get people to understand what they know already. The Movement wants quick results. That's natural, but it won't get them until immensely more effort has been put into it. Imaginative effort. Today was just a sort of red herring. The votometer is just a gadget. This is an age of gadgets, a mechanic answer to every problem. That's where you and it are in conflict. You say, 'The whole of life can't be measured by the machine,' and yet you try to measure public opinion by this votometer. The very thing that's important for you escapes the gadget. You played into the hands of your opponents. By resorting prematurely to this votometer and setting exaggerated store by its findings you were, you see, channelling yourself. Offering Oran, if you like, a single head to chop off. The Movement so far is only leaven. Set occasions, snap votes, mechanic measures, are all against you. Don't you see the very thing you have to break through is the idea that the *whole* of life can be tabulated and docketed and served in a machine, that efficiency is all that matters. For a new idea you've got to have re-orientated minds. The Technical Bureau has used today. You were working for them not for the Movement. It was for Oran —well, just a spyhole. Sfax followed the law of his nature. He can only be loyal to himself. You and he haven't anything in common because he's—not yellow—just gadget-minded. *He's* the thing you've got to break through. He, as much as Oran, is your essential unconscious enemy."

Ren said slowly, "I might understand some day. It's hard to unscrew my head and put it on the other way round."

"Ren, I didn't vote today."

"Yes, I know."

"Can you forgive me?"

Ren found his father's hand in the folds of the cloak and pressed it.

"It wouldn't have made any difference to the result if you had, would it?"

That was all there was to be said about it. After a pause Knarf went on. "There's a long road ahead, Ren, and I think you are committed to it. This thing, liberty, however you like to define it, seems to be one of man's basic impulses. Perhaps it roots down into the gregarious instinct, the desire for the shared life, the brotherhood of man. Power and Liberty. Strophe and Anti-strophe. The word liberty is only a handle. The thing itself has had a thousand manifestations. It is immortal, ever renewing itself. It was in the creative splendour of Greece, the toleration of Rome, the brotherhood of the Christian, England's justice, the ferment of the Renaissance, Revolutionary France, the Red Star of Communism. . . . And every time it was defeated.

Power has always devoured liberty. Because liberty has always called power to its aid it has perished. It has armed itself and fought, only to die of its own violence. Men have thought that liberty and competition could exist in the same world and that war could serve liberty. And so they have defeated themselves. It is the means that should decide the end. Now the struggle is beginning again, but in a new context. For more than a century there has been no war in the world, and competition, as the old world knew it, is no more. The impulses that made these things are not dead but they are present. They are not active and inflamed. The exhausted world is at pause. Now the road is open to the principle of liberty as never before. If men have learned to live at peace they have also learned to be indifferent. The struggle will be against inertia and vested power. It can succeed so long as it does not call in death against life. If you call in violence you may replace one tyranny with another. Means and end are not two separate things. They are one. Means is end in becoming."

Knarf was not talking from any Olympian height. He wanted to reassure Ren, and the only way was through complete sincerity, a striving towards clarity and understanding for their own sakes. No desire to instruct or soothe would serve now, nothing but an act of faith without reserve.

To Ren, these words, whose exact meaning he could not grapple, did bring reassurance. He felt quiet and almost happy. He had come past a crisis and was relieved. He had not been so safe since he was a child. Pain was present but remote. It did not touch his mind or his spirit.

"Dawn can't be long now!" Knarf said. "Drink some more of this." He held the flask to Ren's lips again and the boy drank. "Perhaps you could sleep."

After what seemed a long time while the spirit's warmth fanned through his veins, Ren said, "Perhaps I could."

Tired, safe, and a little drunk, he could not keep awake any longer. The long day was over. Sleep unwound its tension. Knarf watched over his son and his heart was wrung with the most difficult love in the world, the love of a father for his son. It has no code and no ritual, no physical release, it must forever stand by and its way is the way of relinquishment.

He saw the first light of another day creep into the eastern sky. He thought, "This is the beginning," and "The earth remains."

1940-1942.

# M. BARNARD ELDERSHAW

is the pseudonym for Marjorie Barnard and Flora Eldershaw. Marjorie Faith Barnard was born at Ashfield, Sydney in 1897, the year her future collaborator Flora Sydney Patricia Eldershaw was born—in the country in New South Wales. Both graduated from the University of Sydney, though Flora Eldershaw went on to become senior mistress at the Presbyterian Ladies' College, Sydney, while Marjorie Barnard rejected teaching for librarianship, at the Sydney Technical College. Their first novel, *A House is Built,* was published in 1929, winning, with Katharine Susannah Prichard's *Coonardoo,* the *Bulletin* prize for the best novel submitted in 1928.

Their second novel, *Green Memory,* followed in 1931; four years later Marjorie Barnard gave up her job to become a full-time writer and joined the Fellowship of Australian writers, of which Flora Eldershaw was President. The year, too, marked the beginning of Marjorie Barnard's political involvement, reflected in their next novel *The Glasshouse* (1936). This was followed by *Plaque with Laurel* (1937): by now Marjorie Barnard and Flora Eldershaw had become leading literary figures in Sydney. Their partnership extended beyond the field of fiction: they published criticism, including *Essays in Australian Fiction* (1938), and numerous biographical and historical books.

The year 1940 saw dramatic changes in Marjorie Barnard's life: she became a pacifist joined the Australian Labor Party and her father died, leaving her alone with a sick mother. In 1941 Flora Eldershaw moved to Canberra with a new government job, and the next year Marjorie Barnard began work again as a librarian. She also published a volume of short stories under her own name—*The Persimmon Tree* (1942)—and began, largely without help, to write *Tomorrow and Tomorrow and Tomorrow,* published five years later, in 1947, after severe cuts by the government censor. Discouraged by this and the public's cool response M. Barnard Eldershaw write no more fiction, concentrating, instead, on history and criticism. Flora Eldershaw died in 1957; Marjorie Barnard, now eighty-seven, lives outside Sydney.

XAFIC